ECHOES OF HONOR

BAEN BOOKS by DAVID WEBER:

Honor Harrington Novels:
On Basilisk Station
The Honor of the Queen
The Short Victorious War
Field of Dishonor
Flag in Exile
Honor Among Enemies
In Enemy Hands
Echoes of Honor

Edited by David Weber:
More Than Honor
Worlds of Honor (*forthcoming*)

Mutineers' Moon
The Armageddon Inheritance
Heirs of Empire

Path of the Fury

Oath of Swords
The War God's Own

With Steve White:
Insurrection
Crusade
In Death Ground

ECHOES OF HONOR

DAVID WEBER

BAEN

Echoes of Honor

This is a work of fiction. All the characters and events portrayed in this book are fictional, and any resemblance to real people or incidents is purely coincidental.

A Baen Books Original

Baen Publishing Enterprises
P.O. Box 1403
Riverdale, NY 10471

ISBN: 0-671-87892-1

Cover art by David Mattingly

Distributed by Simon & Schuster
1230 Avenue of the Americas
New York, NY 10020

Typeset by Windhaven Press, Auburn, NH
Printed in the United States of America

I would like to express my thanks to
Mark Newman,
Doctor of Maternal-Fetal Medicine.
I think you'll recognize the reason why
when it comes around.

(1) Point Defense Laser Cluster
(2) GRASER main armament
(3) Anti-ship Missile Tube
(4) Anti-ship Missile "Revolver" Magazine Cell
(5) Point Defense Missile Tube
(6) Small Craft Hangar
(7) Folding Wing Cutter/Lifeboat
(8) Anti-ship Missile
(9) Sidewall ("Bow Wall") Generator

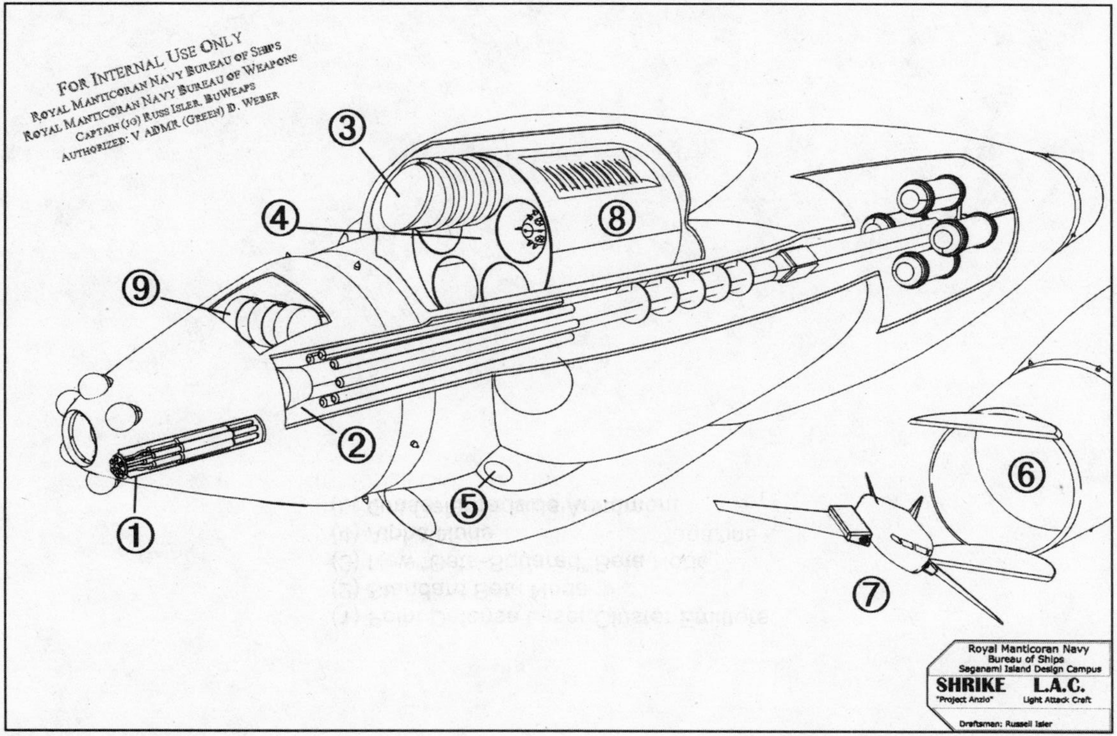
FOR INTERNAL USE ONLY
ROYAL MANTICORAN NAVY BUREAU OF SHIPS
ROYAL MANTICORAN NAVY BUREAU OF WEAPONS
CAPTAIN (JG) RUSS ISLER, BUWEAPS
AUTHORIZED: V ADMR (GREEN) D. WEBER
1
2
3
4
5
6
7
8
9
Royal Manticoran Navy
Bureau of Ships
Saganami Island Design Campus
SHRIKE L.A.C.
"Project Anzio"
Light Attack Craft
Draftsman: Russell Isler

(1) Point Defense Laser Cluster Emitters
(2) Standard Beta Node
(3) New "Beta-Squared" Beta Node
(4) Alpha Node
(5) Graser Broadside Armament

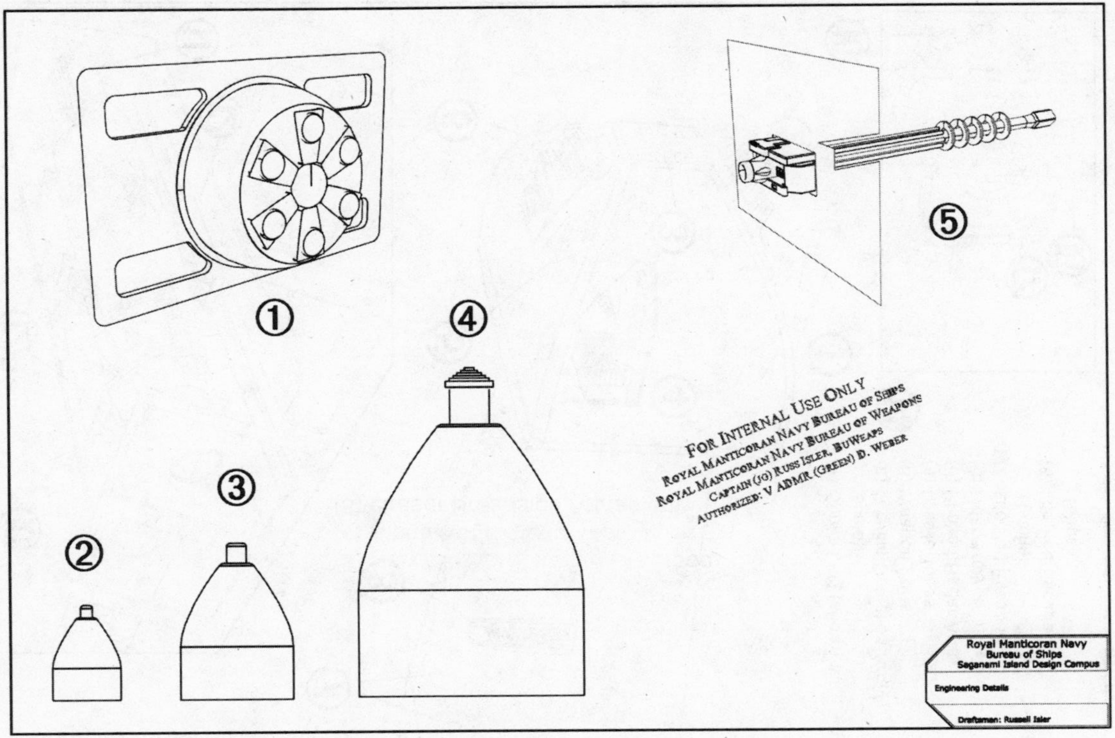
①
②
③
④
⑤
FOR INTERNAL USE ONLY
ROYAL MANTICORAN NAVY BUREAU OF SHIPS
ROYAL MANTICORAN NAVY BUREAU OF WEAPONS
CAPTAIN (JG) RUSS ISLER, BUWEAPS
AUTHORIZED: V ADMR (GREEN) D. WEBER
Royal Manticoran Navy
Bureau of Ships
Saganami Island Design Campus
Engineering Details
Draftsman: Russell Isler

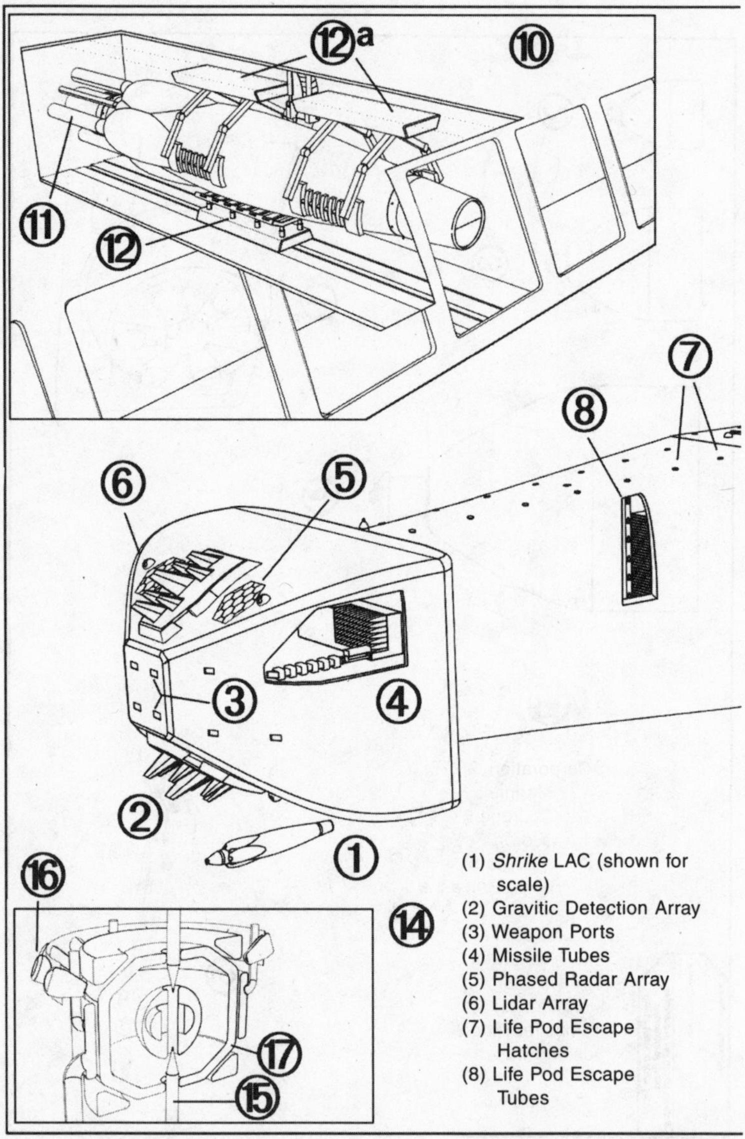

(1) *Shrike* LAC (shown for scale)
(2) Gravitic Detection Array
(3) Weapon Ports
(4) Missile Tubes
(5) Phased Radar Array
(6) Lidar Array
(7) Life Pod Escape Hatches
(8) Life Pod Escape Tubes

Royal Manticoran Navy
Bureau of Ships
Saganami Island Design Campus

H.M.S. Minotaur

L.A.C. Carrier "Project Anzio"

Draftsman: Russell Isler

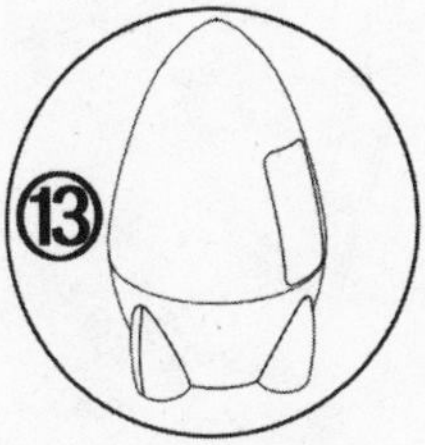

(9) LAC Bay Hatch
(10) LAC Bay
(11) Personnel/Missile Loading Tubes
(12) Docking/Umbilical Cradle
(12A) Docking Arms
(13) Life Pod

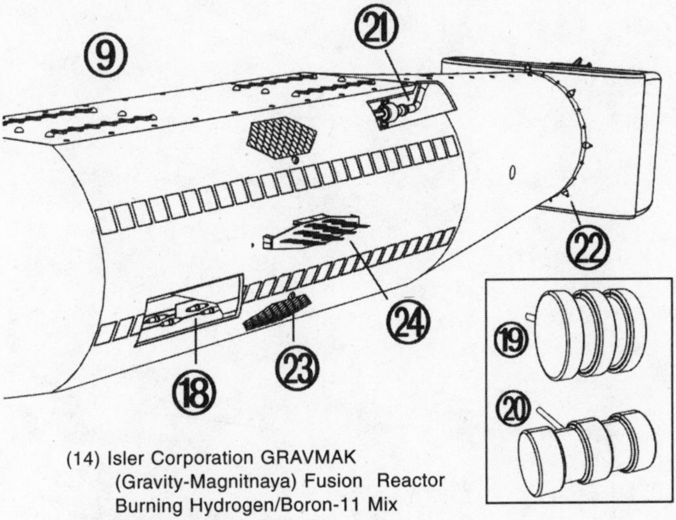

(14) Isler Corporation GRAVMAK (Gravity-Magnitnaya) Fusion Reactor Burning Hydrogen/Boron-11 Mix
(15) Hydrogen/Boron Feed Channels
(16) Gravity Generators
(17) Magnetic Field Housing
(18) Boat Bay
(19) Radiation/Particle Shield Generator
(20) Sidewall Generator
(21) Vectored Thrust Auxiliary Fusion Reactor Thruster
(22) After Impeller Ring
(23) Broadside Phased Array Radar
(24) Broadside Gravitic Array

FOR INTERNAL USE ONLY
ROYAL MANTICORAN NAVY BUREAU OF SHIPS
ROYAL MANTICORAN NAVY BUREAU OF WEAPONS
CAPTAIN (JG) RUSS ISLER, BUWEAPS
AUTHORIZED: V ADMR (GREEN) D. WEBER

Prologue

It was still and very quiet in the palatial room. Four humans and thirteen treecats, four of them half-grown 'kittens, sat silently, eyes locked on the HD which showed only silent swirls of soothing, standby color. The only movements were the slow twitch, twitch, twitch of the very tail-tip of the treecat clasped in Miranda LaFollet's arms and the gently stroking true-hand with which the treecat named Samantha comforted her daughter Andromeda. Andromeda was the most anxious of the 'kittens, but all four were ill at ease, clustered tightly about their mother with half-flattened ears. Their empathic senses carried the raw emotions of the adults in the room—human and treecat alike—to them all too clearly, yet they were too young to understand the reason for the jagged-clawed tension which possessed their elders.

Allison Harrington pulled her eyes from the silent HD and glanced once more at her husband's profile. He stared stonily straight before him, his face gaunt, and Allison needed no empathic sense to feel his tormented grief calling to her own. But he refused to acknowledge the pain—had refused from the very beginning—as if by denying it or battling it in the solitary anguish of his own heart without "burdening" her he could somehow make it not real. He knew better than that. Surgeons learned better, if only from watching patients face those demons alone. Yet that was knowledge of the head, not the heart, and even now he refused to look away from the HD. Both her small hands tightened on the single large one she had captured almost by force when he sat down beside her, but his expression was like Sphinx granite, and she made herself look away once more.

Brilliant sunlight, double filtered through the dome covering Harrington City and then again by the smaller one covering Harrington House, streamed incongruously through the window. It should be night outside, she told herself. Blackest night, to mirror the darkness in her own soul, and she closed her eyes in pain.

Senior Master Steward James MacGuiness saw her and bit his lip once more. He longed to reach out to her, as she had reached out to him by insisting that he be here, "with the rest of your family," for this terrible day. But he didn't know how, and his nostrils flared as he inhaled deeply. Then he felt a soft, warm weight land solidly in his lap and looked down as Hera braced both hand-feet on his chest and reached up to touch his face ever so gently with one true-hand. The 'cat's bright green gaze met his with a soft concern that made his eyes burn, and he stroked her fluffy pelt gratefully as she crooned ever so softly to him.

The HD made a small sound, and every eye, human and 'cat, snapped to it. Very few of the people of Grayson knew the subject of the upcoming special bulletin. The ones in this room, and in a similar room in Protector's Palace, did know, for the chief of the local bureau of the Interstellar News Service had warned them as a matter of courtesy. Not that most Graysons wouldn't suspect its content. The days of instant news had been left centuries behind along with the days when humanity inhabited only a single planet; now information moved between the stars only as rapidly as the ships which carried it. Humanity had readjusted its expectations to once more deal with news that arrived in fits and starts, in indigestible chunks and rumors awaiting confirmation . . . and this story had spawned too many "special reports" and too much speculation for the Graysons not to suspect.

The HD chirped again, and then a message blurb blinked to life, each letter precisely formed. "The following Special Report contains violent scenes which may not be suitable for all audiences. INS advises viewer discretion," it said, then transformed itself into a time and date reference: "23:31:05 GMT, 01:24:1912 P.D." The numbers floated in the HD, superimposed on a slowly spinning INS logo, for perhaps ten seconds, announcing that what they were about to see had been recorded almost a full T-month earlier. Then they vanished, and the familiar features of Joan Huertes, the Interstellar News anchor for the Haven Sector, replaced them.

"Good evening," she said, her expression solemn. "This is Joan Huertes, reporting to you from INS Central, Nouveau Paris, in the People's Republic of Haven, where this afternoon Second Deputy Director of Public Information Leonard Boardman, speaking on behalf of the Committee of Public Safety, issued the following statement."

Huertes disappeared, to be replaced by the image of a man with thinning hair and a narrow face which seemed vaguely out of place atop his pudgy frame. Despite his soft-looking edges, there were deep lines on that face, the sort which came to a man for whom worry was a way of life, but he seemed to have himself well in hand as he folded his hands on the podium at which he stood and gazed out over a large, comfortably furnished conference room crowded with reporters and HD cameras. There was the usual babble of shouted questions everyone knew would not be answered, but he only stood there, then raised one hand in a quieting gesture. The background noise gradually abated, and he cleared his throat.

"I will not take any questions this afternoon, citizens," he told the assembled newsies. "I have a prepared statement, however, and supporting HD chips will be distributed to you at the end of the briefing."

There was a background almost-noise of disappointment from the reporters, but not one of surprise. No one had really expected anything more . . . and all of them already knew from officially inspired "leaks" what the statement would be about.

"As this office has previously announced," Boardman said flatly, obviously reading from a holo prompter no one else could see, "four T-months ago, on October 23, 1911 P.D., the convicted murderess Honor Stephanie Harrington was captured by the armed forces of the People's Republic. At that time, the Office of Public Information stated that it was the intention of the Committee of Public Safety to proceed with the full rigor of the law, but only within the letter *of the law. Despite the unprovoked war of aggression which the elitist, monarchist plutocrats of the Star Kingdom of Manticore and the puppet regimes of the so-called 'Manticoran Alliance' have chosen to wage upon the People's Republic, the People's Republic has scrupulously observed the provisions of the Deneb Accords from the start of hostilities. It is not, after all, the fault of those in uniform when the self-serving masters of a corrupt and oppressive regime order them to fight, even when this means engaging in acts of naked aggression against the citizens and planets of a star nation which wishes only to live in peace and allow other nations to do the same.*

"The fact that, at the time of her capture, Harrington was serving as an officer in the navy of the Star Kingdom, however, further complicated an already complex situation. In light of her repeated claim that under the terms of the Deneb Accords her commission in the Manticoran Navy protected her, as a prisoner of war, from the consequences of her earlier crime, the People's government, determined not to act hastily, requested the Supreme Tribunal of the People's Justice to examine the specifics of the case, the conviction, and the Accords in order to ensure that all aspects of the prisoner's legal rights should be scrupulously maintained.

"Because Harrington's conviction had been returned by a civilian court prior to the commencement of hostilities, the Supreme Tribunal, after careful deliberation, determined that, under the provisions of Article Forty-One of the Deneb Accords, the interstellar protections normally afforded to military personnel did not apply. The Supreme Tribunal accordingly ordered that Harrington be remanded to the custody of the Office of State Security as a civilian prisoner, rather than to the People's Navy as a prisoner of war. In ordering Harrington remanded, People's Justice Theresa Mahoney, writing for the Tribunal in its unanimous opinion, observed that—" Boardman picked up an old-fashioned sheet

of hardcopy from the lectern and read aloud from the obvious prop"—'This was not an easy decision. While both civil law and Article Forty-One are quite clear and specific, no court wishes to establish any precedent which might serve to place our own uniformed citizens at risk should our enemy choose to seek vengeance in the name of "retaliation" or "reciprocity." Nonetheless, this Tribunal finds itself with no legal option but to order the prisoner remanded to the custody of the civilian judicial system, subject to its own legal requirements. Given the peculiar circumstances surrounding this case, and bearing in mind the Tribunal's concern over the possibility of retaliatory acts on the parts of the People's enemies, the Tribunal would respectfully request that the Committee of Pubic Safety, as the People's representative, consider clemency. This consideration is urged not because the Tribunal believes the prisoner deserves it, for she manifestly does not, but rather out of the Tribunal's real, serious, and pressing concern for the safety of citizens of the Republic currently in the hands of the Manticoran Alliance.' "

He laid aside his sheet of paper and folded his hands once more before him.

"The Committee, and particularly Citizen Chairman Pierre, considered the Tribunal's opinion and recommendation most carefully," he said in a solemn voice. "Although the People would always prefer to show mercy, even to their enemies, however, the requirements of the law in this case were, as the Supreme Tribunal noted, quite clear. Moreover, however merciful the People would prefer to be, the People's government cannot show weakness to enemies of the People at a time when the People are fighting for their very lives. With that in mind, and given that the heinous nature of prisoner's crime—the cold-blooded, deliberate, and premeditated murder of the entire crew of the merchant freighter RHMS Sirius—was such as to preclude any reduction in the sentence handed down by the court at the time of her conviction, Citizen Chairman Pierre declined to exercise his pardon authority. Accordingly Harrington was remanded to the appropriate authorities at Camp Charon in the Cerberus System, and at oh-seven-twenty GMT this morning, January twenty-fourth, the Central Headquarters of the Office of State Security in Nouveau Paris received confirmation from Camp Charon that sentence had been carried out, as ordered."

Someone gasped in the quiet, sun-drenched room. Allison wasn't certain who; it could even have been her. Her hands tightened like talons on her husband's, yet he didn't even flinch. The shock seemed blunted somehow, as if their long anticipation had crusted it in scar tissue that deadened the nerves, and neither she nor any of the others could tear their eyes from the HD. There was a dreadful, self-punishing mesmerization about it. They knew what they were going to see, yet to look away would have been a betrayal. They had to be here, however irrational it might be to subject themselves to it, and the demands of the heart had no need for reasons based in logic.

On the HD, the conference room was also utterly silent as Boardman paused. Then he looked straight into the camera, his face grim, and spoke very levelly.

"The People's Republic of Haven cautions the members of the so-called 'Manticoran Alliance' against the abuse or mistreatment of any Republican personnel in retaliation for this execution. The People's Republic reminds its enemies—and the galaxy at large—that this was a single, special case in which a condemned criminal had, for over eleven standard years, evaded the legally mandated punishment for what can only be called an atrocity. Any attempt to mistreat our personnel in response to it will carry the gravest consequences for those responsible when peace is restored to this quadrant. In addition, the People's Republic would point out that any such actions would, almost inevitably, lead to the worsening of conditions for prisoners of war on both sides. Honor Stephanie Harrington was a murderer on a mass scale, and it was for that crime, not any actions she might have performed as a member of the Star Kingdom of Manticore's armed forces since the outbreak of hostilities, that she was executed."

He stood a moment, then inhaled and nodded sharply.

"Thank you, citizens. That concludes my statement, My aides will distribute the video chips. Good day."

He turned and strode briskly away, ignoring the fresh babble of questions which rose behind him, and the HD blanked once more. Then Huertes' image returned, her expression even graver than before.

"That was the scene in the People's Tower this afternoon as Leonard Boardman, Second Deputy Directory of the Office of Public Information, speaking on behalf of the Committee of Public Safety, made the announcement which, frankly, had been anticipated for over two T-months by informed sources here in the People's Republic. What repercussions today's events may have on the military front is anyone's guess, but many usually reliable sources here in the capital have told INS off the record that they anticipate Manticoran retaliation and are prepared to respond in kind." She paused a beat, as if to let that sink in, then cleared her throat. "In the meantime, here is the HD imagery provided by the Office of Public Information. INS wishes once again to warn our viewers of the graphic and violent nature of what you are about to see."

The HD faded to black slowly, as if to give any members of INS' audience time to flee if they wished to . . . or to be sure that anyone who had been temporarily out of the room would have time to get back for the promised tidbit of violence. Then the display glowed back to life.

The scene was very different from the conference room in which Boardman had made his announcement. This room was much smaller, with bare walls and floor of unrelieved ceramacrete. It was high-ceilinged, and a rough wooden platform took up almost all its floor space. A flight of steps ran to the surface of the platform, and a rope—

free end looped into the traditional hangman's noose—dangled from the ceiling above the center of the platform. For several seconds, the HD showed only the empty room and the grimly functional gallows, but then the viewers heard the sudden, shocking sound of a door being thrown open and six people entered the camera's field of view.

Four men in the red-and-black uniform of State Security formed a tight knot about a tall, brown-haired woman in a bright orange prison jumpsuit. A fifth man, in the same uniform but with the insignia of a full colonel, followed them in, then turned to one side and stopped. He stood at a sort of parade rest, one foot beside an unobtrusive pedal set into the floor, and watched the prisoner being led across the room.

Her wrists were chained behind her, and more chains weighted her ankles. Her face showed no expression at all, but her eyes clung to the gallows, as if hypnotized by the sight, as her guards urged her forward. Her hobbled steps became slower and more hesitant as they neared the platform stair, and her expressionless mask began to crack. She turned her head, looking at the guards while desperation wavered in her eyes, but no one would look back. The StateSec men's faces were grim and purposeful, and as her resistance grew, they gripped her arms and half-led and half-carried her up the steps.

She began to pant as they forced her to the center of the platform, and she stared up at the rope, then, with a painful effort every viewer could actually feel, forced herself to look away. She closed her eyes, and her lips moved. She might have been praying, but no sound came out, and then she gasped and jerked as a black cloth hood was pulled down over her head. Her panting breath made the thin fabric jump like the breast of a terrified bird, and her wrists began to turn and jerk against their cuffs as the noose was lowered over the hood, snugged down about her throat, and adjusted with the knot behind one ear.

The guards released her and stood back. Her faceless figure swayed as the fully understandable terror of what was about to happen weakened her knees, and then the colonel spoke. His voice was harsh and gruff, yet there was an edge of compassion in it, like the tone of a man who dislikes what duty requires of him.

"Honor Stephanie Harrington, you have been convicted of the high crime against the People of premeditated murder. The sentence of the court is death, to be carried out this day. Do you wish to say anything at this time?"

The prisoner shook her head convulsively, chest leaping as she hyperventilated in terror, and the colonel nodded silently. He didn't speak again. He only reached out his foot and stepped firmly on the floor pedal with a heavy thrust of merciful quickness.

The sound as the trapdoor opened was a loud, shocking thunk! *and the grisly sound as the prisoner's weight hit the end of the rope was horribly clear. There was a short, explosive spit of air—a last, agonized gasp for breath, cut off in the instant of its birth—and then the brown-haired woman jerked once, hugely and convulsively, as the rope snapped her neck.*

The body hung limp, turning in a slow circle while the rope creaked, and the camera held on it for at least ten seconds. Then the HD went blank once more, and Huertes' soft contralto spoke from the blackness.

"This is Joan Huertes, INS, reporting from Nouveau Paris," it said quietly. The heartrending keen of thirteen treecats answered it, and the soft weeping of Miranda LaFollet and James MacGuiness, and Allison Harrington reached out a trembling hand to touch her husband's hair as his armor of denial crumbled at last and he fell to his knees beside her while he sobbed into her lap.

Book One

Chapter One

A Sphinxian would have considered the raw, autumn wind no more than brisk, but it was cold for this far south on the planet of Manticore. It swept in off Jason Bay, snapping and popping at the half-masted flags above the dense, silent crowds which lined the procession's route from Capital Field into the center of the City of Landing. Aside from the wind noise, and the whip-crack pops of the flags, the only sounds were the slow, mournful tap, tap, tap of a single drum, the clatter of anachronistic hooves, and the rattle of equally anachronistic iron-rimmed wheels.

Captain Junior-Grade Rafael Cardones marched at the horses' heads, his spine, ramrod straight, and his eyes fixed straight ahead as he led them down the stopped-time stillness of King Roger I Boulevard between lines of personnel from every branch of the service, all with black armbands and reversed arms. The crowd watched in unnatural, frozen stillness, and the solitary drummer—a fourth-term midshipwoman from Saganami Island in full mess dress uniform—marched directly behind the black-draped caisson. The amplified sound of her drum echoed back from the speaker atop each flagpole, and every HD receiver in the Manticoran Binary System carried the images, and the sounds, and the silence which somehow seemed to surround and swallow them both.

A midshipman from the same form walked behind the drummer, leading a third horse—this one coal black, saddled, with two boots reversed in the stirrups—and more people followed him, but not a great many. A single, black-skinned woman in the uniform of a captain of the list and the white beret of a starship commander walked behind the horse, gloved hands holding the jeweled scabbard of the Harrington Sword rigidly upright before her. Her eyes were bright with unshed tears, the sword's gems flashed in the fragile sunlight, and eight admirals—Sir James Bowie Webster, CO Home Fleet, and all seven uniformed Lords of the Admiralty—were at her heels. That was all. It was a tiny procession compared to the pomp and majesty the stage managers of the People's Republic might have achieved, but it was enough, for those twelve people and those three horses were the only sight and sound and movement in a city of over eleven million human beings.

Hats and caps were removed throughout the crowds of mourners, sometimes awkwardly, with an almost embarrassed air, as the cortege passed, and Allen Summervale, Duke of Cromarty and Prime Minister of the Star Kingdom of Manticore, stood beside Queen Elizabeth III on the steps of the Royal Cathedral and watched the slow-moving column approach. Very few of those watching the wheeled conveyance pass by had known what a "caisson" was before the newsies covering the funeral told them. Even fewer had known that such vehicles had once been used to tow artillery back on Old Earth—Cromarty had known only because one of his boyhood friends was a military history buff—or the significance they held for military funerals. But every one of those spectators knew the coffin the caisson bore was empty. That the body of the woman whose funeral they had come to share would never be returned to the soil of her native kingdom for burial. But that was not because she had been vaporized in the fury of naval combat or left to drift, forever lost in space, like so many of Manticore's sons and daughters, and despite the solemnity, and the quiet, and the grief flowing on the cold wind, Cromarty felt the anger and the fierce, steady power of the mourner's fury pulsing in time with the drum.

A sound like ripping cloth and distant thunder grumbled down from the heavens, and eyes rose from the procession as five Javelin advanced trainers from Kreskin Field at Saganami Island swept overhead. Bold, white contrails followed them across the autumn-washed blue sky, and then one of them pulled up, climbing away from the others, vanishing into the brilliant sun like a fleeing spirit, in the ancient "missing man" formation pilots had used for over two thousand years to mark the passing of one of their own.

The other four planes crossed directly over the cortege. Then they, too, disappeared, and Cromarty drew a deep breath and suppressed the urge to look over his shoulder. It wasn't really necessary, for he knew what he would see. The leaders of every political party, Lords and Commons alike, stood behind him and his monarch and her family, representing the solidarity of the entire Star Kingdom in this moment of loss and outrage.

Of course, he thought with carefully hidden bitterness, *some of them are here only because it is a funeral. Well, that and the fact that none of them quite dared turn down Elizabeth's "invitation."* He managed not to snort in disgust and reminded himself that a lifetime in politics had made him cynical. *No doubt it has. But I know as well as Elizabeth does that some of those people behind us are delighted by what the Peeps've done. They just can't admit it, because the voters would tear them apart at the polls if they did.*

He drew another deep breath as the procession finally entered the square before King Michael's Cathedral. The Star Kingdom's constitution specifically prohibited the establishment of an official state religion, but the House of Winton had been Second Reformation Roman Catholics for the last four centuries. King Michael had begun the construction of the cathedral which now bore his own name out of the royal family's private fortune in 65 After Landing—1528 Post Diaspora, by the reckoning of humanity at large—and every member of the royal family had been buried there since. The Star Kingdom's last state burial in King Michael's had been thirty-nine T-years before, after the death of King Roger III. Only eleven people from outside the royal house had ever been "interred" there, and of that eleven, three of the crypts were empty.

As the twelfth non-Winton crypt would be, Cromarty thought grimly, for he doubted, somehow, that Honor Harrington's body would ever be recovered, even after the People's Republic's defeat. But she would be in fitting company even then, he told himself, for the empty crypt which would be hers lay between the equally empty crypts of Edward Saganami and Ellen D'Orville.

The procession stopped before the cathedral, and a picked honor guard of senior Navy and Marine noncoms marched down the steps in perfect, metronome unison, timed by the endless, grieving taps of the drum. A petite, black-haired Marine colonel followed them, her movements equally exact despite a slight limp, and saluted the captain with the sword with parade-ground precision. Then she took the sheathed blade in her own gloved hands, executed a perfect about-face while the honor guard slid the empty coffin from the caisson, and led them back up the steps at the slow march.

The drummer followed, still tapping out her slow, grieving tempo, until her heel touched the very threshold of the Cathedral. Then the drumbeats stopped, in the instant that her foot came down, and the rich, weeping music of Salvatore Hammerwell's "Lament for Beauty Lost" welled from the speakers in its stead.

Cromarty inhaled deeply, then turned to face the mourners behind him at last. Queen Elizabeth headed them, with Prince Consort Justin, Crown Prince Roger and his sister, Princess Joanna, and Queen Mother Angelique. Elizabeth's aunt, Duchess Caitrin Winton-Henke, and her husband Edward Henke, the Earl of Gold Peak, stood just behind them, flanked by their son Calvin and Elizabeth's two uncles, Duke Aidan and Duke Jeptha, and Aidan's wife Anna. Captain Michelle Henke joined her parents and older brother after surrendering the sword at the foot of the Cathedral's steps, and the Queen's immediate family was complete. Only her younger brother, Prince Michael, was absent, for he was a Navy commander, and his ship was currently stationed at Trevor's Star.

Cromarty bowed to his monarch and swept one arm at the cathedral doors in formal invitation, and Elizabeth bent her own head in reply. Then she turned, and she and her husband led the glittering crowd of official mourners up the stairs and into the music behind the coffin.

"God, I hate funerals. Especially ones for people like Lady Harrington." Cromarty looked up at Lord William Alexander's quiet, bitter observation. The Chancellor of the Exchequer, the number-two man in Cromarty's cabinet, stood holding a plate of hors d'ouerves while he surveyed the flow and eddy of people about them, and the corners of Cromarty's mouth twitched. Now why, he wondered, was food always a part of any wake?

Could it be that the act of eating encourages us to believe life goes on? Is it really that simple?

He brushed the thought aside and glanced around. The protocolists' official choreography for the funeral and its aftermath had run its course. For the first time in what seemed like days, and despite the crowd about them, he and Alexander actually had something approximating privacy. It wouldn't last, of course. Someone would notice the two of them standing against the wall and come sweeping down on them to discuss some absolutely vital bit of politics or governmental business. But for now there were no eavesdropping ears to fear, and the Prime Minister allowed himself a weary sigh.

"I hate them, too," he admitted, equally quietly. "I wonder how the one on Grayson went?"

"Probably a lot like ours . . . only more so," Alexander replied.

In what was very possibly a first, the Protectorate of Grayson and the Star Kingdom of Manticore had orchestrated simultaneous state funerals for the same person. The concept of simultaneity might strike some as a bit pointless for planets thirty light-years apart, but Queen Elizabeth and Protector Benjamin had been adamant. And the fact that there was no body had actually simplified matters, for there had been no point in arguing over which of Honor Harrington's home worlds she would be buried upon.

"I was surprised the Protector let us borrow the Harrington Sword for our funeral," Cromarty said. "Grateful, of course, but surprised."

"It wasn't really his decision," Alexander pointed out. As Cromarty's political executive officer, he had been responsible for coordinating with Grayson through the Protector's ambassador to Manticore, and he was much more conversant with the details than Cromarty had had time enough to make himself. "The sword belongs to Harrington Steading and Steadholder Harrington, which meant the decision was Lord Clinkscales', not the Protector's. Not that Clinkscales would have argued with Benjamin—especially with her parents signing off on the request. Besides, they would've had to use two swords if they'd kept hers." Cromarty raised an eyebrow, and Alexander shrugged.

"She was Benjamin's Champion, as well, Allen. That made their Sword of State 'hers,' as well."

"I hadn't thought of that," Cromarty said, rubbing one eyebrow wearily, and Alexander snorted softly.

"It's not like you haven't had a few other things on your mind."

"True. Too damned true, unfortunately." Cromarty sighed again. "What have you heard from Hamish about his take on the Graysons' mood? I don't mind telling you that their ambassador scared the hell out of me when he delivered their official condolences, and the Protector's personal message to the Queen could've been processed for laser heads. I was distinctly glad that *I* wasn't a Peep after I viewed it!"

"I'm not surprised a bit." Alexander glanced around again, reassuring himself that no one was in a position to overhear, then looked at Cromarty. "That bastard Boardman played his 'no retaliation' card too damned well for my taste," he growled with profound disgust. "Even the neutrals who are usually most revolted by the Peeps' actions expect us, as the 'good guys,' to refrain from any kind of reprisals. But from what Hamish says, the entire Grayson Space Navy is all set to provide as much grist for the Peep propaganda mill as Ransom and her bunch could possibly hope for."

"Hamish thinks they'd actually abuse prisoners of war?" Cromarty sounded genuinely shocked, despite his own earlier words, for such behavior would be completely at odds with Grayson's normal codes of conduct.

"No, he doesn't expect them to 'abuse' their prisoners," Alexander said grimly. "He's afraid they'll simply refuse to *take* any after this." Cromarty's eyebrows rose, and Alexander laughed mirthlessly. "Our entire population has come together, at least temporarily, because the Peeps murdered one of our finest naval officers, Allen. But Harrington wasn't just an officer, however outstanding, to the Graysons. She was some kind of living icon for them . . . and they aren't taking it very calmly."

"But if we get into some sort of vicious circle of reprisal and counter-reprisal, the situation will play right into the Peeps' hands!"

"Of course it will. Hell, Allen, half the newsies in the Solarian League are already mouthpieces for the Peeps! Pierre's official line on domestic policy is much more palatable to the Solly establishment than a *monarchy* is. Never mind that we've got a participating democracy, as well, and the Peeps don't. Or that the official Peep line bears about as much resemblance to reality as I do to an HD heart-throb! *They're* a 'republic,' and *we're* a 'kingdom,' and any good oatmeal-brained Solly ideologue knows 'republics' are good guys and 'kingdoms' are bad guys! Besides, INS and Reuters funnel Peep propaganda straight onto the airwaves completely uncut."

"That's not quite fair—" Cromarty began, but Alexander cut him off with a savage snort.

"Bushwah, to use one of Hamish's favorite phrases! They don't even tell their viewers the Peeps are censoring every single report coming out of Haven or any other branch of the 'Office of Public Information,' and you know it as well as I do! But they sure as hell scream about it whenever we do the same thing to purely military reports!"

"Agreed, agreed!" Cromarty waved one hand, urging Alexander to lower his steadily rising volume, and the Chancellor of the Exchequer looked around quickly. His expression was a trifle abashed, but the anger in his blue eyes burned as brightly as ever. And he was right, Cromarty thought. Neither INS nor Reuters ever called the Peeps on their censorship . . . or, for that matter, on obviously staged "news events." But that was because they'd seen what happened when United Faxes Intragalactic insisted on noting that reports from the People's Republic were routinely censored. Eleven UFI staffers had been arrested for "espionage against the People," deported, and permanently barred from ever again entering Havenite space, and *all* of their reporters had been expelled from the core worlds of the Republic. Now they had to make do with secondary feeds and independent stringers' reports relayed through their remaining offices in the Havenite hinterland, and everyone knew the real reason for that. But no one had dared report it lest they find themselves equally excluded from one of the galaxy's hottest news zones.

The Star Kingdom had protested the conspiracy of silence, of course. In fact, Cromarty himself had argued vehemently with the Reuters and INS bureau chiefs in the Star Kingdom, but without effect. The bureau heads insisted that there was no need to inform viewers of censorship or staged news. The public was smart enough to recognize a put-up job when it saw one, and standing on principle over the issue would simply get them evicted from the Republic as well. Which, they pointed out somberly, would leave only Public Information's version of events there, with no independent reporting at all to keep its propaganda in check. Personally, Cromarty thought their highly principled argument in favor of "independent reporting," like their supposed faith in the discrimination of their viewers, was no more than a smokescreen for the all important ratings struggle, but what he thought didn't matter. Unless the Star Kingdom and the Manticoran Alliance wanted to try some equally heavy-handed version of "information management"—which their own news establishment would never tolerate—he had no way to retaliate. And nothing short of some sort of retaliation was going to grow the Solarian League's newsies a backbone.

"At least they're giving the funeral equal coverage," the Duke said after a moment. "That has to count for something—even with Sollies!"

"For about three days, maybe," Alexander agreed with another, scarcely less bitter snort. "Then something else will come along to chase it out of their public's infinitesimal attention span, and we'll be right back to the damage those gutless wonders are inflicting on us."

Cromarty felt a genuine flicker of alarm. He'd known the Alexander brothers since childhood, and he'd had more exposure to the famous Alexander temper than he might have wished. Yet this sort of frustrated, barely suppressed fury was most unlike William.

"I think you may be overreacting, Willie," the Duke said after a moment. Alexander eyed him grimly, and he went on, choosing his words with care. "Certainly we have legitimate reason to feel the Solarian news services are letting themselves be used by the Peeps, but I suspect their bureau chiefs are right, at least to an extent. Most Sollies probably do realize the Peeps often lie and take reports from the PRH with a largish grain of salt."

"Not according to the polls," Alexander said flatly. He looked around once more and leaned even closer to Cromarty, dropping his voice. "I got the latest results this morning, Allen. Two more Solarian League member governments have announced their opposition to the embargo and called for a vote to consider its suspension, and according to UFI's latest numbers, we've lost another point and a quarter in the public opinion polls, as well. And the longer the Peeps go on hammering away at their lies and no one calls them on it, the worse it's going to get. Hell, Allen! The truth tends to be awkward, messy, and complicated, but a well-orchestrated lie is almost always more consistent—or coherent, at least—and a *hell* of a lot 'simpler,' and Cordelia Ransom knows it. Her Public Information stooges work from a script that's had all its rough edges filed away so completely it doesn't bear much relationship to reality, but it sure as hell *reads* well, especially for people who've never found themselves on the Peeps' list of intended victims. And in a crazy sort of way, the fact that we keep winning battles only makes it even more acceptable to the Sollies. It's almost as if every battle we win somehow turns the Peeps more and more into the 'underdogs,' for God's sake!"

"Maybe," Cromarty agreed, then half-raised a hand as Alexander's eyes flashed. "All right, probably! But the more industrialized League governments have always been ticked off with us over the embargo, Willie. You know how much they resented the economic arm-twisting I had to do! Do you really think they need Peep propaganda to inspire them to speak up about it?"

"Of course not! But that's not the point, Allen. The *point* is that the polls indicate that we're drawing more fire from the member governments because we're losing support among the *voters* and the governments know that. For that matter, we've lost another third of a point right here in the Star Kingdom. Or we had, until the Peeps murdered Harrington."

His face twisted with the last sentence, as if with mingled shame for adding the qualifier and anger that it was true, but he met

Cromarty's eyes steadily, and the Prime Minister sighed. He was right, of course. Oh, the slippage was minor so far, but the war had raged for eight T-years. Public support had been high when it began, and it was still holding firm at well about seventy percent—so far. Yet even though the Royal Manticoran Navy and its allies had won virtually every important battle, there was no sign of an end in sight, and the Star Kingdom's much lower absolute casualty figures were far higher than the Peeps' relative to its total population, while the strain of the conflict was beginning to slow even an economy as powerful and diversified as Manticore's. There was still optimism and a hard core of determination, but neither optimism nor determination were as powerful as they had been. And that, little though he cared to admit it even to himself, was one reason Cromarty had pressed for a state funeral for Honor Harrington. She'd certainly deserved it, and Queen Elizabeth had been even more adamant than he had, but the temptation to use her death to draw the Manticoran public together behind the war once more—to use a cold-blooded atrocity to make them personally determined to defeat the People's Republic—had been irresistible for the man charged with fighting that war.

I guess that's why the tradition of waving the bloody shirt is so durable, he reflected grimly. *It works.* But he didn't have to like it, and he understood the tangled emotions so poorly hidden behind Alexander's eyes.

"I know," he sighed finally. "And you're right. And there's not a damned thing I can see to do about it except beat the holy living hell out of the bastards once and for all."

"Agreed," Alexander said, then managed a smile of sorts. "And from Hamish's last letter, I'd say he and the Graysons, between them, are just about ready to do exactly that. With bells on."

At that very moment, almost thirty light-years from Manticore, Hamish Alexander, Thirteenth Earl of White Haven, sat in his palatial day cabin aboard the superdreadnought GNS *Benjamin the Great* and stared at an HD of his own. A glass of bonded Terran whiskey sat in his right hand, forgotten while steadily melting ice thinned the expensive liquor, and his blue eyes were bleak as he watched the replay of the afternoon's services from Saint Austin's Cathedral. Reverend Jeremiah Sullivan had personally led the solemn liturgy for the dead, and the clouds of incense, the richly embroidered vestments and sternly, sorrowfully beautiful music, were a threadbare mask for the snarling hatred which hid behind them.

No, that's not fair, White Haven thought wearily, remembering his drink at last and taking a sip of the watered-down whiskey. *The hate's there, all right, but they really did manage to put it aside, somehow—for the length of the services, at least. But now that they've mourned her, they intend to* avenge *her, and that could be . . . messy.*

He set his glass down, picked up the remote, and went surfing through the channels, and every one of them was the same. Every cathedral on the planet, and virtually all of the smaller churches, as well, had celebrated the liturgy for the dead simultaneously, for Grayson was a planet which took its relationship with God—and its duty to Him—seriously. And as White Haven flipped his way past service after service, he felt the cold, hard iron of Grayson deep in his soul, too. Yet he was honest with himself, as well, and he knew why the iron was there. Why he was even more determined than they, perhaps, to avenge Honor Harrington's murder.

For he knew something neither the people of Grayson, nor his brother, nor his monarch, nor anyone else in the entire universe knew, and however hard he fought to, he could not forget it.

He knew *he* was the one who had driven her out to die.

Chapter Two

It was very late, and Leonard Boardman really should have been on his way home for a well-earned drink before supper. Instead, he leaned back in his comfortable chair and felt a fresh glow of pride as he watched the HD in his office replay Honor Harrington's execution yet again. It was, he admitted with becoming modesty, a true work of art—and well it should be, after over two weeks of fine-tuning by Public Information's best programmers. Boardman wouldn't have had a clue where to start on the technical aspects of building something like that, yet it had been his script and direction which the special effects experts had followed, and he was well-satisfied with his handiwork.

He watched it all the way through again, then switched off the HD with a small smile. Those few minutes of imagery not only filled him with a craftsman's satisfaction; they also represented a major victory over First Deputy Director of Public Information Eleanor Younger. Younger had wanted to seize the opportunity to attack Manty morale by having their computer-generated Harrington blubber, beg for mercy, and fight her executioners madly as she was dragged to the scaffold, but Boardman had held out against her arguments. They had plenty of file imagery of other executions to use as a basis, and they'd had stacks of HD chips of Harrington from the imagery Cordelia Ransom had shipped home to Haven before her unfortunate departure—in every sense of the word—for the Cerberus System. The techs had been confident that they could generate a virtual Harrington which would do anything Younger wanted and defy detection as a fake—after all, they'd produced enough "corrected" imagery over the last T-century—yet Boardman had been less certain. The Solarian news services had proven themselves too credulous to run checks on those corrections, but the Manties were much more skeptical. And their computer capability was better across the board than the People's Republic's, so if they saw any reason to subject the imagery to intensive analysis, they were all too likely to realize it was a fraud. But by letting her die with dignity—with just enough physical evidence of terror to undermine her reputation as some sort of fearless superhero—Boardman had executed a much subtler attack on Manty morale . . . and given it that ring of reality which should preclude any analysis. After all, if someone was going to go to all the trouble of producing false imagery, then surely they would have taken the opportunity to make their victim look smaller and more contemptible, wouldn't they? But they hadn't. This imagery felt right, without heaping gratuitous belittlement on Harrington's memory, which meant it offered nothing to make anyone on the other side question or doubt it for a moment.

That was important to Boardman as a matter of pride in workmanship, but even more significantly, his victory over Younger had to have strengthened his chances of outmaneuvering her to succeed Cordelia Ransom as Secretary of Public Information. He didn't fool himself into believing Ransom's successor would also inherit the power she had wielded within the Committee of Public Safety, but just the ministry itself would enormously enhance Boardman's personal power . . . and, with it, his chance of surviving and even prospering in the snake pit atmosphere of the city of Nouveau Paris.

Of course, the additional responsibilities which that power and authority would entail would pose fresh perils of their own, but every member of the bureaucracy's upper echelons faced *that* sort of hazard every day. The Committee of Public Safety and, especially, the Office of State Security, had a nasty habit of removing those who disappointed them. . . permanently. It wasn't as bad as it was in the military (or had been, before Esther McQueen took over as Secretary of War), but everyone knew someone who had vanished into StateSec's clutches for lack of performance in the People's cause.

But blame flowed downhill, Boardman reminded himself. And it would be much easier for Citizen Secretary Boardman to divert blame to an underling—to, say First Deputy Assistant Younger—than it had been for Second Deputy Assistant Boardman to avoid the blame someone else wanted to divert to *him*.

He chuckled at the thought and decided he had time to watch the execution just one more time before he left for the night.

Esther McQueen was also working late.

As a concession to her new job description, she wore sober and severely tailored civilian clothing, not the admiral's uniform to which she was entitled, but the workload hadn't changed, and she pushed her chair back and rubbed her eyes wearily as she reached the end of the most recent report. There was another one awaiting her, and another after that, and another, in a paperwork queue which seemed to stretch all the way from her Octagan office here on Haven to the Barnett System. Just thinking about all those other reports made her feel even more fatigued, but she also felt something she had not felt very often in the last eight years: hope.

It remained a fragile thing, that hope, yet it was there. Not evident to everyone else, perhaps, and certainly not to her civilian overlords, but there for eyes that knew (and had access to *all* the data) to see.

The Manticoran Alliance's momentum had slowed . . . possibly even faltered, if that wasn't too strong a verb. It was as if they'd gathered all their resources for the final lunge at Trevor's Star but now, having taken that vitally important system away from the Republic, they'd shot their bolt. Before her recall to Haven, she had expected Admiral White Haven to keep right on coming and cut the Barnett System off at the ankles, but he hadn't. Indeed, current reports from the Naval Intelligence Section of StateSec had him still in Yeltsin trying to organize a brand-new fleet out of whatever odds and ends the Star Kingdom's allies could contribute. And given all the other reports she now had access to, she could see why.

The door to her office hissed open, and she looked up with a wry smile as Ivan Bukato stepped through it with a folder of data chips under his arm. Under the old regime, Bukato would have been the People's Navy's chief of naval operations, but the CNO slot had been eradicated along with the other "elitist" trappings of the Legislaturalists. Under the New Order, he was simply Citizen Admiral Bukato, who happened to have all the duties and very few of the perks Chief of Naval Operations Bukato would have had.

He paused just inside the door, eyebrows rising as he found her still behind her desk. He wasn't really surprised, for like her other subordinates, he'd long since realized she routinely worked even longer and harder hours than she demanded of anyone else, but he shook his head chidingly.

"You really should think about going home occasionally, Citizen Secretary," he said in a mild voice. "Getting a good night's sleep every once in a while would probably do your energy levels a world of good."

"There's still too much crap to be hosed out of the stables," she told him wryly, and he shrugged.

"That's as may be, but I tend to doubt that you cut yourself this short on sleep at the front."

She grunted like a moderately irate boor in acknowledgment of a direct hit. But there were major differences between running the Republic's entire war office and commanding a front-line fleet. A fleet commander could never be positive when an enemy task force might suddenly appear out of hyper and come slashing in to attack her command area. She always had to be alert, ready for the possibility and with enough reserve energy in hand to deal with it. But a secretary of war was weeks behind the front line. By the time a decision was bucked all the way back to her, there was seldom any point in shaving a few minutes, or hours—or even days—off her response time. If the problem was that time-critical, then either the people at the front had already solved it, or else they were dead, and either way, there was damn-all *she* could do to reassemble Humpty-Dumpty from here. No, McQueen's job was to provide general direction, select officers she thought had the best shot at carrying out the missions assigned to them, pick the targets to aim them at, and then figure out how to keep those homicidal idiots at StateSec off their backs and get them the material support they needed while they got on with said missions. If she could figure out, in her copious free time, how to rebuild the Navy's morale, offset the technological inferiority of its weapon systems, magically replace the dozens of battle squadrons it had lost since the war began, and find a way to divert Manty attention from taking the rest of the Republic away from the Committee of Public Safety, that was simply an added benefit.

She smiled wryly at the thought, tipped her chair back, and folded her arms behind her head as she regarded Bukato with bright green eyes. She was still getting to know him—Rob Pierre and Oscar Saint-Just hadn't been so foolish as to let her shake up the existing chain of command by handpicking her senior subordinates herself—but they worked well enough together. And as his teasing tone had just indicated, he appeared to have begun feeling reasonably comfortable with her as his boss. Not that anyone would be stupid enough to let any *dis*comfort with a superior show in the current People's Republic. Especially when that boss was also a junior member of the Committee of Public Safety.

"I probably should try to keep more regular hours," she agreed, unfolding one arm long enough to run a hand over her dark hair. "But somehow or other, I've *got* to get a handle on all the problems my predecessor let grow like weeds."

"With all due respect, Citizen Secretary, you've already cut through more of the undergrowth than I would have believed possible a few months ago. That being the case, I'd just as soon not see you collapse from overwork and leave me with the job of breaking in still another Secretary of War."

"I'll try to bear that in mind," she said dryly, and smiled at him. Yet even as she smiled, that hidden part of her brain wondered where his personal loyalties lay. It was damnably hard to tell these days . . . and critically important. On the surface, he was as hardworking, loyal, and reliable a subordinate as a woman could ask for, but surface impressions were dangerous. In fact, his apparent loyalty actually made her uneasy, for she was perfectly well aware that most of the officer corps regarded her as dangerously ambitious. She didn't blame them for that—since she *was* ambitious—and she normally managed to win over her direct subordinates despite her reputation. But it usually took longer than this, and she couldn't help wondering how much of his seeming ease with her was genuine.

"In the meantime, however," she went on, letting her chair snap forward and reaching out to rest one hand on the heap of data chips on her desk, "I still have to get the overall situation and its parameters fixed in my mind. You know, I'm still more than a little amazed to discover how true it really is that the people at the sharp end of the stick are too close to the shooting to see the big picture."

"I know." Bukato nodded. "Of course, it's also true that the COs at the front usually do have a much better grasp of their own separate *parts* of the 'big picture.'"

"You're right there," she agreed feelingly, remembering her own mammoth frustration—and fury—with her superiors when she'd been the one fighting desperately to hang onto Trevor's Star. "But the thing that surprised me most was that the Manties aren't pushing any harder than they are. Until I got a chance to review these—" she tapped the data chips again "—and realized just how thinly stretched they are."

"I tried to make that same point to Citizen Secretary Kline before his, um, departure," Bukato said. "But he never seemed to grasp what I was trying to tell him."

He slid his own chip folio into her In basket, walked over to the chair facing her desk, and cocked an eyebrow in question, and McQueen nodded for him to be seated.

"Thank you, Citizen Secretary," he said, folding his long, lanky body into the chair, then leaned back and crossed his legs. "I have to admit," he went on in a much more serious tone, "that was one reason I was glad to see you replace him. Obviously, the civilian government has to retain the ultimate authority over the People's military forces, but Citizen Secretary Kline didn't have any military background at all, and sometimes that made it a bit difficult to explain things to him."

McQueen nodded. Privately, she was more than a little surprised by Bukato's willingness to say anything that could be taken as a criticism of the former citizen secretary. To be sure, Kline's removal from office was a sign he'd fallen out of favor, but Bukato had to be as aware as she was that StateSec must have bugged her office, and anything that even hinted that a senior officer harbored doubts about or contempt for a political superior could have dire consequences. Of course, he *had* covered himself with his pious observation about civilian authority, she reminded herself.

"I'd like to think that that's one difficulty you won't experience in our working relationship," she told him.

"I certainly don't expect to, Citizen Secretary. For one thing, as a serving officer in your own right, you know just how big the galaxy really is . . . and how much defensive depth we still have."

"I do. At the same time, however, I also know that we can't afford to keep on giving ground forever if we don't want morale to crumble," she pointed out. "And that applies to the civilians, as well as the military. The Fleet can't win this thing without the support of the civilian sector, and if the civilians decide there's no point in supporting people who just keep falling back—" She shrugged.

"Of course we can't," Bukato agreed. "But every system we lose is one more the Manties have to picket, and every light-year they advance inside the frontiers is another light-year of logistical strain."

"True. On the other hand, capturing Trevor's Star has already simplified their logistics immensely. Sooner or later, that's going to show up in their deployments."

"Um." It was Bukato's turn to grimace and nod. The capture of Trevor's Star had given the Manticoran Alliance possession of every terminus of the Manticore Wormhole Junction, which meant Manty freighters could now make the voyage from the Star Kingdom's home system to the front virtually instantaneously . . . and with no possibility of interception.

"No doubt it will show up eventually, Citizen Secretary," he said after a moment, "but for the moment, it's not going to help them a whole hell of a lot. They still have to cover the same defensive volume with the same number of available warships. Maybe even more importantly, they have to make certain they *hold* Trevor's Star after all the time and trouble they spent taking it in the first place. From my own reading of the intelligence reports, that's the real reason they sent White Haven off to organize an entirely new fleet at Yeltsin. They're keeping almost all of his old fleet right there at Trevor's Star to protect it."

"You're right," McQueen agreed. "For now, at least, it *is* distracting them from more offensive activities. But it's a dynamic situation, not a static one. By holding the system, they remove the threat of an invasion of the Manties' home system down the Junction. And that means they can start standing down those damned forts they built to cover the central terminus, which is going to free up one hell of a lot of trained manpower."

"But not immediately," Bukato countered with a smile, and McQueen smiled back. Neither of them had yet said anything astonishingly brilliant or insightful, but this sort of brainstorming had become a rarity in the current People's Navy. "Even if they shut the forts down tomorrow—or yesterday, for that matter—they can't actually use the fresh manpower against us until they build the ships for those people to crew."

"Exactly!" McQueen's eyes sparkled. "Of course, they can still build ships faster than we can. But we still have a lot more building slips than they do and our construction rates are going up. It may take us longer to build a given ship than it takes them, but as long as we can work on building more of them at the same time we've got a shot at matching their construction rate in total numbers of hulls. Add that to the fact that we can crew as many ships as we can build, whereas they have a hell of a lot smaller population base, and the 'big battalions' are still on our side . . . for now. But that infusion of additional crewmen from the forts is going to fuel one hell of a growth spurt in their front-line strength a year or so down the line. What we have to do is find a way to use the distraction aspect of their commitment at Trevor's Star against them before they can use the *benefits* of its possession against us."

"Ah?" Bukato cocked his head. "You sound as if you have a way to use it in mind," he observed slowly.

"I do . . . maybe," McQueen admitted. "One of the things I've just been reading over was the availability numbers on our battleships." Bukato grimaced before he could stop himself, and she chuckled. "I know—I know! Every single time someone's come up with a brilliant idea about how to use them, we've ended up with less battleships when the wreckage cooled. And, frankly, we lost an awful lot of them in the run up to Trevor's Star simply because we had no choice but to commit them to defensive actions against dreadnoughts and superdreadnoughts. But I was surprised to see how many we have left. If we strip the eastern sectors down to bedrock, we could assemble quite a fleet of them to support a core of real ships of the wall."

"You're thinking in terms of a counterattack," Bukato said quietly.

"I am," McQueen agreed. It was the first time she'd said a word about it to anyone, and intense interest flickered in Bukato's dark, deepset eyes. "I'm going to keep the exact point where I want to launch it my own little secret for a while longer," she told him, "but one of the jobs Citizen Chairman Pierre gave me was to improve the Fleet's morale. Well, if we can knock the damn Manties back on their heels at a place of our own choosing, even if it's only briefly, we should make a running start on that particular chore. It wouldn't hurt civilian morale, either, and that doesn't even count what it would do to *Manty* morale . . . or their future deployment considerations."

"I'd certainly have to agree with that, Citizen Secretary," Bukato said. "The tech transfers from the Solarian League have helped shake some of our people loose from their sense of inferiority, but most of them are still too defensive minded for my taste. We need more admirals like Tourville and Theisman, and we need to give them the support they require, then turn them loose."

"Um." McQueen nodded, but she couldn't hide a frown of displeasure as mention of Lester Tourville and Thomas Theisman reminded her of the whole Honor Harrington episode. She saw a flicker of concern flash across Bukato's face as her expression altered and quickly banished the grimace before he could decide it was directed at him for some reason.

And it's not as if the affair was a total *disaster*, she reminded herself. *You know damned well Ransom was going to purge Tourville and his entire staff—if not Theisman as well—for trying to protect Harrington from StateSec. At least the paranoid bitch managed to get her worthless ass killed before she did any more damage to the Fleet! And it also means I don't have to fight her tooth and nail over every tiny move I make, either. On the other hand, StateSec is treating Tourville and his people as if* they *were the ones who killed her!* Count Tilly*'s been back from Cerberus for almost four months now, and her entire crew's* still *sequestered while Saint-Just's security goons "investigate" the episode. Idiots!*

"I realize Citizen Admiral Theisman is still a bit . . . old-fashioned," Bukato said, responding to her frown, "but his record in combat is exemplary, Citizen Secretary, and the same is true of Tourville. I hope you don't intend to let any rumors or partial reports keep you from—"

"Relax, Citizen Admiral," McQueen said, waving a hand in the air between them, and he shut his mouth quickly. "You don't have to sell me on Tourville or Tom Theisman—not as fleet commanders, anyway. And I have no intention of making them any sort of fall guys for what happened to Citizen Secretary Ransom. Whatever anyone else might think, I know—and I've seen to it that Citizen Chairman Pierre and Citizen Secretary Saint-Just know, as well—that none of what happened was their fault." *Or I* think *I've made certain of that, at any rate. Saint-Just* says *he's more worried about keeping* Tilly*'s crew "out of the public eye until we make Cordelia's death official," at least. Whether he actually* means *it or not, though . . .*

She studied Bukato a moment, then shrugged mentally. She was doing all she could for Tourville, and it wasn't the very smartest thing she could discuss with Bukato. But perhaps the time had come to test the waters with him in a different way.

"I only wish I could have convinced the Committee to countermand Citizen Secretary Ransom's plans for Harrington," she said. "We might have avoided the entire mess if she'd been willing to let the Navy have custody of Harrington instead of dragging her off to Camp Charon to hang her!"

Bukato's eyes widened at the genuine vitriol in the last sentence. The new Secretary of War was taking a major chance in offering a subordinate access to her inner thoughts—especially if those thoughts were critical of the Committee of Public Safety or any of its members, present or past. Of course, it could also be—in fact, it almost certainly was—a test of him as well. The problem was that he didn't know exactly what he was being tested for. Loyalty to the Committee, which might be demonstrated by denouncing her? Or loyalty to the Navy and his service superior (assuming that those weren't actually two quite different things), which might be demonstrated by keeping his mouth shut?

"I wasn't privy to that decision, Citizen Secretary," he said very slowly, choosing his words with exquisite care. Then he decided to throw out a feeler of his own. "Nonetheless, it did seem . . . questionable to me."

"Not to me," McQueen snorted. She saw a flash of anxiety in his eyes and grinned tightly. "It seemed goddamned *stupid* to me," she said, "and I told Citizen Chairman Pierre and Citizen Secretary Saint-Just as much at the time."

Surprised respect showed in Bukato's expression, and she hid a chuckle. She hadn't expressed herself quite that candidly to them, but she'd come close to it. If StateSec listened to the audio chips she was sure they were making, her version would be near enough to Saint-Just's recollections (or the chips he might have made of *that* meeting, assuming he was sufficiently paranoid for that—and he was) to stay on the safe side of accurate. And from the look on Bukato's face, her willingness to be candid with him on such a topic had just raised her stock with him considerably.

"Mind you, it wasn't their idea, and I don't think they cared for it, either," she went on, always conscious of those hidden microphones. "But she was a member of the Committee, and she'd already dumped the story and her intention to execute Harrington into the Solly news feeds. And that whole Leveler business was barely four T-months old at the time. I don't have to tell you how that had shaken things up, and they felt their only choice was to back her up rather than risk having the rest of the galaxy think we had potentially serious divisions at the top or invite another coup attempt from our domestic enemies. Which is also why they had Public Information fake up that whole hanging scene."

"I have to admit, I didn't quite understand the reasoning behind that," Bukato said. "I hope you'll pardon me for saying this, but it seemed gratuitous to me."

"'Gratuitous,'" McQueen snorted. "In some ways, that's not a bad word for it, I suppose. And I imagine it will motivate at least some of the Manties to seek revenge. But the decision was made over at Public Information, and I'd have to say that PubIn was the proper place for it to be made. They're in a better position to judge its effect on civilian and neutral opinion than those of us in the Navy are."

Somehow the bitter twist of her mouth didn't quite match her thoughtful, serious tone, and Bukato was surprised by the sparkle of laughter he felt deep inside. No doubt anyone listening to the chips would hear exactly what she wanted them to, but she did have a way of getting her actual meaning across anyway.

And I suppose there was *a little rationality in faking Harrington's execution,* he thought. *At least this way we don't have to admit that—what? thirty?—POWs staging an unsuccessful jail break managed to completely destroy an entire battlecruiser all by themselves! God only knows what making* that *public knowledge would do to our morale, even if it* was *only a StateSec ship. Not to mention what the damage to StateSec's reputation for invincibility might do the next time they got ready to suppress some poor bastards. And whether we hanged her or not, she's still dead. We couldn't bring her back even if we wanted to, so I guess we might as well get a little propaganda mileage out of it if we can. And assuming it was the sort of mileage we wanted in the first place. If it was.*

He shook free of his thoughts and looked at the new Secretary of War again, trying to read what was going on behind those green eyes of hers. He knew her reputation, of course. Everyone did. But so far he'd seen remarkably little evidence of her famed political ambition, and she'd accomplished more to straighten out the Navy's mess in the bare six T-months since being officially named Secretary of War than Kline had managed in over four T-*years.* The professional naval officer in Ivan Bukato couldn't help admiring—and appreciating that, yet he sensed a crossroads looming in his own future. She hadn't just happened to come out of her shell tonight. She really was testing him, and if he let himself be drawn into a feeling of loyalty to her, the consequences could prove . . . unfortunate. Even fatal.

And yet . . .

"I understand, Ma'am," he said quietly, and saw her eyes flicker. It was the first time he'd used the traditional, "elitist" courtesy instead of calling her "Citizen Secretary." Technically, she was entitled to it as a member of the Committee of Public Safety, but staying away from the form of address the Navy had been denied among its own ever since the Harris Assassination had seemed the better part of valor.

"I'm glad you do, Ivan," she said after a moment, and saw the answering understanding in his eyes as she used his given name for the very first time. The first step of the intricate dance had been accomplished. Neither of them could be certain yet where the dance would end, but the first step was always the most important one. Yet it was also time to cover her backside just a little more, and she smiled sardonically at Bukato even as she made her voice come out seriously and thoughtfully. "We're going to have to make some pretty tough decisions of our own when it comes to recommending purely military policy. I realize political and diplomatic decisions are going to have an impact on the military equation, but frankly, until we get our own shop up and running properly, I'm delighted that I don't have to concern myself with nonmilitary policy. Time enough to worry about fine-tuning our coordination with the diplomats once we're confident we can hold the Manty bastards where they are!"

"Of course, Ma'am," Bukato agreed, and the two of them smiled thinly at one another.

Chapter Three

Long experience had taught Petty Officer first-class Scott Smith to collect his battered locker from the heap outside the personnel shuttle's cargo tube, activate its counter-grav, and tow it safely out of the way before he did anything else. Only after accomplishing that did he look for the directions board. His searching eyes found it, and he crossed the concourse to it, then kept one hand resting lightly on the locker as he studied the flashing information. There it was: HMS *Candice*, the same name as on his transfer orders. He grimaced. He still didn't have the least damned idea what a "*Candice*" was, but he didn't like the ring of it.

Sounds like the candied-apple kind of name that should belong to some damned armed merchant escort, he snorted mentally. *Or maybe a tender. A tug?* He shrugged irritably. *Hell of a name for a warship, anyway. And why the hell couldn't they just leave me aboard* Leutzen? *It took me three damned T-years to get that slot, and now they yank me out of it for God knows what.*

He grimaced again, but orders were orders. He double-checked the display for the right color-coded guide strip and set glumly off through the bowels of Her Majesty's Space Station *Weyland* for his destination.

Lieutenant Michael Gearman watched the tallish, fair-haired PO 1/c walking down the color guide in front of him and cocked an eyebrow in speculation. He and the noncom had arrived on the same shuttle, and he wondered if they were headed for the same destination. It seemed probable, but *Weyland* was a big place—not as large as *Vulcan* or *Hephaestus*, but still the better part of thirty kilometers long. It was also tucked away orbiting Gryphon, otherwise known as Manticore-B–V, which had caused a few of Gearman's hospital buddies to groan in sympathy when they heard about his travel orders. Gryphon was the least Earth-like of the Manticore

System's three habitable planets. It had required far more terraforming than Manticore or Sphinx, and its extreme axial tilt gave its weather an unenviable reputation among the inhabitants of its sister planets. Worse, from the viewpoint of certain Navy hotshots, its sparsely scattered population was noted for regarding the sissies who lived on the Star Kingdom's other worlds with a certain contempt. That attitude, unfortunately, carried over into the local civilians' attitude towards visiting military personnel in search of diversion and, coupled with the lack of anything like real cities, left those same military personnel with a limited selection of off-duty entertainment possibilities.

But that was all right with Gearman. After nineteen months of regen therapy, he'd had about all the leave he could stand. He was eager to get back to work, and whatever his commiserating friends might have to say about Manticore-B's being the armpit of the Manticore Binary System, he suspected his new assignment might be far more interesting than they expected. It had become traditional over the last twenty or thirty T-years for the Royal Navy to assign its more sensitive R&D prototypes to *Weyland*'s technical support teams, mainly because the secondary component of the binary system saw so much less foreign shipping traffic. Manticore-B's massive asteroid belts supported a very heavy industrial presence, and huge freighters hauled both finished components and massive loads of raw materials from its orbital smelters to Manticore-A. But the main freight transshipment points for the Star Kingdom orbited either Manticore or Sphinx, and that was where the vast majority of the out-kingdom shipping stayed. For the most part, Gryphon was served even in peacetime by short-haul Manticoran-flag freighters which plied back and forth between it and the rest of the Star Kingdom, and the Navy had made the complete prohibition of non-Manticoran hulls in Manticore-B space official once the shooting started.

Which was why BuShips and BuWeaps liked building and testing prototypes at *Weyland*. The Office of Naval Intelligence still couldn't *guarantee* secrecy, but at least the Fleet didn't have to worry about which putatively neutral freighters in the area were actually spying for the Peeps. Not that Gearman had any hard evidence that his assignment was to any such hush-hush project. On the other hand, he'd checked the last available ship list when he got his new orders, and there was no "HMS *Candice*" on it. Of course, the names of new construction were pretty much classified since the war had begun, and someone of his rank hardly had access to the latest, most up-to-date information. But the fact that the name didn't appear on any of the prewar lists suggested that whatever else *Candice* was, she had to be less than eight years old. (*Or*, a corner of his mind insisted upon adding, *a merchant conversion bought in after the war began. Bleh.*) Add that to the fact that his orders had given him absolutely no hint of what his duties aboard her would be (which was, to say the least, unusual), and all sorts of interesting possibilities began to trickle through his mind.

He grinned at his own imagination and walked briskly onward.

"Scooter!"

PO Smith looked up in astonishment as someone shouted his nickname, and then he grinned widely as a familiar face blended out of the crowd. The short, hairy, apelike, amazingly ugly man looked as if he ought to walk on his knuckles. He also wore undress coveralls like Smith's own, with the same three chevrons on his sleeve, and the name patch above his breast pocket said "MAXWELL, RICHARD."

"Well, well! If it isn't the Man Who Dropped the Spanner!" Smith observed, reaching out to shake a hirsute paw, and Maxwell grimaced.

"Give me a break, Scooter! That was—what? Six damn T-years ago?"

"Really?" Smith's gray eyes glinted devilishly. "It seems like just yesterday. Maybe that was because the results were so . . . spectacular. And expensive. I don't get to see a drive room main bus bar short out everyday, you know."

"Oh, yeah? Well, one of these days I'm gonna be there when *you* screw the pooch, Scooter!"

"In your dreams, Silver Spanner. In your dreams."

"Pride goeth, buddy," Maxwell said darkly.

"Ha!" Smith deactivated his locker's counter-grav and let it sink to the deck, then looked around curiously. He'd expected the deck guide to lead him to *Candice*'s slip; instead, it had deposited him in a cavernous boat bay gallery, which indicated his new ship wasn't currently docked with the space station, and he cocked an eyebrow at Maxwell.

"You got any idea what it is we're up to, Maxie?" he asked much more seriously. "I asked around, but the people I talked to knew zero-zip about it."

"Dunno," Maxwell admitted, removing his black beret to scratch the right side of his head. "Friend of mine in BuShips told me the *Candice* is a new, long-range repair ship—a high-speed job, like maybe she's designed to go in the fleet train for a cruiser raiding force or something. Aside from that, I don't know a damned thing. Hell, I don't even know what I'm gonna be doing once I get aboard!"

"You neither, huh?" Smith frowned. RMN personnel orders usually contained at least a brief section on the duty slot one was to be assigned to, not just a ship name with no additional information. Leaving that out of one set of orders could have been simple bureaucratic sloppiness; leaving it out of two started sounding a lot more like a deliberate security measure. But if *Candice* was only a repair ship, even some new, hot-shot model, then what was there to be secretive about? And if—

"Attention Personnel Draft Seven-Seven-Six-Two," the voice of the boat bay officer crackled suddenly from the gallery speakers. "First call for transportation to HMS *Candice*. The shuttle will depart in fifteen minutes from Personnel Tube Blue Four. Repeat. Transportation to HMS *Candice* will depart in fifteen minutes from Personnel Tube Blue Four."

"Guess we better get going," Maxwell observed, and the two of them set off down the gallery, towing their lockers behind them. Smith was in the lead as they approached the designated personnel tube, and he groaned aloud as he saw what rested in the docking buffers on the other side of the thick armorplast wall.

"What?" Maxwell asked, unable to see around his taller friend, and Smith sighed.

"It's a damned trash hauler," he said glumly. "Crap! You'd think they could at least give us a shuttle with *windows!*"

"A shuttle's a shuttle," Maxwell said with a dismissive shrug. "I don't need windows. I've already seen a space station, and I've already seen a repair ship. All I hope is the run over is long enough for me to get a little shuteye."

"Maxie, you're a cretin," Smith said sourly.

"'Course I am!" Maxwell agreed cheerfully, then frowned in sudden suspicion. "What's a cretin?" he demanded.

"Ten-*hut!*"

Captain Alice Truman watched the remote view on her briefing room display as the knife-edged command cut through the confused hum which had filled the gallery of HMS *Minotaur*'s Boat Bay Three. The newest draft of enlisted and noncommissioned personnel for Project Anzio snapped to attention along the lines painted on the deck with spinal reflex suddenness, their speculations about their new assignments slashed off by the familiar command. The woman who had given it had three chevrons and three rockers on the sleeve of her immaculate uniform. The golden anchor of a boatswain's mate floated between them, instead of the star most branches used, and the uppermost rocker carried the embroidered crown which marked her as a senior master chief, the highest noncommissioned rank the RMN offered. Now she looked the block of silent men and women over with an utterly expressionless face, then folded her hands behind her and paced slowly down the length of the block's front row. She reached the end, paused rocking on her heels, then stalked back to the center of the row and smiled thinly.

"Welcome aboard your new ship," she told them in a pronounced Gryphon accent. "My name is McBride. *Bosun* McBride." Her audience was silent, digesting the fact that she had just announced that she was the senior noncommissioned member of their new ship's company and, as such, the direct designated representative of God, and she smiled once more. "For those of you who have not already figured this out, you are *not* aboard a repair ship. Nor *will* you be aboard a repair ship. No doubt this is deeply disturbing to you, and I know all you poor little lost lambs are confused and curious about what you're doing here. Well, I'm sure the Skipper feels nothing in the universe could possibly be more important than explaining it all to you. Unfortunately, she has a ship to run, and she's just a little busy at the moment, so I'm afraid you're going to have to make do with *me*, instead. Does anyone have a problem with that?"

A falling pin would have sounded like an anvil in the silence that answered her, and her smile became something like a grin.

"I didn't think anyone would." She raised her right hand and snapped her fingers, and half a dozen petty officers stepped forward with memo boards under their arms. "When you hear your name called, answer to it and fall in behind whoever called it," she went on more briskly. "They'll get you logged into quarters and give you your slots on the watch bill. Don't drag ass about getting yourselves squared away, either, people! There will be an orientation briefing for all new personnel at twenty-one-hundred, and I *will* be checking attendance."

McBride gazed out over the newcomers for another ten seconds, then nodded, and a brawny senior chief stepped up beside her and keyed his board alive.

"Abramowitz, Carla!" he read.

"Yo!" A woman near the rear of the formation raised a hand and stepped forward with her locker while people moved apart in front of her to let her pass.

"Carter, Jonathan!" the senior chief read, and Truman switched off the display and looked up as her executive officer ushered two lieutenants, one a JG, and a lieutenant commander into her briefing room.

"Our new arrivals, Ma'am." Like the Bosun, Commander Haughton was from Gryphon, although his accent was less severe, and Truman cocked her golden-haired head as the three officers formed a line in front of the clear-topped briefing room conference table and came to attention. She could see burning curiosity in all three sets of eyes and hid a small, amused smile.

"Lieutenant Commander Barbara Stackowitz, reporting for duty, Ma'am!" the gray-eyed, brown-haired woman at the end of the line said crisply, and Truman nodded to her, then looked at the next officer in line.

"Lieutenant Michael Gearman, reporting for duty, Captain," he said. He was dark-haired and eyed, thin and just a little stooped looking, and there was an aura of intensity about him. Truman nodded once more and cocked an eyebrow at the final newcomer.

"Lieutenant Ernest Takahashi, reporting for duty, Ma'am!" Takahashi was small, even darker than Gearman, and wiry, with eyes so dark brown they looked black. He was also the most junior of the three new arrivals, and though his curiosity was as evident as that of the other two, there was a sort of relaxed confidence in his body language. Not complacency, but the look of someone who was used to getting things right the first time.

"At ease, people," Truman said after a moment, and watched their shoulders relax. She smiled and glanced at the exec. "Paperwork all in order, John?"

"Yes, Ma'am. Your yeoman has it now."

"Good." Truman smiled. "I feel confident that Chief Mantooth will dispose of it with all her customary efficiency." She looked back at the newcomers, then waved a hand at the chairs facing her from the far end of the table.

"Sit," she said, and they obeyed.

She tipped her own chair back and let herself consider them afresh while her mind went back over the personnel uploads she'd already studied.

Stackowitz was a tac branch officer who was supposed to be some sort of missile genius. The fact that she'd served a hitch as CO of a light attack craft was icing on the cake. She was earmarked for a slot on Captain (Junior-Grade) Jacquelyn Harmon's staff, but Truman planned to borrow her quite often. Her oval face was strong boned, with a firm mouth and level eyes. At the moment, she seemed a little tense, almost edgy, but that was understandable enough. Not one of these people had been given the slightest hint of what their new assignments were all about, and though the shuttle's lack of view ports had kept them from getting a glimpse of their new ship on approach, they had to have begun to realize they were aboard a most unusual vessel.

Gearman, on the other hand, was almost calm looking. He was clearly curious, but his intensity was a deeper thing, not a reflection of anxiety. Perhaps it would be more accurate to call it focus, Truman mused. He was also deeply and darkly tanned—thanks, no doubt, to the rehab camp to which Bassingford Medical Center's physical therapists had sent him to complete his recovery. She'd watched him carefully when he walked into the office, and there was no limp at all to indicate the left leg he'd lost when Peep fire put the superdreadnought *Ravensport* permanently out of the war at First Nightingale. He'd been *Ravensport*'s third engineer, but before that, as a JG, he'd spent almost a year as a LAC engineering officer.

And then there was Takahashi. Only a lieutenant (junior-grade), he was here because he'd graduated number one in his class from Kreskin Field Flight School (despite an awesome award of demerits over a certain incident concerning the Kreskin flight simulators) and then displayed a dazzling natural ability at the controls of every small craft he'd touched since leaving the Academy. His last post had been as an assault shuttle section leader aboard the big Marine attack transport *Leutzen*, where his piloting virtuosity had no doubt been properly appreciated. Under other circumstances, he would probably have stayed there for at least another year, but Truman and Project Anzio had first call on his talents.

"All right," she said finally, breaking the silence before it became intimidating, "first, allow me to welcome all of you aboard the *Minotaur*." Stackowitz blinked, and Truman smiled crookedly. "There is indeed an HMS *Candice*," she assured them, "but I very much doubt any of you will ever set foot aboard her. She's also a prototype of sorts, but a repair ship, not a warship. She's currently assigned to *Weyland* for evaluation and to serve as the training vessel for similar follow-on units, but she's usually out swanning around somewhere else in the local system to give her trainees lots of practice. She also has a complement of around six thousand, which, coupled with her erratic movement schedule, makes her an excellent cover for us. People don't wonder why new drafts have to be shuttled out to her, and her crew's big enough—and transient enough—that we can cycle quite a lot of people through without anyone noticing it."

Truman let that sink in, and the three junior officers glanced at one another, eyes busy with speculation. She watched them calmly, comparing their reactions to those of all the other officers with whom she'd had this same discussion. So far, they were about standard.

"There really is a reason for all the secrecy, people," she told them quietly after a moment. "In a few minutes, Commander Haughton—" she nodded at the blond, brown-eyed exec, who had seated himself at her right hand "—will see to it that each of you gets introduced to your department heads, who will give you a more detailed description of what we're doing and what your specific duties will be. Given the nature of our job here, however, I prefer to handle my new officers' initial briefings myself, so make yourselves comfortable."

She smiled as they settled back in their chairs. Takahashi was the only one who looked anything like genuinely relaxed, but the other two made a good show of obeying her injunction, and she let her own chair come back upright and folded her hands on the table before her.

"*Minotaur* is the first unit of a new, experimental class," she told them. "I realize you didn't get a look at her before you came aboard, so here she is now." She pressed a button on the keyboard at her data terminal, and a razor-sharp holo image appeared above the table. Heads turned as her newest subordinates looked, and she saw Stackowitz's eyes narrow in surprise.

Truman didn't blame her, for no one had ever seen another ship quite like HMS *Minotaur*. She was obviously a warship—she had the telltale hammerhead ends—and she massed almost exactly six million tons. That put her in the upper third of the dreadnought range, yet even a casual glance was enough to tell anyone that whatever *Minotaur* might be, she was certainly no dreadnought. The rows of enormous hatches on her flanks were much too big to be normal broadside weapons bays, and they were arranged in a pattern whose like none of them had ever before seen.

"People," Truman said softly, "you have just become members of the crew of the first LAC-carrier of the Royal Manticoran Navy." Gearman's head whipped back around. He stared at her, and she smiled crookedly. "That's correct, Mr. Gearman. A LAC-carrier. May I assume you've at least heard rumors about the light attack craft our Q-ships have been using in Silesia?"

"Uh, yes, Ma'am," the lieutenant said after a brief glance at his fellow newcomers. "But 'rumors' are *all* I've heard. Nobody ever said anything about anything like . . . this." He gave a tiny wave towards the holo image, and Truman chuckled, but then her smile faded.

"If anyone had mentioned it to you, Mr. Gearman, he or she would have been in violation of the Official Secrets Act. A restriction, by the way, which now applies to each of *you*. You are now officially assigned to Project Anzio, and our job is to get *Minotaur*—and her LAC wing—on-line, and then to prove the concept. In order to even further safeguard security on this endeavor, we will be leaving for Hancock Station as soon as our first two squadrons of LACs have come on board. The fleet base there will support our efforts, and since ours are the only people with any interest in Hancock these days, sending us there should keep 'neutral' eyes from seeing us and running home to Nouveau Paris to tattle. Clear?"

Heads nodded, and she let her chair tip back once more.

"Good," she said, and waved at the holo image. "As you can see, *Minotaur*—and, by the way, none of you had better let *me* hear you refer to her as 'the *Minnie*'—is an unusual design. Originally, BuShips wanted to build a much smaller experimental model with which to prove the concept, but the projections always called for a dreadnought-sized hull for the final units, and Vice Admiral Adcock sold Admiral Danvers on building her full size. His exact words, I believe, were 'The best scale for an experiment is ten millimeters to the centimeter!' " She smiled again. "So here we are.

"As I'm sure you've noticed," she went on in the tones of a Saganami Island lecturer as she stood and used an old-fashioned light-pointer to pick out details on the holo, "she has no broadside armament at all—aside from her LACs, of course. She masses just under six million tons, with an overall length of two-point-two klicks and a maximum beam of three hundred and sixty-seven meters. Our offensive shipboard armament is restricted to our chase mounts, which, however, are quite heavy: four grasers and nine missile tubes each, fore and aft. On the broadside, we mount only anti-missile defenses and the LAC bays, which—at the moment—are empty."

Lieutenant Commander Stackowitz frowned, and Truman chuckled. The tac officer looked up quickly at the sound, and the captain smiled at her.

"Don't worry, Commander. We do have a main battery . . . and the first part of it is almost ready to embark. But the Powers That Be felt—correctly, I think—that *Minotaur* needed a shakedown cruise of her own. That's what we've spent the last two T-months doing while the Hauptman and Jankowski cartels finished building our LACs at Hauptman's Unicorn Yard."

Understanding flickered in the eyes of all three newcomers. The Unicorn Belt was the innermost—and richest—of Manticore-B's three asteroid belts, and the Hauptman Cartel's Gryphon Minerals, Ltd., subsidiary owned about thirty percent of it outright, with long-term leases on another third. The cartel had built enormous extraction centers and smelters to service its mining operations, and there had been persistent rumors even before the war that Hauptman Yards, Ltd., the shipbuilding unit of the mighty cartel, had been using its Unicorn Yard to build experimental Navy units well away from prying eyes. And the Jankowski Cartel, though far smaller than Hauptman's, was highly specialized and a major player in the Navy's R&D operations in its own right.

In fact, Gearman thought, *Jankowski's who handled the major share of R&D on adapting the Grayson compensator design for the Fleet, aren't they?*

"*Minotaur*'s core ship's company is only six hundred and fifty," Truman went on, and her new subordinates blinked, for that was barely seventy percent of the crew assigned to most heavy cruisers five percent her size. "We've managed this by building in a much higher degree of automation than BuShips was prepared to accept prewar, and, of course, by eliminating all broadside weapons. In addition, we carry only a single company of Marines instead of the battalion normally assigned to a DN or an SD. On the other hand, our current TO&E calls for us to embark approximately three hundred additional shipboard personnel to provide permanent engineering and tactical support to the LAC wing. That, Commander Stackowitz, is where you will come in."

The dark-haired woman cocked an eyebrow and Truman showed her teeth.

"You have a reputation as a real hotshot at missile tactics, Commander, and I understand you spent six months attached to Project Ghost Rider. Is that correct?"

Stackowitz hesitated a moment, then nodded.

"Yes, Ma'am, I did," she said. "But that entire project is very tightly classified. I don't know if I should, well—" She gestured apologetically to the other officers present, and Truman nodded back at her.

"Your caution is admirable, Commander, but these gentlemen will become quite familiar with Ghost Rider over the next few weeks. For our sins, we're slated to play test bed for the first fruits of *that* project, as well. That can wait until later, however. For the moment, what matters is that while you'll be an asset to *Minotaur*'s own tactical department because of your, um, special knowledge, your primary duty assignment will be as Tac-One to the LAC wing."

"Yes, Ma'am."

"As for you, Lieutenant Gearman," Truman went on, turning to the tanned engineer, "you're slated for the squadron engineer's slot in Gold Squadron. That's the command element for the wing, and I imagine you'll be serving as Captain Harmon's engineer aboard Gold One, as well. That seems to be the way things are shaping up, at any rate."

"Yes, Ma'am." Gearman nodded sharply, thoughts already whirring behind his eyes as he contemplated his new, totally unexpected assignment.

"And as for you, Lieutenant Takahashi," Truman went on, fixing the junior-grade lieutenant with a stern eye, "you're slated as Gold One's helmsman. From what I've seen of your record, I expect you'll be playing a major part in setting up the basic software for the simulators, as well, and I strongly advise you *not* to incorporate any elements from that 'surprise scenario' you put together for Kreskin Field."

"Yes, Ma'am! I mean, no, Ma'am. Of course not!" Takahashi said quickly, but he also grinned hugely at the thought of the marvelous new toys the Navy was going to let him play with, and Truman glanced up at Commander Haughton. The exec only shook his head in resignation, and she laughed mentally at his expression as he contemplated the beatifically smiling young lieutenant.

"All right," Truman said more briskly, recapturing her audience's attention, "here's what our LACs will look like."

She punched more buttons, and *Minotaur*'s holo vanished. A new image replaced it almost instantly—a sleek, lethal shape that looked as if it should have come from deep water with a mouth full of fangs—and all three of the junior officers straightened in their chair as its unconventionality registered.

The most immediately obvious point about it was that, except for the absence of anything remotely like an airfoil, the sharp-prowed vessel looked more like an enormously overgrown pinnace than a normal LAC, for it lacked the flared, hammerhead bow and stern of all impeller-drive warships. The next point to penetrate was that it had absolutely no broadside weapons bays—or point defense stations. But perhaps the most astounding point of all almost sneaked past unnoticed, for the vessel in that holo image had only half as many impeller nodes as it should have. No LAC was hyper-capable, so there had never been any need to fit them with the alpha nodes of true starships. But for over six centuries, a full strength drive ring for any impeller warship had mounted sixteen beta nodes. Everyone knew that.

Except that this LAC didn't. There were only eight nodes in each of its rings, although they looked a little larger than they should have been.

"This, people," Truman said, gesturing once more with the light-pointer, "is the lead unit of the *Shrike*-class. She masses twenty thousand tons, and, as I'm sure you've noticed," the pointer reached into the HD, "there have been some changes, including the omission of the standard hammerheads. That's because this vessel's primary energy armament is right here." The pointer touched the small ship's sleek prow. "A one-point-five-meter spinal mount equipped with the latest grav lenses," she told them, watching their eyes, "which permits her to carry a graser—*not* a laser—approximately as powerful as that mounted in our *Homer*-class battlecruisers."

Gearman sucked in sharply at that. Not surprisingly, Truman thought. Chase energy weapons were always among the most powerful any warship carried, but the graser she had just described had an aperture fifty-six percent greater than chasers mounted in most light cruisers six times the *Shrike*'s size. But she'd heard the same reaction from someone in almost every group she'd briefed on the new LACs, and she ignored the sound of surprise and continued in that same Saganami Island voice.

"The power of this weapon is made possible because it is the only offensive energy weapon she mounts, because her missile armament has been substantially downsized, because her impeller node mass has been cut by forty-seven percent, and because her crew is even smaller than that normally assigned to a LAC. Her entire complement will consist of only ten people, which allows a major reduction in life support tonnage. In addition, her normal reactor mass bunkerage has been omitted."

She paused, and Gearman looked at her with a very strange expression. She only waited, and finally he shook his head.

"Excuse me, Ma'am. Did you say her bunkerage had been *omitted?*"

"Aside from that required for her reaction thrusters, yes," Truman confirmed.

"But—" Gearman paused, then shrugged and took the plunge. "In that case, Ma'am, just what does she use to fuel her fusion plant?"

"She doesn't have one," Truman told him simply. "She uses a fission pile."

Three sets of eyebrows flew up as one, and Truman smiled thinly. Humanity had abandoned fission power as soon as reliable fusion plants became available. Not only had fusion posed less of a radiation danger, but hydrogen was one hell of a lot easier and safer (and cheaper) than fissionables to process. And, Truman knew, Old Earth's Neo-Luddite lunatics, who'd been doing their level best to abolish the very concept of technology as somehow inherently evil about the time fusion power first came along, had managed to brand fission power with the number of the beast as *the* emblem of all that was destructive and vile. Indeed, the rush to fusion had been something much more akin to a stampede, and unlike most of the claptrap the Neo-Luddites had spouted, fission power's evil reputation had stuck. Contemporary journalists had taken the negatives for granted at the time, since "everyone knew" they were true, and no popular historian had been particularly interested in reconsidering the evidence since, especially not when the technology was obsolete, anyway. So for most of the human race, the very concept of fission power was something out of a dark, primitive, vaguely dangerous, and only dimly remembered past.

"Yes, I said 'fission,'" Truman told them after giving them most of a minute to absorb it, "and it's another thing we've adapted from the Graysons. Unlike the rest of the galaxy, they still use fission plants, although they've reduced their reliance on them steadily for the last thirty or forty years. But Grayson—and, for that matter, Yeltsin's asteroid belts, as well—are lousy in heavy metals . . . and fissionables. They'd bootstrapped their way back to fission power by the time of their Civil War, and by the time the rest of us stumbled across them again and reintroduced them to fusion, they'd taken their *fission* technology to levels of efficiency no one else had ever attained. So when we added modern, lightweight antiradiation composites and rad fields to what they already had, we were able to produce a plant which was even smaller—and considerably more powerful—than anything they'd come up with on their own.

"I don't expect anyone to be installing them on any planetary surfaces any time soon. For that matter, I doubt we'll see too many of them being installed in capital ships. But one of the new plants handily provides all the power a *Shrike* needs, and despite all the bad-history bogeyman stories about fission, disposal of spent fuel elements and other waste won't be any particular problem. All our processing work is being done in deep space, and all we have to do with our waste is drop it into a handy star. And unlike a fusion plant, a fission pile doesn't require a supply of reactor mass. Our present estimate is that a *Shrike*'s original power core should be good for about eighteen T-years, which means the only practical limitation on the class's endurance will be her life support."

Gearman pursed his lips in a silent whistle at that. One of a conventional LAC's several drawbacks was that its small size prevented it from cramming in anything like the bunkerage of regular warships. RMN battlecruisers could take on sufficient reactor mass for almost four months, but they were specifically designed for long-range, deep penetration raids as well as convoy protection. A light attack craft, on the other hand, was fortunate to be able to stow sufficient hydrogen for a three-week deployment, which made her dreadfully short-legged compared to her betters. But if she only had to refuel every eighteen years—!

"It sounds impressive, Ma'am," he said after a moment, "but I don't know a thing about fission power."

"Neither does anyone else off Grayson, Mr. Gearman—outside the teams which have been developing the new piles for us, that is. We only have fully trained crews for ten or twelve of our LACs; the others will be trained here aboard *Minotaur* and the Hancock Station fleet base, and we've been fully equipped with the necessary simulators. We also have a suitable training cadre from the Jankowski Cartel to help you engineering types ease into things. You'll have about three T-weeks between here and Hancock to get your toes wet, and current plans call for you and your fellow engineers to be properly familiarized with your new equipment within three months, at which time we will begin our actual hands-on training with the LACs." She shrugged. "Ass-backwards, I know. You should have been trained on the new plants before *Minotaur*'s keel was even laid. But even though Project Anzio has been given the highest priority, certain, ah, hardware aspects of it have refused to cooperate as much as we might have wished. And to be honest, some of the security types were always happier with the idea that all the training would take place aboard *Minotaur*, well away from any prying eyes, and not in simulators aboard a shipyard somewhere."

She considered—briefly—mentioning the entrenched opposition of certain senior officers who saw the entire LAC concept as a useless diversion of resources and manpower from more practical (and traditional) weapons mixes. But the temptation was brief. None of this trio had the seniority to become involved in that kind of high-level internecine strife, and there was no point in worrying them over it.

"But if we're not checked out on the power plants, how—?" Gearman began, then cut himself off with a blush. A prudent lieutenant did not press a captain of the list for information she chose not to offer, but Truman only smiled once more.

"How will we get them aboard without power?" she asked, and he nodded. "We won't," she said simply. "We'll be taking eighteen of them aboard before we leave for Hancock; the remaining units of the wing have already departed for that system, tucked away in the cargo holds of half a dozen freighters. Does that answer your question?"

"Uh, yes, Ma'am."

"Good. Now, if you'll look back at the holo," Truman went on, "you'll notice these projections here." The pointer's light beam swept over a series of eight open-mouthed, elongated blisters, just aft of the forward impeller ring and placed so that they aligned with the spaces between the ring's nodes. "These are missile tubes," she told them. "These four big ones—" the pointer tapped "—are anti-ship launchers, each equipped with a five-round 'revolver' magazine. The *Shrike* only has twenty shipkillers, but she can launch one from each tube every three seconds." It was Stackowitz's turn to purse her lips silently, and Truman's pointer indicated the other four tubes. "These are for counter-missiles, and the reduction in normal missile armament lets us fit in seventy-two of those. In addition, if you'll notice here—" the pointer touched the sleek prow again. "These are point defense laser clusters: six of them, in a ring around the graser emitter."

"Excuse me, Captain. May I ask a question?" It was Takahashi, apparently emboldened by her earlier response to Gearman, and she nodded to him. "Thank you, Ma'am." He paused for a moment, as if searching for exactly the right words, then spoke carefully. "What I'm seeing here seems to be a huge pinnace or assault shuttle, Ma'am, with all its armament fixed forward." She nodded again, and he shrugged. "Isn't it just a little, um . . . risky for something as small as a LAC to cross it's own 'T' whenever it fires at an enemy starship, Ma'am?"

"I'll let your department officers handle the nuts and bolts, Lieutenant," she said, "but in general terms, the answer is yes and no. As presently envisioned, doctrine calls for the *Shrikes* to approach regular warships at an oblique angle, denying the enemy anything like a down-the-throat or up-the-kilt shot. One reason they were designed with no broadside armament was to avoid weakening their sidewalls with gunports. In addition, I'm sure you've all noticed the reduced number of drive nodes."

She tapped the forward drive ring with the pointer, and three heads nodded as one.

"These are another innovation—for now we're calling them 'Beta-Squared' nodes—which are much more powerful than older nodes. In addition, they've been fitted with a new version of our FTL com—one with a much higher pulse repetition rate—which should make the *Shrikes* very useful as manned long-range scouts. I imagine we'll be seeing something like it in larger ships in the not too distant future. What matters for our present purposes, however, is that the new nodes are very nearly as powerful as old-style *alpha* nodes, and we've also built much heavier sidewall generators into the *Shrike* to go with them. The result is a sidewall which is about five times as tough as anything ever previously mounted in a LAC.

"In addition, these ships are fitted with very extensive ECM and a suite of decoys which cost almost as much as the main hull does. All our simulations say that they'll be very difficult missile targets even at relatively short ranges, and particularly if they're supported by additional decoy and jammer missiles. We're currently looking at whether it will be more effective to provide conventional warships to supply those missiles or whether it will make more sense to load them into the LACs' own tubes at the cost of reducing their load-outs on shipkillers.

"And finally, the R&D boffins have come up with something really nice for these ships." Truman smiled at her audience like a shark. "As we all know, it's impossible to close the bow or stern aspect of an impeller wedge with a sidewall, right?" Heads nodded once again. "And why is that, Lieutenant Takahashi?" she asked genially.

The lieutenant looked at her for a moment, with the expression of someone whose Saganami Island days were recent enough in memory to make him wary of leading questions. Unfortunately, she was a senior-grade captain and he was only a junior-grade lieutenant, which meant he had to answer her anyway.

"Because cutting off the stress bands' n-space pocket with a closed wedge prevents you from accelerating, decelerating, or using the wedge to change heading, Ma'am," he replied. "If you want the math—?"

"No, that's all right, Lieutenant," she said. "But suppose you don't want to accelerate or decelerate? Couldn't you generate a 'bow' sidewall then?"

"Well, yes, Ma'am, I suppose you *could*. But if you did you'd be unable to change—" Takahashi stopped speaking suddenly, and Lieutenant Commander Stackowitz gave a sharp, abrupt nod.

"Exactly," Truman told them both. "The idea is that LACs will attack single starships in sufficient numbers that it will always be possible for them to close obliquely. The new missile tubes, coupled with the recent improvements in seekers, molycircs that can handle higher-grav vector shifts, and a higher acceptable delay between launch and shipboard fire control's hand-off to the missile's on-board systems, will let them fire effectively at up to a hundred and twenty degrees off bore. That means the *Shrikes* can engage with missiles—and launch countermissiles against incoming fire—even on an oblique approach. Once they reach energy range, however, they turn directly in towards their targets and bring up their 'bow' sidewall . . . which has only a single gunport, for the graser, and is twice as powerful as the broadside sidewalls. That makes it as tough as most dreadnought's sidewalls, people, and according to the Advanced Tactical Course's simulators, a target as small as a bow-on LAC should be much harder to hit than a larger warship engaging broadside-to-broadside even under normal circumstances. When you add the sort of electronic warfare capabilities these ships have, they turn into even harder targets, and the presence—and power—of their 'bow' sidewalls should make them harder to kill even if the bad guys do manage to lock them up."

She paused for a moment, then went on in a much more somber voice.

"Nonetheless, a good shot will hit even a difficult target, and if one of these LACs is hit by almost anything, it will be destroyed. So once we commit them to action, we *will* lose some of them, people. But even if we lose a dozen of them, that's only a hundred and twenty people—a third of a destroyer's crew and less than six percent of a *Reliant*-class battlecruiser's crew. And between them, those twelve LACs will have twenty-one percent more energy weapon firepower than a *Reliant*'s broadside. Of course, they won't have a fraction of the battlecruiser's missile power, and they *have* to get to knife range to really hurt the enemy. No one is trying to say they can magically replace capital ships, but all the projections and studies say that they can be a major enhancement to a conventional wall of battle. They should also be able to provide us with a local defense capability that can stand up to raiding Peep squadrons and let us pull our regular capital ships off picket duty, and their range and endurance on station should also make them invaluable for raids behind the enemy's frontier."

Her three newest subordinates gazed at her, clearly still struggling to take in all the information she'd just dropped on them. But there was a glow in their eyes, as well, as they began to envision the possibilities she'd enumerated . . . and to wonder what else they could figure out to do with the new units.

"Captain?" Stackowitz half-raised a hand, asking permission to speak, and Truman nodded. "I was just wondering, Ma'am—how many LACs will *Minotaur* carry?"

"Allowing for docking buffers and umbilical service points, the total mass cost per LAC, including its own hull, is about thirty-two thousand tons," Truman said in an almost off-hand tone. "Which means we can only carry about a hundred of them."

"A *hun—?*" Stackowitz cut herself off, and Truman smiled.

"A hundred. The wing will probably be divided into twelve eight-LAC squadrons, and we'll carry the other four as backups," she said. "But I think you can see what kind of force multiplier we're talking about if a single carrier *Minotaur*'s size can put that many of them into space."

"I certainly can, Ma'am," Stackowitz murmured, and the other two nodded firmly.

"Good!" Truman said again. "Because now, people, the trick is to make it all work out as nice and pretty as the planners and the sims say it should. And, of course," she bared her teeth at them, "as nice and pretty as *I* say it should, too."

Chapter Four

"Lord Prestwick and Lord Clinkscales, Your Grace," the secretary said, and Benjamin Mayhew IX, by God's Grace Planetary Protector of Grayson and Defender of the Faith, tipped back in the comfortable chair behind the utilitarian desk from which he ruled Grayson as his Chancellor stepped through the door the secretary politely held open.

"Good morning, Henry," the Protector said.

"Good morning, Your Grace," Henry Prestwick replied, and moved aside to allow the fierce-faced, white-haired old man who had accompanied him to enter. The second guest carried a slender, silver-headed staff and wore a silver steadholder's key on a chain about his neck, and Benjamin nodded to him in greeting.

"Howard," he said in a much softer voice. "Thank you for coming."

The old man only nodded back almost curtly. From anyone else, that would have been a mortal insult to Benjamin Mayhew's personal and official dignity, but Howard Clinkscales was eighty-four T-years old, and sixty-seven of those years had been spent in the service of Grayson and the Mayhew Dynasty. He had served three generations of Mayhews during that time, and, until his resignation eight and a half T-years before, had personally commanded the Planetary Security Forces which had guarded Benjamin himself from babyhood. *And even if he hadn't,* Benjamin thought sadly, *I'd cut him all the slack there was right now. He looks . . . terrible.*

He hid his thoughts behind a calm, welcoming expression and waved a hand for his guests to be seated. Clinkscales glanced at Prestwick for a moment, then took an armchair beside the coffee table while the Chancellor sat on the small couch flanking the Protector's desk.

"Coffee, Howard?" Benjamin offered while the secretary hovered. Clinkscales shook his head, and Benjamin glanced at Prestwick, who shook his head in turn. "Very well. You can go, Jason," he told the secretary. "See to it that we're not disturbed, please."

"Of course, Your Grace." The secretary bobbed brief but respectful bows to each guest, then a deeper one to Benjamin, and exited, closing the old-fashioned manual door of polished wood quietly behind him. The soft click of its latch seemed thunderous in the silent office, and Benjamin pursed his lips as he gazed at Clinkscales.

The old man's unyielding, weathered face had become a fortress against the universe, and loss had carved deep new lines in it, like river water eroding bedrock. There was grief behind the old eyes—an angry, furious grief, its expression chained and restrained by sheer strength of will yet seething with power . . . and pain. Benjamin understood not only the sorrow but the anger and the pain, as well, and he'd wanted to give Clinkscales time to deal with them in his own way. But he could wait no longer.

And even if I could have waited, I don't think he ever will *"deal" with them on his own.*

"I imagine you know why I asked you here, Howard," he said finally, breaking the silence at last. Clinkscales looked at him for a moment, then shook his head, still without speaking, and Benjamin felt his jaw tighten. Clinkscales had to know at least roughly what the Protector wanted, and the fact that he'd brought along the staff, which symbolized his duty as Regent of Harrington Steading, only confirmed that he'd guessed the reason for his summons. But it was as if by not admitting that consciously, even to himself, he could make that reason go away, cease to exist.

But he can't, Benjamin told himself grimly, *and neither can I, and we both have duties. Damn it, I don't* want *to intrude on his grieving, but I can't let that weigh with me right now.*

"I think you do know, Howard," he said after a moment, his voice very level, and dark color flushed Clinkscales' cheeks. "I deeply regret the events and considerations which require me to bring it up, yet I have no choice but to deal with them. And neither do you, My Lord Regent."

"I—" Clinkscales' head jerked at the title, as if recoiling from a blow. He looked at his Protector for a brief eternity, and then the fury waned in his eyes, leaving only the grief. In that instant he looked every day of his age, and his nostrils flared as he drew a deep, painful breath. "Forgive me, Your Grace," he said softly. "Yes. I . . . do know. Your Chancellor—" Clinkscales lips twitched in a brief parody of a smile as he nodded at his old friend and colleague "—has been prodding at me for weeks."

"I know." Benjamin's voice had softened as well, and he met Clinkscales' gaze levelly, hoping that the old man saw the matching pain and loss in his own eyes.

"Yes, well. . . ." Clinkscales looked away again, then straightened his shoulders and heaved himself up out of his chair. He took his staff in both hands, crossed to the desk, held it out before him on open palms, and spoke the formal phrases he had hoped never to have to speak.

"Your Grace," he said in a quiet voice, "my Steadholder has fallen, leaving no heir of her body. As her Steading was given into her hands from yours, so the responsibility to govern it in her absence was given into my hands from hers. But—" he paused, the formal legal phrases faltering, and closed his eyes for a moment before he could go on. "But she will never reclaim her Key from me again," he went on huskily, "and there is none other for whom I may guard it or to whom I may pass it. Therefore I return it to you, from whom it came by God's Grace, to hold in keeping for the Conclave of Steadholders."

He reached out, offering the staff, but Benjamin didn't take it. Instead, he shook his head, and Clinkscales' eyes widened. It was rare on Grayson for a steadholder to perish without leaving any heir, however indirect the line of succession. Indeed, it had only happened three times in the planet's thousand-year history—aside from the massacre of the Fifty-Three which had begun the Civil War . . . and the attainting of the Faithful which had concluded it. But the precedent was there, and Benjamin's refusal of the staff had thrown Harrington Steading's Regent completely off balance.

"Your Grace, I—" he began, then stopped himself and looked questioningly at Prestwick. The Chancellor only looked back, and Clinkscales returned his attention to the Protector.

"Sit back down, Howard," Benjamin said firmly, and waited until the old man had settled back into his chair, then smiled without humor. "I see you *don't* know exactly why I asked you to come by."

"I thought I did," Clinkscales said cautiously. "I didn't want to admit it, but I thought I knew. But if it wasn't to surrender my staff, then I have to admit I don't have the least damned idea what you're up to, Benjamin!"

Benjamin smiled again, this time with a touch of true amusement. The acerbic edge creeping into Clinkscales voice, like the use of his own given name, sounded much more like the irascible old unofficial uncle he'd known for his entire life.

"Obviously," he said dryly, and glanced at Prestwick. "Henry?" he invited.

"Of course, Your Grace." Prestwick looked at Clinkscales with something suspiciously like a grin and shook his head. "As you can see, Howard, His Grace intends to leave the scut work and the explanations up to me again."

"Explanations?"

"Um. Recapitulation, perhaps." Clinkscales' eyebrows rose, and Prestwick pursed his lips. "Our situation here may be a bit closer to unique than you actually realize, Howard," he said after a moment.

"Unusual, certainly," Clinkscales replied, "but surely not 'unique'!

I discussed it at some length with Justice Kleinmeuller." His eyes darkened once more as memories of that discussion with Harrington Steading's senior jurist brought the fresh, bleeding pain back, and he swallowed, then shook his head like an angry old bear. "He explained the Strathson Steading precedent to me quite clearly, Henry. Lady Harrington—" he got the name out in an almost level voice "—left no heirs . . . and that means the Steading escheats to the Sword, just as Strathson did seven hundred years ago."

"Yes, and no," Prestwick said. "You see, she did leave heirs—quite a few of them, actually—if we want to look at it that way."

"Heirs? *What* heirs?" Clinkscales demanded. "She was an only child!"

"True. But the extended Harrington family is quite extensive . . . on Sphinx. She had dozens of cousins, Howard."

"But they're not Graysons," Clinkscales protested, "and only a Grayson can inherit a steadholder's key!"

"No, they're not Graysons. And that's what makes the situation complicated. Just as you discussed it with Justice Kleinmeuller, His Grace and I have discussed it with the High Court. And according to the Court, you're right: the Constitution clearly requires that the heir to any steading must be a citizen of Grayson. That, however, is largely because the Constitution never contemplated a situation in which a foreign citizen *could* stand in the line of succession for a steading. Or in which an off-worlder could have been made a steadholder in the first place, for that matter!"

"Lady Harrington was not an 'off-worlder'!" Clinkscales said stiffly, eyes flashing with anger. "Whatever she may have been born, she—"

"Calm down, Howard," Benjamin said gently before the old man could work himself up into full-blown wrath. Clinkscales subsided, and Benjamin waved a hand in a brushing gesture. "I understand what you're saying, but she most certainly was an off-worlder when we offered her her steadholdership. Yes, yes. I know the situation was unprecedented—and, if I recall correctly, *you* were less than enthralled with it at the time, you stiff-necked, reactionary old dinosaur!"

Clinkscales blushed fiery red, and then, to his own immense surprise, he laughed. It wasn't much of a laugh, and it came out rusty and unpracticed sounding, but it was also his first real one in the two and a half months since he'd viewed Honor Harrington's execution, and he shook his head.

"That's true enough, Your Grace," he admitted. "But she became a Grayson citizen when she swore her Steadholder's Oath to you."

"Of course she did. And if I choose to use that as a precedent, then what I ought to do is send for her closest heir—her cousin Devon, isn't it, Henry?—and swear him in as her successor. After all, if we could make her a Grayson, we can make him one, as well."

"No!" Clinkscales jerked upright in his chair as the instant, instinctive protest burst from him, and Benjamin cocked his head at him, expression quizzical. The Regent flushed again, but he met his Protector's gaze steadily. He said nothing else for several seconds while he organized his thoughts, getting past instinct to reason. Then he spoke very carefully.

"Lady Harrington was one of ours, Your Grace, even before she swore her oath to you. She made herself ours when she foiled the Maccabean plot and then stopped that butcher Simmonds from bombarding Grayson. But this cousin—" He shook his head. "He may be a good and worthy man. Indeed, as Lady Harrington's cousin, that's precisely what I would expect him to be. But he's also a foreigner, and whatever his worth in other ways, he hasn't *earned* her Steading."

"'Earned,' Howard?" Benjamin flicked a hand. "Isn't that a rather high bar for him to have to clear? After all, how many steadholders' heirs 'earn' their Keys instead of simply inheriting them?"

"I didn't mean it that way," Clinkscales replied. He frowned in thought for another moment, then sighed. "What I meant, Your Grace, was that our people—our world—still have a great many stiff-necked, reactionary old dinosaurs. A lot of them sit in the Conclave of Steadholders, which would be bad enough if you laid this before them, but a lot more are common citizens. Many of them were uncomfortable with Lady Harrington as a steadholder, you know that at least as well as I do. But even the uncomfortable ones were forced to admit she'd earned her position . . . and their trust. My God, Benjamin—you gave her the swords to the Star of Grayson yourself!"

"I know that, Howard," Benjamin said patiently.

"Well how in the Tester's name is this—Devon, did you say?" Benjamin nodded, and the old man shrugged irritably. "All right, how is this Devon going to earn that same degree of trust? He'll certainly be seen as an off-worlder, and the people who felt 'uncomfortable' with Lady Harrington will feel one hell of a lot worse than that with him! And as for the real reactionaries, the ones who still hated and resented *her* for being an off-worlder—!"

Clinkscales threw up his hands, and Benjamin nodded gravely. He let no sign of it show, but he was privately delighted by the strength of the Regent's reaction. It was the strongest sign of life he'd shown in weeks, and it was obvious his brain was still working. He was following straight down the same chain of logic Benjamin and Prestwick had pursued, and the Protector gestured for him to continue.

"It would have been different if she'd had a son of her own," Clinkscales went on. "Even if he'd been born off world, he still would have been *her* son. It would have been better if he'd been born here on Grayson, of course, but the bloodline and order of succession would have been clear and unambiguous. But this—! I can't even begin to guess where this can of worms would take us if you laid it before the other Keys. And 'Mayhew Restoration' or not, you do realize you'd have no option but to lay it before the other steadholders, don't you?"

"Certainly, but—"

"But nothing, Benjamin," Clinkscales growled. "If you think you could get the hidebound faction in the Conclave to sign off on this, then all that fancy off-world schooling is getting in the way of your instincts again! By your own admission, you'd have to set a new—*another* new—constitutional precedent just to make it work! And whatever Mueller and his crew may have said to her face, they never really forgave her for being a foreigner, and a woman, and the spear point for your reforms. They'd never swallow another foreigner—and one who *doesn't* have the Star of Grayson!"

"If you'll let me finish a sentence, Howard," Benjamin said even more patiently, eyes glinting as the old, irascible Clinkscales reemerged completely once more, "I was trying to address that very point."

"You were?" Clinkscales regarded him narrowly, then sat back in his chair.

"Thank you. And, yes, you're absolutely right about how the other Keys would react to any decision of mine to pass the Harrington Key to an 'off-worlder.' And I don't know enough about this Devon Harrington to begin to predict what sort of steadholder he'd make, either. I understand he's a history professor, so he might do better than anyone would expect. But it might also mean that, as an academic, he's totally unprepared for the command responsibilities a steadholdership entails."

"Well, Lady Harrington was certainly prepared for *that* part of it," Prestwick murmured, and Benjamin snorted.

"That she was, Henry. That she most certainly was, Comforter keep her." He paused for a moment, eyes warm with memory now, and not dark with grief, then shook himself. "But getting back to Professor Harrington, there's the question of whether or not it ever even crossed his mind that he might inherit from her. Do we have a right to turn his entire life topsy-turvy? Even if we asked him to, would he accept the Key in the first place?"

"But if we don't offer it to him, we may open still another Pandora's Box," Prestwick said quietly. Clinkscales looked at him, and the Chancellor shrugged. "Under our treaty with Manticore, the Protectorship and the Star Kingdom are mutually pledged to recognize the binding nature of one another's contracts and domestic law—including things like marriage and inheritance laws. And under Manticoran law, Devon Harrington is Lady Harrington's heir. He's the one who will inherit her Manticoran title as Earl Harrington."

"And?" Clinkscales prompted when Prestwick paused.

"And if he does want the Harrington Key and we don't offer it to him, he might sue to force us to surrender it to him."

"*Sue* the Protector and the Conclave?" Clinkscales stared at him in disbelief, and the Chancellor shrugged.

"Why not? He could make an excellent case before our own High Court . . . and an even better one before the Queen's Bench. It would be interesting to see which venue he chose and how the case was argued, I suppose. But then, I imagine watching a bomb count down to detonation beside you is probably 'interesting' while the adventure lasts, too."

"But . . . but you're the *Protector!*" Clinkscales protested, turning back to his liege, and Benjamin shrugged.

"Certainly I am. But I'm also the man trying to reform the planet, remember? And if I'm going to insist that my steadholders give up their autonomy and abide by the Constitution, then I have to abide by it, as well. And the constitutional precedent on this point is unfortunately clear. I can be sued—not in my own person, but as Protector and head of state—to compel me to comply with existing law. And under the Constitution, treaties with foreign powers have the force of law." He shrugged again. "I don't really think a suit would succeed before our own High Court, given our existing inheritance laws, but it could drag on for years, and the effect on the reforms and possibly even on the war effort could be most unfortunate. Or he could sue in a Manticoran court, in which case he might well win and leave our government at odds with the Star Kingdom's while both of us are fighting for our lives against the Peeps. Not good, Howard. Not good at all."

"I agree," Clinkscales said, but his eyes were narrow again. He put the heel of his staff between his feet and grasped its shaft in both hands, leaning forward in his chair, while he regarded his Protector with suspicion. "I agree," he repeated, "but I also know you pretty well, Your Grace, and I feel something nasty coming. You've thought this through already, and you'd decided what you wanted to do before you ever summoned me, hadn't you?"

"Well . . . yes, actually," Benjamin admitted.

"Then spit it out, Your Grace," the old man commanded grimly.

"It's not complicated, Howard," Benjamin assured him.

"Will you *please* stop trying to 'prepare' me and get on with it?" Clinkscales growled, and added, "Your Grace," as an afterthought.

"All right. The solution is to transfer the Harrington Key to the Grayson who has the best claim on it . . . and the most experience in carrying it, at least by proxy," Benjamin said simply.

Clinkscales stared at him in utter silence for fifteen seconds, and then jerked to his feet.

"*No!* I was her Regent, Benjamin—only her *Regent!* I would never— It would— Damn it, she *trusted* me! I could never . . . never *usurp* her Key! That would—"

"Sit down, Howard!" Command cracked in Benjamin's voice for the first time, and the three words cut Clinkscales off in mid protest.

He closed his mouth, still staring at the Protector, then sank back into his chair once more, and a fragile silence hovered.

"That's better," Benjamin said after a moment, so calmly it was almost shocking. "I understand your hesitation, Howard. Indeed, I expected it—which is the very reason I was trying to 'prepare' you, as you put it. But you wouldn't be 'usurping' anything. Tester, Howard! How many other men on Grayson have given the Sword half—even a tenth!—of the service you have? You're the best possible choice from almost every perspective. You've earned any honor I could bestow upon you in your own right, and you were Lady Harrington's Regent and the *de facto* Steadholder whenever her naval duty took her off-planet. She trusted you, and you know exactly what her plans and hopes were—who else can say that? And she loved you, Howard." Benjamin's voice softened, and a suspicious brightness glistened in Clinkscales' eye before the old man looked away. "I can't think of another man on Grayson whom she would rather have succeed her and look after her people for her."

"I—" Clinkscales began, only to stop and draw another deep breath. He kept his face turned away for several seconds, then made his eyes come back to meet his Protector's.

"You may be right," he said very quietly. "About how she felt, I mean. And I would gladly have 'looked after her people *for* her' to my dying day, Benjamin. But please don't ask this of me. *Please.*"

"But, Howard—" Prestwick began persuasively, only to stop as Clinkscales raised a hand, silencing him with a gesture, and met Benjamin's gaze with infinite dignity.

"You are my Protector, Benjamin. I honor and respect you, and I will obey you in all lawful things, as is my duty. But please don't ask this of me. You said she loved me, and I hope she did, because the Intercessor knows I loved her, too. She was like a daughter to me, and I could never take her place, carry her Key, any more than a father can inherit from his son. Don't ask me to do that. It would be . . . wrong."

Silence hovered once more, and then Benjamin cleared his throat. "Would you consider staying on as Regent, at least?"

"I would—so long as I was sure you weren't trying to ease me into something else," Clinkscales said, and Benjamin looked at Prestwick.

"Henry? Would that work?"

"In the short term, Your Grace?" The chancellor pursed his lips once more. "Probably, yes. But in the long term?" He shook his head and held out both hands, palms uppermost, as he turned to Clinkscales. "If you don't formally accept the Key, then all we've done is defer the crisis, Howard. That by itself would probably be worthwhile, of course. If we could hold it off for another ten years or so, perhaps some of the tension would ease. We might not even have Haven and the war to worry about any longer. But until we have a legal, known, and *accepted* successor to the Harrington Key, this entire uncertainty will simply be hovering over our heads, waiting. And, forgive me, Howard, but you're not a young man, and ten years—"

He shrugged, and Clinkscales frowned unhappily.

"I know," he said. "I'm in decent shape for my age, but even with Manty medical support here on the planet now, I—"

He stopped, eyes abruptly wide, and Benjamin and Prestwick looked at one another. Prestwick started to speak again, but the Protector raised a hand, stopping him from interrupting whatever thought had suddenly struck Clinkscales, and then settled back in his own chair with an expression of intense curiosity. More than two full minutes passed, and then Clinkscales began to smile. He shook himself and made a small, apologetic gesture towards Benjamin.

"Forgive me, Your Grace," he said, "but I've just had an idea."

"So we noticed," Benjamin said so dryly the old man chuckled. "And just what idea would that have been?"

"Well, Your Grace, we *do* have another solution to our problem. One that would accord perfectly with out own law—and, I believe, with Manticore's—*and* keep the Key out of my hands, praise God fasting!"

"Indeed?" Protector and Chancellor exchanged glances, and then Benjamin quirked a polite eyebrow at Clinkscales. "And just what is this marvelous solution which has so far evaded myself, Henry, the High Court, and Reverend Sullivan?"

"Lady Harrington's mother is here on Grayson," Clinkscales replied.

"I'm aware of that, Howard," Benjamin said patiently, frowning at the apparent *non sequitur*. "I spoke to her day before yesterday about Lady Harrington's clinic and her genome project."

"Did you, Your Grace?" Clinkscales smiled. "She didn't mention it to me. But she did mention that she and Lady Harrington's father have decided to remain here on Grayson for at least the next several years. She said—" the old man's smile faded a bit around the edges "—that they'd decided that the best memorial they could give the Steadholder would be to bring Harrington Steading's medical standards up to the Star Kingdom's, so they'd like to move their practices here. And, of course, she herself is deeply committed to the genome project."

"I wasn't aware of their plans," Benjamin said after a moment, "but I don't really see that it changes anything, Howard. Surely you're not suggesting that we offer the Key to one of Lady Harrington's parents? They're not Grayson citizens, either, and the law is quite clear on the fact that parents can 'inherit' titles only when they *revert* to the parent through whom they passed in the first place, and that clearly isn't the case here. If you're about to insist that the Key pass through inheritance, then it has to go 'downstream' from the generation of its creation—which means a child, a sibling, or a cousin—and that brings us right back to Devon Harrington and our original mess!"

"Not necessarily, Your Grace." Clinkscales sounded almost smug, and Benjamin blinked.

"I beg your pardon?"

"You've given a great deal of thought to your reforms, Benjamin, but I think you've overlooked a glaringly obvious consequence of all the changes the Alliance has produced," Clinkscales told him. "Not surprisingly, probably. *I'd* certainly overlooked it—I suppose because I grew up on a planet without prolong and I'd finally gotten it through my head that the Steadholder was in her fifties. Which, of course, means that her parents have to be somewhere around my age."

"Prolong?" Benjamin suddenly sat up straight behind his desk, and Clinkscales nodded.

"Exactly. Her Key could pass to a sibling if she had one, but she doesn't. At the moment."

"Sweet Tester!" Prestwick murmured in something very like awe. "I never even considered that!"

"Nor I," Benjamin admitted, eyes narrow as he pondered furiously.

Howard's right, he thought. *That possibility never even crossed my mind, and it should have. So what if Doctor Harrington—*both *Doctors Harrington—are in their eighties? Physically, Honor's mother is only in her early thirties. And even if they were too old to have children "naturally," we've got all of the Star Kingdom's medical science to draw on! We could have a child tubed, assuming the Harringtons were willing. And if the child were born here on Grayson, then he'd have Grayson citizenship whatever his parents' nationality may have been.*

"It really would tie things up rather neatly, wouldn't it?" he said finally, his voice thoughtful.

"For that matter, there's another possibility entirely," Prestwick pointed out. Both of the others looked at him, and he shrugged. "I'm quite certain Lady Harrington's mother has samples of the Steadholder's genetic material, which means it would almost certainly be possible to produce a child of Lady Harrington's even at this date. Or even a direct clone, for that matter!"

"I think we'd better not start getting into those orbits," Benjamin cautioned. "Certainly not without consulting Reverend Sullivan and the Sacristy first, at any rate!" He shuddered at the mere thought of how the more conservative of his subjects might react to the chancellor's musings. "Besides, a clone would probably only make matters worse. If I remember correctly—and I'm not certain I do, without looking it up—the Star Kingdom's legal code adheres to the Beowulf Life Sciences Code, just as the Solarian League's does."

"Which means?" Clinkscales asked, clearly intrigued by the notion.

"Which means, first of all, that it's completely illegal to use a dead individual's genetic material unless that individual's will or other legal declaration specifically authorized the use. And secondly, it means that a clone is a child of its donor parent or parents, with all the legal protections of any other sentient being, but it is not the *same* person, and posthumous cloning cannot be used to circumvent the normal laws of inheritance."

"You mean that if Lady Harrington had had herself cloned before her death, then her clone would legally have been her child and could have inherited her title, but that if we have her cloned now, the child *couldn't* inherit?" Prestwick said, and Benjamin nodded.

"That's exactly what I mean, although it's also possible—and legal—for someone to stipulate in his will that he be cloned following his death and that his posthumous clone inherit. But no one can make that decision *for* him, which would be essentially what we would be doing if we decided to clone Lady Harrington at this point to solve our difficulties. And if you think about it, there's some sound reasoning behind the prohibition. For example, suppose some unscrupulous relative managed to arrange the death of someone like Klaus Hauptman or Lady Harrington without getting caught. And then that same relative had his victim cloned and himself appointed as the clone child's guardian, thus controlling the Hauptman Cartel—or Harrington Steading—until the clone attained his majority and inherited? And that doesn't even consider the sticky question of when a will would properly be probated! I mean, if a second party could legally produce a posthumous duplicate of the person who wrote the will, would that duplicate's existence supersede the will? Would the clone be entitled to sue those to whom 'his' estate had already legally been distributed—in exact accordance with his 'own' legally written and witnessed directions—for recovery of assets? The ramifications could go on and on forever."

"I see." Prestwick rubbed the end of his nose, then nodded. "All right, I do see that. And it probably wouldn't be a bad idea for us to quietly insert that Beowulf code into our own law, Your Grace, since we now have access to medical science which would make something like that possible. But how would that effect a child born to the Steadholder's parents after her death?"

"It wouldn't," Clinkscales said positively. "The precedents are clear on that point, Henry, and they go back almost to the Founding. It's unusual, of course, and I suppose that to be absolutely legal, the Key should pass to Devon Harrington until such time as Lady Harrington's parents produce a child, but then the Steading would revert to her sibling. In fact, I think there was actually an example of that from your own family history, Your Grace. Remember Thomas the Second?"

"Tester!" Benjamin smacked himself on the forehead. "How did I forget that one?"

"Because it happened five centuries ago, I imagine," Clinkscales told him dryly.

"And because Thomas isn't exactly someone we Mayhews like to remember," Benjamin agreed.

"Every family has its black sheep, Your Grace," Prestwick said.

"I suppose so," Benjamin said. "But not every family has someone who probably had his own brother assassinated to inherit the Protectorship!"

"That was never proven, Your Grace," Clinkscales pointed out.

"Right. Sure!" Benjamin snorted.

"It wasn't," Clinkscales said more firmly. "But the point is that Thomas was actually named Protector . . . until his nephew was born."

"Yeah," Benjamin said. "And if he'd known one of his brother's wives was pregnant and Dietmar Yanakov hadn't smuggled her out of the Palace, his nephew never *would* have been born, either!"

"That's as may be, Your Grace," Prestwick said austerely. "But what matters is that it created a firm precedent in our own law for what Howard is suggesting."

"I should certainly hope that a six-year dynastic war could at least establish a 'firm' precedent!" Benjamin observed.

"Your Grace, it may amuse *you* to dwell on the misdeeds of one of your ancestors, but it really doesn't amuse *us*," Prestwick told him.

"All right. All right, I'll be good," Benjamin promised, then sat for a moment, drumming on his desk while he thought. "Of course," he went on after a moment, "Thomas' sister-in-law was already pregnant when her husband died, but didn't the same thing happen with the original Garth Steading?"

"Not precisely, although that was the original precedent I was thinking of," Clinkscales agreed. "My history's a little rusty, and I can't remember the first Steadholder Garth's given name—John, wasn't it, Henry?" Prestwick flipped a hand to indicate his ignorance, and Clinkscales shrugged. "At any rate, the steading had just been created and he'd been confirmed as its first steadholder when he died. He was an only son, with no sons of his own, and the Garth Key couldn't 'revert' to his parents, so no one had any idea what to do, and they spent the better part of two years wrangling about it. But then the Church and the Conclave discovered that his father's youngest wife was pregnant and agreed that the Key could pass to her child if it was male. Which it was." He shrugged again, holding out both hands palm up.

"Um." Benjamin rubbed his chin. "I remember the details now, and I can see some problems with it now that I look back at it. That predated the Constitution by over two hundred years, and it was pretty obviously an act of political expediency to avoid a war of succession. Still, I imagine we could make the precedent stand up if we asserted it with a straight face. And if we get Reverend Sullivan to sign off on it. But this all assumes Lady Harrington's parents would be willing to cooperate with our plans. Would they?"

"I believe so," Clinkscales said with an edge of caution. "There's no physical reason why they couldn't, and Dr. Harrington—the Steadholder's mother, I mean—has discussed the possibility with my wives in a theoretical sense, at least. And if it would be inconvenient for them to do it, ah, the natural way, they could always tube a child. That wouldn't be a clone of Lady Harrington, so I don't see where it would be a problem."

"We'd still be on slippery ground if either of *them* were dead," Benjamin said thoughtfully, "but let's not go there. They're both alive, both physically able to conceive and bear children, and both on Grayson." He thought a moment longer, then nodded decisively. "I think this could be an *excellent* idea, Howard. If they agree, the child would be a Grayson citizen from birth because he was born here. Would you stay on as Regent in that case?"

"You mean as a caretaker until the child's birth if they agree?"

"Well, yes. And also as Regent for the child after he was born, as well."

"Assuming I last that long, yes, I suppose," Clinkscales said after a few seconds of consideration. "I doubt I'd make it to the child's majority even with Manty medical support, though."

He said it calmly, with the serenity of a man who'd lived a life fuller than the vast majority of other people's. Benjamin looked at him and wondered if he would feel as calm as Clinkscales when it was his turn. Or would the fact that people no more than five or six years younger than he could expect to live two or three centuries longer make him bitter and envious? He hoped it wouldn't, but—

He shook the thought off and nodded.

"All right, gentlemen, I think we have a plan here. There's just one little point about it which still bothers me."

"There is, Your Grace?" Prestwick furrowed his brow. "I confess that I don't see one. It seems to me that Howard has solved most of our problems quite neatly."

"Oh, he has!" Benjamin agreed. "But in the process, he's created a fresh one."

"Indeed, Your Grace?"

"Oh, yes indeed!" Both of Benjamin's advisors looked at him blankly, and he grinned wickedly. "Well, *I'm* not going to be the one to discuss the birds and the bees with Lady Harrington's mother, gentlemen!"

CHAPTER FIVE

"You want me to *what?*"

Allison Harrington shoved herself back in her chair, astonished almondine eyes wide, and Howard Clinkscales blushed as he had not in years. It was the first time since the INS broadcast of the execution that something had driven the quiet, lingering edge of sorrow fully out of Dr. Harrington's eyes, but he would have felt much better about that if he'd been even a little bit less embarrassed. This wasn't the sort of thing a properly raised Grayson male discussed with someone else's wife, and he'd done his best to evade the responsibility. But Benjamin had insisted that he'd thought it up, so it was up to him to enlist the Harringtons' cooperation.

"I realize it must sound impertinent of me to even bring the matter up, My Lady," he said now, his voice gruff, "but it seems the only way to avoid a probable political crisis. And it would be a way to keep the Key in her direct line."

"But—" Allison stopped herself and drew a stylus from her pocket. She shoved it into her mouth, nibbling on it with small, white teeth in a bad habit that went clear back to her hospital residency days on Beowulf, and made herself consider the—request? offer? plea?—as calmly as possible.

It was amazing, she decided, how complex her own reaction was. She and Alfred were finally managing to come to grips with their daughter's death—she better than he, she suspected, but still to come to grips with it. It hurt, and one of her own regrets had been that the two of them had deferred having a second child for so long. Perhaps that had been her fault, she mused. She was the one from cosmopolitan (*read: crowded, stratified, smug, and obsessed with stability,* she thought dryly) old Beowulf, where conspicuous contributions to population growth were more than simply frowned upon. Sphinx, on the other hand, was still a relatively new planet, with a total population of under two billion. Multichild families were the rule there, not the exception, and there was certainly no stigma attached to them.

And I always meant to have more children of my own, now didn't I? Of course I did! That was one of the things that attracted me to Sphinx in the first place, when Alfred proposed. It was just. . . . There were so many other *things I needed to do, and it wasn't like there was any rush.* My *"biological clock" won't run down for another century or more yet!*

But if they'd gone ahead, had those other children sooner, perhaps the savage blow of losing Honor wouldn't have—

She cut that thought off . . . again. What might have happened couldn't change what *had* happened, and even if it could have, producing more children simply as some sort of emotional insurance policy—a way to protect themselves from emotional trauma if one of their brood should die—would have been contemptible. And wouldn't have worked anyway.

Yet now that Clinkscales had brought the idea up—and explained his reasons for it—she felt . . . uncomfortable. Part of it was probably that bone-deep, instinctive reaction of hers which made her dig in her heels whenever anyone tried to tell her she "had" to do something. She'd made a habit of setting herself harder, more challenging goals than anyone else would have dreamed of demanding of her, but let someone—anyone—tell her that she "had" to do something, that something was "expected of her," or her "duty," and her back went up in instant defiance. She felt quite certain that most of it stemmed from her childhood sense that Beowulf's entire population had been out to pressure her into conforming to its expectations. Which was silly, of course. She'd realized that decades ago and worked on overcoming the spinal-reflex reaction ever since, yet it was still there, and she felt it stirring now.

But stronger than that, there was the vague feeling that if she and Alfred decided to have another child now, specifically to inherit Honor's steading, it would somehow be a betrayal of the daughter they'd lost. It would be as if . . . as if she'd been nothing more than a glob of plastic, squeezed out by a robotic assembly line, which could be replaced by any other glob from the same line. It was a ridiculous and illogical way to feel, but that didn't make the emotion any less powerful.

And then there's my own attitude towards inherited titles, isn't there? she asked herself after a moment, and snorted wryly while she nibbled harder on the stylus.

Most off-worlders, impressed with Beowulf's reputation for idiosyncratic personal life styles and sexual inventiveness, never realized how conformist the planet truly was. Allison had frequently wondered if that was because the "norm" to which its citizens conformed was such a liberalized template, but the pressure not to offend the system or offend the preconceptions upon which the template rested was only too evident to a native Beowulfan. A person could be anything she wanted . . . so long as what she wanted to be came off the menu of choices approved by the planet's social—and economic—consensus, and everyone was so damned *smug* about how superior their "open-mindedness" was to all those other, backward planets.

Yet for all its emphasis on stability and orderliness, Beowulf had no such thing as an hereditary monarchy or aristocracy. It was a sort of representative, elective oligarchy, governed by a Board of Directors whose members were internally elected, in turn, from the memberships of an entire series of lower-level, popularly elected boards which represented professions, not geographical districts, and it had worked—more or less, and despite occasional glitches—for almost two thousand years.

Coming from that background, she'd always been mildly amused by the aristocratic Manticoran tradition. It hadn't impinged directly upon her or her yeoman husband and his family, and she'd been willing to admit that it did a better job than most of governing. Indeed, she'd heaved a huge sigh of mental relief when she realized that, aristocratic or not, the Star Kingdom's society was willing to leave people alone. She'd delighted in scandalizing her more staid Sphinxian neighbors for almost seventy years, but very few of them had ever realized that it was because she *could*. That however much some citizens of her adopted star nation might disapprove of her, that mind-numbing, deadly reasonable, and eternally patient Beowulfan pressure to conform to someone else's ideal and "be happy" simply did not exist there. Yet grateful as she was for that, and deeply as she had come to love her new homeland, the notion of inheriting a position of power and authority, however hedged about by the limitations of the Star Kingdom's Constitution, had always struck her as absurd.

Maybe it's the geneticist in me. After all, I know *how much accident goes into anyone's genetic makeup!*

But that absurd notion had become something much less amusing the day Honor became Steadholder Harrington. The notion that her Honor had somehow transmuted into a great feudal lady had taken some getting used to. In fact, she never had gotten used to it—not really—before Honor's murder. But she'd seen the changes in her daughter, recognized the way that something deep inside her answered to the challenge of her new duties. And one thing Honor would never knowingly have done was leave her Harringtons—or her adoptive planet—with a political crisis like the one Clinkscales had just described.

"I don't know," she said finally. "I mean, this isn't the sort of thing Alfred and I ever had to think about before, Lord Clinkscales." She lowered the stylus and glanced at it, smiling crookedly as she saw the deep tooth marks she'd imprinted in the plastic, then looked back up at Harrington Steading's Regent. "It wouldn't be easy to stand the thought that we were somehow trying to . . . replace her," she said much more softly, and Clinkscales nodded.

"I know that, My Lady. But you wouldn't be doing that. No one *could* do that. Think of it instead as helping her see to it that the chain of command for her steading remains intact."

"Um." She realized she was nibbling on the stylus again and lowered it once more. "But that brings up two more points, My Lord," she said. "The first is whether or not it would be fair to my nephew Devon. Not that he ever expected to inherit anything like this, but he's already been informed by the College of Heraldry that he'll inherit her Manticoran 'dignities,' although he won't be officially confirmed as Earl Harrington for several months yet. But if Alfred and I agree to your request, I imagine that title, too, would legally pass to our new child . . . which would mean taking it away from him in the name of someone who hasn't even been conceived yet."

She shook her head and made a face, then sighed.

"I'll be honest, My Lord. I wish to God that Alfred and I didn't have to worry about any of this. That we could be confident that any children we might have would be born because we wanted them for *themselves*, not because there was a slot somewhere they 'had' to fill! And, frankly, a part of me resents the fact that such an intensely personal decision on our part should be of any concern at all to anyone else . . . or have such repercussions for so many other people!"

She brooded down at her blotter for several seconds, then shook herself with another, deeper sigh.

"But however much I may resent that, and however it may affect Devon, there's another, even more important point I think Alfred and I will have to consider."

"And that point is, My Lady?" Clinkscales asked gently when she paused once more.

"Whether or not it would be fair to the child," she said very quietly. "What right do my husband and I have to bring a human being into the universe not for who and what she might become but because a government, or a ruler—or *us*, God help us!—decided what she would have no choice but to become, even before she was conceived. My daughter chose to accept the office of Steadholder; do Alfred and I have a right to unilaterally impose that same choice on someone we haven't even met yet? And how will that someone react when she realizes that we did . . . and why? Will she decide we did it only for political reasons, and not because we wanted or loved her in her own right?"

Clinkscales sat without speaking for several seconds, then leaned back in his chair and exhaled softly.

"I hadn't considered it from that perspective, My Lady," he admitted. "I don't think most Graysons would. Our clan and family structures have been so tightly organized for survival purposes since the early days of the settlement that we'd probably feel at loose ends without that external factor helping us to define who and what we are. But for all that, I've seen the consequences of breeding for an heir solely out of a sense of duty or ambition. Remember the disparity in our male/female birth rates and the fact that up until nine years ago, only males could inherit. So, yes, I've seen the way that knowing his parents conceived him only because the steading or the clan required an heir can sour and scar a man.

"But that doesn't happen often," he went on earnestly. "Children are the most precious gifts the Comforter ever gave us, My Lady. If anyone knows that, it's Graysons. And children who are genuinely loved and cherished, even as the products of pure marriages of state, don't grow up thinking they were born only out of the political needs of their parents."

"Yes, but—" Allison began, but Clinkscales stopped her with a gentle shake of his head.

"My Lady, I knew your daughter," he said quietly. "And anyone who had the privilege of knowing her as well as I did also knew there was never an instant in her life in which she wasn't absolutely secure in her love for you and her father and in your love for her. That gives me a very good opinion of you—and of your ability to raise another child with the same love and sense of self. Don't let your own grief or doubt push you into doubting yourself on that deep a level."

Allison blinked stinging eyes and felt her mouth tremble for just a moment. *My God,* she thought in deep amazement. *I thought he was some kind of museum-exhibit fossil when we first met—some sort of throwback to a time when men walked around on their knuckles in a testosterone haze . . . when they weren't beating their chests and yodeling in triumph. But now—!*

She felt a distant burn of shame for her own past readiness to dismiss him, but it was lost behind a far deeper sense of wonder at the insight and gentleness he'd just displayed. And of how bare it laid the foolishness of her own fears. She still had her doubts about whether or not she and Alfred should produce an heir to the Harrington Key on demand, as it were, but not about whether or not they could raise another child with the same love and welcome they'd shown Honor.

Of course, there is *that other little matter. Clinkscales doesn't know what I've turned up in the genome project . . . and I still haven't decided whether or not to go public with it. I wonder how he and Protector Benjamin will feel about "breeding" a Harrington heir if the Harrington name turns into "Mud" when—*if*—I break the news!*

She pushed that thought aside, shook herself, and stood behind her desk. Clinkscales rose as well, and she smiled at him.

"I'll think about it, My Lord," she told him. "Alfred and I will have to discuss it, of course, and it may take us some time to decide. But we *will* think about it, I promise."

She held out her hand, and Clinkscales bent over it to kiss it in the traditional Grayson fashion.

"Thank you, My Lady," he said quietly. "That's all we could ask of you and your husband. May the Tester help you reach your decision."

"I don't know, Alley."

Alfred Harrington towered over his tiny wife. He was a good four centimeters taller than his daughter had been, and he had the solid muscle and bone of someone born and bred to a gravity ten percent heavier than Beowulf's. Yet despite his impressive physical presence, he'd seemed much the more fragile of the two over the months since Honor's capture, and her death had hit him with crushing force. He was coming back from it at last, and the nights when Allison awoke to his fierce embrace and the hot saltiness of his tears had grown blessedly less frequent, but progress had been agonizingly slow. Now he sank down on the couch beside her in their palatial suite in Harrington House and tucked his right arm around her.

"I told Clinkscales we'd have to think about it," she told him, turning her face up to be kissed and then snuggling down against him.

Bigger may not always be better, but there's definitely something to be said for it when it comes to handing out cuddling, she thought smugly, pressing her cheek luxuriously into his chest, and then smiled as two of the treecats—Nelson and Samantha—flowed up onto the couch to join them. Samantha had brought along Jason, still the most fearless explorer of her children, and the 'kitten came bumbling up to leap upon Allison's free hand and wrestle it into submission. Samantha sat upright on her four rearmost limbs to watch him, tail wrapped around her hand-feet and true-feet while she groomed her whiskers with one true-hand, but Nelson sprawled out across Alfred's lap in companionable, boneless luxury.

"Um." Alfred leaned back, unfocused eyes on Jason while he pursed his lips in thought and rubbed Nelson's ears. The older 'cat gave a deep, buzzing purr and oozed out even flatter in a shameless display of sensuality, but after several seconds, Alfred shook his head.

"You know, this is going to crop up *whenever* we have more children, Alley." She looked up at him, and he shrugged. "They're still going to be Honor's brothers or sisters," he managed to say his dead daughter's name with only the smallest catch in his voice this time, "and that means the whole inheritance thing is going to pop out of the woodwork sooner or later, whatever we want."

"I know," she sighed. Jason had completely enveloped her hand now, wrapping himself around it in a fluffy ball while he fastened all six limbs—and a prehensile tail—about her wrist and forearm, and his own buzz of delight rose as she rolled him over on his back. "I hadn't thought about it before . . . well, you know." Alfred nodded, and she sighed again. "Dynastic inheritance isn't something a good Beowulf girl needs to concern herself about," she said plaintively.

"For better or for worse, I believe you said," he told her, brushing the end of her nose with the tip of his left forefinger while one of the deep chuckles which had become all too rare in the last few months rumbled in his chest.

"And I meant it—then!" she told him pertly. "Besides, you promised the same thing."

"So I did." He returned his left hand to Nelson and ran it slowly down the 'cat's spine, and it was his turn to sigh. "Well," he said very quietly, "I suppose life really does go on, except in bad books and worse holodrama. And we'd always planned on more children. So I guess the real question isn't whether we let 'dynastic' considerations push us into anything but whether or not we let them stampede us *out* of doing what we'd intended to do before they came along."

"True."

His right hand rose to stroke her sleek black hair, and she made a soft sound of pleasure and gave a wiggle at least as feline as any treecat could have managed, and he chuckled again. But then her smile faded.

"Of course, my genome results only make this even more complicated, you know."

"I don't see why," he disagreed. "You didn't have anything to do with it. All you've done is spot it."

"Some cultures have a nasty habit of shooting the messenger when the news is bad, my love. And lest you forget, Grayson tends to be a rather religious planet. And given the Church of Humanity's original take on science in general, I'm more than a little afraid that the locals aren't going to react to the information quite as calmly as you and I did!"

"Well, it's not as if it would be the first time someone named Harrington set them on their ears," he pointed out in return. "They ought to be getting used to it by now. And if they haven't yet, then they'd damn well better get around to it quick if they plan on dumping any steadholders' keys on more of *our* children."

"Goodness, how fierce!" Allison murmured, and giggled as he bared his teeth at her. It felt incredibly good to have him joking with her once more, and her eyes softened as she gazed up at him and saw the man she'd loved for over sixty T-years emerging once more from the stony despair of his grief. She thought about saying something to welcome him back, but it was too soon, and so she only tucked her cheek back against his deep chest with a little sigh of bittersweet joy and concentrated on wrestling with Jason.

"You know," Alfred said after a moment, "what you really ought to do is talk to someone you can trust to be discreet but who can also give you an authoritative read on how the Graysons are likely to react to your findings."

"I thought of that for myself," she told him a bit tartly, "but who did you have in mind? Lord Clinkscales has enough on his mind already, and Miranda—" She shook her head. "Miranda was too close to Honor, and she's grown too close to us. She wouldn't do it on purpose, but she'd filter her response through her feelings for me. Assuming, of course, that she didn't turn out to have a major negative religious reaction to it herself!"

"You don't really think that's going to happen, though," Alfred said confidently.

"No, I don't," Allison admitted. "On the other hand, I've been wrong before, on very rare occasions in my life, and I'd just as soon not find out if this is one of them."

"I can see that." Alfred rubbed Nelson, and then chuckled as Samantha decided the men had been getting too much of the attention. She stood and stalked over to wedge herself down between the two Harringtons, flowing into the space between them like modeling clay and patting Allison's thigh imperiously with one true-hand until the hand Jason hadn't captured came around to pet her.

But then Alfred's chuckle oozed off into a thoughtful silence, and Allison looked up at him with a raised eyebrow.

"You know," he said slowly, "I think I've just had an idea."

"What kind?" she demanded.

"Well, your main concern is over the religious dimension, right? About how the more conservative elements of the Church are likely to react?" She nodded, and he shrugged. "In that case, why not go to the very top? From something Mac said this morning, I understand Reverend Sullivan is going to be here in Harrington in a couple of weeks."

"Rev—?" Allison frowned, furrowing her brow as she thought. "I'd considered that myself earlier, very briefly," she admitted after a moment. "But I chickened out. From all I've seen of him, he's a lot . . . fiercer than Reverend Hanks was. What if that means he's narrower minded or more authoritarian? What if he tries to force me to suppress my findings?"

"What if you're borrowing trouble?" Alfred countered. "I agree he's not very much like Honor described Reverend Hanks to us—or, at least, his public persona isn't. But from what I've seen of the Graysons, I don't think their Sacristy would have been likely to select an idiot or a zealot as Reverend. For that matter, didn't Honor tell us Hanks himself had more or less handpicked Sullivan as Second Elder and groomed him as his successor?"

Allison nodded, and he twitched his left shoulder in another shrug.

"In that case, I'd say you've got at least a better than even chance he'll react reasonably. And even if he doesn't, that's a bridge you're going to have to cross eventually anyway. I mean, you wouldn't really let him stop you from publishing in the unlikely event that he did try to suppress your findings, would you?" She shook her head. "Well, there it is, then. You might as well find out now as later, and going to him first will give you a better chance of enlisting his active support if it's looking iffy. And however individual Graysons may react, there's certainly no one on this entire planet who could give you a better read on the Church's probable official reaction!"

"That's true enough, anyway," Allison agreed. She thought about it for several seconds, then nodded against his chest. "I think you're probably right," she said, "You always did have a better sense than me of how to work a hierarchy."

"All those misspent years of Navy service surviving BuMed's oversight, lovey," he informed her with a smile. "You either learn to work the system, or you wind up a patient instead of a doctor."

"Yeah? I just figured it was that authoritarian, aristocratic, feudalistic throwback of a society you grew up in."

"As opposed to that libertine, lascivious, overstratified and conformist collection of sensualists *you* grew up with?" he inquired sweetly.

"Of course," she agreed cheerfully, then made a little moue of regret and sat up straight as a discreet chime sounded. "Dinner is served," she sighed. "Am I mussed?"

"Not very," he told her after a brief, critical examination.

"Damn," she said. "Now Miranda and Mac are going to know we hadn't even gotten to the good part before they interrupted us. You're simply going to have to do better than this, Alfred! I do have a reputation to maintain, you know."

Her husband was still chuckling when they walked into the dining room two minutes later.

Chapter Six

"Thank you for agreeing to see me on such short notice, Reverend."

"Believe me, Lady Harrington. It is my pleasure to see you at any time, and both I and my office are fully aware of the importance of the work upon which you are engaged. When those factors combine—"

The bald, hook-nosed Reverend and First Elder of the Church of Humanity Unchained tucked Allison's small hand neatly and possessively into his elbow, smiled, and escorted her across the office. They were on the third floor of Harrington Cathedral which, like every cathedral on the face of Grayson, contained a large, comfortable office suite permanently reserved for the Reverend's use on his visits to the steading. Now Sullivan seated his visitor in one of the overstuffed armchairs flanking the polished stone coffee table to one side of the desk and ceremonially poured tea. The silver pot flashed in the sunlight streaming through the huge windows which made up one entire wall of the office, and Allison's nose twitched in surprise as she recognized the aroma rising with the steam. The scent of Sun Plantation Green Tea Number Seven could not be mistaken by anyone who knew their teas, and she was astonished that Sullivan (or someone) had gone to the trouble of discovering her favorite Beowulf blend. It wasn't hard to obtain in the Star Kingdom, but it was decidedly on the expensive side, and she'd already discovered that it *was* hard to find on Grayson.

"Do you take sugar, Lady Harrington?" Sullivan inquired, and this time Allison smiled as her host raised his bushy eyebrows in polite question. If he (or someone on his staff, which seemed more likely, now that she thought about it) had taken the pains to determine what blend of tea she preferred, then she had no doubt that he also knew the answer to that question.

"Yes, thank you, Reverend. Two cubes."

"Of course, My Lady." He dropped them into the steaming liquid, stirred gently, and then handed her cup and saucer. "And like the tea, My Lady, I assure you that the metals levels in the sugar are as low as anything you might encounter back home in your Star Kingdom."

"Thank you," she repeated, and waited while he poured tea for himself, as well, before she sipped. "Ummmm. . . . delicious," she purred, and the Reverend smiled back at her as he enjoyed her sensual delight in the treat.

Allison recognized that smile, for she'd seen it often in her life. Most men seemed to take a simple pleasure in making her happy (*and they darned well* should, *too*, she thought comfortably), but Sullivan's smile still surprised her a bit. Oh, she'd discovered very quickly that Grayson males were much more gallant than most, but she'd known before she ever came to Yeltsin's Star that, however gallant, they could also be smug, patronizing, and paternalistic. She'd come prepared to cut them off at the ankles if necessary to turn that around, and so far she'd never had to squash one of them more than once. On the other hand, she'd spent almost all of her time on Grayson here in Harrington Steading, where public attitudes tended to be a bit more "advanced," and this was the first time she'd actually met Reverend Sullivan, aside from the intensely formal, emotionally shattering day of Honor's funeral.

But even though she hadn't had the chance to form a firsthand opinion of him, she'd gathered from Miranda—and from Honor's letters—that Sullivan was much more conservative at heart than Reverend Hanks had been. No one had suggested that he was anything but committed to supporting Benjamin Mayhew's reforms with the full power of his office, yet he clearly seemed less comfortable with them on a personal level than, say, Howard Clinkscales. Somehow she'd expected that to carry over to the same sort of discomfort with women as authority figures which she'd seen from the more reactionary Grayson physicians. And even if he hadn't been stiff and ill at ease with her, she still would have expected the spiritual head of the Church of Humanity to be more . . . ascetic? Was that the word? No, not quite, but something like it.

Except Reverend Sullivan wasn't whatever it was she'd expected. Indeed, there was a warm appreciation for her attractiveness in his dark eyes, and she sensed a willingness to play the game hiding just beneath his attentive surface. She knew he was married—with all three of the wives Grayson custom enshrined—and she could tell he would never dream of going further than a cheerful flirtation, yet there was an earthy vitality to him which she had never anticipated.

Well, maybe that makes sense after all, she thought. *Honor may not have noticed it*—she felt a pang as she thought of her daughter, but she kept the thought moving despite the hurt—*because, Lord love the girl, the universe had to hit her between the eyes with a brick just to get her to recognize the opposite sex was even out there! But underneath all that gallantry and all those codes of proper behavior and how to act and react around another man's wives, these people are just as "earthy"* (she chuckled mentally at the repeated use of the word) *as my high school sex counselor back on Beowulf. Heavens! All you have to do is poke your nose inside an upper-class lingerie shop to know* that! *That's rather healthy, really.*

But that could also explain Sullivan's attitude towards her. Women like Honor probably did make him uncomfortable—less because they held and wielded "a man's" authority than because the background from which they came was so alien to him. He and other Graysons like him were still in the process of reprogramming themselves around a whole new set of social cues, and it was likely many of them never would learn to truly understand those cues even once they learned to recognize them. But Sullivan had recognized the gleam in her own eye, and it was one he knew how to respond to comfortably as long as they used Grayson rules.

That was good, she decided, sipping more tea while she discarded one strategy for delivering her news and organized an alternative. He looked so forbidding and stern that she'd automatically assumed a certain degree of closed-mindedness, and she'd been wrong. That he had the fierce temper reputation assigned him and did not suffer fools gladly she could readily believe, but there was a much livelier mind behind those eyes than she'd expected, and if he was prepared to be comfortable with her on a personal level, so much the better for the professional one, as well.

She gave a mental nod, set down her cup and saucer, and lifted her small briefcase from its place beside her chair into her lap.

"I realize you have a tight schedule, Your Grace, and that you sandwiched me into it at very short notice, so with your permission, I'd like to waste as little of your time as possible and get straight to the reason I asked to see you."

"My schedule is almost always 'tight' in Father Church's service, My Lady," he said wryly, "but believe me, time with you could never be wasted."

"My goodness!" Allison murmured with a smile and a dangerous set of dimples. "I could wish the Star Kingdom would import a little Grayson manners!"

"Ah, but that would hardly be a fair exchange for your own presence here, My Lady!" Sullivan replied with a broad grin of his own. "Your Kingdom would get only an outward expression of our appreciation for beauty and charm, whereas we would get their reality."

Allison chuckled appreciatively, but she also shook her head and unsealed the briefcase, and Sullivan sat back in his own chair, nursing his teacup. The teasing gallantry faded from his expression, and he crossed his legs and watched alertly as she set out a tiny holo projector and keyed her memo pad to life.

"Your Grace," she said much more seriously, "I have to tell you that I felt some trepidation about requesting this meeting. As you know, I've been working on mapping the Grayson genome for over six T-months now, and I've discovered something which I'm afraid some of your people may find . . . disturbing." The bushy brows knitted together in a frown—not of anger, but of concentration and, possibly, a little concern—and she drew a deep breath.

"How much do you know about your planet's genetic background, Your Grace?"

"No more than any other layman, I imagine," he said after a moment. "Even our doctors were several centuries behind your own in that regard before the Alliance, of course, but we Graysons have been aware of the need to keep track of our bloodlines and avoid inbreeding since the Founding. Aside from that and the genealogical and family health history information my own and my wives' physicians have requested from us over the years, I'm afraid I know very little."

He paused, watching her intently, and she felt the unasked "Why?" floating in the air between them.

"Very well, Your Grace. I'll try to keep this as simple and nontechnical as I can, but I have something I need to show you."

She switched on the holo unit, and a holographic representation of a chromosome appeared in the air above the coffee table. It didn't look very much like an actual magnified chromosome would have, for it was a schematic rather than visually representative, yet Sullivan's eyes flickered with interest as he realized he was looking at the blueprint for a human life. Or, to be more precise, a *portion* of the blueprint for a human life. Then Allison tapped a command into the holo unit, and the image changed, zooming in on a single, small portion of the schematic and magnifying that portion hugely.

"This is the long arm of what we call Chromosome Seven, Your Grace," she told him. "Specifically, this—" she tapped a macro on the holo unit and a cursor flashed, indicating a point on the image "—is a gene with a long and sometimes ugly history in medical science. A single gene mutation at this site produces a disease known as cystic fibrosis, which drastically alters the secretory function of the lungs and pancreas."

It was also, she did not mention, a disease which had been eradicated over a millennium and a half ago on planets with modern medical science . . . and one which still turned up from time to time on Grayson.

"I see," Sullivan said after a moment, then quirked one eyebrow at her. "And the reason for telling me this, My Lady?" he inquired politely.

"The reason for telling you, Your Grace, is that my research and mapping suggest quite conclusively to me that this portion of the genetic code of your people—" she jabbed an index finger at the cursor in the holo image "—was deliberately altered almost a thousand years ago."

"Altered?" Sullivan sat upright in his chair.

"Altered, Your Grace. Engineered." Allison drew a deep breath. "In other words, Sir, you and all your people have been genetically modified."

She sat very still, awaiting the potential eruption, but Sullivan only gazed at her for several seconds without speaking. Then he leaned back, reclaimed his teacup, and took a deliberate sip. She wasn't certain if he was buying time for shattered thoughts to settle or simply deliberately defusing the tension, but then he set saucer and cup back in his lap and cocked his head.

"Continue, please," he invited, and his voice was so calm she felt almost flustered by its very lack of agitation. She paused a moment longer, then glanced down at her memo pad and scrolled through two or three pages of preliminary, hysteria-soothing notes it had just become obvious she wasn't going to need.

"In addition to my purely laboratory research," she said after a second or two, "I've been doing some extensive searches of your data bases." *Which was one* hell *of a lot more work than it would have been back home with proper library computer support.* "In particular, I was searching for the earliest medical records—dating back to your Founding, if at all possible—which might have shed some corroborative light on my lab findings. Unfortunately, while there is a good bit of information, including case history notes on a surprising number of individual colonists, I was unable to find any data on the specific points which concerned me. Which," she said, meeting his eyes with a frankness she had not intended to bring to this meeting before she got a feel for his personality, "was one reason for my concern."

"You thought that perhaps those records had been suppressed?" Sullivan asked her, and chuckled at her expression. "My Lady, for all your frankness, you've been very cautious in your choice of words. Bearing that in mind, did you really think it would require a—what is the Manticoran slang phrase? a *hyperphysicist*, I believe?—to deduce the reason for your concern?" He shook his head at her. "I suppose it's possible, even probable, that Father Church's servants have suppressed . . . unpleasant information from time to time in our history, but if so, they did it without Father Church's approval. Or the Tester's." Her eyebrows rose against her will, and he chuckled again. "My Lady, we believe God calls us to the Test of Life, which requires us to test both ourselves and our beliefs and our assumptions as we grow and mature in His love. How could we do that, and what validity would our Tests have, if Father Church itself distorted the data which forms the basis upon which we are to make them?"

"I . . . hadn't thought of it that way, Your Grace," Allison said slowly, and this time Sullivan laughed out loud.

"No, My Lady, but you've been rather more polite about it than some off-worlders have. We are a people of custom, and one which has traditionally embraced a highly consensual Faith and way of life, yet our Faith is also one of individual conscience in which *no one*—neither a man's Steadholder, nor his Protector, nor even the Reverend or the Sacristy—may dictate to him on matters of the spirit. That is the central dynamic of our beliefs, and maintaining it has never been easy. Which is fair enough, for God never promised us the Test would be easy. But it means that, for all our consensuality, we have experienced many periods of intense, even bitter debate and doctrinal combat. I believe that has ultimately strengthened us, but memories of those periods make some of us uneasy about embracing changes in our Church and society. To be perfectly honest, I myself harbor some personal reservations about at least some of the changes—or, perhaps, about the *rate* of change—which I see around me. Yet not even the priests of Father Church, or perhaps *especially* not the priests of Father Church, may dictate to the consciences of our flock. Nor may we properly decide that this or that bit of knowledge, however unpleasant we may fear its consequences will be, should be restricted or concealed. So continue with your explanation, please. I may not fully understand it, and it may yet shock or concern me, but as a child of the Tester and of Father Church, it is my duty to hear and at least try to understand . . . and not to blame the bearer of the news for its content."

"Yes, Your Grace." Allison shook herself again, then smiled crookedly. "Yes, indeed," she said, and nodded much more comfortably at the holo image.

"As nearly as I can reconstruct what must have happened, Your Grace, at least one person, and possibly several, in your original colonial medical team must have been real crackerjack geneticists, especially given the limitations of the technology then available. As you may be aware, they were still using viruses for genetic insertions rather than the precisely engineered nanotech we use today, and given the crudity of such hack and slash methodologies, his—or their—achievements are truly remarkable."

"I am less surprised to hear that than you might think, My Lady," Sullivan interposed. "The original followers of Saint Austin were opposed to the way technology had, as they saw it, divorced men from the lives God wished them to lead. But they recognized the advances in the life sciences as the gift of a loving Father to His children, and their intention from the beginning was to transplant as much of that gift to Grayson as they could. And that was certainly as well for all of us when our ancestors discovered what sort of world they had come to."

"I believe that probably constitutes at least a one or two thousand percent understatement, Your Grace," Allison said wryly. "One of the things which has puzzled those of us who have studied the situation has been how your colony could possibly have survived for more than a generation or two amid such lethal concentrations of heavy metals. Obviously, some sort of adaptive change had to have occurred, but none of us could understand how it happened quickly enough to save the colony. Now, I think, I know."

She took a sip of tea and crossed her own legs, leaning back in her chair and cradling the tissue-thin porcelain cup between her hands.

"Heavy metals enter the body via the respiratory and digestive tracts, Your Grace, hence your air filtration systems and the constant battle to decontaminate your farm soil. Apparently, whoever was responsible for this—" she jutted her chin at the holo image once again "—intended to build a filtration system into your *bodies* as well, by modifying the mucosal barriers in your lungs and digestive tract. Your secretory proteins are substantially different from, say, my own. They bind the metals—or a large proportion of them, at any rate—which allows them to be cleared from the body in sputum and other wastes, rather than being absorbed wholesale into the tissues. They don't do a perfect job, of course, but they're the reason your tolerance for heavy metals is so much higher than my own. Up until two or three months ago, the assumption, particularly in light of your ancestors' limited technological resources and, um, attitude towards the resources they did have, was that this must represent a natural facet of adaptive evolution, even if we had no idea how it had happened so quickly."

"But you no longer believe this to be the case," Sullivan said quietly.

"No, Your Grace. I've found flanking regions of rhinovirus genetic material around the cystic fibrosis locus indicated in the holo here, and I think I can say with some assurance that it didn't get there accidentally."

"Rhinovirus?"

"The vector for the common cold," Allison said dryly, "which could have offered several useful advantages to the med teams who made use of it. For one thing, with your people so tightly confined in the limited air-filtered habitats they could build, an aerosol vector like this would be very easily spread. Given the fact that I've found absolutely no mention of it anywhere in the records, I might also hazard the guess that the project was kept confidential at the time—possibly to avoid raising hopes if, in fact, it should fail. Or there could have been other reasons. And if there were, spreading the alteration via 'a cold' would have the advantage of maximum concealability, as well."

"Indeed it would have, and there could well have been 'other reasons' to do such a thing quietly," Sullivan agreed, and it was his turn to smile crookedly. "Despite my own analysis of why Father Church does not believe in suppression, not everyone in our history would have agreed with me, and no doubt there *have* been times when our freer thinkers found that . . . discretion was indicated. As I'm sure you've discovered in the course of your research, My Lady, many of our Founders were zealots. Heavens, look at those lunatics who launched the Civil War four hundred years later! However trying our own times may be, they do not compare to the Tests which faced the Founders, and it would certainly have been possible that the Founding Elders might have feared that some of the more blindly faithful among their flock would have reacted badly to the notion of such a thing as permanently modifying their own bodies and those of all their descendants."

"As you say, Your Grace," Allison murmured, then shrugged. "At any rate, we might think of this as a sort of weapon of beneficent biological warfare, an agent designed to modify the genetic material of your people in order to give them a fighting chance at surviving their environment. Unfortunately, it looks like it was a fast and dirty method, even by the standards of then-current technology."

Sullivan frowned, and she shook her head quickly.

"That wasn't a criticism, Your Grace! Whoever managed this was clearly working on a shoestring, with limited resources. He had to do the best with what he had, and what he managed was brilliantly conceived and clearly executed effectively. But I suspect that the need for speed, coupled with extremely limited facilities, prevented his team from carrying out as careful an analysis as they would have wished, and it looks like the vector carried a second, unintentional modification which they failed to recognize at the time."

"Unintentional?" Sullivan's frown was deeper now, not in displeasure but in thought, and Allison nodded.

"I'm certain it was. And the nature of their problem no doubt helps explain what happened. You see, whoever designed this modification had to make the adaptive mutation inheritable. Simply modifying the gene in those actually exposed to the rhinovirus wouldn't work, because it would have been a purely somatic mutation, which means it would have died with the first generation of hosts. To keep that from happening, he—or they—had to cross from the somatic to the germ line—modify the rhinovirus to cross the mucosal barrier and show a predilection for primordial germ cells in the host's ovaries and testes—in order to pass it on to the first generation's offspring. What had to be accomplished was analogous to, oh, the mumps virus. That infects the salivary glands, but also attacks the ovaries and testes and can account for some cases of male infertility."

Sullivan nodded to indicate understanding, and Allison hid another mental smile. Interesting that he showed no discomfort at all with the way the conversation was headed. Of course, with the high percentage of stillborn boys on this planet, Graysons had been fanatical about prenatal care for centuries, and men were just as involved in the process (*at one remove, of course!* she amended) as women.

"They had no real option about that," she went on. "Not if they wanted the change to be a permanent addition to the planetary genome. But in the process, they also got an *unintended* mutation. Their intervention introduced a stable trinucleotide repeat on the X chromosome, which wouldn't have been a problem . . . except that it in turn affected one of the AGG codons." Sullivan looked blank. "AGG codons are adenine-guanine-guanine sequences that act as locks on the expansion of other trinucleotide repeats," she explained helpfully.

"Of course," Sullivan agreed. He didn't look too terribly enlightened, but he nodded for her to continue, and she punched a new command into her holo unit. The imagery changed to a color-coded schematic of nucleotides—an enormous chain composed of the color-coded letters "A," "C," "G," and "T," repeating again and again in jumbled patterns. As Sullivan watched, the image zoomed in on a single section—two three-letter groups of "CGG" in yellow, green, and green, separated by an "AGG" in *red*, green, and green.

"Essentially, it was a very tiny change," Allison told the Reverend. "An adenine here—" she touched another key, and the "AGG" code flashed brilliantly "—mutated to cytosine—" another key, and the flashing red "A" turned into a yellow "C" and the three-letter group to its right grew suddenly into an enormous chain of the same codes, repeating again and again "—which deactivated the lock and allowed unstable expansion of—"

"Excuse me, My Lady," Sullivan interrupted, "but I think we're drifting into deep water here. What, precisely, does that m— No." He stopped and raised one hand. "I'm certain that if you told me what it meant, I would be no closer to understanding than I am now. What I truly need to know, I suppose, is what the consequences of this . . . unstable whatever are."

"Um." Allison sipped some more tea, then shrugged.

"DNA is composed of four nucleotides, Your Grace: adenine, cytosine, guanine, and thymine. They link together in thousands of repeats—codes, if you will—which combine to carry the blueprint for our bodies . . . and transmit it to the next generation. They link in groups of three, hence the term '*tri*nucleotide,' which usually occur in 'runs' of thirty or less, but there are several diseases, such as the one we call 'Fragile X,' in which the number of repeats expands enormously, often into the thousands, effectively . . . well, scrambling a portion of the master code, as it were. Are you with me so far?"

"I believe so," he said cautiously.

"All right. This schematic represents a portion of the nucleotides—in this case cytosine, adenine, and guanine—from the Grayson genome. This trinucleotide here—" she touched her controls and the holo reverted to its original form with the "AGG" flashing once more "—is what we call a 'lock,' sort of a blocker to prevent the CGG repeats on either side of it from expanding in a way that would scramble the code. What happened, though, was that when the adenine mutated into cytosine, the 'lock' disappeared . . . and that allowed an unstable expansion of the CGG chain 'downstream' of it."

"I won't pretend to understand completely, My Lady," Sullivan said after a moment, "but I believe I understand the process, in general terms at least. And just how serious a problem is this 'unstable expansion'?"

"Well, in Fragile X, the consequence is—or was, before we learned to repair it—moderate mental retardation. But what resulted here was worse—much worse. It destroyed a portion of the chromosome necessary for early embryonic development."

"Which means, My Lady?" Sullivan asked intently.

"It means that it produced an embryonic lethal mutation in males, Your Grace," Allison said simply.

This time the Reverend came bolt upright in his chair, and she nodded to the display still glowing above the coffee table.

"Any male embryo with this mutation cannot be carried to term," she said. "Female embryos each have two X chromosomes, however, which gives them the chance for an extra copy of the destroyed gene. And the lyonization process, which inactivates one X chromosome in a female, almost always inactivates the structurally damaged one in cases like this, which means that, unlike males with the same problem, they survive."

"But in that case—" Sullivan stared into the holo for several seconds, then looked back at Allison. "If I understand you correctly, My Lady, you're saying that no male child with this mutation could live?" She nodded. "In that case, how could our ancestors possibly have survived? If everyone who received the benign mutation also received this one, then how were any living male children born at all?"

"The two mutations are linked in that they were both introduced by the same *vector*, Your Grace, but that's the only linkage between them. Everyone got the intended mutation—well, that's probably an overstatement. Let's say that everyone who survived got the intentional one, but the unintentional one, fortunately, had incomplete penetrance. That means that thirty percent or so of the males didn't express the mutation and so survived—but even those who survived could be carriers. To use the Fragile X analogy again, the fragile site from that disease is seen in forty percent of the cells of affected males, but carriers may not show the fragile site at all."

"I . . . see," Sullivan said very slowly.

"There was nothing anyone could have done about it, Your Grace. The original modification was essential if your people were to survive at all. It *had* to be made, and even assuming that any of the original med team were still alive by the time the harmful side effect began to manifest, and even assuming that they still had the technical capability for genetic level examinations, it was too late to do anything about it," Allison said quietly, and sat back to wait.

"Sweet Tester," Sullivan murmured at last, his voice so soft Allison hardly heard him. Then he pushed himself all the way back in his chair and inhaled deeply. He gazed at her for endless seconds, then shook himself.

"I feel certain that you must have felt very confident in your findings before you brought them to my attention, My Lady. May I also assume that your documentation of them will be sufficient to convince other experts of them?"

"Yes, Your Grace," she said positively. "For one thing, it explains the two things about your population which have most puzzled the Star Kingdom's geneticists from the beginning of the Alliance." Sullivan raised an eyebrow, and she shrugged. "I've already mentioned the incredible rapidity with which your ancestors evolved a 'natural' defense against heavy metals. That was number one. But a disparity in male-female birth rates on the scale of Grayson's, while not all that unusual under distressed conditions, seldom lasts as long as yours has."

"I see." He gazed at her meditatively, then drank more tea. "And is there anything which can be done about this, My Lady?"

"It's really too early for me to say yes or no to that one, at least with any degree of confidence. I've isolated two or three possible approaches, but the site of the problem may well make things difficult, because the mutated gene on the X is near the zinc-finger X protein gene. That's a key gene in sex determination, and it's at the Xp22.2—" She paused as his expression began to indicate that he was lost once more.

"It's at a locus where changes can involve literally dozens of disease states, Your Grace," she simplified. "Many of those diseases are lethal, and others can cause disorders of sex determination. We know a lot more about sex differentiation than whoever whipped up your survival modification did, but we still dislike meddling with it, and particularly in this area. There's a lot of room for small errors to have large consequences, and even if we avoid the more dangerous disease states, the Beowulf Code specifically prohibits genetic manipulation in order to predetermine the sex of a child." She grimaced. "There were some very unpleasant—and shameful—episodes relating to that in the first and second centuries Ante Diaspora, and I'm afraid they've been repeated from time to time on some of the more backward colony worlds since. Nonetheless, I think I could probably at least ameliorate the situation. But whatever I do, it will take time to perfect the methodology . . . and probably result in at least some decreased fertility among your planet's male population."

"I see," he said again, and switched his eyes to the holo image above the coffee table once more. "Have you spoken to the Sword's health authorities about this yet, My Lady?" he asked.

"Not yet," Allison admitted. "I wanted to be certain of my data before I did, and then your visit to Harrington gave me the opportunity to speak to you first. Given the role your Church plays in the day-to-day life of Grayson, I thought it might be wiser to speak to you first."

"Obviously Father Church will have to address the issue," Sullivan agreed, "but we who serve him have learned bitter lessons about meddling in secular affairs. I believe you should draw this to the Sword's attention as soon as convenient, My Lady. If my offices can be of assistance to you in this, please tell me."

"I appreciate the offer, Your Grace, but I have the channels to take care of that myself."

"Good. And if I may offer one bit of advice—or, perhaps, make a request?"

"Certainly you may, Your Grace," Allison said. *Of course, I don't have to* follow *the advice if it violates my own professional oaths,* she thought, bracing herself for some last-minute swerve towards suppression of her findings.

"This information must be made public, and the sooner the better," he said firmly, "yet it would be wiser, I think, to allow the Sword to make the announcement." She cocked her head at him, and he twitched his shoulders with a small, apologetic smile. "You remain a woman, a foreigner, and—if you will forgive the term—an 'infidel.' We learned from your daughter that those were not necessarily bad things, yet some of our people, especially the more conservative, remain uneasy with the notion of women in positions of authority. Including, alas, myself from time to time. I wrestle with it in prayer, and with the Comforter's aid, I feel I have made some progress, yet I had hoped that Lady Harrington would—"

He broke off, his expression sad, and Allison felt a brief, terrible stab of hurt deep down inside. *"I had hoped Lady Harrington would live long enough to change our minds,"* she completed the thought for him, and felt her eyes sting. *Well, she didn't. But that doesn't mean other people can't pick up the torch for her, and I can damned well be one of them!* Howard Clinkscales' request flickered in the back of her mind as the thought flashed past, but she only looked at Sullivan and nodded.

"I know, Your Grace." Her voice was just a bit husky. Then she inhaled deeply. "And I understand. I have no problem with allowing Protector Benjamin's people to make the announcement. Besides, there's no huge rush about this—your planet has survived for the next best thing to a thousand years with the problem, and I'm nowhere near devising a corrective procedure that I'd feel comfortable recommending, anyway. Better to go through channels and possibly even give the Sword a little while to consider the best way to go public . . . and what position the Protector should take when it hits the 'faxes."

"That was very much my own thought," Sullivan told her. "Nonetheless, I also believe I'll personally suggest to the Protector that you should be present—and clearly credited with the discovery—when the announcement is made."

"You will?" Allison blinked in surprise, and he shrugged.

"My Lady, you did discover it, and you and the clinic your daughter endowed will undoubtedly take the lead in devising any 'corrective procedure' which may be found. Besides, if we're ever to overcome that 'foreign and female' problem among our more mulish people," he smiled and flicked one finger briefly at his own chest, "then we dare not miss an opportunity such as this."

"I see." Allison considered him with fresh thoughtfulness. Reverend Sullivan was not only less comfortable with the changes in his society, on a personal level, than his predecessor had been; he was also *aware* that he was. His faith and his intellect impelled him to accept and support them, but a part of him longed for the stability and comfortably defined roles of the planet on which he had been raised, and that part resisted his own duty to help demolish those definitions. Which made his last suggestion even more impressive, and she felt a deep, warm rush of affection for him.

"Thank you, Your Grace. I appreciate the suggestion—and the thought."

"You are more than welcome, My Lady," he told her, setting his teacup aside and rising as she came to her feet, switched off the holo projector, and tucked it back into her briefcase. "But no thanks are necessary," he continued, once more capturing her hand to escort her back to the door. "This planet, and all the people on it, are far too deeply in debt to the Harrington family, and especially to the really remarkable women of that name, for that."

Allison blushed, and he chuckled delightedly, then paused as they reached the door. He bent over her hand and kissed it gallantly, and then opened the door for her.

"Farewell, Lady Harrington. May the Tester, the Intercessor, and the Comforter be with you and your husband and bring you peace."

He bowed once more, and she gave his hand a squeeze of thanks and stepped through the door. It closed quietly behind her.

Chapter Seven

The sentries at Harrington House's East Portico snapped to attention with even greater than usual precision as the luxury ground car purred through the dome's main vehicle entrance. A small pennon—a triangle of maroon and gold bearing the opened Bible and crossed swords that were the Protector's emblem, starched-stiff in the wind of its passage—flew from a fender-mounted staff, and two-man grav sleds hovered watchfully above it. Further up, out of sight from the ground, sleek transatmospheric craft kept equally attentive watch, and teams of crack marksmen—some in Mayhew maroon-and-gold, and some in Harrington Steading's green-on-green—stood unobtrusively on vantage points on Harrington House's roof and dome catwalks while sophisticated electronic devices scanned the grounds ceaselessly.

It all seemed just a trifle much to Allison Harrington. She knew about the security features built into Harrington House, and she'd gotten used to the notion that Harrington Steading's armsmen insisted on watching over her and her husband, although she was devoutly thankful that they were less intrusive about it than they had been about guarding poor Honor. More to the point, she supposed, she'd anticipated some of this in advance, given the nature of the occasion. Even if she hadn't, Miranda LaFollet's expression when she suggested it would have offered ample warning. Miranda continued to function as Harrington Steading chief of staff, so it was she who had been responsible for issuing the actual invitation, and she'd shown more than a little trepidation at the prospect. Allison had been confident that the invitees would accept, and she'd been right. But if she'd realized a simple supper invitation was going to put the equivalent of what seemed like a full Marine brigade on alert, she probably wouldn't have had the nerve to issue it in the first place.

Not "nerve," she corrected herself. *Gall.*

The thought helped, and she smiled more naturally as she and Alfred stepped out under the portico with Howard Clinkscales to greet their guests. Miranda and Farragut flanked them on Allison's right, and James MacGuiness, in the civilian clothing he'd worn since returning to Grayson, followed on Alfred's left. At Benjamin IX's personal request, the RMN had granted the steward indefinite leave in order for him to serve as Harrington House's majordomo, and his eyes swept back and forth almost as attentively as the watching armsmen's, searching for any imperfection.

They found none. The green-uniformed men on either side of the doorway stood rigidly to attention, gazes fixed straight ahead, as the ground car slid to a halt. The counter-grav ground effect died, and gravel crunched as the car settled. Then the front passenger door opened, and an athletic major in maroon and gold, with the braided aigulette of Palace Security hanging from his right shoulder, climbed out it.

The Mayhew armsman stood scanning his surroundings while he listened to reports over his earbug. Grav sleds swept through the portal and grounded, and a dozen more men in the same colors joined the major to form an alert, open ring about the car. Then he nodded, and a sergeant opened a rear door and snapped to the salute as Benjamin IX stepped out of it past him.

The Protector waved as Allison, Alfred, and Clinkscales came down the steps to greet him, then turned and handed Katherine Mayhew, his senior wife, from the car. Allison and Katherine had met briefly on several occasions during the days before Honor's funeral, but the demands of protocol and solemnity had kept them from truly getting to know one another. Nonetheless, Allison had sensed a kindred spirit in Katherine, even through the unrelenting formality of those dreary days, and this was one case in which it probably helped that she hadn't been born to an aristocratic tradition. She understood how such traditions worked, and she'd come to respect them—mostly—but they weren't really a part of her cultural baggage. That left her less impressed with Katherine Mayhew's rank than she might have been, and she looked forward to becoming better acquainted with the other woman despite her exalted position, for she suspected they were too much alike not to become friends. They were also very much of a size—which was to say "tiny"—and the First Lady of Grayson held out her hand with a smile as Allison swept down on her.

"Good afternoon, Madam Mayhew," Allison said formally, and Katherine shook her head.

"I would really prefer 'Katherine,' or even 'Cat,'" she said. "'Madam Mayhew' sounds much too formal coming from a Harrington."

"I see . . . Katherine," Allison murmured, and Katherine squeezed her hand and turned to greet Alfred as Benjamin assisted his second wife, Elaine, from the car. Elaine was the shy one, Allison remembered, although the Protector's junior wife seemed to have gained considerably in composure compared to the almost timid person Honor had described from their first meeting, and Allison greeted her warmly.

"Thank you for inviting us," Elaine replied, smiling as she watched Alfred bend over Katherine's hand as gallantly as any Grayson might have. "It's not often we get out for anything except formal occasions."

"This isn't *formal?*" Allison demanded, flicking her free hand at all the punctilious military courtesy and firepower conspicuously displayed about them.

"Oh, goodness no!" Elaine laughed. "With the entire family—except for Michael, of course—all out in the open in one place? This is the lightest security I've seen in, oh, *ages!*"

Allison was certain for a moment that her leg was being pulled, but then she looked back at the major and realized Elaine was dead serious. The major was too well trained to be obvious, but he was clearly unhappy about his charges' potential exposure, and Allison hid a wince of sympathy as he almost visibly swallowed a need to urge the Protector and his wives to get themselves inside Harrington House and under cover. Unfortunately for the major, Benjamin was in no hurry, and Allison chuckled as a torrent of Mayhew offspring poured out of the car on Elaine's heels.

Actually, there were only four of them; they merely seemed like a torrent, and individual armsmen peeled off to attach themselves to each child with the ease of long practice. It seemed dreadfully unfair for children that young to already be burdened with their own permanent, personal bodyguards, but Allison supposed they'd better start getting used to the fanatical way Graysons guarded their steadholders and protectors early. And truth to tell, their armsmen's presence certainly didn't seem to have stunted the Mayhew brood's boisterous development.

The sturdy eleven-year-old in the lead favored Katherine strongly, although she was already as tall as her mother and promised to go right on growing. Rachel Mayhew had been the terror of the palace nursery in her day, and she seemed to be fighting a stubborn rearguard action against the encroachments of civilization. From a few amused comments Clinkscales had let drop, Allison suspected Honor had been a major influence on the taste Rachel had developed for "unladylike" athletics. She was already training as a pilot, as well, and carried a very respectable grade-point average, but her tastes ran to the engineering and hard science courses which had been traditionally male on Grayson. Even worse, in conservative eyes, perhaps, she already held a brown belt in *coup de vitesse.*

The old-fashioned term "tomboy" came to mind every time Allison laid eyes on the girl—who was more likely to be cheerfully engaged in taking an air car's grav generators apart to see how they worked than in learning to dance, giggle over the opposite sex, or any of the other things she "ought" to be doing. At the moment, one of her hair ribbons had come untied, and she'd managed to get a smear of dirt on her cheek. Which, Allison reflected, must have taken some doing, since the ground car had brought her and her family straight here from the shuttle pad. *Funny. I thought* Honor *was the only child who could teleport dirt into otherwise sterile environments!*

Jeanette and Theresa—ten and nine and the biological daughters of Elaine and Katherine, respectively—followed just a bit more sedately. Jeanette had the same dark eyes as Rachel, but her hair was a bright chestnut, whereas Theresa's resemblance to their oldest sister was almost eerie. Except that Theresa was neat as a new pin and obviously hadn't made the acquaintance of Rachel's secret dirt patch.

And finally, Benjamin reached back into the car and lifted out his youngest daughter. The baby of the family—for the moment; that status tended to be transitory in families the size people were raising on Grayson these days—she was only four years old and clearly another of Elaine's. She was tall for her age, with hair much the same auburn as Miranda LaFollet's, and huge sea-gray eyes, and a promise of elegant beauty already showed through her immature child's bone structure. She buried her face shyly against her father when she saw all the strangers, but then she straightened up and demanded to be put down. Benjamin complied, and she reached out and grabbed one of Katherine's hands tightly while she stared curiously at Allison.

"Our youngest," Katherine said quietly, touching the child's curly mop of hair with her free hand. "Your daughter's goddaughter."

Allison had known who the little girl was, but her eyes misted for just a moment anyway. She stooped gracefully, making herself the same height as the child, cleared her throat, and held out her own hand.

"My name is Allison," she said. "What's your name?"

The girl looked gravely at the offered hand for several seconds, then back at Allison's face.

"Honor," she said after a moment. Her Grayson accent softened the name, but she spoke clearly and distinctly. "Honor Mayhew."

"Honor," Allison repeated, keeping the pain from her own voice, and smiled. "That's a very good name for someone, don't you think?" Honor nodded wordlessly. Then she reached out and laid her hand in the one Allison still held extended. She looked up at Katherine and Elaine as if for approval, and Katherine smiled at her. She smiled back, then looked up at Allison.

"I'm four," she announced.

"Four years old?" Allison asked.

"Uh-huh. And *number* four, too," Honor told her with a grin.

"I see." Allison nodded in grave approval and stood back fully erect, still holding Honor's hand. Each of the adult Mayhews had corralled one of the older girls, and Allison dimpled as the major sighed in profound relief when MacGuiness, with the able assistance of Miranda and Farragut, began chivvying people up the steps.

"—so we were *delighted* by the invitation," Benjamin said, leaning back in the comfortable armchair in the Harrington House library while he nursed a glass of Alfred Harrington's prized Delacourt. Allison had decided to use the library instead of one of the grander, more formal sitting rooms the architects had provided. Aside from the huge Harrington seal inlaid into the polished hardwood floor, the library managed not to shout that it was part of a consciously designed "great house," and the titles on its shelves and the relatively simple but comfortable furnishings and efficient data retrieval systems made her think of Honor. Given her determination to keep the night informal, Clinkscales had withdrawn with a gracious smile to join his wives while the Harringtons entertained their guests. Now she and Alfred and the adult Mayhews sat in a comfortably arranged conversational group near the main data terminal, and Benjamin waved his wineglass gently.

"I won't say we never get out—there's always some damned state occasion or another—but just to visit someone?" He shook his head.

"Actually," Katherine said with a wicked smile, "we're all rather hoping some of the other Keys decide to follow your example, Allison. Tester knows half the wives out there are hovering on the brink of death from pure envy over your 'social coup' right now!" Allison's eyebrows rose, and Katherine chuckled warmly. "Of course they are! You're the first hostess outside the immediate Mayhew Clan or one of its core septs who's had the sheer nerve to simply invite the Protector and his family over for a friendly family dinner in over two hundred T-years!"

"You're joking . . . aren't you?"

"Oh, no she isn't," Benjamin said. "She checked the records. What was the last time, Cat?"

"Bernard VII and his wives were invited to a surprise birthday party by John Mackenzie XI on June 10, 3807—um, 1704 P.D.," Katherine replied promptly. "And the experience clearly made a profound impression on Bernard, because I found the actual menu, including the ice cream flavors, in his personal diary."

"Two hundred and eight years?" Allison shook her head, unable to believe it. "*That* long without an invitation for anything but a state occasion?"

"I wouldn't imagine many people just screen Queen Elizabeth and ask her if she'd like to drop by for a beer, Alley," Alfred observed dryly.

"No, but she has to get invitations at least a bit more frequently than once every two centuries!" Allison protested.

"Perhaps so," Benjamin agreed. "But here on Grayson, any informal or personal invitations traditionally go from the Protector to the steadholders, not the other way around."

"Oh, dear. Have we violated protocol that grossly?" Allison sighed.

"You certainly have," Benjamin replied. "And a darned good thing, too." Allison still looked a little concerned, but Elaine nodded in vigorous agreement with her husband even as she removed an old-fashioned printed book from Honor's clutches before it could suffer serious damage.

"Benjamin warned Katherine and me both about protocol before he proposed," Elaine said over her shoulder, leading an indignant Honor firmly back towards where the older Mayhew girls were engaged in a board game with Miranda LaFollet. Rachel had expressed some rather pointed reservations about her younger siblings' level of skill, but she had a basically sunny disposition, and she'd let herself be talked into playing. By now, she'd forgotten to maintain her air of exaggerated patience and entered as fully into the play as Jeanette or Theresa while Farragut watched over them all from the back of Miranda's chair.

The game was one Allison had never heard of before coming to Grayson, but like their peculiar sport of "baseball," it seemed ingrained into Graysons at an almost genetic level. At the moment, Miranda had just thrown the dice and finished moving her token—a scuffed and worn-out-looking antique shoe of cast silver—around the perimeter of the polished, inlaid wood board to a square labeled "VENTNOR AVENUE," and Theresa squealed in triumph.

"I've got a hotel! I've got a hotel!" she announced. "Pay me, 'Randa!"

"I can see taxes are going up if *you* ever become Minister of Finance," Miranda muttered, making all three sisters laugh, and began counting gaily-colored plaspaper strips of play money. Elaine parked Honor on a stool beside her, and Miranda looked up and then smiled at Honor. "I think I'm in trouble here," she confided. "Want to help me and Farragut count all the money I owe your sister?"

Honor nodded vigorously, indignation suddenly forgotten, as Farragut flowed down to sit beside her stool and lean against her, and Elaine returned to join Katherine on the couch facing Allison across a coffee table of beaten copper.

"He warned us about all the protocol," she went on, recapturing the thread of her earlier conversation, "but I don't think either of us really believed him. I know I didn't, anyway! Did you, Cat?"

"Oh, intellectually, maybe," Katherine said. "But emotionally?" She shook her head and leaned back, putting an arm around her sister wife's shoulders, and Elaine leaned comfortably against her. "We both grew up on Grayson, of course, but I don't think anyone who hasn't experienced it from the inside can really understand just how . . . entrenched the protocol at Protector's Palace really is. Not deep down inside."

"We've had a thousand years to make it ironclad," Benjamin said with a shrug. "It's like an unwritten constitution no one would dream of violating . . . except, thank God, for foreigners who don't know any better. That's one reason Honor was such a breath of fresh-filtered air." He smiled a crooked smile of warm memory. "She started out standing protocol on its head during the Masadan War, and she never really stopped. I think she was trying to learn to 'be good' about it, but she never quite got the knack, thank the Tester."

Allison nodded, squeezing Alfred's hand at the mention of her daughter's name, then deliberately changed the subject.

"Given what you've just said, I really hate to mention anything which could be remotely construed as business, Your Grace, but did you have a chance to read the report I sent you?"

"Please, Allison, in private at least," Benjamin protested. Allison glanced at the two armsmen standing just inside the library doors and the second pair hovering watchfully if unobtrusively over the Protector's daughters and their game, then shrugged. "Privacy" was obviously a relative concept.

"Very well. But did you get a chance to read it, Benjamin?"

"I did," he said, his tone suddenly graver. "More to the point, I had Cat read it. She has a better biosciences background than I ever managed to acquire."

"That's because *I* wasn't a stodgy old history and government science major," Katherine told him, and her eyes twinkled at Allison. "And I wanted to thank you for being the one who turned up the truth, Allison. It's exactly the sort of multifunction kick in the seat of the pants I've come to expect from Harringtons!"

"Excuse me?" Allison looked puzzled, and Katherine grinned.

"I imagine you've heard at least a few people muttering about how 'proper' Grayson women don't work?"

"Well, yes. I have," Allison admitted.

"Well, that's one of the stupider social fables around," Katherine said roundly. "Traditionally, women haven't been *paid* for working, but believe me, running a Grayson home requires more than someone to bear and raise children. Of course, most of us were never allowed the formal training men got—Benjamin was dreadfully unconventional in that regard—but *you* try tearing down an air filtration plant, or monitoring the metals levels in the vegetables you're planning on cooking for supper, or managing the reclamation plant, or setting the toxicity alarms in the nursery, or any one of a thousand and one other 'household' chores without at least a practical education in biology, chemistry, hydraulics—!" She snorted with magnificent panache.

"Elaine and I have the degrees that go with what we know; most Grayson women don't have that certification, but that doesn't mean they're ignorant. And, of course, Elaine and I are from the very tip-top of the upper class. We really don't have to work if we don't want to, and most women can at least turn to their families or clans for a household niche to fill even if they never manage to catch a husband, but there have always been some women who've had no option but to support themselves in the workplace. Most people try to pretend they don't exist, but they do, and that's one reason all three of us—" she waved her hand at her husband and sister wife "—were so *delighted* to see women like Honor and yourself. Anyone with a halfway functioning brain knows women can, and have, and *do* 'work' just as hard as any man on this planet, but you and Honor rub their noses in it. You're even more visible than Elaine and I, in some ways, and you and other Manticoran women are one of the big reasons other Grayson women are stepping into the work force at last. In fact, I understand Honor insisted that the Blackbird Yard actively recruit local women, and I hope to goodness other employers have the sense to do the same!"

"I see," Allison said. And, intellectually, she did. Emotionally, the sort of society which could draw such artificial distinctions to start with was too alien for her to truly empathize with. She considered it for several more seconds, then shrugged.

"I see," she repeated, "but I can't really claim any special credit, you know. All I'm doing is going right on as I always have."

"I know," Katherine said. "That's why you're such an effective example. Anyone who sees you *knows* you're more interested in getting the work done than in 'making a point' . . . which, of course, only makes the point more emphatically." She smiled gently. "It was exactly the same thing that made Honor so effective, too."

Allison blinked on unexpected tears and felt Alfred's arm slip around her and tighten. Silence lingered for a moment, and then Katherine went on.

"But as Benjamin says, I did read the report. The appendices were a bit too abstruse for me, but you did an excellent job of explaining the major points in the text, I think." She shook her head with a look of ineffable sadness that sprang from a very different source, and Allison reminded herself that between them, Katherine and Elaine Mayhew had already lost five sons to spontaneous early-term abortion.

"To think that we did it to our birthrate ourselves." Katherine sighed, and it was Allison's turn to shake her head.

"Not intentionally or knowingly," she pointed out. "And if whoever it was hadn't done it, there wouldn't be *any* Graysons today. It was a brilliant approach to a deadly problem, especially given the limitations under which it was implemented."

"Oh, I know that," Katherine said, "and I certainly wasn't complaining."

And that, Allison realized with some surprise, was actually true. She very much doubted that it would have been for her in her guest's place.

"It's just that—" Katherine shrugged. "It comes as a bit of a surprise after all these centuries, I suppose. I mean, in a way it's so . . . prosaic. Especially for something which has had such a profound effect on our society and family structure."

"Um." Allison cocked her head for a moment, then waved a hand in a tiny throwing away gesture. "From what I've seen of your world, you seem to have adjusted remarkably sanely on a family level."

"Do you really think so?" Katherine asked, cocking her head to one side. There was a tiny edge to her voice, and Allison raised an eyebrow.

"Yes, I do," she said calmly. "Why?"

"Because not every off-worlder does," Katherine said. She glanced at her husband and her sister wife for a moment, then back at Allison, almost challengingly. "Some seem to find some of our lifestyle 'adjustments' . . . morally offensive."

"If they do, that's their problem, not yours," Allison replied with a shrug. Inwardly, she wondered which off-worlder had been stupid enough to step on Katherine Mayhew's toes . . . and to hope it hadn't been a Manticoran. She didn't *think* it would have been. For the most part, the Star Kingdom refused to tolerate intolerance, although it was less self-congratulatory about it than Beowulf, but she could call to mind one or two Sphinxians who might have been prudish enough to offend. Given the enormous disparity between male and female births, Grayson attitudes towards homosexuality and bisexuality were inevitable, and Sphinx was by far the most straitlaced of the Star Kingdom's planets. For a horrible moment, Allison wondered if somehow *Honor* could have—? But no. Her daughter might have been more sexually repressed than Allison would have preferred, but she'd never been a prude or a bigot. And even if she had been, Katherine Mayhew certainly wasn't the kind of person to bring it up to hurt Allison now that Honor was gone.

"Of course, I'm from Beowulf, and we *all* know what Beowulfans are like," she went on calmly, and almost despite herself, Katherine chuckled. "On the other hand, genetic surgeons see even more different sorts of familial arrangements in the course of our practices than most family practitioners do; it goes with the sort of diagnostic research we have to do. I've been doing rounds at Macomb General here in Harrington, too, which gives me a pretty good opportunity to compare Manticoran and Grayson norms, and I stand by what I said. Your children are among the most secure and loved ones I've ever seen, and that's comparing them to Beowulf and the Star Kingdom both. That's what matters most, I think, and your traditional family structure—especially in light of your environment—represents an incredibly sane response to your skewed birthrates." Katherine gazed at her for a moment, then nodded, and Allison grinned suddenly. "Now, your *social* responses, as I believe you yourself were just pointing out, might leave just a *tad* to be desired from the viewpoint of a forward, stubborn, uppity wench like myself!"

"You're not the only one of those in this room, believe me!" Benjamin laughed. "And I'm doing the best I can to change the rules, Allison. I figure that if Cat and Elaine and I can kick the door open and keep it that way, those budding real estate tycoons over there—" he twitched his head in the direction of the game board as it became Jeanette's turn to cackle in triumph "—are going to make even more changes. For a bunch as conservative as we are, that's blinding speed."

"So I've seen."

Allison leaned back beside Alfred and looked up at him with a gracefully quirked eyebrow. He looked back down, and then shrugged.

"You're the one doing all the social engineering tonight, love," he told her. "You decide."

"Decide what?" Katherine asked.

"Whether or not to taint the first hooky-playing Mayhew family outing in two centuries with a little business after all, I suspect," Benjamin said lazily.

"Something like that," Allison admitted. "I'd planned on discussing a couple of possible approaches to corrective genetic therapies with you, but that can certainly wait for another time. Besides," she grinned, "now I know which Mayhew I should discuss them with, don't I, Katherine?"

"Science with me and finance with Elaine," Katherine agreed comfortably. "Unimportant things like wars, diplomacy, and constitutional crises you can take up with Benjamin." Her right hand made an airy gesture.

"Oh, thank you. Thank you all so much!" Benjamin said, and shook a mock-threatening fist at his smiling wives.

"Well, leaving genomes and such aside, there are still a couple of things Alfred and I did want to announce tonight," Allison said in a more serious tone, and looked over at the card table in the corner. "Miranda?" she asked.

"Of course, My Lady." Miranda raised her wrist com to her lips—a maneuver made a bit more complicated than usual by the need to reach around Honor, who was now parked firmly in her lap with Farragut clutched in her arms and an enormous smile on her face—and spoke into it quietly. The adult Mayhews looked at one another curiously, but no one said anything for several seconds. Then someone knocked lightly on the door.

One of the Mayhew armsmen opened it, and James MacGuiness stepped into the library.

"You needed something, Milady?" he asked Allison.

"Not something, Mac—some*one*," Allison replied gently. "Please, sit down." She patted the chair beside the couch she and Alfred shared.

MacGuiness hesitated, his natural deference warring with her invitation. Then he drew a deep breath, shrugged almost microscopically, and obeyed her. She smiled and squeezed his shoulder gently, then looked back at the Mayhews.

"One of the things Alfred and I wanted to tell you is that Willard Neufsteiler will be arriving from the Star Kingdom aboard the *Tankersley* next week. When he does, he'll be bringing Honor's will." A chill breeze seemed to blow through the comfortably furnished library, but Allison ignored it. "Because almost half of her financial and business activities were still based in the Star Kingdom, the will has already been probated under Manticoran law, although I understand the portions which affect Grayson will have to be formally probated here, in turn. All the legal details, investment cross links, and tax options make my head hurt—give me a good, simple chromosome to map any day!—but Willard has sent along a *précis*, and Alfred and I wanted to share the rough outlines with you tonight, if no one objects."

Benjamin shook his head silently, and Allison looked at MacGuiness. The steward's face was stiff, and pain flashed in his eyes, as if he'd realized why she wanted him here and wanted nothing to do with yet another formal proof of his captain's death. But then he, too, shook his head, and Allison smiled at him.

"Thank you," she said softly. She took a moment to collect her thoughts, then cleared her throat.

"First of all, I was quite astounded to discover just how large an estate Honor left. Excluding her feudal holdings here on Grayson as Steadholder Harrington, but including the value of her private interest in Sky Domes and your new Blackbird Shipyard, her net financial worth at the time of her death was just under seventeen-point-four billion Manticoran dollars." Despite himself, Benjamin pursed his lips and whistled silently, and Allison nodded.

"Alfred and I had no idea the estate had grown to anything that size," she went on matter-of-factly, with only the pressure of her grip on her husband's hand to show how dearly bought her outer calm was. "For that matter, I'm not at all certain *she* realized it, especially since over a quarter of the entire total was generated out of the Blackbird Yard in the last three years. But Willard had things superbly organized for her, as usual, and he seems to have managed to execute her wishes completely.

"The biggest part of what she wanted done was her instruction to merge all of her personal holdings and funds in the Star Kingdom—exclusive of a few special bequests—and fold them over into Grayson Sky Domes. Lord Clinkscales will continue as CEO, and Sky Domes will be held in trust for the next Steadholder Harrington with the proviso that all future financial operations will be based here, on Grayson, and that a majority of the members of the Sky Domes board of directors must be citizens of Harrington Steading. Our understanding is that Willard will be relocating to

Grayson to serve full-time as Sky Domes' chief financial officer and manager."

"That was very generous of her," Benjamin said quietly. "That much capital investment in Harrington and Grayson—and in our tax base—will have a major impact."

"Which was what she wanted," Alfred agreed. "There are, however, those special bequests Alley mentioned. Aside from a very generous one to us, she's also establishing a trust fund of sixty-five million dollars for the treecats here on Grayson, adding another hundred million to the endowment for the clinic, and donating fifty million to the Sword Museum of Art in Austin City. In addition, she's going to establish a trust fund for the families of her personal armsmen in the amount of another hundred million and—" he looked at MacGuiness "—she's bequeathed forty million dollars to you, Mac."

MacGuiness stiffened, going white with shock, and Allison gripped his shoulder again.

"There are just two stipulations, Mac," she said quietly. "One is that you retire from the Navy. I think she felt she'd dragged you through enough battles with her, and she wanted to know you were safe. And the second is that you look after Samantha and the children for her and Nimitz."

"Of . . . Of course, Milady," the steward husked. "She didn't have to—" His voice broke, and Allison smiled mistily at him.

"Of course she didn't 'have to,' Mac. She *wanted* to. Just as she wanted to leave Miranda twenty million." Miranda inhaled sharply, but Allison went on calmly. "There are some other minor stipulations, but those are the important ones. Willard will bring all the official documentation with him, of course."

"She was a remarkable woman," Benjamin said softly.

"Yes, she was," Allison agreed. Silence lingered for several seconds, and then she drew a deep breath and rose.

"And now, since this *was* a 'supper' invitation, I imagine we should get on to the supper in question! Are we ready, Mac?"

"I believe so, Ma'am." MacGuiness shook himself and rose. "I'll just go check to be certain."

He opened the library doors, then paused and stepped back with a wry grin as a quartet of treecats came through it. Jason and his sister Andromeda led the way, but Hipper and Artemis trailed along behind, keeping a watchful eye on them. The 'kittens scurried forward, with an apparently suicidal disregard for the possibility of being trodden on, but Allison wasn't particularly worried. She had been initially, but treekittens had incredibly fast reaction speeds, and somehow they always managed to be somewhere the foot wasn't at the moment it came down.

Now she watched them stop and sit bolt upright as they caught the emotions of the Protector's daughters. The 'kittens' ears pricked sharply, their green eyes intent, for it was the first time they'd tasted the emotions of human children, and their tails twitched. Artemis plunked down and watched them with a maternal air, and Allison's earlier comments to Katherine flickered back through her brain. There were a great many similarities between treecat and Grayson notions of child rearing, she reflected. And a good thing, too. The Peeps hadn't said a word about it, but every member of Honor's extended family—human and 'cat alike—knew Nimitz had not survived her. More often than not, 'cats suicided when their adopted humans died, yet that was almost beside the point here. For the Peeps to hang Honor, they had to have killed Nimitz first; it was the only way they could have—

Allison's thoughts broke off abruptly as something jabbed at the corner of her attention and pulled her up out of the bitter memories. She blinked, attention refocusing on the library as she tried to figure out what her subconscious had noticed, and then her eyes widened. Artemis was watching the 'kittens as the Mayhew children swarmed forward—suitably cautious after a sharp word from Elaine but still bubbling with delight—to greet the 'kittens. That was hardly surprising, for Honor had told Allison how the children had loved Nimitz, and these were *'kittens*. Brand new, cuddly, *wonderful* 'kittens!

But if Artemis was watching with amused affection, Hipper wasn't. He was crouched on all six limbs, leaning forward almost like a human sprinter poised in the blocks before a race, with his tail straight out behind him. Only the very tip of that tail twitched in quick, tiny arcs; aside from that, he was motionless, and he wasn't even glancing at the 'kittens. His grass-green eyes were locked on the Mayhews.

No, Allison thought with sudden understanding. *Not on* the *Mayhews; on* a *Mayhew*.

The realization flicked through her in an instant and she began to open her mouth, but not quickly enough. Hipper suddenly shook himself and leapt forward in a cream-and-gray blur, streaking across the library towards the children.

Rachel Mayhew's personal armsman saw him coming and reacted with the spinal-reflex quickness of his training. Intellectually, he knew no treecat would ever threaten a child, yet his reflexes were another matter, and his hand flashed out to sweep the girl aside and place himself between her and the potential threat.

But he didn't quite manage it, for even as Hipper had started forward, Rachel's head had snapped around as if someone had shouted her name. Her brown eyes settled on Hipper with unerring accuracy, and as her armsman reached for her, she dodged his arm with astonishing agility. She crouched, opening her arms with a blinding smile of welcome, and Hipper catapulted from the floor into her embrace.

She was only eleven years old, and at 10.3 standard kilos, Hipper was one of the largest treecats Allison had ever met. Which, coupled with Grayson's 1.17 *g* gravity and the conservation of momentum, had predictable results.

Rachel went back on her bottom with a thump as the 'cat landed in her arms, and Allison's hand flashed out. She caught Rachel's armsman's wrist out of sheer reflex, without even thinking about it, and only later realized that she'd stopped his hand on its way to the pulser at his hip. But it didn't really matter. Even as she gripped it, she felt his muscles relax in sudden, explosive relief as everyone in the library heard Hipper's high, buzzing purr of delight and watched the 'cat rubbing his cheek ecstatically against Rachel's.

Rachel's sisters stared at her, stunned, and the adults were little better. Only Miranda moved. She scooped up Farragut and came over to kneel beside Rachel, but the girl never even noticed. At that moment, Hipper was her entire universe, just as she was his.

"Oh . . . my," Katherine murmured finally. She shook herself and looked at Allison.

"This *is* what I think it is, isn't it?" she asked very quietly, and Allison sighed.

"It is. And you have my genuine sympathy."

"Sympathy?" Katherine's brow furrowed. "Surely you don't mean he might hurt her or—?"

"Oh, no! Nothing like that!" Allison reassured her quickly. "But, well, it's very unusual, shall we say, for a 'cat to adopt a child. Not unheard of, of course. The very first adoption on Sphinx was of a child about Rachel's age . . . or Honor's. And it's a very good thing, in most ways, but there are some . . . adjustments."

"What sort?" Elaine asked, moving to stand behind her sister wife, and Allison smiled crookedly.

"For one thing, he's going to be even worse than a Grayson's personal armsman. You're never going to be able to separate them, not even for baths or doctor's visits, and you can forget about leaving him home on state occasions! And she's not going to want to put him down, either."

"Well, I don't see any reason to try to convince her to tonight," Katherine said after a glance at Elaine.

"I didn't mean she won't want to put him down tonight," Allison told her wryly. "I meant she's not going to want to put him down *ever*. Physical contact is very important to both sides of an adoption bond, particularly one where the human half is this young, and especially during the initial several months. I thought Nimitz had been grafted onto Honor for the first T-year or so!"

"Oh, my," Katherine sighed on a very different note.

"And another thing, you'll have to warn the adults who're likely to enter her orbit to keep an eye on their own emotions." Elaine looked at her sharply, and Allison shrugged. "For the most part, a 'cat makes a wonderful babysitter. No abusive personality is going to be able to fool him, and your family knows better than most how effective a protector a treecat can be." Both Mayhews nodded at that, and Allison shrugged again. "Unfortunately, 'cats are also very sensitive to emotions directed at their persons . . . or that they think might end *up* directed at their persons. Which means that he's going to be very tense around people who are angry in Rachel's presence, whether it's at her or something with no connection to her at all. And finally, you're going to have some very interesting experiences when she enters puberty."

Katherine's eyes widened, and Allison chuckled.

"No, no. As far as I've ever been able to determine, 'cats have no interest at all in their people's, um, amatory adventures. But they're empaths. When all those hormonal mood swings start hitting her, *both* of them are going to be irritable as hell. The only good thing about it is that by our best estimate Hipper is about fifty T-years old. That means he's about the age Nimitz was when he adopted Honor. It also means he's got a lot more maturity than Rachel does, and if he's anything like Nimitz was, he won't put up with his person's *whining* at all. Not a minor consideration with a teenager, I think."

"Oh, dear." It was Elaine this time, yet there was a bubble of laughter under her sigh, and she shook her head. Then she sobered. "Actually, that may be the least of our worries, Cat," she said quietly. "What about the other girls?"

"Jealousy?" Allison asked, equally quietly, her eyes back on Rachel and Hipper. Rachel's sisters were coming forward now, going to their knees around her while Jason and Andromeda looked on with bright, interested eyes. Alfred and Benjamin stood to one side, talking softly, and she smiled, then looked back at the Mayhew wives.

"Honor was an only child, so my experiences were undoubtedly different from what yours are going to be, but I don't think that will be a problem," she assured them.

"Why not?" Katherine asked.

"Because Hipper is a 'cat," Allison explained. "He's an empath. He'll be able to feel their emotions as well as Rachel's, and that's one of the very best things about childhood adoptions. They may be rare, but they're *very* good for the child, because their 'cat teaches them to be sensitive to the feelings of others. You'll want to keep an eye on her for a few weeks or so, of course. Even the best kids can get smug and start thinking of themselves as better than anyone else when something this special happens, and the bond is going to take a couple of months to start settling. She could really put the other girls' backs up in that interval, with all kinds of long-term consequences. But unless something like that happens—and I don't think it will—Hipper is going to spend an awful lot of time playing with the others, too." She shook her head with a grin. "For that matter, he's going to think he's in 'cat heaven when he realizes he has *four* of them to spoil him rotten!"

Book Two

Chapter Eight

"Haa-haaaa-*choooo!*"

The sneeze snapped her head back so violently stars seemed to spangle her vision. Her eyes watered, her sinuses stung, and Commodore Lady Dame Honor Harrington, Steadholder and Countess Harrington, hastily dropped the metal comb and rubbed her nose in a frantic effort to abort the next onrushing eruption.

It failed. A fresh explosion rolled around inside her head, trying to escape through her ears, and a cloud of impossibly fine down went dancing and swirling away from her. She waved her hand in front of her face, trying to disperse the cloud like a woman brushing at gnats . . . and with about the same effectiveness. The delicate, fluffy hairs only stuck to the perspiration on her hand, and she sneezed yet again.

The treecat in her lap looked up at her, but without the laughing deviltry his eyes would have held under other circumstances. Instead, it seemed to take all the energy he had just to turn his head, for poor Nimitz was stretched out as flat as his crookedly healed ribs and crippled right mid-limb and pelvis would permit while he panted miserably. Even his tail was flattened out to twice its normal width. Sphinx's winters were both long and cold, requiring thick, efficient insulation of its creatures, and treecats' fluffy coats were incredibly warm and soft. They were also silky smooth and almost frictionless . . . which could be a considerable disadvantage when it came to providing an arboreal's prehensile tail with traction. Having one's grip slip while hanging head-down from one's tail a hundred meters or so in the air was, after all, a less than ideal way to descend a tree.

The 'cats had met the challenge by evolving a tail which was both wider than most people ever realized and completely bare on its underside. Powerful muscles normally kept it tightly curled into a lengthwise tube which showed only its bushy outer surface and hid the leathery skin which gripped even wet or icy branches and limbs without a hint of slippage. It was a neat arrangement which provided maximum heat retention during the icy winter months without depriving a 'cat of the use of his tail.

But that was on Sphinx, and Sphinx was a cool planet, even in summer. The planet Hades (more commonly referred to, by those souls unfortunate enough to have been sent to it, as "Hell") was not. It orbited Cerberus-B, its G3 primary, at a scant seven light-minutes, with an axial tilt of only five degrees, and it had not been designed for treecats. The triple-canopy jungle (although, to be entirely accurate, the local jungle might better be described as *quadruple*-canopy) provided a dark, green-tinted shade which looked deceptively cool, but the current temperature here near Hell's equator was actually well over forty degrees centigrade (close to a hundred and five on the old Fahrenheit scale), with a relative humidity closing in on a hundred percent. It rained—frequently—but none of the rain ever made it straight through that dense, leafy roof. Instead, a constant mist of tiny droplets drizzled to the squelchy ground as the water filtered through the overhead cover. That kind of heat and humidity were enough to make Honor thoroughly miserable, but they had the potential to become actively life-threatening for Nimitz.

Treecats did not put on and shed winter coats on a regular calendar cycle. Instead, the thickness of their triple-layer coats was determined by their environment's current ambient temperature. It was a system which worked well on Sphinx, where a winter which hung on only a little late (relatively speaking) could easily last three or four full extra T-months and where seasonal weather changes were agreeably gradual. But the sudden transition from the moderate temperatures maintained aboard most human-crewed starships to the steam bath of Hell had been far from gradual, and the shock to Nimitz's system had been severe. He had been gradually shedding the innermost, winter-only coat he'd grown during their last stay on Sphinx even before their capture by the Peeps, but the transition to Hell had activated his shedding reflex with a vengeance. He was shedding not simply his winter coat, but also the middle coat of down which the 'cats normally maintained year round (though it grew thinner in warmer weather) with frantic haste, and Honor and her human companions spent their time enveloped in a thin, drifting haze of 'cat fur.

Perhaps fortunately for his continued survival, the two-legged people around him knew he was even more miserable than his shedding was making them. They also recognized the importance of getting his coat thinned down, and that his poorly-healed injuries made it much more difficult than usual for him to groom himself. Despite the billows of fine down which the procedure inevitably entailed, he could always find a volunteer to comb or brush his coat. Under other circumstances, he would have luxuriated shamelessly in all the attention; under these, he was as devoutly eager for the entire process to be completed as anyone could have wished.

Now he blinked up at his person with a soft, almost apologetic "bleek," and Honor stopped rubbing her nose to caress his ears, instead.

"I know, Stinker," she told him, bending over to brush her right cheek against his head. "It's not your fault."

She sat otherwise motionless for several more moments. The warning tingle in her nose refused to—quite—flash over into still another sneeze, yet she knew there was at least one more lurking in there somewhere, and she was determined to wait it out. While she did, she looked up into the branches of the tall, vaguely palm-like almost-tree beside her. The trunk was a good meter across at the base, and she could just pick out Andrew LaFollet amid the foliage thirty meters above her head. Her Grayson armsman had a hand com, a canteen, electronic binoculars, a pulser, a heavy pulse rifle with attached grenade launcher, and—for all she knew—a miniature thermonuclear device up there, and she smiled fondly.

I don't care if he does *have a nuke,* she told herself firmly. *If it makes him happy, then* I'm *happy, and at least "ordering" him to take the lookout slot keeps him from sitting around all day watching my back. This way he can watch* all *our backs . . . and we're*—I'm—*darned lucky to have him. Besi—*

Her thoughts broke off as the anticipated sneeze took advantage of her distraction to rip through her sinuses. For an instant, she thought the top had actually blown off her head, but then it was over. She waited an instant more, then sniffed heavily and leaned to the side, reaching clumsily for the dropped comb. Picking it up without letting Nimitz slide off her lap was an awkward business, for she no longer had a left arm to hold him in place while she did it. He dug the very tips of his claws into her ill-fitting trousers—carefully; the pants had come from the emergency stores of a Peep assault shuttle, and they were not only thinner than the ones she usually wore but effectively irreplaceable—until she managed to snag the comb in the fingers of her remaining hand and straightened with a sigh of relief.

"Got it!" she told him triumphantly, and a fresh wave of fluff rose as she began combing once more. He closed his eyes, and despite his overheated exhaustion and general misery, began to purr. Their empathic link carried her his gratitude for her ministrations—and for the fact that both of them had survived for her to offer them and him to accept them—and the right side of her mouth curled up in an echoing smile, edged with sadness for the men and women who had died helping them escape State Security's custody. He interrupted his buzzing purr long enough to open one eye and look up at her, as if a part of him wanted to scold her for her sorrow, but then he thought better of it and laid his chin back down as he began to buzz once more.

"Is he *ever* going to run out of hair?" a voice asked in tones of wry resignation. She turned to look for the speaker, but he was on her left side (the upwind one), and the Peeps had burned out the circuitry for the cybernetic eye on that side while she was in custody. She began to turn her entire body, but the newcomer went on quickly. "Oh, sit still, Skipper! It's my fault for forgetting the eye."

Feet swished through the low-growing, perpetually wet fern-like growth that covered every open space, and Honor's half-smile grew stronger as Alistair McKeon and Warner Caslet circled around in front of her. Like most of the other members of their small party, both of them had chopped their liberated Peep-issue pants into raggedly cut off shorts and wore only sweat-stained tee-shirts above the waist. Well, that and the ninety-centimeter bush knife each of them had slung over his left shoulder. McKeon also carried a heavy, military issue pulser (also Peep issue) holstered at his right hip, and a pair of badly worn boots—the last surviving element of his Manticoran uniform—completed his ensemble.

"What the stylish castaways are wearing this year, I see," Honor observed, and McKeon grinned as he glanced down at himself. Anything less like a commodore in the Royal Manticoran Navy would be impossible to imagine, he thought dryly . . . except, perhaps, for the woman before him.

"Maybe not stylish, but as close to comfortable as anyone's going to find on this damned planet," Caslet replied wryly. He was a native of Danville, in the Paroa System of the PRH, and his Standard English carried a sharp but oddly pleasant accent.

"Now let's not be unfair," Honor chided. "We're right in the middle of the equatorial zone here, and I understand from Chief Harkness that the higher temperate zones can be quite pleasant."

"Sure they can." McKeon snorted, and flipped a spatter of sweat off his forehead. "I understand the temperature gets all the way down to thirty-five degrees—at night at least—up in the high arctic."

"A gross exaggeration," Honor said. She spoke as primly as the dead nerves in the left side of her face allowed, and a twinkle danced in her remaining eye, but McKeon felt his own smile become just the slightest bit forced and fought an urge to glance accusingly at Caslet. Her captors had burned out her artificial facial nerves at the same time they wrecked her eye, and the slurring imposed by the crippled side of her mouth always got worse when she forgot to speak slowly and concentrate on what she was saying. He felt a fresh, lava-like boil of anger as he heard it, and he reminded himself—again—that Warner Caslet hadn't had a thing to do with it. That, in fact, the Peep naval officer had been headed for something at least as bad as Hell himself because of his efforts to help McKeon and all the other Allied prisoners aboard PNS *Tepes*.

That was all true, and McKeon knew it, but he wanted so *badly* to have someone—anyone—to take his hate out on whenever he thought about what the State Security goons had done to Honor. Ostensibly, deactivating all cybernetic implants of any prisoner had been billed as a "security measure," just as shaving her head had been solely for "sanitary purposes." But despite Honor's refusal to go into details, he knew damned well that neither "security" nor "sanitation" had had a thing to do with either. They'd been done out of sick, premeditated cruelty, pure and simple, and whenever he thought about it he felt almost sorry that the people responsible were already dead.

"All right, *thirty* degrees," he said, trying to sound as light as she did. "But only in the fall and winter."

"You're hopeless, Alistair." Honor shook her head with another of those crooked half-smiles. McKeon was too self-disciplined to let his emotions show, but she and Nimitz had felt his sudden spike of fury, and she knew exactly what had caused it. But talking about it wouldn't change anything, and so she only looked at Caslet.

"And how has *your* day been, Warner?"

"Hot and humid," Caslet replied with a smile. He glanced at McKeon, then held out a hand. "Let me have your canteen, Alistair. Dame Honor obviously wants to talk to you, so I'll take myself off and refill yours and mine both before we head back out."

"Thanks, that's probably a good idea," McKeon said, and unhooked the canteen from the left side of his belt, where it had counterbalanced the pulser. He tossed it underhand to Caslet, who caught it, sketched a jaunty half-salute, and moved off towards the grounded shuttles.

Honor turned her head to watch him go, then looked back up at McKeon.

"He's a good man," she said quietly, with no particular emphasis, and he exhaled noisily and nodded.

"Yes. Yes, he is," he replied.

It didn't sound particularly like an apology, but Honor didn't need Nimitz's empathic abilities to know it was one. In fact, Caslet and McKeon had become good friends during their time aboard *Tepes* and after their escape, but there was still that unavoidable edge of tension. Whatever else Warner Caslet might be, he was—technically, at least—still an officer of the People's Navy. Honor liked him a great deal, and she trusted him, yet that invisible line of separation still existed. And Caslet knew it as well as she did. In fact, he was the one who had quietly suggested to her that it would probably be a good idea if no one offered to issue him a pulser or a pulse rifle, and his departure to refill his and McKeon's canteens was typical of his habit of tactfully defusing potential awkwardnesses. But she still didn't know exactly what they were going to do with him. He'd been driven into opposition to *State Security* because of the way

StateSec had treated her and the others captured with her, yet she knew him too well to believe he could turn his back on the People's Republic easily. He hated and despised the PRH's current government, but like her, he took his oath as an officer seriously, and the time was going to come when he had to make some difficult decisions. Or, more accurately, some *more* difficult decisions, for his very presence here was the result of some he had already made.

And also the only reason he's still alive, she reminded herself. *He would've died with everyone else when Harkness blew up* Tepes *if Alistair hadn't brought him along. And even if the ship hadn't blown, leaving him behind wouldn't have done him any favors. Ransom would never have believed he hadn't helped with the escape, and when she got done with him—*

Honor shivered at her own thoughts, then pulled free of them and nodded for McKeon to sit on the log beside her.

He ran his hands over his dark hair, stripping away sweat, and obeyed the implied command. There was very little breeze under the thick, green ceiling of the jungle, but he was careful to take advantage of what there was and stay upwind from the cloud of drifting treecat down, and Honor chuckled.

"Fritz brought me a fresh water bottle about ten minutes ago," she said, her good eye fixed on Nimitz as she worked with the comb. "It's in the rucksack there. Help yourself."

"Thanks," McKeon said gratefully. "Warner and I finished ours off an hour ago." He reached into the rucksack, and his eyes widened as something gurgled and rattled. He brought the water bottle out quickly, shook it beside his ear, and pursed his lips in delight. "Hey, *ice!* You didn't mention that part!"

"Rank hath its privileges, Commodore McKeon," Honor replied airily. "Go ahead."

McKeon needed no third invitation, and he twisted the cap off the insulated water bottle and raised it to his lips. His head went back and he drank deeply, eyes closed in sensual ecstasy as the icy liquid flowed down his throat. Because it was intended for Honor, it was laced with protein builders and concentrated nutrients in addition to the electrolytes and other goodies Dr. Montoya insisted on adding to everyone else's drinking water. They gave an odd, slightly unpleasant edge to its taste, but the sheer decadence of its coldness brushed such minor considerations aside.

"Oh, *my!*" He lowered the water bottle at last, eyes still closed, savoring the coolness clinging to his mouth, then sighed and capped the bottle. "I'd almost forgotten what cold water tastes like," he said, putting it back into the rucksack. "Thanks, Skipper."

"Don't get too carried away over it," Honor said, shaking her head with just an edge of embarrassment, and he smiled and nodded. A part of her resented the way that Montoya insisted on "pampering" her. She tried to disguise her discomfort with a light manner, but it seemed dreadfully unfair to her, particularly when everyone else in their little party of castaways had done so much more than she to make their escape possible. At the same time, she knew better than to argue. She'd been injured far more seriously than any of the others during their desperate breakout, and she'd been more than half-starved even before that. Despite the difference in their ranks, Surgeon Commander Montoya had flatly ordered her to shut up and let him "fatten her back up," and it often seemed to her that every other member of her tiny command kept saving tidbits from their own rations for her.

Not that "tidbit" was actually a word she would normally consider applying to Peep emergency rations. Prior to her arrival on Hell, she'd thought nothing could possibly taste worse than RMN e-rats.

Well, you learn something new everyday, I suppose, she thought, then changed the subject.

"Anything new from the patrols?" she asked, and McKeon shrugged.

"Not really. Warner and I brought back those specimens Fritz wanted, but I don't think they're going to work out any better than the others. And Jasper and Anson ran into another of those bear-bobcat thingamies that was just as ill-tempered as the other two we've met." He made a disgusted sound. "It's a damned shame the local beasties don't know they can't digest us. Maybe they'd leave us alone if they did."

"Maybe not, too," Honor replied, stroking the comb up and down against her thigh to clear a clot of Nimitz fur from its teeth. "There are quite a few things people—or treecats—can't digest very well, or even at all, that they still love the taste of. For all you know your bearcat might be perfectly happy to spend the afternoon munching on you. It might even consider you a low-calorie snack!"

"It can consider me anything it likes," McKeon told her, "but if it gets close enough to me to be rude, I'm gonna feed it an appetizer of pulser darts."

"Not very friendly, but probably prudent," she conceded. "At least the things are smaller than hexapumas or peak bears."

"True." McKeon turned on the log and glanced over his shoulder at their encampment. Each of their two hijacked Peep assault shuttles was sixty-three meters in length, with a maximum wingspan of forty-three meters and a minimum span of over nineteen even with the wings in full oversweep for parking efficiency. Fervently as every member of their group might curse the hot, wet, rot-ridden, voracious jungle, hiding something the size of those two craft would have been an impossible challenge in most other kinds of terrain. As it was, the individual trees which supported the uppermost layer of the overhead canopy were just far enough apart that the pilots had been able to nudge their way between the thick trunks without actually knocking them over. And once the shuttles were down, the cammo netting which had been part of their standard supplies, coupled with the jungle's vines, lianas, fronds, leaves, branches, and tree trunks had made concealing them a straightforward task. The sheer grunt labor involved in spreading the nets with only seventeen sets of hands and just four portable grav lifters available for the job had been daunting, but the alternative had been a great motivator. They'd all had more than enough of the Office of State Security's hospitality.

"How are the converters holding up?" he asked after a moment.

"Still cranking out the current," Honor replied. She'd gotten the knot of fur out of the comb and went back to work on Nimitz. "The more I see of Peep survival equipment, the more impressed I am," she admitted, not looking up from her task. "I'd expected that most of it would be pretty shoddy compared to our own gear, but somebody in the PRH put some serious thought into equipping those two birds."

"State Security," McKeon grunted sourly. "The SS gets the best of everything else, so why not survival gear, too?"

"I don't think that's what happened here," Honor disagreed. "Harkness, Scotty, and Warner have gone through the operator's manuals, and they're all standard Navy publications. A little more simpleminded than any of ours would have been, but still Navy, not SS."

McKeon made a noncommittal sound, and she smiled down at Nimitz as she tasted the other human's urge to disagree with her. Alistair hated the very thought that anything the Peeps did or had could match the Manticoran equivalent.

"Actually," she went on, "I think their power converters may even be a bit better than ours are. They're a little bulkier and a lot more massive, but I suspect their output's higher on a weight-for-weight basis."

"Oh, yeah? Well at least their *weapons* still stink compared to ours!" McKeon told her, turning on her with a grin that acknowledged her teasing.

"True," she said solemnly. "And I suppose if I simply had to choose between having, oh, a better graser mount for my ships of the wall, let's say, or a more efficient emergency power converter for my lifeboats and shuttles, I guess I *might* opt for the graser. Mind you, it'd probably be a hard choice, though."

"Especially under these circumstances," McKeon agreed much more seriously, and she looked up from Nimitz's grooming to nod soberly.

McKeon had so far given only the most rudimentary consideration to what to do next. Getting the escapees down in one piece, convincing the Peeps they were all dead in order to head off any search parties, hiding the assault shuttles against accidental detection, and exploring their local environs had been quite enough to keep him busy. Yet he suspected Honor was already several steps along in working out their next move, and he was certain those shuttles were central to whatever she had in mind. But Hell's climate could not have been intentionally designed to be more brutal on delicate electronics and machinery. Senior Chief Barstow's work parties were kept busy on a daily business, pruning back the vines and other undergrowth which insisted on trying to infiltrate the intakes for the shuttles's turbines or crawl up into the electronics bays through open landing gear doors. For all that, the shuttles' battle steel hulls were undoubtedly immune to anything even Hell could throw at them, but high humidity, high temperature, and the mold, mildew, and fungus which came with that kind of environment could eat the guts right out of them, leaving nothing but useless shells.

That was why it was as essential to keep their environmental systems up and running as it was to keep the local plant life outside them, but doing that required power. Not a lot of it compared to even a small starship, perhaps, but a *hell* of a lot when it came to hiding a power plant from overhead sensors. Of course, they'd been careful to land on the far side of the planet from the island HQ where StateSec's garrison of prison guards hung out, and so far as Harkness had been able to determine when he raided *Tepes*' computers, the Peeps hadn't planted any of their prison colonies within a thousand kilometers of their present location. All of which meant that, logically, there should be no reason for the Peeps to be looking for anything out here in the middle of the jungle.

Neither Alistair McKeon nor Honor Harrington were particularly fond of including words like "should" in their planning, however. And even if there hadn't been the possibility of detection by satellite or airborne sensors, running the shuttles' onboard fusion plants would quickly have eaten up their available reaction mass even at standby levels.

But the Peeps who'd planned the equipment list for those shuttles had provided them with at least twice the thermal converter capability an equivalent Manticoran small craft would have boasted. Although the intention had probably been for the converters to provide power to recharge weapon power packs and other small items of personal gear, they also produced—barely—enough power to keep both shuttles' environmental plants on-line. Temperatures inside the craft were several degrees higher than anyone would have kept them in regular service, but the interiors felt downright frigid compared to the jungle's external temperatures, and the dehumidifiers kept the all-invasive humidity at bay.

And they also provide just enough power to produce a teeny bit of ice, McKeon thought, wistfully recalling the chill freshness of Honor's water bottle. That coolness was already little more than a memory, and an ignoble part of him wanted to "borrow" her bottle for just one more sip, but he suppressed it sternly. That was *her* water, and so were the nutrients in it, just as the extra ration pack in the rucksack was specifically earmarked for her. *Besides,* he thought with a hidden smile, *Fritz would* hurt *me if I took anything remotely caloric away from her—and well he should!*

The temptation to smile faded, and he shook his head. The enhanced metabolism that went with Honor's genetically engineered heavy-grav muscles had turned her scarecrow-gaunt during her imprisonment. Unlike anyone else in her small command, she was actually gaining weight on a diet of e-rats, which spoke volumes for how poorly her SS gaolers had treated her. But she was still at least ten kilos underweight, and however much she might dislike the notion that her people were "pampering" her or "taking care of her," Alistair McKeon intended to go right on doing exactly that until Fritz Montoya pronounced her fully recovered.

"Have you had any thoughts on our next move?" he asked her, and she raised her right eyebrow at him. It was the first time he'd come right out and asked, and she hid a grin as she realized he must be beginning to consider her truly on the mend if he was willing to push her on command decisions.

"A few," she acknowledged. She finished grooming Nimitz and slipped the comb into her hip pocket, then reached down and removed the water bottle from her rucksack. McKeon suppressed an automatic urge to take it away and open it for her. He might have two hands to her one, but he also had a pretty shrewd notion how she would react if he tried it, and so he sat and watched, instead.

She clamped the bottle between her knees to unscrew the top, then set its cap on the log beside her and held it for Nimitz. The 'cat pushed himself upright, lurching without the use of his crippled limb, and reached for the bottle with both true-hands. He took a long, deep drink of the iced water, then sighed in bliss and leaned back against Honor, rubbing his head against her breastbone as she replaced the cap and tucked the bottle away once more.

She spent a few seconds stroking the angle of his jaw, and his purr was much livelier than it had been. She suspected they were getting towards the bottom of even his ability to shed, and she shared the taste of his pleasure as he realized how much cooler he felt. She chuckled and gave his jaw another rub, then looked back up at McKeon.

"I think I'm beginning to get the rough pieces into place up here," she told him, tapping her temple with her index finger. "We're going to have to move carefully, though. And it's going to take some time."

"Moving carefully is no problem," McKeon replied. "Time, though. *That* could be a bit of a complication, depending on how much of it we'll need."

"I think we'll be all right," Honor said thoughtfully. "The real bottleneck is food, of course."

"Of course," McKeon agreed. Like most small craft aboard a warship, the shuttles had been supplied for use as life boats in an emergency. Normally, that meant a week or so worth of food for a reasonable load of survivors, but the escapees rattled around inside their two stolen shuttles like a handful of peas. What would have carried a "reasonable" number of survivors for a week would feed all of them for months, and his own initial estimate of how long their food would last had been overly pessimistic by a factor of at least forty percent. Yet there was still a limit to how long they could last without some alternate source of food, and he and Honor both felt it creeping up upon them.

"Has Fritz turned up anything at all?" he asked after a moment.

"I'm afraid not." Honor sighed. "He's run everything we could get our hands on through the analyzer, and unless the stuff you and Warner brought back is radically different from anything else he's checked, there's not much hope there. Our digestive systems can isolate most of the inorganics we need from the local plant life, and most of it won't kill us out of hand if we eat it, but that's about it. We don't even have the right enzymes to break down the local equivalent of cellulose, and I don't know about you, but I don't particularly want a big lump of undigestible plant fiber moving through *my* gizzards. At any rate, we're certainly not going to be able to stretch our e-rats by browsing on the local flora or fauna."

"I wish I could say I was surprised," McKeon observed, then snorted a chuckle. "But what the hell, Skipper! If it was going to be easy, they wouldn't have needed *us* to deal with it, now would they?"

"True. Too true," Honor agreed. She wrapped her arm around Nimitz, hugging him for several moments, then looked back at McKeon.

"At the same time, I think it's time we were about it," she told him quietly. "I know you and Fritz are still watching over me like a pair of anxious hens, but I really am recovered enough to get started." He opened his mouth, as if to object, then closed it again, and she reached across to pat him on the knee with her remaining hand. "Don't *worry* so much, Alistair. Nimitz and I are tough."

"I know you are," he muttered, "it's just that it's so damned un—" He cut himself off and twitched a shrug. "I guess I should have figured out by now that the universe really is unfair, but sometimes I get awful tired of watching it do its level damned best to chew you up and spit you back out. So humor me and take it easy, okay?"

"Okay." Her soprano was just the tiniest bit husky, and she patted his knee again. But then she sat back and drew a deep breath. "On the other hand, what I have in mind for starters shouldn't take too much out of me or anyone else."

"Ah?" McKeon cocked his head at her, and she nodded.

"I want Harkness, Scotty, and Russ to break out the satellite com gear and figure out a way to sneak into the Peep com system."

"'Sneak in,'" McKeon repeated carefully.

"For now, all I want to do is find a way to listen to their traffic and get a feel for their procedures. Eventually, we may need to see if we can't hack our way into Camp Charon's computers, as well."

"That's a tall order with the gear we've got here," McKeon warned. "The hacking part, I mean. And unless they're total idiots, there's no way their central systems would accept reprogramming from a remote location."

"I know. I'm not thinking of programming, only of stealing more data from them. And if things work the way I'd like them to, we may never have to do even that. But I want the capability in place if it turns out that we need it. And if Harkness can hack the central computers of a StateSec battlecruiser with only a minicomp, I figure he's got to have a pretty fair shot at infiltrating a simple com net. Especially since the bad guys 'know' no one else on the entire planet has any electronic capability at all."

"A point," McKeon agreed. "Definitely a point. All right, Skipper. I'll go collect the three of them and tell them to get started assembling their gear." He chuckled and climbed to his feet with a grin. "When they figure out they'll get to start spending time in the air-conditioned luxury of one of the shuttles, I probably won't even have to kick any butt to get them started, either!"

Chapter Nine

"You know," Lieutenant Russell Sanko observed, "if these people would just *talk* to each other every so often, we might get something accomplished here."

"I'm sure that if they only knew how much they're inconveniencing you they'd run right out and start gabbing away," Jasper Mayhew replied with a grin. "In the meantime, we've only been listening for two weeks, and—" He shrugged, tipped his comfortable chair well back under the air return and luxuriated in the cool, dry air that spilled down over him.

"You're a hedonist, Mayhew," Sanko growled.

"Nonsense. I'm simply the product of a hostile planetary environment," Mayhew said comfortably. "It's not my fault if that sort of insecure life experience imposes survival-oriented psychoses on people. All us Graysons get horribly nervous when we have to operate out in the open, with unfiltered air all around us." He gave a dramatic shudder. "It's a psychological thing. Incurable. That's the real reason Lady Harrington assigned me to this, you know. Medical considerations. Elevated pulse and adrenaline levels." He shook his head sadly. "It's a terrible thing to require this sort of air-conditioned luxury solely for medical reasons."

"Yeah, sure."

Mayhew chuckled, and Sanko shook his head and returned his attention to the com console. He and the Grayson were about the same age—actually, at twenty-nine, Mayhew was three years older—and they were both senior-grade lieutenants. Technically, Mayhew had about three T-months seniority on Sanko, and he'd been Lady Harrington's staff intelligence officer before they all landed in enemy hands, while Sanko had been HMS *Prince Adrian*'s com officer. By ancient and honorable tradition, there was always an unstated rivalry between the members of a flag officer's staff and the work-a-day stiffs who ran the ships of that officer's squadron or task force, even when they all came from the same navy. But Mayhew was a comfortable person to work with, and however laid back he cared to appear, he was sharp as a vibro blade and, like most Graysons Sanko had met, always ready to lend a hand. He was also some relation to Protector Benjamin, but he seldom talked about it, and he seemed thankfully immune to the arrogance Sanko had seen out of certain Manticorans of far less exalted birth.

Unfortunately, it didn't really matter how pleasant one's partner was if there was nothing for the two of you to work on, and that seemed to be the case here.

It should have been simple, Sanko thought balefully. After all, the Peeps had a planet-wide com net whose security they trusted totally, for reasons which made perfectly good sense. Not only did the StateSec garrison have the only tech base and power generation facilities on the entire planet, but their com messages were all transmitted using the latest in secure equipment. Well, not the *absolute* latest, even by Peep standards, but pretty darn good. Sanko was a communications specialist himself, and the SS's equipment was considerably better than any of the classified Navy briefings he'd attended had suggested it ought to be. Not as good as the Star Kingdom's, but better than it should have been, and Camp Charon had received the very best available when it was built.

Fortunately, Hell seemed to have fallen a bit behind on its upgrades since then. The planetary garrison had an impressive satellite net—why shouldn't they, when counter-grav made it dirt cheap to hang comsats and weather sats wherever you wanted them?—but their ground stations were getting a little long in the tooth. And, of course, the people they didn't know were trying to eavesdrop on them just happened to have a pair of assault shuttles which, up until very recently, had also belonged to StateSec . . . and had been fitted with the very latest in secure communication links. In fact, the systems Sanko was using were probably at least fifteen or twenty T-years newer than the Peep ground stations, and they'd been expressly designed to interface with older equipment as well as their own contemporaries. Which meant Sanko and Mayhew—and Senior Chief Harkness and Lieutenant Commander Tremaine, or Lieutenant Commander Lethridge and Ensign Clinkscales, who'd pulled the other two watches for the same duty—ought to be able to open up that "secure com net" like a pack of e-rats.

Unfortunately, the Peeps didn't seem to *use* the net very much, for aside from routine, automatic downloads of telemetry from the weather sats to Camp Charon's Flight Ops, there was no traffic on it at all. And weather data was completely useless for Sanko's and Mayhew's current purposes.

But I guess it actually makes sense, he acknowledged sourly. *After all, they're all parked on their butts up there at Camp Charon itself. They don't need comsats to talk to each other, and they couldn't care less what happens in any of the prisoner camps, so there's no reason to install ground stations at any of them, either. Hell, their CO can probably just stick his head out the window and* shout *at anybody he actually wants to talk to!*

There wasn't much for the eavesdroppers to do under the circumstances. If they'd just had some decent computer support, there wouldn't even have been any need for them to be here at all—they could have left the routine listening watch up to the computers. Well, to be honest they could probably have trusted a simple listening watch to them anyway, but they were talking about *Peep* computers, which brought the ancient and honorable term "kludge" forcibly to mind every time he had anything to do with them. No wonder Senior Chief Harkness had been able to fry the net aboard that damned battlecruiser! Worse, the shuttles had extremely limited computer support compared to their Allied equivalents. What they needed for flight ops, fire support missions, troop drops, and that sort of thing was adequate—not great, but adequate. But most functions that weren't absolutely essential were done the old-fashioned way . . . by hand, or at least by extremely specific, canned software so limited, and with such crude heuristic functions, it made a man want to sit down and cry. Which meant real live human beings had to sit here to watch over the computers, because their AI functions were so stupid they would have gotten lost in downtown Landing on a night with a full moon if—

"Base, this is Harriman," a bored voice said suddenly, spilling from the com speakers. "You want to give me the count on Alpha-Seven-Niner?"

Sanko's eyes widened, and his hands darted for the console even as Mayhew snapped upright in his chair at the tactical station.

"Harriman, you dickhead!" an exasperated female voice replied in a tone that could have blistered battle steel. "I swear, you are stupider than a retarded rock! How the hell did you lose the numbers *again?*"

Mayhew's fingers flew over the keyboard of the shuttle's main computers while Sanko worked equally frantically at the communications station. All the information on Hades that Horace Harkness had managed to pull out of *Tepes'* data bases before her destruction had been dumped from his minicomp to the shuttle's larger memory, and Sanko heard a sound of triumph from Mayhew as something correlated between the overheard conversation and Harkness' stolen data. At the same time, Sanko himself was working with the comsat serving as the relay link for the exchange between "Harriman" and Camp Charon. His equipment might not be up to the high standards of the Royal Manticoran Navy, but it was newer than the opposition's, and his updated software had let him into the satellite's on-board computers without anyone dirtside knowing a thing about it. The tight-beam tap he'd set up had been cut entirely out of Camp Charon's net, which meant the base's traffic computers didn't even know it was there to log, and his eyes glowed as information from the comsat began downloading smoothly to his own station. All the security and encryption data buried in the transmissions' automatic security linkages spilled over the display before him, and his lips drew up in the snarl of a hunting Sphinx hexapuma.

"How do *I* know what happened to them?" Harriman growled at his critic. "If I knew where the damned grunt list had *gone*, then it wouldn't be *lost*, now would it?"

"Oh, fer cryin' out loud!" Base muttered. "It's in your computers, dipshit—not scribbled down on a scrap of paper somewhere!"

"Oh, yeah?" Harriman sounded even more belligerent. "Well I happen to be looking at the directory right this minute, Shrevner, and it ain't here! So suppose you get off your lazy ass and get it to me? I'm coming up on the drop for Alpha-Seven-Eight in about twelve minutes, and I got lots of other stops still to make."

"*Jee*zus!" the other voice snarled. "You stupid goddamned pilots are so— Oh." It cut off abruptly, and then a throat cleared itself. "Here it is," Base said in a much crisper (and less contemptuous) voice. "Uploading now."

No one spoke for a few seconds, and then a sharp snort came down the link from Harriman.

"Interesting time stamp on that data, Base," he said almost genially. "Looks to me like those numbers were compiled—what? Seventy minutes *after* I left?"

"Oh, screw you, Harriman!" Base snapped.

"In your dreams, sweetheart," Harriman said with cloying sweetness, and Base cut the channel with a click.

"Did you get it?" Mayhew demanded.

"I think so." Sanko punched more commands, calling up a review of the data he'd been too busy downloading to evaluate and felt his face stretch into an exultant grin. "Looking good over here, Jasper! How about your side?"

"Speculative, but interesting," Mayhew replied. He tapped a few queries of his own into the system, then nodded. "I think it's time we got Lady Harrington and Commodore McKeon in here, and then—"

"Base, this is Carson. I'm at Gamma-One-Seven, and I've got a problem. According to my numbers—"

The fresh voice rattled from the speakers, and Sanko and Mayhew dived back into their consoles.

"So that's it, My Lady," Mayhew said. "We've picked up six more complete or partial conversations during the last ninety odd minutes. Of course, we're only working the comsats that are line-of-sight to our own location, so I suspect we've missed others."

"Makes sense," Alistair McKeon rumbled from where he sat beside Honor. He rubbed his jaw, the tip of his tongue probing at the gaps a Peep pulse rifle's butt had left in his teeth. It was a nervous gesture he'd developed aboard *Tepes*, and it seemed to help him think. "You send out that many shuttles, you're going to get com chatter. Especially when half your flight crews don't seem to know their asses from their elbows!"

"Now, now, Alistair. Be nice," Honor murmured with a small smile, and Nimitz bleeked a laugh from her lap. He'd finished shedding last week, and the sauna bath of the local climate was no longer the crushing burden it had been, but he was delighted whenever he and his person entered the shuttle's air-conditioning. Now he showed McKeon his needle-sharp fangs in a lazy smile, and Honor chuckled. She gave the 'cat's head a gentle caress, then leaned forward and peered at the map Mayhew had spread out over the shelf-like fold-down desk. The Peep shuttle's only decent holo imaging capability was in the cockpit, but its tactical section was capable of using the same data that drove that display to print out an old-fashioned plaspaper map that was good enough for her current purposes. Now she bent a little closer, trying to read Mayhew's small, neat handwritten notations, and suppressed another stab of regret for the loss of her cybernetic eye's enhanced vision modes.

She finished deciphering her intelligence officer's notes without it and sat back to ponder them. She'd developed a new nervous habit of her own, and her right palm caressed the stump of her left arm in a futile effort to do something about the "phantom pain" of the missing limb. It was more of a phantom *itch*, really, and she supposed she should be grateful for small favors, but her inability to scratch the darned thing was maddening.

"Well, they *don't* know their anatomical portions apart!" McKeon insisted with a gap-toothed grin. "Hell, from the sound of this crap," he tapped an index finger on a hardcopy transcript of the intercepted com traffic, "these people couldn't even *find* their asses without a detailed flight plan, a dozen nav beacons, and approach radar!"

"Maybe so, but I'm not going to complain about it," Honor replied, and Nimitz made a soft sound of agreement.

"There is that," McKeon agreed in turn. "There certainly is that."

Honor nodded and stopped rubbing at the arm that was no longer there to run her index finger over the map while she considered what they'd learned. *Actually, most of it's more a matter of simply confirming what Harkness already stole for us, but that's worth doing, too,* she told herself.

Contrary to the works of the pre-space poet Dante, Hell had four continents (and one very large island that didn't quite qualify as continent number five), not nine circles. For the most part, neither State Security nor the exploration crews who'd originally surveyed the planet seemed to have been interested in wasting any inventiveness on naming those landmasses, either, and the continents had ended up designated simply as "Alpha," "Beta," "Gamma," and "Delta." Someone *had* put a little thought into naming the island, though Honor personally found the idea of calling it "Styx" a little heavy-handed, but that was about the limit of their imaginativeness. Nor did she find the repetitions on the motif which had gone into naming the planet's three moons Tartarus, Sheol, and Niflheim particularly entertaining. Oh course, no one had been interested in consulting her at the time the names were assigned, either.

Working from the information Harkness had managed to secure before staging their escape, McKeon had grounded the shuttles on the east coast of Alpha, the largest of the four continents. That put them just over twenty-two thousand kilometers—or almost exactly halfway around the planet—from Camp Charon's island home on Styx. Honor had been unconscious at the time, but if she'd been awake, she would have made exactly the same decision and for exactly the same reasons, yet it had produced its own drawbacks. While it was extremely unlikely anyone would over-fly them accidentally here and even less likely that anyone would be actively searching for them, it also deprived them of any opportunity to monitor Camp Charon's short-range com traffic.

But as Honor had hoped, the Peeps seemed to be rather more garrulous when it came time to make their grocery runs to the various camps.

"How many of their birds did you get IFF codes on, Russ?" she asked.

"Um, nine so far, Ma'am," Sanko replied.

"And their encryption?"

"There wasn't any, Ma'am—except for the system autoencrypt, that is. That was pretty decent when it was put in, I suppose, but our software is several generations newer than theirs. It decrypts their traffic automatically, thanks to our satellite tap, and we downloaded all the crypto data to memory, of course." He eyed his Commodore thoughtfully. "If you wanted to, Ma'am, we could duplicate their message formats with no sweat at all."

"I see." Honor nodded and then leaned back, stroking Nimitz's ears while she considered that.

Sanko was undoubtedly right, she mused. However confident the present proprietors of Hell had become, the people who'd originally put the prison planet together eighty-odd years ago for the old Office of Internal Security had built what were then state-of-the-art security features into their installations. Among those features was a communications protocol which automatically challenged and logged the identity of the sender for every single com message, but it appeared the current landlords were less anxious about such matters than their predecessors had been. They hadn't gone quite so far as to pull the protocol from their computers, but they were obviously too lazy to take it very seriously. Camp Charon's central routing system simply assigned each shuttle a unique code derived from its Identification Friend or Foe beacon and then automatically interrogated the beacon whenever a shuttle transmitted a message. All transmissions from any given shuttle thus carried the same IFF code so the logs could keep track of them with no effort from any human personnel.

For the rest of it, rather than bother themselves with changing authentication codes often enough to provide any sort of genuine security, those human personnel relied on an obsolete, canned encryption package which was worse than no security system at all. If anyone ever even bothered to think about it—which Honor doubted happened very often—the fact that they had a security screen in place helped foster the kind of complacency which kept them from considering whether or not it was a *good* screen. And almost as important as that gaping hole in their electronic defenses, only Champ Charon's central switchboard computers worried about authenticating the source of a transmission at all. As far as the human operators seemed to be concerned, the fact that a message was on the net in the first place automatically indicated it had a right to be there.

Actually, they probably aren't being quite as stupid as I'd like to think, Honor told herself thoughtfully. *After all, they "know" they're the only people on the planet—or in the entire star system, for that matter—who have any com equipment. And if there's no opposition to read your mail, then there's no real need to be paranoid about your security or encode it before you send it, now is there?*

She raised her hand to knead the nerve-dead side of her face gently, and the living side grimaced. One could make excuses for the Peeps' sloppiness, but that didn't make it any less sloppy. And one thing Honor had learned long ago was that sloppiness spread. People who were careless or slovenly about one aspect of their duties tended to be the same way about other aspects, as well.

And the Peeps on this planet are way *overconfident and complacent. Not that I intend to complain about that!*

"All right," she said, gesturing for McKeon to come closer and then tapping the map again. "It looks like they're using very simple IFF settings, Alistair . . . and we just happen to have exactly the same hardware in *our* shuttles. So if we can just borrow one of their ID settings—"

"We can punch it into our own beacons," McKeon finished for her, and she nodded. He scratched his nose for a moment, then exhaled noisily. "You're right enough about that," he observed, "but these are assault shuttles, not the trash haulers they use on their grocery runs. We're not going to have the same emissions signature, and if they take a good sensor look at us, they'll spot us in a heartbeat."

"I'm sure they would," Honor agreed. "On the other hand, everything we've seen so far says to me that these people are lazy. Confident, and lazy. Remember what Admiral Courvosier used to say at ATC? 'Almost invariably, "surprise" is what happens when one side fails to recognize something it's seen all along.'"

"You figure that they'll settle for querying our IFF."

"I think that's exactly what they'll settle for. Why shouldn't they? They own every piece of flight-capable hardware on the planet, Alistair. That's why they're lazy. They'd probably assume simple equipment malfunction, at least initially, even if they got a completely unidentifiable beacon return, because they know any bird they see has to be one of theirs." She snorted. "Scan techs have been making that particular mistake ever since a place called Pearl Harbor back on Old Earth!"

"Makes sense," he said after a moment, and scratched his head mentally, wondering where he could track the reference down without her finding out he'd done it. She had the damnedest odds and ends of historical trivia tucked away in her mental files, and figuring out what had called any given one of them to the surface of her thoughts had become a sort of hobby of his.

"The question," Honor mused aloud, "is how often they make their delivery flights."

"I've been running some numbers on that, My Lady," Mayhew offered. He was to her left, and she turned in her chair to look at him with her working eye. "I'm not sure how reliable they are, but I ran some extrapolations based on the data Chief Harkness got for us and what I could glean from the transmissions we monitored."

"Go on," Honor invited.

"Well, Commander Lethridge and Scotty and I have been playing with the stuff the Chief managed to pull out of *Tepes*' secure data base," Mayhew said. "He didn't have the time to pay a whole lot of attention to the planet—he was too busy figuring out how to get to the ship's control systems and get us down here in the first place—but there were some interesting numbers in the dirtside data he'd never gotten a chance to look at. As nearly as Scotty and I can figure out, there are at least a half-million prisoners down here."

"A half-*million?*" Honor repeated, and Mayhew nodded.

"At least," he repeated. "Remember that they've been dumping what they considered to be their real hard cases here for eighty T-years, My Lady. We've got fairly hard numbers on the military POWs they've sent here. Most of them are from the various star systems the Peeps picked off early on, from Tambourine to Trevor's Star. You had to be a pretty dangerous fellow to get sent to Hell, of course—sort of the cream of the crop, the kind of people who were likely to start building resistance cells if you were left to your own devices. Of course, if State Security had been running things at that point, they probably would've just shot the potential troublemakers where they were and saved themselves the bother of shipping them out here.

"At any rate, there weren't very many additions to the POW population for about ten years before they attacked the Alliance, and the nature of the POWs sent here since the war started is a bit different from what I'd expected." Honor raised an eyebrow, and he shrugged. "If I were StateSec, and I had a prison whose security I felt absolutely confident about, that's where I'd send the prisoners I figured had really sensitive information. I could take my time getting it out of them, and I'd have complete physical security while I went about it—they couldn't escape, no one could break them out, and for that matter, no one could even know that was where I had them, since the location of the system itself was classified. But StateSec apparently prefers to do its interrogating closer to the center of the Republic, probably on Haven itself. Instead of using Hell as a holding area for prize prisoners, they've been using it as a dumping ground. People who make trouble in other camps get sent here, where they can't get into any more mischief."

"What sort of 'mischief' were they getting into?" McKeon asked in an interested tone.

"Just about anything you can think of, Sir," Mayhew replied. "Escape attempts, for a lot of them . . . or else they were guilty of being the kinds of officers and noncoms who'd insist on maintaining discipline and unit cohesion even in a prison camp. The trouble-makers."

"And they've been skimming them off and dumping them here, have they?" Honor murmured, and there was a wicked gleam in her good eye. "You could almost say they've been distilling them out of the rest of their prison population, couldn't you?"

"Yes, My Lady, you could," Mayhew agreed. "According to the best numbers Scotty and I could come up with, we figure there are between a hundred eighty and two hundred thousand military prisoners down here. It could run as high as two hundred and fifty, but that's a maximum figure. The other three or four hundred thousand are civilians. About a third of those were shipped out after various civilian resistance groups from conquered planets were broken up, but most are the more usual run of political prisoners."

"Um." Honor frowned at that and rubbed the tip of her nose. After a moment, she moved her hand from her nose to Nimitz, stroking the 'cat's spine.

"A high percentage of them are from Haven itself, with the biggest single block of them from Nouveau Paris," Mayhew told her. "Apparently, both InSec and StateSec concentrated their housecleaning on the capital."

"Makes sense," McKeon said again. "Authority in the PRH has always been centralized, and every bit of it passes through the command and control nodes on Haven. Whoever controls the capital controls the rest of the Republic, so it's not unreasonable for them to want to make damned sure potential troublemakers on Haven were under control. It'd probably work, too. 'Hey, Prole! You get uppity around here, and—*Pffft!* Off to Hell with you!' Except that since the Harris Assassination, they've been sending off 'elitists' instead of 'proles,' of course."

"No doubt," Honor said. "But having them here in such numbers could certainly throw a spanner into the works for us." McKeon looked a question at her, and she made a brushing-away gesture. "I wouldn't want to generalize, but I can't help thinking political prisoners would probably be more likely, on average, to collaborate with StateSec."

"Why?" McKeon's surprise was evident. "They're here because they oppose what's happening in Nouveau Paris, aren't they?"

"They're here because the people who were running the PRH when they were arrested *thought* they were a threat to whatever was happening in Nouveau Paris *at the time*," Honor replied. "It doesn't follow that they really were, and as you yourself just pointed out, things have changed on the domestic front over the last eight or nine years. Some of those prisoners were probably as loyal to the PRH as you and I are to the Crown, whether the security forces thought they were or not. And even if they weren't, people the Legislaturalists sent here might actually agree with what Pierre and his crowd have done since the coup. They could be looking for ways to demonstrate their loyalty to the new regime and possibly earn their release by informing on their fellows. Worse, they could be genuine patriots who hate what's happening in the PRH right now but would be perfectly willing to turn in the Republic's wartime enemies. For that matter, StateSec could probably plant spies and informers wherever it wanted by using the hostage approach and threatening the loved ones of anyone who refused to play its game."

"I hadn't thought of it that way," McKeon acknowledged slowly.

"I'm not saying that there aren't political prisoners who truly do oppose Pierre and Saint-Just and their thugs and who'd stand up beside us to prove it," Honor said. "Nor am I saying that there aren't collaborators among the POWs. There are usually at least some potential weasels in any group, and even the spirits of men and women who would stand up to outright torture can be crushed by enough prolonged hopelessness."

For just an instant, the right side of her face was almost as expressionless as the nerve-dead left side, and McKeon shivered. She was speaking from experience, he thought. About something she'd faced and stared down during her own long weeks in solitary confinement. She gazed at something no one else could see for several seconds, then shook herself.

"Still," she said, "at some point we're going to have to take a chance on someone besides our own people, and I'd think military POWs who were captured fighting against the Peeps in defense of their own worlds or parked here to prevent them from becoming threats after their worlds were conquered are more likely to resist the temptation to collaborate. Not that I intend to leap to any sweeping generalizations. It's going to have to be a case-by-case consideration."

She stroked Nimitz again and the grim look in her eye turned into something almost like a twinkle. McKeon regarded her curiously, but she only shook her head, and he shrugged. He wasn't positive how she did it, but she'd demonstrated an uncanny ability to read people too often in the past for him to doubt her ability to do it again.

"You're probably right," he said, "but Jasper was saying something about how often they make their supply runs?"

"Yes, he was," she agreed, and looked at Mayhew. "Jasper?"

"Yes, My Lady." Mayhew gestured at the map on the fold-down table. "The red dots indicate known camp locations," he explained. "They're not complete, of course. Even if *Tepes* ever had a complete list of camps, her latest data on them was almost two years out of date before Chief Harkness stole it. But we're trying to update, and as you can see, the ones we know about are clustered on Alpha, Beta, and Gamma. Delta's too far into the antarctic to be a practical site, but even with half a million prisoners, they've got plenty of places to put them without sticking them down there. And as you can see, the camps get even thinner on the ground as you move into the equatorial zone here on Alpha."

Honor nodded. Given the climate outside the shuttle, she could certainly understand that. Putting prisoners from most inhabited planets into those conditions would have been cruel and unusual punishment by any standard. While that probably wouldn't have bothered StateSec particularly, the jungle also had a tendency to eat any permanent settlement or base, and that *would* have been a problem for them. Or something that required them to get up off their lazy duffs, anyway. They could force the prisoners to do any maintenance that was needed, but it would still have required them to provide tools and materials and the transport to deliver both. *Unless, of course, they simply chose to let the camps disappear . . . and the prisoners with them*, she thought grimly.

But the near total absence of camps right in the equatorial zone helped explain why she and her fellow escapees were smack in the middle of it, where no Peeps would have any reason to venture.

"As nearly as we can tell," Mayhew went on, "the camp populations average about twenty-five hundred personnel, which means they've got approximately two hundred sites in all. Obviously, there are none at all up here on Styx Island—Camp Charon itself is purely a staging point and central supply depot for the other sites—but the mainland camps are all a minimum of five hundred kilometers from one another. That spreads them out too much for the inmates of any camp to coordinate any sort of action with any other camp, given that the only way they could communicate would be to make physical contact."

"I'd be a little cautious about making that assumption, if I were the Peeps, Jasper," McKeon put in. "Five hundred klicks sounds like a lot, especially when there aren't any roads and the prisoners don't have any air transport, but I have a lot of faith in human ingenuity. For example," he leaned forward and tapped the huge lake scooped out of Alpha Continent's northern quarter, then ran his finger down the rash of red dots along its shore, "if they put camps on a body of water like this, then I'd expect the prisoners to be able to build—and hide—enough small craft to at least open communications with the other camps."

"I wouldn't disagree with you, Sir," Mayhew said with a nod. "And perhaps I should have said that the Peeps seem confident that it would be impossible for them to coordinate any *effective* action, not that all of the camps can be kept totally isolated from one another."

"They could have achieved total isolation on an intercamp basis if they'd been willing to accept larger populations per camp, though," Sanko offered thoughtfully. "That would've brought the total number of camps down, and then they could have put a lot more space between them.

"They could have," Honor agreed. "But only at the expense of making each individual camp a thornier security problem. Twenty-five hundred people are a lot less of a threat than, say, thirty thousand, even if every single person in the smaller camp is in on whatever it is they might try to do. Besides, the larger the total inmate population at any given site, the easier it would be for any small, tightly organized group to disappear into the background clutter."

Sanko nodded, and she returned her one-eyed gaze to Mayhew and gestured for him to go on.

"Whatever their rationale for spreading the prisoners around, and however good or bad their logic," the Grayson officer said, "the point I was going to make is that when this flight—" he tapped the transcript of the first transmission they'd intercepted "—checked in with Charon, Flight Ops sent him the fresh numbers he'd asked for, which tells us how many rations he dropped off at this camp—Alpha-Seven-Niner: just over two hundred and twenty-five thousand. Assuming there are twenty-five hundred prisoners there, that would be enough food for about one T-month, and that checks against this other intercept, which gave us the same kind of numbers for camp Beta-Two-Eight. So it looks like about a once-a-month supply cycle for all of them. What we don't know—and have no way of determining yet—is whether they spread their supply runs out or make them all in a relatively short time window. Given the general laziness with which they seem to operate, I could see them doing it either way. They could make a handful of daily flights and gradually rotate through all the camps, which would let them assign the duty to different pilots every day without overloading any one flight crew. Or they could choose to squeeze all of them into an all-hands operation over just a day or two each month so they could all spend the rest of their time sitting around. At the moment, it looks to me like they've taken the short time frame approach, since we've been listening to their comsats for over two weeks and this is the first traffic we've heard, but there's no way to prove that."

"A month," Honor murmured. She contemplated something only she could see once again, then nodded. "All right, Alistair," she said crisply, "that gives us a time window for any given camp, anyway. And I think Jasper's probably right, that they do make a major supply effort once a month. If so, we've got some idea of the interval we have to work with. All we need to do is figure out what we're going to do with it."

Chapter Ten

"Now *that's* interesting," Lieutenant Commander Scotty Tremaine murmured.

"What is?" a soft Grayson accent asked.

The sandy-haired lieutenant commander took his eyes from his display and turned to look at the other officer in the compartment. Commander Solomon Marchant had been the executive officer of the Grayson heavy cruiser *Jason Alvarez* before they all wound up in Peep hands. Tremaine's slot as Lady Harrington's staff electronics officer had brought him into contact with her flagship's exec on a regular basis, and Tremaine rather liked the black-haired commander. Unlike some of his fellow Graysons, Marchant was singularly free of any special awe for the Royal Manticoran Navy. He respected it, but the RMN had learned just as many lessons, proportionately speaking, from its experience with the GSN, and he knew it. He was also no man to suffer fools lightly, and he could jerk someone up short with the best of them, but he usually assumed you were an adult human being who knew what you were doing until you proved differently.

"I just picked up on something we've all overlooked before," Tremaine said, answering the commander's question. Marchant quirked his right eyebrow, and Tremaine waved a hand at the computer display in front of him. "I should have noticed it sooner, but somehow it went right past me. And Jasper and Anson, I guess."

"So what is it?" Marchant asked with the merest trace of exaggerated patience, and Tremaine hid a mental smile. Everybody was going just a bit stir crazy with so little to do. The classic concept of castaways working diligently—if not desperately—to provide for their continued survival simply didn't apply here. There was no way they could live off the land anyway, so there was no planting or hunting to do. And given the dire necessity of keeping their presence a secret, any avoidable activity which might attract attention was out of the question. Commodore McKeon's patrols had explored the surrounding jungle in all directions for a good thirty klicks, but once that was done and the fiberoptic land lines for a net of undetectable remote passive sensors had been emplaced, their people had been told to stay close to home and keep under cover. Which meant that, aside from those fortunate souls like Senior Chief Linda Barstow, who had been Chief of the Bay in *Prince Adrian*'s Boat Bay Two and had taken over responsibility for maintenance on their shuttles, there was very little to keep a person's brain working. In fact, commissioned officers were almost begging Barstow to let them help out with the grunt work just to avoid sitting around on their hands.

Lady Harrington recognized that, and she'd parceled out assignments in an effort to give everyone at least something to do. Some of it might be little better than make-work, but none of the people who had survived to escape from PNS *Tepes* were idiots, and it couldn't hurt to have as many intelligent perspectives as possible on the raw data they were managing to acquire in dribs and drabs. Which was how Commander Marchant found himself playing fifth wheel and sounding board for Tremaine's analysis sessions while Lieutenant Commander Metcalf and Lieutenant Commander DuChene did the same for Mayhew and Lethridge, respectively.

"Well," he said now, "it seems that there's one prisoner camp here on Alpha that doesn't have a number." Marchant leaned back in his chair with a questioning expression, and Tremaine smiled at him. "It's got a name, instead: Camp Inferno. And it's not exactly prime real estate. As a matter of fact, it's the only camp on the entire planet that's located directly on the equator."

"On the—?" Marchant stood and crossed to the map beside Tremaine's work station to peer at the map he'd called up on his display. "I don't see it," he said after a moment.

"That's because this is our original map, and Inferno isn't on it," Tremaine told him. "When Jasper and I generated the original, we used an old camp survey from *Tepes*' files, and this one wasn't listed. But yesterday Russ pulled a major telemetry download from the weather sats. It included weather maps for Alpha, with the camp sites indicated, including half a dozen that're new since the file survey we used was last updated. Like these." He tapped a key and new red dots appeared on his display, one of them flashing brightly. "And lo and behold, there was this camp we hadn't mapped sitting dead center on Alpha where it shouldn't have been. So when I came on watch this afternoon, I started trying to chase it down. I thought at first that it was just another new camp, but then I found this—" he tapped more keys and the display changed again, transmuting into a terse StateSec internal memo "—in one of *Tepes*' secure files on Hades, and it turns out it's not a new camp at all. The survey just hadn't mapped it—apparently for security reasons."

"I see." Marchant said, and smothered a smile, for Tremaine had added the last phrase in tones of profound disgust that he understood only too well. None of the Manticoran or Grayson castaways had yet been able to figure out what sort of reasoning (or substitute therefor) StateSec called upon when it decided when it was going to get security conscious and when it wasn't, but the logic tree involved promised to be twistier than most.

The Grayson officer stooped to look over Tremaine's shoulder, green eyes flicking over the memo, and then he inhaled sharply.

"I *do* see," he said in a very different tone. "And I think we should get Lady Harrington and Commodore McKeon in on this ASAP."

"My, my, my," Honor said softly, gazing at a hardcopy of the data Tremaine had found. "How very convenient . . . maybe."

"It certainly seems to offer a possibility, at any rate, Ma'am," Geraldine Metcalf observed. The dark-eyed, sandy-blond lieutenant commander had been McKeon's tac officer aboard *Prince Adrian*, and her Gryphon accent was more pronounced than usual as she, too, pondered the data.

"I agree, Gerry," McKeon said, "'but let's not jump to any conclusions here. Scotty's memo is over two T-years old. A lot could've changed in that long, and aside from the food supply, there's no time limit on our operations. If there've been any changes, we could screw ourselves over mightily by jumping too quick. I'd prefer to take it a little slow and check things out first rather than rush in and wind up hanging ourselves."

"No argument from me, Skipper," Metcalf told him. "But if this is right—" she tapped the hardcopy "—then the bad guys just did us a great big favor."

"You're certainly right about that," Honor said. She leaned back and frowned in thought while her hand caressed Nimitz with slow, gentle strokes. The 'cat lay in her lap once more, for his crippled mid-limb made it all but impossible for him to ride in his usual position on her shoulder, but both of them were in much better health than they had been. Her weight was coming back up and his pelt had been reduced to a bearable insulation factor, and although his badly healed bones still hurt whenever he moved, he radiated a sense of cheerful confidence which did more for her own mood than she might have believed possible.

"Of course, they didn't know they were doing us one," she went on after a moment. "And from their perspective, this actually makes sense. Nor is there any reason for them to change a longstanding policy like this one—after all, they don't know we're here, so they can't possibly realize how much this could help us. That's why I'm inclined to go with the data despite its age."

"Um." McKeon scratched his chin and squinted at nothing in particular, then nodded slowly. "I can't fault your logic, but I wish

I had a dollar for every time *I'd* figured something out logically and been wrong."

"True." Honor gave Nimitz another caress, then flipped through the pages of Tremaine's printout one more time. *I wish I could ask Warner about this. Gerry and Solomon are good, and so is Scotty . . . although* he can *get just a little over enthusiastic. But they're all junior to Alistair and me. None of them really want to argue with us.* Alistair *would tell me in a heartbeat if he thought I was wrong about something—God knows he's done it in the past!—but he and I have known each other too long. We each know what the other is going to say before it gets said. That's good when it's time to execute orders, but it can keep us from seeing things in skull sessions. Warner doesn't have that problem, and he's smart as a whip. I found that out in Silesia, and I could really use his perspective here, too . . . if it wouldn't be putting him so much on the spot. And,* she admitted, *if I could be* certain *his sense of duty wouldn't rise up and bite us all on the backside.*

She hated adding those qualifications. Caslet had put himself in his current predicament primarily because that very sense of duty had ranged him against StateSec at the side of Honor's captured personnel, and her link to Nimitz let her sample his emotions. She *knew* he was her friend, that his actions before and during the breakout from *Tepes* had been motivated by stubborn integrity, mutual respect, and fundamental decency. Unfortunately, she also knew that a part of his personality was at war with the rest of him—not over what he had done, but over what he might still do. If he hadn't broken his oath as an officer in the People's Navy yet, he'd certainly come close, and she didn't know how much more cooperation he could extend to her people, for the very traits that made her like and respect him so much gnawed at him with teeth made from the fragments of that oath.

But he wouldn't really know anything more about this than we do, she reminded herself, *so the least I can do is leave him alone where it's concerned.*

"Was Inferno covered in the last supply run?" she asked now.

"We don't know, Ma'am," Anson Lethridge replied. The ugly, almost brutish-looking Erewhon officer who had been Honor's staff astrogator sat with Jasper Mayhew and Tremaine, all three of them facing aft from the shuttle's tactical section hatch to where their superiors sat in the front row of passenger seats. "The only deliveries we can absolutely confirm," he went on in the cultivated tenor which always seemed oddly out of place coming from someone who looked like he did, "were the ones where something came up that required com traffic with Camp Charon that we managed to tap—like the numbers of rations to be dropped off at Alpha-Seven-Niner." He rubbed the neatly trimmed Van Dyke he had declined to shave off despite the climate and shrugged. "If they didn't discuss a particular drop, or we didn't happen to hear it when they did, we can't say for certain that a delivery was actually made. Assuming we're right about the way they schedule the supply drops, then, yes, Inferno probably was covered, but there's no way we can guarantee that."

"I was afraid you'd say that." She gave him one of her half-smiles, then sighed and rocked her chair back and forth in thought. "I think we have to move on this," she said finally, and looked at McKeon. He gazed back for two or three seconds, then nodded.

"All right. Gerry," she turned to Metcalf, "you and Sarah get with Chief Barstow." She turned her head to glance a Tremaine, as well. "Scotty, I'd like you and Chief Harkness to lend a hand, as well. I want both shuttles preflighted by nightfall."

"*Both* shuttles?" McKeon asked, and she grinned wryly.

"Both. There's not much point leaving one of them behind, and having both of them along may give us some extra flexibility if we need it."

"It also puts all of our eggs in one basket," McKeon said. "And two of them are harder to hide than one." It wasn't an argument, only an observation, and Honor nodded.

"I know, but I don't want to split us up. Keeping everybody in one spot will concentrate our manpower, if we need it, and cut down on our com traffic even if we don't. From the looks of the terrain in the area, we can probably hide both of them, if not quite as easily as we could hide a singleton, and keeping them—and us—together cuts the number of potential sighting opportunities in half. And let's be realistic about this. If it all hits the fan so badly that a rescue mission or something like that would be necessary, keeping one shuttle in reserve isn't likely to make that much difference. If Champ Charon figures out that we're here at all before we're ready to make our move, they should be able to handle anything we try without even breaking a sweat."

McKeon nodded again, and she inhaled sharply.

"All right, people. Let's be about it," she said.

It should have been a fairly short hop. Camp Inferno was only about fourteen hundred kilometers from their original landing site, which would have been less than a twenty-minute flight at max for one of the shuttles. But they didn't dare make the trip at max. They thought they'd located all of the recon satellites they had to worry about, and if they were right, they had a three-hour window when they *ought* to be clear of observation. But they couldn't be certain about that. There could always be one they'd missed, and even if there hadn't been, simple skin heat on a maximum-speed run might well be picked up by the weather satellites parked in geosynchronous orbit. So instead of high and fast, they would go low and slow, at less than mach one. Not only that, they would make the entire flight without counter-grav, which would both hide them from gravitic detectors and reduce power requirements enough that there would be no need to fire up their shuttles' fusion plants.

There were, however, some drawbacks to that approach, and Scotty Tremaine and Geraldine Metcalf, tapped as pilots for the trip, spent a great deal of the flight muttering silent curses. Flying by old-fashioned, unaided eye at treetop level above the kind of jungle Hell produced, with all active sensors turned off to avoid betraying emissions, was no picnic. Tremaine almost took the top off a forest leviathan which suddenly reared up right in his flight path, and simple navigation was a pain in the posterior. They'd been able to fix their starting position with suitable accuracy, and the weather map which had first revealed Inferno's existence to them fixed the camp's latitude and longitude. Tremaine and Metcalf had worked out their courses before takeoff using that position data, but there were no handy navigation beacons upon which to take fixes en route, and the idea of using celestial navigation was ludicrous. They could have used the Peeps' satellites as navigation aids—which, after all, was what the StateSec pilots did—but the satellites weren't beacons. They transmitted only when queried from the ground, not continuously, and while hitting them with a tight beam from a moving shuttle was certainly possible, Honor and McKeon had decided that it also increased the chance of giving away their presence by an unacceptable percentage. Which meant the pilots were pretty much reduced to instruments no more sophisticated than a compass and their own eyesight, and over the length of a fourteen-hundred-kilometer flight, even small navigational errors could take them far off course.

That might not have been so bad if visibility had been better, but visibility *wasn't* better. In fact, it stank. True, Hell's trio of moons were all large and bright, but that actually made things worse, not better, for two of them—Tartarus and Niflheim—were above the horizon simultaneously, and the confusion of shadow and brightness those competing light sources cast across the tangled, uneven jungle canopy did bewildering things to human vision. Nor was Camp Inferno likely to offer much in the way of a landmark when they finally reached it. Presumably the jungle had been cut back immediately around it, if only to give the Peep shuttle pilots clearance on their grocery runs, but even a large clearing could disappear without any effort at all against such a confusing sea of treetops and shadow. And without electrical power, the kind of artificial light spill which might have been visible at long range was highly unlikely.

All of which meant the shuttles were going to spend more time than anyone liked to think about cruising around looking for their destination. Which not only increased the possibility that some weather sat or some unnoticed recon sat was going to spot them, but also the possibility that someone on the ground was going to hear them and wonder what SS aircraft were doing overhead in the middle of the night.

Which wouldn't be a problem, Honor thought, sitting in the copilot's seat of Tremaine's shuttle and peering out through the windscreen, *if we could be sure StateSec hasn't planted informers down there. And much as I hate to admit it, if* I *were StateSec, this is one camp where I'd make darn sure I had at least one or two spies in place.*

"We ought to have seen something by now, Ma'am," Tremaine said. Most people would never have noticed the strain in his voice, but Honor had known him since he was a brand-new ensign on his first deployment, and she turned to give him one of her half-smiles.

"Patience, Scotty," she said. "Patience. We've hardly started looking yet."

He grimaced at his controls, then sighed and forced his shoulders to relax.

"I know, Ma'am," he admitted. "And I know anything down there is going to be the next best thing to invisible, but—" He broke off and shrugged again, and she chuckled.

"But you want to spot it anyway and get down on the ground where it's safe, right?" she suggested.

"Well, actually, yes, Ma'am." He turned his head to grin back at her. "I guess I always have been a little on the impatient side, haven't I?"

"Just a little," she agreed.

"Well, I come by it naturally," he said, "and—"

"'Scuse me, Mr. Tremaine," a voice broke in over the com, "but I think I see something."

"And where would that happen to be, Chief?" Tremaine inquired. "You really ought to be a bit more precise in making these minor sighting reports, you know," he added severely.

"Yes, Sir. Sorry 'bout that, Sir. Guess I'm just getting old, Sir," Senior Chief Harkness replied so earnestly Honor had to turn a laugh into a smothered cough. "I'll try not to let it happen again, Sir," Harkness went on. "Maybe next time I can find you a younger, fitter flight engineer, Sir. And then—"

"And then you can tell me where you saw whatever you saw before I come back there and have Master Chief Ascher take care of you for me, Chief!" Tremaine interrupted.

"Ha! Threats now, is it?" Harkness sniffed over the com, but he was tapping keys back in the tac section even as he spoke. A heads-up holo display glowed suddenly, painting a rough map against the windscreen with a blinking icon to indicate the approximate location of whatever Harkness had seen. The icon was well astern and to port of them, and Tremaine brought the shuttle around in a wide curve.

"Is Two still on station?" he asked. Honor leaned to the side, peering through the armorplast on her side of the cockpit, but she couldn't see anything. Senior Chief Harkness, however, had a better view from his location.

"Sticking to you like glue, Sir," he said. "She's dropped back a little on your starboard quarter, but she's holding position nicely."

"That, Chief Harkness, is because she is an officer and a lady. And unlike people who don't tell me they've seen things until we're past them, she's also good at her job."

"You just keep right on, Sir," Harkness told him comfortably. "And the next time you need to find your posterior, you can use your own flashlight."

"I'm shocked—*shocked*—that you could say such a thing to an officer and a gentleman," Tremaine returned in a slightly distracted tone. He was leaning forward, eyes sweeping the night. "I'd think that after all these years, you'd at l—"

He broke off suddenly, and the shuttle's speed dropped still further.

"I do believe I may owe you an apology, Chief," he murmured. "A small one, at least." He glanced at Honor. "Do you see it, Ma'am?"

"I do." Honor raised an old-fashioned pair of binoculars, once more missing her cybernetic eye's vision enhancement as she peered through them with her right eye.. It wasn't much—no more than what looked like a torch or two burning against the blackness of the jungle—and she felt a distant surprise that Harkness had seen it at all. *Of course, he does have access to the tac sensors from back there,* she reminded herself, *but Peep passives are nothing to write home about.*

"How do you want to handle it, Ma'am?" Tremaine asked, and tension burned under his deceptively calm tone.

"Warn Commander Metcalf, and then take us up another few hundred meters," she replied. "Let's see if we can't find another break in this canopy."

"Yes, Ma'am." He thumbed a button on the stick to flash the running light atop the vertical stabilizer once, then eased the stick back and fed a little more power to the air-breathing turbines. The big shuttle angled smoothly upwards while its companion, warned by the flash of light, broke right and stayed low, tracking him visually against the moon-bright sky. He climbed another three hundred meters, then leveled out, sweeping around the dim lights Harkness had spotted.

They were easier to see from the greater altitude, and the live side of Honor's mouth frowned as she studied them through the binoculars. There were actually two double rows of light sources, set at right angles. Most of them were quite dim, but five or six of them flared brighter where the two lines crossed, and she thought she could make out faint reflections of what looked like flat roofs of some sort. She stared at them a moment longer, then laid the binocculars in her lap and rubbed her good eye with the heel of her hand in an effort to scrub away the ache of concentration.

Nimitz bleeked softly at her from where he lay beside her seat in a highly nonregulation nest of folded blankets, and she smiled down at him reassuringly. Then she lifted the glasses again, studying the jungle.

"What's that line to the east?" she asked after a moment.

"How far from the camp, My Lady?" Jasper Mayhew's voice came over the com.

"It looks like—what, Scotty? Twenty or twenty-five klicks?"

"Something like that, Ma'am," Tremaine replied. "Chief?"

"I make it twenty-three from here, Ma'am," Harkness said from the tac section after a moment, studying the frustratingly vague output of his passive sensors.

"In that case, I think it's a river, My Lady," Mayhew said, and she heard the rustle and crackle of plaspaper as he studied the hardcopy map he and Russell Sanko had put together. "The *Tepes* download didn't give any terrain details, but that's what it looked like from the weather sat maps we picked up. If it is a river, it's not much of one, though."

"Um." Honor laid the binoculars back down and rubbed her nose in thought, then looked at Scotty. "Think you could take a shuttle through there without counter-grav?"

"Without—?" Tremaine looked at her for a moment, then inhaled sharply. "Sure," he said, far more confidently than he could possibly feel, and Honor chuckled.

"Don't get your testosterone in an uproar on me now, Scotty. I'm serious. Can you get us in there?"

"Probably, Ma'am," he said after a moment, then added, grudgingly, "but I can't guarantee it. With one of our own pinnaces, yes. But this is a big brute, Ma'am. She's a lot heavier on the controls, and I haven't really experimented with her vectored thrust yet."

"But you think you could do it."

"Yes, Ma'am."

Honor thought for several more seconds, then sighed and shook her head.

"I'd like to take you up on that," she said, "but I don't think we can risk it. Chief Harkness?"

"Aye, Ma'am?"

"Go ahead and fire up the plant, Chief."

"Aye, aye, Ma'am. I'm starting light-off now. We should be nominal in about four minutes."

"Thank you, Chief. Signal Commander Metcalf please, Scotty."

"Yes, Ma'am." Tremaine banked the big shuttle to expose its full wingspan to Metcalf's lower position and flashed both wingtip lights twice.

"Answering flash from Shuttle Two, Ma'am," a Grayson voice reported.

"Thank you, Carson," Honor replied, and leaned back beside Tremaine. Firing up the fusion plants and bringing up the counter-grav added somewhat to the risk of detection if any recon sat happened to be looking their way. She'd hoped to avoid that, but she'd also known she might not be able to. That was why she'd arranged a signal to warn Metcalf without breaking com silence. At least the plants shouldn't be on-line for long, she told herself, and the counter-grav would make it much, much safer—and easier—to get the shuttles down.

"I've got power to the counter-grav, Ma'am," Tremaine reported, breaking in on her thoughts, and she nodded.

"See that 'S'-curve to the south?" she asked.

"Yes, Ma'am."

"It looks like the widest break in the tree cover we've got. See if you can get us in there on its west bank."

"Yes, Ma'am." Tremaine almost managed not to sound dubious, and Honor felt the right side of her mouth quirking in another grin as he banked again and came back around. Her hand dropped down beside her to rest on Nimitz's flank, and she felt a wiry, long-fingered true-hand pat her wrist in reply, and then Tremaine was dumping altitude and speed alike.

Despite his comments about the shuttle's controls, he brought the big craft in with a delicacy a Sphinx finch might have envied. The counter-grav let him fold the wings, which had been swept fully forward for their low-speed examination of possible landing sites, back into their high-speed position without losing control, and she heard turbines whine as he held a moderate apparent weight on the shuttle and vectored thrust downward. The sixty-three-meter fuselage slid almost daintily towards the ground, hovering with ponderous grace, and Honor peered through the armorplast windscreen.

The break in the canopy was a river, and shallow water rushed and tumbled over mossy boulders in a torrent of moon-struck white and black. The trees grew right up to the banks, but the humidity was far lower here in the center of the continent than it had been at their peninsular landing site, and the growth looked less lush and thick. Or she hoped it did, anyway. It was hard to be sure, and the last thing they needed was to suck something into a turbine.

"Over there, Ma'am. To port," Tremaine said. "What about there?"

"Um." Honor twisted in her seat to look in the indicated direction. It looked like one of the trees—and a titan among titans, at that—must have fallen and taken two or three others with it. The result was a breach in the overhead cover that seemed to offer a way under the remaining canopy.

"All right," she said finally, "but take it slow. And take some more weight off her so you can cut back on the VT. Let's try not to kick up trash and FOD a turbine."

"Yes, Ma'am. That sounds like a *real* good idea," Tremaine replied, then grinned tightly despite his gathering tension. "Chief Barstow would appreciate it, too, I'm sure."

"Hey, the heck with Chief Barstow," Harkness growled over the com. "This here is *my* bird, Sir. She can look after Two."

"I stand corrected—or at least chastened," Tremaine said in a somewhat distracted tone, his hands flickering over his controls with the precision of an absent-minded concert pianist while his eyes never left his intended landing site.

The pilot in Honor wanted to help him, but she knew better than to try. Her single hand would make her slow and awkward, and it was better to let him handle the entire load rather than risk getting in his way.

The shuttle came in very slowly, gleaming in the moonlight, and the black shadow of the jungle reached out for it. Tremaine slid it forward, no more than half a dozen meters above the ground, and Honor watched with carefully hidden nervousness as foliage rippled and danced below them. Even with the reduction in downward thrust, there was a lot of small trash flying around down there, and foreign object damage to a turbine could have deadly consequences this close to the ground.

But the turbines continued their whining song of power, and Tremaine eased the shuttle carefully down and forward. The long fuselage slid in under the tree cover, and he fed in some side thrust, edging to port.

"We're not going to be able to get as deep as we were at Site One, Ma'am," he observed through gritted teeth. His voice was still conversational, despite the sweat glistening on his taut face, and his hands moved the stick and thrust controls with smooth delicacy. "Best I can do is scrunch over as far as I can this way and let Gerry have the right side."

"I'll go with your call, Scotty," Honor said softly, without commenting on the fact that he'd given himself by far the tougher landing spot. But he was a better natural pilot than Metcalf—as good as Honor herself, but with more recent practice and two hands—and he brought his shuttle another twenty meters to its left, then nodded to himself.

"Deploy gear, please, Ma'am," he said. That much she could do, one-handed or not, and she pulled the big handle. The landing legs deployed quickly and smoothly, and Tremaine let the shuttle sink slowly down onto them. There was one scary moment as the outboard starboard leg flexed alarmingly and a red light flashed on the panel, but assault shuttles were designed for rough field landings, and the computer controlling that leg adjusted quickly. The red light died, and Tremaine gradually reduced his counter-grav, watching his readouts carefully for several taut seconds. Then he exhaled explosively.

"We're down, Ma'am," he announced. "Chief, kill the fusion plant."

"Aye, Sir," Harkness replied, and Honor reached across her body to pat Tremaine on the shoulder.

"That was good work, Scotty," she told him, and he smiled at her. Then she turned away to watch through her side window as Geraldine Metcalf brought Shuttle Two in on the far side of the opening. From here, it looked almost effortless, but Honor could imagine exactly what it felt like from inside that other cockpit. After all, she'd just experienced it herself.

"All right, people," she said as the other shuttle finally settled and its turbines died. "We're going to have to work faster than we'd expected to get the nets up. Senior Chief O'Jorgenson?"

"Yes, Ma'am?" Senior Chief Tamara O'Jorgenson was a fellow Sphinxian who had been a senior environmental tech aboard *Prince Adrian* but also happened to be a fully qualified small craft gunner.

"You'll man the dorsal turret while we get squared away, Senior Chief," Honor said.

"Aye, Ma'am."

"Very well, then." Honor hit the release on her own straps and stood. "Let's be about it, people."

Chapter Eleven

It was almost dawn before they had the nets in place once more, and Honor was more nervous about the quality of their camouflage than she cared to show. The climate was definitely drier here, and the soil seemed to be less rich. There was far less undergrowth than the ferociously fecund four-canopy jungle in which they had originally landed had offered, and the trees, for the most part, tended to be smaller. It was much harder to snuggle the shuttles in under them, and there were fewer natural vines and lianas to complement the cammo nets. She knew McKeon was as unhappy about the situation as she was, and they'd already made plans for most of their people to spend the coming night weaving more natural elements into the nets, but for now they'd just have to hope the concealment was good enough.

"If things work out, maybe we should consider sending at least one of the shuttles back to Site One after all," she said quietly as the two of them sat under a wing and watched the sun come up. He glanced at her, and she shrugged, knowing that he would recognize her oblique apology for what it was.

"Maybe," he agreed after a moment. "I suppose we could use tight beam off one of the Peeps' comsats to stay in touch without their noticing if we were careful. Bit risky, though."

She made a soft sound of agreement and leaned back against the seat cover Harkness and Andrew LaFollet had removed from the shuttle for her. Her energy levels still hadn't come back up to her precapture standards, and she felt utterly wiped out.

"You shouldn't have pushed yourself so hard," McKeon growled softly as Nimitz limped over to her and curled up on chest. She tucked her arm around the 'cat and closed her eyes wearily.

"Had to do my part. A CO has an example to set. I read that somewhere when I was at Saganami Island," she told McKeon, and he snorted with the fine fervor of an old friend.

"Sure you did. But while I realize you may not've noticed that you're shy an arm, *we* have. So next time Fritz 'suggests' you take a break, you damned well take a break!"

"Is that an order?" she asked sleepily, feeling Nimitz's purr blending into her bones even as his love echoed soothingly about the corners of her soul, and McKeon snorted again, albeit with slightly less panache.

"Actually, I think it is," he said after a moment. "We're both commodores now, after all. You told me so yourself, even if Their Lordships haven't gotten around to making it official. I've noticed that they seem to have lost my address over the last few months." Honor snorted, and he grinned at her. "Besides, Ms. Coup de Vitesse, I can probably beat *you* up in your present condition. Assuming Andrew didn't hurt me first."

"Actually, I'd try very hard not to hurt you, Sir," Major LaFollet called softly from where he sat atop the wing, keeping watch over his Steadholder.

"There, see?" Honor said even more sleepily. "Andrew'll stop you."

"Oh, I didn't say that, My Lady!" LaFollet chuckled. "I meant I'd try not to hurt him while I *helped* him make you take a break."

"Traitor!" Honor murmured, right cheek dimpling with a smile that never touched the left side of her mouth at all, and then she drifted off to sleep.

It was not only drier here, it was also hotter. They were squarely in the middle of the continent, far away from the moderating influence of the oceans, and the aptly named Camp Inferno was, indeed, directly on the equator. It was as well that Nimitz had shed his winter down before they moved, yet even so, he and Honor were driven to retreat into one of the shuttles by noon.

But at least no overflying Peeps seemed to have spotted them, and by late afternoon McKeon, Marchant, and Metcalf had organized work parties to bring in native greenery to supplement the cover of the cammo nets. While they did that, Harkness, Barstow, and Tremaine got all the thermal convertors on-line, and the temperatures in the shuttles dropped dramatically as extra power began to augment their battery backups.

There were about three or four hours of daylight left when Honor found herself back under the wing with LaFollet, Carson Clinkscales, and Jasper Mayhew. Clinkscales fair redhead's complexion had not reacted well to Hell's climate. At least the dense canopy at Site One, coupled with copious use of sun blocker from the shuttles' emergency stores, had protected him from direct sunlight and he hadn't burned—yet—but he tended to stay an alarming, heat-induced beet-red which looked fairly awesome on someone his size. At a hundred and ninety centimeters, he was a good two centimeters taller than Honor, which made him a veritable giant for a Grayson.

At the moment, however, he was standing with crossed arms and regarding her with an expression which looked just as unhappy as Andrew LaFollet's. Or, for that matter, Jasper Mayhew's. *Or*, she reflected wryly, *as Alistair and Fritz are going to look when they hear about this. Fortunately, rank does have its privileges . . . and we'll be long gone by the time they find out what I'm up to.*

"My Lady, Carson and Jasper and I can do this quite well by ourselves," LaFollet said flatly. "Frankly, you'll just be in the way."

"Oh?" She cocked her head. "Let's see, now. Jasper here grew up in Austin City, as I recall. I don't remember seeing any jungles there. And then there's Carson. He grew up in Mackenzie Steading, and I don't remember any jungles there, either. In fact, Andrew, I don't recall *any* Graysons having grown up running around the woods. It's not the sort of thing people do on a planet with environmental hazards like Grayson's. Now I, on the other hand, grew up in the Copperwalls. And if we don't have jungles on Sphinx, we do have picket wood and crown oak and tangle vine, not to mention large and hungry predators, all of which I happen to have learned how to cope with as a wee tiny child."

She raised her hand, palm uppermost, and smiled at them and was rewarded by the audible grinding of LaFollet's teeth.

"Be that as it may, My Lady, this is still no job for you. You're still weak, and you're blind on one side." He didn't mention her missing arm, but his very lack of mention only drew attention to it. "And while you're right about conditions on Grayson, My Lady, and while I may not have known how to *swim* before I entered your service, Palace Security gives its people a thorough grounding in wilderness and rough terrain training, as well as urban environs. In fact, we get exactly the same training the Army's special forces teams get. I haven't had a refresher in the past several years, but I understand it's like riding a bicycle."

"Andrew, stop arguing," she told him, firmly but with a much gentler smile, and laid her hand on his arm. "I'll concede your point about weakness and vision, but I need to be there. There won't be any time to send messages back and forth if decisions have to be made." *And you know I can't send anyone else off to take this kind of risk without taking it myself*, she carefully did not say, but the flicker in his gray eyes told her that he'd heard it anyway.

He glowered at her for another long moment, then sighed and shook his head.

"All right," he surrendered. "All right, My Lady! I suppose that by now I should know better than to argue with you."

"Well, it's certainly not *my* fault if you haven't figured it out," she told him with a chuckle, and smacked him on the shoulder. "On the other hand, I think I've heard it said somewhere that Graysons are just a bit stubborn."

"Not stubborn enough, obviously!" he growled, and this time Mayhew and Clinkscales chuckled as well. "Well, if you're coming,

My Lady, then we'd better get moving before Commodore McKeon or Commander Montoya figure it out. I'm sure you wouldn't let them talk you out of it, either, but by the time they got done trying it'd be midnight."

"Yes, Sir," she murmured docilely, and he glared at her, then bent to pick up the treecat carrier she'd had Harkness run up for her and helped her into it.

Until they could get Nimitz home and into the hands of a good Sphinx veterinary surgeon to fix his twisted limb, it was impossible for him to ride her shoulder as he normally would have. Even if it hadn't been, Honor had none of her custom tunics and vests which had been reinforced to resist a 'cat's claws, and without them, Nimitz would quickly have reduced her tee-shirt to tatters . . . which wouldn't have done her shoulder any good, either. But her own injuries meant she couldn't carry him in her arms the way she would have under other circumstances, so Harkness and Master Chief Ascher had whipped up a sort of lightly-padded knapsack for her. It was just big enough for Nimitz to stand upright in, and it hung from the front of her shoulders, covering her front rather than her back, so that he could look forward from his lower vantage point.

"I still wish you'd stay put, My Lady," LaFollet murmured much more quietly, his voice too low for the other two to here. "Seriously. I don't like you risking yourself this way, and you are still weak. You know you are."

"Yes, I do. And I also know that it's my job as senior officer to be there if you three actually run into someone from Inferno," she said equally quietly. "I'm responsible for whatever decisions get made, so I need to be there when they get made in the first place. Besides, it's going to be essential that I get a . . . feel for anyone we contact."

LaFollet had opened his mouth to try one final protest, but her last sentence closed it with a click. He was one of the very few people who had realized that Nimitz's empathy permitted her to feel the emotions of those about her. He'd seen it save her life on at least one occasion, but even more importantly than that, he knew she was right. If anyone in their group would be able to know whether or not they could trust someone on this Tester-damned planet, Lady Harrington—with Nimitz's help—was that someone.

He helped her adjust the tension of the 'cat carrier's straps, gathered up his pulse rifle, and gave her equipment a quick but thorough examination. All of them carried bush knives, and like himself, she'd hung a pair of Peep-made night vision goggles about her neck against the oncoming darkness. She also wore a heavy, holstered pulser on her right hip to balance her binoculars case and her canteen, and he sighed and looked at the other two. He and Mayhew each carried a pulse rifle and a sidearm, but young Ensign Clinkscales had fitted himself out with a light tribarrel. LaFollet had almost objected to that when he first saw it, but then he'd changed his mind. Clinkscales was big enough and strong enough to carry the thing, and however over-gunned LaFollet might think he was, there were definitely arguments in favor of his choice. The belt-fed infantry support weapon was capable of spitting out as few as a hundred or as many as two or three thousand five-millimeter hypervelocity darts a minute, which would make it awesomely effective as long as the ammo in the tank-like carrier on Clinkscales' back lasted.

"All right, My Lady," the armsman sighed. "Let's go."

Honor did her best to hide her profound relief when LaFollet called another rest stop. She had no intention of slowing the others down—or of giving LaFollet an opportunity for an ever-so-polite, not-quite-spoken-aloud "I told you so"—but her armsman had been right about her physical condition. She was far better than she had been, yet her endurance remained a shadow of its old self. The fact that Hell's gravity was barely seventy-two percent that of her native Sphinx helped, but she wasn't fooling herself. Her current state seemed even worse after a lifetime of regular workouts and the better part of forty T-years of training in the martial arts, and she dropped down to sit with her back against a tree, breathing deeply (and as quietly as possible).

LaFollet prowled watchfully around their resting point for another couple of minutes, and despite her earlier teasing, he moved with almost the silence of a Sphinx snow leopard. *Not that I could hear a herd of Beowulf buffalo through my own pulse just now,* she thought wryly, then looked up as her armsman blended out of the darkness and squatted easily beside her. He turned to look at her, his expression unreadable behind his night-vision goggles. But she didn't need to read his expression. Thanks to Nimitz, she could read his emotions directly, and she felt very much like a little girl under the gaze of a teacher who wondered where her homework had gotten to. Nimitz leaned back against her breasts in his carrier and bleeked softly, and neither his radiated amusement nor the taste of LaFollet's affectionate resignation helped a lot. But she managed a wry half-smile and wiped sweat from her forehead before she let her hand fall to the 'cat's head.

"I hope you're not feeling *too* justified, Andrew," she said quietly, and he chuckled, then shook his head.

"My Lady, I've given up expecting prudence out of you," he told her.

"I'm not that bad!" she protested, and he chuckled again, louder.

"No, you're not; you're worse," he said. "Much worse. But that's all right, My Lady. We wouldn't know what to do with you if you weren't. And all other things being equal, I guess we'll keep you anyway."

"Oh, *thank* you," she muttered, and heard a snort of laughter out of the darkness from roughly Jasper Mayhew's direction. *One thing about being marooned here,* she thought. *There's too few of us for us to go all formal on each other.* That was a vast relief in many ways. She'd grown accustomed to her status as Steadholder Harrington, though it still felt unnatural sometimes, and she'd been a part of the stratified world of the Navy's rank structure since she was seventeen T-years old, and she understood the value of military discipline and authority. But her present "command" was even smaller than the one she'd held when she'd skippered LAC 113 twenty-eight T-years ago, and she'd learned then that informality was just as valuable, as long as the chain of authority remained intact, in a group which must be tight knit and completely interdependent. More to the point at just this moment, it felt good not to be removed or barricaded off from people who were friends as well as subordinates.

"How far have we come, do you think?" she asked after a moment, and LaFollet raised one wrist to consult the dimly glowing readouts on it.

"I make it about nineteen klicks, My Lady."

She nodded and leaned the back of her head against her tree while she thought. No wonder she was tired. The undergrowth here might be sparse compared to that around their initial landing site, but it was still more than enough to pose an exhausting obstacle, especially once night had fallen. It had slowed their pace to a crawl, and even with their night vision equipment, each of them had managed to find more than enough vines, low-growing branches, shrubbery, tree roots, and old-fashioned rocks and holes in the ground to trip over. Honor herself had fallen only twice, but the loss of her arm made it very difficult to catch herself. The first time, she'd come down hard enough to rip the left knee out of her trousers. The heavily scabbed scrape on her kneecap from that was painful enough to give her an irritating limp, but the second fall had been worse. All she'd been able to manage that time was to wrap her remaining arm around Nimitz and tuck her right shoulder under so that she landed on it and rolled rather than crushing the 'cat under her weight. Jasper Mayhew had appeared out of nowhere to help her up after that one, and despite her need to avoid any more "pampering" than she absolutely had to put up with, she'd let herself lean on him for several seconds until her head stopped spinning.

Now she worked the shoulder cautiously, feeling the bruising and relieved she hadn't sprained it as she'd initially feared, while she considered their progress. She couldn't see the sky from where she sat, but here and there the light of Hell's moons spilled through breaks in the tree cover to make small, brilliant patches of silver on tree trunks and undergrowth. Sheol must be almost down by now, she thought, and Tartarus would be setting in an hour or so. They had about three more hours of darkness to cover the last four or five kilometers to Camp Inferno, and she drew a deep breath and pushed herself back to her feet. LaFollet cocked his head and looked up at her, and she grinned again and patted him on the shoulder.

"I may be weak, Andrew, but I'm not decrepit yet."

"I never thought you were, My Lady," he assured her. "I only thought you were too stubborn for your own good." He rose easily, regarding her with that same, measuring air for a few more seconds, then nodded and set off once more without another word.

"So that's Camp Inferno," Honor murmured.

She and the three Graysons lay belly-down on a small, steep hill to the east of their objective, and she rested her chin on the back of her hand as she contemplated the camp. Several tall trees grew on the hilltop, promising both additional cover and at least some shade once the sun came up, but most of the hill was overgrown in head-high, stiff, sword-like grass. The area around the huddle of structures below them, on the other hand, had obviously been completely clear-cut when the camp was put in, although two or three years must have passed since the last time it was brushed back. Clusters of saplings had sprung back up out of the grass of the clearing, and the western side of the fence surrounding the camp was covered in a thick, leafy canopy of vines. It all gave the place a disheveled, somehow slovenly look.

On the other hand, she reflected, first impressions might be misleading. The grass had been cut or trampled down in something almost like a fifteen-meter moat around the enclosed area, and that stuff on the fence might actually have been trained to grow there. Four larger huts, all built out of native materials, were packed tightly along the inner face of the fence there, and unless she was mistaken, that thicket of vines would start offering them shade from very shortly after local noon.

A ceramacrete landing pad and some sort of storage sheds thrust up through the grass about a kilometer north of the camp, and a plastic water tank stood on tall, spindly-looking legs almost at the center of the fenced enclosure. A windmill squeaked with endless, inanimate patience, its plaintive sound clear and forlorn in the predawn stillness, and water splashed from an overflow pipe on the tank. Clearly the windmill powered a pump to keep the tank filled, but it was equally clear that no one had used any of that mechanical power to generate electricity.

The explanation for the lights she'd seen during their approach was obvious enough from where they lay, concealed by yet more of that tall, stiff grass. There were four gates in the fence, located at the four major points of the compass and all tightly closed at the moment, and beaten dirt tracks connected them to form a cross-shaped intersection just south of the water tank. Two rows of dimly glowing lanterns on three-meter posts bordered each lane, and pairs of much brighter lanterns marked their intersection.

"How many do you think, My Lady?" Carson Clinkscales asked quietly. It was highly unlikely that anyone could have heard them from here even if anyone were awake to listen, but all of them spoke only in hushed tones anyway.

"I don't know," she told him honestly. Nimitz lay close beside her, and she took her hand out from under her chin to scratch his jaw while she pondered the ensign's question. Those were big huts down there. Depending on how tightly the prisoners were packed into them, there might be anywhere from fifteen to fifty people in each of them. *So split the difference and call it thirty or so*, she thought. *In that case . . .*

"I'd guess it at about six or seven hundred," she said finally, and turned her head to look at LaFollet, lying on his belly on her right. "Andrew?"

"Your guess is as good as mine, My Lady." He twitched his shoulders in a shrug. "I'd say you're probably close to right, but I thought each of those camps was supposed to have a couple of thousand people in it."

"The others do," she replied, "but this one's not like them. They're mainly just holding areas; this one is a punishment camp."

"Well, they certainly put it in the right place for that, My Lady!" Clinkscales muttered, and she heard the sharp smack of his hand as he swatted another of the insects Sarah DuChene had christened "shuttlesquitos." It was fortunate that they didn't swarm like the Old Terran mosquitos they outwardly resembled, because a "swarm" of blood-drinking predators with wingspans wider than Honor's palm would have been deadly. On the other hand, it would have been even more fortunate if they'd realized that however good human beings might taste, they couldn't live off them. In fact, human blood seemed to kill them quickly . . . which didn't keep their surviving brainless relatives from darting in for their own quick solo drinks.

"I could really learn to hate this place," the ensign added wryly, and she chuckled. Whatever else happened to Clinkscales, he was no longer the shy, clumsy, perpetual accident looking to happen he'd been when he first joined the Eighteenth Cruiser Squadron's staff as her flag lieutenant, and she rather liked the tough young man he'd turned into.

"I suspect that was the Peeps' idea," she told him, and it was his turn for a chuckle to rumble around in his broad chest. "On the other hand, I have no intention of complaining about their logic. Not when they've been kind enough to concentrate the very people I want to meet in one nice, neat spot like this."

Three other heads nodded, and Nimitz bleeked his own agreement. It was clear from the memo Scotty Tremaine had pulled out of the *Tepes* data that StateSec used Camp Inferno as a dumping site for troublemakers from all the other camps. Apparently, prisoners who sufficiently disturbed the status quo to tick their captors off without quite inspiring StateSec to simply shoot them and be done with it were shipped off to Inferno. An average sentence here for a first-time visitor was one local year—a bit shorter than a T-year—with longer terms for repeat offenders, and at least some of the inmates had been sent here permanently. Which, she suspected, was the real reason Inferno existed at all. It was a punishment short of shooting which everyone knew about, and cycling bad boys and girls through it on a semiregular basis would keep its existence—and threat—in the fronts of people's brains. And leaving some of them here permanently was a pointed hint that even on Hell, StateSec could always make someone's life still more miserable . . . and leave it that way.

But the people who ran Hell didn't know there were rats in their woodwork, Honor thought, her remaining eye glinting dangerously in the darkness. They had no idea that a handful of castaways might want to find some local allies for the general purpose of raising all the hell they could. Or that the castaways in question had hijacked a pair of StateSec's own assault shuttles . . . with full arms racks. If there really were six hundred people down there, then Honor had just about enough pulsers and pulse rifles—and grenade launchers, plasma rifles, and tribarrels—to give every one of them at least one weapon each, and wouldn't *that* be a nasty surprise for the Peeps.

Long, sharp fangs those rats have, Mr. Peep, she thought viciously. *If, that is, the people down in that camp really are the troublemakers you seem to think they are. And there's only one way to find that out, now isn't there?*

"All right," she said softly. "Let's pull back under the trees and get some sort of overhead cover rigged. I want plenty of shade for all of us by the time the sun really hits. But keep it unobtrusive."

"Yes, My Lady." LaFollet nodded to her, then jerked his head at Mayhew and Clinkscales, and the other two officers faded back from the lip of the hill. He himself lay motionless beside Honor, watching her peer through her electronic binoculars one more time, then quirked an eyebrow at her.

"Any thoughts on exactly how we go about making contact, My Lady?" he asked, and she shrugged.

"We'll have to play it by ear, but we've got enough food for three or four days, and there's plenty of water." She nodded her head at the stream from the water tank and pump where it snaked under the fence and meandered in their direction. "I'm not in any rush. We'll watch them for a while, see how they spend their time. Ideally, I'd like to catch one or two of them outside the camp on their own and get a feel for how things are organized in there before we jump right in with both feet."

"Makes sense to me, My Lady," he said after a moment. "Jasper and Carson and I will take turns playing lookout once we get the camp set up."

"I can—" Honor began, but he shook his head firmly.

"No," he said in a soft, flat voice. "You were probably right about coming along, My Lady, but we can do this just as well without you, and I want you rested when the time comes to actually talk to these people. And I don't want you dragging Nimitz out of the shade, either."

"You fight dirty," she told him after a moment, and his teeth flashed in a smile.

"That's because you don't leave me much choice, My Lady," he told her, and jerked a thumb in the direction of the trees. "Now march!" he commanded.

Chapter Twelve

"I think those two look like our best bet, Andrew," Honor said quietly. It was the morning of their second day of watching Camp Inferno, and she lay in the fork of a tree four meters above the ground while she peered through her binoculars. LaFollet hadn't liked the notion of letting his one-armed Steadholder climb a tree, and he didn't like the notion of her turning loose of the tree trunk to use her one working hand to hold the binoculars to her working eye, but she hadn't given him much say in the matter. At least she'd let him help her with the climb, and now he hovered over her watchfully. And, he admitted, she wasn't really all that likely to fall. The trees here were very different from the almost-palms where they had originally landed. Instead of smooth, almost branchless trunks, they had rough, hairy bark and thick, flattened branches that shoved out from the main trunk in every direction. Rather than rise to a point, their foliage made them look almost like huge inverted cones, for they grew progressively broader as they grew taller and the individual branches grew thinner but the network of them spread wider and wider. The branch on which his Steadholder lay was fairly near the bottom of that spreading process, and it was two or three times the thickness of her own body, more like a shelf than a "branch."

Not that it kept him from worrying.

He clamped his jaws on a fresh urge to protest and looked up at Nimitz. The 'cat was a couple of meters higher up the central trunk, clinging with his good limbs as he sank ivory claws into the rough bark, and LaFollet had taken a certain perverse pleasure in watching the Steadholder worry over *him* as he hauled himself awkwardly up the trunk. It was the first time he'd attempted any climbing since their arrival on Hell, and he'd done much better than LaFollet had expected from watching his lurching progress on the ground. He still looked undeniably clumsy compared to his usual, flowing gracefulness, and his obvious pain still made something deep down inside the armsman hurt, but there was no self-pity in Nimitz. He clearly considered himself a going concern once more, if on a somewhat limited level, and he flirted his bushy tail with an undeniable air of amusement as he bleeked down at LaFollet.

The armsman looked away, shading his eyes with one hand as he peered at the pair of humans the Steadholder was studying so intently. He couldn't make out many details from here, but he could pick out enough to tell they were the same pair he'd watched yesterday. The man was short and bald as an egg, with skin so black it looked purple, and he favored brightly, almost garishly colored garments. The woman with him was at least fifteen centimeters taller than he was, dressed in somber shades of gray and with a single golden braid of hair that hung to her belt. A more unlikely looking pair would have been hard to imagine, and he'd wondered, that first day, just what they thought were doing as they moved slowly along the very edge of the camp's cleared zone.

He still didn't have an answer for that. It was almost as if they were peering into the forest beyond the open grasslands, searching for something, but there was little urgency in their movements. Indeed, they walked so slowly—and spent so long standing motionless between bursts of walking—that he was half inclined to believe their experiences here on Hell had driven them over the brink.

"You're sure you want to talk to *them*, My Lady?" he asked finally, trying unsuccessfully to keep his own doubtfulness out of his voice.

"I think so, yes," Honor said calmly.

"But . . . they look so . . . so—" LaFollet broke off, unable to find the exact word he wanted, and Honor chuckled.

"Lost? Out of it? Crackers?" she suggested, and he twitched a sour smile at her teasing tone.

"Actually, yes, My Lady," he admitted after a moment. "I mean, *look* at them. If they knew we were out here and were searching for us, that would be one thing, but they can't know it. Or if they do, they're the most incompetent pair of scouts I've ever seen! Walking around out there in sight of the Tester and everyone and staring into the woods—" He shook his head.

"You may have a point, Andrew. After all, a stay on Hell would probably be enough to drive anyone at least a little mad, although I doubt they're as far gone as you seem to think. But that isn't really the reason I picked them. Look for yourself," she invited, rolling over on her side to hand the binoculars up to him and then sweep her arm in an arc across the cleared area. "The only other people out there are all in groups of at least four or five, and each of them is obviously performing some specific task."

LaFollet didn't need the binoculars to know she was right; his unaided vision could see it clearly from here. Two groups of ten or fifteen people apiece were hauling branches and vines and fern-like fronds out of the jungle while another five armed with long, slender spears watched over them protectively. Another group was busy with clumsy looking wooden sickles, cutting back the grass along the edges of the cleared zone about the fence, with another little knot of spearmen guarding them, and others were busy with still more chores, most of them almost impossible to figure out from this distance. Only the pair Lady Harrington had selected weren't obviously embarked on such a task.

"Not only are those two out on their own," she went on, "but they're already headed our way. I think you and Jasper can probably intercept them about there—" she pointed to where a clump of trees thrust out from the base of their hill "—without anyone noticing you, and invite them up here to talk to me."

"'Invite'!" LaFollet snorted. Then he shook his head resignedly. "All right, My Lady. Whatever you say."

Honor sat on a thick, gnarled root, leaning her spine against the tree to which it belonged with Nimitz in her lap, as the two POWs were escorted towards her. They were still too far away for her to feel their emotions with any clarity, but the way they moved proclaimed their uncertainty and wariness. They stayed close together, looking back over their shoulders frequently, and the man had his arm around the woman in a protective gesture which would have looked silly, given the difference in their heights, if it had been even a little less fierce.

Jasper Mayhew followed them, his pulse rifle casually unslung but with the muzzle pointing unthreateningly away from his "guests," and Andrew LaFollet brought up the rear. Her armsman, she saw, had collected the POWs' spears. He'd evidently lashed them together so he could carry both of them in one hand, and he carried his drawn pulser in the other. The spears had long, leaf-shaped heads chipped from a white, milky-looking stone of some sort, and each POW wore an empty belt sheath. She glanced at LaFollet again and saw knives or daggers of the same white stone tucked into his belt.

She watched them come closer, and Nimitz stirred uneasily in her lap. She reached out through her link to him and winced as a fist seemed to punch her in the face. She'd felt fear to match the POWs' often enough, but never such bleak, helpless, terrible fury. The emotion storm was so ferocious she almost expected to see one of them burst into spontaneous flame—or at least turn to charge Mayhew and LaFollet in a berserk suicide attack—but they had themselves too well in hand for that. And perhaps there was another reason beyond self-discipline, for even through their seething rage, she felt a tiny edge of something else. Uncertainty, perhaps. Or curiosity. Something, at any rate, which whispered to them that what was happening might not, in fact, be what they had assumed it must be.

They reached the top of the hill and paused suddenly, stock still as they saw Honor and Nimitz. The two of them looked at one another, and the woman said something too low for Honor to hear, but she felt that spark of curiosity flaring higher, and realized it was the sight of Nimitz which had fanned it. Mayhew said something to her in reply, his tone courteous but insistent, and they shook themselves back into motion and walked straight to her.

She gathered Nimitz up in the crook of her arm and stood, and she felt another, stronger flash of shock and curiosity snap through them as they stepped under the shade of her tree and stopped, staring at her from a distance of three or four meters. Then the woman shook herself and cocked her head to the side.

"Who *are* you people?" she asked in a soft, wondering tone.

Standard English had been the interstellar language of humanity from the earliest days of the Diaspora. It had become that almost inevitably, for it had been the international language of Old Earth and had been carried to the other bodies of the Sol System long before it left them for the stars. Many worlds and even star nations spoke other languages among their own citizens—German in the Anderman Empire, for example, or Spanish on San Martin, French on New Dijon, Chinese and Japanese on Ki-Rin and Nagasaki, and Hebrew in the Judean League—but every educated human being spoke Standard English. And, for the most part, electronic recordings and the printed word had kept its pronunciation close enough from world to world for it to be a truly universal language. But Honor had to concentrate hard to follow this woman's mushy accent. She'd never heard one quite like it, and she wondered what the other's native tongue was. But she couldn't let it distract her, and so she drew herself up to her full height and nodded to them.

"My name is Harrington," she told them calmly. "Commodore Harrington, Royal Manticoran Navy."

"*Royal Manticoran Navy?*" This time the woman's voice was sharp, and Honor felt a fresh stab of anger—and scorn—as the blonde's eyes dropped to the black StateSec trousers Honor wore. "Sure you are," she said after a moment, gray eyes hard.

"Yes, I am," Honor replied in the same calm tones. "And whatever you may be thinking, clothes don't necessarily make the woman. I'm afraid we've had to make do for uniforms with what we could, ah, liberate, as it were."

The other woman looked at her in hard-eyed silence for several more seconds, and then, suddenly, her eyebrows rose in an expression of shock.

"Wait. You said 'Harrington.' Are you *Honor* Harrington?" she demanded harshly, and it was Honor's turn to blink in consternation.

"I was the last time I looked," she said cautiously. She looked past the newcomers at Mayhew, one eyebrow quirked, but the Grayson lieutenant only shook his head.

"My God," the woman muttered, then turned back to the man. He returned her stare without comment, then shrugged and raised both hands palm uppermost.

"May I ask how you happen to know my first name?" Honor asked after a moment, and the woman wheeled back around to face her.

"A couple of dozen Manty prisoners got dumped in my last camp just before the Black Legs sent me to Inferno," she said slowly, narrow eyes locked on Honor's face. "They had a lot to say about you—if you're really the Honor Harrington they were talking about. Said you took out a Peep battlecruiser with a *heavy* cruiser before the war even started, then ripped hell out of a Peep task force at someplace called Hancock. And they said—" her eyes darted to Nimitz "—that you had some strange kind of pet." She stopped and cocked her head aggressively. "That you?"

"Allowing for a little exaggeration in the telling, I'd say yes," Honor replied even more cautiously. It had never occurred to her that anyone on this planet had ever heard of her, and she was unprepared for the fierce, exultant enthusiasm her name seemed to have waked within the stern-faced blonde. "I wasn't in command at Hancock—I was Admiral Sarnow's flag captain—and I had a lot of help dealing with the battlecruiser. And Nimitz isn't my 'pet.' But, yes. I think I'm the one you're talking about."

"Damn," the woman whispered. "*Damn!* I sure as hell knew he wasn't from any evolutionary line on this planet!" But then her exultation faded, and her face turned cold and bitter. "So the bastards got you, too," she half-snarled.

"Yes, and no," Honor replied. "As you may have noticed, we're a little better equipped than you people seem to be." LaFollet had joined her while she and the other woman were speaking, and she handed him Nimitz and then took the lashed-together spears from him. She weighed them in her hand a moment, then passed them back to her armsman and tapped the butt of her holstered pulser, but she was unprepared for the other woman's reaction.

"Oh my God, you *hit* one of them, did you?" she demanded in a tone of raw horror.

" 'Hit one of them'?" Honor repeated.

"Hit one of the supply shuttles," the other woman said harshly, and the horror in her face—and emotions—had turned accusing.

"No, we haven't hit one of the supply shuttles," Honor replied.

"Oh, sure," the blonde said. "You found the guns growing wild in the woods!"

"No, we took these from the Peeps," Honor told her calmly. "But we took them before we ever hit atmosphere." Both newcomers were staring at her now, as if at a lunatic, and the living side of her mouth smiled grimly. "Did either of you happen to see a rather large explosion up there about five T-months ago?" she asked, and jerked her thumb at the sky, invisible beyond the tree branches.

"Yeah," the blonde said very slowly, drawing the word out, and her eyes were narrow again. "Matter of fact, we saw quite a few of 'em. Why?"

"Because that was us arriving," Honor said dryly. LaFollet shifted beside her, and she felt his unhappiness. He didn't want her telling these strangers so much about them so quickly, but Honor only touched him on the shoulder. He stilled his fidgeting, and she gave him a brief smile. Unless she decided that she could trust these two—fully—then they would be returning to the hidden shuttles with her and her companions, at gunpoint if necessary. But for now, she had to convince them she was telling the truth, because if she didn't, they would never trust her, which meant *she* would never be able to trust *them*.

"You?" the woman asked, brow furrowing in disbelief, and she nodded.

"Us. The Peeps captured us in the Adler System and turned us over to StateSec to ship out here. Their plans included hanging me on arrival, but some of my people had . . . other ideas."

"Ideas?" the blonde parroted, and Honor nodded again.

"Let's just say that one of my chiefs has a way with computers. He got access to the ship's net and took the entire system down, and in the confusion, the rest of my people broke me out of solitary confinement, seized control of a boat bay, stole us some transport, and blew the ship up as they left." She felt a fresh, wrenching stab of loss and grief for the people who had died making that possible, but she let none of it show in her face. Not now. Not until she had convinced these people that she was telling them the truth.

"And just how the hell did they do *that?*" the other woman asked in obvious skepticism, and Honor smiled crookedly at her.

"They demonstrated what happens when you bring up a pinnace's impeller wedge inside a boat bay," she said very softly. The other woman showed no reaction at all for two or three seconds, and then she flinched as if someone had just punched her in the belly.

"My *God!*" she whispered. "But that—"

"Killed everyone on board," Honor finished for her grimly. "That's right. We took out the entire ship . . . and no one dirtside knows we got out—and down—alive. With, as I said, somewhat better equipment than you seem to have."

"How do you know?" the man demanded, speaking for the first time. His speech was similar to his companion's, but even more slurred and hard to follow, and he made an impatient gesture when Honor cocked her head at him. "How do you know they don't know?" he amplified in his almost incomprehensible accent, speaking very slowly and with an obvious effort at clarity.

"Let's just say we've been checking their mail," Honor replied.

"But that means—" The woman was staring at her, and then she wheeled back to her companion. "Henri, they've got a pinnace!" she hissed. "Sweet Jesus, *they've got a pinnace!*"

"But—" Henri began, and then stopped dead. The two of them stared at one another, expressions utterly stunned, and then turned back as one to Honor, and this time suspicion and fear had been replaced by raw, blazing excitement.

"You do, don't you?" the woman demanded. "You've got a pinnace, and— My God, you must have the com equipment to go with it!"

"Something like that," Honor replied, watching her carefully and privately astonished by how quickly the other woman had put things together. Of course, it must be obvious that if they'd gotten down without the Peeps knowing about it they had to at least have a lifeboat, but this woman had gotten past her disbelief and shock to put all the clues together far more rapidly than Honor would have believed was possible. Was that because her odd accent made her sound like some sort of untutored bumpkin from a hick planet whose schools couldn't even teach their people to speak proper Standard English?

"But why are you—?" the blonde began, speaking almost absently, as if to herself. Then she stopped again. "Of course," she said very softly. "*Of course.* You're looking for manpower, aren't you, Commodore? And you figured Camp Inferno was the best place to recruit it?"

"Something like that," Honor repeated, astonished afresh and trying not to show it. She didn't know how long this woman had been a prisoner, but captivity obviously hadn't done a thing to slow down her mental processes.

"Well I will be dipped in shit," the other woman said almost prayerfully, and then stepped forward so quickly not even LaFollet had time to react. Honor felt her armsman flinch beside her, but the blonde only held out her right hand, and Honor tasted the wild, almost manic delight flaring through her.

"Pleased to meet you, Commodore Harrington. *Very* pleased to meet you! My name's Benson, Harriet Benson," she said in that slurred accent, "and this—" she nodded her head at her companion "—is Henri Dessouix. Back about two lifetimes ago, I was a captain in the Pegasus System Navy, and Henri here was a lieutenant in the Gaston Marines. I've been stuck on this miserable ball of dirt for something like sixty-five T-years, and I have never been more delighted to make someone's acquaintance in my life!"

Chapter Thirteen

"So that's about the long and the short of it," Benson said fifteen minutes later. Complete introductions had been made all round, and the two POWs sat cross-legged under the shade of the same tree with Honor while LaFollet hovered watchfully at her shoulder and Mayhew and Clinkscales stood guard. "I was dumb enough—and also young, stupid, and pissed *off* enough—to join up with the effort to organize a resistance movement after the surrender, and InSec dumped me here in a heartbeat." She grimaced. "If I'd realized no one else was going to be able to stand up to their goddamned navy for the next half century, I probably would've kept my head down back home, instead."

Honor nodded. She had only a vague notion of the Pegasus System's location, but she knew it was close to the Haven System . . . and that it had been one of the PRH's very first conquests. And from the flavor of Harriet Benson's emotions and the steel she sensed at the older woman's core, she strongly suspected the captain would have attempted to resist the Peeps whatever she had or hadn't known about the future.

"And you, Lieutenant?" she asked courteously, looking at Dessouix.

"Henri got shipped in about ten years after I did," Benson replied for him. Honor was a bit startled for a moment by the other woman's interruption, but Dessouix only nodded with a small smile, and there was no resentment in his emotions. Was it his accent? It was certainly much thicker than Benson's, so perhaps he routinely let her do most of the talking.

"From where?" she asked.

"Toulon, in the Gaston System," Benson said. "When the Peeps moved in on Toulon, the Gaston Space Forces gave them a better fight than we did in Pegasus. Then again," her mouth twisted, "they knew the bastards were coming. The first thing *we* knew about it was the arrival of the lead task force."

She brooded in silence for a few moments, then shrugged.

"Anyway, Henri was serving in the Marine detachment aboard one of their ships—"

"The *Dague*," Dessouix put in.

"Yes, the *Dague*." Benson nodded. "And when the system government surrendered, *Dague*'s skipper refused to obey the cease-fire order. She fought a hit-and-run campaign against the Peeps' merchant marine for over a T-year before they finally cornered her and pounded *Dague* to scrap. The Peeps shot her and her senior surviving officers for 'piracy,' and the junior officers got shipped to Hell where they couldn't make any more trouble. I guess it was—what? About ten T-years, Henri?—after that when we met."

"About ten," Dessouix agreed. "They transferred me to your camp to separate me from my men."

"And how did the two of you end up at Inferno?" Honor asked after a moment.

"Oh, I've always been a troublemaker, Commodore," Benson said with a bitter smile, and reached out to lay a hand on Dessouix's shoulder. "Henri here can tell you that."

"Stop that," Dessouix said. His tone was forceful, and he enunciated each word slowly and carefully, as he if were determined to make his weirdly accented Standard English comprehensible. "It wasn't your fault, *bien-aimée*. I made my own decision, Harriet. All of us did."

"And I led all of you right into it," she said flatly. But then she inhaled sharply and shook her head. "Not but what he isn't right, Dame Honor. He's a stubborn man, my Henri."

"And you aren't?" Dessouix snorted with slightly less force.

"Not a *man*, at any rate," Benson observed with a slow, lurking smile. It was the first Honor had seen from the other woman, and it softened her stern face into something almost gentle.

"I'd noticed," Dessouix replied dryly, and Benson chuckled. Then she looked back at Honor.

"But you were asking how I wound up here. The answer's simple enough, I'm afraid—ugly, but simple. You see, neither InSec nor these new Black Leg, StateSec bastards have ever seen any reason to worry about little things like the Deneb Accords. We're not prisoners to them; we're *property*. They can do anything the hell they like to us, and none of their 'superior officers' are going to so much as slap their wrists. So if you're good looking and a Black Leg takes a hankering for you—"

She shrugged, and Honor's face went harder than stone. Benson gazed into her one good eye for a second, then nodded.

"Exactly," she said harshly. She looked away and drew a deep breath, and Honor could feel the iron discipline it took for the older woman to throttle the rage which threatened to explode within her.

"I was the senior officer in our old camp, which made me the CO," the woman from Pegasus continued after a moment, her voice level with dearly bought dispassion, "and there were two other prisoners there, friends of mine, who both helped me with camp management. They were twins—a brother and a sister. I never knew exactly what planet they were from. I think it was Haven itself, but they never said. I think they were afraid to, even here on Hell, but I knew they were politicals, not military. They really shouldn't have been in the same camp as us military types, but they'd been on Hell a long time—almost as long as me—and InSec hadn't been as careful about segregating us in the early days. But they were both good looking, and unlike me, they were second-generation prolong."

One hand rose, stroking her blond braid. At this close range, Honor could see white hairs threaded through it, though they were hard to make out against the gold, and Benson's tanned face was older than she'd first thought. Small wonder, if she was first-generation prolong, like Hamish Alexander. *Now why did I think about* him *at a time like this?* she wondered, but it was only a passing thought, and she kept her eye fixed on Benson.

"At any rate, about—what, six years ago, Henri?" She looked at Dessouix, who nodded, then back at Honor. "About six local years ago, one of these new Black Leg bastards decided he wanted the sister. He was the flight engineer on the food run, and he ordered her onto the shuttle for the flight back to Styx."

Honor shifted her weight, eyebrows quirked, and Benson paused, looking a question back at her.

"I didn't mean to interrupt," Honor half-apologized. "But it was our understanding that no prisoners were allowed on Styx."

"Prisoners aren't; *slaves* are," Benson said harshly. "We don't know how many—probably not more than a couple of hundred—and I guess it's against official policy, but that doesn't stop them. These sick bastards think they're gods, Commodore. They can do whatever the hell they like—*anything*—and they don't see any reason why they shouldn't. So they drag off just enough of us to do the shit work on Styx for them . . . and for their beds."

"I see," Honor said, and her voice had the frozen edge of a scalpel.

"I imagine you do," Benson said, her mouth twisting bitterly. "Anyway, the son of a bitch ordered Amy aboard the shuttle, and she panicked. No one ever comes back from Styx, Dame Honor, so she tried to run, but he wasn't having that. He went after her, and Adam jumped him. It was stupid, I guess, but he loved his sister, and he knew exactly what the bastard wanted her for. He even managed to deck the Peep . . . and that was when the pilot stepped out of the shuttle with a pulse rifle and blew him apart."

She fell silent once more, staring down at her hands.

"I wanted to kill them all," she said in a voice grown suddenly distant and cold. "I wanted to drag them off their frigging shuttle and rip them apart with my bare hands, and we could have done it." She looked up at Honor with a corpse smile. "Oh, yes, it's been done, Commodore. Twice. But the Peeps have a very simple policy.

That's why I was so upset when I thought you'd attacked one of the food runs, because if you hit one of their shuttle flights, then no more shuttles ever come to your camp. Period. They just—" her right hand flipped in a throwing away gesture "—write you off, and when the food supplies don't come. . . ." Her voice trailed off, and she shrugged.

"I knew that, so I knew we couldn't storm the shuttle, however much the twisted, murdering pieces of shit deserved it. But I couldn't just let them have Amy, either—not after Adam died for her. So when the Black Legs started after her again, I blocked them."

"Blocked them?" Honor repeated, and Dessouix laughed harshly.

"She stepped right into the *bâtards*' way," he said with fierce pride. "Right in their ugly faces. And she wouldn't move. I thought they were going to shoot her, but she wouldn't back off a centimeter."

"And neither would Henri," Benson said softly. "He stepped up beside me, and then a couple more followed him, and then a dozen, until finally there must have been two or three hundred of us. We didn't lift a finger, not even when they tried butt-stroking us out of the way. We only stood there, with someone else stepping into the same place, and wouldn't let them past, until, finally, they gave up and left."

She looked back up at Honor, gray eyes bright, glinting with the memory of the moment, the solidarity of her people at her back, but then her gaze fell once more, and Honor tasted the bitterness of her emotions, like lye in Nimitz's link.

"But they got even with us," she said softly. "They cut off the food shipments anyway." She drew another deep breath. "You've noticed mine and Henri's 'accents'?" she asked

"Well, yes, actually," Honor admitted, surprised into tactlessness by the *non sequitur*, and Benson laughed mirthlessly.

"They aren't accents," she said flatly. "They're speech impediments. You probably haven't been on-planet long enough to realize it, but there actually is one plant we can eat and at least partially metabolize. We call it 'false-potato,' and it tastes like— Well, you don't want to *know* what it tastes like . . . and I'd certainly like to forget. But for some reason, our digestive systems can break it down—partially, as I say—and we can even live on it for a while. Not a long time, but if we use it to eke out terrestrial foods, it can carry us. Unfortunately, there's some kind of trace toxin in it that seems to accumulate in the brain and affect the speech centers almost like a stroke. We don't have a lot of doctors here on Hell, and I never had a chance to talk to anyone from one of the other camps, so I don't know if they've even figured out humans can eat the damned stuff, much less why or exactly how it affects us. But *we* knew, and when the food flights stopped, we didn't have any choice but to eat it. It was either that or eat each other," she added in a voice leached of all emotion, "and we weren't ready for that yet."

"They were in the other camps—the other two the *Tiges-Noires* let starve to death," Henri said softly to Honor, and Benson nodded.

"Yes, they were," she agreed heavily. "Eventually. We know they were, because the Peep psychos made holo chips of it and made all the rest of us watch them just to be sure their little demonstration was effective."

"Sweet Tester," Honor heard LaFollet whisper behind her, and her own stomach knotted with nausea, but she let no sign of it show in her face. She only gazed at Benson, waiting, and felt the older woman draw composure from her own appearance of calm.

"We lasted about three months," the blond captain said finally, "and each month the bastards would fly over as if for a supply run, then just hover there, looking down at us. We all knew what they wanted, and people are people everywhere, Commodore. Some of us wanted to go ahead and hand Amy over before we all died, but the rest of us—" She sighed. "The rest of us were too damned stubborn, and too damned sick of being *used*, and too damned mad. We refused to give her up. Hell, we refused to let her give *herself* up, because we were all pretty sure how they'd treat her once they got her back to Styx."

She fell silent once more, brooding over the cold poison of old memories.

"I think we were all a little out of our heads," she said. "I know I was. I mean, it didn't really make any sense for two thousand people to starve themselves to death—or gradually poison themselves with those damned false-potatoes—just to protect a single person. But it was . . . I don't know. The *principle* of the thing, I suppose. We just couldn't do it—not and still think of ourselves as human beings.

"And then Amy took it out of our hands."

Benson's hands tightened like talons on her knees, and the only sounds were the wind in the leaves and the harsh, distant warbling of some alien creature in the forests of Hell.

"When the shuttle came back the fourth time, she stepped out where the crew could see her." Benson's voice was that of a machine, hammered out of old iron. "She surprised us, got past us to the pad before we could stop her, and just *stood* there, looking up at them. And then, when the shuttle landed, she drew her knife—" Benson jutted her chin at the stone blades still tucked into LaFollet's belt "—and cut her own throat in front of them."

Andrew LaFollet inhaled sharply, and Honor felt the shock and fury lashing through him. He was a Grayson, product of a society which had protected women—sometimes against their own wishes—with near fanaticism for almost a thousand years, and Benson's story hit him like a hammer.

"They left," she said emptily. "Just lifted and left her lying there like a butchered animal. And they waited another month, letting us think she'd killed herself for *nothing*, before they resumed the food flights." She bared her teeth in a snarl. "Eleven of my people died of starvation in that last month, Commodore. We hadn't lost any up until then, but eleven of them died. Another fifteen suicided rather than starve, because they knew the food flights would never resume, and that was exactly what those murdering bastards *wanted* them to do!"

"*Doucement, ma petite*," Henri said softly. He reached out and captured one of her hands in dark, strong fingers and squeezed it. Benson bit her lip for a moment, then shrugged angrily.

"At any rate, that's how Henri and I wound up here, Dame Honor. We're lifers, because they dragged us 'ringleaders' off to Inferno as an added example to the others."

"I see," Honor said quietly.

"I think you do, Commodore," Benson replied, gazing back at her. Their eyes held for several seconds, and then Honor stepped back a bit from the intensity of the moment.

"Obviously, I still have a great many more questions," she said, making her tone come out sounding as natural as her own crippled mouth permitted. *And aren't we all a battered and bedamned lot?* she thought with a flash of true humor. *Benson and Dessouix from their "false-potatoes"and me from nerve damage. Lord, it's a wonder we can understand* ourselves, *much less anyone else!* Nimitz followed her thought and bleeked a quiet laugh from her lap, and she shook herself.

"As I say, I still have questions," she said more easily, "but there's one I hope you can answer for me right now."

"Such as?" Benson asked.

"Such as just what you and Lieutenant Dessouix were doing when my people, um, invited you to come talk to me."

"Doing?" Benson repeated blankly.

"Yes. We could figure out some of what was going on out there," Honor told her, waving her hand in the direction of the camp clearing, "but you and the Lieutenant had us stumped."

"Oh, that!" Benson's expression cleared, and then she laughed with an edge of embarrassment. "We were . . . well, call it bird-watching, Dame Honor."

"*Bird*-watching?" Honor blinked, and Benson shrugged.

"Well, they're not really birds, of course. Hell doesn't have birds. But they're close enough analogues, and they're pretty." She shrugged again. "It's an interest we share—a hobby, I suppose—and yesterday and today were our free days, so we decided to see if we couldn't spot a mated group we've been seeing foraging in the sword grass for the last couple of weeks. You do realize, don't you, that all native life here on Hell is trisexual?" Her expression brightened with genuine interest. "Actually, there are four sexes, but we think only three of them are immediately involved in procreation," she explained. "The fourth is a neuter, but it's actually the one that does the nursing in the mammal equivalents, and it seems to do most of the foraging or hunting for the others. And the birth rates for all four sexes seem to be set by some sort of biomechanism that—"

She stopped abruptly, and blushed. The effect looked fascinating on her stern, captain's face, and Dessouix laughed delightedly.

"You see, Dame Honor?" he said after a moment, "even here in Hell, some people have hobbies."

"Yes, I do see," Honor replied with one of her half-smiles. Then she leaned back against the tree, studying them both for several silent seconds while her mind worked.

Nimitz pressed his chin against her knee, chest rumbling with the merest whisper of his normal buzzing purr. Benson's and Dessouix's emotions had lashed him like a whip during their explanation of how they'd come to Camp Inferno, but he'd weathered that storm, and now he lay calmly in Honor's lap, relaxed in its aftermath.

He was comfortable with these people, she realized. And, truth to tell, so was she. She sensed dark, dangerous currents in both Benson and Dessouix, wounded places deep inside them, and the bleak, unforgiving fury of the berserker lurked somewhere at Benson's heart. But she had it under iron control, Honor knew. *And if she* hadn't *developed something like it in over sixty* years *on this worthless piece of dirt, she'd have to be a psychopath herself.*

And the critical thing just now was that Honor knew through Nimitz that every word they'd just told her was the truth. More, she sensed the curiosity they had somehow managed to lock down, the torrent of questions they longed to pour out at her. And their dreadful, burning hope that perhaps, just perhaps, her appearance in their lives might mean . . . something. They didn't know what that "something" might be—not yet—but they hungered for the chance, however fleeting, to strike back somehow against their captors. And after hearing their tale, Honor could understand that perfectly.

"Are you the senior officer here at Inferno, too?" she asked Benson.

"No," the captain replied, and Honor shrugged mentally. It would have been asking too much of the gods of chance for her to just happen to grab the camp's CO for her first contact, she supposed.

"Actually, I suppose I am the senior officer in some respects," Benson went on after a moment. "I was in the second draft of military prisoners sent to Hell, so technically, I guess, I'm 'senior' to just about everybody on the damned planet! But the senior lifer here in Inferno is a fellow named Ramirez, a commodore from San Martin." She grinned wryly. "In some ways, I think they built Inferno just for him, because he was a very, *very* bad boy while the Peeps were trying to take Trevor's Star. He was the senior surviving officer from the SMN task force that covered the Trevor's Star end of your wormhole junction while the last refugee ships ran for it, too, and he made more waves when they first dumped him on Hell than Henri and I ever did."

"He sounds impressive," Honor mused, then cocked her head and gazed at her two "guests." "Would the two of you be willing to serve as my . . . emissaries to him, I suppose?"

Benson and Dessouix looked at one another for a moment, then shrugged almost in unison and turned back to Honor.

"What, exactly, did you have in mind?" Benson asked with an edge of caution.

"From what you've said, it sounds unlikely that the Peeps have spies in Camp Inferno," Honor told her. "If I were in command, I'd have them there, or at least listening devices, but it doesn't sound to me like StateSec has anything like a real security consciousness."

"Yes and no, Dame Honor," Benson cautioned. "They're arrogant as hell, and God knows Henri and I know they don't give a good goddamn what they do to us or how we might feel about it. And, no, I don't think they have any spies or bugs down in the camp. But they might, and they don't take any chances at all with their personal safety off Styx. Only a camp full of outright lunatics would try to rush one of the supply shuttles. Even if they took it, they couldn't go anywhere with it, and all they'd get would be a month or so of food, whereas everyone in the camp knows that the Peeps would starve them all to death for any attack. But they come in armed, and they'll shoot one of us down for even looking like we might be a threat. We need our spears for defense against the local predators—they haven't figured out they can't digest us—and our knives—" she gestured at the blades in LaFollet's belt "—are survival tools. But if even a single blade is within a hundred meters of the shuttle pad, they'll hose it off with heavy pulser fire and kill every single prisoner inside the landing zone before they touch down." She shrugged. "Like I say, nobody gives a good goddamn what the Black Legs do to us."

"I'll bear that in mind," Honor said grimly, "and the time might just be coming when some of those 'Black Legs' will learn the error of their ways." The right corner of her lips drew up, baring her teeth. "But my point right now is that we can't take the chance that you and I are wrong about whether or not they have Inferno under observation, and I really need to speak to this Commodore Ramirez. Would you two be willing to invite him to come up here to speak with me this evening? And could you convince him to do it without giving anything away if the Peeps *are* bugging the camp?"

"Yes, and yes," Benson said promptly.

"Good!" Honor held out her hand, and the captain from Pegasus gripped it firmly. Then all three of them stood, and Honor smiled at LaFollet.

"Hand our friends back their spears, Andrew. They're on our side, I believe."

"Yes, My Lady." LaFollet bobbed his head in a half-bow to Benson and handed the spears over, then pulled the stone blades from his belt and passed them across. "And may I say," he added, with a confidence born of his faith in his Steadholder and her treecat's ability to read what others felt, "that I'm much happier to have them on our side than the other!"

Chapter Fourteen

The man who followed Benson and Dessouix up the hill just as the sun was setting was enormous. Honor told herself it was only the setting sun behind him as he climbed the slope towards her which made him look like some faceless black giant or troll out of a terrifying childhood tale, but she was forced to reconsider that opinion as he drew nearer. He was over five centimeters taller than she was, yet that only began to tell the tale, for San Martin was one of the heaviest gravity planets mankind had ever settled. Not even people like Honor herself, descended from colonists genetically engineered for heavy-grav planets before humanity abandoned that practice, could breathe San Martin's sea-level atmosphere. It was simply too dense, with lethal concentrations of carbon dioxide and even oxygen. So San Martin's people had settled the mountaintops and high mesas of their huge home world . . . and their physiques reflected the gravity to which they were born.

As did that of the man who reached the top of the hill and drew up short at sight of her. She felt his surprise at seeing her, but it was only surprise, not astonishment. Well, surprise and intense, disciplined curiosity. She didn't know what Benson and Dessouix had told him to get him out here. Clearly they hadn't told him everything, or he wouldn't have been surprised, but he'd taken that surprise in stride with a mental flexibility Honor could only envy.

"And who might you be?" His voice was a deep, subterranean rumble, as one would expect from a man who must weigh in at somewhere around a hundred and eighty kilos, but the San Martin accent gave it a soft, almost lilting air. It was one Honor had heard before—most recently from a since deceased StateSec guard with a taste for sadism. Yet hearing it now, there was something about his voice . . .

She stepped closer, moving slightly to one side to get the sunset out of her eyes, and sucked in a sudden breath as she saw his face clearly at last. He wore a neatly trimmed beard, but that wasn't enough to disguise his features, and she heard an abrupt, muffled oath from LaFollet as he, too, saw the newcomer clearly for the first time.

It can't be, she thought. *It's just— And he's* dead. *Everyone knows that! The possibility never even crossed my mind . . . but why should it have? It's not an uncommon last name on San Martin, and what are the* odds *that I'd—* She gave herself a hard mental shake and made herself respond.

"Harrington," she heard herself say almost numbly. "Honor Harrington."

"Harrington?" The initial "H" almost vanished into the deep, musical reverberations of his voice, and then his dark brown eyes narrowed as he saw her holstered pulser . . . and the salvaged StateSec trousers and tee-shirt she wore. Those eyes leapt to LaFollet's pulse rifle, and beyond him to Mayhew and Clinkscales, and his hand darted to the hilt of his stone knife. The blade scraped out of its sheath, and Honor felt the sudden eruption of his emotions. Shock, betrayal, fury, and a terrifying, grim determination. He started to spring forward, but Honor threw up her hand.

"*Stop!*" she barked. The single word cracked through the hot evening air like a thunderbolt, ribbed with thirty years of command experience. It was a captain's voice—a voice which *knew* it would be obeyed—and the huge man hesitated for one bare instant. Only for an instant . . . yet that was time for the muzzle of Andrew LaFollet's pulse rifle to snap up to cover him.

"*Bastards!*" The voice was no longer soft, and fury seethed behind his eyes, but he had himself back under control. His hatred would not drive him over the edge into a berserk attack, but he turned his head and bared his teeth at Benson and Dessouix in a snarl.

"Just a moment, Commodore!" Honor said sharply. His attention snapped back to her, almost against his will, and she smiled crookedly. "I don't blame you for being suspicious," she went on in a more normal voice. "I would be, too, in your circumstances. But you didn't let me finish my introduction. I'm an officer in the Royal Manticoran Navy, not State Security."

"Oh?" The single dripped disbelief, and he cocked his head. *Am I going to have to go through this with* everyone *I introduce myself to on this planet?* Honor wondered. But she controlled her exasperation and nodded calmly.

"Yes," she said, "and as I explained to Captain Benson and Lieutenant Dessouix earlier, I have a proposition for you."

"I'm sure you do," he said flatly, and this time she let her exasperation show.

"Commodore Ramirez, what possible motive could the Peeps have for 'luring' you out here and pretending to be Manticorans?" she demanded. "If they wanted you dead, all they'd have to do would be to stop delivering food to you! Or if they're too impatient for that, I'm sure a little napalm, or a few snowflake clusters—or an old-fashioned ground sweep by infantry, for goodness' sake—could deal with you!"

"No doubt," he said, still in that flat tone, and Honor felt the anger grinding about in him like boulders. This man had learned to hate. His hatred might not rule him, but it was a part of him—had been for so many years that his belief she was StateSec was interfering with his thinking.

"Look," she said, "you and I need to talk—*talk*, Commodore. We can help each other, and with luck, I believe, we may even be able to get off this planet completely. But for any of that to happen, you have to at least consider the possibility that my men and I are not Peeps."

"Not Peeps, but you just happen to turn up in Black Leg uniform, with Peep weapons, on a planet only the Peeps know how to find," he said. "Of course you aren't."

Honor stared at him for ten fulminating seconds, and then threw up her arm in exasperation.

"Yes, that's exactly right!" she snapped. "And if you weren't as stubborn, mule-headed, and hard to reason with as your son, you'd realize that!"

"My *what?*" He stared at her, shaken out of his automatic suspicion at last by the total *non sequitur*.

"Your *son*," Honor repeated in a flat voice. "Tomas Santiago Ramirez." Commodore Ramirez goggled at her, and she sighed. "I know him quite well, Commodore. For that matter, I've met your wife, Rosario, and Elena and Josepha, as well."

"Tomas—" he whispered, then blinked and shook himself. "You know little *Tomacito?*"

"He's hardly 'little' anymore," Honor said dryly. "In fact, he's pretty close to your size. Shorter, but you and he both favor stone walls, don't you? And he's also a colonel in the Royal Manticoran Marines."

"But—" Ramirez shook his head again, like a punch drunk fighter, and Honor chuckled sympathetically.

"Believe me, Sir. You can't be more surprised to meet me than I am to meet you. Your family has believed you were dead ever since the Peeps took Trevor's Star."

"They got out?" Ramirez stared at her, his voice begging her to tell him they had. "They reached Manticore? They—" His voice broke, and he scrubbed his face with his hands.

"They got out," Honor said gently, "and Tomas is one of my closest friends." She grinned wryly. "I suppose I should have realized you were the 'Commodore Ramirez's Captain Benson was talking about as soon as I heard the name. If Tomas were on this planet, I'm sure *he'd* have ended up in Camp Inferno, too. But who would've thought—?" She shook her head.

"But—" Ramirez stopped and sucked in an enormous breath, and

Honor reached up and across to rest her hand on his shoulder. She squeezed for a moment, then nodded her head at the roots of the tree under—and in—which she had spent the day.

"Have a seat in my office here, and I'll tell you all about it," she invited.

Jesus Ramirez, Honor reflected an hour or so later, really was remarkably like his son. In many ways, Tomas Ramirez was one of the kindest and most easygoing men Honor had ever met, but not where the People's Republic of Haven was concerned. Tomas had joined the Manticoran Marines for one reason only: he had believed war with the PRH was inevitable, and he had dedicated his life to the destruction of the People's Republic and all its works with an unswerving devotion that sometimes seemed to verge just a bit too closely upon obsession for Honor's peace of mind.

Now she knew where he'd gotten it from, she thought wryly, and leaned back against the tree trunk while Tomas' father digested what she'd told him.

I wonder what the odds are? she thought once more. *Ramirez beat the numbers badly enough just to survive to reach Hell, but that I should run into him like this—?* She shook her head in the darkness which had fallen with the passing of the sun. *On the other hand, I've always suspected God must have a very* strange *sense of humor. And if Ramirez was going to get here at all—and not get himself shot for making trouble—it was probably inevitable he'd wind up at Inferno. And given that "troublemakers" are exactly what I need if I'm going to pull this off at all, I suppose it was equally inevitable that we should meet.*

"All right, I understand what you want, Commodore Harrington," the deep voice rumbled suddenly out of the darkness, "but do you realize what will happen if you try this and fail?"

"We'll all die," Honor said quietly.

"Not just 'die,' Commodore," Ramirez said flatly. "If we're lucky, they'll shoot us during the fighting. If we're *un*lucky, we'll be 'Kilkenny Camp Number Three.'"

"Kilkenny?" Honor repeated, and Ramirez laughed with no humor at all.

"That's the Black Legs' term for what happens when they stop sending in the food supplies," he told her. "They call it the 'Kilkenny Cat' method of provisioning. Don't you know the Old Earth story?"

"Yes," Honor said sickly. "Yes, I do."

"Well, *they* think it's funny, anyway," Ramirez said. "But the important thing is for you to realize the stakes you're playing for here, because if you—if *we*—blow it, every human being in this camp will pay the price right along with us." He exhaled sharply in the darkness. "It's probably been just as well that was true, too," he admitted. "If it weren't—if I'd only had to worry about what happened to me—I probably would have done something outstandingly stupid years ago. And then who would you have to try *this* outstandingly stupid trick with?"

A flicker of true humor drifted out of the night to her, carried over her link to Nimitz, and she smiled.

"It's not all *that* stupid, Commodore," she said.

"No . . . not if it works. But if it doesn't—" She sensed his invisible shrug. Then he was silent for the better part of two minutes, and she was content to leave him so, for she could feel the intensity of his thought as yet again his brain examined the rough plan she'd outlined for him, turning it over and over again to consider it from all directions.

"You know," he said thoughtfully at last, "the really crazy thing is that I think this might just work. There's no fallback position if it doesn't, but if everything breaks right, or even half right, it actually might work."

"I like to think I usually give myself at least some chance for success," Honor said dryly, and he laughed softly.

"I'm sure you do, Commodore. But so did I, and look where I wound up!"

"Fair enough," Honor conceded. "But if I may, Commodore, I'd suggest you think of Hell not as the place you 'wound up,' but as the temporary stopping place you're going to leave with us."

"An optimist, I see." Ramirez was silent again, thinking, and then he smacked his hands together with the sudden, shocking sound of an explosion. "All right, Commodore Harrington! If you're crazy enough to try it, I suppose I'm crazy enough to help you."

"Good," Honor said, but then she went on in a careful tone. "There is just one other thing, Commodore."

"Yes?" His voice was uninflected, but Honor could taste the emotions behind it, and the one thing she hadn't expected was suppressed, devilish amusement.

"Yes," she said firmly. "We have to settle the question of command."

"I see." He leaned back, a solider piece of the darkness beside her as he crossed his ankles and folded his arms across his massive chest. "Well, I suppose we should consider relative seniority, then," he said courteously. "My own date of rank as a commodore is 1870 P.D. And yours is?"

"I was only eleven T-years old in 1870!" Honor protested.

"Really?" Laughter lurked in his voice. "Then I suppose I've been a commodore a little longer than you have."

"Well, yes, but—I mean, with all due respect, you've been stuck here on Hell for the last forty years, Commodore! There've been changes, developments in—"

She broke off and clenched her jaw. *Should I tell him I'm a full admiral in the* Grayson *Navy?* she wondered. *But if I do that now, it'll sound like—*

"Oh, don't worry so much, Commodore Harrington!" Ramirez laughed out loud, breaking into her thoughts. "You're right, of course. My last operational experience was so long ago I'd have trouble just finding the flag bridge. Not only that, you and your people are the ones who managed to get down here with the shuttles and the weapons that might just make this entire thing work."

He shook his head in the darkness, and his voice—and the emotions Honor felt through Nimitz—were dead serious when he went on.

"If you truly manage to pull this off, you'll certainly have earned the right of command," he told her. "And the one thing we absolutely can't afford is any division within our ranks or competition for authority between you and me. I may technically be senior to you, but I will cheerfully accept your authority."

"And you'll support me after the initial operation?" she pressed. "What happens then is going to be even more important than the preliminary op—if we're going to get off-planet, at any rate—and no one can command this kind of campaign by committee." She paused a moment, then went on deliberately. "And there's another consideration, as well. I fully realize that you and thousands of other people on this planet will have your own ideas about what to do with the Peeps, and how. But if we're going to carry through to a conclusion that actually gives us a chance to get off Hell, our command structure will have to hold all the way through . . . including the 'domestic' side."

"Then we may have a problem," Ramirez said flatly. "Because you're right. Those of us who have spent years on Hell *do* have scores to settle with the garrison. If you're saying you'll try to prevent that from happening—"

"I didn't say that," Honor replied. "Captain Benson's given me some idea of how badly the Peeps have abused their prisoners, and I've had a little experience of the same sort myself, even before the Peeps grabbed me. But the fact that they've seen fit to violate the Deneb Accords doesn't absolve me, as a Manticoran officer, from my legal obligation to observe them. I almost forgot that once. And even though I felt then—and feel now—that I was completely justified on a personal level, it would have been a violation of my oath as an officer. I'm not going to let it happen again, Commodore Ramirez. Not on my watch."

"Then you *are*—" Ramirez began, but Honor interrupted.

"Let me finish, Commodore!" she said sharply, and he paused. "As I say, I must observe the Deneb Accords, but if I recall correctly, the Accords make specific provision for the punishment of those who violate them so long as due process is observed. I realize that most legal authorities interpret that as meaning that those accused of violations should be tried in civilian courts following the end of hostilities. We, however, find ourselves in a wartime situation . . . and I feel quite sure there are sufficient officers on Hell, drawn from any number of military organizations, for us to empanel a proper court-martial."

"Court-martial?" Ramirez repeated, and she nodded.

"Exactly. Please understand that any court empaneled under my authority will be just that: a court in which all the legal proprieties, including the rights of the accused, will be properly safeguarded. And assuming that guilty verdicts are returned, the sentences handed down will be those properly provided for in the relevant law codes. We will act as civilized human beings, and we will *punish* wrongdoing, not simply compound it with barbarisms of our own."

"I see. And those are your only terms?" Ramirez asked.

"They are, Sir," she said unflinchingly.

"Good," he replied quietly, and her eyebrows rose. "A fair and legal trial is more than any of us ever really hoped these *people* would face," he explained, as if he could see her surprise despite the darkness. "We thought no one would ever speak for us, ever call them to account for all the people they've raped and murdered on this godforsaken piece of hell. You give us the chance to do that, Commodore Harrington, and it'll be worth it even if we never get off this planet and StateSec comes back and kills us all later. But assuming we all live through this, I want to be able to look into the mirror ten years from now and like the man I see looking back out of it at me, and if you let me do what I *want* to do to these motherless bastards, I wouldn't."

Honor let out a long, slow breath of relief, for the feel of his emotions matched his words. He truly meant them.

"And will the other people on Hell share your opinion?" she asked after a moment.

"Probably not all of them," he admitted. "But if you pull this off, you'll have the moral authority to keep them in line, I think. And if you don't have that," his tone turned bleaker, but he continued unflinchingly, "you'll still have all the guns and the only way off the planet. I don't think enough of us will want to buck that combination just to lynch Black Legs, however much we hate them."

"I see. In that case, may I assume that you're in, Commodore Ramirez?"

"You may, Commodore Harrington." A hand the size of a small shovel came out of the darkness, and she gripped it firmly, feeling the strength in it even as she savored the determination and sincerity behind it.

Book Three

Chapter Fifteen

"Thank you for coming, Citizen Admiral. And you, too, Citizen Commissioner."

"You're welcome, Citizen Secretary," Citizen Admiral Javier Giscard said, exactly as if he'd had any choice about accepting an "invitation" from the Republic's Secretary of War. Eloise Pritchart, his dark-skinned, platinum-haired People's Commissioner, limited herself to a silent nod. As the Committee of Public Safety's personal representative ("spy" would have been much too rude—and accurate—a term) on Giscard's staff, she was technically outside the military chain of command and reported directly to Oscar Saint-Just and State Security rather than to Esther McQueen. But McQueen's star was clearly in the ascendant—for now, at least. Pritchart knew that as well as everyone else did, just as she knew McQueen's reputation for pushing the limits of her personal authority, and her topaz-colored eyes were wary.

McQueen noted that wariness with interest as she waved her guests into chairs facing her desk and very carefully did not look at her own StateSec watchdog. Erasmus Fontein had been her political keeper almost since the Harris Assassination, and she'd come to realize in the last twelve months that he was infinitely more capable—and dangerous—than his apparently befuddled exterior suggested. She'd never really underestimated him, but—

No, that wasn't true. She'd always known he had to be at least some better than he chose to appear, but she had underestimated the extent to which that was true. Only the fact that she made it a habit to always assume the worst and double- and triple-safe her lines of communication had kept that underestimation from proving fatal, too. Well, that and the fact that she truly was the best the People's Republic had at her job. Then again, Fontein had discovered that *she* was more dangerous than *he'd* expected, so she supposed honors were about even. And it said a lot for Saint-Just's faith in the man that he hadn't replaced Fontein when the scope of his underestimation became evident.

Of course, if Fontein had recommended I be purged before that business with the Levelers, then there wouldn't be *a Committee of Public Safety right now. I wonder how the decision was made? Did he get points for* not *thinking I was dangerous when I proved my "loyalty" to the Committee? Or for supporting me when I moved against LaBoeuf's lunatics? Or maybe it was just a wash?*

She laughed silently. Maybe it was merely a matter of their sticking her with the person they figured knew her moves best on the assumption that having been fooled once, he would be harder to fool a second time. Not that it really mattered. She had plans for Citizen Commissioner Fontein when the time came . . . just as she was certain he had plans for her if she tipped her hand too soon.

Well, if the game were simple, anyone could play, and think how crowded that *would get!*

"The reason I asked you here, Citizen Admiral," she said once her guests were seated, "is to discuss a new operation with you. One I believe has the potential to exercise a major impact on the war."

She paused, eyes on Giscard to exclude Pritchart and Fontein. It was part of the game to pretend admirals were still fleet commanders, even though everyone knew command was actually exercised by committee these days. Of course, that was one of the things McQueen intended to change. But Giscard couldn't know that, now could he? And even if he did, he might not believe she could pull it off.

He looked back at her now, without so much as a glance at Pritchart, and cocked his head. He was a tall man, just a hair over a hundred and ninety centimeters, but lean, with a bony face and a high-arched nose. That face made an excellent mask for his thoughts, but his hazel eyes were another matter. They considered McQueen alertly, watchfully, with the caution of a man who had already narrowly escaped disaster after being made the scapegoat for a failed operation that was also supposed to have had "a major impact on the war."

"One of the reasons you came to mind," McQueen went on after a heartbeat, "is your background as a commerce-raiding specialist. I realize operations in Silesia didn't work out quite the way everyone had hoped, but that was scarcely your fault, and I have expressed my opinion to that effect to Citizen Chairman Pierre."

Something flickered in the backs of those hazel eyes at that, and McQueen hid a smile. What she'd said was the exact truth, because Giscard was entirely too good a commander to toss away over one busted operation. And it *hadn't* been his fault; even his watchdog, Pritchart, had said as much. And perhaps there was some hope for the Republic still when a people's commissioner was prepared to defend a fleet commander by pointing out that "his" failure had been the fault of the idiots who'd written his orders. Well, that and the

Manty Q-ships no one had known existed. *And,* McQueen admitted to herself, *both of those and Honor Harrington. But at least* she's *out of the equation now . . . and Giscard is still here. Not a bad achievement for the misbegotten system he and I are stuck with.*

"Thank you, Citizen Secretary," Giscard said after a moment.

"Don't thank me for telling him the truth, Citizen Admiral," she told him, showing her teeth in a smile which held a hint of iron. "Just hit the ground running and show both of us that it *was* the truth."

"I'll certainly try to, Ma'am," Giscard replied, then smiled wryly. "Of course, I'll have a better chance of doing that when I at least know enough about this operation to know which way to run."

"I'm sure you will," McQueen agreed with a smile of her own, "and that's exactly what I invited you—and, of course, Citizen Commissioner Pritchart—here to explain. Would you come with me, please?"

She stood, and by some sort of personal magic, everyone else in the room—including Erasmus Fontein—stood aside to let her walk around her desk and lead the way towards the door. She was the smallest person in the room by a considerable margin, a slender, slightly built woman a good fifteen centimeters shorter than Pritchart, yet she dominated all those about her with seeming effortlessness as she led them down a short hall.

I'm impressed, Giscard admitted to himself. He'd never actually served with McQueen, though their paths had crossed briefly a time or two before the Harris Assassination, and he didn't know her well. Not on a personal level, at any rate; only an idiot would have failed to study her intensely since her elevation to Secretary of War. He could well believe the stories he'd heard about her ambition, but he hadn't quite been prepared for the magnetism she radiated.

Of course, radiating it too openly could be a Bad Thing, he reflected. *Somehow I don't see StateSec being comfortable with the notion of a charismatic Secretary of War who also happens to boast an excellent war record.*

They reached the end of the hall, and a Marine sentry came to attention as McQueen keyed a short security code into the panel beside an unmarked door. The door slid open silently, and Giscard and Pritchart followed McQueen and Fontein into a large, well-appointed briefing room. Citizen Admiral Ivan Bukato and half a dozen other officers, the most junior a citizen captain, sat waiting at the large conference table, and nameplates indicated the chairs Giscard and Pritchart were expected to take.

McQueen walked briskly to the head of the table and took her seat, her compact frame seeming even slighter in the comfortable grasp of her oversized, black-upholstered chair, and waved her companions to their own places. Fontein deposited himself in an equally impressive chair on her right, and Giscard found himself at her left hand, with Pritchart to his own left. Their chairs, however, were much less grand than the ones their betters had been assigned.

"Citizen Admiral Giscard, I believe you know Citizen Admiral Bukato?" McQueen said.

"Yes, Ma'am. The Citizen Admiral and I have met," Giscard admitted, nodding his head at People's Navy's de facto CNO.

"You'll get to know the rest of these people quite well over the next month or so," McQueen went on, "but for now I want to concentrate on giving you a brief overview of what we have in mind. Citizen Admiral Bukato?"

"Thank you, Citizen Secretary." Bukato entered a command into the terminal in front of him, and the briefing room lights dimmed. An instant later, a complex hologram appeared above the huge table. The biggest part of it was a small-scale star map that showed the western quarter of the PRH, the war front, and the territory of the Manticoran Alliance clear to the Silesian border, but there were secondary displays, as well. Graphic representations, Giscard realized, of the comparative ship strengths of the opponents on a class-by-class basis, with sidebars showing the numbers of units sidelined for repairs or overhaul.

He sat back, studying the holo and feeling Citizen Commissioner Pritchart study it beside him. Unlike many officers of the People's Navy, Giscard actually looked forward to hearing his citizen commissioner's impressions and opinions. Partly, that was because Pritchart had one of the better minds he had ever met and frequently spotted things which a trained naval officer's professional blinders might prevent him from considering, which helped explain what made her and Giscard one of the PN's few smoothly functioning command teams. There were, however, other reasons he valued her input.

"As you can see, Citizen Admiral Giscard," Bukato said after a moment, "while the Manties have pushed deeply into our territory since the beginning of the war, they haven't pushed very much further into it since taking Trevor's Star. It is the opinion of our analysts that this reflects their need to pause, refit, catch their breath, replace losses, and generally consolidate their position before resuming offensive operations. In addition, a large minority opinion holds that they may be becoming rather less offensively minded now that they've added so much of *our* territory to their defensive commitments.

"Neither Citizen Secretary McQueen nor I believe that they contemplate voluntarily surrendering the initiative, however. We subscribe to the belief that they definitely plan to resume the offensive in the very near future, and that when they get around to it they will go after Barnett from Trevor's Star. To that end, we have been continuing to reinforce Citizen Admiral Theisman. Citizen Secretary Kline's intention—or perhaps I should say 'hope'—was that Citizen Admiral Theisman would attract Manty attention to his command area and hold it there as long as possible in order to divert the enemy from deeper thrusts into the Republic. And, of course, he was to entice the enemy into a battle of attrition in hopes of costing the Alliance more tonnage than he himself lost. What he was *not* expected to do was to defend Barnett successfully."

Giscard managed not to sit sharply upright in his chair or otherwise draw attention to his reaction, but his eyes widened at the acid tone of Bukato's last two sentences. Giscard had known Citizen Secretary Kline was unpopular with his uniformed subordinates—not surprisingly, since the man had been an incompetent political hack with a taste for humiliating any officer he decided was "an elitist recidivist" hungering to restore the officer corps to its old independence of action. But for Bukato to show contempt for even an ex-secretary so openly in front of both Pritchart and Fontein indicated that the changes at the top of the War Office must have been even more sweeping than most people suspected.

"We, however, have somewhat greater aspirations than to achieve another glorious defeat," Bukato continued. "We are reinforcing Theisman in hopes that he will actually hold Barnett—if possible, for use as a springboard to retake Trevor's Star. That isn't something we'll be able to do next week, or even next month, but the time to stop giving ground every time the Manties hit us has come now."

A soft sound circled the table, and something inside Giscard shivered. It had been a long time since he'd heard that hungry growl of agreement from anyone but his own staff, and a part of him wondered how McQueen had put so much iron into her senior subordinates' spines so quickly. *No wonder she's been so effective in combat, if she can do this,* he thought. Then: *And no wonder just thinking about her political ambitions scares the* shit *out of the people's commissioners!*

"Our data on the enemy's currently available fleet strength are not as definite as we'd like," Bukato went on. "Our espionage operations in the Star Kingdom have taken a heavy hit since the war started. Indeed, we now suspect—" he glanced sidelong at Fontein and Pritchart "—that NavInt's major prewar networks there had been compromised even before the start of hostilities. It looks like the Manties actually used our own spies to feed us fabricated information to draw us into false initial deployments."

Again, Giscard kept his face expressionless, but it was hard. Most of the PN's new crop of senior officers must have speculated about that. Giscard certainly had, though, like all the others, he'd dared not say so aloud. But it made sense. Certainly *something* had caused Amos Parnell to radically realign his force structure on the very eve of the war, and no one really believed it had been part of some obscure plot the Legislaturalist officer corps had hatched to betray the People for enigmatic reasons of their own. But the official line had been that the disastrous opening phases of the war had been entirely the fault of that officer corps, and that "crime" had been the pretext for which the new political management had ordered most of its senior members to be shot. So if Bukato was openly saying that it might not have been Parnell's fault—that the disgraced CNO had been snookered by Manty counterintelligence . . .

My God, things really are *changing!* he thought wonderingly, and looked over at Fontein. The Citizen Commissioner hadn't even blinked. He simply sat there impassively, without as much as a frown, and that impassivity told Giscard even more than Bukato's statement had.

"Despite our lack of hard data from covert sources, however," the Citizen Admiral continued, "we've been able to make some estimates based on known enemy deployments. One thing worth noting is that when Citizen Rear Admiral Tourville hit the Adler System, the Manties apparently had not deployed their usual FTL sensor network. From observation of their picket deployments and patrols around Trevor's Star, we think they're still short of a complete network even there, which suggests a production problem somewhere. Any such assumption has to be taken with a grain of salt, but it would appear to be consistent with the building rates we've observed. Their construction tempo has gone up steadily since the beginning of hostilities, but our best estimate is that their yard capacity is now saturated. What we seem to be seeing—not only with the FTL recon satellites around Adler and Trevor's Star, but also in their reliance on Q-ships because of their apparent inability to free up battlecruiser and cruiser elements to police Silesia—is the end consequence of an all-out drive to maximize the production of new hulls. In other words, it looks as if they've overstrained their prewar industrial capacity. If so, then they'll have to build additional yards before they can resume the upward curve in their fleet strength. And it would also help to explain their apparent passivity since taking Trevor's Star."

He paused to take a sip of ice water and give his audience time to digest what he'd said so far. Then he cleared his throat.

"There are other indicators of a lowered tempo of offensive operations on their part," he resumed. "Among others, Admiral White Haven is still at Yeltsin's Star attempting to assemble a new fleet out of Allied units, not simply RMN ships. Also, we're beginning to pick up indications that some of the forward deployed Manty ships of the wall are in increasing need of overhaul. Their systems reliability would appear to be declining."

Well that was good news, Giscard thought wryly. The People's Navy was perennially short of trained maintenance and repair techs, with the result that serviceability rates tended to remain uncomfortably low. The Manties, on the other hand, routinely turned in serviceability rates of well over ninety percent. But doing that relied on more than simply having excellent techs in your shipboard crews. It also required a comprehensive, highly capable, and well-organized base support system . . . and the time to hand ships over to that system when they required overhaul. If Manty systems reliability was dropping, it probably meant they were finding themselves unable to pull their capital ships off the front for scheduled rear area maintenance. And given that staying on top of overhaul needs was as basic an instinct for any Manty commander as topping off his hydrogen bunkers at every opportunity, it was also an even stronger indicator of increasing strain on their resources than anything else Bukato had said.

"Finally," the citizen admiral said, "we need to look at what may be happening a year or so down the road. On our side of the line, our training and manpower mobilization programs mean that we should have all of our presently unused yard capacity up and running, but we're unlikely to have added much additional capacity or significantly improved on our present construction rates. Indications from the Manties' side of the line are that they should have several new yard complexes coming on-line—like their new Blackbird shipyard facility at Yeltsin's Star—*and*, perhaps more ominously, will have the manpower to crew their new hulls, courtesy of the forts they're standing down now that they control all termini of the Manticore Wormhole Junction. So what we seem to have here is a window of opportunity in which their available resources are entirely committed and their basic strategic posture might be accurately described as overextended."

He paused once more, and Citizen Secretary McQueen tipped her chair forward. She leaned her forearms on the table and looked sideways at Giscard with a smile that was simultaneously a challenge, a warning, and somehow . . . impish. As if she were inviting him to share a joke . . . or risk his life beside her on a quixotic quest to save their star nation. And as he saw that smile, he realized there wasn't that much difference between those invitations after all . . . and that some dangerous dynamism within her made him want to accept them.

"And that, Citizen Admiral Giscard," she said to him, "is where you come in. We do, indeed, intend to reinforce Barnett, and I have every confidence that Citizen Admiral Theisman will make the most effective possible use of the forces we send him. But I have no intention of simply holding what we already have until the Manties catch their breath and decide where they're going to hit us next. We still have the numerical advantage in hulls and tonnage—not by anywhere near as much as we did at the start of the war, of course, but we still have it, and I intend to make use of it.

"One reason the Manties have been able to beat up on us so far has been a fundamental flaw in our own strategy. For whatever reason—" even now she did not look at Fontein, Giscard noticed "—our approach has been to try to hold everything, to be strong everywhere, with the result that we've been unable to stop the

Manties cold *anywhere*. We have to take some risks, uncover some less vital areas, to free up the strength we need to take the offensive to them for a change, and that's precisely what I propose to do."

Whoa! Giscard thought. *"Uncover less vital areas"? She knows as well as I do that what we've* really *been covering some of those "less vital areas" against has been domestic unrest. Is she saying she's talked the Committee into—?*

"We will be amassing a strike force and organizing a new fleet," she went on levelly, confirming that she *had* talked the Committee into it. "Its wall of battle will be composed primarily of battleships withdrawn from picket duties in less vulnerable, less exposed, and frankly, less valuable areas. We do not make those withdrawals lightly, and it will be imperative that, having made them, we use the forces thus freed up *effectively*. That will be your job, Citizen Admiral."

"I see, Ma'am," he said, and the calmness of his own voice surprised him. She was offering him the chance of a lifetime, the opportunity to command a powerful force at a potentially decisive point in the war, and patriotism, professionalism, and ambition of his own churned within him at the thought. Yet she was also offering him the chance to fail, and if he did fail, no power in the universe could save him from the people who currently ran the People's Republic of Haven.

"I believe you do, Citizen Admiral," she said softly, still smiling that smile while her green eyes bored into his as if she could actually see the brain behind them. "We'll give you every possible support from this end. You—and, of course, Citizen Commissioner Pritchart," she added, with a nod at the people's commissioner "—will have as close to a free hand in picking your staff and subordinate flag officers as we can possibly give you. Citizen Admiral Bukato and his staff will work with you to plan and coordinate your operations so as to allow the rest of the Fleet to give you the highest possible degree of support. But it will be your operation, Citizen Admiral. *You* will be responsible for driving it through to a successful conclusion."

And I'll give you the best command team I can to pull it off, she thought, *including Tourville, if I can finally pry him loose from Saint-Just! "Investigation"*—ha! *I suppose I should be grateful he's been willing to settle for keeping* Tilly's *crew sequestered so they can't tell anyone what really happened to the bitch, but I* need *Tourville, damn it! And ten months is frigging well long enough for him to sit in orbit and rot!*

"Yes, Ma'am," Giscard said. "And my objective?"

"We'll get to the territorial objectives in a minute," she told him, neither voice nor expression showing a hint of her frustration with Saint-Just's foot-dragging. "But what matters far more than any star system you may raid or capture is your moral objective. So far in this war, we've danced to the Manties' piping. I know that's not the official line, but here in this briefing room, we simply cannot afford to ignore objective realities."

This time she did glance at Fontein, but her people's commissioner only looked back at her without a word, and she returned her own gaze to Giscard.

"That stops now, Javier," she told him softly, using his first name for the very first time. "We *must* assert at least some control over our own strategic fate by forcing them to dance to *our* tune for a change, and you're the man we've picked to play the music. Are you up for it?"

Damn, but she's good, a small voice mused in the back of Giscard's brain. He felt the siren call of her personality, the enthusiasm and hope she'd fanned by the apparently simple yet ultimately profound fact of speaking the truth openly . . . and inviting him to follow her. *And I want to,* he marveled. *Even with all I've ever heard about her, even knowing the dangers of even* looking *like I've committed to "her faction,"* I want *to follow her.*

"Yes, Ma'am," he heard his voice say. "I'm up for it."

"Good," she said, and her smile was fiercer . . . and welcoming. "In that case, Citizen Admiral Giscard, welcome to command of Operation Icarus."

Chapter Sixteen

Citizen Admiral Giscard, CO Twelfth Fleet, stepped through the briefing room hatch aboard his new flagship and looked around the compartment at the equally new staff charged with helping him plan and execute Operation Icarus. Personally, he would have preferred to call it Operation Daedalus, since at least Daedalus had survived mankind's first flight, but no one had asked him.

Besides, I probably wouldn't worry about the "portents" of naming operations myself if the Manties hadn't kicked our asses so often.

He brushed that aside and crossed to the empty chair at the head of the briefing room table, trailed by Eloise Pritchart. She followed him like the silent, drifting eye of the Committee of Public Safety, her public, on-duty face as cold and emotionless as it always was, and slipped into her own seat at his right hand without a word.

By and large, he reflected, he was satisfied with both his flagship and his staff. PNS *Salamis* wasn't the youngest superdreadnought in the People's Navy's inventory, and she'd taken severe damage at the Third Battle of Nightingale. But she'd just completed repairs and a total overhaul, and she was all shiny and new inside at the moment. Even better, Citizen Captain Short, her CO, reported that her upgraded systems' reliability was at virtually a hundred percent. How long that would remain true remained to be seen, but Short seemed pleased with the quality of her Engineering Department, so perhaps they could anticipate better maintenance than usual.

He adjusted his chair comfortably and brought his terminal on-line while he let his mind run over the details about *Salamis*' readiness already neatly filed in his memory. Then he set them aside and turned his hazel eyes on the staffers sitting around the table.

Despite McQueen's promise of as free a hand "as possible" in their selection, he'd been unable to exercise anything approaching the degree of control an officer of his seniority would have wielded before the Harris Assassination. The only two he'd really insisted upon had been Citizen Commander Andrew MacIntosh, his new ops officer, and Citizen Commander Frances Tyler, his astrogator.

He'd never actually served with MacIntosh, but he expected good things from him. Most importantly, the black-haired, gray-eyed citizen commander had a reputation for energy and audacity. Both those qualities would be in high demand for Operation Icarus, and both had become unfortunately rare after the purges.

Tyler was another matter. "Franny" Tyler was only twenty-nine T-years old, young for her rank even in the post-Coup People's Navy, and Giscard had done his best to guide and guard her career over the last five or six years. There was a certain danger in that—for both of them—though Tyler probably didn't really realize the extent to which he'd acted as her patron. Given the vivacious young redhead's attractiveness, some might have assumed he had more than simply professional reasons for sheepdogging her career, but they would have been wrong. He'd seen something in her as a junior lieutenant—not just ability, though she certainly had that, but the willingness to take risks in the performance of her duty. Like MacIntosh, she not only accepted but actually seemed to relish the prospect of assuming additional responsibilities, almost as if (unlike the wiser and more wary of her contemporaries) she saw those responsibilities as opportunities and not simply more chances to fail and attract the ire of her superiors and StateSec. That sort of officer was more valuable than Detweiler rubies to any navy, but especially so to one like the People's Navy.

Physically, Citizen Captain Leander Joubert, Giscard's new chief of staff, closely resembled MacIntosh. He was taller—a hundred and eighty-five centimeters to MacIntosh's hundred and eighty-one—and had brown eyes instead of gray, but both had the same dark complexions and black hair, and they were within four T-years of one another. But physical resemblance aside, Joubert was nothing at all like MacIntosh or Tyler. At thirty-one, he was even younger for his rank than Tyler was for hers, and that would have been enough to pop warning flags in Giscard's mind under any circumstances. Not that the man wasn't good at his job. He was. It was just that when someone catapulted from lieutenant to captain in under four T-years, one had to wonder if there might not be reasons other than professional competence for his extraordinary rise. Add the fact that Joubert had been insisted upon—quite emphatically—by Citizen Commissioner Pritchart with the powerful support of unnamed individuals in State Security, and one no longer had to wonder. Giscard had protested as strongly as he dared, for no admiral could be expected to relish the thought of having a political informer as his chief of staff, but in truth, he was less unhappy with Joubert's presence than his complaints suggested. There were, after all, ways to neutralize one's superiors' spies . . . especially if one knew exactly who those spies were.

The rest of the staff were less known qualities. Citizen Lieutenant Commander Julia Lapisch, his staff com officer, seemed a competent sort, but she was very quiet. Only a couple of years older than Tyler, she appeared to be one of those officers who had found survival by remaining completely apolitical, and she seemed to emerge from her shell only to deal with professional matters. Coupled with the slender, delicate physique her low-gravity home world of Midsummer had produced, she had an almost elfin air of disassociation, like someone not quite completely in synch with the universe about her.

Citizen Lieutenant Madison Thaddeus, his new intelligence officer, was another puzzle. At forty-two, he was the oldest member of Giscard's staff, despite his relatively junior rank. His efficiency reports were uniformly excellent, and he had a reputation as a skilled analyst, with an ability to get inside the opposition's head when it came to drafting enemy intentions analyses, yet he seemed stuck at lieutenant's rank. That probably indicated that somewhere in his StateSec file (which not even Pritchart had yet had the opportunity to peruse) someone had recorded doubts about his political reliability. No other explanation for his stalled promotion seemed likely, yet the fact that he hadn't been purged—or at least removed from so sensitive a slot as staff intelligence—would appear to indicate a rare triumph of ability over someone else's paranoia.

Citizen Lieutenant Jessica Challot, his logistics and supply officer, was in her mid-thirties—again, old for her rank in a navy where the enemy and StateSec had conspired to create so many vacancies in the senior grades. Unlike Thaddeus, however, Giscard had an unhappy suspicion that Challot's lack of promotion was merited on a professional basis. Her accounts were all in order, but she had a bean-counter mentality better suited to a shipyard somewhere than to a fleet duty assignment. Much as Giscard hated admitting it, those charged with overseeing the disbursement of supplies and spare parts at shipyards really did have a responsibility to insure that the materials they doled out were used as frugally as possible—consistent, of course, with efficiency. But it was a staff logistics officer's responsibility to see to it that his CO had everything he needed (and, if possible, a little more, just to be safe) to carry out his mission . . . and to do whatever it took to provide anything his CO *didn't* have. Challot, unfortunately, seemed to have no initiative whatsoever. She certainly wasn't going to stick her neck out by resorting to unofficial channels, and Giscard strongly doubted that she would take the lead in anticipating requirements, either. Well, he could live with that if he had to, he supposed. At the very least, she appeared to be a competent enough supply clerk. If Giscard or someone else—like MacIntosh, perhaps?—did the hard work by figuring out what was needed and where it might be found, she could probably be relied upon to do the paperwork to get it, anyway.

He realized his thoughts had drawn him into contemplative silence and shook himself. It was time to get down to business.

"Good morning, people," he said. "I realize this is the first opportunity we've all had to sit down together, and I wish we had more time to get to know one another before we jump into the deep end, but we don't. The units assigned to Operation Icarus are coming from all over the Republic; just assembling them is going to take better than two T-months. Minimum training and rehearsal time will eat up at least another month, and our orders are to commence operations at the earliest possible moment. That means getting the details and the compositions of our task forces worked out now, not waiting until our squadrons are concentrated."

He gazed around their faces, letting that sink in and noting their expressions while it did. No real surprises there, he decided.

"Citizen Commissioner Pritchart and I have worked together in the past with fair success," he went on after a moment. After all, any admiral who didn't acknowledge his watchdog's presence—and explicitly concede her authority—was unlikely to remain in command for long, despite any changes Esther McQueen might be engineering at the top. "I believe I speak for both of us when I say that we are more interested in initiative, industry, and suggestions than we are with complete observation of all nuances of proper military procedure. Citizen Commissioner?"

He glanced at Pritchart, his expression cool, and she nodded.

"I think that's a fair statement, Citizen Admiral," she said. "What matters, after all, is the defeat of our elitist opponents . . . and, of course, those domestic elements which might conspire against or fail the needs of the People."

A brief chill seemed to sweep the compartment, and Giscard let his mouth tighten. But that was the only expression of disagreement a prudent admiral would permit himself, and he cleared his throat and continued in determinedly normal tones.

"Over the next few days, we'll be taking the War Office's basic ops plan apart, looking at all the pieces, and then putting it back together again. Obviously, each of you will have his or her own spheres of responsibility and areas of expertise. I don't want anyone sitting on any thought or question which comes to mind just because it's not officially in 'his' area, however. The success of our mission matters a lot more than stepped-on toes, and I'd rather have officers who are willing to risk asking potentially dumb questions or make suggestions which may or may not work. Anyone can keep his mouth shut and look wise, citizens; only someone willing to appear foolish in the pursuit of his duty can actually *be* wise. Remember that, and I think we'll get along well."

He deliberately did not look at Pritchart this time. It wasn't precisely a challenge to the people's commissioner, but it was a clear statement of who he expected to exercise authority in the professional sphere.

"Now, then," he said, looking at MacIntosh. "I wonder if you could begin by laying out the basic parameters of Fleet HQ's ops plan, Citizen Commander?"

"Yes, Citizen Admiral," MacIntosh said respectfully. He let his eyes sweep over the notes on his display for another instant, then looked up and met the gazes of his fellow staffers.

"In essence," he began, "Citizen Secretary McQueen and Citizen Admiral Bukato have decided that the Manties' current lack of activity offers us an opportunity to recapture the strategic initiative for the first time since the war began. Our present margin of superiority over the Manties, while still substantial in terms of total tonnage, is much lower than it was before the war, particularly in terms of ships of the wall. That means that scraping up the reserves to make Icarus possible will impose a considerable strain on other operational areas. Nor will the strength which can be committed to us allow us as much margin for error as we might wish. HQ stresses—quite rightly, I think—that we must employ our forces in the most economical possible fashion. Operational losses in pursuit of our objective are to be expected, and those resulting from calculated risks will not be held against us." *And you can believe as much of* that *as you want to*, Giscard thought wryly. "Indeed, Citizen Secretary McQueen specifically directs us to remember that audacity and surprise will be our most effective weapons. But for us to carry Icarus off, we *must* allocate our available strength very carefully."

He paused as if to let that sink in, then glanced back down at his notes again.

"At the present moment, our order of battle is slated to include the equivalent of two dreadnought and four superdreadnought squadrons—a total of forty-eight of the wall—supported by ten squadrons of battleships, for a total of a hundred and twenty-eight capital ships. Our battlecruiser element will consist of three squadron equivalents, for a total of twenty-four units, and Citizen Admiral Tourville will be joining us shortly aboard one of them to serve as Twelfth Fleet's second in command."

Several people looked up at that, and Giscard hid a smile at their expressions. Like Giscard himself, most of the officers in that briefing room were disgusted by Honor Harrington's judicial murder, but the fact that Tourville had captured her in the first place, coupled with his crushing victory in the Adler System, had further enhanced his already high professional stature. Of course, none of Giscard's staffers would find themselves required to ride herd on an officer whose reputation for tactical brilliance was matched only by his reputation as a flamboyant, guts-and-glory adolescent who refused to grow up. But they clearly regarded his assignment to their fleet command structure as a sign that Fleet HQ truly did consider Operation Icarus as vital as HQ said it did, and that wasn't always the case in the People's Navy.

Personally, Giscard had a few private reservations. Not about Tourville's capabilities, but about all the reasons for his assignment to Icarus. There had to have been a reason Tourville and his flagship had been detached from his previous command to escort Citizen Secretary Ransom to the Cerberus System, and he doubted somehow that it had been because Ransom wanted Tourville's opinion on what color to paint her quarters aboard *Tepes*. But no one would ever know for certain now. Giscard was one of only a tiny handful of Navy officers who knew what had happened to *Tepes*—and Citizen Secretary Ransom—and he knew only because he had certain avenues of information very few serving officers could match.

Ten months had passed since *Tepes*' destruction, and he often wondered when the official news of Ransom's long overdue demise would be made public (and exactly how the circumstances of her departing this mortal vale would be structured by PubIn for foreign and domestic consumption). But the people at the top had to realize she'd had a specific reason for dragging Tourville to Cerberus. So did the citizen admiral's continued existence, not to mention employment on a highly sensitive mission, indicate that Ransom's fellows on the Committee of Public Safety questioned her judgment and were less than devastated by her departure? Or that Esther McQueen had managed to protect him because she recognized his value? Or possibly that the success of Operation Icarus was not, in fact, regarded as being quite so vital as McQueen and Bukato had implied?

Any or all of those were certainly possible . . . and if Fleet HQ was setting Tourville up as a fall guy in case this Icarus also flew too close to the sun, might it not be doing the same thing with another officer who had only recently reemerged from the disgrace of a busted operation in Silesia?

"—with at least one light cruiser flotilla and a substantial but probably understrength destroyer screen," MacIntosh was continuing his listing of the resources committed to Icarus, and Giscard shook off thoughts about Tourville in order to concentrate on the ops officer's briefing once more. "All of those numbers are tentative at this point, which is going to make our planning even harder. I have been informed, however, that we may regard the superdreadnought, dreadnought, and battleship numbers as *minimum* figures. The Octagan will be trying to pry still more of each class loose for us. Given that they haven't said the same thing about battlecruisers and how strapped we are for them, I would suspect that BCs are where we're most likely to come up short," MacIntosh went on. "At the same time, however, we're as strapped for light forces as for ships of the wall right now, and pulling together our battleship component will only exacerbate that situation in some respects. The systems we pull them out of will have to be covered by someone—" for, he did *not* add, political reasons "—and it looks like HQ will be tapping tin cans and light cruisers for that, which will cut into what might have been made available to us.

"On the logistical side," he nodded at Citizen Lieutenant Challot, who looked less than delighted to be brought center stage, "we'll be getting very heavy support. In addition to tankers and medical and repair ships, HQ is assigning two complete service squadrons of fast freighters for the specific purpose of assuring us an adequate supply of the new missile pods."

He bared his teeth in a fierce smile as several people around the table made pleased noises.

"The fact that we can finally match the Manties' capabilities in that area is certainly out of the bag by now—they could hardly miss knowing after the way Citizen Admiral Tourville kicked their ass at Adler—but this will be our first mass deployment of the system. In addition, we have upgraded recon drone capability courtesy of, ah, some technical assistance," even here, Giscard noted, MacIntosh was careful not to mention the Solarian League by name, "and our general electronic warfare capabilities will come much closer to matching the Manties' abilities in that area. I won't try to tell any of you that they won't still have a considerable edge, but it's going to be narrower than it's been in at least the last four years, and hopefully they won't even know we're coming. With that kind of surprise working for us, we should cut quite a swathe before they can redeploy their own units to slow us down."

There were more smiles around the table now. Even Citizen Captain Joubert got into the act, although Challot still seemed less enthralled by the prospect than her fellows.

"Now," MacIntosh went on, entering more commands into his terminal, "to look at our ops area. As you know, HQ wanted a zone where things have been rather quiet and the Manties have drawn down their forces to support front-line operations, but important enough to be sure we attract their attention. I think," he smiled and entered a final command, "they've found one."

A holo display flashed to life above the table, and Giscard saw Citizen Commander Tyler sit up straight in her chair as she saw their proposed operational area for the first time. Nor was her reaction unique. Only Giscard, Pritchart, Joubert, and MacIntosh had known where Operation Icarus was aimed before this moment, and eyes narrowed and faces tightened with mingled anticipation and worry as the rest of his staff discovered that information.

Stars were sparse in the holo, but the ones which floated there had a value out of all proportion to the density of the local stellar population. A thin rash of bright red light chips indicated naval bases or member systems of the Manticoran Alliance, but all of them were dominated by the bright purple glow of a single star: Basilisk, the terminus of the Manticore Wormhole Junction where the war had almost begun four T-years early.

"HQ is granting us quite a lot of flexibility in selecting and scheduling our precise targets in this area," MacIntosh went on, "but the basic plan calls for us to begin operations down *here*," a cursor flicked to life in the display, "and then head up in this general direction—"

The cursor crawled upward through the stars, heading steadily towards Basilisk, and Giscard leaned back in his chair to listen as closely as the most junior member of his staff.

"I need to speak with you, Citizen Admiral. Alone."

Citizen Commissioner Pritchart's flat voice cut through the sound of moving people as the staff meeting broke up two hours later. More than one of the naval officers flinched—not because she'd raised her voice, or because she'd said anything overtly threatening, but because she'd said so little during the meeting. People's commissioners weren't noted, as a rule, for reticence. Part of their job, after all, was to ensure that no one ever forgot the living, breathing presence of StateSec as the People's guardian. Which suggested at least the possibility that Citizen Admiral Giscard—or perhaps one of his officers—might have put a foot so far wrong that Citizen Commissioner Pritchart intended to chop the offending leg right off.

"Of course, Citizen Commissioner," Giscard replied after the briefest of hesitations. "Here?"

"No." Pritchart looked around the compartment, topaz eyes flicking over the officers calmly. "Your day cabin, perhaps," she suggested, and he shrugged.

"As you wish, Citizen Commissioner," he said, with an apparent calmness which woke mingled admiration and trepidation in some of his new subordinates. "Citizen Captain Joubert, I'll expect those reports from you and Citizen Commander MacIntosh and Citizen Lieutenant Thaddeus by fourteen hundred."

"Of course, Citizen Admiral." Joubert nodded respectfully, but his secretive eyes darted towards Pritchart for just a moment. The citizen commissioner did not acknowledge his glance, and he turned to address himself to MacIntosh as Giscard waved gently at the compartment hatch.

"After you, Citizen Commissioner," he said coolly.

Chapter Seventeen

There was no sentry outside Giscard's quarters as there would have been on a Manticoran vessel. That was one of the "elitist" privileges the PN's officer corps had been required to surrender under the New Order, but at this particular moment, Javier Giscard was actually quite pleased by his loss. It meant there was one less pair of eyes to watch his comings and goings, although he supposed most people would have considered that having *Salamis*' chief spy and political dictator personally accompanying him more than compensated for the sentry's absence.

They would have been wrong, however. Or, rather, they would have been entirely correct, simply not in any way they might have imagined, for Giscard and his keeper had a rather different relationship from the one most people assumed they had. Now the two of them stepped through the hatch into his day cabin, and Pritchart drew a slim hand remote from her pocket and pressed a button as the hatch slid shut behind them.

"Thank *God* that's over," she sighed, dropping the remote which controlled the surveillance devices in Giscard's cabin on the corner of his desk, and then turned and opened her arms to him.

"Amen," he said fervently, and their lips met in a hungry kiss whose power still astounded him. Or perhaps simply astounded him even more than it had, for the fire between his people's commissioner and himself had grown only brighter in the two T-years since the disastrous collapse of Republican operations in Silesia, as if the flame were expending its power in a prodigal effort to drive back the ever-darker shadows closing in upon them.

Had anyone at StateSec suspected even for a moment that Pritchart and he had become lovers, the consequences would have been lethal . . . and widely publicized. Probably. It might have been a hard call for Oscar Saint-Just, though, when all was said. Would it be better to make their executions a crushing example of the price the People would exact from any StateSec agent who let himself or herself be seduced from the cold performance of StateSec's duty to ferret out and destroy any smallest independence among the Navy's officers? Or better to make both of them simply disappear, lest the very fact that they had kept their secret for almost four T-years now tempt still other people's commissioners into apostasy?

Giscard had no idea how Saint-Just would answer that question . . . and he never, ever wanted to learn. And so he and Pritchart played their deadly game, acting out the roles chance had assigned them with a skill which would have shamed any thespian, in a play where simple survival comprised a rave review. It was hard on both of them, especially the need to project exactly the right balance of distrust, leashed animosity, and wary cooperation, yet they'd had no choice but to learn to play their assumed characters well.

"Ummm. . . ." She broke the kiss at last and leaned back in his arms, looking up at him with a blinding smile which would have stunned anyone who had ever seen her in her people's commissioner's guise, with those topaz executioner's eyes watching every move with chill dispassion. Indeed, it still surprised Giscard at times, for when they'd first met three and a half T-years before, he'd been as deceived by her mask as anyone.

"I'm *so* glad to be back into space," she sighed, wrapping one arm around him and leaning her head against his shoulder. He hugged her tightly to his side, and then they moved together to the small couch which faced his desk. They sank onto it, and he pressed a kiss to the part of her sweet-smelling hair, nostrils flaring as he inhaled the scent of her.

"Me, too," he told her, "and not just because it means we're officially off the shit list." He kissed her again, and she giggled. The sound was sharp and silvery as a bell, and just as musical, and it always astounded him. It sounded so bright and infectious coming from someone with her record and formidable acting skills, and its spontaneity was deeply and uniquely precious to him.

"It does help to be the chief spy and admiral-watcher again," she agreed, and they both sobered. The drafting of Pritchart's official StateSec evaluations of Giscard had become an even more ticklish and delicate task following their return from Silesia. Striking exactly the right note to deflect blame for the commerce raiding operation's failure from him by emphasizing his military skill while simultaneously remaining in character as his distrustful guardian had been excruciatingly hard. As far as they had been able to tell, Oscar Saint-Just and his senior analysts had continued to rely solely on her reports, but there'd been no way for them to be positive of that, and it had certainly been possible that Saint-Just had someone else watching both of them to provide an independent check on her version of events.

Now, at last, however, they could breathe a sigh of at least tentative relief, for they would never have been given their current orders if Pritchart's superiors had cherished even a shred of suspicion as to their actual relationship. That didn't mean they could let their guards down or be one whit less convincing in their public roles, for StateSec routinely placed lower level informers aboard Navy ships. At the moment, all of those informers were reporting to Pritchart—they thought. But it was possible, perhaps even probable, that there were at least one or two independent observers she knew nothing about, and even those she did know about might bypass her with a report if they came to suspect how close to Giscard she actually was.

Yet for all that, shipboard duty offered a degree of control over their exposure which had been completely and nerve-wrackingly lacking since their return from Silesia.

"That Joubert is an even scarier piece of work than I expected," Giscard remarked after a moment, and Pritchart smiled thinly.

"Oh, he is that," she agreed. "But he's also the best insurance policy we've got. Your objections to him were a work of art, too—exactly the right blend of 'professional reservations' and unspoken suspicion. Saint-Just loved them, and you should have seen his eyes just *glow* when I 'insisted' on nominating Joubert for your chief of staff, anyway. And he does seem to know his business."

"In technical terms, yes," Giscard said. He leaned back, his arm still around her, and she rested her head on his chest. "I'm more than a little concerned over how he's going to impact on the staff's chemistry, though. MacIntosh, at least, already figures him for an informer, I think. And Franny . . . she doesn't trust him, either."

"I'll say!" Pritchart snorted. "She watches her mouth around him almost as carefully as she watches it around *me!*"

"Which is only prudent of her," Giscard agreed soberly, and she nodded with more than a trace of unhappiness.

"I realize he's going to be a problem for you, Javier," she said after a moment, "but I'll put pressure on him from my side to 'avoid friction' if I have to. And at least he'll be making any reports to me. Knowing who the informer is is half the battle; surely controlling where his information goes is the other! And picking him over your 'protests' can't have hurt my credibility with StateSec."

"I know, I know." He sighed. "And don't think for a moment that I'm ungrateful, either. But if we're going to make this work—and I think McQueen is right; Icarus does have the potential to exercise a major effect on the war—then I've got to be able to rely on my command team. I'm not too worried about *my* ability to work around Joubert if I have to, but everyone else on the staff is junior to him. He could turn into a choke point we can't afford once the shooting starts."

"If he does, I'll remove him," Pritchart told him after a moment. "I can't possibly do it yet, though. You have to be reasonable and—"

"Oh, hush!" Giscard kissed her hair again and made his voice determinedly light. "I'm not asking you to do a thing about him yet, silly woman! You know me. I fret about things ahead of time so they don't sneak up on me when the moment comes. And you're absolutely right about one thing; he's a marvelous bit of cover for both of us."

"And especially for me," she agreed quietly, and his arm tightened around her in an automatic fear reaction.

How odd, a corner of his mind thought. *Here I am, subject to removal at StateSec's whim, knowing dozens of other admirals have already been shot for "treason against the people"—mainly because "the People's" rulers gave them orders* no one *could have carried out successfully—and I'm worried to death over the safety of the woman StateSec chose to spy on me!*

There were times when Javier Giscard wondered if learning that Eloise Pritchart was a most unusual people's commissioner had been a blessing or a curse, for his life had been so much simpler when he could regard any minion of StateSec as an automatic enemy. Not that he would ever shed any tears for the old regime. The Legislaturalists had brought their doom upon themselves, and Giscard had been better placed than many to see and recognize the damage their monopoly on power had inflicted upon the Republic and the Navy. More than that, he'd supported many of the Committee of Public Safety's publicly avowed purposes enthusiastically—and still did, for that matter. Oh, not the rot Ransom and PubIn had spewed to mobilize the Dolists, but the real, fundamental reforms the PRH had desperately needed.

But the excesses committed in the name of "the People's security," and the reign of terror which had followed—the disappearances and executions of men and women he had known, whose only crimes had been to fail in the impossible tasks assigned to them—those things had taught him a colder, uglier lesson. They'd taught him about the gulf which yawned between the Committee's promised land and where he was right now . . . and about the savagery of the Mob once the shackles were loosened. Worst of all, they'd shown him what he dared not say aloud to a single living soul: that the members of the Committee themselves were terrified of what they had unleashed and prepared to embrace any extremism in the name of their own survival. And so he'd confronted the supreme irony of it all. Under the old regime, he'd been that rare creature: a patriot who loved and served his country despite all the many things he knew were wrong with it . . . and under the new regime, he was exactly the same thing. Only the nature of that country's problems—and the virulence of its excesses—had changed.

But at least he'd known what he had to do to survive. It was simple, really. Obey his orders, succeed however impossible the mission, and never, ever trust anyone from StateSec, for a single mistake—just one hastily spoken or poorly chosen word—to one of Oscar Saint-Just's spies would be more dangerous than any Manticoran superdreadnought.

And then Eloise had been assigned as his commissioner. At first, he'd assumed she was like the others, but she wasn't. Like him, she believed in the things the original Committee had *said* it was going to do. He'd been unable to accept that for months, been certain it was all a mask to entrap him into lowering his own guard, but it hadn't been.

"I wish to hell you were less visible," he said now, fretting, knowing it was useless to say and would only demonstrate his anxiety, and yet unable not to say it. "People's commissioner for an entire fleet *and* an Aprilist . . . they're going to be watching you like hawks."

"An *ex*-Aprilist," she corrected him, much more lightly than she could possibly feel, and reached over to pat his hand. "Don't spend your time and energy fretting about me, Javier! You just pull Icarus off. No one's going to question my support for you as long as you deliver the goods and don't say or do something totally against the party line, especially not with McQueen running the War Office. And as long as the two of us keep up appearances in public and perform effectively in the field, no one's going to worry about my previous affiliations."

"I know," he said penitently. Not because he agreed with her, but because he shouldn't have brought the subject up. There was nothing either of them could do about it, and now she was likely to spend the next hour or so of their precious privacy trying to reassure him that she was completely safe when both of them knew she was nothing of the sort . . . even without her relationship with him.

It was all part and parcel of the madness, he thought bitterly. Eloise had been a cell leader in the action teams of the Citizen's Rights Union, just as Cordelia Ransom had, but the similarities between her and the late Secretary of Public Information ended there. The term "terrorist" had been a pale description for most of the people in the CRU's strike forces, and many of their members—like Ransom—had accepted the label willingly, even proudly. Indeed, Giscard suspected people like Ransom had seen it almost as an excuse, seen the "struggle against the elitist oppressors" primarily as an opportunity to unleash the violence and destruction they craved with at least a twisted aura of ideological justification.

But Eloise's cell had belonged to the April Tribunal, a small but influential (and dangerously efficient) CRU splinter faction which derived its name from an InSec massacre of Dolist protest marchers in April of 1861 P.D. Not even the Aprilists had believed the "April Massacre" was part of a deliberate Legislaturalist policy; it was simply an accident, a botched operation which had gotten out of hand. But the old regime had *treated* it as an accident—and a minor one—as if it regarded the deaths of forty-seven hundred human beings who'd been someone's mothers and fathers or sons or daughters or sisters or brothers or husbands or wives as no more than the trivial price of doing business. Certainly no one had ever suggested that the people responsible for those deaths should be held responsible or punished for them!

Except for the April Tribunal, and that was what had made them fundamentally different from most of the CRU's membership. Whereas the mainstream CRU often attacked civilian Legislaturalist targets—they were, after all, waging a terror campaign—Aprilist attacks had been directed solely against InSec, the military, and official government offices. Their demand had been for justice—which had, by the nature of things, admittedly slipped over into naked vengeance all too often—not power. It was a sometimes subtle distinction, but an important one, and like most Aprilists, Eloise Pritchart had joined the CRU only after suffering a cruel and bitterly personal loss.

But the Aprilists had found themselves in a delicate position following the Harris Assassination. On the one hand, they had enjoyed a reputation, even among people who disapproved of the CRU's violence, as a faction which had fought a "clean" war as urban guerrillas, not terrorists. From that perspective, their inclusion among the Committee of Public Safety's supporters had been invaluable to Rob Pierre and his fellows, for it had brought with it an element of moderation and reason. One might almost say respectability.

Yet the Aprilists had also been suspect in the eyes of people like Cordelia Ransom precisely because of their reputation for moderation, and that had been dangerous, especially as the promises to the Dolists grew more extreme and the pogroms and purges of the "enemies of the People" mounted in intensity.

Fortunately for Pritchart, her pre-Coup prominence had put her in a position to be coopted by Saint-Just's new Office of State Security very early, and she'd been too intelligent to refuse the honor she'd been offered and make StateSec suspicious of her. Which meant that by the time many of the other Aprilist leaders had been made to quietly disappear in favor of more . . . vigorous defenders of the People, she had been firmly ensconced as a people's commissioner.

Her years as an underground fighter had served her well in terms of learning to assume protective coloration, and unlike some of her less wary (and since vanished) companions in arms, she had refused to succumb to the heady euphoria of the Committee's early days. And when the Committee moved to consolidate the cold iron of its power and those less wary companions found themselves quietly detained and "disappeared" by those they had thought were their allies, Pritchart's carefully crafted public persona had already made the transition from apolitical guerrilla fighter to committed guardian of the New Order in the People's name. It had been a dangerous tightrope to walk, but Saint-Just had been deeply impressed by her insightful reports on the relatively junior officers she had initially been assigned to watchdog. Indeed, if the truth be told, he valued her moderation even more because it had been so rare among the people's commissioners. And so she'd been tapped for ever more sensitive duties, rising higher and higher in StateSec without the people who ran that agency's ever realizing what actually went on in the privacy of her own thoughts.

Until she was assigned to Giscard. Had it really been less than four T-years ago? It seemed impossible whenever he thought about it. Surely it had to have been longer than that! The intensity of life on the edge, of finding oneself adrift in the fevered turbulence of Rob S. Pierre's new, improved People's Republic and locked in a war where one's own superiors were as likely to shoot one as the enemy, lent a surrealism to every aspect of existence, and especially to anything as insanely dangerous as a love affair between a Navy officer and his people's commissioner.

And yet, somehow, they'd managed to survive this long. Every day was yet another triumph against the odds in a game where the house always won, sooner or later, but deep inside, both of them knew no streak lasted forever. All they could do was go on as they had, walking their tightrope and dodging each day's bullet as it came at them, and hope that someday, somehow, things would change. . . .

The truly odd thing, though it never occurred to Javier Giscard to see it so, was that even now, neither of them had even once seriously considered defection. A handful of other officers had made that choice, including Alfredo Yu, Giscard's old mentor. Yet much as he respected Yu, that was one example he simply could not follow, and he wondered, sometimes, whether that was a virtue or the ultimate proof of his own idiocy.

"Do you really think McQueen can pull it off?" he asked after a moment. Pritchart drew back enough to look up at him and raise an eyebrow, and he shrugged. "Do you think she can actually reorganize the War Office enough to make a difference without getting herself purged?" he expanded.

"I think she has the ability to do it," Pritchart said thoughtfully. "And she's certainly been given a better opportunity to use that ability than anyone else has had. But whether or not she can make all the pieces come together—?" It was her turn to shrug.

"I'd feel a lot better if I hadn't heard so many stories about her ambition," he sighed.

"Saint-Just has heard them all, too, I assure you," she said much more grimly. "I haven't seen her dossier, of course; she's not my responsibility. But I've heard the scuttlebutt among the other commissioners, and there was a lot of nervousness when Pierre picked her to replace Kline."

"Even after she squashed the Levelers?" He tried to make it a jest, but the joking tone fell flat, and she grimaced.

"Maybe even especially after she squashed the Levelers," she replied. "She did it too well and displayed too much initiative and raw nerve—and ruthlessness. And picked up too much approval from the Mob. Besides, half of them figure she would have kept right on moving herself if her pinnace hadn't crashed. I happen to think they're wrong, and so does Fontein and, I'm pretty sure, Saint-Just himself. I think she recognized that her lack of a power base would have prevented her from supplanting the Committee, and I honestly believe she also would have refused to provoke the kind of anarchy that would have resulted from any failed putsch on her part. But that doesn't mean anyone else trusts her . . . or that even I think she might not make a try if she thought she'd managed to build a strong enough support base to have a shot at success."

"Surely she realizes that, though," Giscard thought aloud. "She has to be smart enough not to do anything that might seem to play into her opponents' hands."

"I'd like to think so, and to give her credit, she has been so far. But she's got some of the same problems we do, Javier. The better she does her job, and the more successful she becomes, the more *dangerous* she becomes."

"Wonderful," he sighed bitterly. "The goddamned lunatics are running the asylum!"

"They are," Pritchart agreed unflinchingly. "But there's nothing we can do about it except survive, and maybe accomplish a little something for the Republic along the way."

Their eyes met once more, and Giscard smiled crookedly. Like himself, she never spoke of "the People" when they were alone. Their loyalty was to the Republic, or at least to the tattered remnants of the ideal of the Republic, which Rob Pierre had promised to restore. And that, of course, would have been the final proof to StateSec that neither of them could be trusted.

He chuckled at the thought, and she raised an eyebrow again, as if asking him to share the joke. But he only shook his head, then bent to kiss her once more. Her lips warmed under his, clinging with desperate longing, and he felt the urgency rising within him. It had been months since they'd last been alone together, and he pulled back from the kiss, just far enough to look deep into her shining topaz eyes.

"Oh, I think there might be a *little* something else we might do, as well, Citizen Commissioner," he murmured, and stood, cradling her in his arms as he crossed to his sleeping cabin's hatch.

Chapter Eighteen

"And come *out* of there, you worthless piece of— Ah *ha!*"

Scooter Smith sat back on his haunches with a triumphant grin as the recalcitrant tracking drive of the LAC's number three laser cluster finally yielded to his ministrations. He didn't know how the defective drive shaft had gotten past the myriad inspections which were supposed to spot such things, but that was less important than that it had. Well, that and the fact that its sub-spec materials had warped and jammed the cluster's training gears solid at a most inopportune moment during yesterday's exercises. It had also managed to splinter and deform itself sufficiently to resist all removal efforts with sullen stolidity for the better part of two hours, and they'd had to strip the entire unit down much further than he'd hoped, but they had it out now.

He tossed it to one of his techs and stood, rubbing the small of his back, then climbed down the side of the work stand.

One of the nicer things about HMS *Minotaur*'s LAC bays was that someone had actually bothered to put some thought into servicing and ammunitioning requirements. Smith's last assignment had been as an assault shuttle section chief aboard HMS *Leutzen*, and, like every other shuttle maintenance specialist, it seemed as if he'd spent about a third of his on-duty time in a skinsuit or a hardsuit floating around in the zero-gee vacuum of a boat bay while he pulled hull maintenance on one or another of the small craft under his care. In most ways, *Minotaur*'s LACs were simply small craft writ large, and he'd expected to face the same problem, only more so. And he *was* spending a good bit of time suited up . . . but nowhere near as much of it as he'd anticipated.

Whoever had designed *Minotaur* had taken extraordinary pains to enhance crew efficiency. Even after five months on board, Smith was still a bit awed by the degree of automation she incorporated. Traditionally, warships had embarked crews which were enormously larger than any merchant ship of equivalent tonnage would have boasted. That was largely because merchant ships tended to be nothing more than huge, hollow spaces into which to stuff cargo, whereas warships were packed full of weapons, ammunition, defensive and offensive electronic warfare systems, sidewall generators, back up fusion plants, bigger Warshawski sails, more powerful beta nodes, and scores of other things merchantmen simply didn't carry and hence had no reason to provide crews for. But it was also true that merchies relied far more heavily than warships on automated and remote systems to reduce manpower requirements still further.

Men-of-war could have done the same thing, but they didn't. Or, at least, they hadn't. The official reason was that large crews provided redundancy. After all, if the fancy automation took a hit that fried it, you needed old-fashioned people with toolkits to fix it. And people were still the ultimate self-programming remotes. If a weapon mount or a critical support system was cut off from the central control net by battle damage, or if the central computers themselves crashed, a warship had the human resources to take over and run things in local control anyway.

That was the official reasoning. Personally, Smith had always suspected that tradition had as much to do with it. Warships always had had enormous crews for their tonnage; ergo they always *would* have enormous crews, and that was simply The Way It Was. Even in the Royal Manticoran Navy, he'd long since discovered, the military mind liked things to stay nice and predictable.

But the Star Kingdom could no longer afford to hang onto tradition for tradition's sake. Smith hadn't seen the figures—first-class engineering petty officers weren't generally invited in by BuPers to study classified manpower numbers—but he didn't have to see them to know the Navy was increasingly strapped for crews. It was also common knowledge that the Navy and Marines between them now had something like twenty million people in uniform, and the Royal Army's appetite for manpower had turned increasingly voracious as the Navy picked off Peep planets and the Army had to provide garrisons. Altogether, there were probably close to thirty million Manticorans in uniform now, and that was the next best thing to one percent of the Star Kingdom's total population.

One percent didn't sound like a lot . . . until you subtracted it from the most productive portions of your economy just as you geared up to fight an interstellar war on a scale the galaxy hadn't seen in at least four hundred years. Then it became a very big thing indeed, and BuShips, under pressure from BuPers to do something—*anything*—to reduce manpower demands, had finally caved in on the automation front. Even with all the personnel for her LAC squadrons on board, *Minotaur* carried a total company of under two thousand, which was less than most battlecruisers a seventh her size. Of course, she didn't mount the normal broadside weapons of a ship of the wall, but Smith figured that even a conventional warship's company could be cut by at least sixty percent if the same standards of automation and remotes were applied to her design. And that could have major consequences for the Navy's front line strength.

Smith supposed it was inevitable—human beings, being human beings—that the new concept would have its critics, and some of the criticisms were no doubt valid. He did tend to get just a bit pissed off with the ones who caterwauled about what a heavy reliance the new design placed on the ship's computers, though. Of course it put a heavy demand on them . . . and anyone but an idiot knew that had always been the case. Human beings could do many of the things their electronic minions normally took care of for them, but they could do very few of those things as well—or in anything like the same amount of time—as their computers could. And there were any number of things people *couldn't* do without computers. Like navigate a starship. Or run a fusion plant. Or any one of a zillion other absolutely essential, extremely complex, time-critical jobs that always needed doing aboard a warship. It probably made sense to minimize total dependency on the computers and AI loops as much as possible, but it simply couldn't be entirely eliminated. And as long as he had an intact electronics shop, with one machine shop to support it, and power, and life support, Scooter Smith could damned well *build* any replacement computer his ship might need. All of which meant he wished the whiners and nitpickers would get the hell out of his way so he could get on with enjoying all the marvelous new features the change in design philosophy had brought with it.

In *Minotaur*'s case, those features meant, among other things, that better than eighty percent of the routine hull maintenance on the carrier's LACs could be performed by cybernetic henchmen without ever requiring a suited human presence. Of course, some people—like "Silver Spanner" Maxwell—could break *anything*, if they put their minds to it, and Maxwell had done just that over on Bay Forty-Six. Smith had never quite understood how someone who was as fundamentally good at his job as Maxwell was could be such a walking disaster area, but there it was. It was almost as if he represented some natural force of chaos or the living personification of Murphy's Law. He always did it by The Book . . . and it always ended up a disaster anyway. Smith only hoped his friend's transfer from *Minotaur*'s deck force to a new slot as LAC 01-001's assistant flight engineer would break the cycle at last, although he had to wonder just what Captain Harmon had been thinking to tap him for her personal bird.

But whatever happened to "Silver Spanner," Smith was delighted with the new remotes. They were almost as impressive as the support a shipyard might have boasted, and he was devoutly grateful to have them. But the designers had gone still further in simplifying his task by designing the LAC bays with outsized bow access tubes. Instead of the standard buffers and docking arms which held a small craft in its boat bay, the LACs' mooring tractors drew them bow-first into a full length docking cradle. In the process, they aligned the little ships' sharp noses with "personnel tubes" fifteen meters across that fitted down over their bows. Since that was where all of the LACs' armament—defensive and offensive alike—was mounted, it let Smith work on things like the jammed laser cluster without suiting up. And additional service tubes to the launchers meant missile reloads could be transported directly from *Minotaur*'s main missile stowage, into the LACs' rotary magazines.

All in all, Smith considered the design concept an enormous improvement over what he'd had to put up with in *Leutzen*. The LACs outmassed the assault shuttles he'd worked with there by a factor of around thirty-five, yet the six-ship section he had responsibility for here was actually easier to stay on top of than the six-*shuttle* section he'd been assigned aboard *Leutzen*. Of course, the thought of what might happen to the ship's hull integrity if some ill-intentioned Peep managed to land a hit on one of these nice, large, efficient, and vulnerable LAC bays hardly bore thinking on, but that was an inescapable consequence of *Minotaur*'s designed role.

"Okay, Sandford. You're on," he said as he stepped from the work stand's last rung to the deck of the access tube. "Get the replacement in and let me know when you're ready to test it. Check?"

The bow of the LAC reared above them, and despite its minuscule size compared to a ship like *Minotaur*, it dwarfed his entire work party. Which put the rest of the ship into a sobering perspective for people who normally saw it only from the inside.

"Aye, PO." The tech who'd caught the warped drive shaft waved it in acknowledgment. "Should take us about another fifty minutes, I guess."

"Sounds reasonable," Smith agreed, arching his shoulders and massaging his aching back again. Getting the damaged component out had been a major pain, but putting the replacement back in should be relatively straightforward. "I'll be around on Thirty-Six if you need me," he went on. "Caermon has something she wants to discuss about the main radar array."

"Gotcha," Sandford agreed, and Smith nodded and headed off. He did have one other little stop to make, but it was on the way to Bay Thirty-Six where Caermon waited for him, and he grinned as he tapped the data chip in his pocket. He liked Lieutenant Commander Ashford a lot, he really did, but there was something undeniably delicious about receiving not simply official sanction but actual orders to put one over on an officer.

Helps keep them humble, it does, he reflected cheerfully. *And humble officers are more likely to remember just who really runs the Queen's Navy. On the other hand, protection from on high or not, I hope to hell he never figures out* I *was the one who did it to him!*

He grinned again and paused as he reached the access tube to Ashford's bird. The LAC sat there all alone, awaiting the service crews who would minister to it in time for the afternoon's exercises, and he nodded to himself. He wouldn't get a better chance, he thought, and sauntered down the tube with a guileless expression.

"And just what the hell did you think you were doing *here*, Ashford?" Captain Harmon inquired genially as she used an old-fashioned, nonilluminated pointer to gesture at the frozen holo display above the ready room tac table. Tiny LACs, no larger than the nail of her little finger, swarmed in it, color-coded by squadron, as they "attacked" a holo of *Minotaur* half again the length of her arm. Most of the thirty-six LACs had altered course in the second or so before she had frozen the display, turning so that their bows were pointed directly at *Minotaur*, but one section of six hadn't, and the dark-haired, dark-eyed captain turned to look at the lieutenant commander who commanded the errant vessels.

"Ah, well, actually, Ma'am—" Ashford began, then exhaled. "Actually," he admitted in an almost but not quite resigned voice, "I was screwing up by the numbers."

"A concise if not particularly helpful analysis," Harmon agreed, but without the biting edge the lieutenant commander had dreaded. His honesty had bought him that much—it was the ones who tried to weasel or excuse their mistakes (or, worse, shuffle responsibility off on someone else) who quickly learned to fear the sharpness of her tongue. Nor did she stop there. Two squadron commanders had already been sent packing, one of them with an efficiency report so scathing it would require a special act of God for her ever to hold a command again.

"Would you happen to know *why* you screwed up?" she asked now, holding the pointer across her body in both hands.

"I'm still trying to track it down, Skipper," Ashford replied. "It looks like we hit a glitch in the tac computer programming. We're pulling the code to run comparisons against the master files just in case, but at this point, my best bet is human error—mine, I'm afraid—on the input from one of the post-launch mission updates. Kelly was busy running an acceleration recompute when the update for this particular maneuver came in, so I took over the computer and input the change. And I must've gotten it wrong, because when we hit the way point for the turn-in, the computers turned us one-eighty in the opposite direction."

"With this result," Harmon agreed, and nodded.

Commander McGyver, effectively her chief of staff (although The Book hadn't yet decided whether or not a LAC wing's commander was supposed to have a staff—officially) keyed the holo back into movement at the unspoken order. Everyone watched Ashford's section turn directly away from *Minotaur* . . . at which point every LAC in it instantly flashed a lurid crimson as they exposed the after aspects of their wedges to the carrier and the point defense laser clusters playing the parts of broadside lasers and grasers took the "up the kilt" shots and blew them away. McGyver hit the freeze key again, stopping all motion, and the "dead" LACs hung in the display like drops of fresh blood.

"Had this been an actual attack, rather than a training exercise," Harmon observed dryly, "the consequences of this little error would have been rather permanent. The good news is that it wouldn't have hurt a bit; the *bad* news is that that's only because every one of Commander Ashford's people would have been dead before they knew it. We can *not* have something like this happen to us on an actual op, ladies and gentlemen."

She held their eyes, her own stern, until every head had nodded. Then her gaze softened as she looked back at Ashford.

"For the record," she told him, "Commander McGyver, Comfmander Stackowitz and I have all reviewed the chips, and your theory about what happened makes sense. It was a long session, and we threw a lot of updates and mission profile plan changes at you, too. We probably wouldn't have to make anywhere near that many changes to the canned profile in a real op."

One or two people nodded again. Training operations were almost always harder—well, aside from the adrenaline rush, the terror, and the dying—than real attack missions. Which only made sense. In actual combat operations, you would almost always carry out only a single attack per launch—assuming that everything went right and you actually found the enemy at all. But on training flights, you were likely to be tasked with several different "attacks" in a single sortie, and the people who'd planned your mission profiles could be counted on to spend at least some of their time throwing in surprise elements specifically designed to screw things up as severely as possible at the least opportune moment.

Everyone understood why that was, just as they understood that the fact that Harmon and her wing command staff were building an entire doctrinal concept from the ground up required her to be even more ruthless than usual. Still, one or two of her section and squadron leaders had been heard to lament the fact that she'd added Ernest Takahashi to her mission planners. Almost everyone liked the cocky young ensign, but his reputation had preceded him. The story of his modifications to the Kreskin Field flight simulators had put all of them on their guards . . . which had proved an unfortunately foresighted reaction.

Jacquelyn Harmon knew exactly what the officers before her were thinking, and she hid an internal smile. Lieutenant Commander Ashford was going to be moderately livid when he and his people finally did track down the problem, she thought. Assuming that they recognized how it had happened when they found it. And, after all, finding it was another part of their exercise mission, even if they hadn't known that when they started looking, and it would be interesting to see if they went the step further to figuring out the "how" and the "why" as well as the "what." Although, she reminded herself, Ernest was too sneaky to make figuring out what had happened easy. She glanced at the bland-faced ensign, shook her head mentally, and then looked away.

So young and innocent looking for such a depraved soul, she thought cheerfully. *And the fact that he and PO Smith served together in* Leutzen *didn't hurt, now did it? But I* do *want to see Ashford's reaction if he ever realizes I had his own section chief slip a deliberately rigged modification into his original mission download.*

Not that recognizing that it had been deliberate was going to be easy. The file corruption which had transposed Ashford's perfectly correct heading change when he punched it in, while freakish, looked exactly like something that could have happened accidentally. Bruce McGyver had bet her five bucks Ashford's crew would never realize they'd been snookered, but one reason Harmon liked Ashford (though she wasn't about to tell him so) was that he was not only smart but as thorough as they came. If anybody was likely to realize he'd been had, Ashford was the one . . . and if he did, he was going to inherit one of the empty squadron commander slots as a reward. But playing with his head to evaluate him for promotion had been only a secondary objective of the exercise, she reminded herself, and cleared her throat.

"Whatever the cause of the problem, however," she went on, "let's look at the consequences, shall we?" She nodded to McGyver again, and someone groaned aloud as the sudden chink in the LACs' attack plan opened the door to a cascade of steadily accelerating miscues by other squadron and section COs . . . none of whom had the excuse that Harmon and Takahashi had jiggered their software.

And that had been the real point of her devious machinations, Harmon thought, watching the carefully orchestrated strike disintegrate into chaos, because one thing was *damned* sure. The first law of war was still Murphy's, and units as fragile as LACs had better learn to show it even more respect than anyone else.

"Well it certainly looked like they got the point, Skipper," Lieutenant Gearman remarked with a grin as the last of the squadron and section commanders departed. "Think any of them have figured out you slipped Commander Ashford a ringer?"

"Now when did I ever say I'd done anything of the sort, Mike?" Harmon asked her personal engineer innocently.

"You didn't have to say a word, Skipper. Not when Ernest was grinning like the proverbial Cheshire Cat!"

"There's nothing feline in my ancestry, Sir," Takahashi objected.

"Of course not," Commander McGyver agreed. McGyver was from Sphinx, a startlingly handsome man with platinum blond hair and a powerful physique who walked with a pronounced limp courtesy of a skiing injury which had stubbornly persisted in refusing to mend properly despite all quick heal could do. Now he smiled, even white teeth flashing in a his tanned HD-star face. "Personally, I've always thought of you as having a bit more weasel than feline, Ernest," he announced. "Or possibly a little snake. You know—" he raised an arm and swayed it sinuously back and forth in mid-air "—the sneaky, squirm-through-the-grass-and-bite-you-on-the-butt-when-you're-not-looking variety."

"I wouldn't know about snakes, Sir," Takahashi replied. "We don't have them on Manticore, you know."

"They do on Sphinx," Stackowitz informed him. "Of course, they've got *legs* on Sphinx, and I don't think Old Earth snakes do. Then again, Sphinx always has been noted for the . . . um, peculiarities of its flora and fauna."

"And people?" McGyver suggested genially, eyes glinting at the ops officer.

"Oh, heavens, Sir! Who would ever suggest such a thing as that?" Like Takahashi, Stackowitz was from Manticore, and her expression could scarcely have been more innocent.

"Personally," Harmon observed, dropping untidily back into her chair and sprawling out comfortably, "I've always figured Carroll must have met a treecat in an opium dream or something when he invented the Cheshire Cat."

"And the lot of you are changing the subject," Gearman pointed out. "You *did* have Ernest cook his software, didn't you?"

"Maybe," Harmon allowed with a lazy smile. Which, Gearman knew, was as close as she would ever come to admitting it.

He shook his head and leaned back in his own chair. Captain Harmon wasn't quite like any other four-striper he'd ever met. She was at least as cocky and confident as any one of the carefully selected hotshots under her command, and she had a wicked and devious sense of humor. She also possessed a downright infectious enthusiasm for her new duties and actively encouraged informality among all her officers—not just her staff—outside "office hours."

She should have been born two thousand years ago, he often thought, in an era when deranged individuals in flying scarves strapped on so-called "aircraft" more fragile than a modern hang glider, but armed with machine guns, and went out hunting one another. Her training techniques were, to say the least, unconventional, as her latest ploy amply demonstrated, yet she got remarkable results, and she was very consciously and deliberately infusing her personnel with what the ancients had called the "fighter jock" mentality.

Stackowitz had been the first to apply the term to her. Gearman had never heard of it before. He'd been forced to look the term up to figure out what it meant, but once he had, he'd had to admit it fitted Captain Harmon perfectly. And given the unconventionality of her assignment, he mused, her command style was probably entirely appropriate. Certainly none of the by-the-book types he'd served under could have accomplished as much as she had in so short a period.

He leaned back and massaged his closed eyes while he reflected on just how much *all* of them had accomplished in the last five months. Captain Truman and Captain Harmon could probably have given lessons to the slave-drivers who'd built Old Earth's pyramids, but they did get the job done. And they'd managed to build a solid *esprit de corps* in the process.

It was a bit confusing to have two Navy captains aboard the same ship, both in command slots, even if one of them was a junior-grade and the other a senior-grade. And it could have led to dangerous confusion as to exactly whom one was speaking to or of in an emergency, which explained why Harmon was almost always referred to as the "COLAC," the brand-new acronym someone had coined for "Commanding Officer, LACs." Harmon had resisted it at first, on the grounds that it sounded too much like "colic," but it had stuck. It still sounded odd, but it was beginning to seem less so, and it certainly made it perfectly clear who you were talking about. (Ernest Takahashi's innocent suggestion that if the Captain objected to "Commanding Officer, LACs," they might try "Commanding Officer, Wing" instead had been rejected with astonishing speed. Even more astonishingly, the lieutenant had survived making it.)

The new title was also only a tiny part of all the adjustments and new departures *Minotaur* and her company had been forced to deal with. For the first time in modern naval history—the first time in almost two thousand years, in fact—the "main battery" of a unit which had to be considered a capital ship did not operate directly from that ship in action . . . and the ship's captain didn't control it. Gearman couldn't imagine a better choice for *Minotaur*'s CO than Alice Truman. She had the flexibility and the confidence, not to mention the experience, to grasp the changes in the RMN's traditional command arrangements which the introduction of the LAC-carrier implied, and he wasn't sure how many other captains could have said the same thing. But the fact was that once *Minotaur*'s LACs were launched, Jackie Harmon—a mere captain (JG)—had under her command twice as many energy weapons and six and a half times as many missile tubes as the skipper of a *Reliant*-class battlecruiser. Not only that, but *Minotaur*'s only real function after launching her brood was to get the hell out of the way while Harmon and her squadron COs got on with business.

That required a genuine partnership between Truman and Harmon. There was no question as to who was in command, but Truman had to be smart enough to know when a call properly belonged to Harmon, and the two of them had worked out the CO's and COLAC's spheres of authority and responsibility with remarkably little friction. More than that, they were the ones who got to make up The Book on carrier ops as they went, and they'd written those spheres into it. By the time the next LAC-carrier commissioned, its skipper would already know how the areas of authority were *supposed* to break down.

And for all intents and purposes, Gearman was getting to write the Book for LAC engineers. His position as Harmon's engineer aboard *Harpy* (still known officially by her call sign of "Gold One") made him her *de facto* staff engineer, as well, and he had to admit that he felt like a kid on Christmas whenever he contemplated the marvelous new toys the Navy had given him.

The *Shrikes* were sweet little ships, with the latest generation of inertial compensator and a max acceleration rate which had to be seen to be believed. And the systems engineered into them—! The demanding cycle of exercises Truman and Harmon had laid on seemed to be demonstrating the fundamental soundness of the doctrine ATC had worked out for them, although a few holes had already been detected and repaired, and the hardware itself performed almost flawlessly.

But what had come as the greatest surprise to him were the differences the change in power plants made. He'd known what they were going to be—intellectually, at least—but that had been very different from the practical experience, and he sometimes found himself wondering just how many other things that everyone "knew" were true were nothing of the sort. In a very real sense, the best thing Grayson had done for the Star Kingdom was to force people in places like the Bureau of Ships to reconsider some of those "known facts" in a new light, he reflected, and wondered how long it would be before BuShips *did* decide to start building fission plants into at least their smaller starships.

Now that he'd been exposed to the theory behind them, he could see why such reactors had been genuinely dangerous in their early, primitive incarnations back on Old Earth (or, for that matter, their reinvented early, primitive incarnations back on Grayson). Of course, *most* new technologies—or even established ones—were dangerous if they were misused or improperly understood. And it was obvious from the history books which BuShips had dug up when it wrote the training syllabus for the new plants that the original fission pioneers on Old Earth had misunderstood, or at least *misestimated*, some of the downsides of their work. Gearman was at a loss to understand how anyone could have blithely set out to build up huge stocks of radioactive wastes when they had absolutely no idea how to get rid of the stuff. On the other hand, he also had to admit that the people who'd predicted that ways to deal with it would be devised in time had been correct in the long run—or would have been, if not for the hysteria of the idiots who'd thrown out the baby with the bath before those ways were worked out—but still . . .

Yet whatever his remote ancestors might have thought of fission, Gearman loved the piles in his new ships. They were smaller, lighter, and actually easier to operate than a fusion plant would have been, and the increase in endurance was incredible. In his previous stint in LACs, he'd been even more paranoid about reactor mass levels than most warship engineers because he'd had so little margin to play with. Now he didn't even have to consider that, and the sheer, wanton luxury of it was downright seductive. Not that there weren't a few drawbacks—including the procedure for emergency shutdown in case of battle damage. If a fusion plant's mag bottle held long enough for the hydrogen flow to be shut off, that was basically that. In a fission plant, however, you were stuck with a reactor core that was its own fuel . . . and which would do Bad Things if the coolant failed. But the Grayson tech reps seemed confident where their fail-safes were concerned. Which wasn't to say that every engineer from the Star Kingdom would agree with them. After all, their entire tech base was so much cruder, accepted so many trade-offs . . .

He gave himself a mental shake. Grayson's technology had been much cruder than Manticore's, yes. But they'd made enormous progress in closing the gap in just the nine and a half years since joining the Alliance, and "crude" didn't necessarily mean the same thing as "unsophisticated," as the new generation of inertial compensators amply demonstrated.

And as these new fission plants are going to demonstrate all over again, he told himself firmly, and looked up as Captain Harmon turned her attention to Lieutenant Commander Stackowitz.

"I've talked Captain Truman into signing off on the expenditure of some real missiles for live-fire exercises tomorrow, Barb," she told her staff operations officer.

"Really, Skipper?" Stackowitz brightened visibly. "Warshots, or training heads?"

"Both," Harmon said with a shark-like grin. "Training heads for the shots at the *Minnie*, of course, but we get to use warshots for everything else. Including," the grin grew even more shark-like, "an all-up EW exercise. Five squadrons worth."

"We get to play with Ghost Rider?" Stackowitz' eyes positively glowed at that, and Harmon nodded.

"Yep. The logistics pipeline just delivered an entire new set of decoy heads with brand-new signal amplifiers—the ones you were telling me about last month, in fact. We've got to share them with Hancock Base, but there're more than enough of them to go around."

"Oh boy," Stackowitz murmured almost prayerfully, and then gave McGyver a grin that eclipsed the COLAC's. "I told you they were going to make a difference, Bruce. Now I'll *show* you. I'll bet you five bucks they cut *Minotaur*'s tracking capability against us by thirty-five percent—and that's with CIC knowing what we're doing!"

"I'll take five dollars of that," McGyver agreed with a chuckle, and Harmon shook her head.

"Some people would bet on which direction to look for sunrise," she observed. "But now that those important financial details have been settled, let's get down to some specifics about said exercise. First of all, Barb—"

She leaned forward over the table, and her staffers listened intently, entering the occasional note into their memo pads while she laid out exactly what it was she wanted to do.

Chapter Nineteen

The Earl of White Haven stood in the boat bay gallery and stared through the armorplast at the brilliantly lit, crystalline vacuum of the bay. It was odd, he thought. He was ninety-two T-years old, and he'd spent far more time in space than on a planet over the last seventy of those years, yet his perceptions of what was "normal" were still inextricably bound up in the impressions of his planet-bound youth. The cliché "air as clear as crystal" had meaning only until someone had seen the reality of vacuum's needle-sharp clarity, but that reality remained forever unnatural, with a surrealism no one could avoid feeling, yet which defied precise definition.

He snorted to himself at the direction of his thoughts while he listened with a minuscule fraction of his attention to the earbug in his left ear that brought him the chatter between the boat bay control officer and the pinnace maneuvering towards rendezvous with his flagship. His mind had always tended to drift through contemplative deeps whenever it had nothing specific with which to occupy itself, but it had been doing it even more frequently than usual of late.

He turned his head to watch the Marine honor guard moving into position. Those Marines comported themselves with all the precision he could have desired, but they wore the brown and green uniforms of Grayson, not the black and green of Manticore, for the superdreadnought *Benjamin the Great*—known informally (and out of her captain's hearing) to her crew as "*Benjy*"—was a Grayson ship. Barely a T-year old, she was quite possibly the most powerful warship in existence. She certainly had been when she'd been completed, but warship standards were changing with bewildering speed. After the better part of seven centuries of gradual, incremental—one might even say glacial—evolution, the entire concept of just what made an effective ship of war had been cast back into the melting pot, and no one seemed entirely certain what would emerge from the crucible in time. All they knew was that the comfortable assurance of known weapons and known tactics and known strategies were about to be replaced by something new and different which might all too easily invalidate all their hard won skill and competence.

And no one outside the Alliance even seems to suspect the way things are changing . . . yet, he thought moodily, turning back to the still, sterile perfection of the boat bay.

A part of him wished the Alliance hadn't thought of it either, although it would never do to admit that. Actually, he'd come close to admitting it once, he reminded himself—at least by implication. But Lady Harrington had ripped a strip off his hide for it, and he'd deserved it.

As always, something twisted deep inside him, like a physical pain, at the fleeting thought of Honor Harrington, and he cursed his traitor memory. It had always been excellent. Now it insisted on replaying every time he and she had ever met—every time he'd counseled her, or chewed her out (though there'd been few of those), or watched her drag what was left of herself home after one of those stupid, gutsy, glorious goddamned attempts to get herself killed in the name of duty, and she'd never been stupid, so why the *hell* had she insisted on *doing* that when she must have known that if she kept going back to the well over and over, sooner or later even the Peeps would get lucky, and—

He jerked his mind out of the well-worn rut, but not before the dull burn of raw anger had boiled up inside him once again. It was stupid—he knew it was—yet he was furious with her for dying, and some deeply irrational part of him blamed her for it . . . and refused to forgive her even now, over eight T-months later.

He sighed and closed his blue eyes as the pain and anger washed back through him yet again, and another part of him sneered contemptuously at his own emotions. Of course he blamed her for it. If he didn't, he'd have to blame *himself*, and he couldn't have that, now could he?

He opened his eyes once more, and his jaw clenched as he made himself face it. He'd known Honor Harrington for nine and a half years, from the day he'd first met her right here in this very system . . . and watched her take a heavy cruiser on a death-ride straight into the broadside of a battlecruiser to defend someone else's planet. For all that time, he'd known she was probably the most outstanding junior officer he had ever met, bar none, yet that was all she'd been to him. Or so he'd thought until that night she stood in the library of Harrington House and jerked him up so short his ears had rung. She'd actually had the gall to tell him his rejection of the Weapons Development Board's new proposals was just as knee-jerk and automatic as the autoresponse pattern in favor of any new proposal which he'd always loathed in the *jeune ecole*. And she'd been right. That was what had hit him so hard. She'd had the nerve to call him on it, and she'd been *right*.

And in the stunned, half-furious moment in which he'd realized that, he'd also looked at her and seen someone else. Someone very different from the outstanding junior officer whose career he had shepherded because it was the responsibility of senior officers to develop the next generation of their replacements. Much as he'd respected her, deeply and genuinely as he'd admired her accomplishments, she'd always been just that: his *junior* officer. Someone to be nurtured and instructed and groomed and developed for higher command. Possibly even someone who would surpass all his own achievements . . . someday.

But that evening in the library, he'd suddenly realized "someday" had come. She'd still technically been his junior—in Manticoran service, at least; her rank in the Grayson Navy had been another matter entirely—but that comfortable sense that there would always be more for him to teach her, more for her to learn from him, had been demolished and he'd seen her as his equal.

And that had killed her.

His jaw muscles ridged and the ice-blue eyes reflected in the clear armorplast burned as he made himself face the truth at last. It was hardly the time or place for it, but he seemed to have made a habit out of picking the wrong times and places to realize things about Honor Harrington, hadn't he? And conveniently timed or not, it was true; it *had* killed her.

He still didn't know what he'd done, how he'd given himself away, but she'd always had that uncanny ability to see inside people's heads. He must have done *something* to give her a peek inside his at the moment all the comfortable professional roles and masks and modes of relationship came unglued for him. It shouldn't have happened. They were both Queen's officers. That should have been all they were to one another, however his perception of her abilities and talents and readiness for high command had changed. But his own awareness had ambushed him, and in that moment of recognition, he'd recognized something else, as well, and seen her not simply as an officer, and his equal, but as a dangerously attractive woman.

And she'd seen it, or guessed it, or felt it somehow. And because she had, she'd gone back on active duty early, which was why her squadron had been sent to Adler, which was how the Peeps had captured her . . . and the only way they could have killed her.

A fresh spasm of white-hot fury went through his misery, and his cursed memory replayed that scene, as well. The falling body, the jerking rope, the creak and sway—

He thrust the image away, but he couldn't push away the self-knowledge he had finally accepted as he stood there in the boat bay gallery, waiting. His awareness of it might have come suddenly, but it shouldn't have. He should have known the way his feelings for her had grown and changed and developed. But it had all taken place so gradually, so far beneath the surface of his thoughts, that he hadn't even guessed it was happening. Or perhaps, if he were totally honest, he'd guessed it all along and suppressed the knowledge as his duty required. But he knew now, and she was dead, and there was no point in lying to himself about it any longer.

Is it something about me? *Something* I *do?* he wondered. *Or is it just the universe's sick joke that makes it the kiss of death for me to love someone? Emily, Honor—*

He snorted bitterly, knowing the thought for self-pity yet unable to reject it just this once. And if he was being maudlin, what the hell business was it of anyone but himself? Damn it, he was entitled to a little maudlinism!

Amber light strings began to blink above the waiting docking buffers, a sure sign the pinnace was on final with the pilot looking for that visual cue, but White Haven didn't even notice. Or perhaps he did, for the blinking lights took him back to that hideous day fifty years before when the supersonic med flight with its strident, eye-shattering emergency lights had delivered his wife's broken and mangled body to the Landing General trauma center. He'd been there to greet the flight, summoned from his office at Admiralty House, but he hadn't been there to prevent the air car accident, now had he? Of course not. He'd had his "duty" and his "responsibilities," and they were both prolong recipients, so they'd had centuries yet to make up for all the time those inescapable concepts had stolen from them.

But he'd been there to see her carried in—to recognize the damage and cringe in horror, for unlike himself, Emily was one of the minority of humanity for whom the regeneration therapies simply did not work. *Like Honor,* a corner of his brain thought now. *Just like Honor—another point in common.* And because they didn't work for her, he'd been terrified.

She'd lived. None of the doctors had really expected her to, even with all of modern medicine's miracles, but they hadn't known her like White Haven knew her. Didn't have the least concept of the dauntless willpower and courage deep within her. But they did know their profession, and they'd been right about one thing. She might have fooled them by living, and again by doing it with her mind unimpaired, yet they'd told him she would never leave her life-support chair again, and for fifty years, she hadn't.

It had almost destroyed him when he realized at last that the doctors were right. He'd fought the idea, rejected it and beaten himself bloody on its jagged, unforgiving harshness. He'd denied it, telling himself that if he only kept looking, if he threw all of his family's wealth into the search, scoured all the universities and teaching hospitals on Old Earth, or Beowulf, or Hamilton, then surely *somewhere* he would find the answer. And he'd tried. Dear *God* how he had *tried.* But he'd failed, for there was no answer; only the life-support chair which had become the lifetime prison for the beautiful, vibrant woman he loved with all his heart and soul. The actress and writer and holo-vid producer, the political analyst and historian whose mind had survived the ruin of her body unscathed. Who understood everything which had happened to her and continued the fight with all the unyielding courage he loved and admired so much, refusing to surrender to the freak cataclysm which had exploded into her life.

The horsewoman and tennis player and grav skier from whose brain stem an artificial shunt ran to her life-support chair's control systems and who, below the neck, aside from that, now had seventy-five percent use of one hand. Period. Total. All there was and all there ever would be again, for as long as she lived.

He'd come apart. He didn't know how Emily had survived his collapse, his guilt, his sense of failure. No one could change what had happened to her or make things "right," but it was his *job* to make things right! It was always anyone's job to make things "right" for the people he or she loved, and he'd failed, and he'd hated himself for it with a bitter virulence whose memory shocked him even now.

But he'd put himself back together again. It hadn't been easy, and he'd needed help, but he'd done it. Of course, it was an accomplishment which had come with a layer of guilt all its own, for he'd turned to Theodosia Kuzak for the help he'd needed. Theodosia had been "safe," for she'd known him literally since boyhood. She was his friend and trusted confidante, and so—briefly—she had become his lover, as well.

He wasn't proud of that, but he'd run out of strength. An Alexander of White Haven understood about duty and responsibility. An Alexander was supposed to be strong, and so was a Queen's officer, and a husband, and he'd tried to be strong for so long, but he just couldn't anymore. And Theodosia had known that. She'd known he had turned to her because he'd had to, and because he could trust her . . . but not because he loved her. Never because of that. And because she was his friend, she'd helped him find the broken bits and pieces of the man he'd always thought he was and glue them back together into something which almost matched his concept of himself. And when she'd reassembled him, she'd shooed him gently away in a gift he knew he could never hope to repay and gone back to being just his friend.

He'd survived, thanks to Theodosia, and he'd discovered something along the way—or perhaps *re*discovered it. The reason for his anguish, the intolerable burden which had broken him at last, was the simplest thing in the world: he loved his wife. He always had, and he always would. Nothing could change that, but that was what had made his agony bite so deep, the reason he couldn't forgive himself for not somehow making things "all right" again . . . and the reason he'd had to turn to someone else to rebuild himself when the collapse came. It had been cowardly of him, in many ways, but he simply could not have made himself dump *his* weakness, *his* collapse on her shoulders while she coped with everything God had already done to her. And so he'd run away to Theodosia until Theodosia could heal him and send him back to Emily once more.

She'd known. He hadn't told her, but he'd never had to, and she'd welcomed him with that smile which could still light up a room . . . still melt his heart within his chest. They'd never discussed it directly, for there'd never been a need to. The information, the knowledge, had been exchanged on some profound inner level, for just as she'd known he had run away, she'd known why . . . and the reason he had come back.

And he'd never run away from her again. There had been a handful of other women over the last forty-odd years. He and Emily were both from aristocratic families and Manticore, the most cosmopolitan of the Star Kingdom's planets, with mores and concepts quite different from those of frontier Gryphon or straitlaced Sphinx. The Star Kingdom had its licensed professional courtesans, but ninety percent of them were to be found on the capital planet, and White Haven had availed himself of their services upon occasion. Emily knew that, just as she knew that all of them had been women he liked and respected but did not love. Not as he loved her. After all these years, it was she with whom he still shared everything except the physical intimacy which they had lost forever. His brief affairs hurt her, he knew—not because she felt betrayed, but because it reminded her of what had been taken from them—and because of that, he was always discreet. He would never let them become public knowledge, never allow even the hint of a possible scandal to expose her to potential humiliation. But he never tried to hide the truth from *her*, for he owed her honesty, and "crippled" or not, she remained one of the strongest people he had ever known . . . and the only woman he loved or had ever loved.

Until now. Until Honor Harrington. Until in some inexplicable fashion, without his ever realizing it, professional respect and admiration had changed somehow, crept inside his guard and ambushed him. However he'd given himself away, revealed at least a little of what he felt, he would never, ever have done anything more than that. But he couldn't lie to himself now that she was dead, and what he'd felt for her had been nothing at all like his friendship for Theodosia or the discreet professionals with whom he'd dealt over the years.

No, it had been far worse than that. It had been as deep and intense—and as sudden—as what he'd first felt for Emily all those decades ago. And so, in a macabre sort of way which no one else in the entire universe would ever realize, he'd betrayed both of the women he'd loved. Whatever he'd felt for Honor hadn't changed the way he felt about Emily; it had been separate from Emily, or perhaps in addition to his love for his wife. Yet letting himself feel it had still been a betrayal that, in many ways, was far, far darker than his affair with Theodosia had ever been. And by letting some hint of his feelings slip, he had driven Honor off to die.

He'd never meant to do either of those things, and even now, he hadn't committed a single intentional act to betray either of them. Indeed, the rest of the universe probably wouldn't even consider that he had, for nothing had ever happened between him and Honor, after all. But *he* knew, and it wounded him deep inside, where his concept of himself lived, in a way his affair with Theodosia never had, for this time he had no excuse. No fresh and bleeding wound which demanded healing. There was only the bewildering knowledge that somehow, without ever meaning to, he had found himself desperately in love with two totally different yet equally magnificent women . . . and that one of them was forever an invalid and the other was dead.

And God how it *hurt*.

The sleek shape of a pinnace appeared suddenly beyond the armorplast, drifting through the silent vacuum towards the buffers, and he sucked in a deep breath and shook himself. He reached up and removed the earbug, dropping it into a pocket, and straightened his tunic as *Benjamin the Great*'s bugler took his place and the honor guard snapped to attention.

The pinnace settled delicately into the buffers, the umbilicals swung up and locked, and the personnel tube ran out to the hatch, and Hamish Alexander, Thirteenth Earl of White Haven, grinned crookedly as he watched the Navy side party muster under the eyes of a harassed, semi-frantic Grayson lieutenant. It wasn't every day that the First Space Lord of the Royal Manticoran Navy and the Chancellor of Her Majesty's Exchequer paid a visit on a neighboring star system in the middle of a shooting war, and *Benjamin the Great*'s crew was determined to get it right.

And so was White Haven. He had that much left, at least, he told himself. The job. His duty. Who he was and what he owed. In that much, he was like Emily and Honor. Neither of them had ever been able to turn their backs on duty, either, had they? So he could at least try to prove himself worthy of the two extraordinary women who meant so much to him, and he gave himself a sharp mental shake.

You do *have a habit of experiencing these moments of personal self-revelation at . . . inopportune moments, don't you, Hamish?* his brain told him mockingly, and the corners of his mouth turned up in a wry, humorless smile.

Many, many years ago, as a fourth-term midshipman, a senior tactical instructor had taken a very young Hamish Alexander aside after a simulator exercise had come unglued. It hadn't been Hamish's fault, not really, but he'd been the Blue Team commander, and he'd felt as if it had been, so Lieutenant Raoul Courvosier had sat him down in his office and looked him straight in the eye.

"There are two things no commander—and no human being—can ever control, Mr. Alexander," Courvosier had said. "You cannot control the decisions of others, and you cannot control the actions of God. An intelligent officer will try to anticipate both of those things and allow for them, but a *wise* officer will not blame himself when God comes along and screws up a perfectly good plan with no warning at all." The lieutenant had leaned back in his own chair and smiled at him. "Get used to it, Mr. Alexander, because if one thing is certain in life, it's that God has a very peculiar sense of humor . . . and an even more peculiar sense of timing."

Raoul, you always did have a way with words, didn't you? Hamish Alexander thought fondly, and stepped forward to greet Sir Thomas Caparelli and his brother as the golden notes of the bugle welcomed them aboard.

Chapter Twenty

"She's a gorgeous ship, Hamish," Lord William Alexander said as Lieutenant Robards, his older brother's Grayson flag lieutenant, ushered them into the admiral's day cabin aboard *Benjamin the Great* at the end of an extended tour. "And this isn't half bad, either," the younger Alexander observed as his eyes took in the huge, palatial compartment.

"No, it isn't," White Haven agreed. "Please, be seated, both of you," he invited, gesturing to the comfortable chairs facing his desk. Robards waited until they'd obeyed and White Haven had seated himself behind the desk, then pressed a com stud.

"Yes?" a soprano voice replied.

"We're back, Chief," the lieutenant said simply.

"Of course, Sir," the intercom said in answer, and another hatch opened almost instantly. This one led to the admiral's steward's pantry, and Senior Chief Steward Tatiana Jamieson stepped through it with a polished silver tray, four crystal wineglasses, and a dusty bottle. She set the tray on the end of White Haven's desk and carefully cracked the wax seal on the bottle, then deftly extracted the old-fashioned cork. She sniffed it, then smiled and poured the deep red wine into all four glasses, handed one to each of White Haven's guests, then to him, and finally to Robards, and then bowed and disappeared as unobtrusively as she'd come.

"So Chief Jamieson is still with you, is she?" William observed, holding his glass up and watching the light glow in its ruby heart. "It's been—what? Fourteen T-years now?"

"She is, and it has," White Haven agreed. "And you can stop hoping to lure her away. She's Navy to the core, and she is *not* interested in a civilian career in charge of your wine cellar." William produced an artfully injured look, and his brother snorted. "And you can stop considering the wine so suspiciously, too. I didn't pick it out; Jamieson selected it personally from a half dozen vintages the Protector sent up."

"Oh, in that case!" William said with a grin, and sipped. His eyes widened in surprised approval, and he took another, deeper sip. "That *is* good," he observed. "And it's a good thing a total ignoramus like you has a keeper like the Chief to watch out for you!"

"Unlike idle civilians, serving officers sometimes find themselves just a little too busy to develop epicurean snobbery to a fine art," the Earl said dryly, and looked at Caparelli. "Would you agree, Sir Thomas?"

"Not on your life, My Lord," the First Space Lord replied instantly, although the corners of his mouth twitched in an almost-grin. Sir Thomas Caparelli had never felt really comfortable with White Haven, and the two of them had never particularly liked one another, but much of their personal friction had been worn away over the last eight or nine years by the far harsher grit of war. There were white streaks in Caparelli's hair now, despite prolong, which had very little to do with age. The crushing responsibility for fighting the war with the PRH had carved new worry lines in his face, as well, and the Earl of White Haven had been his main sword arm against the People's Navy.

"Not a bad strategic decision," White Haven complimented him now, and took a sip from his own glass. Then he set it down and looked up at Lieutenant Robards. "Is Captain Albertson ready for that briefing, Nathan?"

"Yes, My Lord. At your convenience."

"Um." White Haven looked down into his glass for several seconds, then nodded at something no one else could see. "Would you go and tell him that we'll be—oh, another thirty or forty minutes or so?"

"Of course, My Lord." It was a moderately abrupt change in plans, but Robards' brown eyes didn't even flicker at his dismissal. He simply drained his own glass, bowed to his admiral's guests, and vanished almost as unobtrusively as Chief Jamieson had.

"A well-trained young man," William Alexander observed as the hatch closed behind him, then looked at his brother. "May I assume there was a reason you sent him on his way?"

"There was," White Haven agreed. He looked up from his wine and gazed at both his guests. "Actually, there were two, but the more pressing is my feeling that there have to be more reasons for the two of you to come out here than the official communique listed. I also have an unhappy suspicion about what one of those reasons might be. Under the circumstances, I thought I'd clear the decks, as it were, so we could discuss my suspicion from a purely Manticoran viewpoint."

"Ah?" William sipped wine once more, regarded his brother with a half-quizzical, half-wary expression, then crooked an eyebrow, inviting him to continue.

"I've been trying to assemble Eighth Fleet for the better part of a T-year now," White Haven said flatly. "The process was supposed to be complete over nine standard months ago, and I still haven't received the strength my original orders specified. More to the point, perhaps, I have received the units I was promised by Grayson, Erewhon, and the other Allied navies. What I *haven't* seen have been the *Manticoran* units I was promised. I'm still better than two complete battle squadrons—seventeen ships of the wall—short on the RMN side, and nothing I've seen in my dispatches from the Star Kingdom suggests that those ships are going to turn up tomorrow. Should I assume that one reason Allen Summervale sent the second ranking member of his Government and the Admiralty's senior serving officer out here was to explain to myself—and possibly the Protector—just why that is?"

He paused, and Caparelli and William looked at one another, then turned back to him.

"You should," Caparelli said quietly after a moment, "and they aren't. Going to turn up tomorrow I mean, My Lord. We won't have them to send you for at least another two T-months."

"That's too long, My Lord," White Haven said in an equally quiet voice. "We've already waited too long. Have you seen last month's estimates on the Peep strength at Barnett?"

"I have," Caparelli admitted.

"Then you know Theisman's numbers are going up faster than mine are. We're giving them *time*—time to get their feet under them and catch their breath—and we can't afford that. Not with someone like Esther McQueen calling the shots on their side for a change."

"We don't know how free McQueen is to make her own calls," Caparelli pointed out. "Pat Givens is still working on that. Her analysts don't have a lot to go on, but they make it no more than a twenty-five percent chance that the Committee would give any naval officer the authority to build her own strategy. They're still too afraid of a military coup."

"With all due respect, Sir Thomas, Pat is wrong on this one," White Haven replied flatly. "I've fought McQueen, and in my personal opinion, she's the best CO they have left. I think they know that, too, but everything ONI has ever picked up on her has also emphasized her personal ambition. If we know about that, then Saint-Just and State Security know about it, as well. Given that, I can't see the Peeps picking her to head their war office unless they intended all along to give her at the very least a major role in determining their strategy."

"I don't quite see your logic, Ham," William said after a moment.

"Think it through, Willie. If you know someone is a threat to your regime, and you go ahead and put him—or, in this case, her—in a position of power anyway, then you have to have some overriding motive—something which you consider more important than the potential danger she represents. If the Committee of Public Safety called McQueen home and made her Secretary of War, it was because they figured their military situation was so screwed up they needed a professional . . . *even if the professional in question might be tempted to try a coup.*"

White Haven shrugged.

"If they followed that logic, then they'd be not simply fools but *stupid* fools not to make every possible effort to avail themselves of her expertise. And that—" he turned back to Caparelli "—is why giving them this much time is a major, major mistake, Sir."

"I can't fault your reasoning," Caparelli admitted, rubbing a big, weary hand across his face and leaning back in his chair. "Pat's analysts have followed the same trail, and it may be that they're double-thinking themselves into mistakes. They share your opinion as to the reason the Committee recalled her to Haven; they just question whether or not a PRH run by the Committee of Public Safety and the Office of State Security is institutionally *capable* of making use of her expertise. It would require not simply a change but a major upheaval in the entire relationship between their people's commissioners and the officer corps."

"Maybe officially, but it's obvious some of their fleet commanders and commissioners have already made some informal changes," White Haven argued. "Theisman, for example. His tactics at Seabring—and, for that matter, his decision to release their version of the missile pod for use at Adler—all indicate that he, at least, figures he can count on his commissioner to back him up. That's dangerous, Sir. A divided Peep command structure works in our favor; one in which the political and military commanders work together and trust one another is another matter entirely. But the point where McQueen is concerned, is that the Committee may choose to allow an exception—another 'special relationship'—between her and *her* commissioner. Especially since she put down the Levelers for them." He made a face. "I'm not saying that wouldn't come around and bite them on the ass in time, but that doesn't mean they won't try it—especially if the military situation looks bad enough."

"You may be right, Ham," William said, "but there's only so much blood in the turnip. Whatever we'd like, we simply don't have the ships to send you right now. We're trying, but we're tapped out."

"But—" White Haven began, only to stop as Caparelli raised a hand.

"I know what you're going to say, My Lord, but Lord Alexander is right. We simply don't have them. Or, rather, we have too many other commitments and we ran our maintenance cycles too far into the red in the push to get as deep into Peep territory as we are now."

"I see." White Haven sat back, drumming his fingers on the desk in narrow-eyed thought. As a fleet commander, he lacked access to the comprehensive, Navy-wide kind of data Caparelli saw regularly, but the availability numbers must be even worse than he'd thought.

"How bad is it?" he asked after a moment.

"Not good," Caparelli admitted. "As the officer who took Trevor's Star, you must have been aware of how we were deferring regular overhauls on the ships under your command to let you maintain the numbers to capture the system."

He paused, and White Haven nodded. Almost twenty percent of the ships he'd taken into the final engagement had been long overdue for regular maintenance refits . . . and it had shown in their readiness states.

"It hasn't gotten any better," the First Space Lord told him. "In fact, for your private information, we've had no choice but to pull in just over a quarter of our total ships of the wall."

"A *quarter?*" Despite himself, White Haven's surprise showed, and Caparelli nodded grimly. That was seventy-five percent higher than the fifteen percent of Fleet strength which was supposed to be down for refit at any given time.

"A quarter," Caparelli confirmed. "And if we could, I'd have made it thirty percent. We worked the Fleet too hard to get to where we are now, My Lord. We've *got* to take the battle fleet in hand—and not just for routine repairs, either. We've been refitting the new systems and weapons and compensators on an *ad hoc* basis since the war started, but over half our wall of battle units are at least two years behind the technology curve. That's seriously hurting our ability to make full use of the new hardware, especially the compensators, since our squadrons are no longer homogenous. It doesn't do us a lot of good to have three ships in a squadron capable of accelerating at five hundred and eighty gravities if the other five can only pull five-ten! We've got to get all the current upgrades into a higher percentage of the total wall."

"Um." White Haven played with his empty wineglass while his mind raced. The numbers *were* worse than he'd feared, yet he understood Caparelli's logic. And the First Space Lord was right. But he was also wrong. Or, rather, he was running dangerously low on "right" options.

"We're building up our fleet strength as quickly as we can, Ham," William told him, then grimaced. "Of course, that's not as quickly as I'd like. We're beginning to stress the economy pretty hard. I've even got permanent secretaries and undersecretaries in my department talking about a progressive income tax."

"You what?" That brought White Haven upright in his chair once more, and his eyes widened when his brother nodded. "But that's unconstitutional!"

"Not exactly," William said. "The Constitution specifies that any *permanent* income tax must be flat-rated, but it does make provision for temporary adjustments to the rate."

"'Temporary'!" White Haven snorted.

"Temporary," William repeated firmly. "Any progressive taxes have to be enacted with a specific time limit, and they automatically terminate at the time of the first general election after enactment. And they can only be passed with a two-thirds super-majority of both houses in the first place."

"Hmpf!"

"You always were a fiscal conservative, Hamish. And I won't say you're wrong. Hell, *I'm* a fiscal conservative! But we've already quadrupled the transit fees on the Junction and levied special duties on our own merchant shipping, as well—not to mention increasing import duties to a two-hundred-and-fifty-year high. So far, we've managed not to have to rob Peter to pay Paul—or at least not to resort to armed robbery with violence in the process. But without something like a progressive tax, we won't be able to keep that up much longer. We've already had to restrict cost of living increases in government pensions and assistance programs . . . and I'll let you imagine for yourself how Marisa Turner and her bunch reacted to that."

"Not well, I'm sure," White Haven grunted. Then his eyebrows rose. "You're not saying New Kiev went *public* about it, are you?"

"Not directly. She's been more nibbling around the edges—sort of testing the water. The Opposition hasn't come right out and criticized me and Allen over it yet; they're only at the 'we regret the harsh necessity' stage. But I can't guarantee they'll stay there." It was William's turn to snort. "They sure as hell aren't holding their fire on the basis of principle, Ham! They're afraid of what'll happen to them at the polls if they seem to be seeking partisan advantage in the middle of a war."

"Is it really that bad?" White Haven asked anxiously, and this time Caparelli responded before his brother could.

"It is and it isn't, My Lord," he said. "We're doing everything we can at the Admiralty to hold budgets down, and from a purely military perspective, there's lots of slack yet in our industrial capability. The problem Lord Alexander and Duke Cromarty are facing is how we can use that capability without crippling the civilian sector, and even there, we still have quite a lot of slack *in fact*. The problem is that politics is a game of perceptions, and the truth is that we are reaching the point of imposing some real sacrifices on our civilians."

White Haven blinked. The Thomas Caparelli he'd known for three-quarters of a century wouldn't have made that remark, because he wouldn't have understood the fine distinctions it implied. But it seemed his tenure as First Space Lord was stretching his mind in ways White Haven hadn't anticipated.

"Sir Thomas is right," William said before the Earl could follow that thought completely down. "Oh, we're not even close to talking about rationing yet, but we've got a real inflation problem for the first time in a hundred and sixty years, and that's only going to get worse as more and more of our total capacity gets shifted into direct support of the war at the same time as wartime wages put more money into the hands of our consumers. Again, this is for your private information, but I've been in closed-door negotiations with the heads of the major cartels to discuss centralized planning for the economy."

"We already have that," White Haven protested.

"No, we don't. I'm talking about true centralization, Hamish," his brother said very seriously. "Not just planning boards and purely military allocation boards. Complete control of *all* facets of the economy."

"My God, it'll never fly. You'll lose the Crown Loyalists for sure!"

"Maybe, and maybe not," William replied. "They're more fiscally conservative than we are, but remember that the centralization would be under Crown control. That would appeal to their core constituency's litmus test by actually strengthening the power of the Monarch. Where we'd get hurt would be with the independents we might lose, especially in the Lords . . . and the toe in the door it would offer the Liberals and Progressives." He shook his head with a worried frown. "It's definitely not something we're looking forward to, Ham. It's something we're afraid we may not have any choice but to embrace if we're going to make use of the industrial and economic slack Sir Thomas just mentioned."

"I see," White Haven said slowly, and rubbed his lower lip in thought. The Liberals and Progressives had always wanted more government interference in the Star Kingdom's economy, and Cromarty's Centrists had always fought that idea tooth and nail, especially since the People's Republic had begun its slide into fiscal ruin. The Centrists' view had been that a free market encouraged to run itself was the most productive economy available. Too much government tampering with it would be the case of killing the proverbial goose that laid the golden eggs, whereas the very productivity of an unregulated economy meant that even with lower tax *rates*, it would ultimately produce more total tax *revenues* in absolute terms. The Liberals and Progressives, on the other hand, had argued that unregulated capitalism was fundamentally unfair in its allocation of wealth and that it was government's proper function to regulate it and to formulate tax policies to influence the distribution of affluence in ways which would produce a more equitable balance. Intellectually, White Haven supposed both sides had their legitimate arguments. He knew which viewpoint *he* supported, of course, but he had to admit that his own heritage of wealth and power might have a little something to do with that.

Yet whatever one Hamish Alexander might think, Cromarty and William must truly be feeling the pressure to even contemplate unbottling that particular genie. Once the government had established tight centralized control of the economy *for any reason*, dismantling those controls later would be a Herculean task. There were always bureaucratic empire-builders who would fight to the death to maintain their own petty patches of power, and any government could always find places to spend all the money it could get its hands on. But even more to the point, the Liberals and their allies would be able—quite legitimately, in many ways—to argue that if the Star Kingdom had been willing to accept such control to fight a war, then surely it should be willing to accept less draconian peacetime measures in the fight against poverty and deprivation. Unless, that was, the fiscal conservatives wished to argue that it was somehow less moral or worthy to provide its citizens with what they needed when they weren't killing other people?

"We see some other alternatives—and some bright spots on the horizon," William said, breaking into his thoughts. "Don't think it's all doom and gloom from the home front. For one thing, people like the Graysons are taking up a lot more slack than we'd anticipated when the war began. And did you know that Zanzibar and Alizon are about to bring their own shipyards on-line?"

"*Zanzibar* is?" White Haven's eyebrows rose, and his brother nodded.

"Yep. It's sort of a junior version of the Graysons' Blackbird Yard, another joint venture with the Hauptman Cartel. It'll be limited to cruiser and maybe battlecruiser-range construction, at least for the first couple of years, but it'll be top of the line, and the same thing for Alizon. And the Graysons themselves are just phenomenal. Maybe it's because they've already had so many battles fought in their space, or maybe it's simply because their standard of living was so much lower than ours was before the war started, but these people are digging *deep*, Hamish . . . and their civilian economy is still expanding like a house on fire at the same time. I suppose part of the difference is that their civilian sector is still so far short of market saturation, whereas ours—" He shrugged. "And it's not helping a bit that we're still unable to provide the kind of security for our merchant shipping in Silesia that we'd like. Our trade with the Confederation is down by almost twenty-eight percent."

"Are the Andermani picking up what we've lost?" White Haven asked.

"It looks more like it's the Sollies," William said with another shrug. "We're seeing more and more market penetration by them out this way . . . which may help explain why certain elements in the League are willing to export military technology to the Peeps."

"Wonderful." White Haven massaged his temples wearily, then looked back at Caparelli and dragged the conversation back to his original concern. "But the operative point for Eighth Fleet is that it looks like another couple of months before I'll see my other battle squadrons, right?"

"Yes," Caparelli said. "We had to make a choice between you and keeping Trevor's Star up to strength, and, frankly, what happened at Adler is still having repercussions. We're managing to ride them out so far, but the sheer scope of our defeat there has everyone—and especially the smaller members of the Alliance—running more than a little scared. I'm doing my level best to gather back the ships we were forced to disperse in even more penny-packet pickets for political reasons, but Trevor's Star is another matter. If I were the Peeps, that system—and the Junction terminus there—would be absolutely my number one targeting priority, and I have to assume they're at least as smart as I am."

"Um." White Haven considered that, then nodded slowly. If he were Esther McQueen and he had the strength for it, he'd retake Trevor's Star in a heartbeat. Of course, he wasn't Esther McQueen, and so far as he knew, she *didn't* have the strength to retake the system, but he understood why Caparelli was determined to make sure she didn't get the chance. Not that understanding made the implications for his own command area any better.

"All right," he said finally. "I understand what's happening, and I can see why we're where we are on the priorities list. But I hope you and the rest of the Admiralty understand, Sir Thomas, when I say that I'm not trying to set up any sort of preexisting excuses for future failure by saying that I have very deep concerns over our ability to execute our original mission if those ships are delayed for as long as you're suggesting is likely. At the rate they seem to be reinforcing Barnett, what should have given us a very comfortable margin of superiority is likely to provide little more than parity when we actually move. And everything I've seen out of Citizen Admiral Theisman suggests that giving him parity is *not* the way to go about winning a battle."

"I understand, My Lord." Caparelli sighed. "And all we can ask you to do is the best that you can do. I assure you that everyone at the Admiralty understands that, and no one regrets the delay in your buildup more than I do. I'll see what I can do to expedite matters on my return."

"At least the construction rates are still climbing," William observed in the tone of someone looking hard for a silver lining. "And manning requirements should be dropping, if the reports the Exchequer's been getting from BuShips and BuPers hold up."

"That's true enough," Caparelli agreed, "and if Project Anzio—" He cut himself off, then grinned at White Haven. "Let's just say that we've got the possibility for some real force multiplication, My Lord. If the bastards will only give me another four months or so, I think we'll be ready to resume the offensive."

"Remember what Napoleon said about time," White Haven cautioned, and the First Space Lord nodded.

"Point taken, My Lord. But no one's fought a war on this scale in at least three hundred T-years, and even then the *distance* scale was much lower. We're sort of making up the rules for strategic deployments as we go, and so are the Peeps. For that matter, we know what *our* problems are, but let's not make the mistake of assuming the bad guys don't have problems of their own to offset ours."

"Fair enough," White Haven agreed. He tipped his chair back again and sipped wine, frowning as he digested what he'd just been told. His brother watched him for several seconds; then he cleared his throat, and White Haven looked up questioningly.

"You said you had two things you wanted to discuss with us," William reminded him. "Did we already cover the other one, as well?"

"Hm?" White Haven frowned, but then his expression cleared, and he shook his head. "No. No, we didn't actually." He brought his chair back upright and set his wineglass back on the desk. "I wanted to get the official Government impression of the consequences of Ransom's death."

"Ha! You and me both, brother mine," William replied sourly.

"I take it from your response that the whole thing smelled as fishy to you people back home as it did to me?"

"To put it mildly, yes." William glanced at Caparelli, then looked back at his brother. "ONI and Special Intelligence both agree that something about it wasn't kosher, but of *course* they don't agree on what that something was."

White Haven swallowed a snort of laughter at William's expression. The Office of Naval Intelligence and its civilian counterpart had a history of disagreeing with one another, and the turf battles when their areas of expertise intersected could be spectacular.

"Would you care to elaborate on that?" he invited after a moment.

"Well," William leaned back and crossed his legs, "they both agree she must have been dead for some time before the announcement. That 'killed by enemy action while touring the front on Committee business' is pure crap. We know exactly when and where we've knocked out Peep battlecruisers, and none of the dates we have match the one they've given. It's a little more sophisticated than those 'air car accidents' the Peeps' have always favored to explain away disappearances, especially when they've got some reason to want to obscure the exact time they disappeared someone, but it's still a crock, and we know it. As for when she really died, as far as any of our analysts can determine, she hasn't been seen in public in months, and with that as a starting point, we've taken a very close look at the more recent HD imagery of her, as well. At least some of it was faked—and faked very well, I might add—but the earliest example we've been able to positively identify is only a couple of T-months old. She may have been dead longer than that, but we can't be positive."

"At least we know she was alive recently enough to murder Lady

Harrington," Caparelli put in, and the raw, grating anger in his tone snapped White Haven's eyes to him. The earl gazed at his superior for a handful of silent seconds, then nodded without any expression whatever and looked back to his brother.

"Should I take it that the disagreement between ONI and SIS is over the reason the Peeps delayed admitting her death?" he asked.

"You should," William agreed. "SIS thinks she was zapped as part of a personal power struggle between her and Saint-Just or, perhaps, her and the combination of Saint-Just and Pierre. Some of their more . . . creative analysts have actually raised the possibility that she was the senior inside member of the Leveler conspiracy and Saint-Just found out about it and had her popped. I personally find that a little hard to swallow, but it's certainly not impossible, especially when you consider the sort of rhetoric she routinely pumped out. But if that was the case, or if it was simply a case of settling a personal rivalry, the Committee may have wanted to keep it quiet until the winners were confident that they'd IDed—and purged—any of her adherents.

"ONI, on the other hand, is less certain about that. They agree that Ransom was a loose warhead and that deep down inside, at least, Pierre has to be mightily relieved that she's gone. But they don't think it was a *personal* power struggle or that Ransom had anything to do with the Leveler coup attempt. They think it was part of the same process which brought McQueen in as Secretary of War. Everyone knows how bitterly Ransom distrusted the Peep military, and McQueen's reputation for personal ambition would practically make her a poster girl for Ransom's paranoia. So the theory is that Pierre and Saint-Just had decided they absolutely needed a professional to run the military—as you suggested earlier, Hamish—and that McQueen's suppression of the Levelers made her seem an attractive choice . . . to them. But not to Ransom. So either she tried something from the inside to stop the appointment, or else her 'friends' on the Committee figured she might *decide* to try something and chose to play safe by removing her."

William paused and shrugged.

"Either way, the Committee wouldn't have wanted to let the word leak until what they considered the optimum time, hence the delay in announcing her death. As for its supposed circumstances, that's clearly an attempt to paper over whatever intramural conflict led to her removal in the first place and simultaneously gain a little propaganda support for the war. ONI and SIS agree on that, as well, especially given Ransom's continuing popularity with the Mob."

"I see." White Haven rubbed his chin for a moment, then sighed. "I can't say I was sorry to hear about her death," he admitted. *In fact, I was goddamned* delighted *after what she did to Honor!* "But I rather regret the potential consequences." William cocked his head questioningly, and the earl shrugged. "Remember what I said earlier about divided command structures, Willie. Saint-Just and StateSec were only part of the grit in their military machinery, and, frankly, Ransom was a lot bigger problem for them. Whether they recognized that and killed her to remove an obstruction or whether it was purely fortuitous, the fact remains that it's going to make it a hell of a lot easier for McQueen to do whatever she was brought in to do. And that isn't good from our viewpoint."

He brooded pensively down at his blotter for another long moment, then shook himself and climbed out of his chair with a wry smile.

"Well, I suppose that answers my questions, one way or another. But now, gentlemen, my staff and flag captain are waiting to brief you on Eighth Fleet's status. I don't suppose we should keep them waiting any longer than we have to, so if you'll just accompany me?"

He stepped around his desk and led the way from his day cabin.

Chapter Twenty-One

"And that's the lead ship of our new SD class," High Admiral Wesley Matthews told his guests, waving with pardonable pride at the immense, virtually completed hull drifting beyond the armorplast view port. "We've got nine more just like her building as follow-ons," he added, and William Alexander and Sir Thomas Caparelli nodded with deeply impressed expressions.

And well they should be impressed, White Haven thought, standing behind his brother and listening to Matthews' description of the enormous activity going on here in Yeltsin's Star's Blackbird Yard. *Of course, they haven't seen the specs for the class yet, so they don't really know how impressed they* ought *to be,* he reminded himself wryly. *I wonder how Caparelli will react when he does find out?*

The thought came and went, flickering through his brain almost like an automatic reflex without ever diverting his attention from the scene beyond the view port. He'd been here often over the last several months, yet the sights and energy of the place never failed to fascinate him, for Blackbird Yard was totally unlike the Star Kingdom's huge space stations.

For all the relative primitivism of its technology, Grayson had maintained a large-scale space presence for more than half a millennium. Not that it had been anything to boast about in the beginning. They'd had the capability—barely—to exile the losing side of their Civil War to the neighboring system of Endicott, but that was a hop of less than four light-years. Even to accomplish that much had required them to reinvent a cruder form of the Pineau cryogenic process and virtually beggar the war torn planet just to get less than ten thousand "colonists" across the interstellar divide. The strain of it had been almost intolerable for the Civil War's survivors, and it had probably set Grayson's efforts to exploit its own star system back by at least fifty years. Yet it had also been the only way to get the defeated Faithful (and their "doomsday bomb") off the planet, and so Benjamin IV and his government had somehow made it all work.

But that had been six hundred years ago. Since then, and despite ups and downs—and one eighty-year period when the Conclave of Steadholders had been forced to fight bitterly against three Protectors in a row who, with a dogmatism truly worthy of their Neo-Luddite ancestors, had preferred to concentrate on "practical" planet-side solutions to problems and turn their backs on the limitless possibilities of space—the Graysons' off-planet presence had grown prodigiously. By the time their world joined the Manticoran Alliance, the Grayson deep-space infrastructure, while almost all sublight and vastly more primitive than the Star Kingdom's, had actually been almost the size of Manticore-A's, with a far larger work force (almost inevitably, given their manpower-intensive technology base), and they had their own notions about how things should be done.

"Excuse me, High Admiral," Caparelli asked in a suddenly very intense tone, "but is that—?" He was leaning forward, his nose almost pressed against the armorplast, as he pointed at the all but finished hull, and Matthews nodded.

"She's our equivalent of your *Medusa*-class," he confirmed with the broad smile of a proud father.

"But how the devil did you get the design into production this *quickly?*" Caparelli demanded.

"Well, some of our Office of Shipbuilding people were in the Star Kingdom working on the new compensator and LAC projects when the *Medusa* was first contemplated," Matthews said. "Your BuShips involved a couple of them—including Protector Benjamin's brother, Lord Mayhew—in the planning process when they started roughing out the power-to-mass numbers for her impellers and compensator, and they just sort of *stayed* involved. So we had the plans by the same time your people did, and, well—" He shrugged.

"But we only finalized the design thirteen T-months ago!" Caparelli protested.

"Yes, Sir. And we laid this ship down a year ago. She should commission in another two months, and the other nine should all be completed within two or three months of her."

Caparelli started to say something more, then closed his mouth with a click and gave White Haven a fulminating glance. The Earl only smiled back blandly. He'd passed on the information when it came to his attention the better part of nine T-months ago, but it had been evident from several things Caparelli had said that no one had routed a copy of White Haven's report to him. Well, that was hardly the Earl's fault. Besides, the shock of discovering just how far advanced the Grayson Navy really was ought to be good for the First Space Lord, he thought, and returned to his consideration of the differences between Grayson and Manticoran approaches to shipbuilding

The biggest one, he thought as their pinnace drifted closer to the ship Matthews was still describing, was that Grayson yards were far more decentralized. The Star Kingdom preferred putting its building capacity into nodal concentrations with enormous, centralized, and highly sophisticated support structures, but the Graysons preferred to disperse them. No doubt that owed something to the crudity of their pre-Alliance tech base, he mused. Given how incredibly manpower-intensive Grayson shipbuilding had been (by Manticoran standards, at least), it had actually made sense to spread projects out (as long as one didn't get carried away about it) so that one's work force didn't crowd itself. And one thing any star system had plenty of was room in which to spread things out.

But even though the Graysons now had access to modern technology, they showed no particular intention to copy the Manticoran model, and as White Haven could certainly attest from personal experience—not to mention discussions with his brother, who ran the Star Kingdom's Exchequer—there were definite arguments in favor of their approach. For one thing, it was a hell of a lot cheaper, both financially and in terms of start-up time.

The Graysons hadn't bothered with formal slips, space docks, or any of dozens of other things Manticoran shipbuilders took for granted. They just floated the building materials out to the appropriate spot, which in this case was in easy commuting range of one of their huge asteroid mining central processing nodes. Then they built the minimal amount of scaffolding, to hold things together and give their workers something to anchor themselves to, and simply started putting the parts together. It was almost like something from back in the earliest days of the Diaspora, when the colony ships were built in Old Earth or Mars orbit, but it certainly worked.

There were drawbacks, of course. The Graysons had saved an enormous amount on front-end investment, but their efficiency on a man-hour basis was only about eighty percent that of the Star Kingdom's. That might not seem like a very big margin, but considering the billions upon billions of dollars of military construction involved, even small relative amounts added up into enormous totals. And their dispersed capacity was also far more vulnerable to the possibility of a quick Peep pounce on the system. The massive space stations of the Royal Manticoran Navy were at the heart of the Manticore Binary System's fortifications and orbital defenses, with enormous amounts of firepower and—especially—anti-missile capability to protect them. The Blackbird Yard depended entirely upon the protection of the star system's mobile forces, and the incomplete hulls would be hideously vulnerable to anyone who got into range to launch a missile spread in their direction. On the other hand, the Graysons and their allies had thus far successfully kept any Peeps from getting close enough to damage their yards, and the people of Yeltsin's Star were willing to throw an incredible number of workers at the project, which more than compensated for their lower per-man-hour productivity.

"That's an awfully impressive sight, High Admiral," Caparelli said. "And I don't mean just that you've gotten the new design into actual series production while we were still arguing about whether or not to build the thing at all! I'm talking about the sheer activity level out there." He gestured at the view port. "I don't believe I've ever seen that many people working on a single ship at once."

"We almost have to do it that way, Sir Thomas," Matthews replied. "We don't have all the mechanical support you have back in the Star Kingdom, but we do have lots of trained deep space construction crews. In fact, the old-fashioned nature of our pre-Alliance industry actually gives us more trained personnel than we might have had otherwise."

"Oh?" Caparelli turned to raise an eyebrow at me. "Lucien Cortez said something like that to me last week, while I was getting ready to come out here, but I didn't have time to ask him what he meant," the First Space Lord admitted.

"It's simple enough, really," Matthews told him. "Even before the Alliance, we had an enormous commitment to our orbital farms, asteroid extraction industries, and the military presence we needed against those fanatics on Masada. It may not have been all that impressive on the Manticoran scale, but it was certainly more extensive than you'd find in most star systems out this way. But the important point was that we'd put that all together with an industrial base which was *maybe* twenty percent as efficient as yours. Which meant we needed four or five times the manpower to accomplish the same amount of work. But now we're almost up to Manticoran standards, and it's actually easier to train—or *re*train—people to use your hardware than it was to teach them to use ours in the first place. So we took all those people who used to do things the old-fashioned way, trained them to do them the new way, gave them the tools they needed to do it with, and then got out of their way." The High Admiral shrugged. "They took it from there."

"Somehow I don't think it was quite that simple, High Admiral," William Alexander said. "I've certainly had enough experience of the sort of financial strain this level of activity—" he waved a hand at the armorplast "—would entail back home. You've got—what? Three hundred billion Manticoran dollars worth of warships?—building out there, Sir, and this is only one of your yards." He shook his head. "I would dearly love to know how you manage that."

"Actually, we've got closer to *seven* hundred billion dollars worth of tonnage under construction," Matthews said with quiet pride, "and that doesn't even count our ongoing investment in upgrading our orbital forts and expanding our yard facilities and other infrastructure. By the time you put it all together, we probably have something well over a couple of trillion of your dollars worth of construction underway right now, and the new budget just authorized expenditures which should increase that by about fifty percent in the next three T-years."

"My God," Caparelli said quietly. He turned to stare back out the view port for several seconds, then shook his head in turn. "I'm even more impressed than I was a few moments ago, High Admiral. You're talking a good chunk of the Royal Navy's construction budget there."

"I know," Matthews agreed, "and I'm certainly not going to tell you that it's easy, but we do have some offsetting advantages. For one thing, your civilian standard of living and the economic and industrial commitment required to sustain it are much higher than ours." He waved a hand with a crooked smile. "I'm not saying your people are 'softer,' or that ours wouldn't love to have the same standard of living yours do. But the fact is that we never had it before, and we don't have it now. We're working on bringing ours up, but our people understand about making sacrifices to defend themselves—we had enough practice against Masada—and we've deliberately chosen to expand our military capacity at several times the rate at which we've expanded our civilian capacity. Even at the rate of civilian expansion we've allowed, our people's standard of living has gone up by something on the order of thirty percent—that's a planet-wide average—in just the last six years, so we're not hearing a lot of complaints.

"In the meantime," he flashed a smile at Caparelli, "we're actually showing a profit selling warships and components to the Star Kingdom!"

"You are?" Caparelli blinked, then looked sharply at Alexander, who shrugged.

"I haven't looked at the figures lately, Sir Thomas. I do know that whether Grayson is showing a profit or not, *we're* saving something like fifteen percent on the hardware we buy from them."

"I'm sure you are, Lord Alexander," Matthews said. "But when you crank our lower wages into the equation, our production costs are also much lower than yours. In fact, one of the reasons Lady Harrington was able to interest your Hauptman Cartel in investing in Blackbird was to get us more deeply involved in civilian construction, as well." He nodded at the view port again. "You can't see it from here, but over on the other side of the yard, we're building half a dozen *Argonaut*-class freighters for Hauptman. We happen to be building them at cost—as the down payment on a process which will end up allowing Grayson and Sky Domes to buy out Hauptman's share of the yard—but if it works out half as well as we expect it to, we should see orders start to come in from the other cartels over the next T-year or two."

"You're building all this and civilian ships *too?*" Caparelli demanded.

"Why not?" Matthews shrugged. "We're close to the limit of what the government can afford on our current warship programs, but thanks to Hauptman's initial investment—and Lady Harrington's, of course—our total building capacity is considerably higher than that. So we divert some of our labor force to civilian construction and build the ships for about sixty percent of what it would cost to build them in the Star Kingdom—assuming that any of your major builders could find the free yard capacity for them—and then Hauptman gets brand new freighters from us for *eighty* percent of what they would have paid a Manticoran builder. The cartel's actual out-of-pocket cost is only forty percent—the other forty percent goes towards retiring their investment in the yard—but that's enough to cover Blackbird's actual expenses, since the Sword has exempted the transaction from taxes in order to accelerate the buy-out. Meanwhile, the workers' wages go into the system economy, and everyone's happy."

"Except, perhaps, the Manticoran builders who *aren't* building the ships," Alexander observed in slightly frosty tones.

"My Lord, if you could find the free civilian building slips back home, then you might have a point," Matthews said without apology.

"He's got you there, Willie," White Haven observed with a smile. "Besides, isn't it still Her Majesty's Government's policy to help 'grow' Grayson industrial capacity?"

"Yes. Yes, it is," Alexander said after a moment. "If I sounded as if I meant otherwise, I apologize, High Admiral. You simply surprised me."

"We know how much we owe the Star Kingdom, Lord Alexander," Matthews said seriously, "and we have no desire whatsoever to gouge you or suck your financial blood. But our economic starting point was so far behind yours that it provides us with opportunities we'd be fools not to exploit. And for the foreseeable future, it works in both of our favors. The volume of our interstellar trade has risen by several thousand percent in less than a decade, which has produced a boom economy for us despite the cost of the war effort. At the same time, and even allowing for all the loans and trade incentives your government extended to us at the time of the Alliance, you're actually saving money by buying ships and components from us. And speaking strictly for the Grayson Navy," the high admiral's grin bared even white teeth, "I'd like to think that our increased presence adds a little something to the military security of both our nations."

"I'd say there's not much doubt of that, at any rate," White Haven observed, and both Alexander and Caparelli nodded in grave agreement.

And, the Earl thought, *it doesn't even mention things—like the new inertial compensators and the fission piles for the new LACs—which we would never have had without the Graysons. Or the way their habit of charging ahead with things like their own* Medusas *keep pushing us a little harder than we'd push ourselves. No,* he folded his hands behind him and gazed at the enormous superdreadnought, now less than ten kilometers away, *it doesn't matter* how *much we've invested in Yeltsin's Star. Whatever the final total, we've already gotten one hell of a lot more than our money's worth back on it!*

William Alexander had seen entirely too many formal dinners in his life. Unlike his older brother, he actually enjoyed social events, but formal dinners like this one were too much a part of his everyday political life even for him. Most of the time they were just business, about as exciting and enjoyable as a sprained ankle.

But this one was different. It was the first Grayson state dinner he had ever attended, and he was one of the honored guests rather than one of the anxious hosts. That would have been an enormous relief all by itself, but the Graysons' welcome was also genuine and heartfelt. And the dinner gave him a chance to sit here and think about all he'd seen and discovered over the last two days. There was more than enough new information to make his head spin, but he was devoutly grateful that he'd come, and not just to serve as the Prime Minister's personal spokesman when it came to explaining the delay in building up Eighth Fleet. No, he'd learned things from this trip that he could never have learned sitting home on Manticore, and that would have been ample justification for the journey all by itself.

It was odd, he reflected, how many of the Star Kingdom's leaders—himself included, at times—tended to think of Grayson as an immature society still suffering from the barbarism of youth. His tour of the Blackbird Yard had begun undermining that perception in his own mind, but that had been only the start. The whirlwind tour of half a dozen Grayson ships High Admiral Matthews had arranged for Caparelli and himself, the tour of the brand new schools upon which Katherine Mayhew had conducted him, and his intensive conferences with Lord Prestwick and the rest of the Protector's Council had hammered home the fact that whatever else these people were, they were neither crude nor unsophisticated. And here in the planetary capital of Austin, with its ancient stonework and narrow streets, the illusion of a "young" society was particularly hard to sustain.

Unlike many colony worlds, the Star Kingdom had never experienced a neo-barbarian period. Its colonists had picked up exactly where they'd left off, as members of a technic society. Indeed, thanks to the farsighted investments of Roger Winton and the original leaders of the Manticoran expedition who'd set up the Manticore Colony Trust back on Old Earth, they'd actually found instructors waiting for them to bring them up to speed on all the advances humanity had made during the six hundred years of their cryogenic voyage. Not even the Plague of 1454 had seriously shaken their grip on technology—or their fundamental confidence that they were in control of their own destinies.

But Grayson *had* experienced neo-barbarianism. It had been smashed back to its bedrock and begun all over again, and that experience had left its people a legacy of awareness. Unlike their Manticoran allies, the Graysons' ancestors had been forced to confront and resolve the fundamental clash between what they had thought was true and what actually *was* true, and in the process they had developed a mindset in which the question genuinely was the answer. And that, Alexander told himself, was scarcely the mark of "youthful barbarism." The Grayson answers to the questions of how to build a society had been different from those of the Star Kingdom, yet unlike Manticorans, the Graysons, by and large, were willing to go on asking and examining, and Alexander found that a humbling thought. Manticorans seldom really questioned where they were going as a culture, or why. They might argue about their course—as, for example, in the endless, bitter ideological disputes between his own Centrists and Countess New Kiev's Liberals—but that was because both sides were already confident they knew the answers . . . and each was convinced the other didn't. There was a certain smugness (and shallowness) about that narrowly focused certainty and dismissal of any opposing viewpoint, and for all the caricatures some Manticorans drew of Graysons, few of Benjamin Mayhew's subjects could ever be called "smug."

That was even more surprising to Alexander when he reflected that the human civilization on this planet was twice as old as that of the Star Kingdom, and that age showed in the sense of antiquity which clung to the older portions of Benjamin's capital. The narrow streets of the Old Quarter, built to accommodate animal-drawn carts and wagons, and the half-ruinous walls of fortifications built to resist black powder and battering rams still stood in mute testimony to the battle this planet had fought to claw its way back from the brink of extinction to where it now stood, and it had waged that epic struggle all alone. No one had even known its people were here to help—assuming anyone could have been bothered to help them anyway. No doubt that was largely what produced that impression of towering conservatism on casual observers who only skimmed the surface. This planet had found its own answers, developed its own highly distinctive identity without interacting with the interstellar template of the rest of humanity . . . and in a way that no one from the Star Kingdom would ever understand without coming here and seeing it, it was *Grayson* which was the elder partner in the Alliance.

He sat back in his chair and sipped iced tea while he looked around the huge formal setting of the Old Palace's Great Hall. Iced tea was uncommon in the Star Kingdom, where the beverage was usually served hot, but it was a Grayson staple, and he found the flavor added by the sugar and twist of lemon intriguing. It had serious potential as a summer drink back home, he decided, and made a mental note to introduce it at his next political dinner.

But the note was an absent one, and he felt the antiquity of Grayson yet again as he let his eyes wander up the banners hanging from the ceiling. The Great Hall lay at the very heart of the Old Palace, a sprawling stone structure dating from just after the Civil War, built for a warrior king named Benjamin IV. The Civil War had been fought with the weapons of an industrial age, however crude and primitive the tanks and napalm and first-generation nukes of the time might seem by modern standards, but the Old Palace had followed the architectural traditions of an earlier age. In no small part, Alexander suspected, that had stemmed from Benjamin the Great's determination to drive home the lesson that the Sword now ruled—and no longer as first among equals. Like his new Constitution, his palace had been intended to make the Sword's primacy crystal clear, and so he had built a huge, brooding pile of stone whose grim face reflected the iron power of his rule and whose sheer size overwhelmed anything a "mere" steadholder might call home.

He'd overdone it just a bit, Alexander mused. In fairness, expecting a man who had already demonstrated his genius as a warrior, a strategist, a politician, a theologian, and a law-giver to also be a genius in matters architectural would probably have been a bit much, but this hulking stone maze must have been an eye-catching archaism even when it was brand new. And that had been six hundred years ago.

Is it possible Benjamin and Gustav Anderman were both *just a little confused about which age they really lived in?* he wondered. *After all, Anderman thought he was what's-his-name—Frederick the Great, reincarnated—didn't he? I wonder who Benjamin thought* he *was?*

But whoever or whenever Benjamin had thought he was, or the fact that his palace had been modernized several times in the last six centuries—and despite the fact that the Mayhew family had moved delightedly to the much younger Protector's Palace next door sixty years ago—the Old Palace was still older than the entire Star Kingdom of Manticore . . . and its harsh fortress skeleton still showed unyieldingly. The banquet hall's roof towered three stories above the marble-flagged floor, with square-cut rafters a meter on a side and blackened with time. Some of the banners which hung from those rafters were all but impossible to identify, their bright embroidery smoothed away and obliterated by time, but he knew the one which hung directly over Benjamin IX's high seat. Its device was hard to make out, yet it hardly mattered. Benjamin the Great had personally ordered the standard of the vanished Steading of Bancroft hung over his chair here in the Great Hall, and there the trophy had stayed for six hundred T-years.

Yet for all its age, the Great Hall was also strangely modern, with state-of-the-art lighting, central heat (and air conditioning), and air filtration systems which would have done any space habitat proud. And the people sitting at the tables presented an equally odd mixture of the ancient and the modern. The women looked right at home in the Great Hall—like something out of a historical documentary in their elaborately embroidered, tabard-like vests, floor-length gowns, and elaborately coiffured hair—and the men in formal Grayson attire looked almost equally archaic. Alexander had no idea why any society would preserve the "neckties" the men wore (he understood they had gone out of fashion several times over the planet's history; what he didn't understand was why in Heaven's name they'd ever come back *into* fashion again), but it certainly made the Manticorans and other off-worlders scattered through the crowd stand out. Yet here and there among the Graysons were islands which appeared less anachronistic to his Manticoran eyes. Many of the women, including both of the Protector's wives, wore far simpler gowns which Alexander's well-trained fashion sense realized were modeled on those Honor Harrington had introduced. And some of the men had abandoned Grayson attire for more modern garb, as well.

But what really caught the eye was the sheer number of men who wore military uniform of one sort or another . . . and how much smaller the percentage of women in uniform was. Environmental factors had frozen Grayson's population for centuries, but it had been increasing steadily for the last fifty or sixty T-years, and the curve of population growth had shot up sharply in the last decade. By now, the planet's total population was somewhere in the very near vicinity of three billion, which came close to matching that of all three of the Star Kingdom's planets. But given the peculiarities of Grayson birthrates, only about seven hundred and fifty million of those people were male. Which, coupled with the social mores which had banned women from military service ever since the planet's initial colonization, gave Grayson a military manpower pool barely a quarter as big as the Star Kingdom's. Actually, given the impact of prolong on Manticoran society and the higher resulting percentage of its total population which were adults, the differential was almost certainly even higher than that. But it still meant that a far, far higher percentage of Grayson's men were members of the ever-expanding Grayson military.

And at the moment, every one of them seemed to be sitting in the Great Hall for dinner.

It gave Grayson rather a different perspective on the Havenite Wars, Alexander reflected. High Admiral Matthews had touched on it several times during his guided tour of Blackbird, yet it was something else Alexander hadn't adequately considered before this trip. He should have, for Hamish had certainly alluded to it frequently enough, but it was another of those things someone had to see and feel for himself before his mind made the leap to understanding.

The Star Kingdom had spent a half century prior to the outbreak of hostilities building up its navy and alliances against the day of reckoning which had to come. Manticore had approached the battle against the PRH with a long-term wariness, a sense of the inevitable (though some Manticorans—and Alexander could name a few from certain prominent political circles—had done their level best to hide from the truth), which was actually almost a disadvantage, in an odd sort of way, once the shooting started. It was as if certain chunks of the Manticoran public felt that all the time and effort and money they had invested in getting ready for the war should somehow have gone into a metaphysical savings account as a sort of down payment which would somehow excuse them from making still more investment in actually fighting the war now that it had begun. They weren't *tired*, precisely. Not "war weary"—not really, and not yet—but they seemed . . . disappointed. They'd spent all that time getting ready to resist the sort of lightning campaign Haven had used to smash all of its previous opponents, and they'd expected the same sort of quick decision, one way or the other, as in all those earlier campaigns.

But it hadn't worked that way. Alexander and Allen Summervale had known it wouldn't be a short, quick war—not if they were lucky enough to survive at all—as had their monarch and the military, and they'd done their best to prepare the public for the reality of an extended struggle. Yet they'd failed. Or perhaps it was more accurate to say that they hadn't succeeded completely. There *were* people out there who understood, after all, and Alexander suspected the numbers were growing. But that sense that the war should have been over by now, especially with the Royal Navy and its allies smashing Peep fleet after Peep fleet, worried him. It was an unformed groundswell at this point, but William Alexander had been in politics for sixty T-years, and he had developed the discerning eye of a skilled navigator. There was a potential storm out there on the horizon, and he wondered just how well the ship he'd spent six decades helping to build would weather it if—or when—it broke.

But Graysons saw things differently. They'd come to the Havenite wars late . . . yet they'd spent the last six centuries preparing for—and fighting—another war. Looking back, one might call the crushing defeat Honor Harrington and Alexander's older brother had handed the Masadan descendants of the Faithful the true first shot of the current war. But for Grayson, it had been only a transition, a turn from confronting one enemy to confronting another. They knew all about long wars, and they were no more concerned by the potential length of this one than they had been over the interminable duration of the last. It would take however long it took . . . and Grayson was grimly determined to be there until the very end.

And that determination was producing some changes in Grayson society which would have been flatly denounced even as little as five years earlier. There were still no Grayson women in uniform, but the military women "on loan" to the GSN from the RMN and serving in other navies were steadily grinding away that particular prohibition. And Grayson women were beginning to enter the *civilian* labor force in unprecedented numbers. Alexander and Admiral Caparelli had been astonished to discover that over fifteen percent of Blackbird's clerical and junior management staff were women, only a handful of them from out-system. Even more startling, there had been a few women—just a tiny percentage so far, but growing—on the engineering staff, as well. Some of them were actually on the construction gangs! Alexander had no idea who the "Rosie the Riveter" his historian older brother had referred to might have been, but he'd been stunned to see *Grayson women* being allowed into such all-male roles.

Yet the fact was that Grayson had no choice. If it was going to man its military—and "man" was precisely the right term, William thought with a wry, hidden grin—then it had to free up the required manpower somehow. And the only way to do that was to begin making rational use of the enormous potential its women represented. Before the Alliance, that would have been unthinkable; now it was only very difficult, and mere difficulty had never stopped a Grayson yet.

The manpower shortage also explained why Grayson had leapt joyfully at the potential for increased automation aboard warships which the RMN's own Bureau of Ships had found it so monumentally difficult to force through its own ranks. (*I suppose we're just as "traditional" as the Graysons,* Alexander reflected. *Our traditions are simply . . . different. They're certainly not any less bullheaded—or stupid.*) The Royal Navy was still building experimental prototypes to test the new concept, but the GSN had already incorporated it into all their new construction . . . including the new ten-ship superdreadnought class under construction at Blackbird. High Admiral Matthews had been so busy rhapsodizing about how that would reduce the strain where his manning requirements were concerned that he'd completely missed the glance Alexander and Caparelli had exchanged.

Not enough that they're going to have our *new ship of the wall concept in commission at least a full T-year before we do, they had to go ahead and build the new automation into them, too! God, that's embarrassing. Still,* he felt his lips quirk, *maybe if Sir Thomas and I go home and emphasize how "primitive, backward" Grayson is racing ahead of us, we'll be able to get some of our sticks-in-the-mud to get up off their collective asses and authorize* us *to build a few of them, too.*

Unless, of course, they decide that it only makes sense to let the Graysons test the concept in action before we ante up the cash for such "radical, untried, and ill-considered" innovations!

He snorted and reminded himself that he was only the Star

Kingdom's accountant, not a lord of admiralty. He was a civilian, and as such, he should be concentrating on other matters and leaving military concerns up to Hamish and Sir Thomas.

He took another sip of tea and let his eyes travel around the Great Hall again. As a male visitor unaccompanied by any wife, he had been seated at an exclusively male-occupied table just below the Protector's raised dais. The elderly general (actually, he was probably younger than Alexander was, but without the benefits of prolong) seated beside him was more interested in his dinner than in making conversation with foreigners, and Alexander was just as happy. They'd exchanged the proper small talk before the meal began, and then the two of them had ignored one another—in a companionable sort of way—while they addressed the truly delicious dinner. Alexander made a mental note to see if he couldn't extort the Protector's chef's recipe book out of Benjamin at their last formal meeting tomorrow. He was used to the way his older brother twitted him on his "epicureanism," and he couldn't really complain. Hamish was right, after all . . . but just because *he* was an uncultured barbarian who considered anything more complex than a rare steak and a baked potato decadent was no reason for William to reject the finer things in life.

He chuckled to himself and glanced at his brother. White Haven was seated with High Admiral Matthews at the Protector's own table—a mark of the high esteem in which the conqueror of Masada was held here in Grayson. At the moment, his head was turned as he addressed a remark to the exquisitely beautiful woman seated with her towering husband between himself and Katherine Mayhew. Alexander had been introduced to both Doctors Harrington the day before, and he'd been astonished to realize that someone Lady Harrington's size could have had so tiny a mother. And, he admitted, as he chatted with her and discovered the razor-sharp wit of the woman behind that beautiful face, he'd found himself extremely envious of Dr. Alfred Harrington's good fortune.

The general beside him said something, drawing his attention back to his tablemate. But before he could ask the Grayson to repeat his question, the crystal clear sound of a fork or a spoon striking a wineglass cut through the background hum of voices. Alexander's head turned, along with everyone else's, and all other conversation faded as the diners realized Benjamin Mayhew had risen to his feet. He smiled at them, waiting until he was certain he had their full intention, and then cleared his throat.

"My Lords and Ladies, Ladies and Gentlemen," he said then, in the easy tones of a trained speaker, "you were all promised that this would be a 'nonworking state dinner'—meaning that you'd all be spared the tedium of speeches—" that earned him a rumble of laughter, and his smile grew broader "—and I promise not to inflict anything of the sort upon you. I do, however, have two announcements which I believe should be made at this time."

He paused, and his smile faded into a sober, serious expression. "First," he said, "High Admiral Matthews has informed me that the Office of Shipbuilding has elected to name the newest superdreadnought of the Grayson Navy the GNS *Honor Harrington*, and that Lady Harrington's mother," he bowed slightly in Allison Harrington's direction, "has agreed to christen her in our service."

He paused, as a spatter of applause interrupted. It grew louder, and Alexander turned his head to see several men in GSN uniform come to their feet. Other male Graysons joined them, and then women began to stand, as well, and the spatter of applause became a torrent that echoed and resounded from the Great Hall's cavernous spaces. The thunder beat in on William Alexander, and he felt himself coming to his own feet, joining the ovation. Yet even as he clapped, he felt something else under the approval. A hungry something, with bare fangs, that sent a chill through him as he realized how accurately Hamish had read these people's reaction to Honor Harrington's murder.

Benjamin waited until the applause slowly faded and the audience had resumed their seats, and then he smiled again. Despite the harsh wave of emotion which had just swept the hall, there was something almost impish about that smile, and he shook his head.

"You should have waited," he told his audience. "Now you're going to have to do it all over again, because my second announcement is that yesterday morning, Lady Allison Harrington informed my senior wife that she and her husband are expecting." That simple sentence spawned a sudden silence in which a falling pin would have sounded like an anvil, and he nodded much more seriously. "Tomorrow, I will formally inform the Conclave of Steadholders that an heir of Lady Harrington's blood will inherit her Key and the care of the people of her steading," he said quietly.

The previous applause, Alexander discovered, had only seemed thunderous. The ovation which arose this time truly was. It battered him like fists, surging like an exultant sea, and he saw Allison Harrington flush, whether with excitement or embarrassment he couldn't tell, as she stood at the Protector's urging.

It took a seeming eternity for the applause to fade, and as it did, Alexander saw someone else stand at the Protector's table. The wiry, auburn-haired man looked remarkably young to be wearing the uniform of a GSN admiral, and his gray eyes flashed as he faced his ruler.

"Your Grace!" he cried, and Benjamin turned to look at him.

"Yes, Admiral Yanakov?" the Protector seemed surprised at hearing the admiral address him.

"With your permission, Your Grace, I would like to propose a toast," Admiral Yanakov said. Benjamin considered him for just a moment, and then nodded.

"Of course, Admiral."

"Thank you, Your Grace." Yanakov reached down and picked up

his wineglass, holding it before him while the light pooled and glowed in its tawny heart.

"Your Grace, My Lords and Ladies, Ladies and Gentlemen all," he announced in a ringing voice, "I give you Steadholder Harrington . . . *and damnation to the Peeps!*"

The roar which answered should, by rights, have brought the Great Hall crashing down in ruins..

Book Four

Chapter Twenty-Two

"Do you think we'll get the break this month?" Scotty Tremaine asked as he used a brightly colored bandana to mop irritably at the sweat trickling down his face. He tried to keep any trace of anxiety out of his voice, but his audience knew him too well to be fooled.

"Now how would I know that, Sir?" Horace Harkness asked in reply, and his tone, while utterly respectful, managed to project so much patience that Tremaine grinned despite himself.

"Sorry, Chief." He shoved the bandana into the hip pocket of his trousers—no longer StateSec issue, but produced, like the bandana, by Henri Dessouix, who functioned as Camp Inferno's chief tailor—and shrugged. "It's just that all the waiting around is getting to me. And when you add things like *this* to the waiting . . . Well, let's just say my nerves aren't what they used to be."

"Mine either, Sir," the senior chief said absently, then grunted in triumph as the jammed access panel he'd been working on sprang open at last. "Light, Sir?" he requested, and Tremaine directed the beam of his hand lamp up into the shuttle's number one communications bay.

"Hmmm . . ." Like Tremaine, Harkness now wore locally produced clothing, and he obviously favored the same garish colors Dessouix did. In fairness, Dessouix was limited in his choice of dyes by what grew within a reasonable distance from Camp Inferno, but he did seem to enjoy mugging people's optic nerves. So did Harkness, apparently, and he looked more like an HD writer's concept of a pirate than a senior chief petty officer of Her Majesty's Royal Manticoran Navy—especially with the pulser and bush knife he insisted on carrying everywhere with him—as he frowned up into the small, electronics-packed compartment.

Peep installations tended to be bigger than Manticoran ones, largely because they used more plug-in/pull-out components. Peep techs weren't up to the sort of in-place maintenance Manticoran technicians routinely performed, so the practice, wherever possible, was to simply yank a malfunctioning component and send it to some central servicing depot where properly trained people could deal with it. Unhappily for the People's Navy, that assumed one had a replacement unit handy to plug into its place when you pulled it, and that had been a major reason for the soaring Peep unserviceability rates of the first two or three years of the war. The PN had been structured around short, intensive campaigns with plenty of time to refit between gobbling up each successive bite of someone else's real estate. Their logistics pipeline had been designed to meet those needs, and it simply hadn't been up to hauling the requisite number of replacement components back and forth between the front-line systems and the rear area service and maintenance depots over an extended period of active operations.

That, unfortunately, was one problem they seemed to be getting on top of, Tremaine reflected while he watched Harkness pull out a test kit and begin checking circuits. They were finally getting their logistics establishment up to something approaching Allied standards, and—

"Uh-oh." Harkness' mutter pulled Tremaine out of his thoughts and he peered up past the burly senior chief's shoulders. "Looks like we've got us a little problem in the transponder itself, Sir."

"How big a 'little problem'?" Tremaine demanded tersely.

"All I can tell you for certain right this minute is that it ain't working, Sir," Harkness replied. "I won't know more till we pull it, but between you and me, it don't look real good. The problem's in the encryption module." He tapped the component in question and shrugged. "This here's an almost solid cube of molycircs, and I didn't see no molecular electronics shop aboard either of these two birds."

"Damn," Tremaine said softly. "I don't think Lady Harrington is going to like this."

"Is the Chief sure, Scotty?" Honor Harrington asked that evening. She and Alistair McKeon sat with Commodore Ramirez and Captain Benson in Ramirez' hut, and the insect equivalents of Hell's ecology buzzed and whined as they battered themselves with typical buggish obstinacy against the vegetable-oil lamps hanging overhead.

"I'm afraid so, Ma'am," Tremaine replied. "The molycircs themselves are gone, and we don't have a replacement crypto component. He and Chief Ascher are trying to cobble something up from the com gear, but there're all kinds of system incompatibilities. Even if they manage to jury-rig a short-term fix, it won't exactly be what I'd call reliable." He shook his head. "Sorry, Ma'am, but it looks like Shuttle Two's IFF beacon is down for good."

"Damn," McKeon muttered. Honor glanced at him, then looked back at Tremaine.

"Have he and Chief Barstow checked Number One's beacon?"

"Yes, Ma'am. It seems to be fine," Tremaine said, very carefully not stressing the verb or adding *so far* to his reply. Honor heard it anyway, and the living side of her mouth quirked wryly.

"Well, go on back to them, please, and tell them I know they'll do their best for us," she said.

"Yes, Ma'am." Tremaine saluted and turned to leave, and she laughed.

"In the morning will be soon enough, Scotty! Don't go wandering around the woods in the dark—you might get eaten by a bearcat!"

"Drop by my hut, Commander," Harriet Benson put in. After two months of practice, most of Honor's people could follow her slurred speech now without too much difficulty. "Henri and I'll be glad to put you up tonight. Besides, he's been thinking about that last move of yours," she went on when Tremaine glanced at her. "He and Commander Caslet think they've found a way to get out of it after all."

Honor hid a small grimace at Benson's remark. None of the inmates of Inferno ever attached the "Citizen" to the front of Warner Caslet's rank title. None of them were particularly comfortable about having a Peep naval officer in their midst, but they weren't as *un*comfortable about it as Honor had feared they would be, either. Apparently there were enough Legislaturalist ex-officers scattered among Hell's political prisoners for the regular POWs to have developed a live-and-let-live attitude. Indeed, Honor suspected that their term for StateSec personnel—"Black Leg"—had evolved as much as a way to differentiate between the real enemy and Peeps who were fellow inmates as from the black trousers of the SS uniform. Not that Inferno's inhabitants intended to take any chances with Caslet. Everyone had been quite polite to him, especially after Honor's people had had a chance to take them aside and explain how this particular Peep came to be on Hell, but they kept an eye on him. And there was a specific reason he'd been assigned to the hut Benson and Dessouix shared.

"So they're ganging up on me now, are they, Ma'am?" Tremaine asked Benson with a grin, unaware of his CO's thoughts. "Well, they're wrong. I bet I know what they've thought up, and it's still mate in six!"

"Try not to hurt their feelings too badly, Scotty," Honor advised. "I understand Lieutenant Dessouix is quite proficient at unarmed combat." Which, of course, was one of the main reasons Caslet roomed with him.

"Ha! If he doesn't want his feelings hurt, he shouldn't have whupped up on me like that in the *first* two games, Ma'am!" Tremaine retorted with a twinkle, then saluted his superiors and disappeared into the night.

"An entertaining young fellow," Ramirez noted in his deep, rumbling voice, and Nimitz bleeked in amused agreement from his place on the hand-hewn plank table. Benson reached out and rubbed him between the ears, and he pressed back against her touch with a buzzing purr.

"He is that," Honor agreed, watching Benson pet Nimitz.

The 'cat had set about captivating Camp Inferno's inmates with all his customary skill, and he had every one of them wrapped around his thumb by now. Not that he hadn't had more reasons than usual for being his charming self. The seduction process had given him—and Honor—the opportunity to sample the emotions of every human being in the camp. A few of them were hanging on the ragged edge, with a dangerous degree of instability after their endless, hopeless years on Hell, and she had quietly discussed her concerns about those people with Ramirez and Benson, but only one of Inferno's six hundred and twelve inhabitants had been a genuine security risk.

Honor had been dumbfounded to discover that the Peeps really had planted an agent in Inferno, and the other inmates had been even more shocked than she. The man in question had been their resident expert on how to spin and weave the local equivalent of flax to provide the fabric Dessouix and his two assistants used to clothe the inmates. That had made him a vital cog in the camp's small, survival-oriented economy, and almost all of the other prisoners had regarded him as a personal friend, as well. The thought that he was actually a StateSec agent planted to betray their trust had been more than enough to produce a murderous fury in his fellow prisoners.

Only he hadn't actually been an "agent" at all; he was simply an informer. It was a subtle difference, but it had kept Ramirez from ordering (or allowing) his execution when, acting on Honor's suggestion, Benson and Dessouix found the short-range com set hidden in his mattress. Had they failed to find it before the next food drop brought a shuttle into his com range, a single short report from him would have killed them all, and they knew it. But they'd also discovered why he'd become a StateSec agent, and it was hard to fault a man for agreeing to do *anything* which might save his lover from execution.

So instead of killing him, they'd simply taken away his com set and detailed half a dozen others to keep an eye on him. All things taken together, Honor was just as glad it had worked out that way. Whatever else he might have been, too many of the camp inmates had considered him a friend for too many years, and things were going to be ugly enough without having to begin killing their own.

"—on Basilisk Station?"

She blinked and looked up as she realized McKeon had been speaking to her.

"Sorry, Alistair. I was thinking about something else," she apologized. "What did you say?"

"I asked if you remembered what a puppy Scotty was at Basilisk,"

McKeon said, then grinned at Ramirez and Benson. "He meant well, but *lord* was he green!"

"And he was also—what? A couple of hundred thousand richer by the end of the deployment?" Honor shot back with a half-grin of her own.

"At least," McKeon agreed. "He had a real nose for spotting contraband," he explained to the other two. "Made him very popular with his crewmates when the Admiralty started handing out the prize money."

"I imagine it would!" Benson laughed.

"But he's a levelheaded young man, too," Honor said, and her grin faded as she remembered a time that "levelheaded young man" had saved her career.

"I can believe that, too," Benson said. She glanced at Honor as if she'd caught a hint of what had been left unspoken, but she chose not to push for more. Instead, she shook herself, and her expression became much more serious. "How badly is this likely to affect our plans?"

"If nothing happens to Shuttle One's beacon, it won't affect them at all," Honor replied. She held out her hand to Nimitz, and the 'cat rose and limped over to her. She lifted him down into her lap and leaned back, holding him to her chest while her good eye met the gazes of her three senior subordinates. "We were always going to have to task one of the shuttles to deal with the courier boat," she reminded them, "and an IFF beacon won't matter one way or the other for that part of the operation."

"And if something does happen to Shuttle One's beacon?" McKeon asked quietly.

"In that case, we either figure out how to take a supply shuttle intact, or else we abandon Lunch Basket entirely and go for a more direct approach," Honor replied, equally quietly, and the living side of her face was grim.

None of her listeners cared for that, yet none of them disagreed, either. For all its complexity, "Operation Lunch Basket," as Honor had decided to christen her ops plan, offered their best chance of success, and they all knew it. In fact, it was probably their *only* real chance. Trying any of the fallback plans was far more likely to get them killed than get them off Hell, but no one mentioned that either. After all, getting themselves killed trying was better than staying on Hell.

"In that case," McKeon said after a moment, "I guess we'd better just concentrate on not having anything happen to One's beacon." His tone was so droll Honor chuckled almost despite herself and shook her head at him.

"I'd say that sounds like a reasonable thing to do," she agreed. "Of course, exactly how we do it is an interesting question."

"Shoot, Honor—that's *simple!*" McKeon told her with a grin. "We just sick Fritz on it. He'll set up one of his famous preventive care programs, prescribe a little exercise, schedule it for regular office visits, and we'll be home free!"

This time Ramirez and Benson joined Honor's laughter. Fritz Montoya had already proved worth his weight in anything anyone would have cared to name to Camp Inferno. Relatively few medical officers got sent to Hell, and of those who had been sent there, none had been further exiled to Inferno. For the most part, the local germs tended to leave the indigestible human interlopers alone, but there were a few indigenous diseases which were as stubbornly persistent in attacking them as shuttlesquitos or bearcats. And, of course, there was always the potential for food poisoning, accidents, or some purely terrestrial bug to wreak havoc. More than one of Hell's camps had been completely depopulated between supply runs, and Montoya had found himself with a backlog of minor complaints and injuries to deal with.

His facilities were nonexistent, and his medical supplies were limited to the emergency supplies aboard the shuttles, but he was very good at his job. Although he'd been reduced almost to the primitive capabilities of a late prespace physician on Old Earth, he'd handled everything that came his way with aplomb. But he'd also almost had a fit over some of Camp Inferno's routine procedures. He'd completely overhauled their garbage disposal practices, for example, and he'd instigated an inflexible schedule of regular checkups. He'd even rooted out the most sedentary of the camp's inhabitants and badgered Benson into reworking the work assignments to see to it that they got sufficient exercise. For the most part, the camp's inhabitants were still at the bemused stage where he was concerned, as if they hadn't quite decided what to make of this alien bundle of energy, but they were far too glad to see him to resent him.

Honor hid a fresh mental grimace at the thought. That was another thing the Peeps couldn't have cared less about. The way StateSec saw it, it was cheaper for them to lose an entire camp of two or three thousand prisoners than to bother to provide proper medical care. If someone got sick or injured, he or she lived or died on his or her own, with only the crude facilities and resources fellow prisoners might be able to cobble up to keep them alive.

I suppose I should be grateful they even bother to lace the inmates' rations with contraceptives, she thought grimly. *Not that they do it to be nice. Kids would just be more mouths for them to feed, after all. And God only knows what the infant mortality rate would look like in a place like this without proper medical support!*

"I'm sure Fritz would be touched by your faith in his medical prowess," she told McKeon dryly, shaking off her gloomy thoughts. "Unfortunately, I doubt even his superb bedside manner would impress molycircs very much."

"I don't know about that," McKeon argued with a grin. "Every time he starts in on *me* about exercise and diet, I get instantly healthy in self-defense!"

"But you're easily led and highly suggestible, Alistair," Honor said sweetly, and he laughed.

"You are feeling sleepy, *very* sleepy," she intoned sonorously, wiggling the fingers of her hand in front of his eyes. "Your eyelids are growing heavier and heavier."

"They are not," he replied—then blinked suddenly and stretched in a prodigious yawn. Honor laughed delightedly, echoed by Nimitz's bleek of amusement, and McKeon gave both of them an injured look as he finished stretching.

"I, Dame Honor, am neither suggestible nor easily led," he told her severely. "Claims to that effect are base lies, I'll have you and your friend know! However—" he yawned again "—I've been up all day and so, purely coincidentally, I do find myself just a bit sleepy at the moment. The which being so, I think I should take myself off to bed. I'll see you all in the morning."

"Good night, Alistair," she said, and smiled as he sketched a salute and disappeared into the night with a chuckle.

"You two are really close, aren't you?" Benson observed quietly after McKeon had vanished. Honor raised an eyebrow at her, and the blond captain shrugged. "Not like me and Henri, I know. But the way you look out for each other—"

"We go back a long way," Honor replied with another of her half-smiles, and bent to rest her chin companionably on the top of Nimitz's head. "I guess it's sort of a habit to watch out for each other by now, but Alistair seems to get stuck with more of that than I do, bless him."

"I know. Henri and I made the hike back to your shuttles with you, remember?" Benson said dryly. "I was impressed by the comprehensiveness of his vocabulary. I don't think he repeated himself more than twice."

"He probably wouldn't have been so mad if I hadn't snuck off without mentioning it to him," Honor said, and her right cheek dimpled while her good eye gleamed in memory. "Of course, he wouldn't have let me leave him behind if I *had* mentioned it to him, either. Sometimes I think he just doesn't understand the chain of command at all!"

"Ha!" Ramirez' laugh rumbled around the hut like rolling thunder. "From what I've seen of you so far, that's a case of the pot calling the kettle black, Dame Honor!"

"Nonsense. I always respect the chain of command!" Honor protested with a chuckle.

"Indeed?" It was Benson's turn to shake her head. "I've heard about your antics at—Hancock Station, was it called?" She laughed out loud at Honor's startled expression. "Your people are proud of you,

Honor. They like to talk, and to be honest, Henri and I encouraged them to. We needed to get a feel for you, if we were going to trust you with our lives." She shrugged. "It didn't take us long to make our minds up once they started opening up with us."

Honor felt her face heat and looked down at Nimitz, rolling him gently over on his back to stroke his belly fur. She concentrated on that with great intensity for the next several seconds, then looked back up once her blush had cooled.

"You don't want to believe everything you hear," she said with commendable composure. "Sometimes people exaggerate a bit."

"No doubt," Ramirez agreed, tacitly letting her off the hook, and she gave him a grateful half-smile.

"In the meantime, though," Benson said, accepting the change of subject, "the loss of the shuttle beacon does make me more anxious about Lunch Basket."

"Me, too," Honor admitted. "It cuts our operational safety margin in half, and we still don't know when we'll finally get a chance to try it." She grimaced. "They really aren't cooperating very well, are they?"

"I'm sure it's only because they don't know what we're planning," Ramirez told her wryly. "They're much too courteous to be this difficult if they had any idea how inconvenient for us it is."

"Right. Sure!" Honor snorted, and all three of them chuckled. Yet there was an undeniable edge of worry behind the humor, and she leaned back in her chair, stroking Nimitz rhythmically, while she thought.

The key to her plan was the combination of the food supply runs from Styx and the Peeps' lousy communications security. Her analysts had been right about the schedule on which the Peeps operated; they made a whole clutch of supply runs in a relatively short period—usually about three days—once per month. Given Camp Inferno's "punishment" status, it was usually one of the last camps to be visited, which was another factor in Honor's plan.

Between runs, the Black Legs stayed put on Styx, amusing themselves and leaving the prisoner population to its own devices, and despite the guard force's obvious laziness, she reflected, it really was an effective prison system. No doubt the absolute cost of the operation was impressive, but on a per-prisoner basis, it must be ludicrously low. All the Peeps did when they needed another camp was to pick a spot and dump the appropriate number of inmates on it, along with some unpowered hand tools and a minimal amount of building material. Their total investment was a couple of dozen each of axes, hammers, hand saws, picks, and shovels, enough wire to put up a perimeter against the local predators, a few kilos of nails, and—if they were feeling particularly generous—some extruded plastic panels with which to roof the inmates' huts. If a few hut-builders got munched on by the neighborhood's wildlife before they got their camp built, well, that was no skin off the Peeps' noses. There were always plenty more prisoners where they'd come from.

StateSec didn't even carry the expense of shipping in and issuing the sort of preserved emergency rations she and her people had been living on. They grew fresh food on Styx, which, unlike any of the rest of Hell, had been thoroughly terraformed when the original prison was built. To be more precise, their automated farming equipment and a handful of "trustees" did all the grunt work to raise the crops, and the Peeps simply distributed it.

She'd been surprised by that at first, but on second thought it had made a lot of sense. Fresh food was much bulkier, which made for more work on the distribution end of the system, but it didn't keep indefinitely the way e-rats did. That meant it would have been much harder for one of the camps to put itself on short rations and gradually build up a stash of provisions that might let its inmates get into some sort of mischief the garrison would not have approved of. And it made logistical sense, too. By growing their own food here on Hell, the Peeps could drastically reduce the number of supply runs they had to make to the planet. In fact, it looked like they only made one major supply delivery or so a year, now.

But there was more traffic to and from the Cerberus System, albeit on an extremely erratic schedule, than she'd assumed would be the case. For one thing, runs to deliver new prisoners had gone up dramatically after the Committee of Public Safety took over. One of the old Office of Internal Security's failings had been that it hadn't been repressive *enough*. A regime which relied on the iron fist to stay in power was asking for trouble if it relaxed its grip by even a millimeter, and the Legislaturalist leadership had made the mistake of clamping down hard enough to enrage its enemies, but not hard enough to eliminate them outright or terrify them into impotence. Worse, they'd ordered occasional amnesties under which political prisoners were released to placate the Mob, which put people who'd experienced InSec's brutality from the inside back outside to tell their tales of mistreatment—a heaven-sent propaganda opportunity for the agitators of the Citizens Rights Union and other dissident groups. Worse, perhaps, it had suggested a sense of weakness on InSec's part, for why would they have attempted to placate their enemies if they'd felt they were in a position of strength?

The Committee of Public Safety, having been the recipient of such assistance from its predecessors, had decided that *it* would err by going to the opposite extreme. Its determination not to extend the same encouragement to its own enemies went a long way towards explaining the brutal thoroughness which had made Oscar Saint-Just's security forces so widely and virulently hated.

It also explained why the Peeps were dumping even more prisoners on Hell these days. It served them simultaneously as a place to put potential troublemakers safely out of the way and a not-so-veiled threat to keep other troublemakers in line back home. And it was also much thriftier than simply shooting everyone who got out of line. Not that they were shy about summary executions, but the problem with shooting people was that executions were fairly permanent . . . and deprived the state of any potential usefulness the troublemakers might have offered down the road. If you just stuck them on Hell and left them there, you could always retrieve them later if it turned out you needed them for something worthwhile.

In point of fact, StateSec seemed to regard Hell, and especially its political prisoners, as a sort of piggy bank for conscripted labor forces. Even the most modern of industrial bases (which the PRH's was not) had its share of jobs which ranged from the unpleasant to the acutely dangerous. More than that, StateSec had its own highly secret projects, which it preferred to keep as quiet as possible, and there were people among Hell's politicals who had skills those projects sometimes needed badly. For that matter, before the war with the Star Kingdom broke out, StateSec's predecessors in the Office of Internal Security had used Hell as a source of "colonists" (or at least construction crews) for some less than idyllic worlds where the People's Navy needed basing facilities and then returned the workers to Hell when the job was done.

All of which meant that StateSec-crewed personnel transports arrived at Hell, invariably with a warship escort these days, at highly unpredictable but fairly frequent intervals. More rarely, one of StateSec's warships which found itself in the area or passing nearby on its own business might drop by for fresh food, to pick up reactor mass from the huge tank farm StateSec maintained in orbit around Hell, or for a little planetside R&R.

One might not normally think of a "prison planet" as a place where people would want to take liberty, but Camp Charon was actually quite luxurious (InSec had chosen to pamper the personnel who found themselves stuck out here, and StateSec had seen no reason to change that policy), and Styx's climate would have stood comparison with that of any resort world. Which made sense, Honor supposed. It was only reasonable to put your permanent base in the most pleasant spot you could find, and with an entire planet to choose from, you ought to be able to find at least a few spots that were very pleasant indeed.

Besides, she thought grimly, *this is StateSec's planet. They* own *it, lock, stock, and barrel, and they feel safe here. I don't think ONI's ever realized just how important that is to them. It may be off the beaten track, and months may go by with no one at all dropping by, but they always know Hell is* out *here, like some sort of refuge. Or like some nasty little adolescent gang's "clubhouse."*

She snorted at the thought and brushed it aside. It probably had all kinds of psychological significance, but at the moment it was definitely secondary to the problem they faced.

And solving the problem they faced required certain preconditions. Like a Peep supply run to Inferno which happened to arrive when no other supply shuttle had a direct line of transmission to the camp. And which wasn't on the com when it arrived but *had* been on the com at some point prior to its arrival.

So far, they'd been through three complete supply cycles without meeting the conditions they needed, and Honor was honest enough to admit that the strain of waiting was getting to her. At least the rations the Peeps were delivering were sufficient to feed all her people as well as Inferno's "legal" population. The garrison wasn't very careful about counting noses except for the twice-a-T-year prison census, and a dozen or so of Inferno's inmates had died of natural causes since the last headcount, so there was ample food to go around.

Actually, the Peeps were fairly generous in their food allocations . . . when they weren't cutting rations in punishment, at least. Probably because it didn't cost them anything to feed their prisoners a diet which would actually keep them healthy. Honor was almost back up to her proper weight now, and her hair had changed from a short fuzz to a curly, close-growing cap. There was nothing Fritz Montoya could do about her missing arm, blind eye, or dead nerves, and she'd found that the lost arm, in particular, made it very difficult for her to pursue her normal exercise regime. But Montoya was insufferably pleased with the results of the rest of his ministrations, and she had to admit he had cause to be.

She gave herself a mental shake as she recognized the signs. Her thoughts were beginning to wander again, which meant Alistair wasn't the only person who'd stayed up too late.

She stood, holding Nimitz in the crook of her arm, and smiled at the other two.

"Well, whatever happens, we can't do a thing until the next food run. In the meantime, I think I need some sleep. I'll see you both at breakfast."

"Of course," Ramirez replied. He and Benson both rose, and Honor nodded to them.

"Good night, then," she said and stepped out the door into the bug-whining night.

Chapter Twenty-Three

"Commodore Harrington! *Commodore Harrington!*"

Honor looked up and turned quickly. Her missing arm left her unable to help very much with most of the tasks required to keep Camp Inferno's small community alive, but she'd discovered that she had a much better eye for color than she'd ever realized. It wasn't, after all, a subject she'd had a great deal of time to explore prior to her trip to Hell. But since her arrival at Inferno, she'd begun helping Henri Dessouix and his assistants experiment with the dyes they used on their handmade clothing. As Ramirez' exec, Harriet Benson was in charge of managing the camp's manpower pool, and she had detailed Lieutenant Stephenson, late of the Lowell Space Navy, as Honor's assistant. Stephenson had no color judgment at all, but he did have two sound and brawny arms to man the mortar and pestle in which Dessouix crushed roots, berries, leaves, and anything else he could find to provide dyes. He also had a cheerful disposition, and he and Honor had been experimenting with new dye combinations for almost three months now. They were close to producing a green which was almost identical to the dark jade Honor had chosen for the tunics of her Grayson armsmen, but she forgot about that in an instant as she saw the expression on Ramirez' messenger's face . . . and felt the other woman's jagged emotions.

"Yes?" she said sharply, and heard Andrew LaFollet's feet thump on the ground as he slithered down out of the tree from which he had been keeping watch over his Steadholder.

"Commodore Ramirez . . . says to come quick, Ma'am!" the messenger gasped, panting hard after her dead run through the afternoon's searing heat. "He says . . . he says Grandma is inbound!"

Honor's head snapped around, her good eye meeting LaFollet's, and felt the sudden explosive excitement ripping through her armsman. He looked back at her for a second, then unhooked the small com unit from his belt and held it out to her without a word.

She took it and drew a deep breath, then punched the transmit button. It was one of StateSec's own security coms, and they'd chosen a frequency as far as possible from those the SS here on Hell routinely used and set it up for burst transmission. But they hadn't encrypted it, on the theory that if anyone else happened to pick it up anyway, it would be better for Camp Charon to hear a random scrap of chatter which might not make any sense but had to have come from one of their people rather than start wondering why someone was encrypting his traffic.

Not that she intended for the transmission to be long.

"Wolf," she said calmly into the com. "I say again, Wolf."

There was an instant of silence, and then the startled voice of Sarah DuChene came back to her.

"Copy Wolf," DuChene said. "Repeat, copy Wolf."

Honor's fierce half-grin was more of a snarl, baring the teeth on the right side of her mouth, and she tossed the com back to LaFollet, then scooped Nimitz up into his carrier, wheeled, and ran for the main camp as hard as she could.

Citizen Lieutenant Allen Jardine yawned mightily as he swept around in a shallow turn and lined up on the ceramacrete shuttle pad. It was the only break in the sword grass—aside from the POWs' crude village, of course—which made it easily visible even from four or five thousand meters. From Jardine's present low altitude, it showed up still more clearly, and he looked over his shoulder as he dumped forward velocity.

"Coming up on Inferno," he called to his bored three-man crew. "Up top again, Gearing."

"Yeah, yeah, yeah," Citizen Corporal Gearing grumbled. He climbed back into the stirrups of the dorsal turret and twisted the joystick to test the heavy tribarrel. The turret whined as it rotated smoothly, and Gearing's put upon voice sounded in Jardine's earbug. "Turret check. Powered up. Gun hot."

"Confirm turret check," Jardine replied crisply. Despite his own almost unendurable boredom, the citizen lieutenant insisted on following SOP to the letter. That made him unique among the grocery flight pilots (and extremely unpopular with his flight crews), but he'd only been on Hades for about nine T-months, and he was determined to avoid the kind of casual torpor which seemed to infect so many of his fellows. It was also, he suspected, the reason Citizen Brigadier Tresca tended to choose him so often for the run to Inferno. If anyone was likely to make trouble, it was undoubtedly the stiff-necked intransigents here.

Not that even the Inferno inmates would actually be stupid enough to try anything, Jardine reminded himself. All they'd buy if they did was slow starvation, and they knew it. So the other shuttle jocks were probably right when they urged him to ease up on his flight crews. He knew that. It just went against the grain with him to do anything any more sloppily than he had to, and he grinned wryly at his own bloody-mindedness as he flared out, extended his gear, and settled towards the pad.

"Stand by," Honor murmured softly. She sat cross-legged under the cammo net they'd rigged on the hill from which she had first observed Camp Inferno. Her position was a good omen, she reflected . . . and so was the fact that, as closely as she could calculate, the Peeps had captured *Prince Adrian* almost exactly a year ago.

We owe ourselves a little anniversary present, she told herself, and the right side of her mouth twisted in a hungry smile.

Behind her, the satellite com gear they'd lugged from the shuttles and hidden with painstaking care atop the hill was plugged into the Peeps' com net, listening for any scrap of traffic between it and the cargo shuttle settling towards the pad outside the camp. Unlike most of the supply shuttles, this one's pilot had checked in after each landing on his schedule to report his safe arrival, which had given her people plenty of time to steal its IFF settings. That was a sort of adherence to proper operating principles which very few of the Peep pilots ever displayed, and it was almost a pity, she thought regretfully. People who bothered to do their jobs deserved better than for their very attendance to duty to bring destruction down on them.

She raised the binoculars again, listening to the earbug tied into the StateSec net and feeling Alistair McKeon's taut readiness beside her. Nimitz stood upright in the carrier, now slung across her back, pressing his triangular jaw into the top of her shoulder as he stared down at the shuttle pad with her, and the bright flame of his predator anticipation burned at the heart of her own like a fire.

The shuttle settled with neat precision in the center of the pad, and Jardine allowed himself a small smile of self-congratulation. A trash hauler was hardly a sexy mount, but it was nice to demonstrate that he still had the precision of control which had gotten him promoted to Camp Charon.

Yeah, and if I'd known how exciting *it was going to be, you can bet I'd have blown off the chance to get my ass sent here, too, prestige posting or not!* he thought with a silent chuckle, and keyed his com.

"Base, this is Jardine," he reported. "On the ground at Inferno."

"Check, Jardine," Base Ops replied in a voice tinged with ineffable boredom. The woman on the other end of the com didn't quite invite the citizen lieutenant to go away and quit bothering her in so many words, but her tone got the message across quite handily.

And that's exactly why I enjoy reporting in so much, Jardine thought with a nasty smile. Citizen Major Steiner wasn't as bad as a lot of the other base personnel, and she was actually fairly competent. But she was just as set in her ways as anyone else, and she'd leaned harder on Jardine than most about easing up on The Book. She hadn't been confrontational about it, but she'd made her point with a fair degree of emphasis, and she was too senior for him to fire back at her the way he'd wanted to.

But, of course, she can't officially complain if all I do is follow Regs, now can she? And if that just happens to rub it in with a little salt. . . .

He chuckled and looked over his shoulder at his crew.

"He's transmitted," Honor said quietly, good eye aching as she stared through her binoculars.

Come on, Jardine, she thought silently, almost prayerfully, at the pilot. *Be sloppy just this once. Break SOP just a little bit, please. I don't want to kill you if I don't have to.*

"All right, Rodgers. Over to you and Fierenzi."

"Gee, thanks a whole hell of a lot," Citizen Sergeant Rodgers muttered just loud enough for Jardine to hear but not quite loud enough he couldn't pretend he'd thought he was talking only to himself if the citizen lieutenant jerked him up short over it. Not that Rodgers really cared a whole hell of a lot. He was an old Hades hand, and he'd seen a handful of other hotshots like Jardine come and go. The citizen lieutenant's by-the-book, pain-in-the-ass mania for details had lasted longer than most, but sooner or later Hades took the starch out of even the most regulation personality. Still, it would be nice if Jardine would go ahead and get it the hell out of his system and be done with it.

But he wouldn't—or not yet, anyway—and that meant he'd be staying at the controls with the turbines spooling over and Gearing would be staying on the dorsal gun, just in case. And *that* meant it was going to be completely up to Rodgers and Citizen Corporal Fierenzi to unload all the stinking food for the useless bastards here in Inferno.

Of course, there are *some pluses,* Rodgers reminded himself as he hit the button and the big rear cargo hatch whined open. *I may be stuck humping this stuff out, but it'll give me a fresh chance to look over the local talent. If that cute little brunette's still out here, maybe I'll just cut her out of the herd and take her back to Styx with me.*

And maybe he wouldn't, too, he thought. None of the prison bait in Inferno had been sent here for good behavior, after all. Cute as that sweet little number looked, ordering her into his bed might not be the very smartest thing he could possibly do.

He chuckled at the thought and stepped out into the brilliant sunlight with Fierenzi on his heels.

That's funny, he thought. *They had to hear us coming, so why the hell aren't any of 'em already out here to unload their damned food?*

✧ ✧ ✧

"They're following the rules," Honor said, and McKeon heard the sadness in her voice. "Just two of them, and they're already starting to look around," she went on. "I'm afraid we don't have any choice, Alistair." She paused for a heartbeat, then sighed.

"Do it," she said softly.

Commodore Alistair McKeon pressed a button, and a strand of old-fashioned fiberoptic cable flashed the signal to the detonators on five hundred kilos of the very best chemical explosives State Security had once owned. Those five hundred kilos were buried directly under the center of the shuttle pad—beneath, in fact, the exact point on which Citizen Lieutenant Jardine's precise piloting had deposited his shuttle.

The thunderous explosion smashed at Honor's face and eardrums even at a full kilometer's range, and the local equivalent of birds erupted from the trees in a shrill, yodeling chorus of protest as the dreadful sound reverberated. The shuttle vanished in a flaming fountain of dirt and debris, taking its entire crew with it, and Honor felt a stab of terrible guilt. She hadn't had a choice . . . but that made her feel no less like an assassin.

"Cub, this is Wolf. Go," she said into her com, and her calm voice showed no hint of her sense of regret.

"All right, Chief. Let's roll!" Scotty Tremaine snapped.

"Aye, Sir. Everything looks good back here," Horace Harkness replied crisply, and Tremaine glanced out the side window of his cockpit. Geraldine Metcalf and Sarah DuChene had Shuttle Two, with Master Chief Ascher as their flight engineer, but there'd never been any doubt in Tremaine's mind who would draw Shuttle One for Operation Lunch Basket. Now he watched as Solomon Marchant and Anson Lethridge shouted orders to the "ground crew." Muscles strained as the carefully prepared cammo nettings were yanked off, and then the ground crews were streaming aboard Shuttle One.

"Nets clear, Sir," Harkness reported. "Hatches sealing now. Ready when you are."

"Understood," Tremaine said, and the turbines whined as he lifted off.

"IFF code entered, Sir," Senior Chief Barstow's voice came from the tac section. "As far as they know, we're one of theirs now," she added.

"Well that's fair enough, Chief," Lieutenant Sanko said with the sort of cheerfulness that tries to hide gnawing tension. "After all, we *are* one of theirs. We're just under new management."

Honor, McKeon, LaFollet, and Carson Clinkscales jogged down from the hilltop as the big assault shuttle swooped low over their heads and settled in the sword grass just outside the camp's perimeter fence. Ramirez and Benson had already marshaled the assault force, and the first of them were moving towards the shuttle even before Harkness opened the hatches and deployed the boarding ramps. The shuttle's landing gear was tall enough to keep its turbines' intakes clear of the sword grass, and Honor felt the sense of awe rising from many of the prisoners as they actually saw it for the first time. It was one thing to be told that the craft existed; it was another to see it in the flesh and know the moment had arrived.

Marchant and Lethridge were organizing the flow up the ramps by the time she and her companions arrived. The shuttle was big enough to drop one of StateSec's outsized companies—two hundred and fifty troopers strong—in a single flight, and it had been one of *Tepes*' ready shuttles, with fully stocked small arms racks and a complete load of external ordnance. There was only enough unpowered body armor for a hundred and thirty people, but the small arms racks had been intended to provide every member of the company with side arms as well as pulse rifles, plasma rifles, or tribarrels. Transferring any of that hardware to Inferno and running even the tiniest risk of it being spotted by the Peeps before they got a chance to launch Lunch Basket had been out of the question, but Senior Chief O'Jorgenson and Senior Chief Harris stood at the heads of the ramps, handing out armor and weapons to the incoming stream of inmates. By cramming them in with standing room only, Honor could fit three hundred of Camp Inferno's people onboard, and every one of them would have something to shoot with at the other end.

LaFollet broke into the line, clearing a path for Honor and McKeon. One or two people looked irritated at the intrusion . . . but only until they recognized who they were standing aside for. Then they were pushing back against their neighbors, opening the path still wider, and Honor felt a handful of hardier souls reaching out to pat her on the back or simply touch her—as if for luck—as she walked past them. Nimitz shifted in the carrier on her back, true-hands' claws kneading ever so gently at the top of her shoulder as they worked in and out, and the blaze of excitement, fear, anticipation, and dread flowed into him from the humans around them. And over and above all the other emotions there was the eagerness, the flaming need to strike back at least once, however it turned out in the end.

She reached the main troop compartment and picked her way around people strapping into clamshell breast-and-back plates and activating test circuits on their helmet coms and HUDs. She already wore a holstered pulser, but she made no move to collect any additional weapons. A one-armed woman and a crippled treecat had no business in the kind of fight this was likely to be . . . and Andrew LaFollet would have knocked her out and sat on her if she'd even tried to participate in it.

She grinned at the thought despite her tension—or perhaps because of it—and glanced over her shoulder. LaFollet had snagged armor and a helmet of his own and stopped in the tac section to climb into it while she pushed on into the cockpit and settled into the copilot's couch. She actually had no business here, either, since the loss of her arm would hardly make her the ideal pilot to take over if something happened to Tremaine. *On the other hand, if anything happens to Scotty, it'll probably be . . . extreme enough that it won't* matter *how many arms I have,* she reflected, and grinned as the lieutenant commander looked up at her.

"So far, so good, Ma'am," he reported. "Shuttle Two is light on the skids when we need her."

"Good, Scotty. Good. Give me a hand?" She unhooked the chest strap for Nimitz's carrier and turned sideways for Tremaine to help her shift it around in front of her. Then she strapped in—awkwardly with one hand, and careful to keep from crushing the 'cat—and adjusted the powered flight couch to the proper angle.

Someone loomed in the hatch between the cockpit and the tac section, and she turned her head to peer over her shoulder.

"Only me," Alistair McKeon told her. "Jesus and Harriet say another fifteen minutes to get everyone on board."

"Um." Honor checked her chrono. The good news about the late Citizen Lieutenant Jardine's attention to The Book was that no one in Camp Charon was going to expect "his" shuttle to do anything at all untoward upon its arrival. The bad news was that he had told Base Ops exactly when he landed, and given that Camp Charon knew how long it should take him to unload his counter-grav pallets of food, that meant they also knew how soon he ought to be lifting off again. And they should be lifting off right now.

"Tell them to expedite, Alistair," she said calmly, and he nodded and withdrew from the cockpit. Honor returned her attention to the panel in front of her, and the living side of her mouth curled up in a hexapuma's snarl as she keyed the weapons station alive. That was something she *could* do with one arm . . . and she was looking forward to it.

"Checking external ordnance circuits," she told Tremaine calmly, and her good eye gleamed.

Payback time, she thought.

"Come on, come on! Move—*move!*" Captain Harriet Benson chanted, reaching out and physically pushing people up the ramp. It was taking longer than they'd expected. *Should have figured it would,* she thought almost absently. *We thought we'd allowed plenty of time, but Murphy always knows better.* Yet the thought barely touched the surface of her mind. It was an aside, an inconsequential. What mattered was that they were actually doing it. That after the better part of seventy years on Hell, she was about to have her chance at kicking the Black Legs' asses. Personally, she gave Commodore Harrington's plan to actually get anyone off Hell no more than a thirty percent chance of success, but that hardly mattered Whether they managed to escape the prison or not, they were going to make one hell of a hole in the StateSec garrison, and that was good enough for Harriet Benson.

"That's the last, *ma petite!*" Henri told her as he jogged up the ramp.

"Then get aboard, *baudet!*" she told him, and he gave a wild laugh, paused just long enough to drag her head down for a burning kiss, and ran past her. She looked up to see Jesus Ramirez laughing and shook a fist at him, and then the two of them followed Dessouix up the ramp and the hatch hissed closed behind them.

Chapter Twenty-Four

"There it is, Ma'am," Scotty Tremaine said very quietly, and Honor nodded. The island of Styx was a blur of green and brown on the wrinkled blue of the DuQuesne Ocean, named for the powerful Legislaturalist who had been the architect behind the PRH's original plan of conquest.

Funny thing to call an ocean on a planet StateSec owns, she reflected absently. *Wonder why they didn't change its "elitist" name to something more proletarian when they took over the lease?*

Not that it mattered. It was just another of those distractions a human mind sought when the tension ratcheted high, and she knew it.

"I see it, Scotty," she said, and keyed the intercom. "All right, people. We're about five minutes out. Stand by." She released the stud, gave Nimitz a light caress, and looked at Tremaine. "The bird is yours," she said simply.

Citizen Major Cleilia Steiner rubbed the tip of her nose and contemplated the coming change of shift. She and several friends had a date to spend the afternoon surfing, and she was looking forward to trying out that new stud Citizen Captain Harper had brought back from Delta One-Niner last month. He was a political who'd been a big cheese in the Treasury Department under the old regime, and that lent a certain spice to demanding "command performances" from him. Besides, Steiner had always been a sucker for that distinguished, silver-temple look, and if he was even half as good in bed as he was in the looks department, it should be quite an experience.

She smiled lazily at the thought. *I wonder what "the People" would think if they knew how damned much* fun *we have out here?* she wondered. *I know* I *never would've thought there was a post like this one! Sure it's boring when you're actually on duty—too much of the same old, same old to be any other way. But there* are *the off-duty perks, now aren't there? Sort of makes you understand why all those rotten old Legislaturalists got such a charge out of being lords of creation, doesn't it? Well, it's our turn now, and I, for one, intend to enjoy it just as much as they ever did.*

She chuckled, yet in the back of her mind was the memory of the day she'd joined StateSec, all bright and shiny with her desire to protect the People from their enemies. It hadn't taken long for the shininess to rub off, and deep inside she had never stopped mourning the fact that it hadn't. But the real world wasn't like dreams, or the promises people like Cordelia Ransom had made. The real world was where you did the best you could, and you looked out for number one, and you watched your own ass, because it was for damned sure no one else would.

She shook herself and looked out over the neatly parked ranks of shuttles and pinnaces lined up along the parking circles down the side of the main field. Here and there a small cluster of techs labored over one of them in a desultory sort of way. There was no rush. Two things Camp Charon had plenty of were time and—especially—small craft. Steiner sometimes wondered exactly why there were so damned many of them, but no one else seemed to know, either. Of course, they'd already been here when StateSec took over from InSec, and the InSec garrison had been twice as large as StateSec's. Maybe they'd actually needed all those birds for something . . . whatever it might have been. Not that it really mattered. All of them belonged to Steiner—when she had the watch, that was—and they made a satisfyingly perfect geometric pattern, parked side by side with their wings in maximum oversweep, gleaming in the afternoon sunlight. Except that the pattern wasn't quite perfect. There was a hole over there on parking circle twenty-three, and Steiner smiled.

Tsk, tsk, tsk, Citizen Lieutenant Jardine! Is Citizen Perfect running late? Goodness. You'll never hear the last of this!

She chuckled at the thought and checked her approach radar. There he was. The blip of his shuttle traced its course across the holo display, its IFF code blinking beside its icon, and she shook her head. Then she frowned. He was a few degrees off the right heading for a least-time flight from Camp Inferno, and as she watched, he was sweeping still further off. In fact, he was circling around to approach the field from the west, and she rubbed an eyebrow in puzzlement.

There was no operational reason why he shouldn't come in from the west, but, as a rule, pilots did their best to avoid a western approach even when the tower wanted them to use it, because that approach brought them straight in over the base's main installations . . . and over Citizen Brigadier Tresca's personal quarters. Steiner hadn't flown supply runs herself in over three T-years, but she remembered her own experience. Overflying the base's anti-aircraft defenses while they automatically challenged her IFF codes had never bothered her half as much as the possibility that she might disturb the CO while he was napping. After all, even the most wildly errant SAM could only kill you once.

But Jardine was definitely coming around to approach from the west. Not only that, but he was high, and Steiner grimaced, wondering what the hell the Book-loving citizen lieutenant thought he was playing at.

Jardine, you dumb prick, she thought. *Not even your fixation on the Regs is gonna save your ass if you disturb Tresca's afternoon siesta!* She watched his icon a moment longer, then shrugged and reached for the com.

"Jardine, this is Steiner." The voice came from the com, and Tremaine and Honor glanced at one another. "Would you care to tell me just what the hell you think you're doing?" the voice went on. "You *do* realize whose quarters you're about to overfly, don't you?"

"Coming up on Initial Point in thirty-eight seconds," Linda Barstow said from the tac section.

"Understood, Tactical," Honor replied, and flipped up the plastic shield over the master weapons release switch. *What have you got in your basket, Little Red Riding Hood?* a corner of her brain asked her, and she pressed the release button firmly with her thumb, then shifted her hand calmly to the multiposition toggle on the fire control stick and selected missiles.

"Weapons hot," she said.

Steiner frowned, wondering why Jardine hadn't replied, as the shuttle continued its approach. Its icon blipped green as it crossed into the base's anti-air envelope and the computers routinely interrogated its IFF beacon and identified it as a friendly, and her frown deepened. There was still no concern, only irritation, and she keyed the com again.

"Listen, Jardine," the voice from Base Ops said in a much tarter tone. "You can dick around up there if you want, but if you piss off the Old Man, *I'm* not gonna bail your butt out! Now what the hell d'you think you're doing?"

"Looks like they're still buying the beacon, Ma'am," Tremaine observed. His voice was inhumanly calm, but a single bead of sweat rolled down his forehead despite the cockpit's air-conditioning, and Honor chuckled mirthlessly. Her eyes were on the holo image of the base in her heads-up-display. They'd been able to generate fairly detailed topographical imagery from the data Harkness had stolen from *Tepes*, and the shuttle's passive sensors had been updating the HUD by adding specific targeting codes to the display for the last five minutes. Now half a dozen numbered locations were centered in bright red sighting rings, and she smiled.

"They're buying it so far," she agreed. "But it's about time to show them what sharp teeth the Big Bad Wolf has." A soft tone chimed as the range readout to the closest sighting ring dropped to twelve thousand meters, and she straightened in her seat, her voice suddenly cold and crisp.

"Tactical, illuminate Target One," she commanded.

An alarm screamed behind Ceilia Steiner, and something hit the floor with a crunching clatter as she spun her chair to face it. The citizen sergeant on the air-defense console had dropped his book viewer and sat gaping at the brilliant, flashing red light which announced that target designator lasers had just begun illuminating his remote fire stations. He knew exactly what he was supposed to do in that situation, regardless of whether or not the incoming aircraft was friendly, but he'd had absolutely no reason to expect it to happen, and he was as frozen by surprise as Steiner.

Not that it would have mattered anyway. It was already far too late.

"Launch One!"

Honor Harrington's soprano voice was colder than space as she announced the shot and squeezed the trigger on the control stick. A single laser-guided missile dropped from the racks and accelerated at four thousand gravities.

"One away!" she said crisply, confirming the launch

"Target Two up!" Senior Chief Barstow called from the tactical section, illuminating the next target on her queue.

"Launch Two!" Honor replied, and a second missile launched, acquired, and went screaming in on its target.

"Two away!"

"Target Three up!"

"Launch Three!"

Given more launch range to work with, the missiles would have made respectable kinetic energy weapons, but the attackers had had to get in too close for that. Not that it mattered. State Security had very kindly armed those missiles with massive warheads designed to take out hardened targets, and the first missile slammed straight into the primary fire control radar for Camp Charon's air defenses.

A huge ball of fire bloomed against the ground, boiling up into the heavens, breaking windows and sending shockwaves through every structure within a thousand meters. And then the second missile slammed into Radar Two, and the third ripped Number One Missile Battery itself to bits, and the fourth exploded in the exact center of Missile Two. And even as Cleilia Steiner jerked to her feet, staring in numb horror at the destruction marching across the base towards her, missiles five through ten were in the air and streaking for their targets.

A howl of triumph went up from the troop compartment, like the baying cry of a wolf pack, as the passengers nearest the view ports caught a glimpse of the explosions, but Honor had no attention to spare. She was locked into her mission, fused with Chief Barstow and Scotty Tremaine. Barstow was their eyes, peering ahead, finding their prey, marking it for death. And Scotty was their wings, bearing them onward like a falcon stooping upon its victims. And Honor—Honor was the very hand of death, and her hand squeezed again, her one good eye bleak as flint, as she sent a final missile scorching down into the sea of fire and smoke and secondary explosions which had once been Camp Charon's air defenses and the shuttle lined up on the field.

"Designating ready aircraft!" Barstow sang out.

"Acquired," Honor replied as the targeting lasers picked out the ready section of pinnaces. The magnified image in the HUD showed her the missiles tucked under their fuselages, but they were the only armed craft on the entire field, and they'd never been intended for a combat scramble against one of their own shuttles. They were meant as a fire brigade in case some camp full of prisoners went berserk and mobbed a supply shuttle or some equally bizarre occurrence. Yet nothing like that had ever happened . . . and the planners had never even contemplated anything as bizarre as what *was* happening. But for all that, someone down there obviously had her head together, because Honor actually saw a pilot running madly towards one of the ready birds. But whoever she was, she was too late, and Honor thumbed the toggle to select bombs.

Citizen Major Steiner watched in sick, horrified disbelief as the intruder swept over the field.

That's not Jardine! she thought wildly. *It's not even a trash hauler at all! It's a goddamned* assault shuttle! *Where the* fuck *did* that *come from?*

She didn't know where it had come from, yet an assault shuttle it indisputably was, and she could see the StateSec markings on it. It wasn't Jardine, but it *was* one of their own, and what in God's name was *happening* here?

But God didn't answer her, and she flung herself down, trying to burrow into the tower floor, as she saw the ominous shapes detach from the shuttle and go plummeting towards the only armed pinnaces on the entire face of the planet Hades.

The cluster munitions spewed bomblets across the parked pinnaces. They weren't the snowflake clusters designed for anti-personnel use.

These were dragon's teeth, designed to cripple or destroy heavy ground combat equipment. Each bomblet was the size of a Grayson baseball, and hundreds of them rained down across the neatly parked pinnaces.

And then they exploded in a long, incandescent wave that lashed a storm front of destruction across the field. The red and white fury of high-explosives was spalled with the brilliant blue of flaming hydrogen as the pinnaces' fuel tanks let go, and Honor watched a splintered fuselage go smashing across the ceramacrete in an end-for-end tumble, like a toy discarded by some huge, petulant child.

"Put us down, Scotty," she said flatly, then keyed her com. "Cub, this is Big Bad Wolf," she said clearly. "We're inside."

"*What* did you say?" Citizen Lieutenant Commander Proxmire demanded, staring in disbelief at his com officer.

"Camp Charon is under attack, Sir!" Citizen Lieutenant Agard repeated. If he hadn't sounded as shocked and disbelieving as Proxmire felt, the citizen lieutenant commander would have suspected him of trying to pull some macabre kind of practical joke. But if it wasn't a joke, then what the hell was it? How *could* anyone be attacking the base? The prisoners damned straight didn't have the capability to do it, and no one else could possibly even have gotten here without first fighting his way through the orbital defenses!

And if someone was attacking the base, then what the hell was *he* supposed to do?

He scrubbed a hand over his mouth, thinking furiously. His was perhaps the most boring of all the State Security duty assignments in the Cerberus System, for he was Camp Charon's emergency mailman, the only way Hades could get a message out to the rest of the galaxy if it needed to. Someone had to pull the duty, however mind-numbing it was, and Proxmire supposed he shouldn't complain too loudly that his turn had finally come up. He'd spent over four T-years assigned to play diplomatic courier for various embassies before they stuck him here. That had certainly been a cushy slot, and he was due to be relieved from this one in another eight T-months, as he made a habit of reminding himself every morning.

Not that any of those bright and sunshiny thoughts helped a great deal. His forty thousand-ton courier boat was one of the fastest vessels in space, but she was also little more than a pair of Warshawski sails and a set of impellers, with strictly limited living space for her thirty-man crew. That was why half his people were usually down on Styx, rotating through enough liberty to keep bulkhead fever from driving them crazy and simultaneously giving the people still stuck upstairs aboard ship enough extra living space to stay sane. It was strictly against The Book, of course, but no base commander had ever objected. After all, there would be plenty of time to get the rest of Proxmire's crew back upstairs before sending his ship off with a message. Besides, no CO on Hades had ever actually needed to use his communications ship, anyway.

Proxmire scrubbed harder, cursing his own complacency. Yet even as he cursed himself, he realized his error had been all but inevitable. No one had ever threatened Hades. Hell, no one but StateSec even knew where it was! And there had been no point in putting his people to any more hardship than they had to endure simply to satisfy the letter of the Regs. But now this—whatever *this* was!—was happening down there, and he had only half his crew on board and no orders from Citizen Brigadier Tresca. But—

"Start bringing up the impellers," he ordered harshly.

"Yes, Sir."

Proxmire nodded, then jerked his attention back to the display. It would take his ship almost forty minutes to bring her nodes up, and he hoped to hell that by the time they were on-line, the situation would have clarified enough down there that he wouldn't need them after all.

Scotty Tremaine put the shuttle down, and the twin dorsal turrets whined as their heavy pulsers tracked across the base. The single ventral turret joined in, and hangers and parked ground vehicles blew apart under their ravening fire as the troop hatches sprang open.

Three hundred men and women streamed down the ramps, armed to the teeth and carefully briefed on their objectives. They split up into three groups as officers shouted orders, and then they were gone, flowing away into the chaos and flame like vengeful ghosts.

"Last man out!" Horace Harkness announced over the intercom. "Hatch closing . . . *now!* Good seal, Flight!"

"Copy," Tremaine replied, and the shuttle howled back into the heavens. There were no heavy anti-air defenses to challenge it—not anymore—and it took station directly above the heavy vehicle park, prepared to destroy any ground armor the garrison might manage to get into action.

"Move, move, *move!*" Jesus Ramirez bellowed. His team was the truly critical one. Alistair McKeon was leading a second group to seize the vehicle park and appropriate any heavy armor he could find, and Harriet Benson (and, inevitably, Henri Dessouix) led the third group to secure the perimeter of the landing field. Those were both vital missions, but Ramirez's group left them to it and sliced straight across the base, charging for the very heart of the chaos of explosions and flame Commodore Harrington had sown, for their objective lay in the midst of that destruction. It was, in fact, the one defensive installation Commodore Harrington had very carefully left untouched, and the attackers *had* to secure it intact.

A small knot of SS troopers suddenly appeared out of the smoke. One or two of them had side arms; the others seemed to be completely unarmed, but they were in the wrong place at the wrong time, and no one was taking any chances. Pulse rifles whined and a grenade launcher coughed. One of the SS men might have been trying to surrender, but no one would ever know, and Ramirez and his people trampled the bodies underfoot.

Citizen Major Steiner dragged herself to her feet. Her ears rang and her face was bloody, yet she knew she'd been incredibly lucky. The outer crystoplast wall of the control tower had been reduced to splinters and driven across her work area like shrapnel, cutting down and killing every other member of her crew, and she staggered towards the door. She had to get out of here, she thought dazedly. Had to find a weapon. There was only the one shuttle. There couldn't be more than a couple of hundred people aboard it, and the defenders had them outnumbered ten-to-one, with armored vehicles and battle armor to support them. All they needed was time to recover from the shock and get themselves pulled back together, and—

She stepped out the door, moving more briskly, just as Henri Dessouix's twenty-five-man platoon came around a corner, and a dozen pulse rifles opened fire as one.

If anyone had cared, it would have taken a forensic surgeon days to identify the remains.

"Go!" Alistair McKeon shouted, and half a dozen of his people dashed across the open ground towards the vehicle park. A handful of SS types had gotten themselves back together, and a light tribarrel opened fire from somewhere in the enlisted housing blocks facing the main vehicle building. Two of McKeon's people went down, killed instantly, but the others cleared its field of fire before it could engage them.

The gunner would have been better advised to shoot at the hovering shuttle, instead, McKeon reflected grimly. Light as his weapon was, he was unlikely to have brought down the heavily armored assault craft, but he might have gotten lucky. Instead, all he'd managed to do was kill two people and attract the shuttle's attention. It twisted around in midair, the nose dropped slightly, and the building from which the fire had come vomited flame and smoke as Honor put a missile into it and followed up with a half-second burst from her heavy bow-mounted tribarrels.

He waved the rest of his party forward, and they swept across the clear ground. A dozen or so technicians had been working on vehicles or tinkering with the powered armor stored in the base "Morgue," but only about half of them were armed, and those only with side arms. Some of them did their best, with far more guts than McKeon would have expected from SS thugs, and he lost eleven more men and women before he could secure the park. But then he had control of it, and he posted fifteen people to hold the Morgue and keep the garrison from getting to the powered battle armor stored there while the rest of his people began firing up the power plants on armored personnel carriers and light tanks.

McKeon stood on the rear deck of a tank, feeling the armored carapace shudder underfoot as the turbines began to whine, and his gap-toothed grin was a terrifying thing to see.

"Now!" Ramirez barked, and the woman beside him pressed the button. The beehive charge on the armored door ahead of them detonated, blowing the hatch apart, and Ramirez's point team, armed with flechette guns and grenade launchers for this very eventuality, charged through the smoke almost before the debris had landed.

Pulser fire met them, and two of his people went down. But the third triggered a burst from her grenade launcher. The grenades whipped through the opening and exploded in a rippling snarl of light and fury, and the grenadier charged behind them.

They were only flash-bangs, light concussion weapons intended to stun and incapacitate, not to kill. Not because anyone felt any particular compassion for the people beyond that doorway, but because it was absolutely essential that they capture the *equipment* beyond it intact. Jesus Ramirez had already lost nineteen people on his way here, and he was determined to make their sacrifice count.

"Go! *Go!*" someone screamed, and another half dozen men and women lunged through the shattered door on the grenadier's heels. Flechette guns coughed and bellowed, pulsers whined, and a single grenade—not a flash-bang this time, but something heavier—exploded thunderously. And then one of his people poked her head back out.

"Objective secure, Commodore!" she shouted. "We've got some blast damage, but nothing we can't fix!"

"*Maravilloso!*" Ramirez pumped a fist in congratulations and loped forward, already reaching for his hand com.

"Commodore Ramirez has the control site, Commodore!" Senior Chief Barstow announced, and Honor felt the fierce flare of triumph rip through the skeleton crew still aboard the shuttle. It had taken almost twenty minutes longer than the ops plan had hoped for, because Ramirez's group had gotten bogged down in half a dozen tiny, vicious firefights on its way in. But what mattered now was that the commodore had done it! *He* now controlled the ground base to which all of the planet's orbital defenses were slaved. He couldn't use them yet—even if he'd captured the control site completely undamaged, which was unlikely—because none of them knew the security codes. But they would have time to figure the codes out later, especially with Horace Harkness to tickle the StateSec computers, and what mattered for right now was that the Peeps couldn't use them, either.

She stabbed the com stud again.

"Cub, this is Wolf. You are go. Repeat, you are, go!"

"Cub copies go, Wolf," Geraldine Metcalf's voice replied. "We're on our way, Skipper."

Half a planet away from Camp Charon, Shuttle Two screamed straight up with Geraldine Metcalf and Sarah DuChene at the controls. Master Chief Gianna Ascher, who had been the senior noncom in *Prince Adrian*'s combat information center, manned her tac section, with Senior Chief Halburton as her flight engineer. It wasn't the first time Metcalf and DuChene had taken this shuttle into action, but this time they were running late, and they glanced at one another grimly as the sky beyond the cockpit windows began to turn dark indigo.

"*Well?*" Citizen Lieutenant Commander Proxmire snapped at his hapless com officer.

"Sir, I can't get a response from *anybody* down there," Agard replied unhappily. "Base Ops went off the air almost immediately, and all I'm picking up now is a bunch of encrypted transmissions I assume are combat chatter. I can't tell who's saying what to who, but you can see for yourself how it looks."

He gestured at the holo display, and Proxmire bit his lip. The courier boat didn't carry a true tactical section, for she was completely unarmed. But she had a fairly respectable sensor suite, and the sky over Styx was cloudless and clear. That was enough to let them generate a needle-sharp view of events there, and his stomach knotted at what he saw. The fire, smoke, and chaos was even more widespread, but the display projected the icons of armored vehicles moving out of the vehicle park. Unfortunately, they seemed to be firing on SS positions, not the attackers. And if anything had been needed to confirm who was in control of them, that damned assault shuttle wasn't firing at them. In fact, it was providing them with fire support!

He shook his head numbly. Surely this was impossible. It had to be impossible! He still had no idea at all who those people were or where they had come from, but they'd taken barely forty minutes to overrun the most critical sectors of the base. The garrison was cut off from its heavy weapons—for that matter, the attackers were using its own weapons against it!—and simple numbers meant very little against someone who controlled the air and had all the heavy firepower.

But as long as the shuttle stayed occupied down there, it wasn't bothering Proxmire. And as long as he was free to go summon help, it didn't really matter whether or not the enemy—whoever the hell he was—managed to overrun the base.

"Impellers in thirty-five seconds, Skipper!" his harassed second engineer reported, and he smiled thinly.

"There she is, Gerry," Lieutenant Commander DuChene murmured as the courier boat's icon appeared in her HUD.

"Got it," Metcalf acknowledged, adjusting her heading slightly. "Gianna?"

"I've got her, Ma'am," Master Chief Ascher replied, "but these sensors are pure crap." She sniffed disdainfully, and despite her own tension, Metcalf grinned. She and Ascher had worked together aboard *Prince Adrian* for almost two T-years, and she knew how proud the master chief had been of the people and equipment aboard her lost ship.

"Just tell me what you can, Gianna," she said.

"I can't—" Ascher began, then stopped dead. There was a moment of silence, and her voice was flat when she spoke again. "Her impellers are hot, Ma'am. She's already underway."

"Shit!" Metcalf breathed, and looked at DuChene. "Have you got a shot, Sarah?"

"Not a good one," DuChene replied tensely.

"Talk to me about accel curves, Gianna!" Metcalf commanded.

"We've got the velocity advantage now, but she's got a deeper compensator sump and a hell of a lot more brute power than us, Ma'am. She can pull about five hundred and thirty gees to our four hundred, but our present velocity is about four thousand KPH—make it sixty-seven KPS—and hers is only about twenty-seven KPS. Current range is one-three-point-three-five k-klicks, and she'll match our velocity in a little over thirty-one seconds, so we'll equalize at range one-two-point-seven-two k-klicks. After that, she'll pull away from us at one and a quarter KPS-squared."

"Sarah?" Metcalf looked back at DuChene, and the lieutenant commander chewed her lip for a moment, then sighed unhappily.

"These birds weren't designed to kill starships—not even small ones," she said, and Metcalf nodded impatiently. She *was* a tactical officer herself. But she was also a better pilot than DuChene, and the missiles were DuChene's responsibility. "I can take her out, but it'll be an awful long-range shot for our weapons at this range, especially if she knows they're coming and takes evasive action. But if we're only going to close the range by six hundred klicks . . ."

She paused, and Metcalf nodded in grim understanding while her thoughts flickered like lightning, considering options and outcomes, weighing and discarding alternatives.

Courier boats didn't mount point defense, and they weren't equipped with the sophisticated electronic warfare suites of warships. But the shuttle didn't carry the nuclear and laser warheads which warships normally fired at one another, either. Even its limited number of impeller-head missiles, designed for combat with other small craft, had been expended during the breakout from *Tepes*. Those which remained were intended primarily for short-range work against planetary targets, and they all carried chemical warheads, and that was the problem. Although those warheads were many times as efficient as any chemical explosives from pre-Diaspora history, they still required direct hits, and at this range, scoring a direct hit against a *non*evading target would be hard enough with ground attack missiles. Worse, stopping anything the size of that courier boat would require multiple hits, not just one. All of which meant that at this range, they would have to fire without warning to prevent the target from taking evasive action or rolling to interpose its impeller wedge . . . and they couldn't reduce the range enough to change that.

Which meant they couldn't take the risk of even trying to convince the crew to surrender alive.

This wasn't supposed to happen. They were supposed to be too confused to light their drive off this quickly, and we were supposed to get here sooner. It wouldn't matter *how short-legged our birds are if they couldn't move. Hell, for that matter we could've forced them to surrender with plain old* pulsers, *because there wouldn't have been anything else they could do! But now—*

Now if she took a chance, demanded their surrender, gave them even the tiniest warning, they just might get clean away. And if they did, they would bring back enough firepower to turn Hell into a glazed billiard ball. And that meant—

All her flashing thoughts took less than three seconds, and she inhaled deeply.

"Take the shot," Lieutenant Commander Geraldine Metcalf said quietly.

And may God have mercy on us all.

"Sir, I'm picking up something overtaking from astern."

"What?" Proxmire spun his command chair to face his astrogator. "What kind of 'something'?"

"I'm not certain, Sir." The woman was doubling for the courier boat's absent tactical officer (although applying the term "tactical officer" to someone who controlled only sensors and no weapons had always struck Proxmire as a bit ridiculous), and she sounded doubtful as she tapped keys.

"It's some kind of small craft," she announced a second later, "but I'm not getting a transponder code from it."

"No IFF?" Proxmire demanded as an icy fist seemed to grip his stomach and squeeze.

"No, Sir. It's—" The woman froze, and then her head whipped towards Proxmire. "*It's launching on us!*"

But by then the first of sixteen missiles were in final acquisition, and it was much too late.

✧ ✧ ✧

"Wolf, this is Cub." The voice in Honor's earbug sounded drained. "The target is dead. I repeat, the target is dead. We're closing to look for survivors . . . but I don't think there'll be many."

"Understood, Cub," Honor said quietly. She looked down on the carnage below her. The Peeps were falling back—in fact, they were running for their lives—but they still had an enormous advantage in sheer numbers. She needed Metcalf and DuChene to return to Inferno and bring up the rest of the inmates as reinforcements, but she couldn't tell them that. Not yet. Like them, she was a naval officer, and she, too, knew the code. You did not abandon possible survivors—yours or the enemy's—and especially not when you were the one who had killed their ship. And yet—

"Expedite your search, Cub," she said calmly. "We need you down here ASAP."

"Understood, Wolf. We'll make it as quick as we can," Metcalf replied, "and—" She paused suddenly, and then she laughed harshly, the sound cold and ugly with self-loathing. "It shouldn't take long anyway. Her fusion bottle just failed."

Honor winced, but she couldn't let herself think about that just now.

"Understood, Gerry," she said instead. And then she cut the circuit and turned her attention back to her targeting HUD, searching for more people to kill.

Chapter Twenty-Five

A chime sounded, and Honor looked up from the terminal in front of her. She pressed a button on the desk console which had once belonged to Citizen Brigadier Tresca, and the door to the office (which had also once belonged to Citizen Brigadier Tresca, but he was dead and no longer needed either of them) slid open to reveal Alistair McKeon in conversation with Andrew LaFollet. The armsman had left Honor's side long enough to participate in the capture of the vehicle park and picked up a minor flesh wound in the process. But Fritz Montoya had access to a proper base hospital again at last, and LaFollet's injury was responding nicely to quick heal. More to the point, perhaps, his Steadholder had a proper office for him to stand sentry outside of once again, and while he might still be out of his proper uniform, he'd settled back into his appointed role with an almost audible sigh of relief.

McKeon glanced up as the door opened and nodded to Honor over LaFollet's shoulder. He obviously wanted to finish whatever he'd been saying to her armsman, but his expression was grim, and her stomach muscles tightened as she caught the taste of his emotions. Warner Caslet was with him, and the Peep officer looked even grimmer than McKeon.

Nimitz raised his head from where he drowsed on the perch Honor and LaFollet had rigged for him. He'd been napping there a lot over the last five days, and despite her apprehension over whatever had brought McKeon here with such an expression, Honor felt her own spirits lift as she reached up to scratch the 'cat's ears. His buzzing purr and a gentle wave of love answered her caress, and then he rose and stretched deeply but carefully. His crippled mid-limb and twisted pelvis continued to stab him with pain at any injudicious movement, yet he radiated a sense of complacency as he contemplated the change in their circumstances. Not only was Styx much cooler than Camp Inferno had been, but the installations they'd captured from the Peeps even had air-conditioning. And as if that weren't enough, he'd quickly discovered that the huge StateSec farms on the island produced celery.

Actually, it had been Carson Clinkscales who'd discovered that fact. He'd turned up outside Honor's quarters on their second morning on Styx and almost shyly extended a fresh head of celery, still damp with dew, and Nimitz had been in heaven. He'd always been fond of Clinkscales, but the ensign's gift had moved the young Grayson officer into the select circle of his closest friends.

Honor smiled in memory, but then her smile faded. McKeon had finished whatever he'd been saying to LaFollet, and now he and Caslet walked into her office.

"Good morning, Alistair. Warner." She greeted them calmly, allowing herself to show no trace of her reaction to the anxiety they radiated.

"Good morning, Ma'am," Caslet said. McKeon only nodded, which would have been a sure sign of his worry even if she hadn't been able to feel his emotions, and she waved at the chairs which faced her desk.

They sat at her silent invitation, and she tipped back in her own new, comfortable chair to study them briefly. Their sojourn on Hell had given both of them weathered complexions and leaned them down—McKeon, in particular, had lost a good two centimeters of waistline. Well, that was fair enough. Even Honor's normally pale complexion had turned a golden bronze, and she'd actually begun getting back some of her muscle mass despite the awkwardness of exercising with only one arm. Which, a corner of her brain thought dryly, she had just discovered was nowhere near as awkward as trying to operate a console *keyboard* one-handed.

But the other thing Honor and McKeon had in common was the pulser each of them still wore . . . and which Caslet did not.

"You look unhappy about something, Alistair," she said after a moment. "Why?"

"We found two more bodies this morning, Ma'am," McKeon said flatly, and Honor winced at the bleak sense of helplessness behind his words. She quirked the eyebrow above her good eye, and his mouth twisted. Then he sighed. "It wasn't pretty, Honor. Whoever did it took their time with both of them. It looks to me like there must have been five or six killers, and some of the mutilations were definitely sexual."

"I see." She leaned back once more and rubbed her face with her fingers. It seemed almost natural after all these months to feel nothing at all from the pressure on her left cheek, and at the moment she wished she could feel nothing at all deep inside, either. But only for a moment. Then she crushed the self-pitying thought under a ruthless mental heel and lowered her hand.

"Any idea at all who did it?"

"I don't think it was any of our people from Inferno," McKeon replied, and glanced at Caslet.

"I don't think it was, either, Ma'am," the Peep said. In some ways, he had become even more isolated since the capture of Camp Charon, for the flood of SS prisoners they'd taken regarded him with the bitter contempt reserved for traitors, while the island's liberated slaves couldn't have cared less how he came to be here. All *they* cared about was that he was a Peep officer . . . and that was why he had to be accompanied at all times by an armed guard.

"Why not?" Honor asked him.

"Largely because of the mutilations, Ma'am," he replied steadily. "I'm sure some of the people from Inferno would love to massacre every SS thug they could lay hands on, and, to be honest, I don't blame them. But this—" He shook his head grimly. "Whoever did this *really* hated their targets. I'm no psych type, but the nature of the mutilations certainly suggests to me that at least some of the killers were people who'd been hauled back here as sex slaves. And, frankly," he met her gaze levelly, "I blame them even less for wanting revenge than I blame the people from Inferno."

"I see." Honor frowned down at her terminal, rubbing the edge of the console with a long index finger while she considered what he'd said.

He was right, of course. As Harriet Benson had told her that first day, the SS garrison had regarded the prisoners in their charge as property. Worse than that: as *toys.* And too many of them had played with their "toys" like cruel, spiteful children twisting the heads off puppies to see what would happen. Most of the outright sex slaves they'd dragged back to Styx had been political prisoners—civilians from the PRH itself—which had probably indicated at least a modicum of caution on the garrison's part. Most military services gave their people at least rudimentary hand-to-hand training, after all.

But the wheel had turned full circle now. Two-thirds of the SS garrison had been killed, wounded, or captured, but at least six or seven hundred of them had so far escaped apprehension. And on Styx, unlike the rest of Hell, they could actually go bush and live off the land while they tried to keep on evading capture. Honor and her allies had far too little manpower to hunt them down on an island this huge, and Styx had been so completely terraformed that, except for the warmer temperature and lower gravity, it actually made Honor homesick for Sphinx. Fugitives wouldn't even need to know a thing about edible wild plants, for the planetary farms covered scores of square kilometers.

Unfortunately for the Peeps, however, their slaves knew the island even better than they did. There had been a clandestine communication net between the sex slaves and the farms' slave laborers—many of whom had been playthings themselves before their "owners" tired of them—for decades. In fact, over twenty escaped slaves had been in hiding when Honor attacked Styx. They'd contrived their escapes by faking their own deaths—suicide by drowning had been a favorite, given the currents and deep-water predators off Styx's southwestern coast—and the farm laborers had concealed and helped feed some of them for years. But escaping discovery had required them to find hiding places all over the island . . . which meant the liberated slaves were much better than Honor's people at deducing where their erstwhile masters might be hiding now. For that matter, they were better at it than the Peeps were at finding hiding places on the run, and some of them had no interest at all in waiting for the courts-martial Honor and Jesus Ramirez had promised them. Nor were they shy about dumping the results of their grisly handiwork where other fleeing Peeps might find it.

The good news, she thought, *is that sheer terror is probably going to encourage the rest of the garrison to turn themselves in before someone catches up and murders* them. *The bad news is that I never wanted anything like this to happen. I promised them* justice, *not animal vengeance, and I* won't *let myself or people under my command be turned into the very thing I hate!*

She drew a deep breath and looked up from the console.

"I suppose I can't really blame them for wanting to get even either," she said quietly, and saw her friends' eyes flicker to the dead side of her own face. She ignored that and shook her head. "Nonetheless, we have our own responsibilities as civilized human beings, and that means we can't let this pass unchallenged, however much we may sympathize with the killers' motivations. Warner," she turned her good eye on the Peep officer, "I want you to talk to the prisoners. I know they hate you . . . and I know you hate talking to them. But you're the closest thing we've got to a neutral party."

She paused, watching him intently. His expression was pinched, but finally he nodded.

"Thank you," she said softly.

"What do you want me to say to them, Ma'am?"

"Tell them what's been happening. Explain to them that I don't want it to go on, but that I simply don't have the manpower to stop it or patrol the entire island."

McKeon twitched unhappily in his chair at that, and she gave him a crooked half-grin.

"It's not going to come as any surprise to them, Alistair, and it's not like we'll be giving away critical military information! Besides, prison guards are always outnumbered by their prisoners. The whole reason to build a prison is to economize on your guard force, and these people certainly know that if anyone does! And if they get any ideas, all they have to do is look up at the tribarrels in the watch towers around their compound to see why acting on them would be a serious mistake."

She held his gaze for a moment, until he grinned back wryly and shrugged, then returned her attention to Caslet.

"Point out to them that the only way I can possibly guarantee their fellows' safety, even temporarily, is by bringing them in where I can put them under guard to protect them from their ex-slaves. And, Warner," her voice turned much grimmer, "you can also tell them that I really don't especially want to protect any of them, because I don't. But that doesn't change my responsibilities."

"Yes, Ma'am," Caslet said, but he also looked down at his hands for several seconds, then sighed. "I'll tell them, Ma'am, and I know it's the truth," he told her. "But I'll *feel* like a liar, knowing what's waiting for them."

"Should we just let the guilty walk away unpunished then?" she asked gently, and he shook his head quickly.

"No, Ma'am. Of course not. I've seen too much of what StateSec has done—not just to these people, but to you and your people. For that matter, to people I know were loyal officers who did their very best but—" He broke off with an angry grimace. "Someone has to call them to account. I know that. It's just—"

"Just that you feel like you're inviting them to jump out of the frying pan and into the fire," McKeon put in quietly. Caslet looked at the broad-shouldered commodore for a moment, then nodded. "Well, I suppose you are, in a way," McKeon went on. "But at least they'll have trials, Warner. And the sentences of the guilty will be in accord with established military law. They won't be capricious, and you know as well as I do that Honor would never permit the kind of horror you and I just finished looking at. The worst they're looking at is a firing squad or a rope . . . and just between you and me, that's a hell of a lot better deal than some of them deserve."

"I know, Alistair. I—" Caslet stopped himself and gave a tiny shrug. "I know," he repeated, "and I'll tell any of the prisoners who ask exactly that."

"Thank you," Honor said. "And when you do, tell them that I would appreciate the assistance of any of them who would be willing to record orders or pleas for their fellows to surrender themselves. Tell them that I will neither ask nor permit them to make any promises of immunity or pardon. If they wish to include a warning that courts-martial will be convened, they'll be free to do so. But you may also tell them, as Alistair just said, that I will not allow anyone under my command to engage in the sort of atrocities which are now being committed."

"Yes, Ma'am."

"And while Warner does that, Alistair," Honor went on, turning back to McKeon, "I want you, Jesus, and Harriet to try to work out some way to keep tabs on the slaves." Her expression was grim. "I'll speak to them again myself this afternoon, both to remind them that we've promised there will be trials . . . and to tell them that our people will be authorized to use deadly force, if necessary, to prevent this kind of vengeance killing. I hate to come the heavy, but they've been through so much I have to doubt that anything less drastic than that will get through to them. And if you and Jesus and Harriet think it's necessary, I'll be willing to proclaim an island-wide curfew, as well, in hopes of at least cutting down on this kind of thing."

"That may not be a bad idea," McKeon said thoughtfully. "There are almost five hundred of them, counting the farm workers. We've managed to keep any weapons out of their hands—aside from anything they may have 'liberated' from Black Legs they've already . . . dealt with, at least—but there are still as many of them as there are of us."

"I know." Honor sighed. "I just hate the idea of putting them back into some kind of lock-down after everything that's already been done to them. And I'm a little afraid it may turn us into the enemy, as well."

"I wouldn't worry too much about that," McKeon told her with a headshake. "Oh, it'll piss them off, and it may make some of them hate us, at least in the short term. But there's a world of difference between proclaiming a curfew—even one backed up with physical force—and the kinds of things the Black Legs did to them! Things may be tense for a while, but once they realize you're serious about the trials, I think they'll come around."

"As long as we can hold things together until they do," Honor said with another sigh. "We need more manpower, Alistair, and we need it badly."

"Agreed." McKeon slid down in his chair to sit on the end of his spine while he slitted his eyes in thought. "Any progress on the data search?" he asked after a moment.

"There *is* a little progress, actually." Honor tapped her terminal, where she'd just been reviewing the latest memo from her computer attack team.

"Harkness, Scotty, Anson, Jasper, and Ascher are having the time of their lives playing with the Peeps' secure data base, and these people were incredibly overconfident. The possibility of someone's taking the place over from the inside simply never occurred to them. It couldn't happen. And because it couldn't, the only people who could purge their files were Tresca or his exec . . . and they could only do it from the planetary defense command center." She shook her head. "I guess they figured that since the only real threat had to come from the outside, through the orbital defenses, whoever had the duty there would be in the best position to decide when to purge, so that was where they put their central data processing node, as well. But when Jesus took the command center out from the ground before either of the authorized COs could even get there—" She shrugged and held out her hand, palm uppermost.

"So we really did get their records intact?"

"It looks that way to our team of burrowers, anyway. And the security measures are even less sophisticated and up to date than the ones Harkness had to crack aboard *Tepes*. There are a lot more of them, so it's taking some time to work through them, but Anson says it's more time consuming than difficult."

"Do we have a time estimate?"

"Only a rough one. Harkness and Ascher agree that they should be able to generate a complete prisoner list within a couple of local days. How accurate and up to date it is will depend on how well the Peeps did their jobs—" her grimace warned her listeners not to get their hopes up on that score "—but we should have at least a starting point to begin looking for reinforcements."

"Good," McKeon said with a huge sigh of relief. "And with all due respect to Jesus and his people, Ma'am, I'd certainly like to begin with any Alliance personnel we can dig up." Honor gave him a sharp glance, and he shrugged. "I trust our people from Inferno completely," he said, "but we've had months for all of us to get to know one another and for them to learn to trust us. And to accept your authority. But now we're going to have to branch out, and I'd prefer to build up a solid cadre of people who came from our own chain of command before we start trying to weld people from umpteen dozen different militaries into a cohesive force. Especially since you know as well as I do that some of those other people are going to be as hot for vengeance as anyone StateSec dragged back here to Styx to play with."

"He's got a point, Ma'am," Caslet said with quiet diffidence, and his mouth quirked wryly. "I realize I'm sort of the odd man out on this planet right now, but *I'd* certainly like to see you with a force whose loyalty and unity you can rely on . . . if only to protect me from some of the people who want to lump me in with the garrison!"

"Um." Honor swung her chair gently from side to side, chewing on her thumbnail, then nodded. "All right, Alistair. You've got a point. But I want to discuss it with Jesus and Harriet before we move on it. I don't want them thinking we're trying to sneak something past them because we don't trust them."

"I agree completely," McKeon told her, and she nodded, but her mind was already reaching out towards the next worrisome point.

"Have we picked up any more of Proxmire's crew?" she asked.

"Not that I've heard about in the last couple of hours," McKeon replied with a grimace. Metcalf and DuChene were still depressed over the destruction of the courier boat. They knew they'd had no real choice, yet the failure of the boat's fusion bottle had destroyed her with all hands, and they carried a heavy load of guilt. He was confident they'd work through it, and they weren't letting it keep them from doing their duty, but he hated to see them punishing themselves for it this way.

In the meantime, however, they'd picked up seven members of the boat's crew who'd been dirtside when it all hit the fan. Some of them had stubbornly refused to give more than name, rank, service branch, and serial number, but others had been so stunned by the cataclysmic upheaval in their fortunes that they'd started talking as soon as someone asked them a question. Unfortunately, none of the talkative ones were officers, and they didn't really know all that much beyond what their own duties had been. From what they'd told him, he knew there had been eight more crew members on Hell, and he still hoped to pick them up—or identify them from among the mass of other prisoners—but it was entirely possible that all eight were dead. Honor's assault force had taken over a hundred casualties, fifty-two of them fatal, including two of the escapees from *Tepes.* He knew Honor had been privately devastated by the deaths of Senior Chief Halburton and Senior Chief Harris. She'd fought not to show it, yet losing them after they'd come through so much together had struck all of them as bitterly unfair. But StateSec's losses had been at least three times as high as the attackers'. Or, at least, their *known* losses so far had been, he corrected himself. They were still finding bodies and pieces of bodies in the wreckage.

"Keep on that, Alistair," Honor told him. "Without Tresca—" it was her turn to grimace, for Camp Charon's CO had set the standard for his personnel, and his personal slaves had literally ripped him to pieces before he could be taken into custody "—or his exec, we don't have anyone who can tell us how much longer Proxmire was supposed to be assigned here or if he already had orders for another station. If he did have orders and he doesn't turn up on schedule—"

She shrugged again, and McKeon nodded soberly. The possibility that they would have to destroy Hell's courier boat had always existed, but he knew how hard Honor had hoped to take it intact. It couldn't have carried a fraction of their people—which now included everyone from Inferno as surely as it did his own survivors from *Prince Adrian*—away from Hell, but it *could* have been dispatched to the nearest Alliance-held system. The Cerberus System lay deep inside the PRH, but if the Allies knew its coordinates, a convoy of fast transports with a military escort could be in and out again before the Peeps knew a thing about it. The operation would have had to accept a fair degree of risk, but it would have been practical, especially with the People's Navy on the defensive. And the psychological impact of a mass prisoner rescue, both for the Alliance and against the Peeps, would have been enormous.

But without the courier, that possibility went right out the airlock and left them no choice but to fall back on Honor's alternate plan. She'd intended from the beginning to take over Hell's orbital defenses and use them to defend the planet against any SS warships that happened along while they awaited the rescue the courier had been supposed to whistle up. Now she would simply have to use them to acquire her courier in the first place.

Assuming, of course, that she had time to do that before Citizen Commander Proxmire's failure to turn up somewhere else provoked someone into sending a cruiser squadron to see what was keeping him.

That was the real problem, he thought moodily. Massive as the orbital defenses' firepower was, they had serious weaknesses. The biggest was that all of them were fixed, unable to maneuver or dodge, which meant most of them could be killed with long-range, cee-fractional missile strikes by any competent fleet commander who knew what he was up against. McKeon had been enormously relieved—and he knew Honor had been, too—when they discovered that the Peeps had, in fact, at least taken the precaution of putting hardened missile launchers on each of Hell's three moons. It would have made even more sense to put weapons crews up there to operate them under local control if something happened to the central command site here on Styx, but he wasn't about to complain about that. The remotely controlled launchers didn't have much magazine capacity, and light-speed transmission limits meant their fire control was a tad arthritic, given their distances from Styx. Niflheim, the largest and furthest out moon, for example, had an orbital radius of over a light-second and a half, and even Tartarus, the closest, was almost a hundred and fifty-six thousand kilometers out at perigee. But there also hadn't been any Peep gun crews up there to open fire *on* Styx, and they provided at least some long-range defensive firepower which would be extremely difficult for an attacker to neutralize.

Yet most of Honor's defenses were hideously vulnerable . . . if the bad guys knew to attack them in the first place. But that was the up side of the destruction of Proxmire's courier boat. Its failure to escape meant it hadn't been able to tell anyone what had happened, so at least the first few StateSec ships to happen along would have no idea that anyone besides their fellow SS personnel now controlled Hell's orbital weapons. As long as nothing happened to make them suspicious, they ought to make their normal approaches to the planet while Honor and her people waited like the spider at the heart of the web. And once they came in close enough and slow enough for the defenses to engage them, the advantage would swing decisively to *Honor's* side, leaving them no option but to surrender or die.

Which was certainly one way to get their hands on the courier vessel they needed, he thought.

"How many of their communications people did we sweep up?" Honor's question broke into his reverie, and he blinked.

"Uh . . . I'm not sure," he said, shaking his mind back to the present. "I know we've got some of them, but things are still too chaotic—and we're still too shorthanded—to really start sorting people out by category yet."

"I know, but we have to get on top of that as quickly as we can, especially where the com people are concerned," Honor told him. He raised an eyebrow at her, and she shrugged. "As well as we've been able to figure out so far, *Count Tilly* was the only regular Navy ship ever to come here. StateSec seems to have kept the system coordinates completely to itself prior to that. I don't know what's happened to Tourville and his people—I hope to heaven that with Ransom dead someone with a little sanity decided not to come down on them just for being decent human beings—but I rather doubt that Saint-Just is going to encourage them to hand their astro data over to the rest of the Navy. Which means anyone who comes calling out here will almost certainly be StateSec."

She paused, and McKeon nodded, but he still looked puzzled.

"The SS doesn't have all that many warships, Alistair. It can't. Which means that those it does have are part of a relatively small force. Their com people may very well know the Camp Charon com people by name, face, and voice, and if they don't see anyone they know on screen when they come in, they may get just a little suspicious."

"Oh." McKeon nodded and rubbed one eyebrow. She'd done it again, he thought. He was still bogged down in worrying his way through their immediate problems, but she was already two or three moves ahead, considering what they had to do *next*.

"Even if you manage to identify their com people, do you really want to trust them that much?" Caslet asked quietly. The other two looked at him, and he twitched his shoulders. "I don't have a very high opinion of StateSec either, Ma'am, but some of them fought to the bitter end against your people, despite being totally surprised. And quite a few of them did exactly the same thing against LaBoeuf and his Levelers. Some of them might try to warn any incoming ships even with pulsers screwed into their ears."

"They might," Honor agreed. She didn't mention that she and Nimitz ought to be able to sort out the ones likely to do that, but even if Warner had known, he still would have had a point. The unlikliest people could turn on their enemies like lions when the right buttons were punched, and even with the 'cat's assistance, it would be impossible for her to know what those buttons might be for any given person. But she'd already considered that, and she gave him another of her half-smiles.

"They might," she repeated, "but there's some pretty good equipment in the base com center, Warner. In fact, it's substantially better than its software appears to be . . . and I've got a clutch of very capable programmers to teach it all sorts of new tricks. Once they've had a chance to do that, and once we identify the com people we want, I feel confident we can record enough imagery of them for our reeducated computers to let us fake up an acceptable talking head. Harkness has already found an enormous file of what appear to be conversations between Tresca and incoming vessels. We won't know for certain that that's what it is until we get past the security fences, but if it is, we should be able to put together just about anything we want from its contents. It's possible—even probable—that we'll find similar files for the regular communications people, as well, and I hope we will. But I want to be prepared if we don't, too."

"I see." Caslet looked at her respectfully, unaware that he and Alistair McKeon were thinking very similar thoughts at that moment. Honor felt the glow of admiration from both of them, but she allowed no sign of it to show in her expression as she let her chair come back upright. What they were so busy admiring, after all, was no more than the minimum foresight that duty required of her.

"All right," she said crisply. "It sounds like we're as on top of things as we can be with so few people, so our priorities are, first, to get the StateSec stragglers to surrender so we can protect them." She shook her own head wryly at that one, but continued without pausing. "Second, to convince their ex-slaves to stop massacring them and accept our promise that they'll stand their trials. Third, to get into the personnel records and find out where we can scare up some reinforcements—preferably," she nodded to McKeon, "Manticoran, or at least Allied personnel. Fourth, to locate any additional survivors from Proxmire's crew and try to find out when or if he was due to be relieved. And, fifth, to identify and segregate all of the communications staff we can find. Is that about all?"

"Just about," McKeon agreed. "I would like to bring up one other worry, though." She nodded for him to continue, and he shrugged. "The bad guys hiding in the boonies may already know when they expect someone else to arrive, which suggests two unpleasant possibilities to my nasty suspicious mind. One is that if they do know when someone's coming, they may try to come up with some way to warn them. We control the main communications facility, and we think we got all of their vehicles, but we can't be certain that they didn't get away with a few transmitters with more reach than a hand com. If they did, they may try to cobble up something. It wouldn't have to be very sophisticated—even a really crude signal could be enough to make someone suspicious. Bearing that in mind, I think we need to start making some overflights. Peep sensors may not be good enough to spot *people* hiding in the woods, but we ought to be able to detect hidden vehicles or power sources if we look hard enough, long enough, from low enough."

"An *excellent* idea, Alistair," Honor agreed, nodding firmly. "But you said there were two possibilities?"

"Yes." He scratched his eyebrow again. "The second thing that occurred to me is that, under normal circumstances, even the escapees would have as much reason as we do to keep the farms intact—more, actually, since we have control of all the storage facilities. But for all of us, these farms are the only source of food on the planet."

He paused, and Honor nodded to show she was following him. "Well, if they know someone will be along within, say, three to five T-months, they might just decide to take a stab at destroying the crops anyway. Think about it. If they took out all of the food supplies, we'd almost have to surrender ourselves to the first Peep ship to come along or starve right along with them."

"That, Alistair, is a very ugly thought," Honor said quietly.

"Agreed," Caslet put in. "And I think it's something we should certainly take seriously. At the same time, I'd have to say I don't think it's likely." Both Manticorans looked at him, and he chuckled humorlessly. "These are StateSec personnel. I know I just argued that some of them might surprise you with their dedication, but that would be acting as individuals. I still don't see them taking serious chances *as a group*, and any move to destroy their own food supplies along with ours would be a very serious risk indeed. Even if someone out there knows the schedule for the next dozen ship arrivals, they can't be certain it will be kept. And even if it is kept, they have to know there's at least a strong possibility that the ships in question would be either captured or destroyed once they came into range of the orbital defenses, given that you now control them. Besides, I doubt very much that any of them know Proxmire's courier boat was destroyed. They have to allow for the probability that you got it, too, since they obviously know by now that you had at least two assault shuttles. That being the case, for all they know you've already sent for a relief force . . . and if you have, they certainly know what they'd do in your place."

"And what would that be?" McKeon asked when he paused.

"Sail away and leave them here," Caslet said simply. "In your place, they wouldn't worry about anyone but themselves—probably not even the other POWs on the planet. They'd climb aboard the first ship to turn up and run for home just as fast as they could . . . and they might just take out the farms themselves before they left, in hopes that you'd starve to death before anyone else turned up to rescue you."

"You may be right," Honor said after a moment. "In fact, you probably are. Nonetheless, we can't afford to take any chances. Alistair, speak with Harriet and Henri about it. Have them work out some sort of guard schedule—they can use pinnaces and even some of our armored vehicles if they want to—to ensure that no one gets a chance to wreck any of the farm operations. And get your low-level recon flights organized soonest, as well. Put . . . Solomon and Gerry in charge of that. And get Sarah involved, too. Let's keep her and Gerry too busy to beat up on themselves."

"I'll see to it," McKeon promised.

"Good. In that case, I think that just about takes care of everything . . . except for one other little matter."

"Oh? What's that?" McKeon asked.

"I talked to Fritz this morning," Honor told him. "He's just tickled pink to have decent medical facilities again, and he specifically asked me to deliver you into his hands, Commodore McKeon!"

"I beg your pardon?" McKeon blinked, and she chuckled.

"He's got an entire, semicapable hospital over there, Alistair. They don't have regen capability, and, frankly—no offense, Warner—I'm not sure I'd trust myself to Peep regen even if *anyone's* regen worked for me. But they do have a fairly sophisticated dentistry setup." McKeon's hand rose to his mouth, as if suddenly reminded of the jagged gaps the Peep pulse rifle's butt had left in his teeth, and she smiled. "We can't grow you new teeth till we get you home again, Alistair, but in the meantime, Fritz tells me he's read the handbook and he's just itching for a chance to try out his new knowledge on some poor, unsuspecting guinea pig. He's all ready to build you some truly outstanding old-fashioned bridges, so once you've dealt with the things we've been discussing, I want you over at the hospital for him to take impressions."

"But I've got too many other things to—" McKeon began, only to shut his mouth with a click as she cut him off.

"But nothing, Commodore McKeon," she told him firmly. "You and Fritz and Andrew—yes, and you, too, Warner Caslet! Every *one* of you helped Fritz bully me after we got down from *Tepes.* Well now it's my turn, by God, and you *will* report to the surgeon. Do you read me on this, Commodore?"

"You're really enjoying this, aren't you?" he demanded, and the living side of her face smiled serenely.

"Darned right I am," Lady Dame Honor Harrington said smugly.

Chapter Twenty-Six

"Are you out of your *mind?*" Rear Admiral Harold Styles rose from his chair, planted his fists on Honor's desk, and glared at her furiously. "The questionable basis on which you've chosen to insist on retaining command puts you on dangerous enough ground already, *Admiral* Harrington! If you insist on convening courts-martial in time of war on your own authority, then you'd better make *damned* sure all the 'I's are dotted and the 'T's are crossed! Because if they aren't, *Admiral*, I swear to you that I personally will see you prosecuted to the full extent of the Articles of War!"

Nimitz half-rose on his perch, baring snow-white fangs with a warning hiss as Styles' fury flooded his empathic sense, and Honor felt an answering flicker of rage deep within herself. But it was Andrew LaFollet who drew her attention from Styles' outrage-purpled face, and she raised her hand quickly, flicking her fingers in a wave-off just in time to keep her armsman from grabbing the Manticoran by the scruff of his neck and physically expelling him from the office—preferably with a spectacular set of bruises. A part of her longed to let Andrew do just that, but she couldn't, however much she wanted to.

Not yet, *anyway*, she thought coldly. *But if he keeps this nonsense up for one more minute . . .*

"You will sit back down, Admiral Styles," she said instead, and each icy word was a polished chip of clarity, without the slurring her crippled mouth normally imposed. Her single working eye was even colder than her voice, and the right corner of her mouth twitched with a warning tick which made LaFollet almost pity Styles, despite his outrage at the admiral's behavior. But Styles didn't know her as well as her armsman did. He saw that twitch as a sign of nervousness, and awareness that she was in a false position, and the righteous fury he'd felt ever since he arrived on Styx and she refused to yield command to him blazed up in him like fire.

"Like fucking *hell* I will!" he began savagely. "From the first moment I came ashore h—"

He chopped off in mid-word as Honor came to her feet in a movement too graceful to be called an explosion yet too abrupt to be called anything else. He jerked back in alarm, then flushed even darker, shamed by his reaction, and started to snarl something else when her palm came down on the desk surface with the flat, explosive crack of a cannon shot.

"You will shut your mouth *now*, Admiral Styles," she said very softly, leaning forward over the desk in the echoing silence which followed, "or I will have you placed under close arrest, to remain there until such time as we leave this planet and return to Manticoran jurisdiction. Where," she went on even more icily, "I will have you charged with and court-martialed for insubordination, willful disregard of a superior's orders, conduct detrimental to the chain of command, and incitement to mutiny in time of war."

Styles stared at her, and his mouth worked soundlessly, as if he simply could not believe his ears. Two of those charges carried the death penalty if they were sustained, and Honor felt the sudden chill of terror that ran beneath the surface of his fiery bluster as he recognized the uncompromising sincerity of her threat at last. She glared at him for a brief, shivering eternity, then drew a deep breath and straightened her spine.

"I said to sit down," she said, spacing the words out with flat, deadly authority, and the rear admiral sagged back into the chair from which he had hurled himself. She remained standing for a slow ten-count, then lowered herself once more into her own chair much more slowly. She tipped it back and sat there, the right side of her face as expressionless as the left while she regarded him coldly, and a corner of her brain blessed Alistair McKeon's forethought.

She hadn't really considered the possibility before Harkness' team of moles managed to nibble their way through the last Peep security fences, but she wasn't the senior RMN officer on Hell after all. Harry Styles was, and that could have created all sorts of problems. The Inferno inmates had given their trust and loyalty to her, not to some officer they didn't even know, but if Styles had the seniority, then, logically—or, at least, legally—the command was his.

McKeon hadn't said anything in so many words, but he'd made his opinion of that possibility abundantly clear by how he hadn't said it. Honor suspected that he must have served under Styles in the past without enjoying the experience, for it was unlike him to feel such barely suppressed dislike for anyone. He was as capable as the next person of making the occasional misjudgment about a superior officer or succumbing to what was still called "bad chemistry"; Honor knew that even better than most. But she also knew that when it happened, he almost invariably felt uncomfortable, off balance and confused. It was as if he knew something was wrong with his own judgment and simply couldn't figure out what it was.

But whatever his reasons, his obliquely stated warning about Styles had been dead on the money, and she was grateful that she'd taken his advice about how to deal with the rear admiral.

She had been in control of Styx for two local weeks now, and Henri Dessouix had been delighted to discover an entire warehouse full of SS uniforms and, even better, fabric extruders and sewing machines. A little judicious reprogramming of the sewing machines and a few adjustments to the extruders, and he'd been able to turn out proper uniforms for the escaped prisoners.

Some of them—like Harriet Benson or, for that matter, Dessouix himself—had been on Hell so long their memories of what their uniforms should look like had become faded and uncertain. Nor were there any reference works they could consult, since the nations which had once issued those uniforms had disappeared into the ash heap of history . . . and the maw of the all-conquering People's Republic. But Honor felt confident that no one would complain about any minor details which were gotten wrong, and all of them (with the possible exception of Horace Harkness) had felt enormous relief at getting back into uniform once more. It wasn't simply a matter of stepping back into a world they understood, although there was an undeniable edge of that involved. It was more like a punctuation of the change in status they had won under Honor's command, a formal proof of what they had already achieved and a visible expression of what drew them together and forged them into a cohesive whole.

But at McKeon's very strong urging, Honor had not redonned Manticoran uniform. Instead, she wore the blue-on-blue of Grayson, with the five six-pointed stars of her current Grayson rank. Jesus Ramirez's eyes had widened when he first saw it, but he'd been less surprised than he might have been, for there had been more than enough time for Honor's people to fill him and the rest of the Infernoites in on her Grayson career. And then, as quickly as his eyes had widened, they'd sharpened in approval, for McKeon had been right. There could be more than one Allied flag officer on Hell, but there was no way there would be more than one fleet admiral.

Honor had felt ridiculous flaunting her GSN rank that way, however legal it might be and however thoroughly she'd earned it, but only until she met Styles for herself. After no more than five minutes, she'd decided that the People's Navy had done the Alliance an immense favor by capturing Harry Styles and putting him safely on Hell where he couldn't do the war effort any more damage. She had no idea what he was doing here instead of a regular navy-run POW camp somewhere, unless, perhaps, his rank had led StateSec to see him as some sort of prize catch to be kept in its personal trophy case. He was, after all, not merely the highest-ranking Manticoran officer yet captured by the People's Republic but also the only flag officer they'd captured in the entire first six and a half years of the war. They'd had him for over eight T-years, since the day they'd destroyed his entire picket squadron in the Yalta System in one of the probing attacks with which they had opened the present war. They'd actually caught him with cold impellers—which said a great deal about his competence right there—and his subsequent attempt to defend himself had been nothing to write home about.

Not that he saw it that way, of course. As far as he was concerned, he'd simply been the unfortunate victim of Peep treachery, attacked in time of peace and without a formal declaration of war. Apparently he had failed, in those long ago days of peace, to note the minor fact that the Legislaturalists who had run the People's Republic had never once bothered to alert a potential victim by declaring war before they hit it. He didn't seem to have learned much since, either. Added to which, he was arrogant, opinionated, full of his own importance, conceited, and stupid. And those were his good points, she thought acidly.

"I have put up with all the insubordination I intend to tolerate, Admiral Styles," she said into the fragile silence. Her voice was still cold, the words precisely enunciated, and she felt his tooth-grinding hatred flowing over her. "*I* am in command in this star system, and you, Admiral, are *not*. You will remember that at all times, and you will address not simply myself but *any* personnel on this planet who have voluntarily placed themselves under my command with proper courtesy at all times, or by *God* I will have you thrown back into the jungle to rot! Is that *clear*, Admiral Styles?"

He glared at her, then nodded curtly.

"I didn't hear you, Admiral," she said icily.

"Yes," he grated, and flushed still darker as her glacial eye jerked a "Ma'am!" from him, as well.

"Good," she said in a slightly less frozen voice. She knew he hadn't really given up. The fact that he'd been captured so early meant he'd been on Hell since before even the Battle of Hancock or her duel with Pavel Young. More recently captured personnel could have brought him up to date—in fact, for all Honor knew some of them had tried to do just that—but it hadn't taken. In his mind, the Grayson Space Navy was still some sort of comic opera, local-defense fleet and Honor was a mere commodore with delusions of grandeur. He didn't appear to believe that the Fourth Battle of Yeltsin—or, for that matter, the Battle of Hancock—had ever even happened, and he regarded her claim to admiral's rank as an outright lie. As far as he was concerned, it was nothing more than a ploy to allow her to retain the command which should rightfully have been his, and her senior subordinates were all in cahoots with her to make it stand up.

She wondered, sometimes, if perhaps she was wronging him a little. It was possible he'd become unhinged during his long stay on Hell, after all. But she didn't think so. His personality was too narrow, his belief in his own rectitude too unhesitating and unquestioning, for something as minor as eight years as a POW to chip away at.

"Now, then," she went on more calmly. "Whether you care to believe it or not, Admiral, I have given careful thought to your objections. Some of them are well reasoned, even though I may not agree with you, and you are certainly entitled to record them formally and in writing for review by higher authority. For now, however, I am the senior officer present, and it becomes my duty under the Articles of War—Manticoran as well as Grayson—to punish those guilty of criminal conduct in my command area. I do not accept that responsibility lightly, and I do not intend to exercise my authority capriciously. I do, however, intend to empanel courts-martial to consider the charges of criminal conduct leveled against the State Security personnel on this planet."

"With all due respect, Admiral," Styles broke in, "but that's a dangerous and extremely ill-advised decision." His tone didn't sound at all respectful, but she decided to let that pass as long as he watched his word choices. "I have no love for State Security—God knows I was their prisoner longer and suffered more from them than y—"

He chopped himself off again, flushing in embarrassment as she cocked an eyebrow coolly at him. His eyes slipped away from her half-dead face, then bounced off the empty left sleeve of her tunic, and he cleared his throat noisily.

"Well, that's beside the point," he said brusquely. "And the point *is*, Admiral Harrington, that if you go around convening kangaroo courts in the name of the Manticoran Alliance for the sole purpose of shooting Peep personnel as some sort of vengeance play, it won't matter whether you call it a 'court-martial' or simple murder. The propaganda consequences of such an action alone scarcely bear thinking about, and that leaves aside the whole question of its legality! I believe you're exceeding your authority, regardless of your rank, and I seriously question whether or not you can legally apply our Articles of War to the conduct, however reprehensible, of foreign nationals!"

"I don't doubt that you do," Honor said. Nor, though she forbore mentioning it, did she doubt that the true reason he'd objected in the first place was because he saw the supposed illegality of her intentions as a way to undercut the legitimacy of her authority in her subordinates' eyes. Just as he had now convinced himself that the only reason she had promised the courts-martial to the Infernoites and Styx's slaves was as a way to buy their support for her continued usurpation of *his* authority.

"If, however," she continued, "you had bothered to read my memo, or to listen to what I've already said, or, for that matter, even to ask, you would know that I have no intention of applying the Articles of War to them." His face flushed with fresh, wine-dark rage as her cold words bit home, and the living side of her mouth smiled frostily.

"I intend to try them under their own laws, Admiral," she told him.

"You—?" He gaped at her, and she nodded curtly.

"Their own regulations and the People's Uniform Code of Conduct are on file in the Styx data base, Admiral Styles. I will concede that the people who filed those documents there never regarded them as anything other than a propaganda ploy—window dressing to prove how 'enlightened' the current regime is. But they exist, they've never been changed, and they are just as legally binding on StateSec personnel as upon anyone else. *Those* are the laws under which they will be tried, Admiral, and the sentences any convicted parties receive will be strictly in accord with them."

"But—" Styles began, only to be cut off by an impatient wave of her hand.

"I called you here to inform you of my decision, Admiral; not to debate it," she told him flatly. "As the senior Manticoran officer on Hell, you were the proper representative for Her Majesty's Navy on the court-martial board, and I intended to name you to that position accordingly. Since you have so cogently and forcefully stated your objections to the entire proceeding, however, I no longer feel that I can properly ask you to participate in a process to which you are so deeply, morally opposed. Because of that, you are excused from court duty. Commodore McKeon will take your place."

"But if you're going to use their own laws—" Styles began again, almost desperately, and Honor curled a contemptuous mental lip as she felt the chaotic shifting of his emotions. They were too confused and changed too quickly for her to sort them out with any clarity, but she didn't really need to. He'd been prepared to bluster and bully her—and to make his high-minded opposition crystal clear in case higher authority later decided to come down on her over this. But violently as he'd protested, he couldn't stand being shunted aside, either. She'd affronted his dignity yet again, and she felt the hatred welling up inside him afresh.

"No, Admiral," she said firmly. "I will not ask you to compromise your principles in this matter." He opened his mouth yet again, and she shook her head.

"You're dismissed, Admiral Styles," she said softly.

"Whew! You came down on him pretty heavy there, Skipper," Alistair McKeon said.

Styles had left the office like a man walking in a bad dream, so shaken—temporarily at least—that he didn't even look up or glare when McKeon passed him almost in the office doorway. There was very little love lost between him and McKeon, and Honor sometimes wondered how much of that went back to whatever had formed Alistair's initial judgment of him. Not that much previous history was really needed to explain their present hostility. Honor had named

Styles to command the equivalent of her own Bureau of Personnel, which gave him the responsibility for coordinating the shuttle flights busy contacting all of the various prison camps, informing them of what had happened on Styx, and generally counting noses all around. It was an important task . . . but Styles also knew she had deliberately shuffled him off into that job to justify cutting him out of the tactical chain of command. Jesus Ramirez was the present commander of Camp Charon, with Harriet Benson as his exec, but it was Alistair McKeon who was Honor's true executive officer. She'd set things up so that Styles reported directly to her, not through McKeon, but he was the only officer on Hell who did that, and his hatred for his junior was a thing of elemental implacability.

McKeon knew it as well as Honor did, and now she looked up at him sharply, surprised by his comment. He recognized her reaction and smiled crookedly.

"The walls are kind of thin around here, Honor," he pointed out, "and I was next door waiting to see you. Besides, the way he was bawling and bellowing before you performed that double orchiectomy on him, they must've been able to hear him clear over at the landing strip!"

"Oh, dear." Honor sighed. She leaned back in her chair and massaged her forehead with her fingers. "I didn't want that to happen."

"Not your fault it did," McKeon pointed out.

"Maybe not, but I didn't exactly do anything to prevent it, either. And it's not going to help anything for our people to know I'm at dagger-drawing with the second-ranking Allied officer on the planet!"

"First, it wasn't your job to prevent it from happening," McKeon told her sternly. "It's your job to exercise command and keep us alive. If some asshole idiot makes a fool and a laughingstock out of himself, then it's your job to keep his stupidity from hamstringing your efforts to get us off Hell, not to protect him from the consequences he brings down on his own head. Second, it's probably a good thing that this is happening, not a bad one."

"Excuse me?" Honor cocked her head at him in surprise.

"You think maybe our non-Allied personnel aren't going to hear about this?" McKeon shook his head at her. "You know better than that. Walls have ears when something like this happens, and if I could hear it go down, you can be damned sure someone else heard it, too. Which means that it will be all over Styx by the end of the day. And that, in turn, means that our Infernoites, and the ex-slaves, and everyone else will know that you overrode the senior Royal Navy prisoner in order to do what you promised you'd do back at Inferno. Most of these people are—or were—professional military personnel, Honor. They know how the game is played . . . and the way you happen to play it is going to do more to hammer them together than you realize."

"That's not why I'm moving ahead with this, Alistair!" she said sharply.

"Of course it isn't," he said almost sadly. "But they know that, too. And that's exactly why it will have that effect."

She frowned at him, uncomfortable with his argument and also with the emotions behind it, but he only looked back calmly.

"Well, in that case—" she began, only to stop short as someone rapped sharply on the frame of the still open door. She looked up, and both eyebrows rose as she saw Solomon Marchant in the doorway. His face was alight with excitement, and she blinked as she felt his mingled surprise, wariness, and confusion all mixed together with the eagerness of someone with startling news.

"Yes, Solomon?" she said.

"I'm sorry to burst in on you like this, My Lady," he said, "but Senior Chief Harkness and I just cracked another security code, and I thought you'd want to know what we found."

"No doubt you're right," Honor said dryly as he paused for effect, and he blushed, then laughed.

"Sorry, My Lady. It's just that I was so surprised myself, that—" He shrugged. "What we found was a top secret list of Legislaturalist politicals, all of whom were considered to possess such important and sensitive information or to have sufficiently great potential for future usefulness that executing them was out of the question. So instead of being shot, they were declared officially dead and shipped out here under falsified names and prisoner manifests."

"Ah?" Honor tipped back her chair and cocked her head at him.

"Ah, indeed, My Lady. Most of them were high-ranking InSec officials or permanent departmental undersecretaries under the Harris Government—people like that. But a couple of them were military . . . including Admiral Amos Parnell."

"*Parnell?*" McKeon came out of his chair in astonishment, turning to face the Grayson officer, and Marchant nodded sharply.

"Yes, Sir."

"But they shot him years ago—right after Third Yeltsin!" Honor protested.

"They *said* they shot him," Marchant corrected her. "But he's here according to the records, and I've sent a pinnace out to collect him. Ah," he suddenly looked just a little nervous. "I, um, assumed that was what you'd want me to do, My Lady," he added quickly.

"You assumed correctly," Honor said slowly, and then sat for several seconds, considering Marchant's astonishing news. Amos Parnell would never have become Chief of Naval Operations under the old regime if he hadn't been a Legislaturalist, but he'd been extremely good at the job, however he'd gotten it. When she first accepted her Grayson commission, Honor had had a chance to read the classified reports of the Third Battle of Yeltsin, and she'd been deeply impressed by Parnell's performance there. Lured into what was for all intents and purposes a deep-space ambush, then jumped by more than twice the firepower he'd expected to confront, all under the command of no less a tactician than Hamish Alexander, he'd still gotten half his fleet out intact. And like everyone else, she'd assumed he was dead for eight T-years now.

And if he isn't, *who knows where this could lead?* she thought. *He knows where all the bodies were buried under the Legislaturalists, and he's got absolutely no reason to like the present regime! We learned a lot when Alfredo Yu came over to our side, but Parnell could tell us an awful lot more than that if he chose to. Most of it might be dated, but even if it's only deep background . . .*

She shook herself, surfacing from her thoughts as if from deep water, and glanced up at Marchant again.

"Good work, Solomon. And tell Harkness I said the same goes for him, if you would."

"Of course, My Lady."

"And you did the right thing to send the pinnace," she confirmed again, then chuckled.

"What's funny?" McKeon asked her.

"I was just thinking," Honor replied, swinging her chair until she faced him once more.

"Thinking what?"

"That things may be about to change for Warner," she said with a slow, crooked grin. McKeon looked back at her, and then it was his turn to chuckle, and he shook his head.

"You've may just have a point there," he agreed. "Depending on what—if anything—Parnell has to say to us, you may have a point indeed, Lady Harrington!"

Chapter Twenty-Seven

The man Geraldine Metcalf escorted into Honor's office had snow-white hair and a deeply lined face. According to the imagery in his file, he'd had neither of those things before he was shipped out to Hades . . . but, then, neither had all the fingers on his left hand been gnarled and twisted or the right side of his face and what she could see of his right forearm been pocked with the ugly scars of deep, cruel burns. He was also missing even more teeth than Alistair McKeon, and he walked with a strange, sideways lurch, as if there were something badly wrong with his right knee.

But there was nothing old or defeated in the strong bones of his ravaged face or the hard brown eyes which met Honor's as she stood behind her desk in welcome.

"Admiral Parnell," she said quietly.

"I'm afraid you have the advantage of me," he replied, examining her carefully. His mouth quirked as he took in the dead side of her face and her missing arm, and he gave a small snort which might have been either amusement or an acknowledgment that State Security had initiated both of them into the same club. "Grayson uniform, I believe," he murmured. "But a woman?" He cocked his head and looked back at the dead side of her face, and something changed in his eyes with an almost audible click.

"Harrington," he said softly, and she nodded, surprised by his recognition.

"Honor Harrington," she confirmed, "and these are my senior officers—Rear Admiral Styles, Royal Manticoran Navy; Commodore Ramirez, San Martin Navy; and Commodore McKeon, also of the Royal Manticoran Navy. And this—" she nodded to the fourth officer present "—is Citizen Commander Warner Caslet of the People's Navy."

Parnell looked at each of the others in turn, fierce eyes lingering on Caslet for just a moment. Then he nodded to Honor with a curiously courteous choppiness, and she waved at the chair facing the desk.

"Please be seated, Admiral."

"Thank you."

He lowered himself cautiously into the chair with a wince of pain, his stiff knee refusing to bend in the slightest, and leaned back, resting his crippled hand in his lap. He let his gaze run over all of them again, then returned it to Honor and smiled.

"I see you've been promoted since the last time anyone bothered to share news of the war with me, Admiral Harrington," he observed almost whimsically. "The last I remember, you were a captain in the *Manticoran* Navy."

"But you've been out of circulation for some time, Sir," Honor replied with a small, crooked smile of her own.

"True," he said more bleakly. "That, unfortunately, is all too true. But, you know, I spent the entire flight here asking myself what could possibly be going on. This isn't my first return flight to Styx, of course." He raised his smashed hand slightly. "They were quite insistent about seeking certain statements and information from me, and I'm afraid our immunization program works quite well . . . against any of the drugs in our own pharmacopeia, at least.

"But given that the pinnace flight crew wore Manticoran, Grayson, and Erewhonese uniforms—not to mention at least one uniform I didn't even recognize—I was forced to the conclusion that something unfortunate had happened to Corporal Tresca." He saw Honor's eyebrow start up once more and laughed harshly. "Oh, yes, Admiral. 'Citizen Brigadier' Tresca was an InSec corporal before the coup—didn't you know that?"

"According to his personnel file, he was a Marine captain," Honor replied.

"Ah." Parnell nodded. "I don't suppose I should be surprised. He had the access codes to the personnel files, I'm sure, and he was always rather fond of fulfilling his fantasies." The Admiral's tone was light, but his eyes were polished agate, and Honor felt the hatred radiating from him like winter fog. "May I assume something did happen to him?"

"You might say that, Sir," Honor said.

"I do hope it was fatal?" Parnell inquired politely, and his eyes flashed at her small nod. "Oh, good," he murmured. "That's one item out of the way already."

"I beg your pardon, Sir?"

"Um?" The Legislaturalist shook himself. "Forgive me, Admiral Harrington. My attention seems to wander a bit these days." He smiled thinly. "It's just that I made myself a small list of things to do if the opportunity ever came my way, and killing Tresca was the second item on it. Is it to much too hope that he died badly?"

"I think you could say he died about as badly as anyone possibly could, Sir," McKeon answered for Honor, remembering the savagely mutilated lump of once-human meat his people had found in Tresca's blood-spattered quarters.

"Then I suppose that will have to do," Parnell said. An unreadable flash of emotion flickered across Warner Caslet's face, almost too quickly to be seen, but Parnell's alert eyes caught it. He smiled again, and this time there was no humor in expression, only cold ugly hate. "Does my attitude shock you, 'Citizen Commander'?" he asked softly.

Caslet looked back at him for a silent moment, then nodded, and Parnell shrugged.

"It would have shocked me once, too, I suppose. But that would have been before I watched Corporal Tresca personally hammer a six-centimeter nail through the skull of my chief of staff because neither one of us would give StateSec the 'confessions' it wanted." Caslet blanched, and Parnell's nostrils flared. "They'd worked on him for over two hours before they even started on *me* that afternoon, of course," he added conversationally, "and the first nail didn't kill him immediately. Commodore Perot always was a tough man. So Tresca used the same hammer on my hand and my right knee for ten or fifteen minutes before he got around to driving the second one in."

Honor heard a retching sound and looked up to see Rear Admiral Styles dashing from the office, one hand clamped over his mouth. Nausea rippled in her own belly, but she fought it down. In a strange way, her access to Parnell's emotions actually helped, for she felt the terrible, bottomless hatred and the anguish hiding behind his calm demeanor. He and his chief of staff had been close, she realized, perhaps as close as she and McKeon, and she felt her hand clench in an ivory-knuckled fist at the thought of watching anyone do something like that to Alistair.

"Confessions, Admiral?" she heard her own voice ask, and his nod thanked her for her own conversational tone, as if it were a shield against something he chose not to face too closely.

"Yes. He wanted us to confess our participation in the Harris Assassination plot. We'd been sentenced to death for it already, of course, but he wanted chips of our confession for the records. For propaganda, I assume. I could be wrong, though. It may simply have been for his own pleasure." He cocked his head, then sighed. "I suppose there's a certain poetic justice in it. Internal Security did create him, after all. And if we're going to be honest, we brought Pierre and his damned Committee down on our own heads out of sheer incompetence. Didn't we, *Citizen* Commander?"

This time there was a cold, bleak hatred in his voice, and Caslet winced. Parnell's question and the bottomless contempt of his tone—contempt for a traitor who served traitors—cut him like a knife, and he opened his mouth to defend himself. But no words came out. He could only sit there, staring at the fierce, crippled man who had been his uniformed commander-in-chief only eight T-years earlier. The man who had administered his own officer's oath at the Naval Academy so many years before that, though there was no reason to expect Parnell to remember one single midshipman among hundreds.

"I understand your feelings, Admiral," Honor said quietly. The Legislaturalist looked at her, his mouth taut, as if prepared to reject her statement, and she shifted the stump of her left arm ever so slightly. It was a tiny gesture, more imagined than seen, but Parnell's lips relaxed. "I understand your feelings," she repeated, "but you should know that Cit— That *Commander* Caslet is here on Hell because he did his best to see to it that captured Allied personnel were treated properly and humanely by State Security. I assure you, Sir, that to my own personal knowledge, he has always demonstrated all the virtues of the old Havenite officer corps . . . and none of its vices."

She held the ex-CNO's gaze with her own, and it was Parnell who finally looked away.

"I had that coming, Admiral Harrington," he said after a moment, and glanced at Caslet. "I apologize, Commander. I've been stuck here on Hell, but I've talked to other politicals sent here since my own arrival. I know at least a little something about the pressures you and people like you have faced, and in your position I might—" He paused and cocked his head, as if reconsidering something, then shrugged. "No, let's be honest. In your position I *would* have kept my head down and tried to do my duty as best I could and somehow stay alive." He chuckled softly, almost naturally. "I forget sometimes that knowing they're going to kill you in the end anyway tends to make it just a little easier to choose 'death before dishonor.' "

"Sir— Admiral Parnell," Caslet began. He stopped again and closed his eyes, sitting unmoving for several seconds before he could open them again. "We all thought you were dead, Sir," he said finally, his voice hoarse. "You and Admiral Rollins, and Admiral Horner—Vice Admiral Clairmont, Admiral Trevellyn . . . It all happened so *fast*, Sir! One day everything was fine, and then the President and the entire Government were gone, and we were already at war with Manticore, and—" He stopped again, breathing hard, and gazed straight into Parnell's face. "I'm sorry, Sir," he said very softly. "We shouldn't have let it happen, but there was no time, no—"

"Stop, Commander," Parnell said, and this time his voice was almost gentle. "You were too junior to keep it from happening. That was my job, and I'm the one who blew it, not you. And don't shed too many tears for the old regime," he went on. "*I* do, of course—on a personal level, at least. To the best of my knowledge, not a single member of my family survived the purges. I could be wrong. I hope I am. But if any of them lived, they did it by going so far underground that StateSec couldn't find them, and the chance of pulling that off—" He shrugged.

"But the old regime was rotten, too," he went on after a moment. "If it hadn't been, Pierre couldn't have pulled this off. Hell, Commander—all of us at the top knew the system was breaking down! We just didn't know how to fix it, and so we let the rot spread further and further, and in the end, Pierre dragged us all down for the kill. But we knew exactly what we were doing when we sent you and people like you out to conquer other star systems. Don't you ever think for a moment that we didn't. And to be honest about it, I don't really regret it now." He smiled faintly as Ramirez tightened angrily in his chair. "It was the only way out for us," he said, half-apologetically, "the only game we knew, and I'd be lying if I said we didn't take a certain pride in playing it as well as we possibly could."

Ramirez clamped his jaw hard but said nothing. Silence hovered in the office for several moments, and then McKeon leaned back and crossed his legs.

"Forgive me, Admiral Parnell," he said, "but you said that killing Tresca was the second thing on your list." Parnell regarded him with a faint, grim gleam of amusement and nodded. "In that case, would you mind telling us what the first one was?"

"I wouldn't mind at all, Commodore," Parnell said politely. "In fact, this is probably as good a starting place as any. You see, killing Tresca was a purely selfish ambition, something just for me; that's why it was number two on the list. But number one was telling the rest of the galaxy what Tresca told me the day he murdered Russ Perot and smashed my hand to splinters."

"And that was?" McKeon prompted courteously when the Legislaturalist paused.

"That was the identity of the three people who were really the brains behind the Harris Assassination," Parnell said flatly, "because it wasn't the Navy at all." Caslet inhaled sharply, and the ex-CNO glanced at him. "Surely you must have suspected that, Commander. Did you really think we'd do something like that, especially when we'd just gone to war?"

"Not at first," Caslet said in a low voice. "But then all the confessions and all the evidence came out, Sir. It seemed impossible . . . and yet—"

"I know." Parnell sighed. "For that matter, I believed it for a while myself, so I suppose I shouldn't blame you. But it wasn't us, Commander—not the Navy and not the Legislaturalists. It was Pierre himself. He and Saint-Just and Cordelia Ransom set the entire thing up as a means to simultaneously decapitate the government and paralyze the only force that could have stopped them: the Navy."

"*Dios*," Ramirez said softly, but Parnell was looking at Honor, and he cocked his head.

"You don't seem surprised to hear that, Admiral," he observed.

"ONI and SIS have suspected it for quite some time, Sir," she replied levelly. "We had no proof, however, and I believe the decision not to make allegations we couldn't prove was made at the highest levels." She shrugged. "Under the circumstances, I think it was the proper one. Without corroborating evidence, it could only have been viewed as self-serving propaganda and hurt our credibility."

"I see. But you know, don't you, that there are at least a dozen people here on Hell, myself among them, who can 'corroborate' it in considerable detail? For that matter, somewhere in the data base there should be a recording of the interrogation session in which Tresca himself told me."

Warner Caslet inhaled sharply, and Parnell turned to look levelly at him once more. The younger man opened his mouth, then shut it again, and Parnell smiled sadly.

"Treason comes hard even now, doesn't it, Commander?" he asked gently. "Here I sit, aiding and abetting the Republic's enemies in time of war, and that disappoints you. It's not what you expected from an admiral who's sworn an oath to defend it, is it?"

"Sir, your decisions have to be your own," Caslet began. He was white-faced under his tan, and his eyes were troubled. "God knows I have no right to judge you. And from what you've just said, the people running the Republic now are traitors, as well as monsters and mass murderers. I haven't— I mean, I've thought about it myself. But like you, I swore an oath, and it's my *country*, Sir! If I break faith with that, I break faith with myself . . . and then what do I have left?"

"Son," Parnell said compassionately, "you don't have a country anymore. If you ever went home again, you'd wind up right back here—or dead, more likely—because nothing you could possibly say could excuse you for sitting here in this room with these people . . . and me. And I'll tell you something else, Commander. From what you've just said to me, I can tell you that you're better than the Republic deserves, because you're still loyal to it, and it's *never* been loyal to you. It wasn't when people like me ran it, and it sure as hell isn't now."

"I can't accept that, Sir," Caslet said hoarsely, but Honor felt the torment within him. The pain and disillusionment and, even more than either of those things, the agonizing suspicion that he *could* accept it. Indeed, that the core of him already had. And that suspicion terrified Warner Caslet, for if it were true, it would drive him inexorably towards a decision, force him to take control and forge purposefully and knowingly in the direction in which he had so far only drifted.

"Maybe you can't," Parnell said after a moment, allowing him to cling to the lie—for now, at least—if he chose. "But that doesn't make anything I've just said untrue, Commander. Still, I suppose a little of that same idealism still clings to me, too. What an amazing thing." He shook his head. "Forty years of naval service, dozens of cold-blooded campaigns under my belt—hell, I'm the one who drew up the plans to begin *this* war! I screwed them up, of course, but I was damned straight the one who authorized 'em. And eight more years here on Hell, on top of all that. And still there's something down inside me that insists the drunk-rolling whore I served is a great, shining lady who deserves to have me lay down my life in her defense."

He sighed and shook his head again.

"But she isn't, son. Not anymore. Maybe someday she will be again, and it's going to take men and women like you—people who stay loyal to her and fight for her from within—to bring that about. But they'll have to be people *like* you, Commodore. You can't be one of them anymore . . . and neither can I. Because however we may feel about her, she'll kill us both in an instant if she ever gets her hands on us again."

His voice trailed off, and silence hovered in its wake. The other officers in the office looked at one another for several seconds, and then Honor cleared her throat.

"Are you saying that you'll take service with the Alliance, Sir?" she asked in a very careful tone.

"No, Admiral Harrington. Or not directly, at least. I can't help you kill people like him." He nodded his head at Caslet. "I helped train him, shaped his beliefs, sucked him into serving the same system I served. What's happening now is at least as much my fault as it is Pierre's, and I can't be a party to killing officers who are caught up in a mess I made. And for that matter, when you come right down to it, maybe some good will actually come of Pierre's damned 'Committee' someday. God, I *hope* it does! If all of this has been for absolutely nothing . . ."

He shook his head again, eyes lost as he stared at something none of the rest of them could see. Then a shiver seemed to ripple through him, and he was suddenly back with them, his face calm once more as he smiled crookedly at Honor.

"No, I can't do that. I won't," he told her. "But that doesn't mean that I can't hurt Pierre, because that I *can* do, and with a clear conscience. I'm afraid your military intelligence people won't get much out of me, Admiral Harrington—even assuming that anything I once knew is still current—but if you can get me into the Solarian League, I think you'll find it worth your while."

"The League?" Honor's surprise showed in her voice, and he chuckled.

"There are quite a few other people here on Hell who'd be delighted to go with me, I'm sure," he said. "For that matter, there are probably some who can and will offer their direct services to your Alliance. I'd be a bit cautious about accepting them, if I were you—it's never an easy thing to change allegiances. Not for the ones you want on your side in the first place, at least! But those of us who can't do that can still seek asylum in the League. They've got all those wonderful laws covering displaced persons and political refugees, and I rather suspect the newsies will swarm all over us when we 'come back from the dead.' "

He smiled mirthlessly at Ramirez's soft sound of sudden understanding and nodded to the towering San Martino.

"I imagine the very fact that StateSec proclaimed that we were dead will go some way towards undermining the regime's credibility," he said, "and if there is any supporting evidence in the archives here and you'd be kind enough to let us have copies of it, we'll see to it that it gets into the right hands. From a few things I've heard from more recent additions to the population here on Hell, the Sollies have been funneling technology to the Republic for some time now. I'd think a shift in public opinion back home might, ah, adversely impact that practice. And even if it doesn't, news from the League manages to trickle into the Republic despite all Public Information can do. When word of who really murdered the old government gets out, it should help undermine the Committee, I imagine."

"You may be hoping for too much, Sir," Caslet told him soberly. Parnell looked a question at him, and he shrugged.

"There are three kinds of people who support the Committee now, Sir: those who truly believe in its official platform; those who want to prop it up just long enough to replace it with their own idea of the 'right' system . . . and those too terrified to do anything else. The only ones who would even care about something that happened eight T-years ago are the first group, and not even they are likely to do anything about it, I'm afraid. They can't—not without throwing away the very reforms they want, and certainly not in the middle of a war like this one's become."

"You may be right, Commander," Parnell said after a moment in tones of considerable respect, "but I still have to try. In a sense, I'm just as trapped as anybody still in the Navy is. I have to do this, even if it's not going to do any good at all. It's both the most and the least that I *can* do."

"I understand, Sir," Caslet said. He clenched his hands together into a double fist in his lap and stared down at them, his shoulders taut, then sighed. "And I suppose I'm going to have to decide what *I* can do, too, aren't I?" he murmured after a moment.

"Think of it this way, Commander," Parnell replied gently. "I don't know exactly how you landed here, and Hell is hardly the place that anyone I know would choose to go voluntarily, but there are some advantages to being here." Caslet looked up at him, eyes shadowed with disbelief, and the Legislaturalist admiral grinned. "Freedom of conscience, Commander Caslet!" he said, and laughed out loud at Caslet's expression. "You're in such deep shit now that it can't possibly get any deeper, son," the ex-CNO told him, "so the only thing that matters now is what you *choose* to do. It wasn't something we ever encouraged you to do when we were running the Republic, and Pierre and his people would sure as hell never, ever want you to do it now. But between us, we've shoved you into a corner with your back flat to the wall, and in some ways a man with nothing to lose has more freedom of choice than anyone else in the universe. So use what we've given you, Commander." There was no humor in his voice now, and he leaned forward in his chair, brown eyes dark and intent. "You've paid a hell of a price for it, and it's a gift that can kill you in a heartbeat, but it's yours now—all yours. Make up your own mind, choose your own course and your own loyalties, boy. That's all the advice I have left to give you, but you take it . . . and you damned well spit in the eye of anyone who *dares* to fault whatever decision you make!"

Book Five

Chapter Twenty-Eight

"Citizen Saint-Just is here, Citizen Chairman," the secretary announced, and Rob Pierre looked up from behind his desk as his security chief was ushered in. It wasn't the desk in his official office, with all the proper HD props to make it look impressive. This was the one from which he actually ran the People's Republic, with the comfortably shabby furniture and working clutter only his closest allies were ever allowed to see.

And there were far fewer of those allies than there had been eight T-years before.

To the casual observer, Oscar Saint-Just would have looked just as bland, harmless, and unexcited as usual, but Pierre knew him too well. He recognized the acute unhappiness behind those outwardly dispassionate eyes, and he sighed at the sight of it. He'd been fairly certain of why Oscar had wanted to see him, but he'd also hoped that, just this once, he could be wrong.

Unfortunately, he wasn't.

He waved at one of the beat-up old chairs facing the desk and tipped his own chair back with a hidden grimace as Saint-Just sat. For just a moment, Pierre allowed himself to remember another office and another meeting with the man who had then been second-in-command of the Legislaturalists' Office of Internal Security. It provoked mixed emotions, that memory. On the one hand, it reminded him of all the things they had accomplished. On the other, it had been the first step which had landed Rob S. Pierre astride the hungry beast of the PRH, and had he known then what he knew now . . .

Had you known then, you still would have done it, his mind told him severely. *Somebody had to. And be honest, Rob—you* wanted *to do it. You wouldn't be here if you hadn't decided to sit down at the table as a player, so quit whining about the cards you drew and get on with the job!*

"What did you want to see me about, Oscar?" he asked, purely as a way to get things started.

"I just wanted to ask you one more time if you really want to do this," Saint-Just replied. He spoke as calmly as ever, but, then, he'd sounded calm even as LaBoeuf's maniacs fought their way towards the Committee floor by floor, too. Pierre sometimes wondered if some quirk of evolution had simply omitted the standard connection between anxiety and voice pitch built into other people. Or if perhaps someone had foisted one of the mythical androids of prespace fiction writers off on him.

"I presume you mean the devaluation?"

"That's part of what I mean," Saint-Just said. "That part of it certainly worries me. But to be honest, Rob, it worries me a hell of a lot less than the free rein you're giving McQueen."

"We can squash McQueen any time we have to," Pierre retorted. "Hell, Oscar! You're the one who doctored her dossier to make it a slam-dunk in front of a People's Court!"

"I realize that," Saint-Just said calmly. "And I also realize that I'm the one who vetted her, and the one who countersigned Fontein's evaluation, *and* the one who's recording virtually every word she says. Under most circumstances, I'd feel perfectly confident about it. But these aren't 'most circumstances.' You know that as well as I do, and I don't like how . . . comfortable she and her senior officers are starting to sound with each other."

Pierre scowled and started to speak sharply, then made himself stop. Saint-Just's paranoia, both personal and institutional, was exactly what made him so valuable. He distrusted *everybody*, except—perhaps—Pierre. Actually, the Chairman wasn't too certain even about that. Yet paranoid or no, Saint-Just had given Pierre ample proof of the acuity of his perceptions . . . most of the time.

Unfortunately, Pierre had also had proof that the StateSec chief could occasionally go off on tangents all his own, and Oscar Saint-Just was not a great believer in moderation. He believed in playing safe . . . which, from his viewpoint, meant shooting anyone he suspected might even be *contemplating* treason. At least that way he could be sure he got any guilty parties, and if the occasional innocent got blotted out too, well, making an omelet was always hard on a few eggs.

Up to a point, that wasn't such a bad thing—except from the eggs' perspective, perhaps. A certain degree of unpredictability actually made a reign of terror more effective. But that was the point. If they were going to defeat the Manties, they had to begin moving away from outright terror tactics. Oscar himself had agreed with that when they first discussed McQueen's appointment as Secretary of War. The question was whether his present concerns were based in reality or were the result of another of his tangents.

"I don't have any military background myself, Oscar," the Chairman said after a moment. "You know that. But I do have some familiarity with how political figures work with their closest aides and subordinates, and I'd think a certain degree of 'comfort' in McQueen's relationships with her subordinates was actually a good sign. She's always been a leader, not a driver. I know!" He raised a hand before Saint-Just could interrupt. "That's one of the qualities which makes her dangerous to us. But it's the way her command style works, and her command style is what makes her dangerous to the *Manties.* I think we're just going to have to let her do things her way—as we told her we would—while you and your people go on keeping an eye on her. If she gets out of line, of course we'll have to remove her. But in the meantime, let's give her a chance to demonstrate that she can do what we brought her in to do for us."

"And if she can't?"

"In that case, the decision becomes simpler," Pierre said calmly. "If she doesn't produce in the field, then there's no reason to risk letting her build a personal support base in the officer corps."

In which case, he did not add aloud, *she's yours, Oscar.*

"All right," Saint-Just said after a long, thoughtful moment. "I won't pretend I'm happy about it, and Fontein and some of the other commissioners are even unhappier than I am. But I agreed with you about how badly we needed her in the first place, so I suppose bellyaching about it now is a bit childish of me."

"I wouldn't put it that way myself," Pierre told him, prepared to lavish a little stroking now that the decision was made. "You're my watchdog, Oscar. For the most part, I trust your instincts completely, and I know exactly how badly I need them. As for Fontein and the others, I'd be surprised if they *weren't* unhappy. McQueen's cut pretty deeply into their say-so in the operational sphere, and that's bound to have at least a little overlap into the political and policy sides, as well. They'd be more than human if they didn't resent a reduction in their authority."

"I know," Saint-Just agreed. "And in Fontein's case, I suspect a little of it may be overreaction to the way she blind-sided him before the Leveler business. But they're *supposed* to be suspicious of their military counterparts, and I don't want to undercut that. Or make them think I don't give their reports the attention they merit."

"And," Pierre said shrewdly, with just a hint of a twinkle, "you don't like who McQueen chose to head her Operation Icarus, either, now do you?"

"Well . . ." For once, Saint-Just seemed just a little hesitant. He even blushed slightly as he saw the gleam in his superior's eyes, and then he chuckled and shook his head.

"No, I don't like it," he admitted. "'Rehabilitating' one flag officer is risky enough, but rehabilitating *two* of them just in time for the same operation seems to be rushing things just a little."

"Oh, come now!" Pierre chided. "You know what happened in Silesia wasn't really Giscard's fault! The only reason he had to be 'rehabilitated' at all was because Cordelia's handling of the situation meant we needed a scapegoat."

"Agreed. Agreed." Saint-Just waved both hands in the air. "And as a matter of fact, Eloise Pritchart is one of the few senior commissioners who isn't concerned that her charge is succumbing to McQueen's charm. Which, I have to admit, makes me feel a little better about the entire situation. Pritchart's always had a high opinion of his military ability, and she's commented favorably on his political reliability, but she really doesn't *like* him very much. It's like pulling teeth for her to say good things about him in her reports, so I take the fact that she's satisfied as a good sign."

"Well, then," Pierre said with a shrug, but Saint-Just shook his head.

"You're missing my point, Rob. I'm not saying Giscard deserved to be made a scapegoat. I'm just saying he *was* made one, and we still haven't invented a way to see inside somebody's head. Disaffection can begin in lots of ways, and being singled out for public blame and humiliation over something that wasn't your fault is certainly one of them. So however reliable he may have been in the past, I have to bear in mind that the possibility of *future* unreliability may have been planted in there to sprout later."

"But if he pulls this off, we'll slather him with all the praise and positive publicity a man could want. That should help repair any past damage."

"Maybe, and maybe not. But be that as it may, it's a chance I'm willing to take, especially with Pritchart keeping an eye on him. Actually, I'm more worried about Tourville than I am about Giscard."

"Tourville?" Pierre sat back in his chair and tried very hard not to sigh.

"Tourville," Saint-Just confirmed. "You and I both know Cordelia planned to have him purged when she got him back to Haven—probably for trying to protect Harrington from her."

"We know we think she wanted him purged," Pierre corrected, and Saint-Just snorted a laugh.

"Rob, let's be honest with each other here. I mean, Cordelia's gone—and a damned good thing, too—so we don't have to stroke her anymore. And you and I know better than anyone else that she took a personal pleasure out of eliminating anyone she thought was an enemy."

"Yes. Yes, she did." Pierre sighed. *And,* he reflected, *that was the big difference between her and you, wasn't it, Oscar? You're ruthless as hell, and completely* willing *to eliminate anyone you think is even a potential threat. I imagine you sleep a hell of a lot better than I do, too . . . but you don't actually* enjoy *the killing, do you?*

"Damn right she did," Saint-Just said, unaware of the Chairman's thoughts. "The only reason she would have dragged him all the way to Cerberus and then back here with her was to make a big, ugly, public show trial out of it, and you can bet your ass he knew it, too. That's the real reason I sat on him and his crew for so long."

"I know that," Pierre said with a trace of patience he couldn't quite hide.

"No, you don't." It was unusual for Saint-Just to correct him quite so flatly, and Pierre frowned. "I know I told you that I wanted him on ice until we publicly admitted Cordelia's death, but you thought my real reason was that I was being paranoid and trying to decide whether or not to have him eliminated, now didn't you?" the StateSec head asked.

"Well . . . yes, I suppose I did," Pierre admitted.

"Well, you were mostly right, but not entirely. Oh, it really was essential to keep his crew isolated until our version of Cordelia's glorious death hit the 'faxes, but neither of us anticipated initially how long that was going to take." He shook his head. "I never would have believed how useful she could be when we could use her reputation and status with the Mob but not have to put up with her tantrums!"

Saint-Just actually chuckled for a moment, then shook his head. "But even though I know keeping him under virtual ship arrest has to have pissed him off even more than he was, I've never *wanted* to eliminate him, Rob; I've simply been afraid we had no choice. I realize what a tactical asset he is for the Navy, and I'd hate the thought of simply throwing that away when we need it so badly. But in a way, I regard him as a bigger danger than McQueen."

"You do?" Pierre's forehead furrowed in surprise.

"Yes. I've read his dossier and his commissioner's reports, and I've interviewed him myself at least a dozen times since Cerberus. There's a brain behind that cowboy exterior, Rob. He tries like hell to hide it, and he's been surprisingly successful with a lot of people, but he's sharp as a vibro blade. And Citizen Admiral Cowboy doesn't have a reputation for ambition like McQueen's. If *he* decides that his best long-term chance for survival lies in building some sort of cabal out of self-defense, his fellow officers are going to be a lot less wary of getting involved with him.

"So what do I see when I look at him? A man who, right this minute, is being grateful as hell that he dodged a pulser dart while deep inside he has to be wondering if he really did . . . or if he just *thinks* he did. He's been under a microscope for nine T-months, and he's got to know that we know that *he* knows Cordelia was going to have him killed. That means he also knows that we're going to be watching him very, very carefully, even if we have decided to release his flagship and staff for the moment. If he steps out of line again, we'll have no choice but to eliminate him, and he knows that, too. All of which means that he has to have at least considered the possibility of joining up with someone like a McQueen out of sheer self-defense. Or setting up a cabal of his own."

Pierre sat there for a moment, gazing at his security chief with a contemplative expression, then shook his head.

"I'm glad I have you to run StateSec, Oscar. I'd start foaming at the mouth if I had to spend much time concentrating on that kind of triple-think. Are you honestly telling me that you think Lester Tourville is going to take his task force over to the Manties or something like that?"

"Of course not," Saint-Just said with another of those unusual chuckles. "But it's my job, as you just pointed out, to think about the possibilities and then try to disaster-proof our position against them as much as possible. The odds are that Tourville is actually another Theisman. More extroverted and, um, colorful, but essentially nonpolitical and more concerned with getting the job done than he is with personal power. Mind you, I suspect he's even less fond of the Committee right now than I think Theisman is, and, frankly, with better reason. I'll want to keep a close eye on both of them, but we need them both against the Manties, and I know it."

"Well that's a relief!" Pierre said.

"I'm sure," Saint-Just agreed, but then he leaned back and gave the Chairman another sharp glance. "And now that I've aired my concerns about that, I want to ask you one more time if you're determined to carry through with the devaluation and the BLS cuts."

"I am," Pierre said flatly. Saint-Just started to open his mouth, but the Chairman went on before he could. "I realize it's a risk, but we've *got* to put our economic house into some kind of order. That's every bit as important as straightening out the purely military side of the war—and, damn it, it's the reason I went after this stinking job in the first place!"

Saint-Just blinked at the sudden passion in Pierre's voice. The SS chief knew, probably better than anyone else in the universe, how the inability to deal with the PRH's economic woes had eaten at Rob Pierre. And truth to tell, it was the probability of a Republic-wide financial collapse which had brought Saint-Just over to Pierre's side in the first place. As Oscar Saint-Just saw it, his real job was to preserve the power and stability of the state, as the source of authority which held the People's Republic together. In sober fact, he cared less about who exercised that authority than that it be exercised *well*, and the Legislaturalists had failed that critical test.

Yet Pierre's determination to tackle the economy *now* worried him. Too many things would be happening at once, creating too many potential flare-ups of the spontaneous combustion variety. And that was the hardest kind of trouble for a security officer to prepare against, because by the very nature of things, he seldom saw it coming before the flames actually burst out.

"I realize we have to deal with the fundamental problems eventually," he said now, his tone ever so slightly cautious. "I just have to wonder if this is the best time. We're already engaged in one experiment with McQueen and the War Office, after all."

"McQueen is what's *made* this the best time," Pierre replied sharply. "When she took out the Levelers for us, she eliminated by far the most radical element of the Mob." *And*, he added mentally, *you and I used the coup attempt as our pretext to remove some of the more troublesome "moderates" just in case, didn't we, Oscar?* "In the process, she taught the other potential radicals what happens to people who try to overthrow the Committee. And she made it quite clear in the public mind that the military supports us." He smiled thinly. "Even if she's actually trying to build her own power base, the Mob doesn't know that, so it has to assume that if we tell her to go out and kill another million or so of them, she will. Not only that, but the moderate elements of Nouveau Paris' population have had a lesson in what a real insurrection costs everyone in the vicinity, even the innocent bystanders. They don't want to see another one, and the radicals sure as *hell* don't want 'Admiral Cluster Bomb' dropping by to pay them another visit. So if we're going to introduce a policy which risks public repercussions, this is the best possible time for us to do it."

"I understand the reasoning, and I don't question the need to do *something*," Saint-Just said. "The timing does worry me, but that would probably be true whenever we decided to implement reforms. I guess part of it is the notion of deflating the currency and cutting the BLS simultaneously."

"Better to put all the medicine down them in one nasty-tasting dose than to string it out," Pierre disagreed. "Inflation was bad enough under the old regime; it's gotten even worse in the last few years, and it's hurting what foreign trade we've been able to maintain in Silesia and with the Sollies. As I see it, we have two options: we can go whole hog and completely nationalize the economy on the old prespace totalitarian model, or we can begin gradually phasing a true free market back in, but this half-assed socialism-by-regulation is killing us."

"No argument there," Saint-Just agreed when he paused.

"Well, I think we've pretty much demonstrated that the bureaucrats are almost as bad at running the economy under us as they were under the Legislaturalists," Pierre pointed out. "Given their dismal track record, I'm not particularly enamored of the idea of giving them still more control. Which only leaves the free market route, and for that to work we've got to have a stable currency—with at least a passing relationship to its real purchasing power—and a work force motivated to get out there and actually work. Most of the out-planets are in better shape for that than Haven is—they never had the percentage of Dolists we had here to begin with—and even the Nouveau Paris Mob has been reacquiring the habit of work since the war started. If we deflate the currency and reduce the BLS, we'll drag more of them into the nonmilitary labor force, as well. And as I say, this is probably the best time to make the attempt. I know it's risky. I simply don't see how we can avoid this particular risk."

"All right." Saint-Just sighed. "You're right. It's just that knowing how much of it is going to land on my plate if it goes sour makes me . . . anxious. We're playing with several different kinds of fire here, Rob. I only hope I've got enough firemen to deal with things if they get out of hand."

"I realize how much I'm dumping on you," Pierre acknowledged, "and I wish I saw a way to avoid it. Unfortunately, I don't. But the good news is that my analysts' projections suggest that if we get through the next twelve to eighteen T-months more or less intact, we'll actually have turned the corner on the reforms. So if McQueen can just generate some good news on the military front, on the one hand, while the threat of turning her pinnaces loose on the Mob again helps scare the remaining radicals into good behavior and you keep an eye on everyone else, we may actually pull this off."

"And if we don't?" Saint-Just asked very quietly.

"If we don't, then we'll lose the war in the end, anyway," Pierre said just as quietly, his eyes suddenly distant, as if he looked at something Saint-Just couldn't see, "and that will probably be the end of you, me, and the Committee. But you know, Oscar, that might not be such a tragedy. And it certainly wouldn't be undeserved, now would it? Because if we can't manage reform that's even this basic, then we'll have failed ourselves and the Republic. Everything we've done—and all the people we've killed—since the Coup will have been for nothing. And if it was all for nothing, Oscar, then we'll deserve whatever happens to us."

Saint-Just stared at the Chairman while an icy splash of shock went through him. He'd seen Pierre grow more and more brooding as the war dragged on, but this was the first time he'd ever heard him say something like that. Yet the shock wasn't as great as it should have been, he realized. Perhaps a part of him had seen this coming all along. And it wasn't as if he had a lot of choice, even if he hadn't seen it. For better or for worse, he had given his loyalty to Rob Pierre. Not the institutional loyalty he had sworn to the Legislaturalists and then betrayed, but his personal fealty. Pierre was his chieftain, because only Pierre had possessed the vision and the guts to try to save the Republic.

It was time to remember that, Saint-Just told himself. Time to remember how mad most people would have thought Pierre before the Coup, how impossible it had seemed that they could come this far. If anyone in the galaxy could pull the rest of it off, then Rob Pierre was that man. And if he couldn't . . .

Oscar Saint-Just decided not to think about that, and nodded to the man behind the desk.

"If it's all the same to you, Rob, I'll just try to keep anything like that from happening," he said dryly.

Chapter Twenty-Nine

"Signal from *Salamis*, Citizen Admiral," Citizen Lieutenant Frasier announced. "You and Citizen Commissioner Honeker are to report aboard her in twenty-five minutes. Citizen Admiral Giscard requests that you bring your chief of staff and operations officer, as well."

"Thank you, Harrison." Citizen Vice Admiral Lester Tourville glanced at Everard Honeker, then reached inside his tunic to pull a cigar from his breast pocket. The wrapper crackled as he stripped it away, and he looked back at Frasier. "Pass the word to Citizen Captain Hewitt that Citizen Commissioner Honeker and I will be leaving the ship, please. Then inform my coxswain that I'll need my pinnace."

"Aye, Citizen Admiral." Frasier began speaking into his hush mike, and Tourville moved his eyes to the chief of the watch.

"Citizen Chief Hunley, please be good enough to pass the word for Citizen Captain Bogdanovich and Citizen Commander Foraker to join Citizen Commissioner Honeker and myself in Boat Bay Two at their earliest possible convenience."

"Aye, Citizen Admiral."

Tourville nodded dismissal to the petty officer, then took a moment to insert the cigar into his mouth, light it, and be certain it was drawing properly. He removed it to blow a perfect smoke ring at a ventilator air return, gave his fierce mustache a rub, and glanced back at Honeker.

"Are you ready, Citizen Commissioner?" he asked politely.

"I suppose so," Honeker replied, and the two of them walked towards PNS *Count Tilly*'s bridge lift side by side, trailing a banner of fragrant smoke.

Tourville allowed Honeker to precede him into the lift, then punched the destination code and stood back against one bulkhead, drumming thoughtfully on his thigh with the fingers of his right hand.

"I really wish you'd waited to light that thing until I was somewhere else," Honeker remarked after a moment, and Tourville grinned. The people's commissioner had been on his case about the cigars from the moment he first came aboard Tourville's last flagship. It had become something of a joke between them, a sort of game they played, but only when no one was watching. It would hardly have done to let the rest of the galaxy suspect that an admiral and a commissioner had actually become friends of a sort, after all. And especially not at any point in the last nine T-months or so.

"I thought I'd just enjoy it on the way to the pinnace," Tourville told him cheerfully. In fact, he suspected Honeker had realized he rather regretted adopting the damned things as a part of his image. Modern medicine might have virtually stamped out the various ills to which tobacco had once contributed, but it hadn't made nicotine any less addictive, and the ash flecks on his uniform were more than mildly annoying.

"I'm sure," Honeker snorted, and Tourville's grin softened with an edge of genuine affection he would have been very careful not to let anyone else see. Particularly not now. People who'd survived the head-on collision of two air cars didn't light matches to discover whether or not their hydrogen tanks were leaking.

He snorted to himself at the thought. Actually, checking for hydrogen leaks with a match would probably have been considerably safer than what he'd actually done, and he still couldn't quite believe he'd tried it—much less survived the attempt! Defying a member of the Committee of Public Safety for any reason was unlikely to leave a man breathing. Unless, of course, the Committee member in question suffered a fatal accident before she could arrange for him to do the same.

Despite himself, Tourville felt tiny pinpricks of sweat along his hairline as he remembered the way Cordelia Ransom had provoked him. The crazy bitch had actually *wanted* him to challenge her authority. He hadn't realized, then, just how much she hated and feared the Navy, but he'd come to realize that she'd wanted him to do something—anything—she could use as a reason to have him eliminated. It wasn't so much because of who he was as because of *what* he was . . . and because his effort to treat his enemies as human beings rather than vermin to be exterminated had convinced her he could not be trusted.

Well, she'd succeeded in provoking him, but he was still around . . . and she wasn't. Her death hadn't been his doing, but he'd declined to shed any crocodile tears during his interminable "interviews" with StateSec. That would have been as stupid as it would have been insincere, and it would also have been dangerous. So far as he could tell, she'd never passed her specific plans for him on to anyone else, but people like Oscar Saint-Just had to have realized she hadn't ordered him to accompany her ship to Hades and then back to Haven just so she could give him a big, sloppy kiss. And since they had to know that, they would have recognized the falsity of any regret on his part. Worse, they might have wondered if he were displaying regret in an effort to keep them from wondering if perhaps he'd had a little something to do with her demise.

Fortunately, there was plenty of evidence to support his innocence. In fact, he had insisted—with Honeker's strong support—on having a senior member of Hades' SS garrison return to Haven with him as a witness. Citizen Warden Tresca hadn't been happy about that, but he'd known better than to argue, particularly when he himself had downplayed Tourville's initial warnings that something must have gone very wrong aboard PNS *Tepes*. Tresca was going to be in sufficient hot water of his own; SS brigadier or not, he didn't need to borrow trouble by refusing the orders of a senior people's commissioner or looking like he was trying to obstruct the investigation.

And so Tourville and Honeker had arrived at Haven with Citizen Major Garfield in tow. Garfield had brought along Camp Charon's scanner data on the entire episode, as well as a recording of the com traffic between *Count Tilly* and Charon that clearly demonstrated Tourville had been the first to sound the alarm and had done everything in his power to prevent the tragedy. In fact, Tourville and his people had come out looking considerably better than State Security had, and Everard Honeker's reports to Oscar Saint-Just had stressed their exemplary attention to duty.

I wonder if that was part of the reason they held us incommunicado for so long? Tourville mused now. *StateSec belongs to Saint-Just, after all, and it was his personal fiefdom we made look like asshole idiots.* He snorted. *Great, Lester! Now you've come up with* another *reason for the head of State Security, personally, to loathe your ass. Good going.*

Of course, Saint-Just didn't know the full story. Not even Honeker did, for only Tourville and Shannon Foraker had seen the recon drone data Tourville had erased. Camp Charon's sensors had been blinded by EMP at the time, which meant no one else could know what had happened, and Tourville had no intention of ever admitting what he'd seen. But that was one reason he'd insisted so adamantly on bringing along a StateSec witness to explain exactly what had happened . . . and why he'd started sweating bullets after the first five or six months of *Count Tilly*'s confinement to her parking orbit.

Sooner or later they're going to realize Lady Harrington—or some of her people, at least—got out alive. That could have been decidedly dicey if it happened while they still had us all under ship arrest . . . and safely incommunicado. But now, it's going to be StateSec's problem when it dawns on them, not mine. And my people and I aren't going to be anywhere they can quietly *disappear us, either,* he thought with a certain complacency. In fact, he was rather looking forward to watching the SS punish one of its own for such gross negligence, although if the truth were known, he'd really rather that they never caught up with the Manties at all.

And if they do, they'll almost have to kill all *of them this time,* he thought much less cheerfully. *After officially "executing" Lady Harrington just to avoid admitting what really happened, there's no way they'd let any witnesses that inconvenient live.*

He regretted that, but he'd done all he could for them. His conscience was as clear as anyone's could be in today's PRH, and he tucked those thoughts and memories away in a safe place while he considered his present situation.

He supposed some people would consider his promotion to vice admiral a fitting reward for winning the PRH's most crushing victory of the war. Personally, Tourville suspected it was more of a bribe—a tacit payoff for having kept him on ice for so long—and he would much rather have remained a rear admiral. Vice admirals were too senior, too likely to catch the blame if things went wrong for the forces under their command, and for the last eight or nine years, officers who caught that sort of blame had also tended to catch firing squads. That was why he'd devoted so much effort to avoiding promotion, but it had caught up with him at last, and there was nothing he could do about it.

Still, he reflected as the lift reached the boat bay and its doors slid silently open, with Esther McQueen as Secretary of War, the Committee's promise to halt the practice of shooting losing admirals might actually be worth believing. That was the good news. The bad news was that it was Esther McQueen who had chosen Tourville for his current assignment and personally bitched loudly enough at Oscar Saint-Just to get Tourville and *Count Tilly* sprung for the operation. So if she turned out to be up to something ambitious, the fact that he hardly even knew the woman would mean absolutely nothing to StateSec. Whether he liked it or not, he had just been publicly identified as a member of "her" faction . . . which might just turn his release from ship arrest into a case of out of the frying pan.

Another set of lift doors opened, revealing his broad-shouldered chief of staff and his ops officer. Citizen Captain Bogdanovich nodded to Tourville and Honeker with something very like a normal smile, but Shannon Foraker's long, narrow face wore no expression whatsoever. Under normal circumstances, Foraker was rather attractive, in an understated sort of way, but now her features were an icily controlled mask, and Tourville felt a fresh stab of worry. Something inside Foraker had changed after Honor Harrington's capture, and especially during their long confinement, and he was no longer certain what was going on inside her head. She was the only other person who knew any of the Manties had escaped *Tepes'* destruction, and he was confident she would do nothing to jeopardize that secret, but her entire personality seemed to have shifted. She was no longer the cheerful, quintessential techno-nerd, all but oblivious to the interpersonal relationships about her or the political tides sweeping through the Navy. Now she watched *everything* that happened around her, choosing her words as carefully as she had ever laid out an operations plan and never, ever forgetting the proper modes of address.

For anyone who knew Foraker, that last was far worse than merely ominous. It meant the first-class brain which had made her so dangerous to the Manties was now considering other threats and options . . . other enemies.

It was unlikely a mere citizen commander could pose much threat to the Committee of Public Safety, but Shannon Foraker was no ordinary citizen commander. If she decided to do something about the way Cordelia Ransom and StateSec had treated Honor Harrington, the consequences were almost certain to be drastic. It was unlikely she herself would survive, but it was equally unlikely she would go down without inflicting some extreme damage of her own. Intellectually speaking, Lester Tourville no longer had any problem with any damage anyone managed to inflict on StateSec and the Committee. In fact, the more damage someone could do, the better. What he *would* object to would be the loss of Shannon Foraker, who was worth any hundred Committee members he could think of right off hand. And, of course, to the probability that other people in her vicinity—like one Lester Tourville, for example—would go down with her.

All things considered, he mused as he tossed his cigar down a waste disposal slot and led the way towards the pinnace personnel tube, *this assignment looks like being a lot more . . . interesting than I'd really prefer. Ah, well. It beats the alternative, I suppose.*

Tourville sat gazing out the armorplast port as the pinnace maneuvered towards rendezvous with *Salamis*. The view was certainly impressive, he admitted. He hadn't seen this much tonnage in one spot since before the war began. In fact, he wasn't certain he'd *ever* actually seen this heavy a weight of metal.

It was unusual for someone to actually be able to see more than a handful of warships simultaneously with the naked eye. Men-of-war were big, especially ships of the wall, with impeller wedges whose width was measured in hundreds of kilometers. That imposed a certain dispersal upon them underway, and they tended to stay far enough apart to clear their impeller perimeters even in parking orbit. If they didn't, then they had to maneuver clear of one another on reaction thrusters before they could bring their wedges up, and that was costly in terms of both reaction mass and time.

In point of fact, the ships he was seeing now were probably sufficiently dispersed to light off their drives; there were simply so many of them that it didn't look that way. The feeble light of the M2 star known as Secour-C reflected from their white hulls as the units of Twelfth Fleet drifted in orbit around a gas giant almost as massive as its star. A dark haze of upper atmosphere ice crystals provided a bleak, dim background for the assembled fleet, and it looked from here as if he could have walked around the planet by stepping from ship to ship.

Thirty-six superdreadnoughts, sixteen dreadnoughts, eighty-one battleships, twenty-four battlecruisers, and forty heavy cruisers, he thought wonderingly, *and no one even knows they're here.*

That was hard to wrap his mind around, even for a spacer as experienced as Tourville, for Secour was an inhabited system. Of course, everyone in it lived on or near Marienbad, the habitable planet which orbited Secour-A, the F9 star which was the trinary system's primary component. Secour-B was home to a small industrial presence, but Secour-C never approached to within less than thirty-six light-hours of Secour-A even at periastron, and there was nothing of sufficient value to bring anyone here. Which made it a logical place to assemble Javier Giscard's force without anyone's seeing a thing.

And McQueen's done Giscard proud, he mused. *The screen's light—only twenty-three destroyers and light cruisers, all told—but that's still over eight hundred million tons, and that doesn't even count the supply ships and tenders. Pile it all up in one heap, and it's got to come to more than a* billion *tons. In sheer tonnage terms, this has got to be the Navy's biggest concentration in fifteen or twenty years.*

He wondered—again—how McQueen had possibly talked her political masters into letting her assemble a force like this. It had needed doing for years, but she had to have stripped the majority of the PRH's rear area systems to the bone to scare up this much firepower. Even with the new construction beginning to come forward, she had concentrated ten percent of the PN's super-dreadnoughts, fifty percent of its new-build dreadnoughts, and over a third of its surviving battleships into a single fleet. And in doing so, she had created a potentially decisive offensive weapon for the first time since the Third Battle of Yeltsin.

And she'd damned well better produce *something with it. If she doesn't—or if this ends up like another Fourth Yeltsin—after Pierre let her take the risk of reducing rear area security, her head is certain to roll. And ours, of course . . . although in our case the Manties will probably make that a moot point if we screw up.*

He grinned at the thought, despite his tension. Perhaps there was a little more truth to his hard-charging public persona than he cared to admit, because damned if the challenge of helping to wield this much fighting power didn't appeal to him whatever the possible consequences.

Javier Giscard looked up as Citizen Vice Admiral Tourville, Everard Honeker, and Tourville's chief of staff and ops officer entered the briefing room. He saw Tourville's dark eyes narrow as he noted the ice water carafes, glasses, coffee cups, and other paraphernalia of a formal staff meeting and hid a mental smile.

"Please be seated," he invited his guests, and waited until they had taken the indicated chairs. Then he glanced at Pritchart, seated in the chair beside him, before he returned his attention to Tourville.

"As I'm sure you've just realized, Citizen Admiral, we will shortly be joined by the Fleet's other squadron and division commanders. At that time, Citizen Captain Joubert and Citizen Commander MacIntosh will present our general ops plan to all concerned. However, Citizen Commissioner Pritchart and I wanted to speak to you and your senior officers first, since your role in the coming campaign will be particularly critical."

Giscard paused, head cocked slightly to one side, and Tourville fought an urge to squirm in his seat. He glanced at Pritchart, but her face was almost as expressionless as Foraker's, and he repressed a shudder. He'd heard stories about Pritchart. She was supposed to have ice water in her veins and a zealot's devotion to the Committee, and he was devoutly grateful that she wasn't *his* people's commissioner. Honeker had become even more human in the last endless months, but even at his worst he'd never radiated the sort of blank-faced menace which seemed to stream off of Pritchart like winter fog.

"I see," the citizen vice admiral said at last, before the silence could stretch out too far, and Giscard smiled thinly.

"I'm sure you do, Citizen Admiral," he said, with what might have been just an edge of gentle mockery, and then a star chart blinked into existence as he entered a command into his terminal.

"Twelfth Fleet's operational area," he said simply, and Tourville felt Bogdanovich stiffen at his side. Honeker wasn't sufficiently familiar with star charts to realize what he was seeing quite as quickly as the chief of staff, but Shannon Foraker sat upright in her chair, blue eyes narrowing with the first sign of interest she'd shown.

Tourville could understand that. Indeed, he felt his fingers twitch with the desire to reach for another cigar as his own eyes studied the glowing chips of light and read the names beside them. Seaforth Nine, Hancock, Zanzibar and Alizon, Suchien, Yalta, and Nuada. He knew them all . . . just as he recognized the bright scarlet icon of the Basilisk System.

Chapter Thirty

The lift doors opened, and Citizen Captain Joanne Hall—known to friends and family as "Froggie" for reasons which remained a deep, dark secret from the officers and crew of PNS *Schaumberg*—strode briskly through them.

"The Citizen Captain is on the bridge!" a petty officer announced, and Citizen Commander Oliver Diamato, who had the watch, looked up, then rose quickly. Hall gave him a level look, and he swallowed a mental curse. He should have seen her coming, or at least heard the lift door, before the citizen petty officer announced her presence, and he felt quite certain she would find some way to make that point to him in the very near future. She had a habit of doing things like that.

"Good morning, Citizen Commander." Citizen Captain Hall's dark hair and dark complexion were the exact antithesis of Diamato's golden hair and fair complexion, and her dark eyes gazed levelly into his blue ones. Her coloration was perfectly suited to the severe persona she presented to the universe . . . and somehow the "citizen" hung on the front of Diamato's rank title seemed an afterthought the way she said it.

"Good morning, Citizen Captain!" he replied. "I apologize for not noticing your arrival," he went on, taking the bull firmly by the horns. "I was reviewing the chips of yesterday's sims, and I got more immersed in them than I should have."

"Um." She regarded him thoughtfully for several long seconds, then shrugged ever so slightly. "God hasn't gotten around to issuing eyes for the backs of our heads yet, Citizen Commander. Bearing that in mind, I suppose there's no harm done . . . this time."

"Thank you, Citizen Captain. I'll try not to let it happen again," Diamato replied, and wondered if he was the only person on the bridge who found the entire exchange rather antique and unnatural. Not that he expected to hear anyone else say so, even if they did.

Citizen Captain Hall sometimes seemed not to have heard that the old elitist officer corps and its traditions had been overtaken by events, and she was a stickler for what she referred to as "proper military discipline." Then-Citizen Lieutenant Commander Diamato had been less than delighted when he first discovered that fact upon his assignment to *Schaumberg* as the battleship's brand-new assistant tactical officer eleven T-months before. A product of the post-Coup promotions, he had risen from junior-grade lieutenant under the old regime to his present rank in barely eight T-years under the New Order. Much of that was the result of raw ability—he was one of the better tactical officers the PN had produced during the present war—but his political commitment had also been a major reason for his meteoric elevation. The Navy's insidious rot under the Legislaturalist officer corps' iron defense of privilege had inspired him with all the contempt for the old elitist order that any good people's commissioner could have desired, and he had been deeply suspicious of someone as old-fashioned (and probably reactionary) as Citizen Captain Hall.

He had expected Citizen Commissioner Addison to share his reservations about his CO. The slender, sandy-blond people's commissioner was absolutely committed to the New Order, after all. Diamato only had to attend a single one of Addison's regular political awareness sessions to realize that, and his fierce egalitarianism ought to have made him and Hall natural enemies. Yet the commissioner had actually supported her, and as Diamato had watched her in action, her sheer competence had overcome even his doubts.

Yes, she was old-fashioned, and he very much doubted she had the proper political opinions. But in large part, that seemed to stem from the fact that she didn't have *any* political opinions. She did her job exactly as she had under the old regime—far better than most—and let her political superiors worry about policy.

It still struck Diamato as unnatural, but seven months ago she had demonstrated just how well doing things her way worked. Old Citizen Commander Young had been *Schaumberg*'s tactical officer at the time, and Young was the sort of officer who forced Diamato to admit that even the New Order had its weak points. Young's political fervor and patrons had gotten him assigned to a position his ability (or lack of it) could never have earned, and Hall and Addison hadn't managed to get rid of him. Which was why the Citizen Captain had taken personal command of the ship and proceeded to give Citizen Lieutenant Commander Diamato a rather humbling lesson in just how good he himself truly was.

Everyone knew battleships couldn't fight proper ships of the wall and that battlecruisers were even more outclassed by battleships than battleships were by superdreadnoughts. Fortunately, ships of the wall usually couldn't catch battleships, and battleships usually couldn't catch battlecruisers. Unfortunately for the Royal Manticoran Navy, that rule didn't always hold true. It especially didn't hold true when the battleship's captain had the nerve to take her own impellers off-line and just sit there like a hole in space until the Manties were actually in extreme missile range. Hall had that kind of nerve, and less than a month after Citizen Rear Admiral Tourville blew out the Adler System picket, she had neatly ambushed a trio of raiding Manty battlecruisers. They hadn't had the remotest suspicion she was even there until they'd built vectors which gave them no choice, even with their superior acceleration rates, but to come into her engagement range.

RMN battlecruisers were tough customers, especially given the superiority of the Star Kingdom's EW and missiles. Many Republican officers would have hesitated to engage three of them at once, even if she did out-mass them by almost two-to-one. That, in fact, had been Citizen Commander Young's earnest recommendation. Hall hadn't taken it, however . . . and she'd blown two of her enemies right out of space. The third had gotten away, but with enough damage to keep her out of action for months, whereas *Schaumberg*'s repairs had required only five weeks of yard time. It had been a small-scale action, but it had also been a very difficult assignment, and Diamato had been on the bridge when it all went down. Despite the Manties' numerical advantage—not to mention the two destroyers screening them—Hall had made it seem almost routine. The only people who'd appeared more confident than her of her ability to handle it had been her bridge crew (aside from Young), and as Diamato watched their crisp efficiency, he had realized something he'd never quite grasped before.

A military organization was not the best laboratory for working out the proper forms of egalitarian social theory. The defense of a society which enshrined economic and political equality had to be undertaken by an authoritarian hierarchy with the clear, sharply defined sort of chain of command that put a single person ultimately in control, for combat operations were not a task which could be discharged by committee. The fact that, even after she won the battle by doing the exact opposite of what Young had recommended, it had still taken her and Addison another seven months to overcome the old tac officer's political influence in order to get rid of him had only made that even more obvious to Diamato.

That thought had caused him a few anxious moments when he reflected upon the existence of the *Committee* of Public Safety, but he'd soon realized that it was a false comparison. Military operations were a specialized and limited sphere of human activity. The larger macrocosm of the entire People's Republic required a different approach, and the combination of centralized power and multiple viewpoints represented by the Committee of Public Safety was undoubtedly the best possible compromise.

But Citizen Captain Hall's firm, demanding command style certainly had its place in the military. That, Diamato had come to realize, was the reason Addison supported her to the hilt. The people's commissioner didn't actually seem to like her very much, but he respected her, and the record of *Schaumberg*'s accomplishments under her command was the reason Citizen Rear Admiral Kellet had chosen the battleship as Task Force 12.3's flagship.

"Don't beat your apology to death, Citizen Commander," Citizen Captain Hall said now, with a slight smile that took most of the sting from the words. "You *are* my tac officer. I suppose it's not totally unreasonable for you to spend some time reviewing tactical problems . . . even when you have the watch."

She stepped past him and seated herself in the command chair, and Diamato folded his hands behind his back while she ran her eyes over the readouts to catch herself up on the state of her command.

"Did Engineering find out what was causing that harmonic in Beta Thirty?"

"No, Citizen Captain." Diamato was glad he'd checked the status of the after impeller room with Citizen Lieutenant Commander Hopkins less than fifteen minutes ago. Letting the Citizen Captain catch one less than fully informed was a seriously unpleasant experience, and Citizen Commissioner Addison wouldn't do a thing to preserve one from the consequences. *In fact,* Diamato thought, *he usually gets behind her and* pushes *when she comes down on someone.*

"Um," she repeated. Then she leaned over and tapped a command code into the touchpad on her chair's arm. Her tactical repeater came on-line, and she frowned pensively at the data codes moving across the display. Diamato glanced inconspicuously over her shoulder and realized she was rerunning the same sim he'd been reviewing when she arrived. She let the one-on-one duel play through on a six-to-one time compression, then looked up so quickly she caught him watching her. He tensed for an explosion, but she only smiled.

"I see why you were so intent on this, Citizen Commander," she told him, and waved him over to stand beside her chair, then restarted the sim again.

"I hadn't realized at the time quite how neatly you pulled off this maneuver here," she went on, freezing the display, and Diamato nodded cautiously. He'd been rather proud of the shot himself. It wasn't one that was likely to prove practical in a fleet action, of course. Walls of battle didn't take kindly to units which suddenly pitched up perpendicular to their original vectors while simultaneously rotating on their long axes *and* turning through a radical skew turn. Doing that usually caused Bad Things to happen when impeller wedges collided, but the sim had been a single-ship duel, not a fleet action, and the unorthodox maneuver had given him an up-the-kilt shot at his simulated opponent that had inflicted extremely heavy damage.

"The question," Hall went on, leaning back and crossing her legs while she regarded him with an almost whimsical smile, "is whether you saw it coming or simply reacted on instinct." Diamato felt his expression try to congeal, but she shook her head. "Either possibility still puts you well ahead of the normal performance curve, Citizen Commander. I simply want to know which it was for future reference. So which was it?"

"I'm . . . not certain, Citizen Captain," he admitted after a moment. "It all came together without my consciously considering it, and I suppose you might call that instinct. But it wasn't all automatic. I . . . Well, I saw the pattern coming and recognized the possibility, so I had the whole thing sort of waiting in the back of my mind in case it actually happened, and—"

He shrugged helplessly, and she chuckled.

"So you do have the eye, Citizen Commander! I rather thought you might. Good. That's very good, Oliver." Diamato managed not to blink. He'd been her second officer for just under a T-month now and her tactical officer for over three, yet this was the first time she had ever used his first name. In fact, it was the first time she'd ever indicated she even knew what his first name *was*. Yet what truly astounded him was how good it felt to hear her use it with approval.

She cocked her head, watching him as if she were waiting for something, and his mind raced as he wondered what the hell he was supposed to say now.

"I'm glad you approve, Citizen Captain," he said finally.

"Ah, but you may not be for long, Oliver," she told him with something which looked unaccountably like an actual grin. "You see, now that you've demonstrated that you have it, you and Citizen Commander Hamer and I are going to be spending at least four extra hours a day developing it." Her grin grew broader at his expression, and she reached out and patted him on the elbow. "I'll have the Citizen Exec whip up half a dozen new problems for you in Simulator Seven," she promised. "I'll be interested to see your solutions to them by your next watch."

"Do you really think we can pull this off?" Everard Honeker asked very quietly. Lester Tourville almost gave a snort of laughter, but then he looked up with a much more serious expression as the people's commissioner's tone registered.

"That hardly sounds like the proper attitude for one of the New Order's forward-looking leaders of the People's vanguard," he said. His voice was more confident than the look in his eyes, and he watched Honeker closely, waiting for his reaction with an outward assurance he was far from feeling. He and his people's commissioner had been edging closer and closer to a true partnership for the better part of a T-year, yet this was the first time the citizen vice admiral had dared to expose his own contempt for his political masters quite so clearly.

It wasn't the best possible moment he could have picked, either, he reflected wryly. He'd retained *Count Tilly* as the flagship of Task Force 12.2 of the People's Navy, and Giscard's entire Twelfth Fleet had just departed the Secour System. In almost precisely twenty-four T-days, the various task forces would arrive simultaneously at their objectives and Operation Icarus would be on. Under the circumstances, this was scarcely a propitious moment to risk fracturing TF 12.2's command team. Then again, he'd been making a habit of doing things at less than optimum moments for quite some time now, and despite his apparent rehabilitation, he was hard pressed to think of a way he could dig his current hole much deeper. Besides, he was confident that Cordelia Ransom had disgusted Honeker just as much as she had disgusted Tourville himself.

The question, the citizen vice admiral thought, *is whether or not his disgust with* her *is going to carry over to the rest of the Committee now that she's gone? It could be very . . . useful to me if it does. Maybe. Especially if Giscard and I are going to end up labeled as two of "McQueen's Men" whether we want to or not!*

"Those of us in the vanguard of the People seem to spend a great deal of time looking over our shoulders to see who's following us," Honeker said after several silent seconds. Which, Tourville thought, could be taken several ways. The people's commissioner let him stew for a couple of more seconds, then produced a wintry smile. "Given the fact that some of those people tend to react just a little unreasonably where failure is concerned, my interest in the outcome of our assignment is more than simply academic, however. And, frankly, the thought of heading this deep into Manty space makes me nervous. *Very* nervous."

"Oh, well, if *that's* all that's worrying you, put your mind at ease, Citizen Commissioner," Tourville said with a broad grin, trying to hide his vast relief. "Unreasonably" wasn't a word people's commissioners were supposed to use—or not, at least, in connection with their political superiors—when speaking to the officers on whom they rode herd. Honeker's use of it constituted a major advance in the cautious dance they'd been dancing since Honor Harrington's capture, and hearing it made such things as the possibility of being blown to bits by the Manties seem almost minor.

"I'm sure I appreciate your display of confidence, Citizen Admiral," Honeker said dryly. "If it's all the same to you, however, I think I'd prefer something a little more detailed than 'put your mind at ease' when we're headed over two light-centuries into Alliance-held space to hit one of the Manties' allies' home systems with only thirty-six capital ships! If you'll pardon my saying so, this sounds entirely too much like what happened to Citizen Admiral Thurston at Yeltsin's Star, and I'd really rather not reprise his role there. As I recall, there were very few survivors from the first performance."

"There are some differences, Sir," Tourville said mildly, hiding raised mental eyebrows. Honeker's openness had just escalated his own probe by a few thousand percent, and he leaned back in his chair to consider how best to respond to it. The good news was that the two of them sat alone in Tourville's flag briefing room, and he had to assume Honeker would never have voiced his concerns unless he'd either disabled the bugs or else had complete confidence in his ability to control any access to the recordings.

Of course, the fact that he's confident wouldn't necessarily mean he has reason *to be. And I suppose I still shouldn't overlook the possibility that he's trying to set me up, get me to say something he can use to nail my ass for StateSec. On the other hand, why wait this long or go to elaborate lengths when all he'd have had to do was remind someone back on Haven of just how splendidly Ransom and I had gotten along before her untimely departure? Besides, I've got to take some chances somewhere along the line.*

The thoughts flicked through his brain in a heartbeat, and he smiled at Honeker.

"First of all, Sir, there are some substantial differences between Zanzibar and Yeltsin's Star. Zanzibar has a much larger population, but it's a largely agrarian world. The system's asteroid belts are richer than most, and it's developed a respectable extraction industry in the last thirty or so T-years, but it's primarily an exporter of raw materials—definitely still a third-tier economy. By this time, Yeltsin is at least second-tier, and I think an argument could be made for its rapidly approaching first-tier status. More to the point, the Zanzibar Navy is still essentially a sublight self-defense force which requires a substantial Manty picket for backup, whereas the *Grayson* Navy has turned Yeltsin into some kind of black hole for our ships."

He paused again, and Honeker nodded. But the people's commissioner still looked unconvinced, and Tourville couldn't really blame him.

"There are also differences between both the operational planning and the leadership of Dagger and Icarus," he went on, "and that's probably even more important than the inherent toughness of the objectives. I never served with Citizen Admiral Thurston, but I knew his reputation. He was a fairly good strategist on paper, but he was pretty much a headquarters type. A 'staff puke,' if you'll pardon the expression. Citizen Admiral Giscard is a shooter, not a chip-shuffler, and he and Citizen Secretary McQueen between them have avoided the weakest parts of Thurston's strategy for Yeltsin's Star."

"Which were?"

"Which were his elaborate maneuvers to draw the Manties and Graysons out of position prior to the attack," Tourville said without hesitation. "He got too clever and tried to manipulate them—to suck them out of his way so as to give himself a virtually unopposed shot at his objective. Worse, he seems to have fallen in love with his own plan. When he finally hit Yeltsin, he'd spent so much time convincing himself his preliminary operations had worked perfectly that he came in fat, dumb, and happy. Granted, he was up against an opponent with better electronic warfare capabilities, which contributed materially to his misappreciation of the enemy's forces when he finally saw them, but the *mindset* to be misled was implicit in his entire approach. So he walked right into the concentrated firepower of six superdreadnoughts at minimum range."

The Citizen Vice Admiral shrugged and moved his hands as if he were tossing something into the air above the briefing room table.

"If he'd come in more cautiously, kept the range open, he still had more than enough missile power to take the system. His battleships were no match for SDs on a one-for-one basis, but he had thirty-six of them, with two dozen battlecruisers to back them up. If he'd held the range open and pounded the Graysons with missiles, he would've had an excellent chance of annihilating the defenders anyway, but he didn't.

"That was a tactical failure on his part once all the pieces were in play, but, frankly, any strategist who *depends* on convincing his adversaries to do what *he* wants has made the kind of mistake even amateurs should know enough to avoid. Oh, it's always worth trying to mislead the other side, convince him you're going to hit him at Point A when you actually intend to blow hell out of Point B, but you should never—ever—set up a strategy under which the enemy *has* to do what you want if your own operations are going to succeed."

"But wasn't that what Thurston did? You just said he'd brought along enough firepower to win if he'd used it properly even when the enemy didn't do what he wanted."

"He did, but he lacked the will and preparedness to use it properly because his entire strategy had been built towards avoiding the need for a real fight. Frankly, he may have figured he had no option but to set it up that way if he was going to convince his superiors to let him try it. I once met Citizen Secretary Kline on a visit to the Octagan, and I hope you won't take this wrongly, Sir, but he was one of the worst arguments for civilian control of the military you could imagine."

He watched Honeker's eyes as he spoke, but the people's commissioner didn't even blink.

"Citizen Secretary Kline's biggest problem as a war minister," the citizen vice admiral went on after a moment, "was that he was too afraid of losing to let himself have a real shot at winning. To be fair, the Navy wasn't doing all that well in stand-up fights at the time—we were still reorganizing after the Harris Assassination, and we had a lot of people getting on-the-job training—but Kline's idea was to stand on the defensive and let the enemy come to us. I think he hoped that if we did that, the Manties would make the mistakes instead of us, but you may have noticed that they don't seem to make all that many mistakes. Besides, a primarily defensive strategy has to be a losing one when your operational area is two or three light-centuries across. You can't possibly picket every single star system in sufficient strength to defeat a determined attack, and trying to simply guarantees your opponent the right to pick his fights. Which, if he has a clue as to what he's doing, means he'll hit you in one of the places where you're too weak to stop him. If you hope to give yourself any kind of chance of actually winning a war, you simply have to take some chances in order to act offensively. I think some old wet-navy admiral from Old Earth said something along the lines of 'He who will not risk cannot win,' and it's still true today.

"So if I thought that what had actually happened was that Thurston had structured his proposals to understate the probability of a real fight in order to, um, entice the Octagon and the Committee into letting him try it despite the fact that he actually planned on fighting a serious battle, I'd have a lot more respect for him. Citizen Admiral Theisman or Citizen Admiral Giscard—or Citizen Secretary McQueen—might have done that. But if they had, they also would have carried through even if they knew their official diversionary strategy hadn't completely succeeded. Unfortunately, I think what happened was that Thurston really came up with a bad operational concept—or a weak one, at least—which simply happened to fit the profile of the 'low risk' counterattack for which his superiors were searching. He wasn't looking for a fight; he genuinely believed he could avoid one—have his cake and eat it too, if you will—and put his foot straight into it.

"The difference here is that Citizen Secretary McQueen isn't particularly interested in tricking the enemy into doing anything. Instead, she intends to take advantage of things the enemy's already *done*. And unlike Thurston or Citizen Secretary Kline, she's willing to take a few risks to win. So she expects us to actually do some serious fighting when we reach our objectives, but she's picked those objectives to give us the best shot of achieving our mission goals anyway."

"But Zanzibar has been a Manty ally for almost ten T-years now," Honeker pointed out. "That's why the Alliance put its new shipyard there, and they've picketed it since before Parks took Seaforth Nine away from us."

"They certainly have," Tourville agreed, "but at the moment, they're in very much the position *we* were in when Thurston launched Operation Dagger, if for rather different reasons. They've got an awful big chunk of their wall of battle in for overhaul at the very moment when they're strategically overextended by their successes. That means they can't possibly be strong everywhere—just as we couldn't—because they simply don't have the ships for it. And that means that someplace like

Zanzibar, which is so far behind the front, and where there have been no active operations by either side for over eight years, is going to be lightly covered. They'll have enough firepower on call to deal with a raiding battlecruiser squadron or two . . . but that's why we have three battle*ship* squadrons along for support."

Tourville paused once more, watching Honeker's eyes, then shrugged.

"Frankly," he said, "this is something we should have done years ago, Sir. We lost a lot of battleships trying to stop the Manties short of Trevor's Star, but we've still got over two hundred of them, and our superdreadnought strength has been rising again for the last T-year or so. That means we ought to be using the battleships as aggressively as possible. Since they aren't suitable for the wall of battle—and since our growing SD strength means we can finally stop putting them into it anyway—they should be committed to a strategy of deep raids. They've got the accel to run away from SDs and dreadnoughts and the firepower to squash battlecruisers. That makes them pretty damned close to the ideal tool to keep the Manties thinking about the security of *their* rear areas. And every ship of the wall we can force them to divert to guarding a star twenty or thirty light-years behind the front is just as much out of action as one we've blown apart. That's what Icarus is all about. What we'd prefer to do is to actually gain the initiative for the first time since the war began, but even if we don't, we should at least take the initiative away from the Manties. And that, Citizen Commissioner, is a damned sight better than anything we've managed yet!"

"So you actually have confidence in the ops plan?" Honeker sounded almost surprised, and Tourville gave a short, sharp bark of a laugh.

"I've got a hell of a lot of confidence in the plan, Sir," he said. "I think we'll probably lose some ships—the Manties may be out of position, but anyone who's ever fought them knows they won't go easy—but their forces are too light to stop us from getting in and doing one hell of a lot of damage. We'll take out more of their ships than they'll knock out of ours, and that doesn't even count the potential damage to their infrastructure . . . or their morale." He shook his head. "If this succeeds even half as well as Citizen Secretary McQueen hopes, it will have a tremendous effect on the future course of the war."

And, he added silently, *McQueen is also avoiding the* other *two mistakes Thurston made. She's staying the hell away from Yeltsin's Star . . . and she's not sending us up against Honor Harrington.*

"I hope you're right, Citizen Admiral," Honeker said quietly. He still looked anxious, but he seemed less so than he had, and Tourville decided not to broach the subject of whether or not the people's commissioner's superiors might decide to consider the two of them members of any "McQueen Faction" if it came to fresh purges.

Let the poor bastard worry about one thing at a time, the Citizen Vice Admiral thought.

"Well, Sir, we'll know one way or the other in about three T-weeks," he said instead, and he smiled.

Chapter Thirty-One

"So here we are . . . at last."

Earl White Haven knew the words sounded almost petulant, but he couldn't help himself. Admiral Caparelli's two-month delivery time for Eighth Fleet's Manticoran superdreadnoughts had turned into five, which meant White Haven was almost exactly fifteen months late assembling his assigned striking force. Or would be, when the last two RMN SDs actually arrived the day after tomorrow.

And I wouldn't be up to strength now *if the GSN hadn't anted up three more of its SDs to replace Manticoran ships which won't be arriving at all,* he thought, looking at the staffers assembled around the briefing room table. *Well, I suppose I should be grateful for small favors. At least it means I got the* Harrington *and one of her sisters.*

He glanced at the plot of his assembled fleet displayed on his terminal, eyes automatically seeking out the icons of the Grayson contingent. The GSN had worked like demons to get the *Harrington* ready to christen on schedule. There had been a delay in the fabrication of her beta nodes, and they'd had to divert half a dozen from one of her sisters to meet their deadline, but they'd met it . . . and a noticeably pregnant Allison Harrington had pressed the button that detonated the champagne bottle affixed to the ship's prow on the first anniversary, to the minute, of Grayson's receipt of INS's broadcast of Honor Harrington's execution.

I doubt the symbolism was lost on anyone, White Haven reflected with an edge of grimness. *It certainly wasn't lost on me, at any rate, or on Judah Yanakov when he chose the* Harrington *as his flagship. But I'm delighted to have her. And I might as well admit I'm eager to see how the concept actually works out in action.*

The corners of his mouth quirked wryly at the last thought, but he banished any hint of a smile instantly. Not that any of his staff would have noticed. They were all still busy looking down at the table rather than meet his eyes.

Hmm . . . maybe I let myself sound just a bit too *petulant there. Or could it be that I've been acting just a little more like a hexapuma with a sore tooth than I thought I had? Possible. Entirely possible. Even probable.*

"All right, ladies and gentlemen," he said in a much lighter tone. "They say late is better than never, so let's just see if we can't put some teeth into that old cliché. Jenny, what's the status of Barnett?"

"Our last scouting report is a week old, Sir, but the numbers hadn't changed since the probe before it."

Jennifer O'Brien, White Haven's intelligence officer, was a red-haired, blue-eyed native of Manticore. She was also only a senior-grade lieutenant and a third-generation prolong recipient. At thirty-one, the slender lieutenant looked like a pre-prolong seventeen-year-old, but despite her youth and junior rank, White Haven had specifically requested her for his staff. Just before the First Battle of Seabring, then Ensign O'Brien had strongly dissented from the enemy forces appreciation of the full commander who'd been White Haven's intelligence officer at the time. As it happened, she'd been right and the commander had been wrong . . . and Thomas Theisman had inflicted enough damage on the task force White Haven had sent to take Seabring to force its humiliating retreat. White Haven hadn't blamed his intelligence officer—he'd seen the same reports and drawn the same conclusions—but neither had he forgotten that O'Brien had been right when both of them had been wrong. *And* that she'd had the nerve to disagree with both her own immediate superior and the commander of an entire fleet.

"Run back over it for us again, please," he requested now, and O'Brien keyed her terminal.

"Our current strength estimate gives him twenty-six of the wall, twenty-eight battleships, twenty battlecruisers, thirty to forty heavy cruisers, thirty-five to forty light cruisers, and at least forty destroyers. We don't know how many LACs he may have, but Enki and DuQuesne Base were very heavily fortified prior to the war, and we have to assume they'll use missile pods to thicken their orbital launch capability. Call it a hundred and ninety hyper-capable units and six or seven times that amount of firepower in fixed defenses and/or LACs." She made a small face. "I'm sorry we can't be any closer to precise on that latter figure, Sir, but we simply don't know the present condition of their fortifications. We know they've had their own maintenance problems, and it's always possible a goodly percentage of their fixed weapons are down, but I wouldn't count on it. My own view is that if they were willing to reinforce him this heavily in mobile units, they would also have made every effort to put his permanent defenses on-line, and they've got the techs for that if they're willing to take them away from other, less important systems."

"Um." White Haven turned that over in his mind. He was inclined to agree with her, but he looked at his chief of staff. "Alyson?"

"I agree with Jenny," Captain (Junior Grade) Lady Alyson Granston-Henley said firmly. "All our sources confirm that McQueen has been sweeping with a new broom ever since she took over their war office, and she has to know Theisman is one of her best fleet commanders. Whatever Kline might have done, there's no way McQueen will stick him out at the end of a limb and saw it off behind him. She *has* to have made a major push to put his forts on-line. If she hadn't, she certainly would have sent him more mobile units—and heavier ones—to make up the difference. Either that, or reduced his strength still further to make it hurt less when we punch the system out."

White Haven nodded slowly and glanced around the table, seeing agreement on most of his other officers' faces. Commander Yerensky, his RMN astrogator, seemed a little doubtful, and Commander Yanakov, his Grayson logistics officer, appeared to share Yerensky's reservations.

"What's your feeling, Trev?" he asked his operations officer, Commander Trevor Haggerston of the Erewhon Navy. The heavyset commander scratched an eyebrow for a moment, then shrugged and grinned crookedly.

"I think Jenny and Captain G are both right," he said. "God knows we've taken long enough to assemble Eighth Fleet, and McQueen can't be certain we're not planning on diverting additional units to it from Third Fleet before we move on Barnett. And while Theisman has fifty-four capital ships to our forty-nine, twenty-eight of his are only battleships. We've got a fifteen-percent tonnage edge in capital ships—exclusive of battlecruisers—and a forty-seven-percent edge in genuine ships of the wall. We could just about double those numbers with diversions from Third Fleet, and he and McQueen must know it. Under the circumstances, someone as cagey as McQueen would have been pulling ships *out* of Barnett before we killed them—or at least replacing SDs and dreadnoughts with battleships she could better afford to lose—unless she figured his fixed defenses were good enough to even the odds."

"With all due respect, Admiral, that assumes McQueen is in a position to act on her judgment," Commander Yanakov put in. The sandy-haired Grayson officer was thirty-one, young enough that he'd received the first-generation prolong treatments shortly after Grayson joined the Alliance. He was a third cousin of Admiral Yanakov's, and he also had remarkably handsome features and intriguing, gold-flecked brown eyes which had cut a devastating swath through the female Allied officers who'd crossed his path.

"I think we have to assume she is, Commander," O'Brien said quietly. She, at least, seemed impervious to his looks and undeniable charm, although, to do the Grayson officer credit, he himself seemed unaware of his attractiveness.

"I realize all the analyses point that way," Yanakov said calmly, "and they may very well be accurate. In fact, I think they are. But we have to remain open to the possibility that they aren't. Giving her the authority to call the shots without civilian interference represents a major departure from the Peeps' established policies. I believe we ought to allow for the chance that they haven't changed directions as completely as we believe. At the very least, we have to be cautious about making operational assumptions based on an unquestioning belief that they have."

"Your point's well taken, Zack," White Haven agreed. "However, I believe ONI and SIS are correct about the extent of McQueen's authority."

"As I said, Sir, I'm inclined to think that myself," Yanakov said with deferential stubbornness. "But assuming she *is* in charge of their deployments, why hasn't she reinforced Theisman even more heavily? ONI's lost track of at least three squadrons of their SDs, not to mention all those other battleships. If I were McQueen and I was serious about holding Barnett, some of those missing ships would have turned up down here months ago. They haven't."

He shrugged and held out his hands, palm uppermost.

"The Commander has a point, Sir," Lieutenant O'Brien admitted. "I've asked myself that question. As you know, I've also asked Captain Leahy—" Leahy was Third Fleet's senior intelligence officer "—and both Grayson and Manticoran naval intelligence for their views. Unfortunately, the only answer they've been able to give me is that they don't know." It was her turn to shrug unhappily. "The only thing we know so far is that they haven't turned up anywhere else, either, and ONI's best estimate is that the SDs have probably been recalled for refit. Given the fact that Solarian League technology seems to be continuing to leak through the embargo to them, it would make sense for them to upgrade their ships of the wall in rotation to take advantage of whatever they've gotten. And, frankly, we've been so busy consolidating our own positions for the last eighteen months or so that we've given them the opportunity to do just that."

"I know, Jenny." White Haven rubbed his chin and glanced at the hologram floating above the briefing room table. It was a split image: a chart of the Trevor's Star System juxtaposed to an actual repeat of the flag bridge's main visual display, and the visual was even more impressive, in some ways, than the plot on his terminal.

Eighth Fleet floated before him—two hundred ships in all, headed by thirty-seven Manticoran and Grayson SDs and twelve Erewhonese dreadnoughts—maintaining station forty-five light-seconds off the Trevor's Star terminus of the Manticore Junction while White Haven awaited the arrival of the last of his superdreadnoughts via the Junction. The massed, massive firepower of the fleet gleamed in the display like tiny, fiery sparks of reflected sunlight, nuzzling relatively close (in deep-space terms) to the terminus, but the star chart showed what else they shared the system with. Third Fleet's fifty-five SDs hung in San Martin orbit, permanently on guard to protect the system and the thick clutch of half-complete deep-space fortresses being assembled under their watchful eye. Eventually, half those forts would be left to cover San Martin while the other half were towed out to cover the terminus directly. They could have been finished long ago if the Peeps had done even a tiny bit less effective job of destroying San Martin's orbital industry before they gave up the system. As it was, the Alliance had been forced to ship in the equipment to build the facilities needed to assemble the prefabricated components of the bases. It was taking far longer than it should have, but current projections called for the first group of forts to be finished within six or seven T-months—at which point everyone would no doubt heave a sigh of profound relief. But for now the solid ranks of capital units held their watchful orbit, proudly protecting what had been won at such terrible cost in lives and ships, and White Haven let his eyes rest upon their icons.

He hated the sight. Not that he didn't feel a deep sense of pride whenever he saw them and remembered the savage fighting which had finally taken the system. Nor did he have anything but respect for Theodosia Kuzak, who had replaced him as CO 3 FLT on the new Trevor's Star Station. No, what he hated was the way the terminus acted as an anchor on Third Fleet. The idea had been for the conquest of Trevor's Star to free up fighting power, not glue it in place, but until the forts were ready, the Admiralty refused to reduce Third Fleet in any way.

No, that's not fair, he reminded himself. In fact, Kuzak's command had already been reduced by over twenty ships of the wall, but those units had all been returned to the RMN's central dockyards for desperately needed maintenance. None had been released for operations elsewhere . . . and none of Theodosia's remaining units would be detached to Eighth Fleet, either. Trevor's Star was the prize for which the RMN had fought for over three years, and no risk of surrendering it back to the Peeps could even be contemplated.

It'll be all right, he told himself. *We're about to take the offensive again, and whatever McQueen and Theisman are thinking about, they've waited too long. Theisman doesn't have the mobile firepower to stop us—not with our advantages in EW and missiles, even if he does have their own version of the pods. Once we punch out Barnett, anything else they may be thinking about will have to be rethought in reaction to Eighth Fleet's operations. We've taken far too long about it, but it looks like we've preempted them after all.*

"All *right*, people! Now *that*'s the way an op is supposed to go!"

Jacquelyn Harmon smiled hugely at her assembled staff and squadron commanders—including newly promoted Commander Stewart Ashford. The holo above the briefing room table was very different from the one which had shown the "dead" icons of Ashford's section six months earlier. Instead, it showed the spectacular (if simulated) wreckage of three battlecruisers, twelve destroyers, and all thirty-three of the merchantmen those warships had been escorting. A tabular sidebar showed the LAC wing's own losses: six ships destroyed, eight more damaged beyond *Minotaur*'s on-board repair capability, and lighter damage to another thirteen. The tonnage ratio was appallingly in the LACs' favor: two hundred and eighty thousand tons of LACs lost or seriously damaged in return for the complete destruction of almost four million tons of warships and a staggering quarter of a *billion* tons of merchant shipping.

"The LAC concept certainly seems to have been proved . . . in sims, at least," Captain Truman observed. *Minotaur*'s skipper had been invited to the wing debrief, and she, too, smiled at the exultant young LAC COs, but there was a note of warning in her voice.

"It certainly does, Ma'am," Commander McGyver replied. "I make it a tonnage ratio of just about eight hundred to one, and God only knows what the casualty ratio was!"

"Roughly a hundred-and-fifty-two-to-one," Barbara Stackowitz put in promptly. "We suffered one hundred and twelve casualties, ninety-three of them fatal, and they lost sixteen thousand nine hundred and fifty-one, but over eleven thousand of them were aboard the escorts."

"In a simulation," Rear Admiral of the Green George Holderman pointed out sourly. Unlike Truman, Holderman hadn't been invited to the debrief; he'd invited himself. That was something Manticoran flag officers simply didn't do, yet no one had possessed the seniority to tell him no, and his personality had done its best to put a damper on *Minotaur*'s mood ever since his arrival. He was one of the officers who had fought the entire LAC-carrier concept from the beginning, and he continued to fight on with dogged persistence. His own battle record was good enough to give his opinions a solid weight, and he'd become one of the leading spokesmen for the "missile-deck admirals," as the traditionalist opponents of the LACs had been dubbed. He considered the idea a worthless diversion of desperately needed resources and everyone knew it. Yet despite Admiral Adcock's best efforts, he'd possessed sufficient seniority—and allies within the service—to get himself named to head the special board empaneled to evaluate *Minotaur*'s effectiveness.

"With all due respect, Admiral," Truman said flatly, "until the Admiralty is willing to turn a LAC wing loose on a live target, the only way we can test the concept is in simulations. Where, I might add, the LACs have won every engagement to date."

Holderman's beefy face darkened as the golden-haired captain looked him straight in the eye. She hadn't cared for the fashion in which he'd bulled his way into the debrief, and she didn't particularly care for him as a human being, either. Nor did she like the way he'd begun tinkering with the simulations, convincing the umpires to incorporate "more realistic" assumptions . . . all of which just happened to pare away at the LACs' advantages in speed, nimbleness, and smaller target size.

The rear admiral knew exactly what she was implying, and he didn't care for her tone of voice. Nor had he ever liked uppity juniors who expressed disagreement even privately—far less publicly—with flag officers, and anger sparkled in his eyes. But the Honorable Alice Truman was no ordinary uppity junior. She was a captain of the list with a reputation—and allies (and patrons)—of her own, and he knew she was on the next short list for rear admiral. It was unusual to jump an officer straight past commodore to rear admiral, even in wartime, and Holderman gritted his teeth as he wondered if she knew it was going to happen to her. That would certainly be one possible explanation for the challenge in her tone and eyes.

But whatever she might become in the future, she was only a captain at the moment, and he let himself lean towards her, using his twenty-centimeter height advantage to loom pugnaciously over her.

"Yes, it's all been in simulations, *Captain*," he said even more flatly than she'd spoken. "And it will stay that way until this board and the Admiralty are convinced the concept merits testing in action. And, frankly, the unrealistic assumptions so far applied to the operational parameters of the exercises have done very little to convince me to recommend approval."

"Unrealistic, Sir?" Truman's blue eyes were hard, and several of her juniors glanced apprehensively at one another as they felt the thunderheads gathering. "Unrealistic in what way, if I may ask?"

"In *every* way!" Holderman snapped. "The exercise parameters assumed none of the escort captains assigned to it had ever encountered one of the new LACs before. They were forced to engage them in total ignorance of their actual capabilities!"

"I see, Sir." Truman cocked her head and bared her teeth in a tight almost-smile. "May I ask if any of the captains involved actually did have any knowledge of the *Shrike*'s capabilities?"

"Of course they didn't! How could they have when it's still on the Official Secrets List?" Holderman demanded.

"An excellent point, Sir," Truman shot back. "But unless I misread my own briefing from the umpires, that was the objective of the exercise: to see how a force which had never encountered them would fare against them. Was I, perhaps, in error in that interpretation?"

Holderman turned a dangerous shade of red. Truman's words were respectful enough, but the tone in which she'd delivered them was cold as a frozen razor. Worse, she was completely right about the simulation's purpose.

"Whatever the object of the *simulated* exercise," he grated, "the true test of the concept will be how it works in real space, in real time, against people who *do* know what's coming, Captain. Eventually someone on the other side is going to figure out what they can do, after all, and begin taking steps to attack their weaknesses, now aren't they? So don't you think it might be a good idea to try and figure out those weaknesses for ourselves before we throw lives away against the Peeps? The Fleet *would* like to use these vessels—and their crews—more than once each, you know!"

"Certainly, Sir," Truman agreed. "I only point out that the object of *this* exercise was to determine how we can expect them to fare in their initial employments."

"'Initial employments'!" Holderman half-spat, and his lip curled. "Even granting that you're correct in this instance, Captain, no simulation is going to prove much until its assumptions bear at least some resemblance to reality. Obviously anyone can stack the odds in an exercise to favor one side or the other!"

"Indeed they can, Sir," Truman agreed in tones of deadly affability. "Of course, sometimes they fail to dictate the outcome they desire no matter how thoroughly they stack the odds, don't they, Sir?"

Holderman went puce, and someone sucked in air audibly, for everyone in the briefing room knew what she was referring to—they just couldn't quite believe she'd had the nerve to do it.

Rear Admiral Holderman had convinced the umpires to alter the immediately previous exercise's ground rules by giving the officers assigned to command the simulated superdreadnought division opposed to *Minotaur* a detailed briefing on the *Shrike* and its capabilities. The briefing had been a major change from the original exercise plan approved by BuShips, Admiral Adcock's BuWeaps, and the Bureau of Training, and everyone knew it had been intended to give the SDs a clear advantage. Despite that, however, both ships of the wall had been destroyed, although they had managed to take thirty of *Minotaur*'s LACs with them and damaged another eleven. It had been the carrier's worst losses to date . . . and had still cost the defenders seventeen million tons of capital ship in return for only six hundred thousand tons of LACs. Not to mention twelve thousand crewmen as opposed to only three hundred and thirty-two from the LAC wing.

"You may think these . . . these *toy boats* are warships, Captain, but they'll be worth damn all against an alert wall with its sensor and fire control net intact!" he snapped.

"I'm sure loss rates will climb against a prepared opponent, Sir," Truman conceded. "No one has ever claimed they wouldn't. Nor, to the best of my knowledge, has anyone ever suggested that 'these toy boats' can substitute in close action for properly handled ships of the wall. But so far they've met every challenge thrown at them and performed even better than expected in almost every case. I submit to you, Sir, that Captain Harmon and her people have amply proved the first-stage practicality of Anzio."

"You can submit whatever you like, Captain!" Holderman spat, and his eyes blazed dangerously. "Fortunately, the decision is the board's, not yours, and we'll continue testing the concept until my colleagues and I are convinced these things have some *real* value."

"I see." Truman regarded him with calm, cold dispassion, then shrugged. "Very well, Sir. I cannot, of course, fault your determination to do a full, complete, and impartial job of evaluating the concept." Her voice might be cold, but the vitriol dripping from it could easily have stripped paint off a bulkhead. "In the meantime, however, Captain Harmon and her officers have a great deal to do to prepare for tomorrow's exercises. May I suggest that you and I leave them to it?"

Holderman glared at her, but there was little he could say in reply. More to the point, she was *Minotaur*'s captain, and he, despite the difference in their ranks, was only a visitor aboard her ship. If she chose to, she had the legal authority to order him out of the compartment—or entirely off the ship. It would be a suicidal career move, regardless of whatever sponsors or patrons she might have attracted, but the look in her eyes suggested she might not care a great deal just at the moment. Nor would being the subject of such an order do very much for Holderman's career. At the very least, it would make him a laughingstock. At worst, it might even convince people Truman was right about the LACs and that *he* was the one who'd been out of line. Which was ridiculous, of course, but not something he could afford to ignore.

"No doubt you're correct, Captain," he said, and if her tone could have stripped paint, his was a flat declaration that she'd just made a mortal enemy. "If you'll have my pinnace called away, I'll return to the orbital base to consult with the umpires about tomorrow's exercise."

"Of course, Sir. It will be my pleasure." Again, the words were harmless . . . and the tone in which they were delivered was deadly. He glared at her, then turned and stamped out of the compartment.

Truman watched the hatch close behind him, then turned to give her breathless juniors a crooked smile.

"If I could have one more moment of your time, Jackie?" she asked politely, and twitched her head at the hatch.

"Certainly, Ma'am," Harmon replied, and the two of them stepped out into the passage beyond the briefing room. Holderman had already vanished, and Truman smiled again—more nearly naturally—at *Minotaur*'s COLAC.

"I suppose I might have handled that just a *bit* more tactfully," she observed, "but the son of a bitch pissed me off."

"Me, too," Harmon agreed. "All the same—"

"All the same, nothing we could possibly do could make him any more determined to scrub the entire project," Truman interrupted. "Although," she added judiciously, "I did do my best to inspire him to greater efforts."

"You—?" Harmon blinked, then shook her head. "Would you care to explain that?"

"It's simple enough, Jackie," Truman said with a chuckle. "He and Commodore Paget are the board's senior officers, and they've been sitting on the sim results for months. You and your people have blown the other side out of space over and over again, but they're damned if they'll admit it. Surely you've noticed that?"

"Well, yes. Of course I have," Harmon admitted.

"Then what makes you think they'll *stop* sitting on the results?" Truman demanded. "Worse, the two of them will go right on tinkering with the sim parameters until they manage to come up with a way for the defenders to swat your people in droves. And they're not idiots. In fact, both of them are superior conventional tacticians, however stupidly they may be acting in this instance. They *will* find a way, and you and I know it, because they're right about how fragile your LACs are. Sooner or later, they'll devise a setup which will require you to accept catastrophic losses to accomplish your mission. It won't have to be a reasonable scenario, or a situation likely to recur in action. All it has to do is be theoretically plausible and inflict massive losses on the wing for minimal results. Because when they pull it off, *that's* the exercise they'll use as the baseline for their report to the Admiralty."

Harmon stared at her, and Truman sighed. The LAC wing's CO was a brilliant officer in her own iconoclastic way, but she came from a non-naval family. In many ways, she reminded Truman of Honor Harrington, for despite Alfred Harrington's career as a Navy surgeon, Honor had also come from a family with few or no naval ancestors and accomplished all she had on the basis of raw ability. Alice Truman, on the other hand, was the daughter of a vice admiral, the granddaughter of a captain and a rear admiral, and the great-granddaughter of a commodore, two rear admirals, and a first space lord. She understood the Byzantine feuds and machinations of the Royal Navy's great dynasties as Jacquelyn Harmon never would, and she knew exactly how Holderman and his fellows could—and would—go about killing or delaying Operation Anzio. She even understood that they'd do it because they honestly believed it to be their duty. The only problem was that she couldn't let them, for the Navy desperately needed the potential the *Shrikes* represented.

"Trust me on this, Jackie," she said as gently as she could. "I don't say they can kill the concept outright, because I don't think they can. It makes too much sense, we need it too badly, and it's got too many supporters. But they *can* delay it by another year or even two, and we can't afford that."

"But how will pissing them off stop them?"

"Because unless I miss my guess, Holderman is so hot right this minute that he can hardly wait to get back to Hancock Base, call in the umpires, and start twisting tomorrow's exercise like a pretzel," Truman said cheerfully. "By the time he's done, the sim's outcome will be the worst disaster for your LAC wing since Amos Parnell left a month early for the Third Battle of Yeltsin."

"And that's a *good* thing?" Harmon demanded, her expression aghast, and Truman chuckled.

"It's a wonderful thing, Jackie, because I've already drafted a dispatch to Admiral Adcock's attention at BuWeaps—with information copies to Admiral Caparelli, Vice Admiral Givens at BuPlan, Vice Admiral Danvers at BuShips, and Vice Admiral Tanith Hill at BuTrain—expressing my concern that the sims are being written unrealistically."

Harmon's eyes widened, for that was five of the Space Lords of the Board of Admiralty. In fact, it was *all* of them except for Admiral Cortez and Vice Admiral Mannock, the heads of BuPers and the Surgeon General, respectively. Truman saw her expression and smiled.

"Naturally I would never attribute intentional bias to anyone," she said piously, "but for whatever reason, I feel I've discerned a . . . failure to fully and fairly examine the capabilities of the LAC-carrier concept in the last few exercises. In fact, I'm afraid the problem is becoming more pronounced, and so I've brought it to the attention of all the relevant authorities, exactly as I'm supposed to. Unfortunately, Chief Mantooth somehow neglected to forward a copy to Admiral Holderman or any other member of the evaluation board here in Hancock. A terrible oversight, of course. Doubtless the board's copies simply got lost in transit someplace."

"You mean—?" Harmon stared at her in something very like awe.

"I mean the Powers That Be are going to have ample reason to look very, very carefully at the parameters of the sims and how they came to be written as they are. And what they're going to find is a steady procession of successes by the LACs followed—hopefully—by a single, crushing, overwhelming failure. Which will cause them to look even more carefully at that particular exercise, talk to the umpires . . . and discover just how the parameters were changed, and by whom." Truman smiled nastily. "I suspect Admiral Holderman and Commodore Paget will have just a *little* explaining to do after that."

"Jesus, Alice," Harmon said. She was silent for several seconds, then she shook her head. "I see what you're up to, but what if he doesn't bite? What if he just bides his time? And what if he decides to get even with you down the line? He *is* a rear admiral, after all."

"First, I think he's too pissed off—and too convinced he's right—to resist the bait," Truman replied. "Second, the seed is planted. Even if he waits another few days—or even longer—sooner or later he'll push a little too hard, and when he does, the trap will spring. And as for getting even with me—" She shrugged. "If he reacts the way I expect him to, he'll cut his own throat. His career may survive it, but any move he ever makes to hit back at me will be seen as a vengeful senior trying to use his position to punish a junior who was simply doing her job when he made himself look like an idiot. Oh, sure, some people will figure out what really happened—and a few will probably realize it from the very beginning—but I'm not worried about them. The ones who figure it out will also know why I did it. They may not be exactly delighted by the spectacle of a captain helping a rear admiral shoot his own . . . foot off, and I could find myself in trouble at some point if one of them ends up on a promotion board evaluating me for my own flag, but I'll cross that bridge when I reach it. Besides, I figure most of them will have realized how valuable the LACs are long before that happens."

"And if you're wrong?" Harmon asked quietly.

"If I'm wrong, my career is going to be very disappointing, by my family's standards," Truman said much more lightly than she felt. "I won't like that, and neither will my parents. But they'll know why I did it, and that's enough for me. Besides," she smiled, this time completely naturally, "at least this way I'll still be able to sleep with myself . . . and I'll still get that asshole Holderman, whatever happens. Believe me, Jackie—that by itself would be almost enough to make the whole thing worth it!"

Chapter Thirty-Two

The alarm buzzed very quietly. Lieutenant Gaines would always remember that—how *quiet* it had been, how civilized. As if the central computer were merely clearing its throat politely to get his attention.

It was only later, in the nightmares that lasted for so many years, that he realized how utterly inappropriate that peaceful sound had been.

He reached out and killed the alarm, then checked the master plot. The cool K2 primary of the Seaford Nine System floated at the holo tank's center, and he frowned as his eyes swept the sphere indicating the star's hyper limit, searching for the icon that had to be there. Then they found it, and he nodded and began punching commands into his console.

The computers considered his instructions and obediently lit a smaller holo directly in front of him. It didn't have much detail yet—just a single blur of light blinking the alternating red and amber of an unknown, possibly hostile contact. His gravitic sensors had picked up the FTL hyper footprint, but at anything over two or three light-minutes, even the best sensors couldn't tell much about the sizes or numbers of ships which had created any given footprint. He needed individual impeller signatures before he could make that sort of estimate, and he waited patiently for the newcomers to light off their drives.

It was most probably simply an unscheduled friendly arrival, he thought, although, failing that, it might be one of the increasingly infrequent Peep scout ships. Gaines almost hoped it was. The Peeps seemed to pick their hottest hotshots for the occasional, screaming sensor pass, and watching Admiral Hennesy maneuver to try to intercept them had always been entertaining and sometimes downright exciting. He hadn't seen Admiral Santino in action yet, either, and he was curious about how well he'd stack up against the officer he'd relieved.

Then again, he reflected, *the duration figure on the footprint would almost have to indicate a multiship transit, now wouldn't it? Hmmm . . .*

That made the unscheduled friendlies rather more likely, he judged. Still, he couldn't rule out the possibility of three or four scout ships intended to work in concert, and a multibogie intercept of that sort would be even more entertaining than most, but it was going to take a while to figure out which it was. He nodded to himself as symbols began to blink beside the fuzzy haze in his display. They were picking up impeller drives now, but the range was still long, and he waited as the system began painstakingly enhancing the faint emissions which had attracted the computer's attention.

There were reasons it took so long. Not *good* ones, in Gaines' humble opinion, but reasons nonetheless. There had once been plans to provide Seaford with an FTL sensor shell as good as any other Manticoran fleet base outside the home system, but somehow those plans had gone awry. Personally, Gaines suspected the paperwork was simply lost somewhere in the bowels of BuShips' Logistics Command. He'd always figured Logistics was the closest humankind was ever likely to come to producing a genuine black hole, because any work orders or parts requests that came within shouting distance of it were doomed to be sucked in, mangled, and forever vanish from the known universe.

Of course, he could be wrong in this instance. Despite the mammoth orbital facilities the Peeps had put in before Sir Yancey Parks took the system away from them, Seaford had never had all that high a priority for the Royal Manticoran Navy. BuShips and BuWeaps had spent a year or two going absolutely wild over the opportunity to get a detailed look inside the Peeps' tech establishment. But once they'd finished crawling through every nook and cranny of the repair bases and parts storage depots and asteroid smelters, and inspecting the contents of the magazines, and carting off samples of the latest Peep computer hardware, the Star Kingdom really hadn't had all that much use for the base.

Oh, it was bigger than Hancock. In theory, the RMN could have taken over the old Peep shipyards and used them for its own construction programs. And if the Star Kingdom didn't want to do that, even the limited portions of the repair facilities it had chosen to crew could have supported a considerably larger local defense force than Hancock Station did. Unfortunately, Seaford Nine's equipment was crap compared to Manticoran hardware, and the system had no local population or even habitable planets. Upgrading the yard to Alliance standards and shipping in a work force large enough to operate it would have cost almost as much as it would have cost to build new building slips from scratch, and the system itself was badly placed as a major defensive node. Hancock was in a much better position for that, and the only reason Parks had wanted Seaford in the first place was to eliminate its threat to the long-haul Manticore–Basilisk hyper route and deny the Peeps a springboard against Hancock, Zanzibar, Alizon, Yorik, or any of the other Allied systems in the area.

Plans had been drawn at one point to upgrade at least the repair portion of the system's infrastructure to Manticoran standards despite the cost, and those plans were taken out and dusted off periodically. But the Navy was stretched too tight to make the project worthwhile. The Admiralty had acknowledged that months ago when it began pulling out picket ships for refit at Hancock or the home system without bothering to replace them. If there was anyplace the Star Kingdom had decided it could do without, Seaford Nine was it. And so there wasn't really very much here: a fairly good-sized caretaker detachment of techs to keep the huge, mostly empty main repair base more-or-less operational, two squadrons of heavy cruisers, and a reinforced division of superdreadnoughts, supported by a half-squadron of battlecruisers and a couple of destroyers. And, of course, one Lieutenant Heinrich Gaines, Senior Officer Commanding Her Majesty's Sensor Station, Seaford Nine.

It sounded impressive as hell, he thought with a chuckle, but the same considerations which gave the system such a low priority for modernization and enlargement had also reduced its priority for first-line sensor equipment. He had an extremely limited FTL net, built mostly on first- and second-generation platforms only a very little better than those Lady Harrington had employed in the Second Battle of Yeltsin. They had a far slower data transmission rate than the new third-generation systems he'd heard rumors about, and—

His ruminations chopped off as the holo at his console sudden dissolved and reformed. He stared at it, feeling his eyebrows try to crawl up into his hairline, and his mouth was suddenly dry.

The information wasn't complete. Over half the identifying data codes continued to blink, indicating that the computers had been forced to assign tentative IDs pending better data resolution, and the emission sources were still right on the K2 primary's 16.72 LM hyper limit, which put them over ten light-minutes from Gaines' main sensor arrays. That meant everything he did know—aside from the impeller signatures, which were FTL themselves—was better than ten minutes old by the time he saw it. But even the limited data he had was enough to turn his belly to frozen lead.

He looked at the display a moment longer, then punched a priority code into his com. The delay seemed interminable, though it could not in fact have been more than five or ten seconds, and then a voice spoke in his earbug.

"Task Group Combat Information Center," it announced in professional tones that still managed to sound ineffably bored. "Commander Jaruwalski."

"CIC, this is Sensor One," Gaines said crisply. "I have unknown—

repeat, unknown—vessels entering the star system, bearing one-seven-seven zero-niner-eight relative from the primary, range from base ten-point-seven-seven light-minutes. They have not transmitted an FTL arrival report."

"Unknown vessels?" The boredom had vanished from Jaruwalski's voice, and Gaines could picture the commander snapping upright in her chair. "Class IDs?" she demanded.

"I'm working with light-speed sensors here, Commander," Gaines reminded her. "My gravitics make it—" he double-checked to be certain "—fifty-four point sources. At present—" He paused and cleared his throat. "At present, the computers are calling it fifteen to twenty of the wall and at least ten battleships. That's based solely on the strengths of their impeller signatures, but the data enhancement looks solid, Ma'am."

For just a moment, there was total silence from the other end of the com, but Gaines could almost hear the thoughts flashing through Jaruwalski's brain. Twenty-five capital ships—minimum—was hardly a typical raiding force. And the three superdreadnoughts and four battlecruisers of the Seaford Picket could never stand up to what was headed for them.

"Understood, Sensor One," Jaruwalski said after several seconds. "Patch your output straight through to me and do what you can to refine it."

"Aye, aye, Ma'am." Gaines felt immensely relieved to have passed the knowledge on to someone else—someone senior to him, who had become responsible for dealing with it. All *he* had to do now was keep the information flowing . . . and hope he could somehow survive what he knew was about to happen.

"Well, if they didn't have us on sensors before, it's clear they have us now," Citizen Vice Admiral Ellen Shalus remarked to her people's commissioner as the sparks of Manty impeller drives began to appear in the flag deck plot. She watched them carefully, then reached up and scratched an eyebrow while she frowned. Citizen Commissioner Randal saw the frown and cocked his head.

"Something is bothering you, Citizen Admiral?" he asked, and she shrugged.

"I don't see enough impeller signatures, Sir," she replied, and looked over her shoulder at her ops officer. "What did HQ say we were supposed to hit here, Oscar?"

"According to the analysts' best estimates, at least six or eight of the wall, plus a dozen battlecruisers, Citizen Admiral," Citizen Commander Levitt replied instantly. From his tone, he knew he was answering the question for the official record, not because his admiral hadn't already had the information filed away in her head, and Shalus looked back at Randal and pointed at the plot with her chin.

"Whatever that is—and we're still too far out for good reads—

it sure as hell *isn't* a squadron of the wall, Citizen Commissioner. And I'll be very surprised if there are a dozen battlecruisers out there, either. It looks to me more like three or four of the wall with a screen of heavy cruisers."

"Could the other units be hiding in stealth?" Anxiety honed the edges of Randal's question, and Shalus smiled thinly. The same thought had already occurred to her, because it was just the sort of thing those sneaky Manty bastards liked to do.

"I don't know, Sir," she said honestly. "It's certainly possible. On the other hand, Citizen Admiral Giscard and Citizen Lieutenant Thaddeus did warn us that a lot of our data was out of date. We haven't exactly swamped this area with scout ships since the war began, after all. That's one of the reasons we figure the Manties are probably feeling smug and secure about it. And I suppose the answer could simply be that they've pulled the missing SDs home for refit. Intelligence said they have a lot of capital ships in the body and fender shop."

"Um." Randal moved to stand beside her and folded his arms, gazing down into the plot. "Can you make any estimate of what they're up to?" he asked after a moment.

"Right now, running around like headless chickens, I imagine," Shalus replied with a cold smile. "Even if they are hiding people in stealth, they can't have enough firepower to stop us—not this far from the front line. My gut feeling is that what we see is what they've got; they're just trying to get it all concentrated while they figure out what to do with it. As for what they can do—" She shrugged. "We've got the pods on tow, and we've got the advantage in numbers, and in tonnage, and in surprise, Sir. All I really see that they can do is run away . . . or die. And frankly," her smile turned even colder and a predator glow flickered in her eyes, "I don't really much care which."

"I want *options*, people!" Rear Admiral of the Red Elvis Santino snapped.

In that case, you should have gotten off your fat ass and spent at least a few hours thinking about this sort of situation ahead of time! Andrea Jaruwalski thought coldly.

Santino had succeeded Vice Admiral Hennesy two and a half months earlier when the picket was reduced to its present strength, and he had not impressed Jaruwalski. He'd made a big deal out of retaining Hennesy's staff when he took over Hennesy's flagship, treating their retention as a generous sign of his trust in them. After all, if he hadn't trusted them, he would have brought in his own command team, wouldn't he?

Unfortunately, Jaruwalski didn't believe for a moment that that was what had happened or why. Personally, she suspected Santino had been sent here because the system, however prestigious command of it might look on paper, was about as much use to the Star Kingdom as a screen door on an air lock. It was a supremely unimportant slot, suitable for shuffling off nonentities who might have been embarrassments in significant assignments. And Santino hadn't retained Hennesy's staff because he trusted them; he'd retained them because he didn't give a good godamn. He certainly hadn't bothered to set up anything remotely like an exercise schedule, after all. Or even arranged regular planning sessions, for that matter!

She let no sign of her contempt shadow her expression, despite her thoughts, but she knew she wasn't the only one who felt less than total confidence in the CO of Seaford Station.

"Sir," she said in her most reasonable tone, "assuming Sensor One's figures on enemy strength are accurate—and I feel confident that they are—we don't *have* a lot of options. There are at least twelve superdreadnoughts and eight dreadnoughts out there; we have three ships of the wall. They have twelve battleships and four battlecruisers; we have five battlecruisers." She gave a tiny shrug. "We don't have the firepower to stop them, Sir. In my opinion, our only real option is to order the immediate evac of the orbit base technicians and pull out."

"Not acceptable!" Santino snapped. "I'm not going to be another Frances Yeargin and let the goddamned Peeps take out *my* command area without a fight!"

"With all due respect, Sir," Jaruwalski said, "we cannot go toe-to-toe with these people, and they know it." She checked the tactical data CIC was relaying to her briefing room terminal as further updates became available from Sensor One. "They've been in-system for eleven a half minutes, and they're now nine light-minutes out, moving at over forty-five hundred KPS. Assuming they're headed for a zero-zero intercept with the main orbital facilities, they should hit turnover in another hundred and seventeen minutes and reach the base in two hundred and fifty-nine. That's only a little over four hours, Admiral, and it leaves the evac ships very little time to get moving."

"Goddamn it, you're supposed to be my frigging *operations* officer, not some gutless civilian! Or don't you *care* about showing cowardice in the face of the enemy?" Santino snarled, and Jaruwalski's eyes snapped up from her display. Anger smoked like liquid nitrogen at their cores as they locked with Santino's, and the staffer next to her shrank away from the sudden ferocity which filled the air about her.

"Nothing in the Articles of War requires me to listen to that, Admiral Santino," she said in a tone of chipped ice. "My duty is to give you my best assessment of the tactical situation, and my assessment is that we have a hundred and forty-seven million tons of ships of the wall coming at us and that we have just over *twenty-five* million tons with which to face them. That works out to an enemy tonnage advantage of just about six to one, Sir—and completely ignores the twelve battleships supporting them."

"You'll listen to whatever I goddamned *tell* you to listen to, Commander!" Santino bellowed, and pounded a meaty fist on the table. Jaruwalski half-rose and opened her mouth to say something career-ending as answering fury flashed through her, but then she stopped, frozen in mid-movement, as she recognized what lay behind Santino's belligerent choler.

Fear. And not just the totally rational personal fear any sane person would feel as that juggernaut roared down upon her, either, the commander realized. It was the fear—almost the terror—of responsibility. That, and the fear of what retreating without firing a single shot might do to his career.

She swallowed hard while tension roared and sang in the silence of the emotion-lashed briefing room. Nothing in her training told her how to deal with a commanding officer so consumed with moral panic his brain had ceased functioning, yet that was what she faced.

I suppose any CO could be excused for being afraid of her duty in this situation, she thought almost calmly, *but it's worse for Santino after the way he shot his mouth off about Adler and Commodore Yeargin. And the way he just sat on his butt and vegetated out here. He's always been a sanctimonious pain in the ass, but all those lordly pronouncements about what* he *would have done if* he'd *been in her position—*

Nor had Santino been alone in that. The total destruction of Yeargin's task force had shaken the Royal Manticoran Navy to the core, however little it cared to admit it, because Peeps weren't suppose to be able to do things like that. Not to *them*. The official Board of Inquiry had delivered its verdict six months ago, following its painfully emotionless analysis of Yeargin's (many) mistakes with a scathing condemnation of the mindset which had let her make them. The Board had pulled no punches, and that was good. The last thing the Fleet needed was some whitewash which would allow other station commanders to make the same mistakes. Yet the report had its downside, as well, for in its wake, some officers had become more terrified of being labeled "unprepared" or "insufficiently offensive-minded" or "lacking in the initiative properly expected from a flag officer" than they were of dying.

And Elvis Santino had just proved he was one of those terrified officers. Worse, he *had* been caught unprepared, and insufficiently offensive-minded, and lacking in initiative . . . and whatever he chose to admit to his staff, inside he knew he had. Which only made his terror worse . . . and his desperate determination to prove he hadn't been still stronger.

"Sir," Jaruwalski said after a moment, her voice as calm and unchallenging as she could possibly make it as she sought another way to get through to him, "whatever you or I may want can't change the facts of the tactical situation. And the facts of the situation are that our capital ships are outgunned by theirs by approximately five-to-one in grasers, five-and-a-half-to-one in lasers, and well over six-to-one in missile tubes . . . and that, of course, assumes they don't have still more units hiding under stealth out there somewhere. Under the circum—"

"I am not giving up this system without firing a shot, Commander," Santino said, and the sudden flat intensity of his voice was more frightening than his bellow had been. "I'll evacuate the noncombatants, but there is no way—no way in hell, Commander!—that I am giving them Seaford Nine without a fight. I know *my* duty, even if other officers may not know theirs!"

"Sir, we can't fight them broadside-to-broadside! If we try—"

"I'm not going to," Santino said in that same flat tone. "You're forgetting our missile pods and our edge in electronic warfare."

"Sir, they have pods, too!" Jaruwalski tried to keep the desperation out of her voice and knew she was failing. "And ONI believes they've been using Solly technology to upgra—"

"Their pods aren't as good as ours," Santino shot back obstinately. "And even if they were, their point defense and ECM suck. We can close with them, fire at extreme range, and break off, and all of our superdreadnoughts have the new compensators. They'll never catch us in a stern chase, and if they try to overhaul, it will only divert them from pursuing the evac ships."

Jaruwalski felt a chill of horror as his eyes brightened with the last sentence. *Oh my God,* she thought despairingly, *now he's come up with a tactical justification for this insanity! He's going to get us all killed because he's too stupid—too afraid of showing lack of fighting spirit—to do the sensible thing, and now he's found a "logical reason" he thinks he can use in his after-action report to justify his stupidity!*

"Sir, it doesn't matter if our pods have an edge if they have enough more of them than we do," she said as reasonably as she could. "And—"

"You're relieved, Commander," Santino grated. "I need advice and some offensive spirit here, not cowardice."

Jaruwalski jerked as if he'd slapped her, and her face went white—not with shame or fear, but with fury.

"Admiral, it's my duty to give you my best est—" she began, and his hand slapped the tabletop like a gunshot.

"I said you're relieved!" he shouted. "Now get the hell out of here! In fact, I want your gutless ass the hell off my flagship right now, Jaruwalski!" She stared at him, speechless, and his lip drew up in a snarl. "I'll pass the evac order to the base in five minutes—now get the hell out of here!"

"Sir, I—"

"*Silence!*" he bellowed, and even through her own anger and sense of despair, she knew she was simply the focus his panic-spawned rage had fastened upon. But the knowledge helped nothing, for he could not possibly have chosen a worse one. She was his ops officer, his staff tactician, the one officer he absolutely *had* to listen to in this situation, and he refused to. She stared at him, trying to think of some way—of any way at all—to reach him, and he punched a com stud savagely.

"Bridge, Captain speaking," a voice replied.

"Captain Tasco, I have just relieved Commander Jaruwalski of duty," Santino said spitefully, his burning eyes locked on the ops officer. "I want her off this ship—now. You will provide a pinnace to deliver her to one of the evac ships immediately. I don't care which. Just see to it. And, Captain—" He paused briefly and let his lips curl with contempt before he resumed. "If necessary," he said coldly, "you will have Colonel Wellerman remove her from *Hadrian* under guard."

The com was silent for at least ten seconds. Then—

"Sir," Tasco said in a voice which was just that little bit too unshaken, "are you certain about this? I—"

"*Dead* certain, Captain," Santino said icily, and took his thumb from the com stud.

"Get out," he said flatly to Jaruwalski, and then turned his back on her and turned to the rest of his white-faced staff.

The ops officer stared at him a moment longer, then let her gaze sweep the other officers in the compartment. Not one of them would meet her eyes. She had become a pariah, her career ended in that single instant. It wouldn't matter in the end if she'd been right or wrong; all that would matter was that she had been relieved of duty for cowardice, and her fellow staffers—her friends—refused to look up, as if they feared the same leprosy would infect them if their gazes should touch.

She wanted to scream at them, to demand that they support her, present a united front against Santino's insanity. But it was useless. Nothing she could say would move them, even though they had to know she was right, and she felt her own anger flood out of her as suddenly as water from a shattered pot. They would sooner risk their own deaths, and the deaths of thousands of others, than Santino's rage . . . and their careers.

She gazed at them for one more second, some corner of her mind already knowing she would never see them again, and then turned and walked silently from the compartment.

At least the evacuation plan seemed to be working, Lieutenant Gaines thought thankfully as he swam quickly down the pinnace's personnel tube to HMS *Cantrip*'s boat bay. Unfortunately, that seemed to be the only thing that was.

He reached the end of the tube, caught the grab bar, and swung himself into the heavy cruiser's internal gravity.

"Gaines, Heinrich O., Lieutenant," he told the harassed ensign waiting by the tube. The young woman's fingers flew over her portable touchpad, feeding the name into the ship's computers to check against the current personnel list Orbital Base Three's computers had transmitted twenty-three minutes ago.

The touchpad beeped almost instantly, and she turned to look over her shoulder at the lieutenant serving as boat bay officer.

"Last man, Sir!" she announced. "Everyone's confirmed aboard."

The lieutenant nodded and bent over his com.

"The last evac ship is underway, Sir," Captain Justin Tasco told Admiral Santino. He knew his voice sounded flat and unnatural, yet he couldn't seem to do anything about it. He'd tried to argue with Santino only to be chopped off with a violence as extreme as it was sudden and unexpected. Now he was trapped by his own duty, his own responsibilities, and knowing it was stupid did absolutely nothing to change any of it.

"Good," Santino said, and his broad face smiled fiercely on the small com screen linking Tasco to *Hadrian*'s flag bridge. Then the admiral's smile faded. "You got that bi—" He clamped his jaws and drew a deep breath. "Commander Jaruwalski is off the ship?" he demanded after a moment.

"Yes, Sir," Tasco said woodenly. He'd been Vice Admiral Hennesy's flag captain for two years and worked closely with Jaruwalski all that time, but he was only a captain and Santino was an admiral, and the Articles of War forbade "comments detrimental to the authority of superior officers," so he couldn't tell the fatheaded, pig-ignorant fool what he really thought of him. "Our pinnace put her aboard *Cantrip* eighteen minutes ago."

"Excellent, Justin! In that case, put us on course and let's get underway."

"Aye, aye, Sir," Tasco said flatly, and began giving orders.

Despite his relatively junior rank, Gaines was able to fast-talk his way into the heavy cruiser's CIC on the basis of his status as the senior sensor officer for Seaford Station. *Or at least my* recent *status as SO,* he thought with graveyard humor as the ship's assistant tactical officer nodded him into the compartment and then waved him back out of the way. Gaines found a position against a bulkhead from which he could see the master plot's holo sphere and took a moment to orient himself to the smaller display. Then he stiffened in shock.

"What the—?!" He shook his head and leaned forward, watching in horror as the main body of the system picket began to move at last. Not to escort the ships detailed for evacuation clear of the system, but to advance towards the Peeps!

"What the *hell* do they think they're *doing?*" he muttered.

"They think they're going to 'distract' the enemy," a drained-sounding soprano said from beside him, and he turned his head quickly. The dark-haired, hawk-faced woman wore a skinsuit with commander's insignia and the name JARUWALSKI, ANDREA on its breast, and her eyes were the weariest, most defeated-looking eyes Gaines had ever seen.

"What do you mean, 'distract'?" he asked her, and she turned her head to look at him with a considering air. Then she shrugged.

"Are you familiar with the term 'For the honor of the flag,' Lieutenant?"

"Of course I am," he replied.

"Do you know where it came from?"

"Well, no . . . no, I don't," he admitted.

"Back on Old Earth, one of the old wet navies had a tradition," Jaruwalski said distantly, returning her eyes to the display. "I can't remember which one it was, but it was way back before they even had steam ships. It doesn't matter." She shrugged. "The point is, that when one of their captains found himself up against an enemy he was afraid of engaging or figured he couldn't fight effectively, he'd fire a single broadside—frequently on the disengaged side, so as to avoid pissing the enemy off so badly they shot back—and then haul down his flag as quickly as he could."

"Why?" Gaines asked, fascinated somehow despite the disaster brewing in the display.

"Because hauling down his flag was the same as striking a wedge is today," Jaruwalski said in that same detached voice. "It was a signal of surrender. But by firing a broadside first—'for the honor of the flag'—he covered himself against the charge of cowardice or surrendering without a fight."

"He—? That's the stupidest thing I ever heard of!" Gaines exclaimed.

"Yes, it was," she agreed sadly. "And it hasn't gotten any less stupid today."

"What the devil do they think they're doing?" Citizen Commissioner Randal demanded.

"I'm not certain," Citizen Vice Admiral Shalus replied, her eyes fixed on her plot. Then she looked up with a bone-chilling smile. "But I'm not complaining, either, Citizen Commissioner." She looked at her ops officer. "Time to optimum launch range, Oscar?"

"Seven minutes, Citizen Admiral," Levitt responded instantly.

"Good," Shalus said softly.

"We're in range now, Sir," Captain Tasco told Admiral Santino. "Shall I give the order to fire?"

"Not yet, Justin. Let the range close a little more. We only get one shot here, so let's make it a good one."

"Sir, from their acceleration curve they have to be towing pods of their own," Tasco pointed out.

"I'm aware of that, Captain," Santino said frostily, "and I will pass the word to fire when I am prepared to do so. Is that understood?"

"Aye, aye, Sir," Tasco said bleakly.

"They must think they can hit us with one or two heavy salvos, then pull away with their compensator advantage," Citizen Commander Levitt said quietly, and Shalus nodded.

She could scarcely believe anyone—especially a Manty—could be that stupid even when she saw it happening, yet it was the only explanation for their antics. They'd come to meet her decelerating task force, then executed a turnover of their own. The range was coming down on six and a half million kilometers, and her overtake speed had reduced to only four hundred kilometers per second. She could never overtake them if they chose to go to a maximum safe acceleration, which meant they were deliberately allowing her to edge into range of them.

Are they that *confident of the superiority of their systems?* she wondered. *Nothing in our intelligence briefings indicates that they* ought *to be . . . but, then, we don't know all there is to know about their R&D, now do we? But I simply can't believe they could possibly have a big enough tactical advantage to justify letting us into range! At max, they can't have more than forty-five or fifty pods on tow . . . and* I've *got three hundred and twenty-eight!*

"Dead meat," she heard someone mutter behind her, and nodded.

"Let the range drop a little more," Santino said quietly. "I want the best lock-up fire control can give us. And when we launch, I want all our fire concentrated on their two lead SDs."

"Aye, aye, Sir," Captain Tasco said, and Santino smiled nastily. Even after detaching a full squadron of heavy cruisers for the evacuation, he had fifty-four pods. Adding his ships' internal launchers, he could put almost nine hundred missiles into space, and his lip curled as he contemplated what that would do to ships with Peep missile defense systems.

I'll blow those two fuckers right out of space, he told himself. *And, really, everything else in the system combined is hardly worth two of the wall. Oh, it might be worth something to the* Peeps, *but this junk is hardly worth our time. Everyone will understand that. Nobody'll be able to say I didn't make the bastards pay cash to take over* my *command area, and—*

"Enemy launch!" someone shouted. "Multiple enemy launches! Multi— *My God!*"

"*Launch!*" Citizen Vice Admiral Shalus snapped, and three hundred and twenty-eight missile pods belched fire. The People's Navy's missiles were less individually capable than the RMN's, with slightly shorter range, but to make up for it, each of their pods had sixteen launchers to the Manticorans' ten. Now all of them vomited their birds, and TF 12.1's internal launchers sent another fifteen hundred along with them. All together, over six thousand seven hundred missiles went screaming towards the outnumbered Manticoran task force.

Elvis Santino clung to his command chair arms with white knuckles, his eyes pits of horror as he saw the solid wall of missile icons streaking towards him. It wasn't possible. He knew it wasn't. But it was happening, and he heard orders crackling over the com link to *Hadrian*'s command deck as Captain Tasco fought frantically to save his ship.

Lieutenant Commander Uller, Santino's acting ops officer after Jaruwalski's eviction, barked the command to flush their own pods without Santino's orders, but the Manticoran response seemed feeble in the face of the Peep tsunami, and Santino closed his eyes, as if he could somehow evade his hideous responsibility by shutting the sight away.

ONI had warned him, and so had Jaruwalski, but he hadn't believed it. Oh, he'd heard the reports, nodded at the warnings, but he hadn't *believed*. He'd seen the Manticoran missile storm loosed upon the Peeps, but he had never seen an answering storm front, and somewhere deep down inside him, he'd believed he never would. Now he knew he'd been wrong.

Yet he'd been *almost* right, after all; he would only see it once.

Heinrich Gaines and Andrea Jaruwalski huddled together as if for warmth, their sick eyes locked to the display. *Cantrip* was safely beyond the Peeps' reach, with a velocity advantage which would take her across the hyper limit and to safety long before any Havenite ship could even think about interfering with her. But none of the Peeps were thinking about anything as unimportant as a fleeing heavy cruiser. Their attention was on more important prey, and Gaines groaned as he read the data codes beside the icons.

ONI was wrong, Jaruwalski thought detachedly. *They said the Solly systems had probably improved the Peeps' point defense by fifteen percent; it's got to be closer to twenty. And their penaids must be better than we thought, too. Of course, with that many incoming birds to swamp the systems—*

Her detached thoughts froze as the Peep missiles reached attack range. Santino's desperate point defense had thinned them, but no force as small as his could possibly have killed enough of those missiles to make any difference. Almost four thousand of them survived to attack, and a holocaust of bomb-pumped X-ray lasers ripped and tore at impenetrable impeller bands, all-too-penetrable side walls . . . and the wide open bows and sterns of Santino's wedges.

It was over quickly, she thought numbly. That was the only mercy. One moment, three RMN superdreadnoughts led four battlecruisers and eight heavy cruisers on a firing run; nineteen seconds after the first Peep laser head detonated, there were two damaged heavy cruisers, one crippled hulk of a battlecruiser . . . and nothing else but wreckage and the eye-tearing fury of failing fusion bottles. She heard someone cursing in a harsh, flat monotone—heard the tears and rage and helplessness behind the profanity—but she never looked away from the display as the Peeps' internal launchers dealt with the cripples.

Santino's return fire hadn't been entirely futile, she saw. A single Peep SD blew apart as violently as his own flagship had, and a second reeled out of formation, her wedge down, shedding lifepods and wreckage. But the rest of the Peep armada didn't even hesitate. It just kept driving straight ahead, and she looked away at last as the missile batteries which had massacred men and women she had known and worked with for over two T-years came into range of the orbital facilities. Old-fashioned nuclear warheads bloomed intolerably bright as the enemy fleet methodically blew the abandoned, defenseless installations into half-vaporized wreckage, and Andrea Jaruwalski felt old and beaten and useless as she turned her back upon the hideous plot at last and made her way from *Cantrip*'s CIC.

Chapter Thirty-Three

"Do you *believe* this crap, Maxie?" Scooter Smith demanded in a disgusted mutter. He and PO Maxwell sat in the rear of the briefing room, listening while Lieutenant Gearman explained the day's program to the wing's engineering staff. Commander Stackowitz and Captain Harmon would brief in the squadron and section leaders a bit later, but as always, everyone else's efforts ultimately depended on the engineers. Which meant they had to get the word first, and at the moment, Smith wanted to spit as he glanced at Maxwell.

"What's not to believe?" his hirsute friend replied, using the junior officers and senior noncoms seated between him and the briefing lectern for cover as he scratched his ribs industriously. Then he shrugged. "The brass has decided to screw the *Minnie* over. You gonna try to tell me you've never been part of that procedure before?"

"Is that all you have to say about it?" Smith regarded him with pronounced disfavor, and Maxwell shrugged again.

"Hey, what I say—or you say—don't matter squat, Scooter. What matters is that that asshole Holderman's decided we're gonna blow this exercise. I don't know why he's so hot to make us look bad, but there's damn all you or I can do about it, so how's about you vent with just a little less fervor? Or on someone else, at least."

"You never look outside your toolbox, do you?" Smith snorted.

"Nope," Maxwell agreed, then grinned crookedly. "Course, that *could* be because I've had a little more experience dodging official displeasure than you have, Scooter m'boy."

"Well, that's true enough, anyway!" Smith grunted with a laugh. "You've had more experience at that than just about anyone else in the Service, 'Silver Spanner.'"

"A low blow," Maxwell observed sadly, "but no lower than I'd expect from someone like yourself."

Smith grinned, left more cheerful by the exchange despite his disgust with the briefing. But Maxwell was obviously correct about what was happening here. Rear Admiral Holderman had leaned on the umpires hard, and the result had been an order for the LACs to make their approach on Hancock Base without utilizing their stealth systems at all. They could come in at whatever acceleration they liked, on whatever vector they wished, from a starting point that would be completely their own choice. But they could not take advantage of a single aspect of their powerful EW suites on the approach. Worse, the umpires had decided to reduce their *active* missile defenses' efficiency by forty percent in order to "reflect probable enemy upgrades in scan data enhancement and fire control," which was bullshit if Smith had ever heard it.

But at least they'd get to try it in real space, not the simulators, he reminded himself. If nothing else, that would prevent Holderman and his merry band from fudging the exercise's parameters still further once it was actually underway—and Scooter Smith wouldn't put even that past this bunch. Unlike Maxwell, he had at least a suspicion of what had punched Holderman's buttons, and he wondered what in heaven's name had possessed the Skipper to do something that dumb.

Well, I guess even captains can fuck up, he thought as philosophically as he could, *and at least there won't be all that many "bad guys" looking for us. Aside from the base itself, there's only five SDs and the battlecruisers. That's a lot of sensor ability, but Captain Harmon's a sneaky one. I'll bet she and Commander Stackowitz will figure out a way to get a hell of a lot closer in before detection than old Holderman even dreams is possible!*

"Time to translation?" Citizen Rear Admiral Kellet asked her staff astrogator quietly as she and Citizen Commissioner Ludmilla Penevski stepped onto PNS *Schaumberg*'s flag deck.

"Approximately six hours, forty-three minutes, Citizen Admiral!" Citizen Commander Jackson announced crisply.

"Good." She acknowledged his report with a nod and looked at Penevski. The other woman looked back impassively, then produced a smile.

"Our people seem confident, Citizen Admiral," she remarked quietly as the two of them walked towards the master plot, and Kellet shrugged.

"They should be, Citizen Commissioner. I could wish for a little more tonnage and a few ships of the wall, but I'm confident we can hold our own against any picket we're likely to hit."

"Even if, unlike us, they *do* have superdreadnoughts?" Penevski asked still more quietly, and this time it was Kellet who bared even white teeth in a thin smile. It was hungry, that smile, and most unpleasant despite its whiteness, and her dark eyes gleamed.

"The gap between our onboard systems efficiency and the enemy's has fallen since the war began, Citizen Commissioner," she said. "Oh, they still have an edge, but our best estimate is that our technology transfers have reduced it by at least fifty percent. What's really made them so dangerous to us for the last several years has been the fact that they had missile pods and we didn't. The overwhelming advantage that gave them in the initial missile exchanges would be very difficult to exaggerate. Certainly the sheer volume of a pod salvo was enough to make any real difference between our missile defense capabilities largely irrelevant. But now we have pods of our own, with a sixty percent edge in the number of birds per pod, and that means the playing field just got leveled big time, Ma'am."

"So I understand," Penevski replied. "But there's no point pretending I'm as technically informed as you are, Citizen Admiral. I suppose it's just a little harder for me to accept the projections when I don't fully understand the basis upon which they were made . . . especially when you seem to be saying that we've reached a point at which the relative capability of our defenses does count once more."

"Understandable enough, Ma'am," Kellet said. Penevski had been assigned as her people's commissioner only three months earlier, and they were still learning to know one another. One thing she had already discovered, however, was that Penevski was at least willing to admit when she didn't know something. Jane Kellet was prepared to forgive any superior for a great many other failings when that was true, and she turned to face Penevski squarely.

"In the end, missile engagements come down to numbers, Citizen Commissioner," she said, "because probability theory plays no favorites. Differences in electronics warfare, jammers, and decoys can divert fire from a target, thus reducing the number of birds which become actual threats, but if a missile achieves lock, and if it retains maneuver time on its drive, only active defenses can stop it."

She paused for a moment, and Penevski nodded to show she was following her.

"Any ship, or squadron, or task force has only a finite active antimissile capability," Kellet resumed, "and that capability is defined by the interplay of scanner sensitivity, the sophistication of the defenders' fire control and supporting ECCM, and the effectiveness and numbers of the weapons systems the defender can bring to bear upon incoming fire.

"Since the war began, the Manties have held a considerable advantage in scanners, fire control, and ECCM. Their missiles' onboard seekers and penaids are also better than ours, but that's a separate issue and harder to quantify, anyway. Our countermissiles and laser clusters are roughly comparable to theirs, and it appears that we do a little better job with our main battery energy weapons when we use them in counter-missile mode, as well. But the Manties' electronics superiority, coupled with their previous monopoly on the missile pod, has given them a very substantial edge in missile engagements.

"But now our Solly . . . associates have helped us upgrade our electronics and reduce their superiority in that area from probably a thirty to thirty-five percent or so advantage to no more than fifteen or sixteen percent. Even more importantly, however, we can now swamp *their* fire control with massive salvos, just as they've been doing to us ever since the Battle of Hancock.

"What that means becomes apparent when we look at the probable numbers here. Intelligence estimates that the Manties have a maximum of a heavy battle squadron, with screen, waiting for us—call it twelve SDs, maybe the same number of battlecruisers, and twenty or thirty cruisers and destroyers. Assuming previous engagements are any meterstick, they'll choose a compromise between the maximum numbers of pods they can tow and their acceleration curves. They don't like to reduce their max accel, so their superdreadnoughts will be good for ten to twelve pods each, but their battlecruisers will probably have a maximum of four on tow, with perhaps two more for each heavy cruiser. Taking the worst case estimate, then, they'll have a hundred forty-four behind the SDs, forty-eight behind the battlecruisers, and call it thirty-two behind heavy cruisers.

"That gives them two hundred twenty-four pods, with a total missile load of about twenty-two hundred. *We* on the other hand, have a lot more tractor capability than they do, and the new *Mars*-class heavy cruisers have more brute impeller strength than their compensators can handle anyway."

She chose not to complicate her little lecture by explaining that that was because the People's Navy had hoped that either they would have captured intact samples of the Manties' new inertial compensator technology or that their Solarian suppliers would have figured out how they worked by now. Neither had happened, which left the *Mars*-class ships ridiculously overpowered. But that had its good points, as well. For one thing, they could lose quite a few beta nodes before their maximum attainable acceleration dropped. For another, they could tow twice as many pods as a Manty *Star Knight* could for the same acceleration loss. And as far as the People's Navy knew, the Manties didn't yet have a clue that that was the case. Of course, if they'd had the compensator efficiency the Manties had, they could have towed *three* times as many pods, but who knew? The Republic might yet manage to acquire that efficiency somehow, and then . . .

"What all that means, Ma'am," she went on, shaking off the reflexive thoughts, "is that we'll be going in with twelve pods behind each battleship and six behind each heavy cruiser. It'll reduce our max acceleration substantially—by about twenty percent for the cruisers—but it will give us four hundred fifty-six pods and well over *seven* thousand missiles in our opening salvo. Which," she smiled again, with that same pearlescent ferocity, "is the reason I'm so looking forward to the *Second* Battle of Hancock."

◈ ◈ ◈

"Coming up on translation in forty-five minutes, Citizen Admiral." The tone in which Citizen Commander Lowe made the announcement carried that unmistakable edge of professional calm—the sort pilots or surgeons always seemed to drop into when things threatened to fall into the crapper. Lester Tourville recognized it, but the rules of the game required him to pretend he hadn't, and so he simply nodded.

"Thank you, Karen," he replied with a sort of absent-minded courtesy . . . which sounded much more absent than he felt. To be sure, his attention was distracted by his plot and the serried icons of Task Force 12.2, but under the surface his thoughts tried to whiplash out in all directions. He was glad Lowe could sound so composed and collected, yet a part of him fretted that her apparent composure might mask some error in her calculations until it was too late. And the fact that his was by far the smallest of Twelfth Fleet's four task forces—in tonnage terms, at least; he had five more ships than Jane Kellet's TF 12.3, but she had nine more battleships than he did—and also had the farthest to go to launch its initial attack wasn't calculated to make him feel any calmer. Despite his earlier conversation with Everard Honeker, he couldn't help feeling more than a little nervous at the thought of hitting the home system of an important Manty ally when he was this far from Republican-held territory, and—

Stop it, Lester, a corner of his mind scolded while his eyes and the rest of his brain sorted out the icons and checked vector notations. *So they're going to have at least some sort of picket there to support the Zanzibarans. They still aren't going to have the least idea you're coming, and if they turn out to have ships of the wall on station, you've sure as hell got the acceleration to pull away from them!*

"Are the pods ready, Shannon?" he asked without looking up from the plot.

"Yes, Citizen Admiral," Citizen Commander Foraker replied in the carefully correct voice she had acquired since the Battle of Adler. Tourville regretted the wariness in it, but she'd been her old self—sort of—when it came to planning the actual attack, and whatever was going on in her head hadn't affected her flair for sneaky tactics. Or her willingness to make the case for her chosen approach with the sort of blunt succinctness which left no room for misunderstanding . . . although it sometimes left those who argued with her feeling as if they'd been run down by an out-of-control ground car.

For one thing, she'd argued for a high-speed run-in from the very start, despite some other officers' fear that such an approach could leave them with a dangerously high velocity if there were, in fact, Manty ships of the wall in-system. Their concern had been that a high initial velocity would leave them with too much momentum to kill quickly if an evasive vector change were required, but

Foraker had shown even less patience than usual with that argument. Even if there were ships of the wall present, she'd pointed out arctically, they would still have to generate an intercept vector, and the less time TF 12.2 took reaching its objective, the less time the Manties would have in which to intercept. In fact, the only way they could guarantee to intercept an attack on the planet Zanzibar would be for them to be in orbit around it and stay there . . . in which case, TF 12.2 should see them long before they entered engagement range and would have a much higher base velocity from which to evade the defenders and go after its secondary objective: the system's asteroid extraction industry. Besides, a higher approach velocity would not only face the Manties with more difficult interception acceleration curves but force them to commit sooner and at higher power settings, which would degrade the efficiency of their stealth systems and make them far easier to detect early enough for it to do some good.

In keeping with that recommendation, she'd also argued that the retention of their own ships' full acceleration capability was more important than putting the maximum possible number of pods in space. That liveliness in maneuver, after all, was the one advantage battleships held over ships of the wall, and she refused to throw it away. So rather than tow the pods astern, she'd suggested, they should take a page from the Manties' book in the Fourth Battle of Yeltsin and tractor the pods inside the wedges of their battleships, where they would have no effect on their acceleration curves. Their battlecruisers could tractor only two pods inside their wedges, and the heavy cruisers and destroyers lacked the tractors and wedge depth to tractor any inside at all, but that was fine with her.

Some of the squadron ops officers had hit the deckhead at the very suggestion, but she had simply waited them out with a cold, almost mechanical patience. And when the hubbub had settled, she'd pointed out that battleships had been designed as general purpose workhorses, which meant, among other things, that they had more tractors on a ton-for-ton basis than any other ship type in the Republican order of battle. Each of them could tractor eleven pods—more than most superdreadnoughts, actually—tight in against their hulls. That meant that when they actually deployed them, they could still put over forty-two hundred missiles into space at once, with another three hundred eighty from the battlecruisers. In the meantime, their entire task force's ability to maneuver at full acceleration would not only make them fleeter of foot but might actually convince the defenders that they hadn't brought along *any* pods until it was too late.

Most of the doubters had acquired suddenly thoughtful expressions at that, and those who hadn't had shut their mouths anyway when Tourville glared at them. This was the command team which had produced the Battle of Adler, after all. And even if it hadn't been,

Lester Tourville was a citizen vice admiral who clearly enjoyed the full-bodied support of his people's commissioner.

Now Tourville grinned crookedly at the memory. Perhaps there were some advantages to promotion after all, he mused. But then his thoughts slipped back to the little matter of astrogation, and he leaned back in his chair with a quiet sigh which he hoped concealed the tension coiling tighter in his midsection from any of his juniors.

Karen Lowe was an excellent astrogator, but a hyper voyage this long provided a great deal of scope for minor astrogation errors to produce major results. Overshooting their intended n-space translation point wouldn't be all that terrible . . . unless, of course, they overshot it *too* badly. A ship which attempted to translate out of hyper inside a star's hyper limit couldn't. As long as it made the attempt within the outer twenty percent of the hyper limit, all that happened was that it couldn't get into n-space. If it made the attempt any further in than that, however, Bad Things happened. Someone had once described the result as using a pulse cannon to fire soft-boiled eggs at a stone wall to see if they would bounce. Lester Tourville rather doubted they would, and even if he was wrong, it was a proposition he had no desire at all to test firsthand.

And that was what made the nervous serpent shift and slither in his belly as the digital display counted down towards the translation, because after a voyage of over a light-century and a half, it would take an error of only one five-millionth of a percent to give them all an egg's-eye view of that stone wall. He trusted Citizen Commander Lowe implicitly . . . but he couldn't quite shut his mind off when it yammered about teeny-tiny errors and misplaced decimal points.

And, he thought dryly, *your having supported Shannon's insistence on coming in fast and hot won't make things any easier for Karen, now will it?*

It wouldn't, and he knew it. But he wasn't about to change his mind, either, because his tac witch was right. His task force was in the lowest alpha band, traveling at .6 *c* and headed for a crash translation. He knew what most of his crews were going to have to say about that, but they should have plenty of time to stop throwing up before the Manties could come into range. And by hitting the wall at roughly a hundred and eighty thousand kilometers per second, he would carry an n-space velocity of a bit more than fourteen thousand KPS across it with him.

The system's G4 primary had a hyper limit of just over twenty light-minutes, the planet Zanzibar orbited it at nine light-minutes, and their course had been chosen to drop them into n-space at the limit's closest approach to the planet. All of which meant that if Lowe hit her translation point exactly right, they should drop into n-space almost exactly eleven and a half light-minutes from their target. And with an initial velocity of 14,390 KPS and a maximum fleet acceleration of 450 gravities, they could reach Zanzibar's orbit in one hundred and sixteen minutes. They'd be moving at over forty-five thousand KPS when they crossed it, and decelerating and coming back to tidy up would be a time-consuming pain, but the advantages of a high-speed pass more than compensated. Even if the Manties and Zanzibarans were there in sufficient strength to stand and fight, his velocity would be such as to make their engagement window very brief. And whatever happened, his units would pass close enough to the planet to take out its orbital installations with missiles without hitting too many neutral merchantmen . . . or the planet itself.

He damned well hoped so, anyway. If he launched missiles that went wild and hit the surface of an inhabited planet in the middle of a civilian population somewhere, even by accident—

He shuddered. He would never forgive himself if he let something like that happen. But more important than any personal guilt he might feel, however traumatic, violation of the Eridani Edict's ban on indiscriminate planetary bombardment was the one thing *guaranteed* to bring the Solarian League Navy down on any star nation like a hammer. There wouldn't be any internal Solarian debate, no arguments or resolutions or declarations, for none would be needed. Enforcement of the Eridani Edict had been part of the League's fundamental law for five hundred and three years, and the League Navy's standing orders were clear: any government or star nation or rogue mercenary outfit which indiscriminately bombarded an inhabited planet or directed a bombardment of any sort against a planetary population which had not first been summoned to surrender would be destroyed.

It was probably the closest the Sollies would ever come to a clear-cut foreign policy decision, at least in his lifetime, Tourville reflected. But it was one they came by naturally . . . and one they had implemented five times since 1410 P.D.

The first two centuries after the Warshawski sail had rendered interstellar warfare practical had seen more than their share of atrocities, including ruthless attacks on defenseless planetary populations. It had been bad enough then; with the weapons available now, it would be far worse. A single superdreadnought—for that matter, even a single battlecruiser—could exterminate every city, town, and village on any planet once the target's defenses had been suppressed. These days, they could do it with kinetic missile strikes, duplicating on a far grander scale the so-called "Heinlein Maneuver" Old Earth's rebellious colonists had employed in the Lunar Revolt of 39 A.D. The Lunar rebels had settled for dropping cargo shuttles loaded with rock into Old Earth's gravity well; a missile capable of eighty or ninety thousand gravities of acceleration was incomparably more effective than such crude, improvised weapons. And a kinetic strike would do minimal damage to the rest of a planet and leave it suitably empty for the attacker's own colonists.

Except that the Solarian League, having experienced the bitter horrors of trying to clean up after such an atrocity on one of its member worlds, had not only unilaterally issued the Eridani Edict but incorporated it as Amendment Ninety-Seven of the League Constitution. Seven billion human beings had died in the Epsilon Eridani Massacre. The Solarians had not forgotten them, even today, and no one who was still in shouting distance of sanity wanted to remind them once again and bring the League Navy down on his head by violating the edict.

He pushed the thought to the back of his brain with an impatient flick of a mental hand. The Eridani Edict had no bearing on today's mission, and it was time he stopped fretting about the Sollies and started concentrating on the Manties.

"Well, you *said* you wanted to push him into cooking the exercise," Jackie Harmon observed to Alice Truman as the two captains rode the lift down to Harmon's wing briefing room.

"I did," Truman agreed calmly. "On the other hand, I'm a little disappointed in him if this is the best he can do."

"'Best he can do'?" Harmon echoed. The COLAC shook her head. "Let's see, he's increased our vulnerability to detection by about eighty-five percent, reduced our EW's ability to confuse his fire control by the same amount, *and* reduced the effectiveness of our active defenses by forty percent. Just what exactly did you expect him to do for an encore?"

"Oh, I admit it should do the job," Truman agreed with a chuckle. "He's going to wax most of our wing, though your people are enough better than he's willing to admit that I think he's still going to get hurt a lot worse than he expects. But it's a purely brute force approach . . . and one he's going to find extremely hard to justify when Admiral Adcock and Admiral Caparelli start asking pointed questions."

The lift came to a stop and the doors slid open, and she went on speaking—in a lowered voice—as she and Harmon stepped out into the passage.

"Reducing your EW is the most arbitrary change he could possibly have made—and it's also one which is totally unjustifiable on the basis of ONI's estimates of Peep capabilities, present or near-term future. He's being so ham-handed I almost feel guilty . . . as if I've just pushed a baby chick into a pond full of Sphinx near-pike."

"Oh?" Harmon cocked her head to regard *Minotaur*'s captain sidelong, and her smile was wry. "Well, just at the moment, *I* feel more like the chick, knowing what's coming. So I hope you'll excuse me if I don't feel a great deal of sympathy for the good admiral?"

"I suppose I'll have to," Truman agreed with a theatrical sigh as they reached the briefing room hatch and it opened before them.

"Attention on deck!" Commander McGyver barked as the two

captains appeared. He and Barbara Stackowitz had been conducting the preliminary brief, and Harmon smiled again, more wryly even than before, as she sensed her officers' reaction to what they had already heard.

"At ease," Truman told them, and they settled back in their chairs, regarding their superiors warily. Truman took her own seat without another word—she was still the senior officer present, but this was Harmon's domain—and the COLAC folded her arms as she faced her people.

"All right," she said, "the XO and Commander Stackowitz have already given you the bad news. Yes, we're going in with our electronics artificially degraded, and, yes, we're going to get our butts kicked. But along the way, we're going to do a little—"

A sharp, shrill sound interrupted her, and she turned her head quickly. Stackowitz was already reaching for the acceptance key, and she cut the priority com signal off with a sort of dying *wheep!* The screen lit, and the commander's eyebrows arched in surprise as she recognized *Minotaur*'s executive officer on the display.

"Briefing Four," she told him. "Commander Stackowitz. How can I help you, Sir?"

"I need the Captain, Commander," Commander Haughton replied crisply, and his Gryphon accent was much more pronounced than usual. Truman frowned as she heard it, then crossed to stand beside Stackowitz' chair and lean into the com pickup's field.

"Yes, John? What is it?"

"Captain, we need you on the bridge," Haughton told her flatly. "The FTL net's just reported a bogey, Ma'am—a *big* bogey, that hasn't pulsed us an arrival notification—and it's headed straight in system at ten thousand KPS, accelerating at four-point-zero KPS squared." He paused and cleared his throat. "I don't know who they are, Ma'am, but they sure aren't ours."

Chapter Thirty-Four

"Captain is on the br—" the quartermaster began, but Alice Truman's curt wave cut him off as she stormed out of the lift onto HMS *Minotaur*'s command deck.

"Talk to me, Tactical!" she snapped, continuing in a straight line for her command chair.

"They came out of hyper five minutes ago, Ma'am," Commander Jessup replied quickly. "They made translation just above the ecliptic and just outside the hyper limit and headed straight in. Present range to the primary is six-five-six-point-six light-seconds. Bearing from Hancock Base is zero-zero-three zero-niner-two relative, range to orbit shell intercept three-five-one-point-eight-five light-seconds, closing at one-one-two-zero-one KPS and accelerating at four-point-zero KPS squared."

"Um." Truman had continued across the deck as Jessup spoke. Now she threw herself into the command chair McGyver had vacated at her approach. Her eyes darted down to the plot, and she frowned at the vector projections. Then she punched for a readout on the probable enemy types, and her frown deepened.

Thirty-plus battleships, ten or twelve heavy cruisers, and a half-dozen destroyers, she thought, fingers drumming nervously on the arm of her command chair. Individually, nothing in that force could stand up to Rear Admiral Truitt's superdreadnoughts; collectively, they could demolish everything Truitt had in twenty minutes of close action. They'd get hurt in the process, but they could do it. And their low acceleration made her wonder if they'd need even twenty minutes . . . or get hurt all that badly. They had to be towing heavy loads of pods to account for that acceleration, and Adler had proved Peep missile pods were not to be taken lightly. Which meant Hancock was going to fall, and that was more than just a disaster because there wasn't enough shipping with enough life support in the entire system to take off the personnel assigned to the steadily expanding fleet base. And—

Her fingers stopped drumming suddenly, and her eyes narrowed as a thought struck her. It was preposterous, of course. Or was it? She turned it over in her mind, examining it from all angles with feverish haste while the Peeps' vector built steadily towards Hancock Base. Could it really be—?

She began punching rapid-fire numbers into her plot.

"Could they have seen *Minnie* yet?" she demanded of the tac officer, using the nickname she'd done her level best to stamp out in her distraction.

"No way, Ma'am," Jessup replied confidently, and she nodded at the confirmation. Not that she'd expected anything else. *Minotaur* had been running silent under stealth for the point from which she and Harmon had decided to launch their "attack" on Hancock Base's defenders—which wasn't all that far, on the scale of deep space, from where the Peeps had actually appeared—and anything that could hide from the Hancock sensor net wouldn't be picked up by Peep sensors even if the damned Sollies had doubled their efficiency. And that meant . . .

She stopped, looking at the results on her plot, and swore silently. She couldn't quite pull off what she'd hoped for, but the fallback looked good.

"Check me on this, Alf," she said, turning to face the tactical section. "I make it that they're on course for a speed-zero/range-zero intercept with the orbit base. Do you concur?"

"Yes, Ma'am," Jessup replied. "Assuming accelerations remain constant at four KPS squared, they'll hit turnover in approximately forty-five minutes at just under six-zero-point-six million klicks from the base. Time to zero/zero intercept from now is one-three-six-point-seven-niner minutes."

Truman nodded again as he confirmed her figures. Of course, if the Peeps decided to, they could simply maintain a constant acceleration, in which case they would cross the base's orbital shell in only eighty-three minutes. They'd be well "ahead" of the base at the time if they stuck with their current heading, but they'd have plenty of time to adjust their course for a missile pass.

But whichever option they pursued, they would certainly remain on their current heading at their current acceleration at least to the turnover for the zero/zero approach, and that gave her forty-five minutes with which to work. She turned to look down at her plot again, then looked at her helmsman.

"Bring us to zero-one-zero zero-seven-eight at three-zero-zero gravities," she said.

"Aye, aye, Ma'am. Zero-one-zero zero-seven-eight at three hundred gravities," the helmsman replied, and Truman punched a com stud.

"LAC Control, COLAC speaking," Harmon's voice responded instantly.

"We're going to get a live-fire test of your birds after all, Jackie," Truman said with a tight smile. "Are they prepping?"

"Yes, Ma'am! We're loading the mags with war shots now. We'll be ready to launch in four minutes."

"Um." Truman punched a fresh set of assumptions into her plot and scowled. It would stretch the range envelope still further and require a higher acceleration from the LACs than she really liked, EW or no EW, but it would be possible. Probably.

"All right," she said. "Here's what we're going to do. . . ."

"Here come the Manties, Citizen Admiral," Citizen Commander Morris called out, and Jane Kellet looked up quickly. She'd known the defenders would have the precious advantage of near real-time data on her command thanks to their FTL sensor net, but her own gravitics were quite capable of picking up impeller signatures at this range. Now she saw them on her plot, coming at her, and her eyebrows rose at the data codes beside their icons.

"Are you certain about those class IDs, Olivia?" she asked her tac officer.

"CIC's confidence is high, Citizen Admiral," Citizen Commander Morris replied. "We see no evidence that they're trying to spoof us, nor are they running under stealth. Of course, with that much power to their wedges, even Manty stealth systems would be pushed to the max. Our best count makes it five superdreadnoughts and eleven battlecruisers with eight light cruisers or destroyers screening them."

"And they're accelerating at four hundred and thirty-five gravities?"

"Aye, Ma'am. CIC makes it . . . four-point-two-six KPS squared. That's why their signatures are so clear."

"I see." Kellet leaned back in her command chair, stroking her chin, and Citizen Commissioner Penevski looked a question at her.

"I'm a bit surprised by their tactics, Citizen Commissioner," Kellet admitted. "Given their acceleration, they must have cut their pod strength to the bone. Everything they've got has to be inside their wedges, and that means we can't be looking at more than a hundred pods or so."

"Why would they do that?" Penevski asked.

"That's what I don't quite understand," Kellet said. "Unless . . ." She tapped some numbers into her plot and frowned at the vectors the display obediently generated. "Well, I suppose that could be it," she said finally.

"What could?" Pevenski's tone was that of a woman who was reining in her own frustration to be polite . . . and wanted the Citizen Rear Admiral to know it. Kellet's mouth quirked wryly at the thought, and she looked up at the people's commissioner.

"Their current course and acceleration will intercept our projected vector well before the point at which we'd make turnover for a zero-speed intercept of their base," she said. "They probably figure we have to maintain our profile that far whatever we intend to do—and they're right," she admitted. "I suppose what they could be hoping to do is to blow past us with the maximum velocity differential they can generate and rake hell out of us in a passing engagement, but I wouldn't have thought they'd try something like that."

"Why not?"

"Because it buys them the worst of all worlds, Ma'am. Their current acceleration indicates that they're light on pods, so they've sacrificed a lot of firepower to achieve it. At the same time, *our* accel curve almost has to have told them we're coming in heavy with pods—on the battleships, at least; they probably figure the heavy cruisers are light, since they can't know how much reserve impeller strength the *Mars*-class has. Our closing speeds won't really matter very much to the kind of missile exchange they're inviting, and we'll hurt them badly at the very least. And after we do, they'll be behind us, headed out-system and unable to kill enough velocity to stay with us while we go sailing merrily inward and blow their fleet base to dust."

"Could they be intending to reverse acceleration before we actually intercept them?" Penevski asked.

"Certainly they could, and it's what I would have expected them to do, assuming they intended to fight us at all," Kellet agreed. "But in their place, I'd want to do that at some point after we've made turnover . . . especially since that would've let them pull a lower acceleration. Which, in turn, would have meant they could have brought along a maximum pod load—and used their EW to hide their signatures longer to keep us guessing—instead of stripping down and coming in wide open this way."

"Could it be that they just want to engage as far from their base as possible?" Penevski wondered.

"It could," Kellet conceded, "but, again, I can't see a reason they should. Their accel will let them come further out to meet us and match vectors sooner—and further from their base—than they could have otherwise if that's what they want to do, Ma'am. What it *won't* do, however, is give them any particular advantage. Even with maximum pod loads, they'd have been able to match vectors far beyond our missile range of the base. Meeting us further out of range of it doesn't offer any advantage commensurate with the sacrifice in firepower they've accepted."

"Maybe surprise just panicked them into making a mistake, then," Penevski suggested.

"I suppose it's possible. . . ."

"What do you make of it, Ira?" Citizen Captain Hall asked calmly.

"Beats me, Citizen Captain," Citizen Commander Hamer replied from her com screen. The XO was in Auxiliary Control, as far away from the bridge as he could get, ready to take over in the event that something unfortunate happened to *Schaumberg*'s command deck, but he had the same displays Hall did, and his expression was puzzled on the small com screen.

"Do you have any suggestions, Oliver?" the Citizen Captain asked next, glancing at her tactical officer, and Citizen Commander Diamato shrugged to indicate his matching bafflement.

As promised, Citizen Captain Hall and Citizen Commander Hamer had kept Diamato thoroughly busy with tactical problems in his putatively free time. Along the way, he had come to admire both of them—and especially the citizen captain—intensely. He still had some qualms about their possible political opinions, but they made a brilliant command team. And in another five or six years, Diamato calculated, he might be as good a tactician as the Citizen Captain, assuming she and Hamer kept hammering away at him hard enough. For the moment, however, he was devoutly grateful he was only third in *Schaumberg*'s chain of command, for working so closely with Hall had shown him the weak spots in his own experience. He'd come up too quickly, been driven up the rank ladder too rapidly, to acquire the sort of foundation he truly needed, and he was grateful to the Citizen Captain for showing him that.

"I think someone over there's screwed up, Ma'am," he said, and felt his face stiffen, his eyes darting towards Citizen Commissioner Addison as he realized how he'd addressed her. Addison gave him a dagger-sharp glance, but then the Citizen Commissioner looked away without saying anything, and Diamato sighed in relief.

"You may be right," Citizen Captain Hall said, her voice as calm as if she hadn't heard anything at all out of the ordinary. "But while I have no objection at all to seeing the Manties screw up—and God knows Adler proved they can screw up just as badly as anyone else—I don't think I'm quite ready to leap to any conclusions here. Stay on your sensors, Oliver. I've got a feeling something nasty is headed our way. We just haven't seen it yet."

"So far, so good," Alice Truman murmured to herself. *Minotaur* had swept in from the side, angling to cross the Peeps' course well behind them. Her EW was the best in the RMN, which (presumably) meant the best in space, at least for the moment, and she was using it for all she was worth. Not that the Peeps would worry too much if they did see her. She would cross directly astern of them in a little over twelve minutes, but she would also be something like eight million kilometers from them, well beyond effective missile range, especially for missiles trying to overtake them from astern.

Of course, there were a few other things the Peeps didn't know about. Like the ninety-six LACs which had launched from the big carrier over half an hour ago and darted away on a radically divergent course. Their impellers were far more powerful than any previous

LAC's, but they were still much weaker than any conventional warship's. Coupled with their EW, that let them move at almost five hundred gravities and remain undetected at a range as low as thirty light-seconds. They could probably get even closer than that under ideal circumstances—like against Peep-quality sensors manned by people who had no idea they existed. Their acceleration rates were rather lower than that by now, however, for this was no time to take unnecessary chances, and they were slicing in toward the Peeps on a sharply converging angle. In fact, they ought to be cutting their acceleration back to zero any moment now.

"Any sign they've spotted us?" Captain Harmon asked quietly.

"Negative, Skipper," Ensign Thomas, Gold One's tactical officer said. "They're sticking with their original flight profile. They'll cross our course starboard to port at a range of two-eight-four thousand klicks in—" he tapped on his key pad "—nine minutes. The angle won't be all that good, but our closing velocity at course intersection will be right on two hundred KPS."

"And their decoys and jammers are still down?"

"That's affirmative," Thomas replied. Then he grinned tautly. "Makes sense, doesn't it, Skipper? They've still got their share of maintenance problems, and they probably don't want to put any more time on their decoys' clocks than they have to. But we're well inside our own missile envelope, so the fact that they figure they don't have to bring their systems up yet has to indicate they don't have a clue we're here."

"Good." Harmon glanced across at her engineer. Lieutenant Gearman sat at his console, hands resting lightly on its edge. He looked almost calm, but a trickle of sweat down his right temple gave lie to that impression. "I'll want full power on the wedge and the forward sidewall the instant I give the word, Mike," she reminded him.

"Aye, Skipper. You'll get it."

"Good," she repeated, then glanced further aft to the second engineer's station and directed a ferocious mock glower at the hairy-armed first-class petty officer who manned it. "And as for *you*, PO," she said tartly, "I don't want any dropped spanners on *my* bridge!"

"No, Ma'am," PO Maxwell replied quickly, and rolled his eyes at his own console. He'd always suspected his nickname had made it to the officers' ears, but this was the first time the Skipper had ever used it. He had absolutely no doubt who'd passed her the word, and he resolved to do something to thank PO Smith properly for seeing to that little detail when he got back to the ship. Something humorous, he thought, with boiling oil or molten lead. . . .

"I'm picking up something a little odd, Citizen Cap—" Diamato began, then interrupted himself. "Unknown ship astern of us!" he announced sharply. "She's running under stealth, Citizen Captain!"

"What is she?" Citizen Captain Hall's deliberate tone was pitched to remind him to calm himself, and he drew a deep breath.

"I can't say for certain, Citizen Captain," he told her in a more nearly normal voice. "She's extremely hard to hold even now. I don't think we've encountered ECM this good before. She's about to cross our course about eight million klicks back, but it looks like she's altering heading to follow us in. CIC's calling her a dreadnought, but that's tentative."

"And she's all alone back there?" Hall's eyebrows rose in surprise, and Diamato nodded.

"She's all we see, Citizen Captain."

"Well, she's too far back to engage us even if she wasn't alone," the Citizen Exec murmured from the com screen. Hall had it in split-screen mode, with Hamer on the left side and Citizen Rear Admiral Kellet on the right.

"I agree with Citizen Commander Hamer," Kellet said now, "but what the hell is she doing swanning around all by herself? Why not shape a course to join the rest of them ahead of us? If her ECM's this good, she should have been able to do that."

"Unless she's coming in from the outer system," Hall pointed out, and tugged at the lobe of one ear, frowning down at her own plot. She didn't like the timing on this. The Manties coming out from the base had reversed course after all. At the moment, they were six-point-eight million kilometers directly ahead of TF 12.3, allowing the Republican ships to overtake them at a little over ninety-four hundred kilometers per second. That would let her into extreme missile range of them in another twelve minutes, and now this. . . .

"They're up to something, Citizen Admiral," she said softly, but try though she might, she couldn't figure out what that something was. Yet that was hardly her fault, for Manticoran security had held. No one in the People's Navy had yet heard even a whisper about the *Shrike*-class or HMS *Minotaur* and their capabilities.

"Agreed," Kellet said flatly, and looked over her shoulder. "Pass the word to finish prepping the decoys, Olivia," she ordered. "I want them ready to go on-line in five minutes."

"Aye, Ma'am. Shall I initiate jamming?" Citizen Commander Morris asked.

"Not yet," Kellet said after a moment's thought. "They haven't begun jamming yet, either—or deployed their own decoys, for that matter. Given the difference in the number of birds we've each got, I don't want to push them into starting to screw with our tracking capability any sooner than necessary."

"Understood, Citizen Admiral," Morris said.

"And in the meantime, Citizen Captain," Kellet went on, glancing back at Hall, "I think I want to have a little talk with Citizen Rear

Admiral Porter." The two women didn't—quite—grimace at one another. That would have been prejudicial to good discipline, after all, for Porter *was* Kellet's official second-in-command . . . even if he did need an instruction manual to pour piss out of a boot.

"If you'll excuse me?" Kellet said. Hall nodded, and TF 12.3's CO looked at her com officer. "Get me Citizen Rear Admiral Porter."

"By God, it's going to work!" Alice Truman whispered to herself. She hadn't really believed it would when she'd thought it up, but it had seemed the only possibility worth trying, and so she'd done it. And to her astonishment, Rear Admiral Truitt had accepted her recommendation. He must have, although he hadn't commed her to say so, for his ships were doing precisely what she'd suggested.

Passing that suggestion had worried her. Not the mechanics of the transmission; *Minotaur* had been within less than two light-seconds of one of the FTL com platforms, easily close enough to hit it with a whisker laser and let it transmit her message in-system. Nor had she worried about the Peeps detecting the grav-pulse message and realizing someone was behind them. By now they had to be able to recognize such transmissions—any decent gravitic sensor could detect them; the trick was learning how to *generate* them . . . or read them—but the entire FTL scanner net had been yammering away with enough data transmissions to hide a broadcast of the annual Address from the Throne in the background chatter.

No, what had worried her had been that she'd had to commit her ship and Jackie Harmon's LACs to her plan immediately if they were to get into position. And that meant that if Truitt had rejected her suggestion, the LACs could have found themselves pitted against the Peeps all alone. But that wasn't going to happen, and she smiled evilly as she watched the time display tick downward.

"Got 'em, Skipper!" Ensign Thomas announced.

"Well enough to guarantee lock-on?" Harmon asked sharply.

"I'll have to go active to guarantee that, Ma'am," Thomas said a little less exuberantly, and Harmon grunted. Her LACs were almost at their prebriefed attack points, coasting in ballistically with their wedges up but at minimum power. The range was a little under a light-second, and grasers were light-speed weapons. If everything worked perfectly, the Peeps would have no more than two seconds—certainly no more than four—to realize what was coming.

"All right," she said. "Stand by for energy weapons and missiles. Mike, I want the bow sidewall first, then full power to the rest of the wedge. Bring the wall up the instant Tommy gets his missiles away."

"Understood, Skipper," Gearman replied tautly.

A light began to blink on Citizen Commander Diamato's panel, and he frowned. He punched a query into the board, and his frown deepened as CIC responded.

"We're picking up something to port, Citizen Captain," he said.

"Something?" Citizen Captain Hall spun her command chair to face him. "What sort of 'something'?"

"I don't really know, Citizen Captain," he admitted. "It's too weak to be a ship's impeller signature or an incoming missile, and we're picking up at least a dozen point sources . . . unless it's some sort of scatter?" He frowned, then shook his head. "No, Ma'am," he said, this time using the old style address without even thinking about it. "It's definitely separate sources; I'm confident of that. But there's nothing like it in our sensor or threat files."

"Could it be some sort of drone?" Hall asked intently.

"That's what CIC thinks, Ma'am," Diamato said. "But I don't think so. It doesn't . . . *feel* right, somehow. And faint as it is, it's too strong for a stealthed Manty recon drone."

"Bring the jammers and decoys up *now!*" Hall snapped, and Diamato's thumb jabbed at the button.

"What the—?" Citizen Captain Hector Griswold, CO of PNS *Citizen Admiral Tascosa*, frowned as *Tascosa*'s sister ship *Schaumberg* suddenly brought her defensive electronic systems fully on-line. He looked at the readouts for a second or two, then switched his eyes to his com officer.

"Anything from the Flag?" he asked.

"No, Citizen Captain," the com officer replied, and he turned towards Tactical.

"Why did the flagship bring her EW on-line?" he demanded.

"I don't know, Citizen Captain," the tac officer replied.

"Damn!" Ensign Thomas swore as a single Peep battleship suddenly lit off every defensive electronics system she had. Those systems remained considerably inferior to the Manticoran equivalents, but they were an awful lot better than they'd been eighteen or twenty T-months earlier, and he swore again as the single ship vanished into a ball of electronic fuzz which made it impossible to see anything as small as a train of towed missile pods.

He started to report it, but Jacquelyn Harmon had already seen it.

"Engage now!" she barked.

"She did *what?*" Citizen Rear Admiral Kellet looked up from the com screen and blinked at Citizen Lieutenant Commander Morris.

"She brought up our EW without orders, Citizen Admiral," Morris repeated, and Kellet frowned.

"Excuse me, Ron," she said to Citizen Admiral Porter and reached for the interrupt switch. But the display blanked, banishing Porter's image before she could hit the button, and then it lit once more and Citizen Captain Hall's face looked out of it.

"Froggie, just what the h—" Kellet began.

"Ma'am, CIC has just—" Hall said simultaneously, but a third voice cut them both off before she could explain.

"We're being hit with lidar!" Olivia Morris shouted. "Multiple emitters—very close, Citizen Admiral!"

"Locked up!" Thomas snapped as the ranging and targeting pulses from his lidar came back to *Harpy*. "Firing—*now!*"

Ninety-six LACs fired ninety-six grasers within the space of barely two seconds. Their angle of closure was too broad for them to get shots up the open after aspects of the Peep ships' impeller wedges, but they weren't shooting at ships. They were firing at *missile pods*, and they killed ninety-three of them in the first salvo.

The pods were utterly defenseless, following docilely along behind their mother ships, and grasers which could blast through a ship of the wall's armor ripped them to splinters with dreadful ease. When a weapons-grade energy beam hit a target, it didn't melt that target. The energy transfer was too enormous, too sudden. Natural alloy or synthetics, ceramics or human flesh, it vaporized explosively, literally blowing itself apart with fearsome force, and some of the first salvo's targets' sister pods succumbed to proximity damage as fragments blasted into them like old-fashioned prespace armor-piercing shot.

But the LACs weren't counting on that sort of fortuitous kills. Their fire control lashed the other pods viciously, despite the fact that the laser emissions were giving the Peeps' targeting beacons of their own, and a second fusillade of grasers ripped out even as the *Shrikes*' missiles tubes went to maximum rate fire.

"*What's out there?*" Jane Kellet demanded harshly. She felt the edge of panic trying to ooze into her own voice and throttled it savagely before anyone else heard it.

"I don't know, Citizen Admiral!" Morris replied, fingers flying over her console as she, CIC, and Oliver Diamato all tried to make sense of the preposterous readings. "There are—"

"LACs!" another voice came over the circuit, and Kellet's eyes snapped back to her com as a sidebar identified the speaker as Citizen Commander Diamato.

"Explain!" she snapped.

"It has to be LACs, Citizen Admiral," Diamato said urgently. "It'd take a dozen Manty battlecruisers to produce that much graser fire, but not even Manties could get something that big this close. And if they were battlecruisers, they'd be firing lasers, as well. And all the point sources, it—"

"Missiles incoming!" CIC reported.

✧ ✧ ✧

Alice Truman watched the Peeps' jammers and decoys coming frantically on-line and bared her teeth at her plot. *Minotaur* was too far away to pick up any sort of accurate read on the Peeps' missile pods, but her sensors had reported the first tsunami of graser fire and hits on *something* astern of the enemy ships. And now the diamond-dust glitter of the LACs' outgoing missiles speckled her display against a background holocaust of independently firing grasers still ripping pods to pieces.

"All right, Alf," she said to Jessup. "Let's you and Commander Stackowitz just see what you can do to help out."

"Aye, *aye*, Ma'am! Firing now!"

Minotaur twitched ever so slightly as her bow missile tubes opened fire. She was nine million kilometers astern of her enemies and losing ground steadily. Her superior acceleration would change that shortly, but it hadn't yet, which should have made the launch a futile gesture. But she had the first fruits of Project Ghost Rider in her magazines, and the missiles she fired in salvos of nine were like none that had ever been fired in anger before.

"Bow wall up!" Michael Gearman barked as the last of twelve shipkillers erupted from *Harpy*'s bow-mounted tubes.

"Wedge nominal!" PO Maxwell snapped almost simultaneously.

"Ready to answer the helm on reaction thrusters, Skipper!" Lieutenant Takahashi said.

"Very good," Harmon acknowledged, watching her small plot, and her lips curled back from her teeth. The wing had already gutted the Peeps' pods—they might have a dozen or so left, hiding amid the wreckage, but certainly not enough to have any great impact on the coming engagement—and now the *Shrikes*' missiles were howling in on their targets. The angle was still bad, but the range was down to only 220,000 kilometers, and the closure rate at launch was close to three hundred KPS. That would leave the birds plenty of time on their drives, and with an acceleration of 85,000 *g*, their flight time was barely twenty-two seconds.

Oscar Diamato watched in horror as the huge cloud of missiles flashed towards TF 12.3. He was right, he thought numbly. Those had to be LACs out there—the individual missile salvos were too small and coming from too many dispersed points to be from anything larger. But there were so *many* of them! Worse, they'd launched from such short range, and from so many places on so many vectors, that point defense was caught hopelessly flatfooted. CIC and the sensor crews did their best, but the target environment was too chaotic. They needed time for their plots to settle, only there was no time.

The Manticoran missiles came howling down on their targets, in final acquisition before more than a handful of counter-missiles could launch, and laser clusters and main energy mounts vomited beamed energy in a desperate effort to pick them off. PNS *Alcazar*, senior ship of the task force's understrength destroyer screen, took a direct main battery hit, squarely amidships, from *Tascosa*. The battleship was only trying to protect herself, but *Alcazar* was in the wrong place at the wrong time, and the hapless ship blew up with all hands as the massive graser ripped contemptuously through her sidewall.

Schaumberg was firing as desperately as anyone else. Diamato's hands flew over his console, his entire universe focused on his responsibility to somehow break through the Manties' EW and find them for his own weapons, yet he felt the ship shudder and buck as the first bomb-pumped lasers tore at her. Citizen Captain Hall's orders to bring Diamato's ECM up on her own initiative made the flagship a much harder target than the other battleships, but with so many missiles flying some of them simply had to get through, and alarms wailed as she jerked again.

"Graser Three down! Direct hit on Lidar One, switching to backup! Citizen Captain, we're taking hits forward! Beta Thirteen and Fourteen are out of the ring! Heavy casualties in Point Defense Five!"

Diamato cringed as the litany of damage reports rolled through the bridge, yet even as he cringed, he knew it could have been far, far worse—*would* have been worse, if not for Citizen Captain Hall. But that was cold comfort as—

"Direct hit on Auxiliary Control!" someone shouted, and despite himself, Diamato looked up from his own displays at the damage schematic. Auxiliary Control turned bright, blazing crimson as he watched, and he darted a look at the citizen captain. Hall's face was a mask etched from stone, her presence an eye of calm as she forced her bridge crew to hold together by sheer willpower, yet he saw the pain—the loss—in her eyes as she realized Ira Hamer was dead.

"Find me those LACs, Oliver!" she commanded, her voice very nearly as even as it had been before the Manties launched, and he wheeled back to his display.

Reaction thrusters flared, pushing LAC Wing One's bows sideways with old-fashioned brute power. It was slow and ponderous compared to maneuvering on impellers, but it let them maintain their powerful bow sidewalls as they simultaneously turned and rolled to present the bellies of their wedges to the enemy.

Jacquelyn Harmon watched the maneuver with fierce elation. That asshole Holderman might have hung them up out here for months while he tried to sabotage Operation Anzio, but at least his machinations had given her people plenty of time to train. They were reacting like veterans, bringing themselves far enough around to deny the Peeps down-the-throat shots so they could go in pursuit, and she felt herself leaning forward against her shock frame as if to physically urge *Harpy* on.

But then something caught her eye, and she blinked, lips pursing in surprise, as HMS *Minotaur*'s first nine missiles came shrieking in from astern. They'd taken one hundred and forty-three seconds to overhaul their targets, and their overtake velocity was over a hundred and twenty-six thousand kilometers per second. No other missile in space could have done that; simply to get the burn time would have required a thirty-five-percent reduction in maximum acceleration, which would have put it three million kilometers behind these birds with a velocity almost twenty thousand KPS lower. More to the point, any other missiles would have been ballistic and unable to maneuver by the time they overhauled their prey, whereas *these* birds would still have close to forty seconds on their drives.

No one in TF 12.3 saw them coming—not even Oliver Diamato. The PN tactical crews could be excused for that. There was so much other confusion on their displays, so many other known threats scorching in on so many different vectors, that none of them had any attention to spare for the single dreadnought so far behind them that it couldn't possibly represent a danger.

And because none of them did, *Minotaur*'s first salvo came slashing in completely unopposed.

All nine missiles were locked onto a single target, and they had not only plenty of power for terminal attack maneuvers but a straight shot directly up the after aspect of its wedge. Two of them actually detonated *inside* the wedge, and the other seven all detonated at less than eight thousand kilometers. The hedgehog pattern of their X-ray lasers enveloped the stern of PNS *Mohawk* in a deadly weave of energy, and the battleship's after impeller room blew apart, and her wedge faltered. Unfortunately, however, it didn't *fail* . . . and every man and woman aboard her died almost instantly as one laser scored a direct hit on her inertial compensator and two hundred gravities smashed the life from them like an enraged deity's mace.

That caught the attention of the tactical officers aboard *Mohawk*'s sisters, and a fresh surge of consternation washed through them as they realized the Manties had just hit them with yet another new weapon. Their counter-missiles and laser clusters trained around onto the threat bearing, firing furiously at the followup salvos, and at least they had plenty of tracking and engagement time against *this* threat.

"Admiral Truitt is coming back at them, Skipper!" Evans reported, and Harmon nodded. Truitt's task group had reversed acceleration, charging to meet the Peeps now that their pods had been mostly destroyed, and his own pods launched as he entered attack range. They flew straight into the Peeps' faces, and ships slewed wildly as they tried to turn the vulnerable throats of their wedges away from the incoming fire. But that turned them almost directly away from Harmon's LACs, exposing their vulnerable after aspects, and her people had turned far enough away that they were no longer crossing their own "T"s for the enemy. That meant they'd been able to take down their bow walls, unmasking their missile tubes once more

"Reengage with missiles! Flush the reserves now!" she ordered over the wing command channel, and the missiles she'd held back from the initial attack for just this moment went roaring out.

It was a nightmare for Jane Kellet—or would have been, if she'd had even a single microsecond to dwell upon it. But she didn't have that microsecond. Her task force writhed at the heart of a deadly ambush, with missiles flying at her seemingly from every possible direction, and the Manty SDs were closing on her battleships. They couldn't fight those leviathans—not in energy range—and win . . . and that didn't even count the damned LACs. Her tac people could find them now that they'd made their presence felt and brought their wedges up, but their decoys and jammers were hellishly effective for such small vessels. Locking them up for fire control should have been easy at this short range, but it wasn't. Worse, they were splitting into two forces which angled away from one another, obviously intending to race out on either flank before they turned and scissored back towards one another with her in the middle. She could see it coming, but the maneuver had turned the bellies of their wedges towards her, which meant she could engage only with missiles.

"All ships, stand by to come to course oh-niner-oh by two-seven-oh!" she barked. It wasn't much, but it would turn her sterns at least a little further away from the LACs and twist her vector violently away from the Manty SDs. Even with their new compensators, those SDs had a lower max accel than her battleships, and if she could just draw out of *their* range—

"Flush remaining pods at the LACs!" she snapped, her brain whirring like a computer as she considered options and alternatives. She didn't know how many missiles she had left, but she had a decent chance of keeping the ships of the wall from getting into energy range. That meant it was the damned LACs which were the real threat. They, and they alone, had the acceleration and, more importantly, the position from which to overtake her fleeing units. Which meant that every one of them she killed would be—

The incoming missile from Rear Admiral Truitt's superdreadnoughts detonated nineteen thousand kilometers in front of *Schaumberg*, and the battleship writhed like a tortured animal as two massive X-ray lasers, vastly more powerful than anything the LACs could have fired, slashed into her. One destroyed three missile tubes, breached a magazine, demolished a graser mount and two of the ship's bow lasers, and killed eighty-seven people. The other smashed straight through armor and blast doors and bulkheads with demonic fury, and Citizen Rear

Admiral Jane Kellet and her entire staff died as it blew her flag deck apart.

Joanne Hall felt her ship lurch, heard the alarms, saw the flag bridge com screen go blank, and knew instantly what had happened. Disbelief and horror foamed up inside her, but she had no time for those things. She knew what Kellet had been thinking and planning, and as the crimson bands of battle damage flashed in her plot, ringing the icons of the task force's ships, she had no idea who was the surviving senior officer. Nor was there time to find out.

"Message to all ships!" she told her com officer without even looking away from her plot. "'LACs are primary targets. Repeat, LACs are primary targets. All ships will roll starboard and execute previously specified course change.'" She looked over her shoulder at last, meeting the white-faced Citizen Lieutenant's eye. "End it Kellet, Citizen Rear Admiral," she said flatly.

The Citizen Lieutenant's eyes darted to Calvin Addison. The citizen commissioner looked at Hall for one brief instant, then back at the com officer and nodded sharply.

"They're turning away from us, Skipper," Ensign Thomas reported. "Looks like they're trying to evade Admiral Truitt."

"I see it," Harmon replied. She gazed at her plot with narrow eyes, her mind racing. The Peeps were clearly trying to run for it, and after the hammering they'd already taken, they wouldn't be back any time soon. All she and her LACs really had to do was chase them; catching them was no longer necessary to save Hancock, because those ships weren't going to stop running as long as a single Manticoran starship or LAC appeared on their sensors.

But her plot showed their projected vector, and she swore silently. It was going to take them out of Truitt's envelope—not without giving him the chance to batter them with missiles, but staying well out of his energy range—and that meant a lot of them were going to get away. Only three battleships, two destroyers, and six heavy cruisers had actually been destroyed so far, and she gritted her teeth at the thought of letting all those cripples get away. But the only Manticoran ships which could possibly overtake them and *keep* them from escaping were her LACs, and they were out of missiles. Which meant graser-range attacks on targets which were individually enormously more powerful than her ships were. And which also meant turning the wing's bows dangerously close to its enemies as it pursued.

And they're learning, she thought grimly as two LAC icons flashed crimson on her plot. One broke off, limping away from the battle while the data codes of severe damage blinked beside it; the other simply vanished. *They know we're out here, and they're not running scared or shocked anymore, so if we do follow them up, it's going to* *get ugly. Ugl*ier, *that is,* she corrected herself grimly, for she'd already lost four ships—five with the latest casualty.

She didn't have to do it. Not to save the system. And what had already happened was a brilliant vindication of Operation Anzio. But that wasn't the point, was it?

"The LACs are pursuing, Citizen Captain," Diamato reported.

"The superdreadnoughts?"

"They're turning to cut the angle on us as well as they can, but they're not going to be able to overtake, Ma'am. I make their closest approach something over a million and a half klicks—well outside effective energy range, anyway. Whoever that is out-system of us could, but she's not trying to." He actually managed a death's head grin. "I don't think I would, either, if I had her missile range," he added.

"Understood," Hall grunted. She glanced at the damage report sidebar scrolling down her plot and winced. A third of the surviving battleships had been hammered into wrecks. And despite what Diamato had said, two of them, at least, weren't going to make it clear after all. They'd taken too much impeller damage to stay away from the Manty capital ships, yet the task force had no choice but to leave them behind and save as many other units as it could.

I hope to hell the other attacks are doing better than we *are,* she thought bitterly.

"Citizen Captain, I have a com request from Citizen Rear Admiral Porter. He wants to speak to the Citizen Admiral," the com officer said quietly.

He would, Hall thought, watching the missiles fly. *And I have to give him command . . . which I wouldn't mind at all—at least I could also let him have the responsibility!—except that he doesn't have a clue what to do with it.*

She darted a look at Addison.

"Citizen Commissioner?" She couldn't ask him for what she really wanted, not in so many words. But he recognized her expression and drew a deep breath. He looked back at her for several seconds, then spoke to the com officer without even glancing in the young woman's direction.

"Inform the Citizen Rear Admiral that Citizen Admiral Kellet is . . . unavailable, Citizen Lieutenant," he said flatly. "Tell him—" He paused, thinking hard, then nodded once. "Tell him our com systems are badly damaged and we need to keep our remaining channels clear."

"Aye, Sir," the Citizen Lieutenant said in a tiny voice, and Hall turned back to her plot.

"All right!"

Michael Gearman heard Ensign Thomas' cry of delight as *Harpy* and the rest of Gold Section concentrated the fire of their grasers on one of the Peep cripples. The battlecruiser-weight weapons blasted through armor and structural members like battleaxes, and their target heaved, belching atmosphere and debris and bodies. Gearman shared Thomas' exultation, but he remembered another battle, another ship—this one a superdreadnought—heaving as she was battered to wreckage and her people were slaughtered . . . or maimed. His hand went to the thigh of his regenerated leg, and even in the heart of his own battle fury, his lips murmured a silent prayer for their victims.

"We've drawn out of range of their superdreadnoughts, Ma'am," Diamato reported hoarsely.

"Understood." Hall nodded. Yes, they'd left the ships of the wall behind, but not before their fire, coupled with those incredible missiles coming in from the lone dreadnought so far astern of her—and, of course, the LACs—had killed another four battleships. That made nine gone out of thirty-three, with all of the survivors damaged. All the tin cans were gone, as well, and only two heavy cruisers remained to her, both badly damaged.

Which means I have no screen at all, she thought coldly as the LACs raced back up on her flanks like shoals of sharks. She had a count on them now, and her people had managed to destroy sixteen of them outright and drive another five off with damage. But that left seventy-five, and their acceleration was incredible. The bastards were hitting her with what was obviously a well-thought-out maneuver; charging up on TF 12.3's flanks, taking their licks from her missiles—which were far less effective than they ought to be—until they reached their attack points, and then slashing in in coordinated runs from both sides. They were scissoring through her formation, firing as they came, and the damage they were doing was immense.

But they lost ground and velocity on her each time they crossed her base course. For some reason, they appeared to completely stop accelerating each time they turned in for a firing pass, but they were turning out over six hundred and thirty gravities of acceleration *before* they turned in, and they snapped right back up to it as they turned back to parallel her course once more at the end of each pass. Which meant they had more than enough maneuvering advantage to continue battering away at her remaining twenty-six ships all the way to the hyper limit.

Which meant the only way out was going to be through them.

"All right," Jackie Harmon told her squadron and section commanders. Her voice was still relaxed, almost drawling, but her face was taut. She'd lost three more LACs, two of them on cowboy solo attacks they should never have attempted, on the last firing run.

She was down to seventy-two effectives now, and she tried not to think of all the people who had died aboard the LACs she no longer had. "Admiral Truitt's lost the range, so it's all up to us, now. I want full squadron attacks—no more individual horse shit, here, people, or I will provide some unfortunate souls with new anal orifices!" She paused a moment to be sure it had sunk in, then nodded. "Good! Ensign Thomas will designate targets for the next attack run."

"They're turning in on us again, Ma'am!" Diamato snapped.

"I see them, Oliver," Hall said calmly. "Citizen Admiral Kellet's" orders had already gone out, and she bared her teeth at her plot. She knew what was going through the mind of whoever was in command over there. The LACs were enormously outmassed and outgunned, despite TF 12.3's damage. But her opponent simply couldn't stand to see her getting away, and the Manties were clearly out of missiles. They had to come into knife range and engage with energy weapons, where they should have been easy meat for battleships, but she and Diamato had already deduced that there was something very peculiar about these particular LACs. Not only did their acceleration fall to zero whenever they fired their grasers, but even the accel for their lateral maneuvers dropped enormously, almost to what she would have expected out of old-fashioned reaction thrusters. She didn't know precisely what it meant, but they were incredibly resistant targets—extremely difficult just to lock up on fire control and almost as hard to actually kill even when Tracking had them firmly. Could they be generating some sort of shield forward? Something like a sidewall? But how was that possible?

A vague suspicion glimmered at the corner of her adrenaline-exhausted brain, but there was no time to follow it up now. She'd have to be sure she mentioned it to NavInt later, though, and—

"Here they come!"

LAC Wing One altered course and came slashing in, firing savagely. Another Peep battleship blew up, and one of the surviving cruisers, but the enemy had been waiting for this, and their own energy batteries replied savagely. Even more dangerously, the Peeps were firing missiles *past* them now, as if someone on the other side had figured out about their bow walls. A passing shot was always a harder targeting solution, but the laserheads exploding astern of the LACs probed viciously at their wedges' open after aspects. One of them died, then two more, then a fourth, but the others held their courses, unable to accelerate as they locked their bow walls and poured fire into the enemy.

Too many! Jacquelyn Harmon thought. *I'm losing too many! They're running now, and their fire's too heavy for us to take them alone.*

"Last pass, boys and girls," she announced over the com. "Make it count, then break off and head back for the *Minnie*."

Another battleship blew up, then yet another, and she stared into her plot as *Harpy* reached her own turn-in point and began to pivot.

PNS *Schaumberg* staggered drunkenly as three grasers burned through her port sidewall like red-hot pokers. The sidewall flickered and died, then came back up at half strength, and four of her energy mounts and two missile tubes were torn to wreckage by the same hits.

But then a fourth graser struck home, and Oscar Diamato slammed his helmet shut as the port bulkhead shattered and air screamed out of the breached compartment. Fragments of battle steel blasted across the bridge, killing and wounding, but Diamato hardly noticed. His eyes were on the lurid damage codes for the port sidewall, and he darted a desperate look at the plot. There! If he rolled ship just right—

"Roll ship twelve—no, *fourteen* degrees to port!" he shouted.

"Rolling fourteen degrees port, aye!" the helmsman's voice replied over his suit com, and Diamato gasped in relief as the ship turned. But then a sudden, icy shock washed through him as he realized he hadn't heard the Citizen Captain confirm his order.

He turned his head, and his face twisted with horror as he saw thick, viscous blood bubbling from Citizen Captain Hall's skinsuit as the last of the bridge's air fell away into vacuum.

"Damn, I didn't think she could do that," Jackie Harmon muttered as she watched her target roll. Whoever was in charge over there must have ice water in her veins. She'd managed to roll at exactly the right angle to turn her weakened port sidewall away from the LACs following Lieutenant Commander Gillespie in from port for a followup shot. Unfortunately for the Peep, however, it had forced her to give *Harmon's* group an almost perpendicular shot at her other sidewall, and that was about as good as it was going to get this side of a hot tub, a good-looking man, and a chocolate milkshake.

"Stand by to take us in, Ernest," she told Lieutenant Takahashi.

"Aye, Ma'am." Takahashi checked his own plot, then looked up at *Harpy*'s engineers. "Watch the power to the forward nodes when I call for the wall, PO," he reminded Maxwell.

"I'll watch it, Sir," Maxwell promised him.

"Yeah, I've *heard* about you and forward nodes, 'Silver Hammer,'" Takahashi said with a grin, and the hirsute petty officer chuckled.

"Take us in—*now!*" Harmon snapped as the numbers matched on her plot.

"Captain! Captain Hall!"

Diamato knelt beside the command chair while fat, blue-white sparks leapt and spat silently in the vacuum. Citizen Captain Hall sat upright on the decksole, but only because he held her there, bracing her shoulders against his body while he tried desperately to get her to respond. By some miracle, his tactical section was untouched, and so was the com and the helm. Everything else was gutted, and he fought nausea as he tried to ignore the slaughterhouse which had engulfed his fellow officers and friends.

Citizen Commissioner Addison had been torn almost in half, and most of the rest of the bridge personnel were just as dead. But Citizen Captain Hall was still alive . . . for the moment.

He'd slapped patches over the worst holes in her skinsuit, but her life-sign readouts flickered on the med panel. Diamato was no doctor, but he didn't need to be one to know she was dying. There was too much internal bleeding, and no one could do anything about it without taking her out of her suit . . . which would kill her instantly.

"*Captain!*" he tried again, and then froze as the dark eyes inside the blood-daubed helmet opened.

"O-Oliver." It was a faint, thready sound over his suit com, with the bubbling sound of aspirated blood behind it, and his hands tightened on her shoulders.

"Yes, Skipper!" He felt his eyes burn and blur and realized vaguely that he was crying. She must have heard it in his voice, for she reached out and patted his skinsuited thigh feebly.

"Up . . . to you," she whispered, her eyes burning into his with the fiery power of a soul consuming itself in the face of approaching death. "Get—" She paused, fighting for breath. "Get my people . . . out. Trust . . . you, Oli—"

Her breathing stopped, and Oliver Diamato stared helplessly into the eyes which had suddenly ceased to burn. But something had happened to him, as if in the moment of Joanne Hall's death, the spark had leapt from her soul into his, and his nostrils flared as he drew a deep breath and laid her gently down.

Then he rose and crossed almost calmly to his panel. Half his starboard energy weapons were gone, he noted, and most of the other half were in local control. But that meant half of them remained, with on-mount crews to fire them, and he bared his teeth as his gloved fingers flew. There was no time to set it up with proper double-checks, and his internal data transmission links had taken too much damage for him to rely on computer target designation. He was going to have to do this the hard way—the deep-space equivalent of shooting from the hip—but his eyes were cold and very still.

There, he thought. *Those two.*

He laid the sighting circles by eye, hit the override button that stripped the targeting lidar away from the central computer's command, and painted his chosen targets for his energy battery crews' on-mount sensors. Green lights blinked—he couldn't tell exactly how many—as at least some of his crews picked up the designator codes and locked onto them. However many it was, it would have to do.

See you in hell, Manty! he thought viciously, and pressed the fire key.

A fraction of a second later, LAC 01-001, call-sign *Harpy*, exploded in an eye-wrenching flash as Oliver Diamato's crews sent two capital ship grasers cleanly through her bow wall.

Chapter Thirty-Five

"Citizen Admiral Kellet should be hitting Hancock about now, and Citizen Admiral Shalus should already have hit Seaford Nine," Citizen Commissioner Honeker observed. Tourville nodded but said nothing. Of course, Honeker hadn't really expected him to reply. The people's commissioner was just making conversation while he tried to ignore the worm of tension which had to be eating at his own belly.

"Twelve minutes to translation, Citizen Admiral." Citizen Commander Lowe sounded as professional as ever, but there was a certain undeniable edge even in her voice.

"Thank you, Karen." Tourville made his tone as calm and confident as possible. It wasn't much, but when it came right down to it, that was about all any admiral could really do at a time like this.

Rear Admiral of the Green Michael Tennard bounded out of the flag deck lift still sealing his skinsuit. Alarms blared throughout the eight-and-a-half-million-ton hull of his flagship, and he swore vilely as he saw the master plot.

Fifty-plus bogies were scorching in towards Zanzibar. Their velocity was already close to fifteen thousand KPS, and it was climbing at a steady four hundred and fifty gravities. That acceleration meant the intruders couldn't have anything heavier than a battleship, but he had only his own six ships of the wall, six RMN battlecruisers, and a handful of cruisers, destroyers, and obsolete LACs of the Zanzibar Navy to stop them.

"At least they can't be towing pods," his chief of staff observed beside him. "Not with that accel."

"Thank the Lord for small favors," Tennard grunted, and the chief of staff nodded soberly, for the unhappy fact was that Tennard didn't have anything like a full load of pods for his own ships, either. He could put a total of only seventy-three on tow, and that wasn't going to give him anywhere near the salvo density he wanted for his first strike. On the other hand, the Peeps wouldn't have anything at all to respond with, and his SDs had immeasurably better point defense. If he could take out a half dozen battleships in the first strike, then match courses and maintain separation for a classic missile duel, his people would have a fairly good chance of shooting the survivors up badly enough to make them think very hard about breaking off. Of course, the Peeps would be shooting up *his* ships in the meantime, and those damned missile-heavy battleships of theirs were just the thing to do it with. But—

He chopped his thoughts off and began issuing a steady stream of orders, and even as he gave them, he tried to pretend he didn't know what was going to happen. Not that it would have made any difference if he had chosen to admit it to himself. There was no way he could withdraw without at least attempting to defend Zanzibar. Even if the honor of the Royal Navy hadn't made that unthinkable, the act would devastate the faith of the Star Kingdom's other allies in the worth of a Manticoran guarantee of protection. But the truth was that if the Peeps were willing to take their losses and keep coming, they had the numbers to weather his understrength pod salvo, cripple or destroy his ships of the wall, and still carry through to take out every ship and structure in Zanzibar orbit.

All Rear Admiral Tennard could really hope to do was make it expensive for them, and he set grimly out to do just that.

"Coming up on translation in thirty-one minutes, Citizen Admiral," the voice over the com said, and Javier Giscard reached out to press the stud.

"Understood, Andy," he told Citizen Commander MacIntosh. "Citizen Commissioner Pritchart and I will be up to the flag deck shortly."

"Aye, Sir," MacIntosh said, and Giscard smiled crookedly at Pritchart as he released the stud.

"I do believe Andy has his suspicions about us," he remarked.

"You do?" Pritchart looked at him sharply, and he nodded.

The two of them sat in his day cabin, already skinsuited while they waited for the alarms which would summon *Salamis*' crew to action stations. No doubt most of their subordinates thought they were deeply immersed in some last-minute planning session—and so they were, in a sense. But none of their subordinates would have expected to see People's Commissioner Pritchart sitting in Citizen Admiral Giscard's lap, nor guessed exactly what sort of plans they were laying. Or so Pritchart had thought, and Giscard's remark touched her topaz eyes with alarm.

"Why do you say that?" she demanded.

"Because he's gone out of his way to tell a few stories about incidents between us, love," Giscard said with a slow smile. "Incidents which never happened—or not, at least, quite the way he describes them—and all of which emphasize the 'tension' between us."

"You mean—?"

"I mean I think he's covering for us," Giscard told her. She gazed into his eyes for several seconds, chewing her lower lip with even white teeth, then sighed and twitched her shoulders in a shrug.

"I'm grateful to him if he is," she said unhappily, "but I'd be even more grateful if he'd never guessed. And he'd better be careful about his stories, too. If he gets too creative and StateSec starts comparing his versions with those of some other informer. . . ."

She let her voice trail off, and Giscard nodded again, this time soberly.

"You're right, of course. But I don't think he'll let himself get carried away. And don't forget—you and I *are* exhibiting a lot of 'tension' in our official relationship. What he's doing is mostly a matter of . . . emphasizing that tension, and I suspect most of his embroidery is the sort that could be put down to someone exaggerating for effect. Or possibly an amateur angling for a job as an *official* informer."

"Um." Pritchart considered that, then sighed in resignation and leaned back against his shoulder. "Well," she said in a determinedly brighter tone, "at least you came up with a brilliant way to get rid of Joubert, Javier!"

"I did, didn't I?" Giscard said rather complacently. He had no doubt that StateSec would figure out that getting rid of Joubert was exactly what he'd done, but, then, he'd made it plain from the beginning that he'd accepted the chief of staff only under protest. And although Pritchart had argued strenuously against his decision to reassign Joubert to command PNS *Shaldon*, not even a commissioner as vigilant in the People's service as she could argue that it had been a demotion. No one had expected Citizen Captain Herndon to drop dead of a heart attack en route to the target, but his exec had been far too inexperienced to command a dreadnought in action, whereas Citizen Captain Joubert had both the experience and the seniority for the spot. And so Citizen Admiral Giscard had regretfully deprived himself of his services by transferring him to Citizen Rear Admiral Darlington's Task Group 12.4.2 and tapped Citizen Commander MacIntosh to fill both the chief of staff's slot and the ops officer's, and everyone—except, of course, for Citizen Commissioner Pritchart's official persona—was delighted with the change.

He chuckled quietly at the thought, and Pritchart smiled, following the direction of his mind with her usual uncanny acuity. His arms tightened about her for a moment, and his mood darkened. *At least I can say one thing for worrying about StateSec's reaction if they find out they've got an unregenerate Aprilist watching over a rogue admiral,* he thought. *It puts the thought of such minor things as being killed in action into their proper, unimportant perspective!*

"We'd better go," he said quietly, and she turned to kiss him with fierce, quiet desperation before they stood and donned their masks once more.

"They're going for a straight-up duel," Citizen Captain Bogdanovich said, and shook his head.

"Why not?" Tourville replied quietly. The two of them stood gazing down into the master plot, hands clasped behind them, and the citizen vice admiral shrugged. "Thanks to Shannon, they may figure we forgot to bring any pods along, and their missiles—and point defense—have always been better than ours. In their place, I think I'd want to get to energy range as quickly as possible, but then, I do know about our pods. Even if I try to forget it, I can't, which may be affecting my opinion."

"No it's not," the chief of staff said with a wry smile. "You'd want to charge in and get it done anyway."

"I'm not *that* bad," Tourville protested. He turned to frown quellingly at Bogdanovich, but the chief of staff only grinned. "Am I?" the citizen vice admiral asked rather more plaintively, and Bogdanovich nodded.

"Oh, well. Maybe you're right," Tourville conceded. *But maybe you* aren't, *too, my friend,* he added silently. *I may believe in getting in and getting it done, but I'm not prepared to be stupid about it. And I didn't just happen to decide to keep* Count Tilly *as my flagship, either. She's more fragile than a battleship, but battlecruisers are going to draw a hell of a lot less fire than the battleships are, too!*

He smiled at the thought, then turned and walked back to his command chair.

Rear Admiral Tennard waited tautly as the range continued to drop. He'd gone out to meet the Peeps, then turned to decelerate back the way he'd come. The range was down to only a little more than six-point-seven million kilometers now, and he was letting it drop by a steady eight hundred KPS. They'd be in long missile range in a little over four minutes, at which point he would attack and then increase his accel to hold the range open as long as possible.

"Stand by to launch," he said in a firm, quiet voice.

"Recommend we deploy the pods, Citizen Admiral," Shannon Foraker said. The tension everyone else felt burned in her voice, as well, but on her it had a curious effect. It was almost as if *this* tension were a familiar one—even a welcome one—which displaced that other tension which had gripped her for so long. In that moment, she sounded more like Lester Tourville's old tac witch than she had since Honor Harrington's capture, and he turned his head to look at her. She glanced up, as if she felt his eyes upon her, and then, to his astonishment, she actually smiled and *winked* at him!

"Recommendation approved, Citizen Commander," he told her, and Citizen Lieutenant Frasier passed the order over the intership net.

"Sir! Admiral Tennard, they're—"

"I see it," Tennard said, and the sound of his own voice surprised him. It was even, almost relaxed, when every cell of his brain screamed his fatal mistake at him. It hadn't even occurred to him that they might have held their pods inside their wedges, and it should have. Such a simple thing to do . . . and he'd never seen it coming, never even considered it.

But it was always the simple things, wasn't it? And he knew now. The long, lumpy trails of pods deployed astern of the battleships and battlecruisers in ungainly tails, revealing themselves to his sensors, and there were far more of them than he had.

"Course change," he said. "Let's close the range."

"*Close* the range, Sir?" his chief of staff asked as Tennard's flag captain acknowledged the order.

"Close it," the rear admiral confirmed grimly. "Those people are going to blow the ever living hell out of us when they launch. And then, if they have a clue at all, *they'll* be the ones holding the range open. They'll stay outside our energy envelope and pound us with more missiles until we're scrap metal."

"But—"

"I know," Tennard said softly. "But our best shot is going to be to get in close enough to land a few good licks with our energy weapons before they take us out." He managed a tight, bitter smile. "I screwed up, and I'm going to lose this system, but nothing I can do will get our people out of the trap I walked them right into," he said almost calmly. "That being the case, all we can do is try to take some of them with us."

"They're altering course, Citizen Admiral," Foraker reported, and studied her plot carefully. "They're coming to meet us again," she announced after a moment.

"Trying to get into energy range," Tourville grunted. He rubbed his luxuriant mustache for a moment, then shrugged. "Bring us about as well, Karen," he told Citizen Commander Lowe. "They must have figured out how Shannon suckered them, but there's an old, old saying about suckers and even breaks."

The two forces continued to close, but at a much lower rate, and as the range fell below six and a half million kilometers, both opened fire almost simultaneously. Rear Admiral Tennard's missiles slashed out, driving for the solid core of Tourville's battleships. But unlike Alice Truman, he had none of Ghost Rider's experimental missiles. Those he possessed had marginally greater range and marginally greater acceleration than the People's Navy's, coupled with superior penaids and seekers, but not enough to make up the difference in numbers. Even with his internal tubes to thicken the launch, he could put only twelve hundred missiles into space; Lester Tourville and Shannon Foraker replied with almost six *thousand*.

The two salvos interpenetrated and passed one another, and both admirals turned their walls of battle broadside-on to one another, swinging the most vulnerable aspects of their wedges away from the incoming fire . . . and also clearing their broadside tubes to pour maximum-rate fire into one another.

The displays in CIC showed the holocaust reaching out for both of them, showed the fury hurtling through space, and yet there was something unreal, almost dreamy about it. There were only the light dots of hostile missiles, not the reality—not yet. For now, for a few seconds still, there was only the professional tension, the slivered edges of what they had thought was fear only to feel the reality of that emotion trying to break loose within them, and wrapped about it all the quiet hum of ventilators, the beep and murmur of background chatter, and the flat half-chants of tracking officers.

They seemed to last forever, those last few seconds, and then the illusion shattered with the silence as counter-missiles began to launch and the reality of megatons of death howling towards rendezvous burst in upon them.

Incoming fire began to vanish from the plot as counter-missiles blotted it away, tearing great holes in the shoals of destruction. And then laser clusters began to fire, and broadside energy mounts, and both sides ripped great swathes through the other side's fire. But it was not the sort of battle the Royal Manticoran Navy had become accustomed to fighting. TF 12.2's point defense was far better than the People's Navy's had been, its Solarian enhanced ECM was more effective . . . and there were far fewer missiles coming at it. The counter-missiles killed almost half of them, and the laser clusters killed a third of those that remained. Scarcely four hundred broke through to actually attack, and half of those were spoofed and confused by decoys and false targets far superior to anything the people who'd launched them had expected.

Two hundred missiles plummeted inward, targeted on thirty-three battleships, but those battleships turned as one, in the exquisitely choreographed maneuver Shannon Foraker had conceived and Lester Tourville had ruthlessly drilled them upon all the way here. The maneuver which turned the entire wall up on its side, showing only the bellies of its wedges to the missiles.

There were chinks in that wall of wedges—huge ones, for battleships required wide safety perimeters for their wedges—but it was far tighter than anything a Havenite fleet had assembled in over eight T-years. It was a Manticoran-style defense, one only a superbly drilled formation could attain, and the chinks in it were fewer, and smaller, and further apart than they ought to have been. Missile after missile wasted its fury on the unyielding defenses of the wedges of which it was built, and Lester Tourville smiled savagely as he watched it.

He lost ships anyway, of course. He'd known he would. Manticoran missiles were too good, their warheads too powerful, for it to have been any other way. But as he had told Everard Honeker three T-weeks before, Esther McQueen and Javier Giscard—and Lester Tourville, for that matter—had allowed for that. They had *expected* to lose ships . . . and to keep coming anyway.

Two battleships were destroyed outright, with two more driven out of the wall in a debris-shedding slither, but that left twenty, and they rolled back down to pour fire into what remained of their opponents.

Not that there was much left to shoot at. TF 12.2's fire had been five times as heavy as Rear Admiral Tennard's, and every missile had been concentrated solely upon his superdreadnoughts. Nine hundred and sixty missiles roared in upon each of them, and Tennard's ships were too far apart to duplicate Tourville's maneuver and build a wall in space with their wedges. The Manticoran admiral had never anticipated such a weight of fire. Against what he'd *thought* he faced, it had made sense to maintain unit separation, give each ship room to maneuver independently within the envelope of the task group's combined point defense. There had been no time to close up his formation when he realized what he actually confronted . . . and even if there had been, the galling truth was that his force was insufficiently drilled for it. This time, at least, it was the despised Peeps who possessed the superior training, the superior weight of fire . . . and the superior command team.

Michael Tennard knew that. He admitted it to himself, draining the bitter cup of his own assumptions as he watched a corona of fire envelop his lead superdreadnought. It flashed back along his formation, reaching for his flagship like some monstrous dragon from Old Earth's legends, and then there was only the terrible, unending, world-shattering succession of blows as laser after laser blasted into his flagship. He clung to the master plot, fighting to stay on his feet, watching the lights flicker, the dust filter from the overhead, and then there was a final, smashing concussion and a brilliant flash of light . . . and darkness.

"My God," Yuri Bogdanovich muttered. "It's like Adler all over again!"

"Not quite, Yuri," Tourville said grimly, looking at the icons of his dead and wounded ships. Three of the twenty battleships he'd taken into the final exchange had suffered severe damage. All told, the enemy had put twenty-nine percent of his wall out of action . . . but they'd completely ignored his battlecruisers to do it. Now those ships joined their fire with that of the remaining seventeen battleships, battering the Manty battlecruisers into wreckage one by one with merciless concentration. Here and there a Manticoran missile still got through to wreak more damage, but there weren't enough of them . . . and there were still fewer in each successive salvo as Shannon Foraker's precise fire demolished the enemy launch platforms in ruthless succession.

Nausea stirred in Tourville's belly as he looked out at the spreading patterns of wreckage, the life pods and unidentifiable debris which had once been megaton ships of the wall, each with a crew of over five thousand, and wondered how many of them had survived.

Not many, he thought. *No, not many at all. And what the hell am I thinking of? Would I rather it was* my *people who'd died out there in such numbers? Hell, I* have *lost eight or nine thousand of my own! I should be* glad *the bastards who killed them are dead.*

But he wasn't. Proud of his own people, yes, and grimly determined to carry through with the job for which so many had paid so much. But no one could look at that display and count all those dead and be *glad*. Or not anyone Lester Tourville ever wanted to know, at any rate.

He shook himself as the last Manticoran battlecruiser blew apart. The surviving cruisers and destroyers and LACs kept boring in, trying to get to energy range with utter gallantry and total despair, and he turned away, unable to watch their dying.

"Put us on course for Zanzibar again, Karen," he told his astrogator quietly, and looked at Shannon Foraker.

"Start calculating your fire patterns, Shannon," he said. "I hope to God they're smart enough to surrender, and if they are, I'll give them up to twelve hours to evacuate their orbital installations before we take them out. But I don't intend to spend much time discussing it with them." He produced a wintry smile. "If *this* can't convince them to accept sanity, then nothing I can say will, now will it?

He sat down in his command chair, tipped it back, crossed his legs, and felt in his breast pocket for a cigar, and all the time he wanted to weep.

Chapter Thirty-Six

"Stand by for translation on my mark," Citizen Commander Tyler said. "Coming up on translation in five . . . four . . . three . . . two . . . one . . . *mark!*"

Task Group 12.4.1, composed of Task Force 12.4's superdreadnoughts and their screening light cruisers, exploded out of hyper into n-space in brilliant, multipeaked flashes of azure transit energy barely a hundred and eighty thousand kilometers outside the twenty-two-light-minute hyper limit of the G0 star known as Basilisk-A. It was a phenomenally precise piece of astrogation, but Javier Giscard was unable to appreciate it properly as he fought the mind-wrenching, stomach-lashing dizziness the crash translation sent smashing through him. He heard others on *Salamis*' flag bridge retching and knew thousands of other people throughout his flagship's huge hull were doing the same, and even through his own nausea, he reflected on how vulnerable his task group was in that moment. His ships' crews were as completely incapacitated as he himself for anywhere from ten seconds to two full minutes, depending on the individual. During those seconds and minutes, only the ships' automated missile defenses were available to stave off attack, and had any hostile vessel been in position to take advantage of that brief helplessness, the price could have been catastrophic.

But no hostile ship was. Nor was one likely to be, for a star system was an immense target, and he had deliberately avoided a least-time course to the planet Medusa. Not that he was far off one. He intended to waste no time carrying out his mission, but even a slight diversion vastly increased the n-space volume into which his units might make translation. He preferred to have some room to work with . . . and it wasn't as if he was going to manage to evade the sort of sensor net the Manties must have assembled here. The PN had no hard data on the Basilisk net, but Giscard knew what the Republic's Navy had assembled to watch over its own core systems. The huge, sensitive, deep-system passive sensor arrays standing sentry over the Haven System for the Capital Fleet, for example, measured something on the order of a thousand kilometers in diameter and could detect the footprint of even a normal hyper translation at a range of up to a hundred light-hours. He had to assume the Manties' arrays were even better—after all, every other sensor they had was—which meant there was no point trying to sneak up on them with a slow, furtive approach.

Besides, the Manties were *supposed* to see him. If the timing worked properly, they would have almost an hour to react to his presence before Citizen Rear Admiral Darlington arrived. Which should give the defenders time to let themselves be well and truly caught between stools when they realized what was actually happening.

Of course, trying to achieve that sort of coordination comes awfully close to asking for the impossible, he acknowledged as his body's protests began to subside and his vision cleared enough for him to see his plot once more. *But the beauty of it here is that we don't really* have *to achieve it. It'll be nice if we pull it off, sort of like frosting on the cake, but we should be all right either way. Should.*

"Talk to me, Franny," he said.

"Uh, yes, S— Citizen Admiral." The astrogator shook herself and looked down at her readouts. "On profile, Citizen Admiral," she reported in a brisker, more normal-sounding voice. "Present position is three hundred ninety-five-point-niner million klicks from Basilisk-A, bearing oh-oh-five by oh-oh-three relative. Velocity is . . . fourteen-point-one KPS, and task force acceleration is three-point-seven-five KPS squared. Range to Medusa orbit is two hundred twenty-nine-point-niner-five million klicks. On current heading and acceleration, we should reach a zero-range intercept with the planet in one hundred thirty-two minutes, with a crossing velocity of forty-three-point-eight-two thousand KPS at the moment we cut its orbit."

"Andy? Anything headed our way yet?" Giscard asked.

"Not yet, Citizen Admiral," MacIntosh replied promptly. "We've got a lot of impeller signatures running around in-system, and some of them are almost certainly warships, but nothing seems to be heading our way yet. Of course, we *are* being just a bit visible, Citizen Admiral. Their sensor net has to have us, and I expect we'll be seeing a reaction soon."

"Thank you." Giscard glanced at Pritchart, then plucked his lip while he considered the two reports. Tyler's only reconfirmed the superb job of astrogation that she'd done to hit her intended n-space locus so closely. The acceleration numbers made Giscard a little nervous, however, even though he'd ordered them himself, for they were higher than was truly safe. Not that the PN found itself with a great deal of choice about cutting safety margins. Like the Royal Manticoran Navy, the prewar People's Navy had restricted its ships' top drive settings to a maximum of eighty percent of their full officially rated inertial compensator capacity. That was because the only warning a compensator usually gave that it was thinking about failing was the abrupt cessation of function . . . which instantly turned a ship's crew into goo. Since higher power settings were more likely to result in failure, most navies (and all merchant shipping lines) made a habit of limiting their ships to a comfortable safety margin of around twenty percent.

Unfortunately, the new Manty compensators made that unacceptable to the People's Republic. Unable to match the new compensators' power levels, they had opted both to begin building dreadnoughts for the first time in eighteen T-years and to cut their prewar compensator safety margins in half. The new dreadnoughts were considerably less powerful than superdreadnoughts would have been, but their lower tonnage gave them something approaching the acceleration curves a Manty *super*dreadnought could pull with the RMN's new compensators. By the same token, cutting the safety margins let the People's Navy steal back most of the Manties' advantage across the board. Which didn't help a whole lot when the Manties decided to go to full military power and toss *their* safety margins out the airlock, but at least it reduced the differential a little.

But MacIntosh's report was the really interesting one. Giscard hadn't expected to hear anything just yet, for any defensive picket would need at least ten or fifteen minutes just to get organized . . . and as much as forty if its CO had been so overconfident he'd let his units sit in orbit with cold impellers. For that matter, Giscard probably wouldn't know for some time even once the Manties began responding, given the quality of their stealth systems. Still, he'd be happier when MacIntosh's sensor crews finally detected some reaction to their arrival. In no small part, that was simply because he always hated waiting for the other shoe to drop, but there was more to it this time. Until he had some sign of what the Manties intended to do, he would have no idea whether or not the diversionary effort had worked . . . or just what sort of hornet's nest he might be sailing into.

Vice Admiral Michel Reynaud, Manticore Astro-Control Service, looked up and quirked an eyebrow as a distinctive three-note alarm chimed. It wasn't a particularly loud alarm, but it didn't have to be, for the master control room buried deep at the heart of the multimegaton space station that housed Basilisk ACS was a calm, quiet place. Not that it wasn't busy. Basilisk ACS oversaw all the traffic passing through the Basilisk terminus of the Manticore Wormhole Junction. A single mistake by one of its controllers could result in the complete loss of several million tons of shipping, not to mention the human cost to the crews of the ships involved, and that was the very reason the main control room was kept calm and quiet and efficient.

It was also the reason the lighting was intentionally adjusted to be on the dim side, the better to make the various displays visible, and why, in a practice dating back to the earliest days of electronic watch standing on Old Earth, the temperature was kept decidedly cool. (*Except*, Reynaud reminded himself wryly, *for the handful of Sphinxians on staff;* they *insist it's like a balmy spring day . . . the showoffs!*) The deliberate chill was carefully designed to prevent people from becoming so comfortable they dozed off on duty. Not that anyone on Reynaud's staff was likely to have enough idle time to doze off. He snorted at the familiar thought, but his eyebrow didn't come down, for he didn't recall any scheduled exercises with the picket force or Basilisk Station Command, and those were the only people who ever used that particular com circuit.

He turned his well-padded command chair to watch the com officer of the watch kill the alarm and begin inputting the primary authorization code. It always took a fair amount of propitiating with codes and responses to various challenges to convince the FTL com systems to disgorge their contents. Of course, that was to be expected. In Reynaud's humble opinion, most people who went into the Navy tended to be on the anal retentive side (ACS personnel were civil servants, not military—and proud of it—despite their uniforms and rank insignia), and they were especially retentive about toys like their FTL com. Except under very special and carefully defined conditions, ACS was absolutely forbidden the use of its own FTL transmitter, and the fact that only Manticore knew how to read the grav pulses hadn't prevented the RMN from insisting on all sorts of internal security fences.

But despite his private conviction that it was unnecessary, Reynaud was perfectly content to wait out the delay. For that matter, he didn't really mind any of the military-style crap he had to put up with, because he remembered when he and his people had been left all on their own out here. Michel Reynaud was an old Basilisk hand—he had fourteen T-years on the station, longer than anyone else aboard the huge base—and there had been a time when he'd felt nothing but contempt for the Navy. Which had been understandable enough, he reminded himself, considering the useless screw-ups and idle layabouts who used to be exiled to Basilisk. But these days—

A bright red light began to blink on the master communications panel, and Vice Admiral Reynaud never remembered getting out of his command chair. He simply found himself suddenly standing behind the com officer, as if the blood-red flash that announced an emergency Priority One signal had teleported him there. And perhaps it had, a distant corner of his brain thought as he watched over the com officer's shoulder and the message began to appear on her display. But that thought was far away and unimportant compared to the content of the short, terse sentences, and his thoughts reeled as he read the estimate of what was headed for

Medusa and all the orbital warehouses, freight transfer points, repair shops, and supply bases that served the commerce which poured through Basilisk daily.

He stared at it for one more moment, mouth dry, then wheeled to face the rest of his staff.

"Listen up, everybody!" he snapped, and heads turned throughout the control room, for they had never heard that particular harshness from him. "There's an unidentified task force headed in-system. Vice Admiral Markham estimates it at a minimum of twenty super-dreadnoughts and fifteen to twenty light cruisers."

Someone gasped in horror, and Reynaud nodded grimly.

"I'm sure the terminus picket will be getting underway shortly," he went on, "but even if they could get there in time, there aren't enough ships in the system to stop this kind of attack. Which means—" he inhaled deeply "—that I am declaring Case Zulu. Jessie—" he looked at his senior watchkeeper "—you're in charge of organizing the evac queue. You know the drill: neutrals and passenger ships first, bulk carriers last."

"I'm on it, Mike." The woman waved for two assistants to follow her and headed for the huge holo tank that plotted every ship movement within five light-minutes of the junction, and Reynaud laid a hand on the com officer's shoulder.

"Pass the word to the standby courier, Angela. Download Markham's dispatch and my own Case Zulu, and get it on its way. Jessie—" he looked back over his shoulder "—clear a priority route for the courier as soon as Angela's finished."

Jessie nodded, and Reynaud wheeled and beckoned to another controller.

"Al, you and Gus are in charge of short-range com traffic from here on out. I want Angela undisturbed on the Fleet com, just in case." Al, the senior of the two nodded, and Reynaud went on in a voice which was both calm and urgent. "There's going to be hell to pay when some of the merchant skippers figure out what's going on. We're ten light-hours from Medusa out here, but they're not going to be thinking about that, and they're going to demand priority to get their own precious asses out of here. Don't let them browbeat you! Jess will give you the movement schedule as soon as she's got it organized. Stick to it."

"Yes, Sir," the senior man said, almost as if he meant to salute—which simply wasn't done in the ACS. But Reynaud had already turned away, eyes searching for yet another officer. She had to be here somewhere, but he couldn't seem to spot her.

"Cynthia?" he called.

"Yes, Admiral?"

Reynaud almost levitated, for the reply came from directly behind him. He wheeled quickly—so quickly, in fact, that Lieutenant Carluchi stepped back to avoid him—and managed, somehow, not to glare at the speaker. It was his own fault, he told himself. Carluchi had commanded Basilisk ACS's Marine detachment for almost five months now, and he should have had plenty of time to get used to the silent, catlike way she moved.

"Oh, *there* you are," he said with just enough emphasis to make her blush. At any other moment, he would have taken time to enjoy his minor triumph, for Lieutenant Carluchi was as perpetually self-controlled and composed as she was attractive and young. But he had other things on his mind today, and he looked grimly down into the slim, wiry Marine's huge aqua eyes.

"You heard what I told Al and Gus?" he asked, and she nodded without the usual trace of discomfort she felt at ACS' casual, highly unmilitary modes of address. "Good," he said even more grimly, "because it's going to be up to you to put some teeth into their orders if some of those skippers out there actually panic. Can do?"

"Can do, Admiral," Carluchi said flatly.

Unlike the others, she snapped him a sharp salute, and Reynaud actually found himself returning it, albeit with much less precision. Then she turned and left at a trot he knew was going to turn into a run the instant she was out of his sight. Well, that was all right with Michel Reynaud. Lady Harrington had begun a tradition when she detached two of her pinnaces to support ACS' antismuggling inspections twelve years ago. But these days there were twelve pinnaces, not two, and the personnel to man them were assigned directly to Basilisk ACS by the Royal Marine Corps. A pinnace's twin pulse cannon and single light laser weren't even popguns compared to the weapons carried by real warships, but they were more than powerful enough to deal with unarmed, unarmored merchantmen who got out of hand. More than that, Reynaud knew beyond a shadow of a doubt that Cynthia Carluchi and her Marine crews would use those weapons in a heartbeat if the situation required it.

He just hoped the merchies knew it, too.

Vice Admiral of the Red Silas Markham managed to keep himself in his seat aboard the pinnace only by main force of will. Eleven minutes ago, he had been ensconced in his comfortable office aboard Medusa Gold One, the Navy's relatively new orbital HQ for the Basilisk Station. He'd been buried to the elbows in boring, frustrating paperwork and feeling ticked off—as usual—by the way the picket had been reduced over the last seven T-months. He'd understood the logic. Hell, he'd even agreed with it! But that hadn't make it any more pleasant to hold what was supposed to be a vice admiral's billet and see the forces assigned to him reduced to something a *rear* admiral would probably have been too senior to command had it been located anywhere other than a single junction transit from the Manticore System.

But he hadn't been able to argue. The Peeps hadn't even sniffed around the perimeter of the Basilisk System for a standard decade. This was a routine, unthreatened sector, much too far behind the front for someone as defensive-minded as the post-Coup Peep Navy had proven itself to hit. And if that should change, the entire strength of Home Fleet was only a transit away. There would be plenty of time to adjust deployments to beef up his task force if the Peeps ever seemed to be headed this way.

Only now it looked as if no one had remembered to tell the Peeps they were too defensive-minded and timid to try a deep-strike raid like this, because as sure as Hell had a monopoly on brimstone, *somebody* was headed in to blow the holy howling bejesus out of Markham's command area. And all the comfortable assurance—his, as well as the Admiralty's, he admitted bitterly—about redeployments from Home Fleet were crap in the face of something like this. Even battlecruisers would require almost nineteen hours just to reach the Basilisk terminus from Manticore orbit; SDs would take almost twenty-two . . . and that was for ships with the latest-generation compensators. Ships could make the actual transit from Manticore to Basilisk in mere seconds, but to do that they first had to get to the central Junction terminus in Manticore. And even after they hit Basilisk space, they would be another twenty-two and twenty-six hours respectively from Medusa. Which meant that getting any reinforcements out here was going to take time. Virtually none by the standards of normal interstellar movement, but tactical combat within a star system operated on another scale entirely. And on that scale, forty-one hours was a very long time indeed . . . especially with the enemy barely two hours out from Medusa and coming hard.

The pinnace was running flat out, straining to catch up with HMS *King William*. The flagship, known affectionately to her crew as *Billy Boy*, was holding her accel down enough for the small craft to overhaul, and Markham watched out the port as the pinnace maneuvered to dock. He didn't think of himself as a particularly brave man, and his belly knotted with tension as he thought of what *King William* and the rest of his understrength force was going out to face. But heroic or not, Silas Markham was a vice admiral of the Royal Manticoran Navy, and his place was aboard his flagship when she faced the foe, not in some damned office light-minutes behind the battle.

The superdreadnought's tractors reached out to the pinnace, capturing it and easing it into the brilliantly lit cavern of a boat bay, and Markham stood. It was against Regs, of course. Passengers were supposed to remain seated and strapped in during any approach maneuver, but he was in a hurry . . . and he was also a vice admiral, which meant no one was going to tell him no.

He snorted at the thought, bending to keep peering out the view port as the pinnace settled towards the docking buffers. His eye caught the ship's crest, painted on the outer face of the docking gallery below the armorplast viewing area, and his mouth twitched. The crest was built around the personal seal of King William I, for whom the ship was named, and Markham wondered once again how many of *Billy Boy*'s crew ever considered the fact that their namesake had been assassinated by a psychotic.

It was not a thought he particularly cared to contemplate at a moment like this.

"They're coming out, Citizen Admiral," Citizen Commander MacIntosh announced. Giscard held up his hand, interrupting a report from Julia Lapisch as he turned to face the ops officer.

"Strength estimates?" he asked.

"Still too far for any sort of positive count, Citizen Admiral, but it looks like they're present in considerably lower strength than predicted. We make it six to eight of the wall and an unknown number of battlecruisers. They seem to be headed our way at about three hundred gravities."

"Thank you." Giscard turned his chair towards Citizen Lieutenant Thaddeus. "Reactions, Madison?" he asked the intelligence officer.

"Our estimates were the best we could give you from the data we had when Icarus was planned, Citizen Admiral," Thaddeus said.

There was an edge of something almost like challenge in his voice, but Giscard was prepared to let that ride as long as Thaddeus kept it under control. He'd wondered why someone of the citizen lieutenant's obvious ability had not been promoted; now he knew, for the answer had been in the StateSec files Pritchart had received just before their departure from Secour. Thaddeus' older sister had been denounced to the People's Courts by a vengeful lover—falsely, as it turned out—as an enemy of the People. The lover had hanged himself when his anger cooled and he realized what he'd done, but his remorse had come too late to save Sabrina Thaddeus' life, and the SS feared that his sister's fate might turn the citizen lieutenant against the New Order. From what Giscard had seen of the man, they were right to be afraid of that. But it had never affected his work for the Citizen Admiral, and Giscard was hardly in a position to fault another over divided loyalties.

"I know the analysts' data was limited, Madison," the citizen admiral said now, putting just enough patience into his tone to remind the intelligence officer to watch his manners in front of others. "But this is a considerably lighter force than we anticipated, and I'd prefer not to find out the hard way that they actually have all those other ships we expected headed at us in stealth somewhere. So if there was any information, even questionable information, that could shed some light on this, I'd like to hear it."

"Yes, Citizen Admiral. Sorry," Thaddeus apologized, and leaned back in his chair, thinking hard. Finally he shook his head. "I can't really think of anything concrete that could explain it, Citizen

Admiral," he said in a very different voice. "But that doesn't mean as much as I'd like. We haven't made any scouting sweeps of Basilisk since the war started and the Manties blew out Seaford Nine. Instead, we've relied on covert intelligence gathered by merchant skippers on our payroll. For the most part, they're foreign nationals, not our own people, which means any report from them has to be taken with a grain of salt, but they're the best we've had."

He paused, glancing at Giscard, and the Citizen Admiral nodded in combined understanding and an order to go on.

"Within those qualifications, they've been able to give us a pretty solid count on the forces deployed to watch over the terminus itself," Thaddeus said. "Those units are easily inside the sensor reach of any merchie using the Junction. But the numbers have always been a lot more . . . amorphous for the rest of the picket."

"Why is that, Citizen Lieutenant?" Pritchart asked in neutral tones. "My understanding was that over half the traffic passing through this system transships at least some cargo at the warehouses in Medusa orbit before continuing through the terminus."

"That's correct, Ma'am," Thaddeus said much more stiffly. Pritchart, after all, was the enemy as far as he was concerned, yet he seemed a little baffled by his own reaction to her. It appeared that he couldn't quite work up the hate for her that he felt for StateSec's other minions, and that seemed to puzzle him.

"In that case, wouldn't they have been able to observe the other portion of the picket in some detail, as well?"

"Yes and no, Ma'am," MacIntosh said, coming to Thaddeus' aid. "They'd get a good look at anyone in close proximity to Medusa, but not at any units that were further out—on patrol, say, or conducting exercises. And the Manties are as sensitive to the possibility of espionage here as we would be in their place. They don't exactly encourage through traffic to use active sensors in areas like this, and there are limits to what merchant-grade passives can pick up. Unfortunately, part of the inspection the Manties have been insisting on since the war started includes a very close look at the sensor suites of visiting merchantmen, and if they find something more sophisticated than they feel is appropriate, the ship in question better have a very good justification for it. If she doesn't—*pffft!*" The Citizen Commander made a throwing away gesture with one hand. "That ship and that merchant skipper are banned from any use of the Junction for the duration of hostilities, which leaves them no real legitimate reason to be anywhere in the Basilisk System, much less anyplace they could see something that would do us any good to know about. Sort of cavalier of them, I suppose, but effective, and I'd do the same thing in their position."

"The Citizen Commander is correct, Ma'am," Thaddeus added. "We've had some reports that they've been drawing down the strength of the picket for the past several months, but no hard evidence to support them. Under the circumstances, NavInt—" it wasn't actually Naval Intelligence anymore, but Thaddeus, like a great many naval officers (and with more personal reason than most), still referred to the military intelligence section of State Security by the old pre-Coup name "—went with the last definite numbers we had. I suppose the theory was that it was better to make a worst-case assumption. And according to those figures, there ought to have been at least twelve of the wall assigned to the inner-system picket here."

"I see. Thank you, Citizen Lieutenant. And you, Citizen Commander." Pritchart gazed down into the master plot for several seconds, then looked at Giscard. "Does this change your intentions in any way, Citizen Admiral?"

"I think not, Citizen Commissioner," he replied with the exquisite courtesy he habitually used in public to depress her pretensions to interference in his tactical decisions. "There may be less opposition than we expected, but there's still enough to hand us some nasty lumps. And their Home Fleet is still no more than forty to forty-eight hours from Medusa even if it has to come all the way from Manticore orbit." He shook his head. "Hopefully their units will try to come through piecemeal and let Citizen Rear Admiral Darlington chop them up, but if anything goes wrong at that end, they can put a hell of a lot more firepower into this system than *we* have. I think we'll just continue the profile and head straight for a fly-by firing run on Medusa. Unless, of course, you wish to proceed in some other fashion, Ma'am?"

"No, Citizen Admiral," she said in chill tones.

"Excellent," he replied, and folded his hands behind him and turned back to the plot.

Chapter Thirty-Seven

Despite the temperature setting, most of the people in Basilisk ACS' central control room were sweating hard as they tried to cope. The initial reaction of the merchant traffic awaiting transit had been confusion, promptly followed by a panic that was as inevitable as it was irrational. They were ten light-hours from the Peeps' obvious objective, and every hostile starship in the vicinity was headed for Medusa, which meant almost directly away from them. There was ample time to get every one of them through the Junction and safely out of harm's way, and even if there hadn't been, they were far outside the Basilisk hyper limit. The FTL sensor net would give plenty of warning if any of the Peeps turned around and headed this way, and it would be relatively simple to duck into hyper and vanish long before the enemy could possibly get here.

Those comforting reflections, however, did not appear to be foremost in the minds of the merchant skippers arguing vociferously with Michel Reynaud's controllers. Lieutenant Carluchi and her pinnaces had already been required to physically intervene to keep a big Andermani ore ship and a Solarian freighter loaded with agricultural delicacies for the inner League worlds from jumping the queue.

Despite his fury with both skippers and a personal dislike for the Solarian League which had grown with each report of technology transfers to the Peeps, Reynaud could summon up rather more sympathy for the Solly than for the Andy. Asteroid ore was scarcely a perishable commodity, and the skipper's flight plan indicated he was on a fairly leisurely routing anyway. But while the Solly was less than two hours out of Sigma Draconis on a direct transit via the Junction, she would add over two T-months to her voyage just to reach Manticore the long way if she was forced to run for it in hyper. And her cargo was about as perishible as they came. Understanding the reasons for the woman's blustering anxiety hadn't made him any more patient with her, however, and he'd watched with satisfaction as Carluchi's pinnaces chivvied her ship back into line.

That was the *only* satisfaction he was feeling at the moment, however, and he darted a look at the main plot. The six dreadnoughts and eight battlecruisers composing the terminus picket had headed in-system at maximum acceleration the instant the first report came in. They couldn't possibly arrive in time to intercept the Peeps before they hit Medusa, but their CO could hardly just sit here and watch the system fall. The dreadnoughts had all received new compensators, but they were only second-generation upgrades with no more than a six percent efficiency boost over the old style. Nonetheless, Rear Admiral Hanaby was running them at full military power—right on four hundred and eighty gravities—and she'd been underway for ten minutes now. She was over eight hundred thousand kilometers from the terminus, up to a velocity of twenty-eight hundred kilometers per second and still accelerating at 4.706 KPS^2, and as he watched the icons of her ships moving further and further from his command area, Michel Reynaud felt a chill of loneliness.

Hanaby's departure didn't leave the terminus completely unprotected. But the outbreak of hostilities and the more immediate needs of the Fleet had cut deeply into the funding originally appropriated to pay for the deep-space fortresses that had been supposed to protect the Basilisk terminus . . . and into the priority assigned to their construction, as well. What had been planned as a shell of eighteen sixteen-million-ton forts had been downgraded to ten . . . and only two of those had actually been completed. The other eight were anywhere from six T-months to a T-year from readiness—which put the most advanced of them something like five T-years behind the prewar schedule—and Reynaud gritted his teeth at the thought. Two fortresses should be ample to stand off any Peep battlecruisers which might be hiding out there to come running in and jump on the terminus from which Hanaby had withdrawn, but if there was something bigger and nastier in the offing . . .

He turned his mind away from that thought once again and concentrated on his own job.

"*What?*" The Earl of White Haven jerked around to face Commander McTierney. His com officer's face was pale, and her right hand pressed against her earbug as if she thought screwing it physically inside her head could force what it had just told her to make sense.

"The Peeps are attacking Basilisk, Sir," she repeated in shock-flattened tones still echoing with disbelief, and for once her Sphinxian accent did not remind White Haven painfully of Honor. "ACS has declared Case Zulu and began clearing the terminus of shipping six—No," she glanced at the time display, "*seven* minutes ago. Enemy strength estimate when Vice Admiral Reynaud dispatched his courier was a minimum of twenty superdreadnoughts with a light cruiser screen."

"My *God*," someone whispered behind White Haven, and he felt all expression vanish from his own face as the implications hammered over him. Basilisk. They were hitting *Basilisk*, and not with any raid-and-run force of battlecruisers, either. Twenty superdreadnoughts were more than enough to take out the entire Basilisk picket, given the way its strength had been drawn down—*in no small part to build up* your *wall of battle, Hamish!* a corner of his brain whispered—even if it hadn't been spread between Medusa and the terminus itself.

And after they punch out Markham's task force, they'll destroy every single installation in Medusa orbit, he thought with a dull sense of horror. *Will they give the orbit bases' personnel time to evacuate? Of* course *they will . . . unless their CO is one of the new regime's fanatics. But even if they do allow an evac, that's still sixty* T-years' *worth of infrastructure. My God! Who* knows *how many trillions of dollars of investment it represents? How in* hell *will we manage to replace it in the middle of a damned war?*

The ringing silence about him returned no answers to his questions, but then another, even uglier thought suggested itself to him.

"Did Reynaud say anything about Admiral Hanaby's intentions?" he demanded.

"No, Sir." McTierny shook her head, and White Haven scowled. Reynaud should have passed that information along, but the earl reminded himself to cut the ACS man some slack. For what was basically a uniformed civilian, he'd already done more than White Haven had a right to expect. Which didn't make the lack of information any more palatable.

Still, he thought, *you already know what Hanaby is doing, don't you? Exactly what any admiral worth her gold braid would do: steering for the sound of the guns.*

Which may be exactly what the enemy wants her to do.

He frowned down at the plot that showed his own command still holding station forty-five light-seconds from the Trevor's Star terminus of the Junction, and his thought stream flashed too rapidly for him to split it down into its component parts. His staff stood behind him on *Benjamin the Great*'s flag deck, staring at his back, with no idea what thoughts were pouring through his head. Their own brains were still too shocked to think coherently, but they could see the weight of his conclusions pressing down on him, see his broad shoulders slowly hunching to take the weight. And then he turned back to them once more, his face set and hard, and began to snap orders.

"Cindy, record the following message to Admiral Webster. Message begins: 'Jim, keep your ships where they are. This could be a trick to draw Home Fleet into Basilisk to clear the way for an attack on the capital. Eighth Fleet will move immediately to Basilisk.' Message ends."

Someone hissed audibly behind him, and his mouth twitched without humor at the reaction. *They should have thought of that possibility for themselves*, he thought distantly, but his eyes never moved from McTierney.

"Recorded, Sir," she replied. Her voice was still shaken, but her eyes were coming back to life and she nodded sharply.

"Good. Second message, this one to CO Manticore ACS Central. Message begins: 'Admiral Yestremensky, upon my authority, you will clear all traffic—I repeat, *all* traffic—from the Manticore–Basilisk queue immediately and stand by for a Fleet priority transit.' Message ends."

"Recorded," McTierney confirmed again.

"New message," White Haven rapped, "this one to Rear Admiral Hanaby via Basilisk ACS. Message begins: 'Admiral Hanaby, I am headed to relieve Basilisk at my best speed from Trevor's Star via the Junction with forty-nine of the wall, forty battlecruisers, and screen.'"

"Recorded, Sir."

"Very well. I want information copies repeated to the Admiralty, special attention Admiral Caparelli and Admiral Givens, to Vice Admiral Reynaud, and to Vice Admiral Markham," White Haven went on with staccato clarity. "Standard encryption and code, Priority One. As soon as you've got them coded up, transmit them to Admiral Reynaud's courier boat."

"Aye, aye, Sir."

White Haven gave her a curt nod, then turned to his chief of staff and his ops officer.

"Alyson," he told Captain Granston-Henley, "I want you to grab that courier boat and send it straight back to Manticore as soon as Cindy's transmitted my message. Then I want you and Trevor to build me a transit plan: Trevor's Star to Manticore to Basilisk."

"Yes, Sir." Granston-Henley shook herself, as if to clear the last echoes of stupification from her brain and glanced at Commander Haggerston, then looked back at White Haven. "Standard translation order, Sir?" she asked.

"No." The earl shook his head curtly. "There's no time for a nice, neat, orderly transit; we'll send them through as fast as we can, in whatever order they reach the terminus. If it's a choice between a capital ship and a screening unit, the capital ship goes first; otherwise, it's strictly on an 'on arrival' basis. And, Alyson—" he looked straight into her eyes "—I want this set up to go quickly. Ships will move to the terminus at maximum military power, and transit windows are to be cut to the minimum *possible*, not the minimum allowed. Use the courier boat to inform Manticore ACS of that intention, as well."

"I—" Granston-Henley began, then stopped herself. "Yes, Sir. Understood," she said quietly, and White Haven nodded and turned back to his plot once more.

He understood Granston-Henley's reaction, but he had no choice. His fleet was forty-five light-seconds from the Trevor's Star terminus. A destroyer with the latest compensator could accelerate at six hundred and twenty gravities with its safety margin cut to zero, but his superdreadnoughts could manage only four hundred and sixty-six with the same generation of compensator. That meant his destroyer screen could reach the local terminus on a least-time course in approximately thirty-five minutes while his SDs would need closer to forty-one. But a least-time course allowed no room for turnover and deceleration, and this large a force would have no choice but to decelerate to zero relative to the terminus before making transit, however urgent the crisis. And *that* meant those same destroyers would take fifty minutes while the SDs took just over fifty-seven. And once they'd gotten there, they still had to make transit—not once, but twice—just to get to the Basilisk terminus.

Nor could they go through together. Oh, it was tempting. There was an absolute ceiling on the amount of tonnage which could transit through any wormhole junction. In the case of the Manticore Junction, the maximum possible mass for a single transit was approximately two hundred million tons, which meant he could put that much of Eighth Fleet's wall—twenty-two SDs, for all practical purposes—through the junction in one, convulsive heave. Unfortunately, any wormhole transit destabilized the termini involved for a minimum of ten seconds, and vessels which massed more than about two and a half million tons destabilized it for a total interval proportional to the square of the transiting mass . . . which meant a maximum-mass transit would lock the route from Manticore to Basilisk solid for over seventeen hours.

If twenty-two superdreadnoughts were sufficient to deal with what White Haven feared the Peeps might be up to, that would pose no problem. But they might not be, and he had fifteen more of them, plus twelve dreadnoughts, under his command. They were the only ships which could possibly reach Basilisk in less than thirty hours, and he dared not leave any of them behind.

But that meant sending them through one by one. As long as there were no hostile units in range to engage them as they threaded the needle back into n-space, there was no tactical reason why he shouldn't do that, and he should know whether or not any bad guys were likely to be in range before he began sending them through. Yet each individual transit would *also* destabilize the junction route, even if for vastly shorter periods.

His screening units, up to and including his battlecruisers, would each produce a ten-second blockage of the route for whoever came next in line, but his dreadnoughts would close the route for almost seventy seconds and each superdreadnought would shut it down for a hundred and thirteen. Which meant that cramming his entire fleet through would require a minimum of a hundred and eight minutes. Add in the time required just to reach the Trevor's Star terminus, and it would be over a hundred and sixty-six minutes—over two and three-quarters hours—before his last ship could possibly reach Basilisk.

That was an immensely shorter response time than for anyone else, but it was still too long to save Medusa. And to achieve even that, he had to cut the transit windows to the bare minimum, which was going to give ACS fits. Under normal circumstances, the minimum allowable transit window was one minute. Usually the windows actually ran considerably longer than that, since the number of ships awaiting passage was seldom large enough to cause ACS to push the minimum. But that limitation had been adopted for a very simple reason: to give people time to get out of the way.

A ship made transit under Warshawski sail. Those sails provided no propulsion in n-space, but a wormhole junction was best thought of as a frozen funnel of hyper-space which happened to connect to n-space at either end. That meant sails not only could be used in a junction transit, but that the transiting vessel had no option but to use them. And that, in turn, meant each ship had to reconfigure its impeller nodes from sail to wedge as it emerged from the far side of the wormhole. Its sails would leave it with some momentum, but not very much, and if the lead ship in a transit was even a little tardy reconfiguring and the one astern of it ran up its backside—

White Haven shuddered at the thought, but he knew how *he* would have set up this attack, and knowing that, he had to get into Basilisk as quickly as he possibly could. And so he watched his plot, his face grim and set, as Eighth Fleet began to accelerate towards the local terminus at its best possible speed.

Admiral Leslie Yestremensky, Manticore ACS, stared at the message on her display in disbelief. Forty-nine ships of the wall? He was going to bring *forty-nine ships of the wall* through her wormhole at minimum intervals? He was insane!

But he was also the third-ranking serving officer of the Royal Manticoran Navy, and in wartime that gave him the right to be just as crazy as he wanted. Which wasn't going to make the disaster one bit less appalling if anyone's numbers were off by as little as one ten-thousandth of a percent.

She shook herself and checked the time. At least she still had over half an hour before the first of the lunatic's destroyers arrived. Maybe she could do a little something to reduce the scale of the catastrophe she felt coming.

"All right, people," she announced in a clear, ringing voice which showed no sign of her own horror. "We've got a Category One Alpha emergency. Manticore ACS is proclaiming Condition Delta. All outgoing merchant shipping will be cleared from the Junction immediately. Dispatch, tag a message to that courier boat before you let it go back to Basilisk. Inform Vice Admiral Reynaud that he will halt all outbound traffic from Basilisk thirty minutes from now. There will be no exceptions, and he may inform any merchant master who objects that he is acting under my authority as per Article Four, Section Three, of the Junction Transit Instructions."

"Yes, Ma'am," Dispatch said. Manticore ACS tended to be rather more formal than the crews who worked the Junction's secondary termini, but it was stunned shock, not discipline, that wrung that "Ma'am" from Commander Adamon.

"Jeff, Sam, and Serena," Yestremensky went on, her index finger jabbing like a targeting laser as she made her selections. "The three of you turn your boards over to your reliefs. We've got a two-hundred-ship, minimum-window, double transit coming at us, and you're elected to supervise it. Get started planning now."

"Two *hundred* ships?" Serena Ustinov repeated, as if she were positive she must have misunderstood somehow.

"Two hundred," Yestremensky confirmed grimly. "Now get cracking. You're down to . . . forty-three minutes before the first one comes in from Trevor's Star."

Michel Reynaud listened to Admiral White Haven's clipped, gunshot voice and pursed his lips in a silent whistle. He'd never participated in a transit of such magnitude. For that matter, no one had, and relieved as he was by the thought of reinforcements, the potential for disaster twisted his stomach into an acid-oozing ball of lead. But no one had asked him, and he turned to his staff.

"Heavy metal coming through from Manticore in thirty-eight minutes," he told them. "All outbound transits are to cease twenty-five minutes from now. Anyone we can't get through in that time frame is to be diverted immediately. I want the holding area as well as both the inbound and outbound lanes cleared in precisely twenty-six minutes, 'cause we're sure as hell going to need the space to park warships. Now move it, people, and don't take any crap!"

The emergency had already stretched the voices that replied too wire-thin for them to register fresh shock, but he felt the disbelief under the surface and his mouth twitched in a wry grin. But then the grin faded as he glanced back into the master plot. Rear Admiral Hanaby had been underway for nineteen minutes now. She was over three million kilometers away . . . and message or no message, she showed no signs of slowing down.

Well, I suppose it makes sense, he thought. *We've got the two forts to watch out for us till White Haven gets here, and with someone coming in behind to watch the back door, she must feel even more pressure to get into the inner system ASAP. She can't change what happens to Markham, but if she gets there quick enough, close enough on the Peeps' heels, they may not have enough time to wreck the orbital stations completely.*

He snorted contemptuously at his own desperate need for optimism, and returned to his duties.

"Time to Medusa intercept, Franny?" Giscard asked quietly.

"Fifty-nine minutes, Citizen Admiral," Tyler replied. "Current closing velocity is thirty-point-niner-two thousand KPS; range one-fifty-point-two-five-five million klicks." The Citizen Admiral nodded and looked at MacIntosh.

"Are we ready, Andy?"

"Yes, Citizen Admiral," the ops officer said. "The enemy's velocity is up to just over nine thousand KPS—closure rate is . . . twenty-three-point-one-five-two KPS, and range is just under a hundred thirty-nine million klicks. Assuming all headings and accelerations remain constant, we'll hit a zero-range intercept in almost exactly forty-six minutes."

"Very good." Giscard nodded and glanced at Pritchart from the corner of one eye. At moments like this, he almost wished he had one of the other people's commissioners—the sort he wouldn't miss if *Salamis* happened to take a hit on Flag Bridge. And also at moments like this he bitterly resented the game they had to play, the way it kept him from looking at her, holding her while they waited for the missile storm. But wishing and resenting changed nothing, and he locked his eyes resolutely on his plot.

The Manties were coming hell for leather, and he didn't blame them. Even with their present high accel, his task group would be only thirteen minutes' flight from Medusa when their vectors converged. *If* their vectors converged. It was hardly likely that the Manties would break off at this late date, but they had to survive clear across his missile zone to get to energy range . . . and even with a closure rate of over sixty thousand KPS, he doubted very much that any of them would.

He grimaced at the thought, already feeling the weight of all the deaths about to occur. Yet what made him grimace was the fact that even knowing the nightmares he would face in years to come, he was eager for it. His Navy had been humiliated too many times. Too many men and women he'd known and liked—even loved—had been killed, and he was sick unto death of the handicaps under which he had taken other men and women into battle so many times. Now it was his turn, and if his execution of Esther McQueen's plan was working even half as well as the two of them had hoped, he was about to hurt the Royal Manticoran Navy as it had never been hurt. Hand it not one but an entire series of simultaneous defeats such as it had not known in its entire four-hundred-year history.

Yes, he thought coldly. *Let's see how* your *damned morale holds up after this, you bastards.*

Chapter Thirty-Eight

Michel Reynaud heaved a sigh of relief as the last protesting merchant skipper moved aside before the implacable approach of Cynthia Carluchi's pinnaces. A good quarter of the waiting merchantmen had already taken themselves off into hyper, where they were undoubtedly putting as many light-seconds as possible between themselves and Basilisk. The others—less than twenty ships all told, now—remained, hovering just beyond the half light-second volume of the terminus in hopes that normalcy would be restored and they would still be able to make transit to Manticore.

Personally, Reynaud didn't think there was a chance in hell "normalcy" would be restored to Basilisk any time soon.

He grunted at the thought and checked his plot once more. Almost exactly one hour had passed since the Peeps first turned up, and they were considerably less than nine light-minutes out from Medusa. Admiral Markham's horribly outnumbered task group was headed to intercept them, and Reynaud's stomach churned every time he thought of what would happen when they met.

Admiral Hanaby had been underway for forty-four minutes now, which put her over sixteen million klicks from the terminus, with her velocity up to 12,424 KPS. Which sounded impressive as hell, he thought bitterly, until he reflected that it meant she'd covered almost exactly one-and-a-half percent of the distance between the terminus and Basilisk. But at least the first of White Haven's destroyers should be arriving within another thirteen minutes, and—

An alarm shrilled. Michel Reynaud jerked bolt upright in his chair, and his face went paper white as the blood-bright icons of unidentified hyper footprints blossomed suddenly on his plot.

Citizen Rear Admiral Gregor Darlington swore with silent savagery as the plot stabilized. He felt his astrogator cringing behind him, and he wanted to turn around and rip the unfortunate citizen commander a brand-new rectum. It would have done the citizen admiral an enormous amount of good to vent his fury, but he couldn't. It wasn't really Citizen Commander Huff's fault, and even if it had been, Darlington would never have raked him down in front of a people's commissioner. The People's Navy had given up enough martyrs as scapegoats.

"I see we seem to have misplaced a decimal point, Gorg," he said instead, unable to keep an edge of harshness out of his voice, however hard he tried. Then he cleared his throat. "How bad is it?"

"We . . . overshot by one-point-three light-minutes, Citizen Admiral," Citizen Commander Huff replied. "Call it twenty-three-point-seven million klicks."

"I see." Darlington folded his hands behind him and rocked on his toes, digesting the information. Of course, it wasn't quite as simple as "overshot" might be taken to imply, he thought grimly. Task Group 12.4.2 had been *supposed* to emerge from hyper four million klicks from the Basilisk terminus, headed directly towards it with a velocity of five thousand kilometers per second. That would have put them in missile range and firing by the time the defenders could realize they were coming. And with any luck at all, the picket force normally stationed on the terminus would have been headed in-system at max for a full hour, which would have put those ships safely out of the way and left only the two operational forts to deal with. Thirty-two million tons of fort would still have been a handful, but he had eight dreadnoughts, twelve battleships, and four battlecruisers—a better than three-to-one edge in tonnage—and he should have had the invaluable advantage of complete and total surprise, as well.

But Citizen Commander Huff had blown it. In fairness, it was expecting a great deal to ask anyone to cut a hyper translation that close, but that was exactly what he'd been trained for years to do . . . and the reason TG 12.4.2 had dropped back into n-space less than two light-months out to allow him to recalibrate and recalculate. And he hadn't actually missed it by all that much, had he? His error was—what? Less than two-thousandths of a percent of the total jump? But it was enough.

"Time to decelerate and return to the terminus?" the citizen rear admiral demanded after a moment.

"We'll need about twenty-one minutes at four KPS squared to decelerate to relative zero," Huff said, watching the back of the citizen admiral's neck carefully. He saw its muscles tighten, and though there was no explosion, he decided not to mention that the battleship component could have decelerated considerably faster than that if they left the dreadnoughts behind. Citizen Admiral Darlington knew that as well as he did; if he wanted the numbers for just the battleships, he'd ask.

"After that," the citizen commander went on, working furiously at his console as he spoke, "we'll be just over thirty million kilometers out. A zero/zero intercept with the terminus would take us a hundred and eleven minutes from now, with turnover for the original braking maneuver at twenty-one minutes and for the intercept at sixty-six minutes from now. A least-time course would get us to range zero in . . . eighty-four-point-three minutes from now, but our relative velocity at intercept would be almost sixteen thousand KPS."

"Um." Darlington grunted and bounced on his toes once more. The Manties had seen him now; their forts were bringing up every jammer they had, including some remote platforms that seemed to be doing things the PN had never heard of before, and decoys were lighting off all over the place, as well. The entire area of the terminus was disappearing into a huge ball of electronic and gravitic fuzz that his sensors would be unable to penetrate at ranges much above four million kilometers. That was bad. On the other hand, he had a fix on the Manty dreadnoughts and battlecruisers normally assigned to watch the terminus, and they were a hell of a lot further from it than he was.

"Time for the Manty picket force to return to the terminus?" he demanded of his ops officer.

"Forty-five-point-two minutes just to kill their present in-system vector, Citizen Admiral," the ops officer said instantly. Clearly he'd been anticipating his CO's thoughts . . . and had no intention of being caught out like the unfortunate Huff. "At that point, they'll be almost two light-minutes in-system, and they'll need ninety more minutes to get back here. Assuming they begin decelerating immediately, call it a hundred and thirty-five minutes.

"Thank you." Darlington pondered a moment longer. He didn't like closing into all that jamming. Even with his Solarian-upgraded ECM and sensors, he'd have to cross something just under a million kilometers in which they'd be able to shoot at him, but he couldn't pick out a clear target to shoot back at. At the relatively low closing velocity he could generate between now and then, it would take him almost a minute to cross that fire zone. Which wouldn't have been all that bad if he hadn't been confident those forts were going to have missile pods—*lots* of missile pods—deployed and waiting for him.

He considered nipping back into hyper and trying to micro-jump his way to the terminus, but he rejected the notion almost instantly. Superficially appealing though it might be, a hyper jump this short was actually more difficult for an astrogator to calculate, not less. That, no doubt, was the reason the Manty picket commander was headed for Medusa in n-space instead of hyper. Control had to be so fine at such low ranges that something as small as a tiny difference in the cycle time of the hyper generators of two different ships could throw their n-space emergences off by light-seconds and hopelessly scramble his formation. No, either he pulled out completely, or he went back the hard way. Dicking around with still more hyper jumps would simply invite the ancient curse of order, counter order, disorder, and he had enough crap to deal with already.

He glanced at Citizen Commissioner Leopold.

"With your permission, Sir, I believe we should reverse course immediately and come back at the terminus."

"Can we still defeat the fortresses?" Leopold asked, not even glancing at Huff—which, Darlington reflected, boded ill for the citizen commander when Leopold turned in his report.

"I believe so, Sir. We'll take heavier losses than the ops plan originally contemplated, but we should be able to secure control of the terminus. Whether we can carry through and maintain control until Citizen Admiral Giscard rejoins us is another matter, however. The terminus picket has almost as many dreadnoughts as we do. They can be here well before Citizen Admiral Giscard if they reverse course promptly, and if they do that and we've taken heavy damage from the forts, then I doubt we could stand them off *and* pick off anything making transit from the Manties' Home Fleet. On the other hand, we're well outside the hyper limit here. If we see a force we can't fight coming at us, we can retreat into hyper immediately. That," he added quietly, "was the reason Citizen Admiral Giscard was willing to contemplate this maneuver in the first place, Sir. Because we can always run away if the odds turn to crap on us."

"I see." Leopold considered for several seconds, then nodded. "Very well, Citizen Admiral. Make it so."

"Citizen Commander," Darlington said, turning to Huff, "we'll go with the least-time course. We should have time to decelerate and come back again—" he managed, somehow, not to stress the adverb "—if their terminus picket wants a fight, and I want to cross their forts' missile zone as quickly as possible."

"Aye, Citizen Admiral," Huff said, and began passing maneuvering orders to the rest of the task group.

Reynaud smothered a groan as the fresh Peep force began to decelerate. He knew exactly what they'd intended to do, and exactly how it had gone wrong, but the fact that it had didn't make him feel much better. He could run the numbers just as well as they could, and his fingers flew as he punched them into his plot. But then he felt his spine slowly stiffen as the new vectors blinked in the plot before him.

The Peeps could be here in roughly eighty-five minutes—into missile range, even with the jamming, in about eighty-four—and unlike the Peeps, Reynaud knew that the operational forts' supply of missile pods was dangerously low. The two of them together probably couldn't put more than a hundred and fifty into space. But Eighth Fleet's first destroyer would arrive in eleven minutes . . . and its first *super-dreadnought* would be here in twenty-six. And assuming White Haven could actually pull it off without turning his capital ships into billiard balls (or expanding plasma), another SD would arrive every one hundred and thirteen seconds after that. So he could have . . .

The Astro Control vice admiral's fingers flashed, and a most unpleasant smile appeared on his face.

Vice Admiral Markham felt his heart spasm as the FTL net reported the arrival of still more enemies. He realized as quickly as Reynaud what the original Peep intent had been, and the bitterness and despair he fought to keep out of his expression deepened at the fresh proof of how utterly the RMN had underestimated the "defensive minded" People's Navy.

But he also knew, thanks to the FTL com relays between the terminus and Medusa, that Eighth Fleet was on its way, and he bared his teeth in a death's head grin as he, too, worked the numbers on its arrival time. It didn't change what was going to happen to his own task group, of course. Nothing short of a direct act of God could have changed that. But it *did* change what was going to happen to the Peep bastards who thought they were going to kill the terminus forts and then wait to ambush Home Fleet if it tried to respond.

"Missile range in thirty-nine minutes, Sir," his ops officer said quietly, and he nodded.

"I wonder how Citizen Admiral Giscard is making out," Citizen Commisioner Leopold said quietly, and Darlington turned his head to meet his eyes. The people's commissioner had spoken softly enough no one else could have heard, and the citizen admiral replied equally quietly.

"Probably just fine, so far, Sir," he said. "I doubt he's made contact with their main force yet."

"I wish we could know what was happening to him," Leopold said, and Darlington shrugged.

"If we had the FTL relays the Manties have, we could, Sir. Without them, we can only guess. But it doesn't really matter. Nothing that happens that far in-system can have any immediate effect on us, and even if the Medusa picket turned out to be a hell of a lot heavier than we thought and it killed every one of the Citizen Admiral's ships and then came after us, we'd have plenty of warning to hyper out before it got here."

He glanced back up, and his mouth twitched as he saw the stricken look on Leopold's face.

"I didn't mean that I think anything of the sort is going to happen, Citizen Commissioner," he said with a barely suppressed chuckle. "I only meant to present a worst-possible-case scenario."

"Oh." Leopold swallowed, then smiled wanly. "I see. But in future, Citizen Admiral, please tell me *ahead* of time that that's what you're doing."

"I'll remember, Sir," Darlington promised.

✧ ✧ ✧

The air-conditioned chill of Basilisk ACS' control room was a thing of the past. Vice Admiral Reynaud felt the sweat dripping down his face as his controllers hovered over their consoles, and even though he saw it with his own eyes, he could scarcely believe what was happening.

Thirty-nine destroyers hovered just beyond the terminus threshold. They'd come through in a steady stream, as rapidly and remorselessly as an old, prespace freight train, and Reynaud had felt like some small, terrified animal frozen on the rails as the train's headlamp thundered down upon him. But he'd handed each warship off to its own controller, cycling through the available list with feverish speed, and somehow—he still wasn't sure how—they'd managed to avoid outright collisions.

But not all damage. HMS *Glorioso* had been just a fraction of a second too slow reconfiguring from sails to wedge, and HMS *Vixen* had run right up her backside. Fortunately, perhaps, the second destroyer *had* gotten her wedge up quickly, for it had come on-line one bare instant before *Glorioso*'s had, but without building to full power. Which meant that only *Glorioso*'s after nodes had blown. The resultant explosion had vaporized two-thirds of her after impeller room, and Reynaud had no desire at all to think about how many people it must have killed when it went, but it hadn't destroyed her hull or her compensator, and the fail-safes had blown in time to save her forward impellers. Momentum, coupled with instantaneous and brilliant evasive action on *Vixen*'s part, had been just sufficient to carry her clear of an outright collision, and two of her sisters had speared her with tractors and dragged her bodily out of the way of *Vixen*'s next astern. But for all that, it had been impossibly close. A thousandth of a second's difference in when either wedge came on-line, a dozen meters difference in their relative locations, a single split-second of distraction on the part of *Vixen*'s watch officer or helmsman, and not only would *they* have collided, but the next ship in line would have plowed straight into their molten wreckage in the beginning of a chain-reaction collision that could have killed thousands.

But they'd avoided it, and now the first superdreadnoughts were coming through. The huge ships were much slower on the helm, but they were almost as quick to reconfigure from sails to wedge, and their longer transit windows gave them precious additional seconds to maneuver. They were actually easier to handle than the destroyers had been, and Reynaud leaned back in his chair and mopped the skim of sweat from his forehead.

"Did it, by God," someone whispered, and he looked over his shoulder. All four watches had assembled, which meant he had more controllers than he did consoles, and the off-duty people with nothing to do were probably in the least enviable position of all. They knew how insanely dangerous this entire maneuver was, but there was nothing they could do about it except hold their breaths and pray whenever things looked dicey. But now Neville Underwood, the number-three man on the fourth watch, stepped up beside his own command chair and shook his head as he gazed down into the plot.

"Maybe yes, and maybe no," Reynaud replied. "We've got three—no, four—SDs through with no collisions so far. But if two of *those* babies bump—" He shuddered, and Underwood nodded soberly. "And even if we don't have any collisions, there's always the chance the Peeps'll detect them and stay the hell out of range."

"Maybe," Underwood conceded. "But they'll need damned good sensors to pick up their arrivals through all the jamming the forts are putting out. And once our people maneuver clear and take their wedges down to station-keeping levels, they should be downright invisible at anything above a few light-seconds. Besides," he summoned up a ragged smile, "at this point I'll be delighted to settle for the Peeps staying the hell away. It beats the crap out of what I *thought* was going to happen to us, Mike!"

"Yeah," Reynaud grunted, turning back to his console. "Yeah, I guess it does, at that. But I want these bastards, Nev. I want them bad."

Underwood eyed him sidelong. Michel Reynaud was one of the easiest going—and least military—people he knew. In fact, Underwood had always suspected that the reason Reynaud had gone ACS instead of Navy in the first place was his deep-seated, fundamental horror at the thought of deliberately taking another human being's life. But he didn't feel that way now, and when Underwood glanced at the display tied into the FTL sensors, he understood exactly why that was.

Vice Admiral Markham's gallant charge was less than twenty minutes from contact with the main Peep force, and Reynaud and Underwood both knew what would happen then.

"Their EW is getting even better, Citizen Admiral," Darlington's ops officer reported. The citizen rear admiral walked over to stand beside him, looking down at the hazy sphere that had enveloped the terminus, and frowned.

"Are their jammers hitting us harder?" he asked.

"No, Citizen Admiral. Or I don't think so, at least. But look here and here." The ops officer keyed a command, and the plot blinked as it replayed what had happened over the last several minutes at a compressed time rate. "See?" He pointed at the flickering shift of questionable icons in the display. "It looks to me like their decoys must be considerably more advanced and flexible than we'd thought, Citizen Admiral. We've still got probable fixes on the forts themselves, but our confidence in them is degrading steadily because they're throwing so damned many false impeller signatures at us."

"Well, we knew it was going to happen." Darlington sighed after a moment. "Do your best, Citizen Commander."

"Yes, Citizen Admiral."

White Haven stood stock still on *Benjamin the Great*'s flag bridge and stared at the order slowly gelling in the depths of the master plot. He'd brought his Grayson SDs through first, because even if it might hurt the Royal Navy's pride to admit it, they were newer, more powerful units than most of his Manticoran ships. Eight of them were through the Junction now, with three more to go and the first Manticoran units following on behind them. He'd gotten here in time to defend the terminus against the second prong of the Peep attack, but his pride at his achievement tasted of ashes and gall.

It wasn't because of the damage to *Glorioso*, or even the loss of life entailed. The destroyer's list of known dead already stood at thirty-five, and dozens of people remained unaccounted for, dead or trapped in the tangled wreckage of her after half. He felt the weight of those deaths, knew they were his responsibility and his alone. But in eight bloody years of war he had learned that there were *always* deaths. The best a wartime commander could hope for was to minimize the toll, to lose no more than he could possibly avoid . . . and to make certain the lives he could not save were not bartered away too cheaply.

Nor did this leaden fist crush down upon his heart because Rear Admiral Hanaby hadn't even tried to reverse course. That was her smartest move, he conceded—for all the good it would accomplish. The only thing she could realistically hope to do now was to put some sense of time pressure on the main Peep force, and she could never have gotten back to the terminus in time to affect the outcome there, anyway.

But she wasn't going to save Vice Admiral Markham . . . and neither was White Haven's brilliant transfer from Trevor's Star.

He drew a deep breath and made himself turn away from the main plot to look at the smaller display tied into the in-system FTL net. He didn't want to. There was a peculiarly detached, mesmerizing horror about seeing something like this in real-time and yet not being close enough to somehow forbid it or alter the outcome. But he could no more not have looked than he could have stopped it from happening.

Diamond dust icons speckled the plot as both sides flushed their pods and the missiles went out. Markham launched first, and his fire control was better, but the Peeps had many more birds than he did. There was a mechanistic inevitability to it, a sense that he was watching not the clash of human adversaries, but some dreadful, insensate disaster produced by the unthinking forces of nature.

A distant corner of his mind noted the huge numbers of incoming missiles Markham's ships picked off or fooled with their ECM and decoys, but it wasn't enough. It couldn't have been, and he bit his lip until he tasted blood as the first Manticoran superdreadnought vanished from the plot. Then another died—a second. A third. A fourth. A fifth. Three of them survived the opening exchange, led by *King William*, but the flickering sidebars of damage codes told how savagely wounded they were as they closed to energy range of the Peeps behind their flagship. The butchery grew suddenly even worse, yet no one flinched, no one surrendered—not on either side.

Two Peep superdreadnoughts had died with *King William*'s consorts, and others had been damaged, if none had been hurt so dreadfully as the Manticoran ships of the wall. Now the two forces slammed together and interpenetrated, short-range weapons ripping and tearing with brief, titanic fury.

It took only seconds, and when it was over, two more Peep SDs had been destroyed. At least three more were severely damaged . . . and every single ship of Vice Admiral Silas Markham's task group had been obliterated.

A spreading lacework of life pods beaded the display, Manticoran and Havenite alike. The pattern they made was less dense than the missile storms had been, and here and there one winked out as battle-damaged life-support systems or transponders failed. White Haven's lips worked as if to spit, but then he wrenched his eyes away from the secondary plot as the first Manticoran superdreadnought of Eighth Fleet came out of the Junction behind him. He darted a bitter, hating look at the dreadnoughts and battleships accelerating steadily towards him, and his face was hard.

"*Our* turn now, you bastards," he murmured to himself, so softly no one else ever heard at all, and beckoned Commander Haggerston over beside him.

Javier Giscard handed the memo board back to the skinsuited yeoman. The hammering *Salamis* had taken in the last few seconds of the engagement made him wonder if the Manties had somehow deduced that she was the task group flagship, but it turned out that Citizen Captain Short had had good reason to feel confident about the quality of her techs back in Secour. Giscard intended to have a little talk with her, find out just how she'd managed to pull the strings to get her hands on a fully qualified engineering department in the present day People's Navy, but for now it didn't really matter. What mattered was that, according to the report he'd just been handed, *Salamis* would have all of her alpha nodes back within twenty-five minutes. That was good. In fact, it was outstanding, for it meant his flagship—unlike her consort *Guichen*—would be able to withdraw if that became necessary.

He sighed and lowered himself into his command chair, then raised a hand at Julia Lapisch. The com officer looked up, then trotted over to him.

"Yes, Citizen Admiral?" she asked. That withdrawn, disconnected edge remained somewhere inside her, but her gray-green eyes glowed with a sort of dark fire. Giscard wasn't certain what that meant. It was almost as if in the last few minutes she had seen something more terrifying than even StateSec could be, a threat which had put the relative threat of the SS into a different perspective in her mind. Or it could simply be that she had just discovered that, as someone on Old Earth had once put it, "Nothing in the world is so exhilarating as to be shot at . . . and missed."

"Are you ready to transmit?" he asked her now, and she nodded. "Yes, Citizen Admiral."

"Then do so," he instructed, and she nodded again and headed back towards her console, right hand above her head while she whirled her index finger in a "crank it up" signal to her assistants.

Giscard leaned back in his chair and rubbed his closed eyes. His ships had been decelerating from the moment they opened fire on the Manties, and they were still decelerating hard. But their base velocity was too high to kill. He was going to slide right past Medusa, and all he could do was slow it down, stretch the pass out a bit . . . and give the Manties a little longer to evacuate their orbital installations.

He sighed. This was what he had come for, the part he had most looked forward to and, conversely, dreaded. The destruction of eight Manticoran SDs had been worth accomplishing, even if he had lost four—five, probably, as he would have to leave *Guichen* behind if he was forced to pull out—of his own to accomplish it. But it was the devastation of Basilisk Station, the utter destruction of Medusa's orbital bases and Gregor Darlington's destruction of their incomplete fortresses and Basilisk Astro Control, which would strike the true blow. It would be a shot not to the body of the Star Kingdom, but to its soul, for this was no frontier fleet base or allied system. Medusa was *Manticoran* territory, as much an integral part of the Star Kingdom as Sphinx, or Gryphon, or Manticore. For eight years, the Manticoran Alliance had taken the war to the Republic, fought its battles on Republican territory, smashed and conquered *Republican* planets. But not this time. This time it was *their* turn, and Javier Giscard was too good a strategist—and too hungry for vengeance—not to long to drive that lesson home with all the brutal power Esther McQueen or Rob Pierre could have desired.

Yet the waste of it appalled him. The lives he had squandered, Havenite and Manticoran alike, and the untold trillions of dollars of material he was about to destroy. He knew many of his fellow officers saw it *only* as material, and the true believers among them undoubtedly saw it as the best, most fitting way possible to punish their "plutocratic" enemies. But it wasn't as simple as "hitting them in the pocketbook" for Giscard. He couldn't help seeing his target in terms of all the time and effort, the labor and sweat and hopes and dreams, as well as the monetary investment, which had gone into building it. He would be smashing livelihoods, even if he took no more lives at all, and deep inside, he knew there *would* be more deaths. The message Julia Lapisch was broadcasting ordered the immediate evacuation of every orbital structure. It warned the people who crewed them to abandon ship and gave them the precise timetable on which his missiles would launch, and he knew anyone but an idiot would have begun evacuating to the planetary surface an hour before, when it became obvious the defending task group couldn't stop him.

But he also knew some of them hadn't left. That some of them would not . . . and that others *could* not. They had their own duties, their own responsibilities, and despite all the planning that might be done, and all the exercises which might be held, it would be physically impossible to get everyone off of some of those bases. They would do their best, and he would hold his fire until the very last moment, until the instant before he lost lock and range to hit them. He would do all that the Deneb Accords and the Epsilon Eridani Edict required of him and more, and still some of them would not get out . . . and he would kill them.

He longed not to, yet he had no choice. If Darlington had won against the forts and the terminus picket, if the Manty Home Fleet would be unable to come charging through the Junction after him, then he could afford to take the time. To decelerate and come back at a lower rate of speed, to wait and be sure there were no civilians still aboard his targets. But he couldn't know what was happening out there for at least another six hours, and he dared not squander that time if it turned out that Darlington had lost, or that they had been wrong about the strength of the terminus picket, or that Home Fleet had already made transit into the system to come rushing up behind him.

And so he sat back in his chair, watching the time display tick downward while elation and shame and triumph and grief warred within him.

"They're fourteen minutes out from the terminus, Sir," Captain Granston-Henley said quietly, and White Haven nodded.

He clasped his hands behind him and turned his back on the main plot. He no longer needed to see it to know what was happening, anyway. He had twenty-three superdreadnoughts in the system now, and they were as ready as they were going to get.

The Peep commander obviously intended to make a maximum-velocity pass, flushing his pods as he came and hoping to saturate the forts' defenses. He must have what he considered to be damned reliable intelligence about the status of the other forts, or he would never have risked it. Unfortunately, he *was* risking it, and White Haven was relieved that the work crews had managed to abandon the incomplete fortresses. Those unfinished hulls were sitting ducks, with neither active nor passive defenses. Their only protection would be the decoys and jamming of their active sisters—and Eighth Fleet—and any missile which acquired them was virtually guaranteed to hit.

More losses, he thought, gritting his teeth. *I'll be amazed if even one of them comes through this intact enough to make it worthwhile bothering to finish the damned thing. And* that, *of course, will make a continuing—and heavily reinforced—Fleet picket here absolutely unavoidable.*

He shuddered at the thought, already hearing the strident demands that the Fleet provide sufficient protection to stop this sort of thing. If the Peeps were smart and audacious enough to try similar raids against another system or two, they could throw a monumental spanner into the works for the RMN. It had been hard enough to scrape up the forces for offensive action before; now it would get astronomically harder. Yet if they *didn't* resume the offensive, they only gave the Peeps time to pick their spots with even more care, land their punches with even more weight behind them, and that—

He jerked his mind back from useless speculation and inhaled deeply. The active forts had strictly limited numbers of pods—*another point to take up with Logistics Command,* he thought grimly; *when a fort is declared operational, then it should damned well receive its full ammunition allocation* immediately, *not "as soon as practical!"*—but, fortunately, the *Harrington* and her two sisters were another story. Built to the radical new design proposed by the Weapons Development Board, they'd been constructed around huge, hollow cores packed full of missile pods and ejection racks to deploy them. Between the three of them, they carried no less than fifteen hundred pods, and they'd been busy launching them into space ever since their arrival. Unlike older ships of the wall, they also had the fire control to handle a couple of hundred pods each, and they'd been handing the other eleven hundred off to the two forts and to their fellow SDs. But it was the *Honor Harrington* and Admiral Judah Yanakov who would call the shot for them. Not only did he have the best fire control equipment, but they were his navy's pods . . . and the Grayson Navy had earned the right.

"Any sign they've detected us?" he asked Granston-Henley.

"No, Sir," she said firmly, and Commander Haggerston shook his head in support of her statement.

"I don't think they'll be able to see us much above three or four million klicks, Sir, and they're still thirty-nine light-seconds out," he said. "The forts' EW isn't as good on a ton-for-ton basis as our latest mobile refits, but they've got an *awful* lot of it aboard each of those platforms, and their decoys are a lot bigger—and better—than anything a warship could deploy. I figure those people are going to have to keep coming for another nine and a half minutes before they have a chance of picking us out of the clutter. Whereas we—"

He shrugged and nodded to the crimson display burning in one corner of his plot. It said TIME TO LAUNCH 00:08:27, and as White Haven followed his nod, another second ticked inexorably away.

"Citizen Admiral, we seem to be picking up something new from the Manty decoys," Darlington's ops officer said.

"What sort of 'something'?" the citizen rear admiral demanded testily. They were only a little more than a minute outside their own effective engagement range—which probably meant they were already inside the Manties', if only barely—and they'd managed to lock up the two forts again. Or they thought they had, anyway. They couldn't be sure, and anticipating a tidal wave of missiles while he sailed straight into the teeth of launch platforms he wasn't even certain he'd found well enough to shoot back at was not making him feel any more tranquil.

"I'm not really certain, Citizen Admiral," the ops officer said slowly, shaking his head. "We've had impeller ghosts coming and going inside the jamming all along, of course. Now more of them seem to be hardening up simultaneously, and there's something else going on. It's almost as if we were taking lidar and radar hits from a lot more units all of a sudden."

"*What?*" Darlington spun to face the tactical section, but it was already too late.

"Sir, I've just picked up something I think you should hear," Cynthia McTierney said.

"What?" White Haven looked at her irritably. "Cindy, this is hardly the time—"

"It was an all-ships transmission from Admiral Yanakov to all Grayson units, Sir," McTierney said with stubborn diffidence, and then, before White Haven could respond, she pressed a stud and Judah Yanakov's harsh recorded voice echoed in White Haven's earbug.

"Admiral Yanakov to all Grayson units," it said, and White Haven could almost hear the clangor of clashing swords in its depths. "The order is—*Lady Harrington, and no mercy!*"

"*What?*" White Haven spun towards his own com, but it was already too late.

Sixteen hundred and ninety-five missile pods fired as one, and broadside launchers fired with them. The next best thing to nineteen thousand missiles went howling towards the Peeps at 95,000 gravities, and the range was only five million kilometers and the Peeps were headed straight to meet them at over fourteen thousand kilometers per second.

"Take us into hyper!" Darlington shouted, but flight time was under ninety seconds, and he'd wasted four responding.

Counter-missiles launched desperately, and laser clusters trained onto the incoming fire, but there simply wasn't time. His engineers needed at least sixty seconds to bring their generators on-line, and by the time Darlington snapped the order to Citizen Commander Huff, and Huff relayed it to the captains of the other ships, and *they* relayed it to their engineers, time had run out.

Space itself seemed to vanish in the titanic violence as thousands upon thousands of laserheads exploded in a solid wall of fury. At least a thousand of the Allies' own warheads killed one another in old-fashioned nuclear fratricide, but it scarcely mattered. There were more than enough of them to deal with eight dreadnoughts, twelve battleships, and four battlecruisers. Amazingly, and against all apparent reason, two of Darlington's six destroyers actually escaped into hyper. Because no one was intentionally wasting missiles on such small fry, no doubt.

Alexander Hamish grabbed for his own com with frantic haste with Judah Yanakov's order still ringing in his ears. He was horrified by the implications, and his horror grew as the Graysons' fire control continued to sweep the tumbling wreckage and the handful of life pods which had escaped. But none of them fired, and as he slowly relaxed in his chair once more, his memory replayed the words once more. "No *mercy*," Yanakov had said, *not* "No quarter," and a long, quavering breath sighed out of him as he realized he was not about to see a vengeful atrocity by units under his command.

He inhaled slowly, then looked at Granston-Henley.

"Remind me to have a little discussion with Admiral Yanakov about communications discipline," he said, and his mouth quirked in a wry, exhausted grin that might actually hold true humor again someday.

Book Six

Chapter Thirty-Nine

The conference room was silent as the four other members of the court filed into it behind Alistair McKeon. The door closed after them, shutting off the humming background murmur of the hearing room conversations, and McKeon led the way to the table at the center of the room. He and his fellows took their seats, and he tipped back in his chair with a weary sigh.

He was not the senior member of the court . . . but he was its president. That unusual arrangement had been adopted at the unanimous vote of the rest of the board, and he wished it hadn't been. Honor was right, of course, but however much he might agree with her, he didn't have to like the logic which had put him in charge.

If anything like justice was to be done where StateSec's atrocities on Hell were concerned, it would have to be done by a military court whose members, by definition, had been SS victims. That was the reason the other members had insisted that he, as not simply the sole Manticoran member of the court but also as the only one who had never been in SS custody here on Hell, must preside. They were as determined as he or Honor that their proceedings should be seen as those of a court, not a mob seeking vengeance, which was the main reason they had recorded every moment of the trials themselves. No one in the People's Republic or the Solarian League was likely to be convinced the difference was real, however careful they were or however many records they had, and they knew it, but that wasn't really the point. These people wanted posterity, and their own people, to know everything had been done legally, properly, as impartially as possible under the circumstances, and by The Book. That was important, for it would make the difference between them and their victimizers crystal clear for *themselves*, and at the moment, that was all they really cared about.

After all, McKeon thought mordantly, *if we blow this thing, the Peeps will take this planet back over. In which case all of us will undoubtedly be dead . . . and the only chance we had to punish the guilty will have been lost forever. And bottom line,* that's *what really matters to these people.*

He let his eyes slide over the other four members of the court. Harriet Benson and Jesus Ramirez had both turned down invitations to sit on it—wisely, in McKeon's opinion. Honor had had no choice but to extend the invitations, given the roles they had played in making the capture of Styx possible, but both of them knew they had too much hate inside to be anything like impartial, and so they had withdrawn themselves from the temptation. Instead, Commander Albert Hurst of the Helmsport Navy represented the inmates of Camp Inferno while Captain Cynthia Gonsalves of Alto Verde and Commodore Gaston Simmons of the Jameston System Navy represented the other military POWs on Hell. Simmons was senior to McKeon . . . and so was Admiral Sabrina Longmont, who undoubtedly had the hardest duty of all the members of the court.

Unlike any of the others, Longmont was—or had been, at least—a citizen of the People's Republic and a fervent supporter of the Committee of Public Safety from the earliest days of the New Order. She hadn't cared for its excesses and purges, but she'd been too intimately acquainted with the old regime to miss it, and at least the Committee had appeared to be open and above board about its objectives and tactics, which the Legislaturalists had not. Unfortunately, Longmont had been defeated in battle by the Alliance, which had given her a much closer view of the Committees "excesses" than she'd ever wanted. Indeed, she was extremely fortunate that her previous exemplary political record had bought her a mere trip to Hell instead of a firing squad.

Unlike most of the other prisoners on the planet, she'd been housed in Camp Delta Forty, where conditions had been far better than anywhere else on the planet. Indeed, Longmont had had no idea what StateSec was doing to its other prisoners, because Delta Forty had been a sort of holding point for Peep officers who hadn't blotted their copybooks beyond all hope of redemption. Since it had always been possible the Committee would choose to reach out and pardon one or more of Delta Forty's inmates in order to make use of their skills once more, the SS had been careful not to permanently embitter them against the regime. As a result, Longmont, like most of her fellows, had come to the conclusion that the horror stories about Hell they'd heard before being sent here had been just that: stories. They certainly hadn't seen any sign of the abuse and casual cruelty rumor assigned to the planet . . . which meant that the discovery of what had been happening elsewhere shocked them deeply. The more so because they blamed themselves for being credulous enough to let StateSec deceive them so completely.

Not all of them saw it that way, of course. Some had been delighted at being granted even a slim chance to escape Hell and strike back at the New Order and all its minions. A surprisingly large majority of Delta Forty's inmates, however, had wanted no part of the escape effort. In some cases, that was because they expected the attempt to fail and preferred to survive, but most of them remained genuinely loyal to the Republic (if not necessarily to the Committee of Public Safety) despite all that had happened to them. By refusing to cooperate with Honor's efforts, they demonstrated that loyalty with the clear hope that if and when the PRH retook Hell, they would be given a chance for rehabilitation among their own people, not foreigners.

McKeon could respect that . . . but he respected Longmont more. The Peep admiral (actually, she still insisted on being addressed as "Citizen Admiral Longmont") found her own loyalties badly torn. In the end, McKeon suspected, she would be one of the ones who threw in with Admiral Parnell and went into exile in the Solarian League. But unlike Parnell, who had declined any role in the trials for much the same reasons as Ramirez and Benson, Longmont had chosen to serve, and she had made no bones about her reasons.

"What's happened here on Hades have been atrocities, and the guilty parties must be punished," she'd told Honor frankly, brown eyes bleak in a face of stone, when she accepted a position on the court. "But that doesn't mean you and your people have carte blanche to convict and hang everyone who comes before your tribunal, Admiral Harrington. I will serve on your court, but on only one condition: any guilty vote on a capital offense must be sustained by a unanimous vote, not a simple majority."

"But that's—" Jesus Ramirez had begun, only to close his mouth with a click as Honor raised her hand without ever looking away from Longmont's granite expression.

"I agree that it has to be a court, not a source of hunting licenses," she'd said quietly, "but I'm not prepared to give you a license to hang any verdict that comes along, either, Citizen Admiral."

"Nor would I ask you to," Longmont had replied. "I will give you my word—under a lie detector, if you wish—that I will vote in accordance with my honest understanding and interpretation of any evidence presented to me. If I believe a death sentence is merited under our own Uniform Code of Conduct and the Field Regulations, I will vote to impose it. But I won't lie to you, Lady Harrington. I am willing to accept this role only because I believe that it is also my responsibility and duty to be the voice of doubt, the one who speaks for the accused at least until your prosecutors and the evidence absolutely convince me of their guilt."

McKeon hadn't known how Honor would respond to that. He'd sat beside her at the conference table, trying to ignore the silently fuming Rear Admiral Styles at the table's foot, and watched the composed expression on the living side of her face while she considered what Longmont had said. She'd scooped Nimitz up in the crook of her arm, holding him to her chest while she gazed at the Peep officer, and McKeon had been able almost to feel the intensity of her regard. And then, to the amazement of every other person in the conference room, she'd nodded.

"Very well, Citizen Admiral," she'd said simply, and so it had been decided.

Now McKeon gave himself a mental shake, returning himself to the present and letting his chair come back upright. He could readily understand why Longmont had disqualified herself as president of the court, despite her rank, but he knew most of the liberated prisoners on the planet must have been as surprised as Commodore Simmons when she kept her promise to Honor. She was tough minded, skeptical, and hard to convince, but she also voted to confirm the death sentence when the prosecutor convinced her it was justified.

"All right," he said into the silence. "Who'd like to start the ball rolling this time?" No one answered, and he cocked his head and looked at Captain Gonsalves. "Cynthia?"

"I'm not sure," the dusky-skinned Alto Verdan said after a moment. She glanced sideways at Longmont, and McKeon suppressed a wry smile. In an odd way, they had all come to use the board's single Peep member as a sort of ethical sounding board. That was largely due to the ample proof she'd given of her integrity, but there was another dimension to it, as well. All of them had come to recognize the agonizing position in which Longmont had put herself. If she could accept that sort of responsibility out of a sense of moral obligation, then none of the others were willing to come up short against her measure.

Longmont and Honor have a great deal in common, he mused, not for the first time. *Especially the way they get the rest of us to live up to their standards simply by assuming that we will . . . and daring us to disappoint them.*

"The evidence of what actually happened at Alpha Eleven is pretty clear," Gonsalves went on in a troubled tone, "but there are too many holes in the documentation for what happened here on Styx for me to feel comfortable, Sir."

"We have eyewitness testimony from Jerome, Lister, and Veracruz, Captain," Hurston pointed out. "They all saw Mangrum order Lieutenant Weiller aboard the shuttle, and Mangrum has admitted forcing her to have sex with him. That's rape, at the very least. And two of the other slaves both testify that he's the one who killed her."

"They did testify to that effect," Commodore Simmons observed, "but Mangrum's counsel did a pretty fair job of demonstrating the probability of bias against him on their part. Mind you, I don't think I can blame them for that—*I'd* sure as hell be prejudiced against him in their place, and I'd do my dead-level best to get him hanged, too—but the fact that we sympathize with them doesn't absolve us from the responsibility of considering whether or not their prejudice is affecting their testimony's reliability."

"Agreed." Gonsalves nodded, her expression troubled, and then looked back at Hurston. "I agree that the rape charge has been clearly demonstrated, Commander. But rape isn't a capital crime under the Havenite Uniform Code of Conduct unless accompanied by actual violence, not simply the threat of it. Murder *is* a capital crime, but we have no physical or documentary evidence to support that charge. For that matter, not even the slaves who claim he killed her agree on whether or not he committed forcible rape as defined under the UCC. The woman—Hedges—says Weiller had bruises on her face and that—" the captain tapped a command into her memo pad to refresh her memory, then read aloud "— 'She limped pretty bad the next day.' But even Hedges goes on to say that 'She wouldn't talk about what the bastard did to her.' "

Gonsalves shrugged unhappily, and McKeon concealed a mental grimace. The fact that Gonsalves was right about the terms of the Uniform Code of Conduct didn't make him like it. Under the Manticoran Articles of War, forcible rape was a capital offense whether force was actually used or simply threatened, and given the situation here on Hell, any demand a Black Leg made had to be considered to be backed by the threat of force. Given his druthers, McKeon would hang Citizen Lieutenant Mangrum in a heartbeat and then go back to piss on his grave, but Honor had been right. They *had* to proceed under the basis of the Peeps' own rules. Otherwise Section Twenty-Seven of the Deneb Accords—which neither he nor Honor had any intention of infringing in any way, given their own experiences—would have prohibited any trial of enemy personnel in time or war. Subsection Forty-Two specifically provided for wartime trials of individuals for alleged violation of local laws (in this case the Peeps' own UCC, since Hell had been sovereign territory of the People's Republic of Haven at the time) predating their capture, but prohibited *ex post facto* trials under the municipal law of whoever captured them.

"I believe Captain Gonsalves has a point," Citizen Admiral Longmont said after a moment. "In my judgment, the charge of rape is clearly sustained, not simply by Mangrum's own admission, but by the physical evidence. The charge of murder, however, is not."

"It would have been if the security imagery hadn't been lost," Hurston grumbled.

"You may be right," Longmont conceded. "In fact, my own feeling is that you probably are. Mangrum was just a bit quick to confess to rape for my taste, and I suspect he did it in hopes of convincing us to accept his 'honesty' and 'contrition' so that we would believe him when he denied the murder charge. But what you or I suspect is not evidence."

"There *is* the testimony of the other two slaves, Hedges and Usterman," McKeon pointed out.

"There is," Simmons agreed. "However, they've contradicted one another on several other points, and Usterman actually contradicted himself twice. Nor could he or Hedges explain how Mangrum got from the Morgue to his quarters during the time in which Weiller was killed without being seen by anyone else or any of the base security systems."

"Um." Hurston's grunt was unhappy and angry, but not at Simmons. The problem was that the commodore was right. None of the escaped prisoners had expected to discover that the SS's security systems here on Styx had actually kept tabs on their own personnel round the clock. Not that they should have been surprised by the discovery, McKeon thought. The surveillance systems appeared to have been installed to keep track of the sex slaves and farm "trustees" for their masters, but anything with that sort of coverage was bound to catch most of the Black Legs' day-to-day activities, as well. When Harkness and his team of moles broke into those files, they'd found themselves with a huge treasure trove of evidence. Not only did they have audio recordings of people casually discussing things they had done to the prisoners under their control, but they had actual imagery of many of the guards in the very act of committing the crimes of which they stood accused. And the Republic's UCC included none of the Star Kingdom's prohibitions against admitting electronic evidence gathered without benefit of a court order.

Unfortunately, the very wealth of those records worked against a sense of sureness in the instances in which there was no recorded evidence. And in this instance, it did more than that, because they did have imagery—complete with time and date stamp—of Mangrum reporting to the storage area for the garrison's powered armor for a routine day of scheduled maintenance. What they did *not* have was imagery of him actually working on the armor . . . or of him crossing the base to his quarters, where Weiller's body had been discovered that afternoon. The pickups inside the Morgue had been few and far between, and no one had bothered too much over whether or not they were in working order. Which made sense, since no slaves were ever permitted anywhere near the battle armor, and the main function of the system was to keep an eye on them. But if they didn't have Mangrum on chip performing the scheduled work, they did have his log sheets for the day, and they seemed to support his claim that he'd been in the Morgue all day.

"Of course," McKeon murmured, "we only have his logs' word for the fact that he actually performed any maintenance checks. He could have falsified them. God knows it wouldn't be the first time someone did that to get out of a little work!"

"I know," Longmont said, her expression as troubled as Gonsalves' had been. "And the fact that he didn't log a single component replacement is certainly suspicious. According to his records he worked on—what?" She consulted her own memo pad. "Here it is. According to his log sheets, he up-checked fourteen sets of battle armor . . . and he did all that without finding a single faulty component?" She shook her head. "I find that highly suspicious, but it's not enough to offset the fact that we don't have any evidence that positively places him at the scene of the murder."

"He knew about the pickups in his quarters," Hurston pointed out. "We know he deliberately disabled them on at least four other occasions, and *someone* sure as hell disabled them the afternoon Weiller was killed. What makes you think it wasn't him that time?"

"What proves it *was* him?" Simmons countered. "Certainly the fact that he knew where they were and had previously shut them down indicates he could have done the same thing again. But each of the four times we know the pickups were down as the result of his actions and not a genuine malfunction were very shortly after he brought her back to Styx. It certainly looks like he was shy about being recorded having sex with her—"

"*Raping* her, you mean, Sir," Gonsalves said grimly. Simmons paused, then nodded.

"Raping her," he agreed, and Longmont nodded sharply.

"You're quite correct, Captain," she said, and managed a wintry smile. "Neither Commodore Simmons nor I ever said he wasn't a loathsome, revolting piece of human garbage. I simply said we don't have any supporting evidence of Hedges and Usterman's contention that he's the one who murdered her. And the point I believe the Commodore was going to make is that he'd become increasingly less shy about performing for the cameras."

She glanced at Simmons, who nodded as if to resign the ball to her, then continued.

"In fact, he hadn't shut them down for over three local months prior to Weiller's death. So unless we're going to stipulate that he knew ahead of time that he was going to kill her—that it was a carefully planned murder, not unpremeditated or an accident—and wanted an alibi, why should he have disabled them on arrival *this* time? And why should he worry about establishing an alibi when Citizen Commander Tresca had made it abundantly clear that no one would be prosecuted for something as 'inconsequential' as the murder of helpless prisoners?"

The loathing contempt in the Citizen Admiral's overcontrolled voice underlined her disgust at having to make any sort of argument in Mangrum's defense, but ultimately, that only gave it more power.

"She's got a point there, Cynthia," Hurston said, manifestly against his will, and Gonsalves nodded unhappily.

"I know," she confessed. "That's what I meant when I said there were too many holes in the documentation. I just hate the very thought of letting him walk away from the hangman. Whether he actually killed Weiller or not, he's the sick animal who dragged her back here, raped her, made her his toy, and put her in a position for *someone* to murder."

"I don't like it either," Longmont said. "And just among the five of us, I wish to hell the UCC made any case of rape a capital offense. But it doesn't. And if these trials are going to be justifiable under the Deneb Accords—"

She shrugged, and McKeon nodded with an unhappy sigh.

"I think I'm hearing a consensus here," he said. "Does anyone want to call for secret ballots, or is a voice vote acceptable?"

He looked around the table, then directly at Longmont as the senior officer present.

"A voice vote is acceptable to me," the citizen admiral replied, and he glanced at the others.

"Voice," Simmons said, speaking aloud for the recorders faithfully taking down everything that happened in the conference room.

"Agreed," Gonsalves sighed.

"Agreed," Hurston said more grudgingly.

"Very well. How vote you on the charge of second-degree rape, Commander Hurston?" McKeon asked formally, beginning—in age-old military tradition—with the junior member of the court.

"Guilty," Hurston said flatly.

"On the charge of kidnapping?

"Guilty."

"On the charge of abuse of official authority for personal advantage?"

"Guilty."

"On the charge of murder?"

"Guilty."

"On the charge of second-degree rape, Captain Gonsalves?" McKeon went on, turning to the next most junior member of the court.

"Guilty," Gonsalves replied in a voice of cold certainty.

"On the charge of kidnapping?"

"Guilty."

"On the charge of abuse of official authority for personal advantage?"

"Guilty."

"On the charge of murder?"

"Abstained," Gonsalves said with a grimace, and McKeon turned to Simmons.

"On the charge of second-degree rape, Commodore Simmons?"

"Guilty."

"On the charge of kidnapping?"

"Guilty."

"On the charge of abuse of official authority for personal advantage?"

"Guilty."

"On the charge of murder?"

Simmons opened his mouth, then closed it. He sat hunched in his chair for several seconds, glaring down at the table top, then raised his eyes and looked at McKeon and Longmont almost defiantly.

"Guilty," he said in a hard, cold voice.

McKeon nodded. He wasn't really surprised, despite the discussion which had preceded the vote, and he simply looked at Longmont.

"On the charge of second-degree rape, Citizen Admiral Longmont?" he asked.

"Guilty," Longmont said without hesitation.

"On the charge of kidnapping?"

"Guilty."

"On the charge of abuse of official authority for personal advantage?"

"Guilty."

"On the charge of murder?"

"For acquittal, due to lack of evidence," Longmont said unhappily, and McKeon nodded once more.

"The vote on the first three charges being unanimous, and the vote on the sole capital charge being divided, the president of the court accepts the decision of the court's other members without casting a vote," he said for the record. "It is now the responsibility of this court to recommend a sentence to Admiral Harrington, however. The UCC provides for up to twenty-five years in prison for second-degree rape, fifty years for kidnapping, and two for abuse of official authority for personal advantage. By my math, that means Citizen Lieutenant Mangrum is theoretically subject to seventy-seven T-years at hard labor. To impose such a sentence, however, will require his return to Alliance space with us at such time as we leave the planet."

He didn't add "assuming we *can* leave the planet," but the other four heard it anyway, and he smiled wryly. Then he looked back at Hurston.

"Commander Hurston, what is your recommendation?"

"The maximum penalty—seventy-five T-years without possibility of parole," Hurston said harshly.

"Captain Gonsalves?"

"The maximum," she agreed, her expression murderous. "God knows the bastard has it coming . . . and I only wish we could leave him here on Hell to serve it!"

That wasn't exactly proper etiquette or procedure, but McKeon had no intention of pointing it out. He simply nodded and turned to Gaston Simmons.

"Commodore Simmons?"

"The same." His voice was hammered iron, even colder than Gonsalves', and McKeon looked at Longmont.

"Citizen Admiral Longmont?"

"I concur with the recommendations of my fellows," she said flatly.

"And so also says the president of the court," McKeon told them. "The vote being unanimous, this court will recommend to Admiral Harrington that Citizen Lieutenant Kenneth Mangrum be kept in close confinement for the duration of our time on Hell, to be returned with us to Alliance space, there to serve the full term of his sentence. Is there any exception to or disagreement with the court's statement of its recommendation for the record?"

No one spoke, and he nodded one last time, then sighed and let his shoulders slump.

"Well, that's one more out of the way," he said in a much less formal tone, and rubbed his face with both hands. "God, will I be glad when this is finally over!"

"I'm sure all of us will be, Commodore," Longmont told him, then shook her head sadly and looked at the other three members of the court. "I'm sorry we couldn't find the evidence to let me agree to hang him," she said. "But—"

"Don't be sorry, Sabrina!" Somewhat to McKeon's surprise, it was Simmons, interrupting the Havenite before she could finish. "I think he did it, Cynthia and Albert and Alistair all think he did it, and you think he did it. But you were right. We can't *prove* it, and if we ever start rubber-stamping execution orders, we'll be just as bad as the people we're hanging." He smiled sourly as Longmont raised an eyebrow at him, and then shrugged. "I know. I voted guilty. And in this case, I would cheerfully have hanged him if the rest of you had gone along, holes in the evidence or not. I would've slept soundly tonight, too. But that's why there's more than one person sitting on this court, and I was the one who held out against hanging Citizen Major Younce last week. As long as every one of us votes his or her conscience every time, then we've done both the best—and the least—we can do under the circumstances."

"You know," Longmont said after a moment, "it's really a pity we're on different sides. If the politicians—especially mine—would just get the hell out of the way and let the five of us deal with it, we could hammer out a peace settlement and end this whole damned war in a week."

"I wouldn't bet on that, Citizen Admiral," McKeon told her wryly. "Compared to the war, the things we're looking at here are pretty cut and dried. At least we've all agreed whose rules we're going to use as the basis for our verdicts! But when we started hammering away at each other about things like who owns which planets . . . well—"

He shrugged, and Longmont gave a snort of half-bitter, half-amused laughter.

"It's not polite to go around destroying a lady's daydreams, Commodore!"

"My commission says I'm an officer and a gentlemen, Ma'am; it never said I was a *polite* gentlemen!" The citizen admiral chuckled appreciatively, and McKeon grinned at her. "And however unlikely I may think it is that we could negotiate an end of the war, I'd much rather hammer away at you with words than laserheads any day, Citizen Admiral!"

"Amen to that," Commodore Simmons said fervently, then pushed his chair back. "And given that we've just concluded our judicial duties for the day, I move that we adjourn, deliver our verdict and recommendations to Admiral Harrington, and then go find a nice, thick steak and a good beer. Takers?"

"Me, for one," Longmont told him. "Assuming that an unregenerate Peep is welcome in your company, of course?"

"This particular unregenerate Peep is welcome anytime," Simmons said graciously. "As long as she agrees to lose at darts after supper, that is!"

"Of course I'll agree to lose," Longmont promised. "Of course, I am an *unregenerate* Peep, servant of an order which you all insist is corrupt and venal."

"Are you saying your agreement would be a *lie?*" Simmons demanded.

"Of course not," the Citizen Admiral said sweetly. "I'm simply saying that despite Commodore McKeon's rudeness where my dreams were concerned, I would never even contemplate damaging our close working relationship by overturning your concepts of proper Peep-like behavior." She smiled. "And, of course," she added, "the loser *does* get to buy the beer. Coming, Commodore?"

Chapter Forty

The harsh buzzer woke her.

Nimitz complained sleepily as she sat up, and she didn't blame him. They'd just gotten to sleep, but as she always seemed to do in the morning, she'd forgotten she was missing an arm. She woke with the instant awareness—mostly—that forty years of naval service had trained into her, only to try to push herself upright with two hands, not one, and overbalance. The sheets half-wrapped around her, spilling the 'cat over onto his back, and she felt his drowsy indignation as he opened one eye. It glinted like a lost emerald in the reflected light flashing from atop the bedside com unit, and she sent him a silent apology and reached for the acceptance key. The accusing emerald blinked, and then its neighbor opened and a slightly less sleepy sense of amused forgiveness came back to her.

She found the key and pressed it, accepting the call audio-only, then ran her hand over her tousled hair.

"Yes?" Her voice came out clogged with sleep, and she cleared her throat.

"Sorry to disturb you, Admiral, but this is Commander Phillips," a soprano voice said, and Honor felt her pulse stir as she registered the tension trying to crackle in its depths. She knew Phillips was one of Benson's watch officers, but there were over five thousand ex-prisoners on Styx now. She'd been too busy with her own duties—and especially the courts-martial—to pay as much attention as she would have liked to other matters, and she wasn't certain exactly which watch slot Phillips held.

"Captain Benson instructed me to alert you," the commander went on, then paused as if to await her reaction.

"Alert me to what, precisely, Commander?" she asked a bit more testily than was her wont.

"Sorry, Ma'am," Phillips said in a chastened tone. "I didn't mean to sound obscure. I'm the XO on Captain Benson's watch, and she asked me to tell you that the sensor net's picked up a hyper footprint at roughly twenty-one light-minutes."

Honor stiffened, and Nimitz rolled over and heaved himself upright in the tangled bedclothes beside her. Her gaze dropped to him again as he reached out and touched her thigh with a wiry true-hand, and his emotions reached out to hers as well, meeting her sudden tension head-on.

"I see," she told Phillips after only the briefest pause, her voice calm. "How long ago did they arrive? And has the challenge been transmitted?"

"We picked up the footprint about five minutes, Ma'am. We don't have it on light-speed sensors yet, but our near-space gravitic arrays say it's a single impeller source. We don't have a definitive mass, but it's accelerating in-system at over three hundred and ninety gravities, so it's not using a merchant-grade compensator. And, yes, Ma'am. Captain Benson instructed me to order the recorded challenge transmitted just over three minutes ago."

"I see," Honor repeated. She wished Benson had commed her sooner, but that was only because of her perennial dislike for delegating authority, and she knew it. Harriet had done exactly what she was supposed to do by sending the "StateSec" challenge on her own initiative immediately, as the real Black Legs would have done, rather than waiting until she could get word to Honor. And given that sending the challenge had initiated at least a twenty-nine-minute com loop, there had been no logical reason for her to rush reporting anything to Honor before her tracking team had been given time to refine their initial data as far as they could.

"Current range from Hades?" Honor asked after a moment.

"They're fourteen-point-six light-minutes from a zero/zero intercept with the planet, Ma'am," Phillips replied promptly. "They made a low-speed translation—about eight hundred KPS—and their current velocity is up to just over nineteen hundred. That puts them right at a hundred and twenty-nine minutes from turnover with a decel period of a hundred and thirty-eight minutes. Call it four and a half hours from now."

"Thank you." Honor sat for a moment, considering the numbers, then nodded to herself in the darkened bedroom. "Very well, Commander. Tell Captain Benson I'll be there presently. In the meantime, she's to use her own judgment in responding to any additional com traffic. Is Commander Tremaine there?"

"He is, Admiral. And Senior Chief Harkness is on his way. I expect his arrival momentarily."

The undamaged corner of Honor's mouth quirked as the slight, prim note of disapproval in the other woman's voice brought her memory of the officer at the other end of her com suddenly into sharper focus. Commander Susan Phillips had been a computer specialist in the Sarawak System Navy. But she had also been on

Hell for over forty T-years, and her training had been sadly out of date, even for Peep equipment, when her camp was liberated and she reached Styx. She'd done extremely well in the quickie refresher courses Honor had organized, but she was still rusty compared to Honor's people from *Prince Adrian* and *Jason Alvarez*—or, for that matter, most of the other Allied POWs from the current war.

Phillips knew that, and for the most part, she accepted it with a good grace. But a part of her couldn't help resenting the fact that Tremaine, who was both junior to her and young enough to be her son, had been assigned to her watch specifically to handle any creative communication or electronic warfare requirements which might arise. Honor suspected she would have minded it less if Scotty had been even a little older, although the fact that he was third-generation prolong while Phillips was only second-generation must make it seem even worse to her. The Commander might have found it easier to have Anson Lethridge ride herd on her—he was only two T-years older than Scotty, but he, too, was second-generation prolong and looked considerably older. Unfortunately, Honor needed Anson on first watch.

But the same part of Phillips that resented Tremaine *really* resented the fact that Harkness, a mere senior chief, had become the chief cyberneticist of Hell.

Well, Honor sympathized in many ways, although she considered the commander's belief that officers could always do things better than senior noncoms foolish. Of course, Phillips came from a very different naval tradition—that of the Sarawak Republic, one of the liberal-thinking targets the Peeps had gobbled up in the early days of the DuQuesne Plan. The SSN had relied upon a professional officer corps, but Sarawak's advanced, egalitarian social theories had inspired it (unlike the dangerous, elitist plutocracy of Manticore) to use short-service conscripts to fill its enlisted and noncommissioned ranks. The result had produced something very like the present-day People's Navy, in which the service simply hadn't had its enlisted draftees long enough to train them up to Manticoran standards. Which meant that Phillips' ingrained belief that officers ought to be better at their jobs than petty officers represented her own experience, not blind prejudice. And to be fair, she was less resentful of Harkness' status than many of Honor's other non-Manticoran officers. Not to mention the fact that she was working diligently at getting rid of the resentment she still harbored. It just seemed to come a bit hard for her.

Which was too bad, Honor thought with a crooked grin, because Harkness wasn't going away. The senior chief might not have a commission, but he'd been doing his job considerably longer than Honor had been doing hers. Besides, after the better part of seven months crawling around inside Camp Charon's computers, Harkness knew them better than anyone else on Hell—including the SS personnel Honor and her people had taken them away from. If any emergencies came up, she wanted the best person for the job—which meant Harkness—there to handle it.

"I understand, Commander," she said now, silently scolding herself for judging Phillips overly harshly. After all, they *were* from different navies, and it was as unrealistic for Honor to blame Phillips for having different traditions and expectations as it would have been for the commander to hold the same thing against Harkness. "I'll be there shortly. Harrington, clear."

She killed the com and reached for the bedroom light switch, and excitement burned within her.

Honor missed James MacGuiness even more than usual as she dressed. The fact that she had only one hand made things awkward at the best of times; when she tried to hurry herself, it only got worse. And what made her particularly irritated with herself was that she *knew* it did . . . and tried to rush herself anyway.

Nimitz chittered in amusement at the taste of her emotions, and she paused to shake a fist at him, then resumed her efforts more deliberately. She knew LaFollet, for one, thought she was foolish not to have selected another steward from among the prisoners her people had liberated, and she more than suspected that several of her senior officers agreed with him. McKeon certainly did, although Honor regarded Alistair's judgment as just a little suspect where the concept of her "pushing herself too hard" was involved. More than that, however, she knew most—not all certainly, but most—of the enlisted or noncommissioned personnel she might have chosen would have been delighted to fill the role for her.

Yet despite her frustration with things like fastening the waist of her trousers one-handed, or sealing the old-fashioned buttons the GSN had insisted on using for its uniform blouses—and which Henri Dessouix, after discussions with LaFollet, had insisted with equal stubbornness upon using in the name of "authenticity"—she simply couldn't bring herself to do it. It was foolish, and she knew it, which only made her even more stubborn about refusing. But she simply couldn't.

Rear Admiral Styles was one reason, and she grimaced even now as the thought of him flickered across her brain. He continued to feel she had improperly usurped the authority which was rightfully his. And however inept he might be as a tactician or strategist (and she was coming to suspect that her original caustic estimate of his probable capabilities in those areas had been entirely too generous), he was obviously a genius at bureaucratic infighting. He reminded her irresistibly of a plant Grayson's original colonists had, for reasons none of their descendants could imagine, brought with them from old Earth. The vine, called kudzu, made an excellent ground cover, but it was almost impossible to get rid of, grew with ferocious energy, and choked out all competing flora with ruthless arrogance. Which was a pretty fair metaphor for Styles.

She found herself compelled to cut the Admiral back to size at least once per local week or so. The fact that he possessed far more bluster than backbone helped on those occasions, and he never persisted in attempting to undercut her authority twice in the same fashion once he'd pushed her to the point of bringing the hammer down on him for it the first time. Unfortunately, he'd played what McKeon scathingly called "pissing contests" for much too long to stay crushed. He either didn't believe she really would squash him once and for all, or else he was so stupid he genuinely didn't realize how much grief he was storing up for himself. Whatever his problem, he seemed capable of learning only one lesson at a time, and he was endlessly inventive when it came to finding new ways to goad her into the sort of temper explosions she hated.

She disliked admitting it even to herself, but that was one of the more ignoble reasons she refused to select a steward. Styles obviously wished to return to the lifestyle to which he had become accustomed as an RMN flag officer, with all the perks and privileges attached thereunto. The fact that he had done absolutely nothing to earn those perks or privileges was beside the point; he had the rank for them and so he was *entitled* to them. Except that if Honor chose not to claim them when her missing arm gave her such a good pretext for doing so, then he could hardly insist upon them without looking utterly ridiculous, and she took a spiteful pleasure she knew was petty in denying them to him.

And he should be grateful it's the only *pleasure I allow myself where he's concerned*, she thought grimly as she managed to get her blouse's collar buttoned. *If I did what I'd* like *to do to him, they'd never find the body!*

Nimitz yawned, baring sharp, white canines in a lazy grin while he radiated approval of that thought. Then he concentrated hard, and Honor smothered a sudden, sharp bark of laughter as he radiated the image of a Sphinx chipmunk with an unmistakable, if very chipmunkish, caricature of Styles' face, fleeing for its wretched life. She looked down at the 'cat in astonishment, for this was the first time he'd ever attempted to send her an image which obviously was not something he'd actually seen and simply stored in memory. But her astonishment turned into a helpless, fiendish giggle as the chipmunk vanished out one "side" of his projected image . . . and a brown-eyed treecat with bared claws, an eye patch, an RMN beret, and the red-and-gold shoulder boards of a commodore went bounding past in hot pursuit.

She half-sat, half-fell back down onto the edge of the bed, laughing delightedly, and Nimitz bleeked his matching delight at having gotten her to laugh. He sat up as straight as his crippled limb permitted, curling his tail primly around his true-feet, and groomed his whiskers at her with insufferable panache.

"You," she said severely, as soon as she could master her voice once more, "are a dreadful person and no respecter at all of rank or position, aren't you?"

He nodded complacently, and she smiled and reached out to caress his ears, then bent to pull her boots on. Despite Nimitz's opinion of Styles, however, she knew he was more dangerous than she cared to admit. Not because she thought anyone but him took him seriously, but because whatever else, he was the second-ranking Allied officer on the planet. Which meant that unless she was prepared to officially remove him, she couldn't cut him out of the chain of command, and he was quite capable of doing something outstandingly stupid in a fit of pique just to show her he wasn't to be taken lightly. Which probably meant that rubbing his nose in her opinion of him, however obliquely, wasn't the smartest thing in the entire universe that she could do. Unfortunately, just this once, and despite what Machiavelli had said about doing enemies small injuries, she couldn't help it. He was such a poisonous, irritating, pompous, stupid, officious, *toadlike* nonentity of an incompetent that she simply had to do something about him, and the fact that this particular response was almost as petty as he was made it so appropriate it was inevitable.

Besides, she told herself, whatever pleasure she might find in denying Styles the luxuries he coveted, there were other factors, as well. One was that she would have felt pretentious . . . which was also her less spiteful reason for refusing Styles. She had little doubt that most of the liberated POWs would have considered a steward her due. But she had no intention of building any walls between her and the people under her orders. It was bad enough that she'd been forced to claim her fleet admiral's rank to keep Styles in his place without assembling the sort of personal staff which would insulate her from the people who depended upon her leadership.

And there was a final reason, she admitted as she stood and collected her necktie. MacGuiness was her steward and she was his admiral, and she refused to allow anyone else to intrude into that relationship even temporarily.

Nimitz bleeked another laugh behind her, but it came with a wave of approval. MacGuiness was his friend, too, and, like Honor, he missed the steward badly. Besides, MacGuiness knew exactly how he preferred his rabbit roasted.

Honor looked back at the 'cat with one of her crooked grins, then crossed to her bedroom door and hit the open button with her elbow. It slid quietly aside and, as she had known she would, she found Andrew LaFollet already waiting, immaculate in one of the Harrington Guard uniforms Henri Dessouix had produced for him.

You know, Honor thought, *I bet that's another reason Phillips waited five minutes to com me. I'll bet Harry had her—or someone—com Andrew first.*

She'd never considered it before, but now that she had, she wondered why it hadn't occurred to her much earlier. LaFollet had been willing to allow handpicked (by him) Marines from Hell's liberated POWs to spell him on guard duty when his Steadholder was asleep, but every single time something roused Honor in the middle of the night, he was always awake and waiting for her, as if he never slept at all. But he did, so the only way he could have managed to pretend he didn't was to make certain that anyone who contemplated waking her knew to wake him first. In fact, it was possible—no, knowing him it was *probable*—that he'd been vetting her calls and diverting any he felt someone else could handle just to ensure she got her sleep!

The thoughts flickered through her brain while the door was still opening, but she let no sign of them touch her expression. She intended to ask a few discreet questions to confirm her suspicions first. Of course, if she did find out that he'd been diverting calls, they were going to have to have one of their periodic little talks.

Not that she expected it to do a great deal of good. They never had before, after all.

I may not have Mac or Miranda along, but I'm sure both of them would approve of the way Andrew's taken over to mother-hen me for all of them, she thought wryly, and held out the tie.

"Help," was all she said, and then raised her chin so he could loop the ridiculous thing around her neck and knot it for her. *I should have insisted that Henri make this thing a clip-on, whatever Andrew and Solomon had to say about it,* she thought darkly, and waited patiently while LaFollet worked.

"There, My Lady," he said after a moment, and folded her collar down and buttoned it for her, as well.

"Thank you," she said, and returned to the bedroom for her tunic. She supposed there was no real reason she had to be properly uniformed in the middle of the night, but she refused to come running in half-dressed and out of breath. She'd always felt that taking the time to present the proper appearance was an important leadership function, however trivial it might seem to others. It was one way of demonstrating one's composure, a sort of subliminal statement of an officer's ability to exert control over the situation around her which her subordinates absorbed through their mental pores without really thinking about it. Or even if they did think about it and recognized it as a bit of subtle psychological warfare on their CO's part.

Of course, it was also true that she sometimes wondered how much of her belief in the importance of a proper appearance stemmed from personal vanity, she admitted with a small smile.

She collected her gold-braided Grayson cap from the top of her dresser, settled it on her head, and held out her arm to Nimitz. The 'cat still couldn't leap to it as he once would have, but he managed to walk up it to the crook of her elbow. She knew he felt her desire to pick him up like a kitten to make it easier on him, and she tasted the soft undercurrent of his gratitude when she refrained.

"Ready, Stinker?" she asked, and he nodded again, this time with an ear-flick of agreement.

"Good," she said, and headed back out the door to her waiting armsman.

"Good morning, Admiral," Harriet Benson said formally as Honor walked into the Styx command center. Honor glanced at the time and date display and grinned wryly.

"I guess it is," she agreed, and Benson chuckled.

The blond captain did a lot more of that since they'd taken Styx . . . and even more since the courts-martial, Honor thought, trying not to feel bitter about it. It was hard, sometimes, and she knew she'd made it harder by establishing from the outset that she personally would review and confirm every sentence handed down by the tribunal. It had never been easy for her to accept responsibility for death, yet confirming those verdicts was her responsibility. She could have avoided it legally, but not if she'd wanted to live with herself afterwards. Which was perverse of her, she thought mordantly. Surely she'd assumed "responsibility" for deaths enough by now! Yet it sometimes seemed to her that she would never escape that crushing weight—that her life had made her the very Angel of Death. Wherever she went, it followed, among her own people as well as the enemy, and there were times the memory of all her dead ambushed her with crushing force in her dreams.

And yet she couldn't walk away. It was the paradox of her own nature that the one thing she found even more impossible to face than the blood upon her hands was what would happen if she refused to shed it. She knew that, but she also knew it stemmed from more than a simple, stubborn inability to shove her duty off onto another or turn her back on those who depended upon her. Whatever she wanted, whatever she *thought* she wanted, she was a killer because she was . . . good at it. She had the gift—the tactician's eye and the strategist's mind and the talent no one could quite define. In some strange way, that gift had *required* her to become a killer. Duty. Honor. Loyalty. Patriotism. She might call it by any name she chose, but in the dark hours of the night she knew she had become what she was not simply because someone had to but because she did it so much better than most.

She knew her own weaknesses: the temper which had once almost ended her career, the inability to stop or relent that sometimes verged all too closely upon obsession, and the aptitude for violence that, in an even slightly different personality, would have created a monster.

She wasn't a . . . safe person, and she knew it, so she had found a way to turn that dangerousness into a virtue by dedicating her life to defending the people and beliefs she held dear.

The majority of people were decent enough human beings. Not saints most of them, no, but not monsters either. If anyone in the universe knew that, she did, for her link to Nimitz gave her an insight and a sensitivity no other human had ever possessed. But she also knew that the two-legged animals who had raped and tortured and murdered here on Hell for StateSec were not unique . . . and that as someone had said long, long ago on Old Earth, all that was necessary for evil to triumph was for good men—and women—to do nothing.

Honor Harrington could not be one of those who "did nothing." That was the dreadful, simple and inexorable center of her life, the source of all the paradoxes. Someone had to resist the State Securities and Committees of Public Safety and the Pavel Youngs and William Fitzclarences, and whatever made her who and what she was forced her to be that someone. And when her dead came to her in her dreams, she could face them—not without sorrow and guilt, but without allowing those things to conquer her—because she'd had no choice but to try. And because if she'd attempted to evade her duty, tried to divert it to someone who lacked her killer's gift, she would have broken faith with the superiors who had trusted her to honor her oath as a Queen's officer and with the subordinates who'd trusted her to keep them alive . . . or at least make their deaths mean something.

That was the reason she had made herself review those sentences, despite how dreadfully she'd longed to evade the task. Because it was her job. Because she was the one who'd seen no option but to order those trials held, and she would not shuffle the weight of that decision off onto Alistair McKeon or any of her other subordinates. And because she had to be certain the sentences she confirmed were justice, not mere vengeance. It was another of those things she had no choice but to do, whatever the rest of the universe might think, and so she'd done it. But the burden of still more death—and the courts-martial had hanged fifty-eight StateSec troopers over the last six months—was the reason a small corner of her mind, raw and wounded, felt bitter at Harriet Benson's laughter. The captain wasn't gloating over the destruction of her enemies; she was simply a human being who could not avoid a deep sense of satisfaction that those who had thought themselves above all laws, immunized against any day of reckoning, had discovered they were wrong.

Nimitz made a soft, scolding sound, and she blinked, then gave herself a mental shake and sent him a silent apology. It was getting up in the middle of the night, she told herself. The darkness outside the command center made her more vulnerable than usual to the other darkness brooding within her, but Nimitz's soft touch in her mind was like a bright light, chasing shadows from the corners of her soul. Unbiased he certainly was not, but he knew her far better than anyone else did. Indeed, he knew her better than *she* did, and his uncomplicated love echoed his verbal scold as he took her to task for being so hard on herself.

"Honor?" She looked up and saw Benson regarding her with a slightly worried frown.

"Sorry," she said, and smiled almost naturally. "Nimitz and I had just dropped off when you had Commander Phillips screen me. I'm afraid we're not quite fully awake yet, and I wandered off into a mental blind alley."

"You're not old enough to be doing that sort of thing yet, Admiral," Benson told her severely, and grinned at Honor's chuckle. "Better!" Benson approved, and laughed when Honor gave her a mock serious glare.

That laugh snuffed Honor's petty bitterness like a stiff breeze, and she was glad. It was utterly unfair of her to resent the fact that Harriet had become more relaxed, less driven and less haunted by her own demons. Besides, Honor suspected that at least as much of the change in the captain came from Fritz Montoya's activities as from the executions. The doctor had run an entire battery of tests on her and Henri Dessouix—and the others from their original camp who had been affected by eating "false-potatoes"—and managed to isolate the neuro-toxin which had affected their speech centers. He'd found it in several other places in their nervous system, as well, and some of its other potential effects concerned him far more than slurred speech did. He was still figuring out exactly what it was, but he'd been able to use the SS hospital's facilities to design a special nanny to go in after it. The molycirc machines had been scavenging it out of Benson's brain for a full month now, and her speech was far clearer than it had been.

In fact, Honor thought wryly, *it's at least as clear as* mine *is now, but I don't suppose Fritz can be expected to do a lot about destroyed nerves with such primitive facilities.*

"What's our situation?" she asked, and Benson nodded to the oversized holo sphere of the system.

Honor glanced at it and cocked her head as she absorbed its contents.

The display was centered on Cerberus-B, Hell's G3 primary, rather than on Cerberus-A, the F4 primary component of the trinary system. Cerberus-B orbited its more massive companion at an average distance of six hundred and eighty light-minutes, with an orbital eccentricity of twelve percent. At the moment, it was just past apastron, which meant Cerberus-A was almost exactly ten light-hours away. Cerberus-C—a cool, barren, planetless M9—had a much more eccentric orbit, but its average orbital radius was approximately forty-eight light-hours, and it never approached within less than thirty-three and a half light-hours of Cerberus-A. Which meant, of course, that it occasionally passed considerably closer than that to Hell, although such near approaches were centuries apart. And, Honor reflected, she was just as glad that her own stay would be far too short (one way or the other) for her to get a firsthand look at the next one.

But at the moment, local astrography was less important than the bright red icon blinking in the display to indicate a hostile impeller signature, and she watched the red bead tracking down the white vector projection that intersected Hell's orbit.

"So far, everything seems to be just where it ought to be," Benson said while Honor absorbed the plot's details. "They've been in-system for twenty-one minutes now, and their arrival message crossed our challenge—we received it . . . nine minutes and twenty-one seconds ago," she said, checking the time chop on a hardcopy message slip. "They should have received ours fifteen seconds after that, and they're still following straight down the least-time profile for a zero/zero intercept. Assuming they continue to do so, they'll make turnover in another hundred and thirteen minutes."

"Good," Honor murmured. She gazed at the plot a moment longer, then turned and walked over to stand behind Commander Phillips and Scotty Tremaine at the main com console. Horace Harkness sat to one side with two other electronics techs to assist him. Harkness himself was watching two displays simultaneously, and he spoke to Tremaine without looking away.

"I think we can lighten up on 'Citizen Commander Ragman's' mood in the next transmission, Sir," he said, forgetting his normal "lower deck" dialect as he concentrated.

"Sounds good to me, Chief," Tremaine replied, and Harkness grunted. He watched the display a moment later, then glanced at one of his assistants.

"See if this lousy excuse for an AI can get her to smile just a little, but don't get carried away. Throw her up on Three here for me to look at ASAP."

"I'm on it, Senior Chief," the assistant said, and Honor looked at Benson again.

"What is she?" she asked.

"According to her initial transmission, she's a StateSec heavy cruiser—the *Krashnark*—headed in with a fresh shipment of prisoners," Benson replied, looking down at the hardcopy. "I didn't recognize the name, but I found it in their Ship List data base. *Krashnark* is one of their new *Mars*-class CAs. From what I could find on their capabilities, they look like nasty customers."

"They are that," Honor agreed softly, remembering a deadly ambush, and the right corner of her mouth smiled slightly. She was going to enjoy getting a little of her own back from a *Mars*-class . . . and the fact that this ship belonged to the SS would only make it sweeter.

But slowly, she reminded herself. *Let's not get cocky and blow this, Honor!*

"Commander Phillips, has *Krashnark* ever visited Hell before?" she asked.

"No, Ma'am," Phillips answered promptly. "I ran a data search as soon as we had the name. Neither she, nor her captain—a Citizen Captain Pangborn—nor her com officer have ever been to Cerberus before this visit. I can't vouch for her other officers, but everyone who's been identified in their com traffic is a first-timer."

"Excellent," Honor murmured. "And very promptly done. Thank you, Commander."

"You're welcome, Admiral," Phillips replied without a trace of her earlier resentment, and Honor smiled down at her before she looked back at Benson.

"If they're all newcomers, we don't need 'Commander Ragman's' familiar face, so let's get Harkness' artificial person out of there and replace it with a live human being," she said. "Who do we have who sounds like a Peep?"

"You've got me, Dame Honor," another voice said quietly, and Honor turned towards it in surprise. Warner Caslet smiled crookedly and walked towards her from where he'd stood unobtrusively against one wall.

"Are you sure about that, Warner?" She spoke even more quietly than he had and felt a dozen other people fighting the urge to turn and look at the two of them.

"Yes, Ma'am." He met her single working eye levelly, and she and Nimitz tasted the sincerity and certainty at his core. He was hardly what she would call calm, but for the first time since their arrival on Hell, she felt no doubt at all in him, and the 'cat sat straighter in the bend of her elbow to consider the Citizen Commander with bright green eyes.

"May I ask why?" she inquired gently, and he smiled again, more crookedly than ever.

"Admiral Parnell is right, Ma'am," he said simply. "I can't go home because the butchers running my country won't let me. Which means the only thing I can do for the Republic is fight it from the outside. Didn't someone once say that we always hurt the one we love?"

The tone was humorous; the emotions behind it were not, and Honor wanted to weep for him.

"And if the Committee and State Security are overthrown?" she asked. "You're starting down a dangerous slope, Warner. Even if the 'butchers' are thrown out of office, the people who replace them will probably never trust you again. Might even consider you a traitor."

"I've thought about that," he agreed. "And you're right. If I cross the line to active collaboration with you, I'll never be able to go home. But if I don't cross it, all that's left for me would be to stand around doing nothing, and I've discovered I can't do that." Honor felt a stab of surprise as he echoed her own thoughts of only moments before, but he didn't seem to notice.

"That's the downside of the freedom of choice Admiral Parnell was talking about," he went on. "Once you've got it, you can't live with yourself very comfortably if you refuse to exercise it." He drew a deep breath, and his smile turned almost natural. "Besides, I've heard a lot about Captain Yu from Admiral Parnell in the last few weeks. If he could have the guts to not only take service with the Allies but actually go back to Grayson to do it, then so can I, by God! If you'll let me, of course."

Honor gazed at him for several seconds while silence hovered in the control room. She felt the emotions of the watch personnel beating in on her, and at least a third of them were convinced she'd have to be out of her mind even to contemplate trusting him so deeply. But Benson, Tremaine, and Harkness—the three people present, besides Honor, who knew Caslet best—were almost completely calm about the possibility. And Honor herself hesitated not because she distrusted Caslet in any way, but because she sensed at least a little of what this decision would cost him.

But he had the right to make up his own mind about the price his conscience required him to pay, she thought sadly, and nodded.

"Fine, Warner," she said, and looked at Harkness. "Can you put Cit—" She paused. "Can your little box of tricks put *Commander* Caslet in SS uniform for *Krashnark*'s edification, Senior Chief?"

"In a skinny minute, Ma'am," Harkness confirmed with a grin.

"Then sit down, Warner." She pointed to the chair in front of the main com console. "You know the script."

Chapter Forty-One

Caslet did his job to perfection.

The incoming cruiser never suspected a thing, and there was no reason she should have. After all, what could possibly go wrong on StateSec's most secure prison and private base? The orbital defenses were intact, so clearly no outside enemy had attacked the system. Every com procedure was perfect, for it was carried out in accordance with the instructions logged in the SS's own computers and every message carried all the proper security codes. And the wreckage of Citizen Lieutenant Commander Proxmire's courier boat had long since dispersed.

And so PNS *Krashnark* followed Caslet's instructions without question, for they, too, were precisely what they should have been. The cruiser passed through the safe lane Honor's people cleared through the mines for her and assumed the parking orbit Honor's people assigned her. And then *Krashnark* stood by to receive the three shuttles Camp Charon sent up to take off the Alliance POWs she'd come to deliver.

Citizen Sergeant Maxwell Riogetti, State Security Ground Forces, stood in the boat bay gallery with his back to the personnel tubes, cradling his flechette gun in his arms and watching the Manty prisoners narrowly. They weren't really all Manticorans, of course. There were Zanzibarans, and some Alizonians—even twenty or thirty Graysons and a handful of Erewhonese who'd been unfortunate enough to be serving aboard picket ships assigned to Zanzibar—but Riogetti thought of them all as Manties. And he heartily hoped that every single one of them was sweating bullets at the thought of being sent to Hell.

They damned well ought to be, the Citizen Sergeant thought with bitter satisfaction. *But it's okay with me if they aren't. Maybe it's even better that way. Citizen Brigadier Tresca will sort the bastards out soon enough!*

He smiled thinly at the thought. The damned Manty plutocrats were not only greedy bastards who hoarded the enormous wealth they'd stolen from the People, they were also pains in the ass every step of the way. It was as if they were absolutely determined to prove they were every bit as much enemies of the People as Citizen Secretary Ransom had always insisted they were.

Riogetti's smile turned into a frown at the thought of Cordelia Ransom's death. Now there had been a true heroine of the People! And horribly though her loss had hurt, it was fitting that such a courageous and charismatic leader should have died in mortal combat with the People's enemies as she would have wished. Yet her death had left a tremendous hole on the Committee of Public Safety and in the People's hearts. The Citizen Sergeant had tried hard, but he couldn't bring himself to think very highly of Citizen Secretary Boardman. He'd done his best, no doubt, but no one could have filled Ransom's shoes after her tragic death. Still, Boardman's heart was in the right place, and he knew how dangerous scum like these prisoners were to the People. Why, the bastards weren't even grateful to Citizen Vice Admiral Tourville and Citizen Admiral Giscard for picking up their life pods! They seemed to think that had been no more than their due, the very minimum the Navy could have done for them, despite the way their kind had callously abandoned Republican life pods in battle after battle—when they weren't using the pods for point defense practice!

Riogetti felt rage trembling in his muscles and made himself take his finger out of the flechette gun's trigger guard. It was hard. What he really wanted to do was switch to full auto, drop the muzzle, and empty the magazine into the handcuffed garbage waiting for the shuttles. But he couldn't, however much they deserved it.

Not without orders, anyway, he thought longingly.

He should have been given those orders, too. Oh, sure. Some people—even some of his fellows in StateSec—actually believed the Manty propaganda claims that they always picked up Republican survivors. But Riogetti knew better than to be fooled by such clumsy lies. He'd heard the truth from Public Information often enough. Hell, PubIn had even broadcast actual Navy sensor recordings that *showed* the Manties shooting up life pods! It was going to take more than plutocratic lies to explain away that kind of hard evidence, and—

A chime sounded, and he glanced over his shoulder as the shuttles from Camp Charon settled into the docking buffers. The mechanical docking arms engaged, and a green light blinked as the personnel tubes pressurized.

Now that's the way a maneuver should be performed, the Citizen Sergeant thought. *All three of them docked in less than a ten-second spread!*

It never occurred to him to wonder why bored shuttle pilots from a prison planet should care enough to make their approach with such perfect coordination. Not until the first battle-armored border emerged simultaneously from each personnel tube.

The Citizen Sergeant gawked at the apparitions in confusion, wondering what the hell was going on. He didn't feel alarmed, precisely, despite the new arrivals' abrupt appearance, for their armor carried standard StateSec rank emblems and unit flashes and they'd arrived aboard StateSec shuttles cleared by Charon Central and *Krashnark*'s own CIC. That meant there had to be a reasonable explanation, but hard as Riogetti might think, he could come up with no reason for prison guards to strap on the equivalent of old prespace main battle tanks just to go up and fetch a bunch of unarmed, handcuffed POWs!

Eight or nine armored troopers had disembarked from each shuttle by the time Citizen Lieutenant Ericson, the boat bay officer, got over his own shock enough to react.

"Just a minute—*just a minute!*" he shouted over the bay intercom. "What the hell is going on here? Nobody said anything about this to me! Who's in command of you people, anyway?"

"I am," an amplified voice replied over a suit speaker, and someone stepped to the front of the newcomers. It was a man's voice, deep but very young, Riogetti thought, and there was something about its soft accent. . . .

"And who the hell are you?" Ericson demanded, storming out of his control cubicle to glare at the newcomer. The very *tall* newcomer, Riogetti realized. Battle armor made anyone look tall, but this fellow must have been a giant in his bare feet. And he and most of his fellows were armed with flechette guns, not pulse rifles. Well, that made more sense than most of what was happening. The flechette guns were much more effective than pulse rifles for prisoner control—and much less likely to blow holes in shuttle hulls or other important equipment.

The giant turned, gazing thoughtfully at the boat bay officer through his armorplast visor while still more armored troopers emerged from the shuttles. There must have been forty-five or fifty of them in the bay gallery by now, and then the giant smiled thinly, and somehow his flechette gun was in his armored hands and the safety was off.

"In answer to your question," he told Ericson flatly, "my name is Clinkscales. Carson Clinkscales, Ensign, Grayson Space Navy, and this ship is no longer under StateSec command."

The citizen lieutenant gaped at him, and so did Riogetti and every other guard in the boat bay. The words were clear enough, but they made no sense. They couldn't make sense, because they were manifestly impossible. But then, suddenly, one of the guards shook herself and reacted. She wheeled with her flechette gun, reacting out of pure instinct, not reason, and hosed a vicious stream of flechettes at the nearest boarder.

The razor-edged projectiles whined uselessly off her target's armor, ricocheting wildly, and another SS guard screamed as three of them chewed into his back. One of the boarders jerked up his own weapon and triggered a single shot back at the guard who'd opened fire, killing her instantly, and a StateSec officer shouted something frantically. Perhaps it was an offer to surrender, or an order for the boat bay guards to lay down their weapons. But whatever it was, it came too late. Other guards were following the dead woman's example while prisoners flung themselves desperately to the deck to get out of the line of fire, and the rest of the borders responded with lethal efficiency.

Citizen Sergeant Riogetti saw Citizen Lieutenant Ericson reach for his holstered pulser, saw him jerk it free, saw the giant's gun come up, and saw the citizen lieutenant's mangled body fly backward under a blast of flechettes. And then the citizen sergeant saw the same flechette gun swinging towards him, and another muzzle flash.

And then he never saw anything at all again.

"I should have called on them to surrender before the shuttles docked," Honor said with quiet bitterness. She, McKeon, Ramirez, and Benson sat in the small briefing room off the main control center, viewing Solomon Marchant and Geraldine Metcalf's report from *Krashnark*. Marchant was safely in command of the ship, and there had been remarkably little fighting after the initial outbreak in the boat bay. Or perhaps not so remarkably, given that *Krashnark*'s skipper had been given his options by Charon Central just about the time that idiot guard opened fire. With the equivalent firepower of three or four squadrons of the wall locked onto his ship, Citizen Captain Pangborn had recognized the better part of valor when he saw it.

Unfortunately, twenty-nine members of his crew—and eight POWs—had been killed in the boat bay bloodbath first.

"Anyone can be wise after the fact, Honor," Jesus Ramirez said almost gently.

"But if they'd waited to board until Pangborn had agreed to surrender, none of this would have happened," Honor replied, jabbing her index finger at the casualty figures on the terminal before her.

"Maybe, and maybe not," McKeon said before Ramirez could respond. "Don't forget that Pangborn was up against a two-pronged threat—boarders inside and weapons platforms outside—and we really don't know which was the decisive factor for him. Without the boarders, he might have tried to bluff or threatened to kill the prisoners. Hell, he might have figured you wouldn't dare push the button, since you couldn't kill him without killing the POWs as well!"

"But—"

"Don't second-guess yourself!" Ramirez rumbled more forcefully. "Alistair is right. It wasn't your fault, and it wasn't young Clinkscales' fault, either. It was that idiot Black Leg. Once the first shot was fired—"

He shrugged, and Honor sighed. He and Alistair were right, and she and Nimitz could both feel Benson's firm agreement with her superiors. But still. . . .

She sighed again, then made herself nod unhappily. Yet despite Ramirez's firmness, she knew she was going to go right on second guessing herself, and knowing he was right wouldn't change a thing. She'd made the call hoping the double threat would minimize any temptation to resist, and it should have worked—*had* worked, once the initial firefight (if you could call such a one-sided massacre that) was over. But she was the CO. It was her job to get things right, and she hadn't, and whether it was reasonable or not, she blamed herself for it.

Still, she couldn't afford to brood on it, either, and she opened her mouth to speak, then looked up as the briefing room door opened to admit Geraldine Metcalf and a stranger in an orange jumpsuit. Honor felt a spasm of confused emotion—distaste, anger, and an undeniable stab of fear—as she saw the jumpsuit, for she had worn one just like it in PNS *Tepes*' brig, but the jumpsuit hardly registered, for it was buried in her surprise at seeing Metcalf. The situation aboard *Krashnark* had only just started settling down, and she'd expected Metcalf to remain aboard the cruiser as Marchant's XO until they had everything buttoned up. But she hadn't . . . and Honor stiffened in her chair as Metcalf's emotions hit her like a hammer.

"Gerry?" she asked, half-raising a hand to reach out to the other woman before she could stop herself.

"Excuse me, Ma'am," Metcalf said, her voice curiously flat and almost stunned sounding. She didn't even seem to see Honor's hand, and she clasped her own hands behind herself, coming to a sort of parade rest and straightening her spine. "I realize I shouldn't have burst in on you like this, Milady," she went on in that same flat voice, "but this is Commander Victor Ainspan. He was the senior Manticoran POW aboard *Krashnark*, and Solomon and I thought you should hear his news as quickly as possible."

"What news would that be?" Honor's voice sounded almost calm, but that was solely because decades of command experience had control of her vocal cords. Underneath her apparent composure the jagged spikes of stress and shock radiating from Metcalf twisted her nerves like taut cables, and she kept herself in her chair only by sheer force of will.

"The prisoners aboard *Krashnark*, Ma'am," Metcalf told her. "They're all military POWs, not politicals, and fifteen of them are from the Zanzibaran Navy."

"Zanzibaran?" Honor's eyebrows furrowed. The Caliphate's navy didn't have anything bigger than a heavy cruiser, and its units were assigned almost exclusively to the defense of their own home system, so how—

"Zanzibaran," Metcalf confirmed harshly, and her nostrils flared. "Milady, according to the prisoners, the Peeps hit Zanzibar hard two T-months ago." Alistair McKeon muttered a disbelieving imprecation behind Honor, but she couldn't look away from Metcalf's face. "They rolled right over it—sucked the picket into a head-on pass, blew it out with missile pods, and then went on and took out every industrial platform in the system."

Ramirez and Benson looked perplexed. They'd been on Hell too long, and they were too unfamiliar with the members and dynamics—not to mention the astrography—of the Manticoran Alliance to realize how far into the Allies' rear the Peeps had gone to strike at Zanzibar. But Honor and McKeon knew.

"My God, Gerry," the commodore said. "Are you *sure?*"

"Whether I am nor not, the prisoners are, Skipper," Metcalf told him, her expression grim. "But that's not the worst of it. Commander Ainspan?"

The dark-faced, whippet-thin commander stepped forward, and Honor shook herself.

"Excuse me, Commander," she said. "It was rude of us to ignore you."

"Don't worry about that, Milady," Ainspan said, and Honor's eyebrows flipped back up as she truly concentrated on him for the first time and the boiling confusion of his emotions reached out to her. His eyes were fixed on her ravaged face, and they positively glowed with some deep reaction she couldn't even begin to sort out. Whatever it was, it wasn't the same as Metcalf's—which was reasonable enough. Gerry's news was no surprise to him, after all. But even so, he radiated a sense of shock almost as great as the lieutenant commander's. It was just a different kind of shock. One that was almost . . . reverent, and he seemed unable to go on after his first short sentence.

"Are you all right, Commander?" Honor asked after a few seconds of silence, and the liberated prisoner flushed darkly.

"I— Yes, Milady. I'm fine," he said. "It's just that . . . well, we all thought you were dead."

"Dead?" Honor frowned for a moment, then nodded. "So they admitted what happened to *Tepes*? I didn't think they would."

"Tepes?" Ainspan blinked at her. "No, Milady. They never said anything about anyone named Tepes."

"It wasn't an 'anyone,'" Honor explained. "It was a ship—Cordelia Ransom's ship." This was insane, she thought. The fact that the Peeps had hit Zanzibar was incomparably more important than discussing the names of blown up StateSec battlecruisers, yet Ainspan seemed almost more concerned about her than he was about the fact that he himself had just been rescued from Peep custody!

"It was—?" the commander began, then stopped and shook himself. "INS didn't give the name of her ship, Milady. But how did *you* know it? It only happened nine months ago."

"What?" It was Honor's turn to feel confused. "I don't know what happened nine months ago, Commander, but we've been on Hell for a T-year and a half, and Commodore McKeon and his people blew *Tepes* up before we ever landed!"

"A year and a—?" Ainspan blinked, then stopped again, thinking furiously, and Honor turned to look at her subordinates at last. McKeon still seemed almost too stunned for coherent thought, but Ramirez and Benson looked just as perplexed by Ainspan's odd behavior as Honor felt.

"I guess that *would* make sense," he said finally, and Honor frowned.

"*What* would make sense, Commander?" she asked rather more sharply than she'd meant to, and he gave himself a shake.

"I'm sorry, Milady. It's just that I never expected— I mean, we all thought— And Commander Metcalf didn't even mention your name to me until just before we grounded, so I didn't—" He stopped again, drew a deep breath, and visibly got a grip on himself. "Lady Harrington, the reason we thought you were dead is that the Peeps told everyone you were. More than that, they broadcast the video of your execution over INS."

"They *what?*" Honor stared at him in disbelief.

"They broadcast the video of your execution—your hanging—Ma'am," Ainspan said. "They said they'd executed you for that business on Basilisk Station, and they showed everyone the imagery to prove it."

"But why?" Surprise startled the question out of Honor, but she knew it was a foolish one even as she asked it. Ainspan couldn't possibly know why they'd done it. He hadn't even known she was alive until Metcalf told him!

"Actually," Jesus Ramirez said slowly, "it could even make a kind of sense, in a sick, Peep-minded sort of way."

"Sense?" Honor turned to him, still grappling with the news, and a darker thought hit her with sudden, sickening force. Her parents! If the Peeps had broadcast her "hanging" and done it so realistically that no one in the Alliance had even questioned it, then her mother and father must have seen—

"In a way," Ramirez repeated. His voice jerked her free of the horrifying image of her parents watching her "death" on HV, and she felt a stab of gratitude so powerful it was almost painful. She clung to his words, using them as a shield against her mother's and—especially!—her father's probable reaction to that imagery and nodded choppily for him to go on.

"You hadn't heard anything about the *Tepes*, had you, Commander?" the San Martino asked Ainspan, and the Manticoran shook his head. "Then I suspect that's the explanation, Honor," Ramirez said, turning back to her. "They think you *are* dead, as well as Alistair and anyone else who was with you and could ever dispute their version of what happened. And they damned well wouldn't want to admit that twenty or thirty POWs broke out of StateSec custody and blew an entire battlecruiser to hell in the process! Even announcing that they'd destroyed your shuttle as you 'fled' wouldn't make up for the kind of black eye that would give them—and especially if this Ransom was aboard her at the time. So they decided to cover it all up and carry through with your execution for the record because they'd already told everyone they were going to and it was one way to keep anyone from continuing to ask questions about you. Which meant they still had to explain what had happened to Ransom *and* her ship, so they announced her death after they'd had time to decide exactly how they wanted to handle the fallout. And when no one would have any reason at all to associate *her* death with yours." He snorted bitterly. "Legislaturalist or 'New Order,' Public Information's thinking doesn't seem to change very much, does it?"

"Um." Honor gazed at him a moment longer, then nodded again, more normally. It did make sense, in an insane sort of way, and she should have seen it for herself. But she knew why she hadn't, and she reached out to gather Nimitz close as the 'cat walked down the table to her. She held him against her breasts, clinging to the comfort of her link to him even more tightly, and forced herself to put all thought of her parents out of her mind for the moment. Then she turned back to Ainspan and somehow summoned up a smile.

"As you can see, Commander, the reports of my death have been somewhat exaggerated. That, however, is less significant than your other news. What, exactly, happened in Zanzibar?"

"We got our asses kicked, Milady," Ainspan said bitterly. He, too, seemed to have struggled past the initial shock of finding her alive, but there was no relief in that for him, and his poison-bleak emotions washed into her. "The Peep CO—according to their propaganda, it was Tourville, the same bastard who captured *Prince Adrian*—completely wiped out our picket force, then carried through and destroyed the system's deep-space infrastructure, just like Commander Metcalf said. And after he'd done that, he moved on and did exactly the same damned thing to Alizon."

"Jesus *Christ!*" McKeon breathed, and Honor fought to keep the shock out of her own expression. It was hard—and even harder because she was still tapped into Ainspan's emotions.

"Why do I have the feeling there's more, Commander?" she asked flatly.

"Because there is, Milady," Ainspan replied just as flatly. "They also hit Hancock and Seaford Nine. I don't know exactly what happened at Hancock. I'd guess they got *their* asses kicked there, because I haven't run into any of our people who were captured there, and the Peep propaganda's made a big deal out of all the naval losses they supposedly inflicted but never claimed that they'd taken the system. They did take Seaford, though, and punched out another picket squadron and all the fleet facilities, as well. But that's not the worst of it."

He drew a deep breath, as if stealing himself. Then—

"They hit Basilisk, too, Milady," he said quietly. "They killed Admiral Markham and destroyed the inner-system picket, then went on and wrecked everything in Medusa orbit."

"*Basilisk?*" McKeon sounded strangled. "They hit *Basilisk*, too?!"

"Yes, Sir," Ainspan looked as if he wanted nothing in the universe more than to give McKeon a different answer, but he couldn't. "I don't have anything like official numbers, Milady," he went on, turning back to Honor, "but I know we got hurt and hurt bad. According to the Peeps, we've lost sixty-one of the wall, plus most of their screening units. I think that has to be an exaggeration, but I've personally met prisoners who can confirm the attacks on Zanzibar, Alizon, and Seaford Nine. I think—" He drew another deep breath. "I think this time they're actually telling the truth, Milady—at least about the systems they hit."

Honor felt Ramirez and Benson flinch at last as the number sixty-one hit them. They might not be sufficiently familiar with the Alliance's astrography to know where Zanzibar was or what the significance of an attack on it might be, but they thought they knew how hard the Alliance had been hit if the Peeps' claims about Allied ship losses were anywhere near accurate.

Only they were wrong, she thought, and her brain was so numb she felt almost calm. The ship losses and loss of life were serious enough—even assuming the Peeps had inflated them by thirty or forty percent, they were still the worst the Royal Manticoran Navy had suffered in its entire four hundred-year history—but the impact of that paled beside the sheer audacity of the Peep attack.

It must have hit the Admiralty like a thunderbolt, she thought. *After all this time, no one could have anticipated the possibility that the Peeps might try something like this.* I *certainly never would have! But if they've really punched out Zanzibar and Alizon and hit* Basilisk, *then—*

She closed her eyes, and despite the insulation of her shock, her thoughts raced. Even the total destruction of all industry in Zanzibar and Alizon would be a relatively minor blow to the industrial base of the Alliance as a whole, and the civilian loss of life wouldn't have been too bad—not if Ainspan was right about who'd commanded the raids. Lester Tourville would have done everything humanly possible to hold down the noncombatant death count. And from an industrial viewpoint, the RMN satellite yard at Grendelsbane Station alone had more capacity than Zanzibar and Alizon combined. All of which meant the Alliance could take up the slack without dangerously overstraining itself.

But that hardly mattered, for the political and diplomatic consequences of a successful strike of this magnitude upon two allies of the Star Kingdom must have been devastating. And the destruction of the Basilisk support structure must have been even worse. Basilisk was Manticoran territory, and no one had dared to attack the Star Kingdom's home space in three hundred and seventy years. The economic cost alone had to have been catastrophic, at least as bad as the Zanzibaran and Alizonian losses combined, but the other consequences of such an attack must have cut deeper than any financial loss. And—

"We're on our own," she said softly, not even aware she'd spoken aloud.

"What did you say?" It was McKeon. He sounded far more abrupt than usual, but at least he was beginning to fight sufficiently clear of his own shock to think again, and she looked at him.

"I beg your pardon?" she said.

"You said 'we're on our own,'" he told her. She looked at him blankly for a moment, then nodded. "So what did you mean?" he asked.

"I meant that we can't whistle up a rescue expedition after all," she told him bleakly. He cocked his head as if to invite fuller explanation. The beginnings of understanding already showed in his eyes, but she went on anyway, looking up at Ainspan while she explained it to him, as if using the words to hammer home her own acceptance of them.

"We thought we could send a ship like *Krashnark* back to Alliance space if we could ever take her in the first place," she said. "Then all we'd have to do would be sit tight while the Admiralty organized a convoy and escorts and came to get us out. But if the Peeps have hit us that hard back home, the Alliance couldn't possibly justify sending a force big enough to lift us all out of here. Even if the Admiralty were willing to, the Government would never authorize it—not when every voter in the Star Kingdom and every member government of the Alliance has to be screaming for ships of the wall to reinforce *their* picket forces!"

McKeon's gaze met hers. He started to open his mouth, but she'd read the thought behind his eyes and gave a sharp, tiny shake of her head. His mouth closed again, and she looked away, watching her non-Manticoran officers grapple with the news. It didn't seem to have occurred to any of them that the Allies certainly *would* send a ship to pick up Steadholder Harrington if they knew she was alive, and Honor hoped it never did occur to them. Sending a single fast ship to collect one person—or even a few dozen people—was one thing. Sending enough personnel lift to take everyone else off Hell as well was something else entirely.

"But if we can't call for help," Harriet Benson said at last, speaking very quietly, "then we're screwed, aren't we? We *needed* that support, Honor. What the hell do we do if we can't get it?"

"Do, Harry?" Honor turned to look at her, and the living side of her mouth turned up in a grim, cold smile. "We do what we have to do," she said in a voice that matched the smile perfectly. "And if we can't do it the easy way, then we do it the *hard* way. But I'll tell you this now—all of you. There aren't enough Peeps in this galaxy to keep me from taking my people home, and I am not going to leave a single person I promised to get off this planet behind me when we go!"

Chapter Forty-Two

"So that's what I intend to do," Honor told the officers around the conference table. "I know it's risky, but given Commander Ainspan's news—" she nodded her head courteously at the Commander, who sat at the foot of the table, where he'd just finished briefing her senior officers "—I don't see that we have any choice."

"*Risky?* That plan isn't 'risky'—it's insane!" Rear Admiral Styles' voice was flat and hard. No doubt he meant for it to sound firm, decisive and determined, but she heard the naked terror behind it only too clearly. And when she glanced around the conference table at the expressions of her other senior officers, she knew that impression was neither her imagination nor solely due to her link to Nimitz.

"Keeping *Krashnark* here in the Cerberus System is the worst thing we could possibly do," he went on, turning slightly away from her to address her other officers as if lecturing a crowd of school children. "I've never heard a senior officer suggest anything so reckless and ill-considered! I remind you all that she is the only means of communication with the Alliance we have! If we don't use her to send for help, no one can have the least possible idea that we're even here awaiting rescue!"

"I'm aware of the risks, Admiral." Honor managed—somehow—to keep her voice level and wondered if she were being wise to do so. Speaking around a senior officer to her subordinates, especially when criticizing that senior officer's plan in such immoderate language, constituted a serious offense by RMN standards. At the very least it was insubordinate; at worst, it was an attempt to undermine the chain of command, and she knew she ought to bring the hammer down. But Styles remained the second-ranking Allied officer on Hell and this was no time for divisiveness, and so she gritted mental teeth and made herself speak to him as reasonably as if he had a functioning brain and a desire to use it.

"Risk or no, however, I don't believe the Alliance could possibly justify sending a sufficient force to lift all of our people off this planet so far from the front under the circumstances. Even assuming that there haven't been still more raids on Allied systems since Commander Ainspan was captured, the threat of such attacks has to have thrown all our dispositions into confusion. Allowing for the inevitable communications delays, the Joint Chiefs and Admiralty probably don't even know where all our vessels are at the moment! And even if they decided that they could risk uncovering the core systems just to send an expedition out here after us, it would be criminal for us to ask them to." She shook her head. "No, Admiral Styles. We have to accomplish whatever we can on our own, and that means I can't possibly justify sending *Krashnark* to ask for help."

"That's one opinion," Styles shot back, "and I suggest that the decision as to what the Alliance can and can't do ought to be made at a much higher level than this. More than that, allow me to point out—in case it's slipped your own attention—that by keeping *Krashnark* here you're probably throwing away our only chance to get at least some of the people on this planet to safety! If we stripped her down and cut her life-support margins to the minimum, we could get forty percent of the people currently on Styx aboard her. Surely getting at least some of us out is better than having StateSec recapture all of us!"

"And just which forty percent would you advocate we get out, Admiral?" Alistair McKeon asked flatly. The other officers present—Jesus Ramirez, Gaston Simmons, Harriet Benson, Cynthia Gonsalves, Solomon Marchant, and Warner Caslet—all looked acutely uncomfortable, and their expression got still more uncomfortable at McKeon's question. None of them were Manticoran and all were junior to Styles, and they looked like family friends trying to stay out of a domestic quarrel. But they'd also come to know Styles much better than any of them would really have preferred, and, like McKeon, they knew exactly which forty percent of the eight thousand people actually on Styx Styles would advocate sending to safety. After all, it just happened that approximately forty percent of those people were members of one or another of the Allied militaries . . . just as forty percent of the people in this conference room were.

But however furious and terrified he might be, the admiral seemed unwilling to be quite that explicit.

"That's neither here nor there," he said instead. "Obviously some sort of screening or selection process would have to be worked out. But the point is that we could get at least that forty percent—whoever it was—to safety *and* inform higher authority of the situation here at the same time. Given that, it would be the height of irresponsibility even to contemplate holding *Krashnark* here! And," he took his eyes from McKeon's just long enough to dart a sideways glance at Honor but went on as if speaking solely to McKeon, "I suspect a board of inquiry might well conclude that it went beyond simple irresponsibility into criminal disregard of duty and—"

"That will be enough, Admiral Styles." Honor's voice had changed. Unlike Styles', her tone was now cool and calm, almost conversational, but Andrew LaFollet smiled coldly when he heard it. He stood against the conference room wall behind her, able to see and hear everything yet so unobtrusive no one even noticed his presence after so many weeks, and he watched Styles' choleric face with anticipation. The Steadholder had put up with more than enough from this bigmouthed fool, and LaFollet felt himself silently urging Styles to misread her tone and manner.

"I beg your pardon, *Admiral* Harrington, but it is *not* enough!" the Manticoran said sharply, and satisfaction widened LaFollet's smile. The idiot *had* misread her voice. He actually thought her apparent calmness was a good sign. Or perhaps he simply thought it indicated that she was uncertain and trying to hide it, or that he finally had a pretext he could use to undercut her authority in the eyes of her subordinates for his own gain.

"I have questioned the wisdom of many of your decisions here on Hades," he went on, "but this one goes beyond unwise to insane! I have accepted your command authority despite the . . . irregularity of your claimed seniority in a non-Manticoran navy, but your current course of conduct leads me to seriously question my own wisdom in doing so. Whatever the actual status of your commission—or even the legality of your holding commissions in two different navies simultaneously—this decision absolutely proves you lack the experience for your supposed rank!"

Alistair McKeon had started to lunge furiously up out of his chair when Styles began. Now he sat back instead, regarding the Rear Admiral with the same sort of fascination with which people watched two ground cars slide inexorably towards one another on icy pavement. Honor sat very still in her chair beside him, watching Styles with her single hand flat on the table before her and her head tilted slightly to one side. Her only expression was the small, metronome-steady tic at the living corner of her mouth, and Nimitz crouched on his perch, as motionless as she . . . except that the very tip of his tail flick-flick-flicked in exact rhythm with the tic of her mouth.

McKeon looked away from Honor long enough to glance at the others around the table and felt reassured by what he saw. None of them really understood why Honor hadn't already crushed Styles, and while none of them wanted to get involved in a fight between her and an officer of her own navy—or one of her own navies, at least—they were entirely prepared to support her against him now. McKeon happened to agree with them that Honor should have stepped on the loathsome bastard the first time he got out of line, but he also knew (far better than they) that she didn't do things that way. Sometimes—as in McKeon's own case, once upon a time—that could be a good thing. This time, as far as he was concerned, she'd waited far too long, and he felt an anticipation very much like Andrew LaFollet's as Styles went right on running his mouth.

"I'll accept that you believe you're doing the right thing and performing to the very best of your ability," the Manticoran went on, his voice oozing damning-with-faint-praise scorn, "but one of the things experience teaches is the ability to recognize the limitations of reality. Yes, and the true nature of responsibility, as well! Your primary duty as a Queen's officer is—"

"I don't believe you heard me, Admiral Styles," Honor said, still in that conversational tone, her body language completely relaxed. "I said I had heard enough, and I remind you—for the final time—of the penalties laid down by the Articles of War for insubordination."

"*Insubordination?*" Styles glared at her, apparently oblivious to the dangerous glitter in her single working eye. "It's not 'insubordination' to point out to a manifestly inexperienced officer that her conception of her own duty and importance is obviously and completely divorced from reality and—

"*Major LaFollet!*" Honor's voice was no longer calm. It was a blade of chilled steel, cutting across Styles' hotter, bombastic bellicosity like a sword.

"Yes, My Lady?" LaFollet snapped to attention behind her.

"Do you have your side arm, Major?" she asked, without so much as looking over her shoulder or taking her steely gaze from Styles' congested face.

"I do, My Lady," her armsman replied crisply.

"Very good." The right side of her lips curled up in a thin, dangerous smile, and Styles' eyes began to widen as the fact that she had been anything but intimidated by his bluster finally started to seep into his awareness. LaFollet was already moving, circling the table towards Styles in anticipation of Honor's orders, but the rear admiral didn't even notice that. He stared at Honor instead, opening his mouth as if to speak, but it was much too late for that.

"You will place Rear Admiral Styles under arrest," Honor went on to LaFollet in that arctic voice. "You will escort him immediately from this conference room to the brig, and you will there place him under close confinement on my authority. He will not be allowed to return to his quarters. He is not to be permitted contact with any other individual between this conference room and his cell."

"This is preposterous—an *outrage—!*" Styles lunged to his feet and started to lean threateningly towards Honor, only to break off with a gurgle as Andrew LaFollet's left hand caught the collar of his tunic from behind. LaFollet no more believed Styles had the courage to physically assault his Steadholder than anyone else in that conference room did . . . but he didn't very much care. It was far too good a pretext to pass up. He was a good five centimeters shorter than Styles, but he was all wiry muscle and bone, and he got his back and shoulders into it as he pivoted and heaved.

Styles pitched backward, arms windmilling. He sailed through the air, crashed down on his back with a grunt of anguish, and slid across the floor until his head slammed into the wall and stopped him. He lay for an instant, half-stunned, then blinked and started to push himself back up—only to freeze as he found himself looking into the muzzle of Andrew LaFollet's rock-steady pulser from a range of two meters.

His eyes went huge. Then they traveled slowly up the Grayson's arm to the armsman's face, and his heart seemed to stop as he recognized LaFollet's complete willingness to squeeze that trigger.

"I have tolerated your gross insubordination, incompetence, cowardice, defiance, and disrespect for as long as I intend to, Admiral Styles," Honor told him coldly. "You have been warned dozens of times, and you have steadfastly declined to amend your behavior, despite repeated warnings that my patience was not without limit. Very well. I will not warn you again. You will now accompany Major LaFollet to the brig, where you *will* be held in close confinement until such time as formal charges are preferred against you before a court-martial board of Her Majesty's Navy. I have no doubt that those charges will be sustained . . . and you know as well as I what the penalty attached to them will be."

Styles seemed to wilt down inside himself, his normally dark face turning a sickly paste-gray, and she watched him with the dispassion of a scientist gazing at some particularly revolting new bacterium. She gave him time to speak, if he should be foolish enough to want to make things still worse, but he said nothing. From the taste of his emotions, he was probably physically incapable of making his vocal apparatus work at the moment, and she forced her mouth not to twist with contempt before she glanced back at LaFollet.

"Carry out your orders, Major," she said quietly, and her armsman nodded and stepped back from Styles. His pulser twitched commandingly, and Styles came to his feet as if the weapon were a magic wand that had cast a spell of levitation upon him. He stared at LaFollet, unable to take his eyes from the Grayson's implacable expression, and swallowed hard as the contempt and loathing discipline had prevented LaFollet from displaying earlier looked back at him. The last thing in the universe that he wanted to do, Harry Styles realized in that instant, was to give Andrew LaFollet even the smallest excuse to do what the armsman wanted so badly to do.

"After you, Admiral." The major spoke almost courteously and flicked a nod at the conference room door. Styles stared at him a moment longer, then darted one dazed look around the conference room only to see unwavering support for Honor on every other face, and all life seemed to ooze out of him. He turned without another word and shuffled out, followed by LaFollet, and the door closed silently behind them.

"I apologize for that unseemly episode," Honor said to the officers still seated around the conference table. "If I'd dealt with the situation more effectively sooner, I could have avoided such an undignified confrontation."

"Don't apologize, Admiral Harrington." Jesus Ramirez used her rank title with quiet emphasis. "Every military organization in the galaxy has its share of fools who manage to get promoted far beyond their abilities."

"Perhaps." Honor drew a deep breath, more than a little ashamed of herself now that LaFollet had marched Styles off. Whatever Ramirez might say, she knew she could have handled things better than this. At the very least, she could have ordered Styles to place himself under quarters-arrest after any of a dozen earlier, less virulent confrontations. She hadn't had to let it get to this stage, or to humiliate him so utterly in front of others, and she wondered if she'd let it go so far deliberately. She knew how badly a part of her had wanted to crush him like a worm. Had her subconscious always hoped the opportunity to act as she just had would eventually present itself if she just gave him enough rope?

She didn't know . . . but she suspected she wouldn't have liked the truth if she had.

She closed her eyes for a moment and inhaled deeply once more, then made herself put Styles' fate out of her mind. She would have to return to it eventually, for she'd meant exactly what she said. Whatever her own motives, she simply could not let this most recent behavior pass, and she had more than enough witnesses—not simply to this episode, but to others—to guarantee that his career was over. The Judge Advocate General might allow him to resign rather than prosecute, given the circumstances which had put him on Hell for so long, but either way he would be disgraced, dishonored, and ruined. Yet she couldn't let herself be distracted by that just now, and her expression was calm when she opened her eyes once more.

"Whatever my opinion of Styles may be," she said calmly, "he did make at least two accurate statements. If I hold *Krashnark* here, I deliberately turn down a chance to alert the rest of the Alliance to the situation on Hell, and I may be wrong about their ability and readiness to cut loose the forces needed to lift us off this planet. Even if I'm not, my action will effectively make that decision for them, without ever giving them the opportunity to consider it. And he's also right that holding her throws away the near certain chance of getting two or three thousand people to safety in Alliance space."

"If I may, My Lady?" Solomon Marchant half raised one hand, forefinger extended, and Honor nodded for him to go on.

"In regard to your first concern, My Lady," Marchant said very formally, "I would simply like to point out that whatever Admiral

Styles may believe, you *are* the second-ranking officer of the Grayson Navy, which happens to be the second largest navy of the Alliance—and the third largest in this entire quadrant, after the RMN and the Havenite Navy. As such, you would be one of the people who would normally help make any decision as to whether or not the Alliance could safely divert shipping on such a mission. Under the circumstances, I believe it's entirely appropriate for you to exercise your own judgment in this situation."

An almost inaudible murmur of agreement supported his argument, and Honor felt the sincerity of the emotions behind the murmur.

"And as to your second concern, My Lady," Marchant went on, "you say we could get two or three thousand people off Hell." He glanced at Cynthia Gonsalves. "Could you tell us what the current total number of evacuees is, Captain Gonsalves?"

"Three hundred ninety-two thousand, six hundred and fifty-one," Gonsalves replied with prompt precision. Since the courts-martial had wound down, she had taken over as Styles' second-in-command . . . which meant she'd actually been doing virtually all of the work in coordinating the prisoner contact and census project. "To date, two hundred seventeen thousand, three hundred and fifty-four have formally declined to collaborate with us. Most of those are Peep politicals, of course, but some of them are military or ex-military POWs."

Her voice hardened and flattened with the last sentence, and Ramirez stirred in his chair.

"It's hard to blame them, Cynthia," he said, his deep voice oddly gentle. "Most of them have just run out of hope after so long on Hell. They don't believe we can possibly pull this off, and they don't want to be part of the reprisals the Black Legs are going to carry out when and if they come back."

"I understand that, Sir," Gonsalves replied, "but understanding it doesn't change the consequences of their decision—for them, as well as for us."

"You're right, of course, Ma'am," Marchant said, reclaiming the floor. "But my point, My Lady," he turned back to Honor, "is that while Admiral Styles was correct that we could cram forty percent of the people on *Styx* aboard *Krashnark*, even packing her to the deckheads would account for less than one percent of the total on *Hell*."

"Which is still a lot more than none at all, Solomon," Honor replied quietly.

"It is," McKeon agreed before the Grayson officer could speak again, "but I think you're missing Solomon's point—or simply choosing not to admit it." He smiled wryly as her eye flashed at him, then continued more seriously. "Whichever it is, though, the question you have to ask yourself isn't whether or not holding *Krashnark* here throws away the certainty of getting eight-tenths of a percent of us out, but rather whether or not it ups the odds of getting *more* than eight-tenths of a percent out by a large enough factor to justify accepting the *risk* of getting no one out."

"Alistair is right, Honor," Ramirez said before she could reply. "Certainly there are going to be people—like Styles—who second-guess you however things work out. And some of the people who criticize you *won't* be idiots, too, because it's a question that can be legitimately argued either way. But the bottom line is that for everyone else, it would be a hypothetical question . . . and for you, it isn't. You're the one who has to make the call, and you have to make it now. So make it. In your considered judgment, does holding this ship in Cerberus improve your odds of success more than sending her for help the Alliance may or may not be in a position to extend to us?"

Honor sat back in her chair, feeling Nimitz's warm, supporting presence at her shoulder, and gazed into the mouth of Ramirez's stark options. She'd already considered the consequences and the odds, of course. If she hadn't, she never would have stated the intention which had so horrified Styles. But she knew herself too well—knew that this time was different, for Marchant and McKeon and Ramirez were right. It *was* her call, and they were waiting for her to make the decision which would commit them all not to an "intention" which left room to wiggle later but to a hard and firm plan they would all carry through together . . . or die trying to.

"If we were talking about a lighter ship," she said finally, "my decision might be different. But this is a *Mars*-class. She masses six hundred thousand tons—almost as big and tough as most of their prewar battlecruisers—and if we're going to make this work, we've *got* to have some mobile combat units with real fighting power." Her nostrils flared. "Which means I can't justify sending her off."

"I agree," Ramirez said softly, and other heads nodded around the table.

Honor felt their support and knew how much it meant to her, but she also knew it was only support. The responsibility was hers, and the responsibility for the deaths of all of them would also be hers if she blew it.

Yet she had no choice. She simply could not abandon the POWs who hadn't run out of defiance for their captors after their time on Hell, just as she could not abandon the non-Allied POWs who had actively aided her in capturing and securing Camp Charon in the first place.

A "calculated risk," she thought. *Isn't that what they called a decision like this back at Saganami Island? And they were right, of course. But it's an awful lot easier to analyze past examples of them in a classroom and decide where the people who took them screwed up than it is to take responsibility for them yourself!*

"All right, then," Admiral Lady Dame Honor Harrington said with calm, confident assurance, "we keep her. Alistair, I want you and Harry to grab Gerry Metcalf and Master Chief Ascher. We're going to need as many people trained to combat-ready status on Peep hardware as we can get, because if this is going to work at all, we'll need a lot more hardware than a single heavy cruiser. But she's got simulators on board as well as complete manuals on all of her hardware in her data banks. So we'll use her for a training ship while we start getting our people brought up to speed."

"Yes, Ma'am." McKeon tapped a note to himself into his liberated Peep memo pad. "I'll snag Gerry as soon as the meeting breaks up. Harry," he looked at Captain Benson, "can you free up Commander Phillips and . . . Lieutenant Commander Dumfries, I think, to help Gerry and me with the initial planning?"

"I'll have to rework the watch schedules a little, but I don't see a problem," Benson said after a moment.

"Be sure you're comfortable with that before you give them up, Harry," Honor warned her. "Because once Alistair's got that running, you and Jesus and I are going to have to put our heads together and start thinking seriously about genuine tactics. I've got a few thoughts, but to make this work, we may well be going to have to get a lot more performance out of the orbital defenses than I'd initially planned on. If you give up Phillips and Dumfries, do you have someone else who can replace them?"

"I do," Benson replied firmly.

"All right, in that case—"

Honor turned to Cynthia Gonsalves, her expression calm and focused, and her brain ticked smoothly and efficiently. There were no more doubts. She was committed now, her mind and thoughts reaching out to the challenge without a shadow of uncertainty, and her concentration was so complete she never even noticed Alistair McKeon and Jesus Ramirez grin broadly at one another across the table.

Chapter Forty-Three

Citizen Lieutenant Commander Heathrow hadn't been at all happy when he received his latest orders, but he hadn't been sufficiently unhappy to let it show. That was a bad enough idea for a Republican officer when it was merely Navy orders he objected to.

Still, it did seem unfair to pick on him for this. State Security had skimmed off large enough numbers of badly needed warships for its own private use, and the SS was notoriously secretive about its affairs. Those were two good reasons they should have been able to send one of their own courier boats right there!

But they hadn't, for whatever reason. Officially (and it might even be true) the problem was shortage of time and resources in the wake of the Navy's achievements at the front. Heathrow was too junior an officer to have access to any of the classified briefings, but even peasants like him knew Citizen Secretary McQueen's enormously successful offensives had thrown the Republic's naval forces into utter confusion. In some ways, following up success had wreaked more havoc with their deployments than years of slow, steady retreat had, and Heathrow supposed StateSec might be experiencing echoes of that same mad scramble to reorganize on the fly.

But whatever the reason, the StateSec CO in Shilo had needed a courier—fast—and he hadn't had any courier boats of his own immediately available. What he *had* had, however, was the standing SS authority to requisition the "support" of any Navy or Marine units which he might happen to decide he needed, and so Heathrow and his crew had ended up stuck with the job. Which explained why he was sitting *very* nervously in his command chair and watching Citizen Lieutenant Bouret follow Camp Charon's extremely specific helm instructions. Given the number of targeting systems currently illuminating his command and StateSec's obsessive suspicion of the regular Navy, neither Heathrow nor Bouret had the least intention of straying so much as a meter from their cleared flight path. Besides, the damned mines out there looked thick enough to walk on.

Heathrow made himself sit back and ease his death grip on the chair arms. It wasn't easy, and he tried to distract himself by studying his plot. Camp Charon had warned him in brusque, no-nonsense tones that Navy ships were not encouraged to use active sensors this close to StateSec's private little planet, but even passive sensors and old-fashioned visuals were enough to show Heathrow that he wanted nothing to do with this place. Seeing all that orbital firepower made his skin crawl. This was supposed to be a *prison*, not some kind of fortress against the universe, for God's sake! What did they expect? That the prisoners were somehow going to signal an enemy fleet to come charging in and attack the system? It had to be something like that—or else sheer, paranoid distrust of the Republic's own Navy—because there was no way in hell StateSec needed remote missile platforms, graser and laser platforms, and minefields against anyone on the surface of Hades.

I just hope that the fact that they had to tell me the system's coordinates so I could get here in the first place doesn't come back to haunt me, Heathrow thought mordantly. *I can see it now: "We can tell you how to get there, but then we'll have to kill you. Here, take Citizen Warden Tresca this message, then report back for . . . um, debriefing. Thank you very much, and remember—StateSec is your friend!"*

"We're coming up on our designated orbit, Skipper," Bouret reported.

"Good. We're a lot more likely to attract some loose mine when we're moving under power," Heathrow muttered. "Time to thruster shutdown?"

"Eight minutes," Bouret replied.

"Very well."

Heathrow watched the plot as the courier boat's icon drifted ever so slowly towards precisely the proper spot. They'd been on reaction thrusters with their wedge down for the last hour, as per instructions from Camp Charon. His mission brief had warned him that would be SOP once he arrived; apparently StateSec imposed it on everyone who came to Cerberus, though for the life of him Heathrow couldn't understand the reasoning behind that particular bit of idiocy. But as with all the other foolishness which had come his way, he'd known better than to argue. Nonetheless, he would have felt much more comfortable with the wedge up. At least it would have offered his ship *some* protection if one of those hordes of mines took it into its idiot-savant brain that she was a hostile unit.

And after associating with StateSec for so long, the poor things probably think everybody *is "the enemy,"* the citizen lieutenant commander thought moodily.

"Done with thrusters, Skipper," Bouret reported finally.

"Very good." Heathrow looked over his shoulder at the com section. "Are you ready to transmit, Irene?"

"Yes, Sir," Citizen Ensign Howard replied promptly.

Heathrow glanced over at Bouret with a grin, but he didn't correct her. One of the few things that made the cramped confines of a courier boat endurable was that such vessels were considered too small and unimportant to require their own people's commissioners. Which meant there was still one place in the Navy where officers could be *naval* officers.

"Request authorization and validation for download, then," Heathrow instructed her after a moment.

"Transmitting now," Howard said, and punched a key at her console. She watched her display, listening to her earbug carefully, then grunted in satisfaction. "Receipt code validation confirmed, Sir," she said. "The crypto files are unlocking now." She sat for several more seconds, watching the display flicker and dance as her onboard computers communed with those on the planet below in a cyber-speed game of challenge and response. Then a bright green code flashed, and she looked over her shoulder at Heathrow.

"Master encryption unlock confirmed, Sir. The message queue is uploading now. Time for full data dump nine minutes, ten seconds."

"Excellent, Irene. That was smoothly done."

"Thank you, Sir!" Howard beamed like a puppy with a new chew toy, and Heathrow made a mental note to speak to her about her mode of address after all. She was a good kid, and he wouldn't be doing her any favors if he got her into the habit of using recidivist modes of address. At the same time, it wouldn't do to hammer her hard over it all of a sudden. Better to wait and speak to her off-watch—or better yet, let Bouret talk to her. He was closer to her rank and age, and it wouldn't sound as threatening coming from him. Besides, if Heathrow spoke to her himself, he'd almost have to sound as if he were reprimanding her for something . . . or else risk sounding as if he thought the whole "Citizen This" and "Citizen the Other" business was stupid. Which he did, but letting anyone else know that wouldn't be the very wisest thing he could possibly do.

He frowned and rubbed his chin, letting his mind play with the best way to go about it, then shrugged. He'd find an approach that worked . . . and he'd have plenty of time to hunt for it, too. They had two more stops after Hades before they returned to Shilo and hoped Shilo State Security would finally release them for their interrupted trip to the Haven System, after all.

Yeah, and we're not going to get offered any R&R at this *stop,* he thought. *Not that I really want to complain.* Voluntarily *spend leave time surrounded by an entire island full of SS goons? Uh-uh, not Ms. Heathrow's little boy Edgar! I'm sure there have to be some perfectly nice people in State Security. It's just that I've never* met *any of them*

. . . and somehow I doubt I'd run into them among the garrison of a top secret, maximum security prison!

He chuckled at the thought, then stirred as Howard spoke again.

"Message dump complete, Sir."

"Was there any 'reply expected' code on the message queue?" Heathrow asked.

"Uh, yes, Sir. Sorry, Sir. I should have reported that already. I didn't—"

"When I think you need chewing out, Irene, I'll chew you out all on my own," Heathrow said mildly. "Until that happens, take it a little easy on yourself."

"Yes, Sir. Thank you, Sir." Despite her thanks, the citizen ensign's face was still red, and Heathrow shook his head. He'd been twenty-two once himself, he was sure. He simply didn't seem to remember when it had been.

But the important thing was that at least some of the traffic he'd just delivered to Hades—whatever it had been—required an immediate response. That was unfortunate. It might mean he and his crew had to hang around for several hours, or even a day or two, waiting while Dirtside got its act together. With no idea of what had been in the encrypted message files, he couldn't even make an estimate of how long he might be hung up. Not that there would have been anything he could do to shorten the time requirement even if he'd known what it was, he thought with a mental sigh.

"Is anyone down there asking us to receipt anything?" he asked, trying not to sound too hopeful that no one was. After all, it was possible some regular SS courier had just happened to wander by and deal with the problem before he got here. That wouldn't be asking too much, would it?

"No, Sir," Howard told him, and he started to smile. But then the citizen ensign went on. "They have transmitted a request to hold while they read the traffic, though."

"Great," Bouret muttered under his breath, and Heathrow heartily endorsed the astrogator's disgusted tone. God only knew how long it would take for Groundside to read its mail and then record a response.

"Well, there's nothing we can do about it except wait," he said as philosophically as possible, and leaned back in his command chair.

Lieutenant Commander Geraldine Metcalf tried very hard not to swear. She'd felt badly enough out of place as officer of the watch in Command Central without having the responsibility for *this* dumped on her shoulders! She'd already put in a call for Commodore Simmons, but he was halfway around the planet with Captain Gonsalves, interviewing people over a problem which had arisen at Beta Eleven, one of the camps to which they'd transferred the prisoners who intended to remain behind on Hell. Beta Eleven, unfortunately, was also one of the camps whose inmates had decided that as part of their proof that they'd had nothing to do with events on Styx, they didn't even want to be part of the "rebels" communications net. Which meant Simmons was out of immediate contact until someone from his shuttle crew got word—and a hand com—to him. . . and that the hot potato was all Metcalf's in the meantime.

She paced slowly up and down behind the operators' consoles, hands clasped behind her, and concentrated on looking calm while Anson Lethridge worked on decoding the message traffic. The homely Erewhonese officer had the com watch, which, up until—she checked the time display—eleven minutes ago, had been one of the more pleasant aspects of her present duty. The two of them had been seeing a good deal of one another lately, although they'd been careful not to go too far too fast in light of the provisions of Article 119. Of course, Article 119 didn't actually apply to Anson, since it was a purely Manticoran regulation, but that was a gray area they'd preferred not to get into. Not that they weren't both aware of how that was going to change once they could get out of the same chain of command and out from under 119's restrictions.

She knew some people wondered what she could possibly see in the brutish-looking Lethridge, but that was because they'd never bothered to look past the face at the man. Metcalf had, and—

"Oh, shit!" The soft expletive was almost a prayer, and she turned quickly as she heard it. Lethridge sat back in his chair, looking down at the lines of text glowing on his display, and she walked quickly towards him.

"What is it?"

"We've got a 'response required' message," he replied.

"What about?" she asked.

"They've missed Proxmire's courier boat," he said grimly, and she felt her face lose all expression.

"And?" Her voice was flat, impersonal, and Lethridge looked up at her quickly. He opened his mouth, then closed it again, discarding whatever he'd been about to say as he recognized the grimness in her dark eyes.

"And it's just about what the Admiral figured it would be," he said after a moment instead. "His next duty station's sent a routine missing ship inquiry up the line."

"Is this one his replacement?" Metcalf asked. It was unlikely, of course. If the new boat was carrying a shipping inquiry, then obviously someone expected it to report back instead of settling into orbit here.

"No." Lethridge shook his head. "There's an attachment to the inquiry, though—something about another message that explains why Proxmire's replacement has been delayed. It's listed as . . . Alpha-Seven-Seven-Ten." He looked at the petty officer who shared his com watch with him. "Anything on that one, Alwyn?"

"Sorry, Sir. I'm still working through the queue directory. There's an awful lot of routine stuff in here—requests for reports, new regulations, all kinds of crap. Just looking at all of it is going to take a couple of hours, I'd guess, and I haven't started any actual decoding of the lower priority messages yet."

"Find it now," Metcalf directed, much more curtly than she'd intended to, and resumed her pacing as PO Alwyn called up message A-7710 and he and Lethridge dove into the task of decoding it.

She hadn't thought about Proxmire and his crew in months now. Part of her had felt almost guilty about that, but the rest of her had recognized it as a healthy sign that she'd finally accepted that she'd truly had no choice but to kill him and that it was time to put it behind her. But they never had located anyone on Hell who'd known exactly how long he was supposed to have the Cerberus courier duty, and Citizen Brigadier Tresca's sloppy com staff had never bothered to enter that information into their computers.

Once Harkness and his team had broken into the secured data they'd at least been able to check the records for how long courier boats were normally assigned to Camp Charon, but the information hadn't helped much. The duration of courier assignments tended to be erratic—in some cases, the records suggested, because assignment here was considered punishment duty, which meant that how long a crew had it depended on how seriously they'd pissed off their superiors. The shortest duration they'd found had been five T-months, and the longest had been just over a T-year and a half. They'd also been able to establish that Proxmire had been here for only three months, and they'd hoped that meant he'd had enough time left on his assignment for them to do what they had to do before someone came looking for him.

Only they'd been wrong.

"Got it!" Lethridge announced suddenly, and Metcalf found herself back beside his chair. "It says here—" the Erewhonese officer began, then paused in surprise as he looked up and discovered that Metcalf had somehow teleported herself across to him without making a sound. He blinked, then shook himself.

"It says here," he resumed with a slightly lower volume, "that Proxmire failed to check in with Shilo Sector SS for his next assignment. They sound concerned, but not terribly so; this is just a request that Camp Charon confirm that he hypered out on time. But it also says his replacement won't be here for another two T-months—which means he'll be almost four months late by the time he actually gets here." The Erewhonese officer smiled wryly. "Whoever drafted this message seems to've figured Tresca would be bouncing off the walls by now over the delay. He went to some lengths to explain the courier net's been all screwed up lately. Apparently StateSec doesn't have as many boats of its own as we'd thought. They seem to rely on Navy couriers a lot, but the Navy's been whipping their own boats all over the PRH to coordinate all the ship movements Citizen Secretary McQueen's been ordering."

"Well thank God for small favors," Metcalf muttered.

"Agreed. But that leaves the problem of what I tell *this* courier," Lethridge pointed out. "Should I go with the canned response?"

"Um." Metcalf frowned again, hands still clasped behind her, and bounced slowly up and down on the balls of her feet while she thought. It would have been so much nicer to be able to ask Admiral Harrington about it, but that was impossible for the same reason she couldn't ask Commodore Ramirez or Captain Benson: none of them were on Hell at the moment.

Ramirez and Benson were off reacquiring their command skills aboard *Krashnark* in company with the ex-StateSec light cruiser *Bacchante*, and Admiral Harrington had gone along to observe and possibly throw a few unplanned tactical problems at them. That was one reason Metcalf had designed the courier boat's inbound routing so carefully—to keep her well clear of the exercise area—and she hoped the CIC crews she and Senior Chief Ascher had been training aboard *Krashnark* had made use of the opportunity to run a passive plot on a live target. And that they weren't embarrassing their teachers.

Her mouth moved again, this time in a grimace. They were making enormous progress, but aside from about four thousand Manticoran and Grayson POWs, none of whom had been dirtside on Hell for more than five T-years, the best of their personnel were at least a decade out of date. Some of them, like Benson, were more like half a *century* out of date, and blowing that kind of rust off their skills required something on the order of an old-fashioned nuke. Of course, Benson was a special case, Metcalf admitted. The captain had a genuine gift—she might even be as good in the captain's chair as Admiral Harrington was reputed to have been—and her skills were coming back with astonishing speed. But a lot of the others were still pretty pathetic by RMN standards.

Which was the reason Metcalf prayed they wouldn't have to deal with any regular navy crews that approached the quality of, say, Lester Tourville's people. It would not be a pleasant afternoon in space if they did.

Now stop that, she told herself with absent severity. *So far, things have gone better on the retraining front than you could ever have expected, now haven't they?*

And so they had. *Bacchante* had come swanning along as innocently and unsuspectingly as *Krashnark*, and Warner Caslet had talked her skipper through the minefields and energy platforms just as smoothly as he'd talked Citizen Captain Pangborn through them. The actual capture of the ship had been a little trickier, since *Bacchante* had just stopped in for a little R&R and a broader selection of fresh vegetables. Since she hadn't been delivering any prisoners, finding a justification for sending multiple shuttles full of boarders up to meet her had been much harder. In fact, it had been impossible . . . but it hadn't been necessary, either. Citizen Commander Vestichov hadn't been able to surrender fast enough when the targeting systems of a dozen graser platforms locked his ship up at a range of less than twelve thousand kilometers.

And so the light cruiser had become the second unit of what Commodore Ramirez had christened the Elysian Navy. She was nowhere near as powerful as *Krashnark*, and Metcalf knew the Admiral had been tempted to turn her loose as a courier to the Alliance, but the lieutenant commander was grateful she hadn't. Having two ships with which to exercise against one another had increased the effectiveness of their quickie training program by at least a hundred percent.

And now the fact that we have two ships means the Admiral is off in one of them, and Commodore McKeon is off in the other one, and they've taken Ramirez and Benson with them. Which means I *get to make the call on this, unless I want to drag Simmons into it. And I can't do that until they get him to the other end of a com link, and I really shouldn't shuffle the decision off onto him even then. Because the longer that boat sits up there, the more likely it is that something will blow up in our faces, isn't it?*

"Dust off the stored response, Anson," she said, and to her own surprise, her voice sounded almost as calm as the Admiral's would have. "Transmit it, and let's get that boat out of here before its crew notices something they shouldn't."

"Yes, Ma'am," Lethridge said formally, his eyes showing his respect for how quickly she'd decided, and nodded to PO Alwyn. "You heard the Commander, PO. Let's send them on their way."

"Aye, aye, Sir."

The petty officer entered a command sequence on his board, and Metcalf watched a green light blink, confirming transmission of the stored message Admiral Harrington had ordered Harkness and Scotty Tremaine to create six months earlier. It wouldn't tell anyone at the other end anything very exciting—only that Proxmire and his crew had pulled out on schedule for their next destination. The message was from Camp Charon's chief com officer, courtesy of Harkness' computer generation efforts. The real com officer had hanged herself five months ago rather than face court-martial on charges of murder and torturing prisoners. Metcalf didn't quite understand the logic behind that, but in light of the evidence against her, she'd simply advanced the date of her demise by a few weeks without altering its manner in the slightest.

Thanks to Harkness, however, they hadn't really needed her, and now the message flicked up to the courier boat. The time and date stamp had been left blank when the message was recorded, but the computers automatically entered today's as they transmitted it. A little more worrisome was the fact that it didn't say where Proxmire had been supposed to go, since no one they'd managed to take alive appeared to have known what his next assignment was, and Metcalf was tempted to update the recording now that they knew he'd been supposed to go to Shilo. But that shouldn't be important enough to justify futzing about with the message and possibly screwing something else up. The people who'd sent the inquiry knew where Proxmire had been bound, and a simple "departed on schedule" ought to more than suffice.

"Message receipt confirmed, Ma'am," PO Alwyn announced, and Metcalf nodded.

"Anything else in the queue require an immediate response?"

"Nothing else," Lethridge told her. "Of course, we haven't opened most of the mail yet," he added.

"Understood. But I want that boat out of here ASAP, and if nothing else is marked urgent, no one's going to be upset if we don't answer it before we boot them out. Send the release, Anson."

"Yes, Ma'am."

"Message coming in from Charon Control," Citizen Ensign Howard reported. Heathrow turned his chair to look at her, but she was busy inputting commands at her console. Then she looked up. "One return transmission received and stored in the secure banks, Sir. No other return traffic or outgoing messages. We're cleared to depart."

"Flight plan information?" Bouret asked.

"Coming through now, Sir," Howard replied. "I'm dumping to your console."

"Got it," Bouret confirmed a moment later. He studied the vectors and accelerations displayed on his maneuvering plot, then made a small sound of mingled satisfaction and disgust. "Pretty straightforward, Skipper. We go back the way we came, for all intents and purposes, except for a couple of little dog legs."

"Dog legs?" Heathrow repeated with a raised eyebrow.

"It's just dirtside bullshit, Skipper," Bouret assured him—being very careful to use the spacer's generic term for planet-bound idiots rather than call the idiots in question StateSec. "They're just flexing their muscles. Citizen Commander Jefferies warned me they liked to do that when he gave me the system coordinates."

"All right." Heathrow sighed. "If that's the way the game's played here, then that's the way it's played. Are we cleared to head out now?"

"Yes, Sir," Howard said.

"And according to this, we can even use impellers, Skipper," Bouret told him.

"Oh frabjous day!" Heathrow muttered under his breath, and pressed a com stud on his chair arm.

"Engineering," a voice replied.

"They're going to let us have our impellers back, Andy," Heathrow said. "How soon can you have the nodes back on-line?"

"Give me seven minutes, and you're hot, Skipper," Citizen Lieutenant Anderson assured him.

"Good." Heathrow released the stud and looked back at Bouret. "All right, Justin, we've got reaction mass to burn, so let's get the hell out of here now. We'll transition to impellers as soon as Andy can bring them up."

"You got it, Skipper," Bouret said with fervent agreement, and began tapping commands into his console. Then he closed his hand on the joystick. "Coming about to new heading of one-seven-eight relative, same plane," he announced, and the courier boat quivered as her thrusters began to fire.

"And so we say farewell to sunny Hell," Heathrow muttered under his breath.

"Well, at least he made out better than the last one," Metcalf said softly to herself as she watched the courier boat's wedge come up. The little craft went scooting away from Hell, accelerating hard down the flight path that would take it well clear of the Admiral's exercise area, and she smiled crookedly. Those people had no idea at all of how close to annihilation they'd just come, she thought, and more power to them.

More than one person in the control center let out a sigh of relief as the boat headed outward. Of course, some of those present didn't, too. Not all of Admiral Harrington's people were happy with the thought of letting any ship depart, however unsuspicious it might appear to be.

Personally, Metcalf agreed with the Admiral, especially in this case. It was far smarter to let courier traffic in and out of Cerberus with the word that everything was normal there than it would have been to turn the system into a complete black hole. And that was a regular Navy vessel, not a StateSec courier, which meant its crew was much less likely to notice any little glitches which might have crept into the behavior of Camp Charon's new managers. For that matter, if they were like many of the officers Metcalf had met during her incarceration aboard Lester Tourville's flagship, they wouldn't want to learn any more about StateSec than they had to. Once upon a time, Metcalf had thought some of her fellow RMN officers took their traditional rivalry with the Royal Marines to ridiculous extremes, but even the worst of them had grudgingly conceded that Marines also belonged to *homo sap*. The People's Navy's jury still seemed to be out on that question in StateSec's case.

Her mouth twitched a wry smile, but she didn't mention the thought to anyone else.

Still, she admitted, if it hadn't been for that inquiry about Proxmire's boat, she might have been more inclined to argue for hanging onto this courier, regular Navy or no. Deciding to send an unarmed courier with neither the firepower for combat nor the life support for large loads of passengers to the Alliance would have been an easy call . . . if they hadn't known someone was anticipating that courier's immediate arrival with the reply to that inquiry. The nearest piece of real estate they could be certain the Alliance would have held onto in the face of the Peeps new, aggressive stance was Trevor's Star, which happened to be a hundred and thirty-five-plus light-years from Cerberus. Even a courier would take over two weeks to make a voyage that long—more like twenty days, unless it wanted to play some really dangerous games with the iota wall in h-space—and that was for a one-way trip. If somebody who was closer than that—say a half-dozen or so light-years—was expecting the courier to come tell it about Citizen Lieutenant Commander Proxmire and it didn't turn up, then that somebody might just decide to come see what it was about the Cerberus System that was being so hard on the SS's mailmen. In which case they would almost certainly get here well before anything from Trevor's Star could.

"Got something else interesting here, Gerry."

She turned, pulled back out of her thoughts by Lethridge's voice, and raised an eyebrow. His tone was very different this time, and his expression could have indicated excitement, trepidation, anticipation, or a combination of all three.

"What is it?" she asked, walking back across the control room towards him.

"The computers just finished decoding the next message in the queue," he told her, "and it looks like we're about to have company."

"Company?" her voice was sharper, and he gave her a tight smile.

"Company," he confirmed. "The Peeps have hit the Alliance again. This time they took back Seabring, and it looks like they're going to try to hold it. They're planning to ship in a shit pot full of mines and energy platforms to thicken the defenses, anyway, and they need a lot of workers to put them on-line."

"And?" Metcalf encouraged when he paused.

"And StateSec has decided to temporarily 'rehabilitate' some of the politicals here on Hell. They're planning to stop by with a flotilla of transports and collect seventy thousand or so of them as a deep-space work force to emplace all that hardware for them."

"Transports?" Metcalf straightened, eyes bright. "Hey, that's great! Exactly what we need!"

"Sure," Lethridge agreed grimly. "Except that they're not coming alone."

"What do you mean?" Metcalf's brows furrowed as his tone registered.

"I said they were planning on holding the place, Gerry," he reminded her. "And one of the things they seem to be worried about is that the locals apparently preferred our occupation to the old management. So StateSec is sending in one of its major generals with the equivalent of two divisions worth of intervention battalions supported by full combat equipment, including battle armor, assault boats, and heavy tanks, to 'repacify' them if necessary. And since the entire force is being dispatched under StateSec control from their sector HQ at Shilo, they figured they might as well keep everything together so they could send it with a single escort force."

"You mean we've got two *divisions* of SS goons headed *here?*" Metcalf asked very carefully.

"That's exactly what I mean," Lethridge said flatly. "And they'll be arriving with an escort of StateSec battlecruisers and heavy cruisers."

"Sweet Jesus," Metcalf murmured prayerfully.

"I hope He's listening," Lethridge told her with a mirthless smile, "because we're going to need Him. According to the alert message, we can expect them within three weeks. And with that many senior SS officers all in one place, somehow I don't think they'd settle for long-range virtual handshakes with our cyberspace version of Brigadier Tresca even if they *didn't* expect us to be ready to hand seventy thousand slave laborers over to them!"

Chapter Forty-Four

"That's a lot of firepower, Honor," Harriet Benson observed soberly. "And a lot of chances for something to go wrong if even one unit doesn't do what we expect her to."

"Agreed," Honor said.

She sat with her inner circle, studying the readouts on the ships due to arrive so shortly from Shilo. Two of the new *Warlord*-class battlecruisers—the *Wallenstein* and *Farnese*—were confirmed, as were the heavy cruisers *Ares, Huan-Ti,* and *Ishtar*, and the light cruiser *Seahorse.* They didn't have classes on the cruisers, but from the names the heavies were both probably *Mars*-class ships, like *Krashnark*, and *Seahorse* was probably one of the Peeps' new "frigate-class" light cruisers, like *Bacchante.* The rest of the escort, or even if there would *be* any additional escorts, had still been up for grabs when the courier boat sailed, but there would probably be at least a few more ships. Had it been a Navy escort for troopships destined for a front-line system, there would have been, at any rate, and the additional units would have included a minimum of two or three destroyers for long-range scouting. But this was an SS operation, and StateSec had been uninterested in smaller men-of-war when it started collecting its private fleet. Honor wasn't sure why that was, though she suspected that a great deal of the reason had to do with State Security's institutional egotism. Although, she conceded, the Black Legs' apparent belief that sooner or later they would confront mutinous ships of the People's Navy might also help explain it. It did make sense to go for a tonnage advantage if you could get one, after all. Although that left the interesting question of why StateSec hadn't been interested in dreadnoughts or superdreadnoughts.

Too much manpower tied up in crewing ships that size? Honor wondered. *Could be, I suppose. Or it might just be that someone on the Committee of Public Safety recognized the insanity implicit in allowing the head of its "security forces" to assemble an actual battle fleet that answered only to him. Not that it matters right this minute.*

"Harry's right, Ma'am," Warner Caslet said quietly. "The *Warlords* are big ships—at least as big as your *Reliant* class. I know you didn't get to see a lot of *Tepes*, but I did, and she was more heavily armed on a ton-for-ton basis than your ships are. Of course, their systems aren't as capable as yours, so they need the extra brute firepower to equalize the odds, but they're still bad medicine."

"I don't doubt it," Honor replied, "and I know Harry is right about the sheer number of hulls confronting us with more possible things to go wrong. But I think you're both missing the point. For the initial grab, at least, it wouldn't matter whether they were sending in superdreadnoughts or destroyers *or* how many of them there are. If they follow SOP, the entire force—escorts and transports alike—will stay together and come in close enough for our orbital weapons to get the drop on them. In that case, we can take out anything we have to, so the worst result from our viewpoint will be that we blow a ship away rather than taking her intact. But if even a single destroyer *doesn't* follow SOP and come in that close, all she has to do is run away and get help and we're all dead."

She shrugged, and Alistair McKeon nodded. He looked like a man sucking sour persimmons, but he wasn't alone in that. No one at the conference table looked particularly cheerful . . . except, perhaps, Honor.

I really do *feel cheerful, too,* she thought with some surprise. *Because I'm as confident as I try to pretend? Or is it because I'm just grateful to have the other shoe drop at last?*

Of course, she reminded herself, it wasn't really "the" other shoe. It was simply the first shoe—or the third, if she wanted to count *Krashnark* and *Bacchante* as the first two—and there were likely to be others before this was all over.

"On a brighter note," she went on, "look at all the personnel lift we get our hands on if we manage to pull this off." She nodded at the data on the five *Longstop*-class transports the warships would be escorting. "They're providing enough lift for a full seventy thousand slave laborers, assuming Tresca could find that many in so short a time, plus another forty-one thousand technicians and supervisory personnel and twenty-four thousand SS ground troops—and that doesn't even count the additional eight thousand SS support personnel attached to the intervention battalions. That's over a hundred and forty thousand total, and according to the readouts, these ships are actually designed to provide life support for forty thousand people each, exclusive of their own crews, so StateSec is planning on running them light."

"Was there anything in the message about *why* they're running so light?" Benson asked.

"No," Honor replied. "My best guess is that they expect to pick up some more warm bodies further down the line to Seabring. But what matters most to us right now is that we can grab off the personnel lift for two hundred thousand of our people aboard the transports alone. Then each of the battlecruisers has a normal complement of twenty-two hundred, so that's another forty-four hundred, plus a thousand each in the heavy cruisers—counting *Krashnark* and the three we know are coming, that's another four thousand. So we're looking at enough life support for—what? Two hundred and eight thousand of our people?"

"Which still leaves us a hundred and eighty-six thousand short of the numbers we need," McKeon pointed out in the tones of a man who hated being the voice of cold reason.

"Looking at the numbers from The Book, you're right, Sir," Fritz Montoya said. Honor had called the doctor in for the meeting expressly to address the life support question, and now he turned to look at all of them. "But the transports were designed around a lot of reserve environmental capacity. We could increase a *Longstop*'s load from forty thousand to about fifty without stretching its life support dangerously. In a pinch, I'd be willing to call it fifty-six or maybe even fifty-seven. I wouldn't want to go much over that unless it was for a very short hop, but the enviro plants should carry the atmospheric load for that many as far as we need. The worst problem will be physical overcrowding, because that many people need a lot of cubage, and the ships' other waste processing systems will be heavily strained. But these are military transports. They're also designed to carry heavy combat equipment, and we could probably beef up the reclamation equipment by cannibalizing all the shuttles and pinnaces sitting here on Styx and adding their enviro plants as strap-on backups in their cargo spaces. It wouldn't be pretty or elegant, but there ought to be enough air to go around when we finish."

"I hadn't thought about the shuttles, Fritz," McKeon admitted, and pursed his lips with a faraway look.

"You're right about the *Longstops*," he went on. "They're way too slow to be used as anything we'd consider a true assault transport, but they are configured to carry all of their embarked troops' equipment as well as just the personnel. If we dump all the other hardware out of their vehicle holds, we could probably pack three or four dozen shuttles and pinnaces into each of them. For that matter, they've probably got around that many of their own already stowed in their boat bays, and if we've got 'em, we could even park a lot of them on the hull exteriors. Remember that Peeps go in for a lot more small craft docking ports than we do."

"You're thinking about putting people aboard them instead of the transports?" Ramirez asked.

"No, I was thinking more of connecting all of them to the ships' internal environmental systems as sort of secondary plants, or maybe booster stages."

"But even without that, Fritz's numbers would get us up to over two hundred and eighty-five thousand," Honor said, looking up from where she'd been scribbling numbers on an old-fashioned scratchpad.

"It would," Cynthia Gonsalves agreed. "But I don't like it. Even assuming Alistair's notion about using the shuttles and pinnaces works, it'll be a fragile, jury-rigged piece of work. And if we go with no safety margin, we create a situation in which if any part of the environmental plant does go down, people die." She sounded troubled, and Honor opened her mouth to reply, but Jesus Ramirez spoke up before she could.

"You're right," he agreed soberly. "On the other hand, if the plant holds, we get them all out. And if we don't get them out somehow, they die eventually anyway. Unless anyone in this room thinks we can hold this planet indefinitely against StateSec . . . or maybe even the regular Peep Navy, if we prove too tough for the Black Legs to handle on their own."

"Of course we can't," Gonsalves acknowledged. "And I know it. I just hate stressing the plants to the max with no reserve at all."

"I agree," Gaston Simmons said. "But to be honest, I'm more worried about the hundred thousand plus we still won't be able to cram aboard them." Eyes turned to him from all around the table, and he shrugged. "I think Dame Honor is right to expect that we can take all of the ships we know Shilo is sending this way. We have to figure we can, at any rate, or else we might as well go ahead and give up right now. But even assuming we pack every soul we possibly can aboard those ships, what do we do with the people we *can't* stuff on board? Leave them behind?"

"No," Honor said so flatly that every eye snapped to her. "We're not abandoning a single person who's told us he or she wants off this rock."

"But if we can't lift them all out—" Gonsalves began.

"We can't lift them all out at once aboard the shipping we expect to be available," Honor said. "So we send out as many as we can in the first flight."

"*First* flight?" McKeon repeated very carefully.

"Exactly." Honor smiled thinly, with no amusement at all. "Assuming that we take the shipping from Shilo intact, we load the transports up and send them off with everyone we can fit aboard, but we hold the warships here."

McKeon frowned. He could feel where she was headed, and he didn't like it. Which didn't mean he saw an alternative he liked better.

"Hold the warships here?" Jesus Ramirez cocked his head at Honor and scratched his chin thoughtfully. "Are you thinking what I think you're thinking?"

"Probably." This time there was a bit of true humor in Honor's crooked half-smile. "We don't know who or what will be coming along after this first lot, but if we can grab off both battlecruisers and all three heavy cruisers, plus whatever else they send along for escort, we'll have the beginning of a fair little squadron of our own. If we can put even skeleton crews aboard each of them, we'll have the capability to run down and intercept later arrivals even if they get hinky and refuse to come into the orbital weapons' envelope. They'll also give us a mobile combat element that should let us think about some much more flexible defensive plans if the bad guys come calling in force."

"I like the thought, Honor," Benson said, "but do you think you might be getting a little overly ambitious? I know how rusty *I* am, and we've only got three more weeks to train in. Where do we get the people to man that many ships?"

"Warner?" Honor turned to Warner Caslet and crooked an eyebrow. "You're more familiar with Peep crewing requirements than any of us are. What's the minimum crew that could fight a *Warlord* effectively?"

"That's a little hard to say, Ma'am, since I never actually served aboard one of them," Caslet replied. But he also rubbed his left eyebrow while he thought hard. "You could start by forgetting the Marines," he said thoughtfully. "Our—I mean the People's Navy's—Marines don't have any real role in ship-to-ship combat, except to back up damage control, so we carry smaller Marine complements than Manty ships. We'd save about three hundred there, which would get us down to around nineteen. Then we could probably cut Engineering about in half and save another two-fifty."

"Cut Engineering in *half*?" McKeon sounded doubtful, and Caslet shrugged.

"You're going to have to take chances somewhere," he pointed out, "and our engineering departments are heavily overstaffed compared to yours because our people aren't as good. The worst part would be the loss of warm bodies for damage control—which would only be aggravated by leaving the Marines out, of course."

"True," Honor agreed. "On the other hand, I think any fighting we got involved in would have to be fairly short and decisive if it was going to do us any good. Damage control might be fairly immaterial under those circumstances."

"That seems a little optimistic to me, Honor," McKeon said, but then he shrugged. "On the other hand, Warner's right. We've got to take some chances somewhere. So how much more can we cut the designed complements, Warner?"

"We've already cut them by over five hundred," Caslet said, "and if we thin out the energy mount crews to the absolute minimum needed to fire them in local control if we lose the central fire control net, then do the same for the missile tubes, and then gut the boat bay department completely, we can probably save another . . . three hundred to three hundred twenty-five per ship. I don't see how you could reduce a *Warlord*'s crew by much more than that and still have an efficient fighting machine."

"So five-fifty plus three-twenty-five, then?" Honor asked, and he nodded. "All right, call it eight hundred and seventy-five, so the complements come down to thirteen hundred per ship."

"Thirteen hundred and *twenty-five* by my math," McKeon told her with a slow grin. "But, then, who's counting?"

"I am," she said, "and it's not polite to call attention to the problems I have with math."

"I didn't; you did," he said, and she chuckled. Her other officers looked puzzled, sensing a bit of byplay they hadn't known her long enough to understand, but she felt their moods lighten anyway.

"Yes, I suppose I did," she admitted after a moment, "but using your numbers, then, two *Warlords* would require a total crew strength of twenty-six hundred and fifty."

"I believe they would," McKeon agreed with a twinkle. She smiled back, then returned her attention to Caslet

"And how far could we cut the crews for the *Mars*-class ships, Warner?"

"About the same ratio, Ma'am. Call it roughly forty percent."

"So that drops them to around six hundred each," she murmured, scribbling on her pad again. "Which makes twenty-four hundred for the four of them. Twenty-four plus twenty-six . . ." She jotted a total and cocked her head to consider it. "Excluding *Bacchante* and this *Seahorse*, I make it five thousand and fifty warm bodies," she said. "Adding the two light cruisers at just under five hundred each, that brings the total to right on six thousand. Does that sound fair?"

"I don't like cutting their companies by that much," McKeon said with a frown, "but Warner's probably right that we could get by with that sort of stretch if we absolutely had to. Especially if we can manage to engage with only one broadside per ship." He rubbed his jaw, then shrugged. "All right, six thousand sounds reasonable . . . under the circumstances."

Ramirez and Benson nodded sharply, followed a little more slowly by Gonsalves and Simmons. Gonsalves looked less happy than any of the others about it, but her nod was firm.

"Well, we've got roughly five thousand Allied POWs whose training is still reasonably up to snuff, in light of how recently they were dumped here," Honor pointed out, "and we've got another eighteen hundred we've been retraining in *Krashnark* and *Bacchante.* By my count, that's sixty-eight hundred . . . which is eight hundred more than we'd need."

"And what do we do with any other warships they send along?" Benson asked. Everyone turned to look at her, and she grinned. "I mean, while we're sitting here being so confident, let's assume they increase the escort and we get all of it intact. If we manage to pull that off, I'd purely hate not making maximum use of everything we can grab."

"I doubt we could come up with the people to fight more ships effectively," Simmons put in. "Oh, give us another three or four months, and we could probably change that. Most of our people were trained military personnel before they were sent here, so we know they could handle the load. Assuming we had time to bring them up to speed on modern hardware and put them all through refresher training . . . which we don't. For that matter, even a fair percentage of those Allied POWs you mentioned are going to need at least a quick refresher before we commit them to action, Dame Honor."

"True," Honor agreed. "But we probably can come up with enough people to run the power plants and actually man the cons on anything else we can grab—we wouldn't need more than forty or fifty people per ship for that. And that would let us pack still more evacuees into their crew quarters."

"And don't forget that warships always have more reserve life support than anything else in space, even military transports," Montoya pointed out. "The RMN's designers always assume warships are going to take damage, for example, so they build as much redundancy as they can into the core survival systems. We could increase nominal crew sizes by at least fifty percent and still have some reserve. In fact, we'd probably run out of places to put people well before we maxed out their enviro."

"So that would let us get at least another four or five thousand out," Ramirez mused. He gazed into the distance for several seconds, the nodded. "I like it," he said crisply.

"I wouldn't go quite that far in my own case," Benson said with a small smile. "But I don't think I see any alternative I'd like better—or as well, for that matter. But assuming this all works, where do we send the transports once we capture them?"

"Trevor's Star," McKeon suggested. "We know our people aren't going to take any chances with that system's security—not after how much it cost us capture it in the first place—so we can be fairly confident it's still in friendly hands. Or, at least, if things have gotten so bad that it isn't, we might as well stay here in the first place, because the Alliance is screwed."

"I don't know, Alistair." Honor leaned back and rubbed the tip of her nose. "I agree with your logic, but don't forget that we'll be sending in Peep military transports, possibly with Peep warships as escorts. Trigger fingers are going to be awfully itchy at someplace like Trevor's Star after what happened at Basilisk."

"I would very much like to go home," Jesus Ramirez said softly, the ache in his deep, rumbling voice reminding them all that San Martin was the planet of his birth, "but I believe you may have a point, Honor."

"That's probably true enough," McKeon acknowledged, "but it's also going to be true in just about any Allied system by now. At least Trevor's Star is the closest friendly port we know about, which means less time in transit and less opportunity for life support to fail."

"That's certainly a valid point," Gonsalves said. "And look at the compensators and hyper-generators on those transports. They're basically converted longhaul bulk freighters the Peeps have been using to transport work forces or haul peacekeeping troops to domestic hot spots for decades. That's probably why StateSec had them immediately available, but like Alistair said, they're a hell of a lot slower than anything a regular navy would consider using that close to a combat zone. They can't even climb as high as the top of the delta band, so their max apparent velocity isn't going to be any more than a thousand lights or so, and we're an awful long way from friendly territory. Even the voyage to Trevor's Star would take the next best thing to fifty days base time. The dilation effect will shrink that to about forty days subjective, but that's still over a full T-month for something to go wrong with their life support. If we send them still further to the rear—" She shrugged.

"I know." Honor frowned and rubbed her nose harder, then sighed. "I was hoping to send them clear to Manticore, or at least Grayson," she admitted, "but you and Alistair are right, Cynthia. The shorter the flight time the better. But in that case, they're going to have to be *very* careful how they approach the system perimeter."

"Careful I think we can manage," McKeon assured her. "I know abject, quivering terror tends to make *me* cautious as hell, anyway."

"All right, then." Honor looked around the table. "In that case, I want you and Fritz to take care of making the most careful estimates we can of our actual life-support capacity on a ship-by-ship basis, Cynthia. Gaston," she looked at Commodore Simmons, "you're in charge of drawing up the evac priority lists. I need three of them immediately: one of the people who should go in the first lift, assuming we use only the *Longstops*; one of the people best suited to crew any warships we take; and one that lists every soul who wants off this rock but who isn't on the first two. In addition, I want the last one organized to indicate the order in which they'll be moved out as extra lift becomes available. I don't want there to be any room for panic and fighting for places in the evac queue."

"Yes, Ma'am. Should I consider some sort of lottery for the evacuation lists?"

"I'll leave that up to you, at least until I see how they break down. As for the second list, I want all-volunteer crews for the warships if at all possible, but if we've got *anyone* with recent experience, I need them. Try and talk any reluctant heroes into volunteering. If you can't, give me a list of their names and let me have a go at them."

"Yes, Ma'am."

"Alistair, you and Jesus are in charge of accelerating the retraining program as much as possible, because Gaston is right; we do need to get in at least a quickie refresher for everyone. I want to cycle the current batch of trainees out of *Krashnark* and *Bacchante* within the next seventy-two hours, and I want the designed training cycle cut to one week."

"That's not very long," McKeon protested.

"No, but it's all the time we've got," Honor told him flatly. "Increase the percentage of people with recent experience in each cycle. They can help train the people who are completely out of date at the same time they dust off their own skill levels, and, frankly, I'll settle for half-trained companies to take over the escorts if we manage to capture them in the first place. We can arrange for additional training onboard the ships themselves later, if the Peeps give us the time, but I want them able to at least defend themselves—or run away, if the odds go to crap on us—ASAP."

"Understood," McKeon said.

"Good. Harry," she turned to Benson, "I wish I could leave you aboard *Krashnark*, but I need you for Control Central, at least for now. We need to start pushing training harder there, as well. We've let ourselves slow down once we had four complete watch crews trained, but the control consoles for the orbital weaponry are very similar to the weapons controls aboard the Peeps' warships. Let's get as many people trained on them dirtside as we can."

"Yes, Ma'am." Benson nodded sharply, and Honor turned to Caslet with another of her crooked smiles.

"As for you, Warner, I want you to make yourself available to everybody, everywhere, at every single instant, twenty-six hours a day. I realize we're talking about State Security and not the People's Navy, but you still know more about the ships and the procedures involved than any of the rest of us. I'm sure all of us will have specific questions for you in the next few days, and if you think of anything—anything at all—that could be a worthwhile suggestion, don't hesitate to make it."

"Yes, Ma'am." He returned her smile, and she felt a deep sense of personal satisfaction as she tasted the change in his emotions. The wounded anguish the "desertion" of his country had wakened at his core had diminished. It hadn't vanished, and she doubted it ever would, for he was a decent and an honorable man. But he had come to terms with it, accepted it as the price he must pay for doing what he believed to be right, and she could feel him reaching out to the challenge.

Admiral Lady Dame Honor Harrington let her eye sweep around the conference room one last time. Her entire plan was insane, of course . . . but that was nothing new. And crazy or not, she'd brought them all this far.

Yes, I have, she thought, *and I will by God take every single one of them home with me in the end, as well!*

"All right, then, people," she said calmly. "Let's be about it."

Chapter Forty-Five

Citizen Lieutenant Commander Heathrow leaned back in his command chair and smiled as Lois, the sole inhabited planet of the Clarke System, fell away astern. He hadn't enjoyed dealing with Citizen Colonel White, the system's senior StateSec officer, but at least there were other people on Lois. More to the point, perhaps, Lois had some of the most glorious beaches in the entire People's Republic. He and his crew had been made welcome in traditional Navy style by Citizen Captain Olson, CO of the small PN patrol detachment, and his engineering staff had managed a little creative reporting to justify a full extra twenty-three-hour day of sun and sand.

There were, he thought smugly, occasional advantages to courier duty after all.

Yeah, sure. "Join the Navy and see the Galaxy!" He snorted suddenly. *You know, that's probably truer for the courier crews than it is for anyone else, now that I think about it!*

He chuckled, but then he let his chair come back upright with a sigh as his mind reached out to their next destination. He wasn't looking forward to his stop in the Danak System. Clarke had a relatively small SS detachment, which spent most of its time fulfilling regular police functions. Personally, Heathrow suspected that the warm, languid tranquility of Lois had infected them, as well. The system's Navy personnel were crisp and efficient enough when onboard ship or crewing the planet's orbital HQ base, but they tended to go native, all crispness vanishing into a sort of planetwide, laid-back surfer culture, the instant they hit groundside, and the same seemed to be true of the SS.

Danak was different, however . . . and not just because of the weather. Granted, Danak Alpha, the inhabited half of the double-planet pair of more or less terrestrial worlds was considerably further out from its G8 primary than Lois was from its G1 primary. That gave it a much cooler climate, and its weather was characterized by clouds and rain liberally seasoned with various objectionable atmospheric compounds from volcanic outgassing. At that, it was a nicer place than Danak Beta. Beta was only technically habitable, and to the best of Heathrow's knowledge, no one had ever expressed any particular desire to visit it, much less live there.

But Danak, unlike Clarke, had been settled for four hundred years, and where Lois had been a resort world catering to the tourist trade before the Republic annexed it, Danak had been a heavily industrialized system for more than two T-centuries. More than that, its current population was up to something approaching four billion, which was extremely large for a system this close to the frontier. All of which meant that miserable as Danak Alpha was, and dour as people assigned here tended to become, the system was very important to the powers that were.

As a consequence, Danak System Command had always been home port to a largish fleet presence, and State Security had made Danak Alpha the HQ for its intervention forces here in the Danak Sector, just as Shilo was in the Shilo Sector. Needless to say, the presence in force of StateSec had not increased the attractiveness of gray and miserable Danak Alpha when it came to choosing someplace as a potential retirement address.

Or, for that matter, one to visit on courier duties.

Heathrow grimaced. *Ah, well. We had our run ashore on Lois; I suppose it's inevitable that we pay for it on this end. I just hope Citizen General Chernock has been replaced.*

He checked the time and date display on his console. His command was fourteen days, sixteen hours, and thirty-three minutes (base-time reckoning) out of Cerberus. Of course, given relativity's input into things, that worked out to only ten days, twenty-two hours, and some change for Heathrow and his crew, which seemed like a particularly dirty trick. The rest of the universe got to enjoy the full fourteen days between the time he touched base with two different groups of sourpuss, pain in the butt SS types, while his people got cheated out of almost three whole days.

Oh, well. No one had ever said the universe was fair.

Citizen Major General Thornegrave swung himself out of the personnel tube and into PNS *Farnese*'s shipboard gravity. The StateSec ground forces citizen lieutenant assigned to greet him snapped to attention and saluted, and Thornegrave returned the courtesy brusquely.

"*Sir!* May the Citizen Lieutenant have the honor of escorting the Citizen General to his quarters, *Sir?*"

The citizen lieutenant had an unfortunately round and puffy, rather dissipated looking face, crowned by the sort of carefully-sculpted hairstyle Thornegrave had always disliked. Despite his immaculate uniform, he didn't look much like the popular concept of an officer, and he seemed determined to overcompensate by demonstrating more than his fair share of panache. His eyes were parked a good fifteen centimeters above Thornegrave's head, and the third-person form of his address, while militarily correct, sounded just a little too studied. As a rule, the citizen major general approved of junior officers who greeted their seniors with proper respect. But everything about this one's manner—from the parade ground punctilio Thornegrave suspected had been learned more from HD than basic training to the powerful hint of apple-polishing obsequiousness in his patently false smile of greeting—irritated him immensely.

He started to say something, then stopped. First impressions could be misleading, and the kid might just be nervous at greeting such a senior officer with so little warning. With that in mind, he rejected any of the several cutting remarks which had sprung to mind and settled for a simple, if curt, nod. The citizen lieutenant seemed not to notice any curtness and turned to lead the way to the lifts.

I really should have read his name patch, Thornegrave mused. *He* was *on Harris' staff, so I suppose he's on mine, as well. Ah, well. They're all the same when they're that new. And I'm not really certain I* want *to know the name of one who seems so much more eager to . . . please than most.*

He followed his guide, then paused, hands clasped behind him, and indulged in a mild, moderately pleasant spasm of guilt as he watched the citizen lieutenant punch a code to summon a lift car.

He really shouldn't be aboard this ship, he thought cheerfully, and StateSec General Headquarters back on Nouveau Paris would probably be irritated when it learned he was. He was officially assigned to command the Shilo Sector, which meant overseeing the deployment of all the sector's people's commissioners, intervention battalions, spacegoing security detachments, and all the billion-plus-one other details involved in riding herd on so many different star systems in the Committee's name. And to be fair, he enjoyed the responsibility and authority which were his. But there were times when it could get deadly dull, and the best a sector CO this far from the front—or the Capital Sector—could realistically hope for was that things would stay so quiet no one on Nouveau Paris even noticed he was out here. If the capital did notice him, it would almost inevitably be because he'd screwed up in some spectacular fashion, since, by definition, no one ever noticed the places where things went right. Which meant that those who wished to be promoted still higher in StateSec's hierarchy sought to avoid postings to places like Shilo like the very plague.

Thornegrave had recognized the danger when Citizen General Tomkins invited him to a personal meeting at GHQ and begun by describing his new assignment as "not flashy to the untrained eye, maybe, but critically important to the war effort. The sort of post where we need the best man we can possibly find—which was the reason we immediately thought of you, Prestwick. I can call you Prestwick, can't I, Citizen Major General?"

Unfortunately, his best efforts to evade Shilo had failed, and he'd been stuck here for close to two T-years while men and women junior to him were promoted past him. There hadn't seemed to be anything he could do about it, either . . . until, that was, Citizen Major General Harris (no relation to the defunct Legislaturalist clan of the same name) had been obliging enough to drop dead of a cerebral hemorrhage. Thornegrave had never wished the woman any harm, and to be fair, his initial reaction had been one of dismay. But that had only lasted long enough for him to realize that the projected expedition to Seabring was inarguably a two-star command. And since he'd been the only SS two-star available . . .

He chuckled gleefully at the thought of his coup. He supposed it could be reasonably argued that the Shilo Sector was also at least a two-star command . . . and the one to which he had been assigned. But that was the point. It could be *argued* either way, and he was the senior officer on the spot who had to decide the argument. And so, regretfully, he had concluded that Seabring's proximity to the front, coupled with the reported refractory attitudes of its citizens, gave it priority over a quiet sector a light-century and a half from the nearest fighting. That being the case, there was no way he could justify remaining in the safety of his formally assigned billet, which had left him no choice but to turn Shilo over to his exec and take command of the Seabring expedition. If Citizen General Tomkins disagreed, he could always tell him so . . . in about six and a half months, when the reply to Thornegrave's first report from Seabring got back to him from Nouveau Paris.

The chuckle he couldn't quite suppress threatened to turn into a gleeful cackle, but only until the citizen lieutenant darted a look over his shoulder at him. For a moment, the bland-faced young man looked frightened, but then he began to chuckle himself and gave the citizen major general the broad, vapid smile of someone "sharing" in a joke he didn't have a clue about. That, unfortunately, was one of the things Thornegrave could not abide. It was one thing for a senior officer to invite a junior to share a joke; it was quite another for some kiss-ass young prick who thought he was showing his sophistication to deal himself into a joke he didn't even begin to comprehend.

The citizen major general cut his own chuckle off instantly and gave the citizen lieutenant—Rodham, Guillermo, the kid's name patch said, he noticed—a sudden, cold glance. The citizen lieutenant immediately stopped laughing, swallowed hard, turned away, and punched the lift button again, as if that could somehow magically conjure the slow-arriving car into existence. He stood absolutely silent, as erect as if someone had inserted a broom handle up his backside, while small beads of perspiration dewed his hairline, and Thornegrave looked away once more, satisfied with the effect.

Unfortunately, in looking away his eye fell on *Farnese*'s crest, and he felt a familiar sour distaste as it did. The crest said "PNS *Farnese*," and that always irritated him. After all, the battlecruiser wasn't a Navy ship; she belonged to State Security, and her designation should reflect that. Except that the Navy's position was that she was only a Navy ship which was *assigned* to StateSec, as if the true guardians of the People's safety had no right to put on the airs of "real" warriors.

Of course, Thornegrave conceded, *hanging SSS on the front of a ship's name would probably look a little funny, but it's the principle of the thing! The Navy and the Marines represent vestigial holdovers from the decadent elitism of the Old Regime. It's past time that State Security absorbed them both into a single organization whose loyalty to the People and State can be absolutely relied upon. The people's commissioners are a move in the right direction, but there's still too much room for recidivists to secretly sabotage the war and the Revolution alike. Surely Citizen Secretary Saint-Just and Citizen Chairman Pierre realize that, don't they?*

No doubt they did, he told himself once more as the lift finally arrived and Citizen Lieutenant Rodham bowed and scraped him into it. And he had no doubt that, in time, they would act upon their realization. But timing continued to be the problem. Making changes like that in the middle of a war fought on such a scale would always be difficult, and the fact that McQueen and her uniformed, elitist relics had finally knocked the Manties back on their heels made it even more difficult now . . . for the moment, at least. Well, he'd seen to it that the Navy knew who was in charge here in Shilo, at any rate! And he supposed StateSec would have to settle for a gradualist approach . . . at least until McQueen overstepped and gave Saint-Just an excuse.

And for now, he thought with a lazy sense of triumph as the lift door slid closed and the car moved off, *at least I've put that poisonous little fart Citizen Commodore Yang in her place. Argue that convoy escort is a "Navy responsibility" indeed! Hah! One star loses to two stars any day, Citizen Commodore, especially when the two-star in question is SS!*

Citizen Commodore Rachel Yang nodded to acknowledge the report of Citizen Major General Thornegrave's arrival. She actually managed not to spit on the decksole at the news, too, which she considered a major triumph of self-discipline. Citizen Major General Harris had also been SS, and no doubt the woman had had her faults, but at least she'd recognized that running warships was a job for someone trained to run them. Thornegrave didn't. Or perhaps he simply believed that someone whose devotion to the Revolution was pure as the driven snow and utterly devoid of personal ambition (*Hah! I'll just* bet *it is!*) was automatically more competent than someone who'd merely spent thirty-three years of her life training for the duty in question.

Damn it, I believe in the Revolution, too! she thought viciously. *All right, maybe I do think there've been excesses, but you can't build an entire New Order without some individual cases of injustice. Who was it back on Old Earth who said that liberty was a tree which had to be watered occasionally with the blood of patriots? So where does Thornegrave get off climbing into my face this way? Why does he think Citizen General Harris specifically* asked *for a Navy officer to command the escort? Does he think my staff and I* like *being stuck here on an SS ship where we're the only regulars aboard? Does he think we actually* requested *the duty or something? And he's a frigging* ground-pounder, *for Christ's sake—not even trained as an air-breathing pilot, much less a naval officer—so what does* he *know about escort tactics and convoy security? Zip-zero-zilch-nada,* that's *what!*

Unfortunately, he'd also dealt himself the command slot, and all Yang could do was accommodate herself to his demands as unconfrontationally as possible and hope it did some good.

"Has *Mardi Gras* finished loading?" she asked her com officer.

"No, Citizen Commodore. Citizen Commander Talbot reports that he'll have his last vehicles aboard by twenty-two hundred."

"Very good. But send him another signal. Tell him that the convoy is leaving for Cerberus at twenty-two-thirty and not a moment later."

"At once, Citizen Commander!"

Yang nodded and returned her attention to her plot.

"The convoy is underway, Citizen General."

"Very good, Citizen Commodore. Thank you for informing me. Please let me know a half hour before we cross the hyper limit. I'd like to be on the flag bridge when we make translation."

"Of course, Citizen General."

The expression of the face on his com screen didn't even flicker, but Thornegrave heard the gritted teeth Yang didn't display and hid a smug smile of his own. God, the woman was easy to goad. And he was taking careful note of her behavior, as well as her words, naturally. Every little bit of ammo would help justify decisive action when the time came for the regular officer corps to be completely suppressed at last.

"Thank you, Citizen Commander," he replied with a graciousness as false as her own, and cut the com link.

Citizen Lieutenant Commander Heathrow sat up in bed when the com warbled at him. The CO and XO of a courier boat were the only members of its complement who actually had cabins to themselves, which was a luxury beyond price. Unfortunately, the designers had been forced to squeeze those cabins into an oddly shaped section where the hull narrowed dramatically towards the after impeller ring, with the result that the curved deckhead offered barely sixty centimeters of headroom above Heathrow's bunk. Under normal circumstances, it was second nature to remember that and allow for it when getting up. He had a tendency to forget when awakened in the middle of the night, however, and he yelped as his skull smacked into the deckhead.

Fortunately, the designers had padded it—presumably to avoid killing off captains in job lots. He smothered a curse as he rubbed the point of contact, but he hadn't done himself any lasting damage, and he reached for the audio-only com key.

"Yes?" he growled.

"Sir, it's Howard. I— Sir, we've got a problem up here, and I—"

The citizen ensign broke off, and the ache in Heathrow's head was suddenly forgotten as he heard the barely suppressed panic in her voice. He could actually hear her breathing—she sounded as if she was about to go into hyperventilation any moment—and he slammed the visual key.

Howard blinked as her skipper's bare-chested image appeared on her screen. It was highly irregular for the citizen lieutenant to accept a visual com connection out of uniform, and the fact that he'd overlooked the minor consideration that he slept in his briefs, not pajamas, added to the irregularity, but vast relief bloomed in her eyes as she recognized the supportive concern in his expression.

"What's wrong, Irene?" he asked, racking his brain for possible answers to his own question even as he spoke. But nothing came to him. After all, what *could* be wrong sitting here in Danak orbit?

"Sir, it's Groundside," Howard said. "I told them we didn't have any— But they wouldn't *listen*, and now Citizen Colonel Therret says Citizen General Chernock himself is— But I don't *have* any more traffic for them, Sir! I sent it all down yesterday, when we arrived! So—"

"Hold it. Hold it, Irene!" Heathrow managed to sound soothing and firm and commanding all at the same time, though he wasn't quite certain how he'd pulled it off. Howard slithered to a stop, staring at him pleadingly, and he drew a deep calming breath. For both of them, he thought wryly.

"All right," he said then. "I want you to begin at the beginning. Don't get excited. Don't run ahead. Don't assume that I know anything at all about whatever is going on. Just tell me what's happened step by step, okay?"

"Yes, Sir." Howard made herself sit back and took a visible grip on herself. Then she, too, inhaled deeply and began in a voice of determined calm.

"I didn't want to disturb you, Sir, or . . . or make you think I wasn't willing to take responsibility, and everything started out sounding so routine that I thought I could handle it." She swallowed. "I was wrong, Sir."

Her expression showed the humiliation of a bright, eager young officer who'd wanted to do her job and win her CO's approval only to see the attempt blow up in her face, but her voice was unflinching as she admitted her failure.

"As you know, Sir, we transmitted all the message traffic for Danak on our arrival in Danak Alpha orbit." She paused, and Heathrow nodded encouragingly. "Well, that was all the traffic there was, Sir. There wasn't any more at all, but they don't believe me Dirtside."

"They don't?" Heathrow raised a perplexed eyebrow, and she shook her head.

"No, Sir. First, I got a standard request from StateSec Sector HQ for a recheck of the message storage files to be sure everything had transmitted. So I did that, and told them everything had gone, and they went away. Only then, about fifteen minutes later, some SS citizen major turned up and *demanded* another recheck. And when I told him I'd already done it, he insisted on remote access to the message files. But he didn't find anything either, and when he didn't, he accused me of having somehow screwed up the message storage. But I told him I couldn't screw it up, that it was all automated. So then he accused me of having done it on purpose, if it couldn't happen by accident, so I told him that I couldn't deliberately tamper with the files because I didn't have a list of their contents—that I didn't even know how many messages had been loaded to the Danak queue, much less what those messages were about! Sir, I can't even unlock the central directory without the authenticated security code from the ground station the traffic is intended for—you know that!"

"Of course I do, Irene," he said soothingly, drawing her gently back from the brink of fresh hysteria.

"Well, I told him all that over and over—I don't know, maybe as much as nine or ten times and in five or six different ways—and he finally went away. But then this Citizen Colonel Therret called. He's Citizen General Chernock's chief of staff, and he started out just like the Citizen Major. Sir, he *insists* there has to be a message we haven't delivered, and . . . and he says he's sending a full security detail up here to 'talk' to me about it!"

She stared at him with huge eyes, panic once more hovering just under the surface, and now Heathrow understood completely. He didn't understand what was happening, or why—or even how, for that matter—but he understood Howard's terror only too well. And, truth to tell, he felt a swelling panic of his own, for if StateSec decided something had happened to its secure traffic aboard Heathrow's ship, there was no way their headhunting would stop with the lowly citizen ensign serving as his com officer.

"All right, Irene," he said after a moment of furious thought. "I want you to pull a complete copy of all com traffic between you and Dirtside on this. I'm going to get dressed while you do that. When I've got my clothes on, I'll buzz you to pipe the copies down here and let me view them. Then I'll want you to connect me directly to this Citizen Colonel Therret. I'll take it from there, and any further traffic from on this is to be routed directly to me as it comes in. Is all that understood?"

"Yes, Sir. It's on the com log, Sir." He heard the enormous relief in her voice, but her eyes were troubled. "Sir, I swear I didn't do anything to their message files. You know that."

"Of course I do, Irene. Hell, like you already told them, you *couldn't* have done anything without their own authentication codes!"

"I just— I'm sorry, Sir," she said in a small voice. "Whatever happened, it was my job, and—"

"Irene, we don't have time to sit here and let you beat yourself up for something you didn't do, couldn't have helped, and aren't responsible for," he told her. "So hush and get started on those copies ASAP."

"Yes, Sir."

He killed the com, rolled out of his bunk, and reached for the uniform he'd discarded three hours earlier.

"—so I assure you, Citizen Colonel, that I've looked into the matter thoroughly. There are no additional messages for Danak in our banks, no messages for Danak have been erroneously transmitted at any of our earlier stops, and no messages have been tampered with in any way."

"So your citizen ensign has already told me, Citizen Commander," Citizen Colonel Brigham Therret said coldly. "I must say, I find this all extremely suspicious."

"If I may be so bold, Sir, could you tell me anything at all to explain what, precisely, you're looking for?" Heathrow asked as courteously as he possibly could. "At the moment, we're shooting blind up here. We know you're looking for something, but we've checked all the places that something ought to be without finding it. Maybe if we had a better idea of what we were trying to find, we could make some educated guesses as to where and how it might have been misdirected, mislabeled, or misfiled."

"Um." Therret frowned, but his expression actually lightened a tiny bit, as if he hadn't considered that. He pondered for several moments, then made a face that might have indicated either indecision or annoyance. "Hold the circuit," he said abruptly, and his face disappeared, replaced by a standard COM LINK ENGAGED, PLEASE STAND BY image.

Heathrow looked up from it to smile encouragingly at Howard. After viewing her message logs, he'd decided to conduct this conversation from the bridge rather than his cabin terminal for several reasons, not the least of which was a desire to place himself in as official a setting as possible. Not that he expected an SS citizen colonel to be particularly impressed by a Navy citizen lieutenant commander, bridge environment or not, but it could hardly hurt. More to the point, he wanted immediate access to Howard and her console in case other questions came up . . . and, he admitted, exercising a soothing influence on the distracted citizen ensign seemed like a good idea, too.

He only wished someone could exercise one on him.

The standard holding pattern vanished, and Heathrow blinked at the face which had replaced it. It wasn't Therret. This man also wore StateSec uniform, but he had three stars on his shoulder boards, and Heathrow swallowed hard as he realized he was looking at Citizen General Chernock himself. The Citizen General had a dark face, a strongly hooked nose, and eyes that looked as if someone had figured out a way to carve the vacuum of deep space to order.

"Citizen Lieutenant Commander," the sector CO said flatly, and Heathrow nodded. He knew it looked jerky, despite his effort to appear calm, but all he could do was the best he could do.

"Yes, Citizen General?" he said. "How can I help you, Sir?"

"You can give me my goddamned mail, that's how you can help me!" Chernock growled.

"Sir, I have personally checked Citizen Ensign Howard's documentation on your message traffic—the upload logs, as well as the download logs. And every single message file logged in for you here on Danak has been delivered, Sir. We aren't privy to the contents of those files. Couriers never are, as I'm sure you're aware, so I can't say unequivocally that you received every individual message you should have. But I *can* tell you that no message with a Danak header is still aboard this ship."

"I would like to believe you, Citizen Commander," Chernock said flatly. "But I find that very difficult to do."

"Sir, if you could see your way to giving me even the smallest hint as to where this message might have originated, at least, then I might be able to shed some additional light on the situation. Without that, there is literally nothing I can do. And, Sir—" Heathrow drew a deep, anxious breath "—I must respectfully point out that State Security regulations pertaining to the safeguarding of classified traffic mean that I cannot give you access to any other addressee's message files." Chernock's brow darkened thunderously, and Heathrow hurried on quickly. "I didn't say I refused to, Sir; I said I *couldn't*. It's physically impossible for me or anyone else in this ship to open those files or even their directories without the addressee's authorization codes."

"I see." Chernock regarded him with lowered eyebrows, long, tapering fingers drumming fiercely on the edge of his own com console, then twitched his shoulders in a shrug. There might even have been an edge of grudging respect in those flat, cold eyes.

"Very well, Citizen Lieutenant Commander," he said after an endless, thoughtful moment. "I understand from certain other messages in your download to me that you were also scheduled for a stop at Cerberus."

"Yes, Sir," Heathrow said when Chernock paused. "We went directly there from Shilo. I realize it was irregular to use a Navy courier for Cerberus, but the State Security courier who'd been supposed to report to Shilo was late, and Citizen Major General Thornegrave insisted on commandeer—er, assigning us to the duty."

"And from Cerberus you went to Clarke, and from Clarke you came directly here?"

"Yes, Sir. I can download a copy of our astro log, if you'd care to review it."

"That won't be necessary, Citizen Lieutenant Commander. I'm simply endeavoring to be certain I have your itinerary firmly fixed in my brain." The citizen general smiled thinly. "You see, the problem I'm having down here is that there should have been a message—an eyes-only, personal one—directed to me from Citizen Brigadier Tresca."

"From Citizen Brigadier Tresca?" Heathrow blinked again, then looked at Howard. She looked back helplessly and shook her head. But he hadn't really needed that, for his own memory of their (very) brief stop at Hades was quite clear.

"Sir, there was no message from Citizen Brigadier Tresca," he said. "We receipted only a single transmission from Camp Charon, and it was directed to Citizen Major General Thornegrave in Shilo."

"Are you positive about that? There couldn't have been some mistake in the routing?"

"I don't see how, Sir. It wasn't addressed specifically to Citizen Major General Thornegrave, just to 'Commanding Officer, State Security Headquarters Shilo Sector,' but the destination code was clear. That much I can pull up for your review if you wish."

"Please do so," Chernock said, and for the first time it actually sounded like a request.

"Make it so, Citizen Ensign," Heathrow said quietly, and Howard complied instantly. The record was part of the information she'd already pulled together at Heathrow's instruction, and they watched together as Chernock considered it on his own com screen.

"I see," he said after what seemed a very long time to read such a short string of letters. "There appears to have been some confusion here, Citizen Lieutenant Commander. Do you have any idea what this message concerned?"

"None, Sir," Heathrow said very firmly indeed. Even if he'd had any idea, admitting it would have been a very bad move. Regular Navy courier COs who waxed curious about secure StateSec communications tended to end up just plain waxed. "All I can tell you," he went on, trying not to sound cautious, "is that one of the messages in the Hades queue specifically requested a response. It's SOP for the courier to be informed whenever that's the case, Sir, in order to ensure that we don't hyper out before someone groundside reads all of his or her mail and realizes a response is necessary. We aren't normally informed which message requires an answer or what that answer's content or subject might be, of course, and never when the subject is classified. In this case, however, my assumption would be that, since the only message we received from Camp Charon was coded for delivery to Shilo, Citizen Major General Thornegrave must have requested the response."

"I see," Chernock repeated. He gazed unreadably out of the screen for several seconds, then nodded. "Very well, Citizen Commander. You've been most responsive. I believe that will be all . . . for the moment."

He added the final qualifier almost absently, as if the need to intimidate regular officers was so deeply ingrained it had become reflex, and Heathrow nodded.

"Of course, Sir. If I can help in any other way, please let me know."

"I will," Chernock assured him, and cut the circuit.

"My God," Justin Bouret said fervently from where he'd lurked outside the pickup's range. "I thought for a while they were going to come up here and demand to take the message banks apart!"

"Wouldn't have done them any good, and Citizen General Chernock knew it," Heathrow said in an oddly detached tone. He felt the tremors of relief tingling in his fingertips and toes and raised one hand to mop sweat from his forehead without even trying to conceal it from his subordinates. "Even if they did take the banks apart, they couldn't make any sense of them," the citizen lieutenant commander went on. "Unless they have either Shilo's authentication codes or a copy of StateSec GHQ's override software, that is."

"You know," Bouret said thoughtfully, "I'll bet that if they did have it, they *would* have been up here."

"Maybe." Heathrow tried to make his tone final enough to end the conversation before Bouret said something unfortunate, then shook himself and smiled at Howard. "You did well, Irene. Very well," he said, reaching out to squeeze her shoulder.

"Thank you, Sir," she said softly, looking at the deck. Then she raised her eyes to his and smiled suddenly. "And you did pretty well yourself, Sir!" she added daringly, and blushed dark crimson.

"Do you think they're telling the truth, Brig?" Citizen Major General Seth Chernock asked.

"I think . . . yes," Citizen Colonel Therret said after a moment. Chernock's eyes asked the silent question, and he shrugged. "Everything Heathrow said or offered can be checked from hard records, Sir—if not here and now, then certainly as soon as his other messages are unlocked for delivery." He shook his head. "I don't see him exposing himself that way if he were actually up to something. If he hadn't known it would all check out—which it wouldn't, unless he was telling us the truth—he' would've made us dig it out of him rather than offering it before we could even ask."

"But that's impossible," Chernock said. "It was Dennis' move."

"Sir, I realize how important your chess games are, but—"

"You don't understand, Brigham. Or you're missing the point, at least. Dennis and I have been playing chess by mail for nine T-years. It was his move, he knew Heathrow's routing would bring him here, and he would never have passed up the opportunity to send it."

Therret kept his mouth shut. He had never understood the odd bond between Chernock and the brutish, self-indulgent Tresca. Obviously Tresca possessed both patrons and an excellent performance record, or he would never have been selected for a post as sensitive as Camp Charon's warden. But Therret had seen enough evidence to make some pretty accurate guesses about the sort of gross sensuality and permissiveness Tresca had extended to his Hades personnel. Nor did the citizen colonel doubt the rumors of prisoner abuse and mistreatment. And while Therret would shed no tears for enemies of the New Order, he considered that sort of behavior destructive of discipline.

None of that should have been tolerable to Seth Chernock. The citizen major general was an intensely self-disciplined man, and one of the few true intellectuals who had served State Security since the very beginning of the New Order. He'd been a sociology professor before the Harris Assassination, with a tenured position as assistant department head at Rousseau Planetary University in Nouveau Paris. As such, he'd needed all his self-discipline under the old regime to conceal his disaffection with the Legislaturalists and his disgust over their insistence on propping up the moldering remnants of capitalism and its unequal distribution of the fruits of society's productivity. Not only had the RPU faculty senate never realized his true feelings, but he'd also managed to conceal his membership in the Citizens' Rights Union from Internal Security. After the Harris Assassination, he'd emerged as one of the leading intellectual supporters of the Committee of Public Safety, although Therret suspected his enlistment in State Security represented a sense of disappointment with the Committee. Chernock obviously realized that Citizen Chairman Pierre was unwilling or (more probably) unable, in the middle of a war, to complete the sweeping program of change Chernock had endorsed. But his own zealous commitment to it had never wavered, and State Security was certainly the logical place for someone committed to preparing the groundwork for his grand plan.

Since joining StateSec Chernock had become even more disciplined . . . and much colder. Therret had known him for only six T-years, but he'd seen the change in him even over that time period. The citizen major general remained capable of astounding warmth and friendship, but it was as if he were rationing the ability to feel human emotions solely to those in his inner circle. As far as the rest of humanity was concerned, he had retreated behind the icy armor of his intellect and his commitment to the ends of the Revolution, deliberately making himself hard as the accepted price of achieving his goals.

All of that should have made Chernock loathe Tresca, who was certainly no intellectual, about as undisciplined as a man could be, and (as Therret felt certain Chernock recognized) far more committed to the cause of Dennis Tresca than that of the People. Yet the citizen major general had taken to the ex-noncom the first time they met. In fact, Chernock was one of the patrons who had gotten Tresca his current assignment, and he looked forward eagerly to the slow, stretched-out moves of their interstellar chess games. And crude as Tresca might be, he did play an extremely good game of chess, Therret admitted. But then, the citizen colonel had never thought there was anything wrong with Tresca's basic intelligence; Therret's problem was with how the citizen brigadier used it . . . or didn't.

"No," Chernock went on, rising to pace back and forth, "Dennis would have sent his move. But he didn't—not unless Heathrow and that hysterical citizen ensign are both lying, and as you just pointed out, that would be incredibly stupid of them when we could check their stories so easily. Hell, all we'd have to do is ask Dennis to verify their version of events in our next dispatch to him!"

The citizen general fell silent, hands clasped tightly behind him while he paced faster and harder. Therret watched him moving back and forth, back and forth, until he felt like a spectator at a tennis match. Finally he cleared his throat.

"So what are you saying, Sir?" he asked.

"I'm saying something is wrong on Hades," Chernock said flatly. His voice was decisive, and he turned to face Therret as if grateful to the citizen colonel for pushing him into stating his conclusion out loud.

"But what could be wrong, Sir?" Therret asked, honestly bewildered. "Heathrow was just there. Surely he would have known if anything hadn't been kosher!"

"Not necessarily," Chernock said in a more reluctant tone. "He would have known if anyone had attacked the planet from space and captured it, yes. I'm sure there would almost have had to be gaps in the orbital defenses, wreckage, any number of things to suggest combat, if that were the case. But if the attack didn't come from outside . . ."

His voice trailed off, and Therret blanched.

"Sir, are you suggesting the prisoners somehow—? But that's impossible, Sir!"

"I know. But so is the idea that Dennis didn't send me a chess move—or at least a reason for why he didn't send it. I'm telling you, Brigham; something had to happen to prevent that. And if it wasn't an external attack, then somehow the prisoners must actually have gotten to Camp Charon. And they must have done it successfully, too. If they'd attacked and been suppressed, Dennis—or his XO, if Dennis had been killed—would surely have reported it to the next competent authority on Heathrow's flight plan. And that competent authority would have been Danak HQ, which means me."

"Sir, you realize what you're saying here?" Therret said very carefully. "You're telling me, on the basis of a chess move that wasn't sent, that the inmates of the most escape-proof prison in the history of mankind have somehow overpowered their guards and taken possession of the planet."

"I know it sounds crazy," Chernock admitted. "But I also know it must have happened."

Therret looked at him for a small, endless eternity, then sighed. "All right, Sir. I don't know if I agree with you—not yet, anyway—but I can't refute your reasoning based on anything we know at this moment. But assuming the prisoners have taken the planet, what do we do about it? Alert Nouveau Paris and the other Sector HQs?"

"No," Chernock said decisively. "We move on this ourselves, Brig. Immediately."

"Sir, we only have two or three of our own ships here in Danak right now. And if the prisoners have managed to take Styx, I think we have to assume they've also taken over the armories, the battle armor storage and vehicle parks. . . . We'll need troops and additional firepower, not to mention a way to deal with the orbital defenses."

"Orbital defenses?" Chernock looked startled by the citizen colonel's last remark.

"Sir, it's a logical consequence of your basic assumption," Therret pointed out. "Assuming they've actually taken Styx, then they must have taken the central control room pretty much intact—and broken most of the security codes—because they were able to receive, read, and respond to the message traffic Heathrow delivered. That being the case, can we afford *not* to assume they have control of the orbital defenses, as well?"

"No. No, you're right," Chernock said, and grimaced sourly. "All right, we need a ground combat element—probably a good-sized one—and an escort capable of taking on the orbital defenses. Damn!" He slammed a fist down on his com unit. "That probably means we *do* have to send all the way back to the capital!"

"Not necessarily, Sir."

"What do you mean?" Chernock turned back to the citizen colonel, and Therret shrugged.

"I read a report on the Cerberus defenses a couple of months ago, Sir. It was generated by the NavInt Section after that disgrac—" He stopped himself as he remembered who had been responsible for the tardy response to another escape attempt to which he had been about to apply the adjective. "After that unfortunate business with Citizen Secretary Ransom and the *Tepes*," he went on after only the tiniest hesitation.

"And?" Chernock chose to ignore his chief of staff's self-correction.

"It pointed out that the system was much more vulnerable to external attack than anyone with InSec or, for that matter, with our own HQ staff had ever realized. Apparently there's some way to attack unmanned orbital weapons from long range and take them out without ever entering their own engagement envelope." He shrugged again. "I didn't understand it all—it was written from a naval perspective—but the conclusion, I believe, was that even a few battlecruisers could probably blow a way through the defenses. Our own ships here in Danak might not have enough firepower, but if we conscripted a few naval units, we could almost certainly shoot our way in if we had to."

"We could?" Chernock looked disturbed by the thought that Hades was so much more vulnerable than he'd assumed. Or perhaps he was disturbed by the notion that he might have to become the one responsible for blowing a hole in the defenses StateSec had always thought were impregnable . . . and use units of the distrusted regular Navy to do it. He frowned in silence for several long seconds, then sighed.

"All right. If that's what we have to do, then that's what we have to do. But it's going to take time to organize all this."

"It is that, Sir," Therret agreed grimly, then smiled crookedly. "On the other hand, we should have some time in hand. Hades isn't going anywhere!"

"No, but if they get their hands on a ship or two, the prisoners might," Chernock pointed out.

"Not very many of them," Therret countered respectfully. "It would have taken thousands of unarmed people to overrun the garrison. I'll grant they might grab off the odd ship arriving solo, but they'd need more life support than they could possibly have captured that way to get any significant percentage of the prison population off-world."

"And if they sent a courier to the Manties to request a relief convoy?"

"They may have done that, Sir," Therret conceded after a moment. "I don't know if the Manties are in a position to respond to a request like that after the hammering the Navy's finally given them, but it's certainly possible. In that case, though, I doubt very much that we have enough firepower in-sector to meet them in a stand-up fight. So either they'll have come and gone before we get there, or they'll be there and we'll have to avoid action, or they haven't come yet and we'll get in in front of them, or else they're not coming at all. That's a fifty-fifty chance of accomplishing something even if the prisoners did manage to get their hands on some sort of courier, and if we send dispatches to GHQ, we can certainly get a relief force to Cerberus a hell of a lot quicker than the Manties could."

"Yes, and then we might as well post the system's coordinates on a Navy info site," Chernock sighed.

"We can't have it both ways, Sir," Therret said almost gently. "Either there's a serious problem, and we need Navy help to deal with it, or there isn't."

"I know. I know." Chernock frowned into the distance, then shrugged. "All right, Brig. Before we do anything else, check our force availability. We've certainly got the manpower to restore control of Camp Charon. I don't know if we've got enough intervention battalions ready to go, but I'm sure we can draft enough Marines from the Fleet base to do the job, especially with orbital fire support available as needed. What I'm not sure about is the availability of transport and/or naval escort shipping. I want a complete report on my desk within three hours. Can you do it that quickly?"

"Almost certainly, but this is coming at everyone cold, Sir. I'd estimate that it will take at least a standard week—probably a little longer—to get a troop movement organized on the scale we're projecting. And I have no idea at all how quickly the Navy can respond."

"Then I guess we're about to find out," Chernock said grimly.

Chapter Forty-Six

"Welcome to Flag Bridge, Citizen General," Citizen Commander Yang said pleasantly.

"Thank you, Citizen Commodore," Citizen Major General Thornegrave responded, as politely as if they both meant a word of it, and they smiled at one another.

"As I explained when I screened you, we're just coming up on our alpha translation, Sir," Yang went on. "We'll reenter n-space in—" she glanced at the date/time display "—eleven and a half minutes."

"Excellent, Citizen Commodore. And from there to Hades orbit?"

"We're making a fairly gentle translation, Sir." Yang smiled again, this time with genuine humor. "There's no need for what a crash translation does to people's nerves and stomachs, after all. That means we'll hit normal-space with a velocity of only about a thousand KPS, and we'll be about fourteen and a half light-minutes from Hades on a direct intercept course. Unfortunately from the prospect of a fast passage, however, the *Longstops* can only manage about two hundred and twenty gravities. That gives us a total flight time of almost exactly six hours, but the decel leg will be eight minutes—and about a hundred and fifteen thousand klicks—longer than the accel because of the velocity we'll take across the alpha wall with us."

"I see." Thornegrave nodded gravely, and despite his antipathy for regular officers in general and his awareness of the need to put this regular officer in particular in her place and keep her there, he was grateful for her apparent tact. No doubt a Navy officer, or even a Marine, would have realized what bringing an initial velocity across from hyper-space would have meant for their passage time to Hades. Thornegrave hadn't, but Yang had found a way to give him the information without drawing any attention to the fact that he'd needed it. That might not matter in the long run, but her explanation might also keep him from saying something which would sound at best ill-informed and at worst stupid in front of some junior officer.

Yang saw the flicker of awareness in his eyes, but she had no intention of indicating that she had, for she'd long since decided Thornegrave needed regular stroking to keep him off her back. It wasn't even really because he was StateSec, either. She'd had regular Navy superiors who were just as compulsive about controlling everything and everyone around them, and she sometimes wondered if that sort of personality was what had propelled them to senior rank in the first place.

Of course, she didn't dare forget his SS connections for a moment, either, and he'd seen to it that she hadn't. The one good thing about her current assignment was that there was no people's commissioner attached to her staff. The downside of that was that the reason for it was that she was, in effect, simply attached to Thornegrave's staff, which left him filling the role of watchdog himself. Worse, the *Longstops* couldn't climb above the delta bands (which was why no Navy officer would have even considered using them to deliver so many troops so close to the front line of a serious war), so the piddling little 33.75 light-year-voyage from Shilo to Cerberus had required over two hundred and ninety-five hours, base-time. Relativity had reduced that to just under ten days subjective at the transports' best speed, but that had still given him entirely too much time to make himself totally unbearable. Of course, she thought moodily, a man with his immense native talent could have done that in just a few hours. Nine days had simply given him the time he needed to achieve complete artistry.

But they were coming up on Cerberus at last, thank God. She could at least hope that the chance to boss around more of his red-coated SS minions would distract him from badgering her for the next couple of days. *On the other hand, we're scheduled to ship everyone on board and be out of here within seventy-two hours, and it's going to take us over five and a third T-weeks subjective to reach Seabring.* She shuddered at the very thought, but shuddering wouldn't change anything.

"The actual translation from hyper to n-space is quite visually spectacular, Sir," she went on in her most pleasant voice. "Have you ever had the opportunity to observe it?"

"No. No, I haven't," Thornegrave replied after a moment.

"If you'd like a ringside seat for it, Sir, you can watch the main plot here on Flag Bridge. CIC will be keeping an eye out for Tactical, and I'm sure Citizen Captain Ferris will be watching his maneuvering plot carefully. But I rather enjoy watching the translation bleed myself, so I normally have the main plot configured to take a visual feed from the forward optical heads. Or you can also watch it directly with the naked eye from the observatory blister."

Thornegrave regarded her thoughtfully. He more than half suspected she was looking for any excuse to tempt him off "her" flag bridge, but if she was she'd certainly found a bait that piqued his interest. And she *had* covered his ass for him with that smoothly slipped in little explanation, so he supposed he could argue that he owed her some small triumph in return. He weighed silent pros and cons for several seconds, then shrugged mentally. He had no intention of spending the next six hours standing around on Flag Bridge. Yang was going to, but it was her job to play chauffeur. In his own case, however, he could use the observation blister as an excuse to leave now, then come back several hours later to fulfill his role as the expeditionary CO without losing face.

"I believe I *will* watch it from the observation blister, Citizen Commodore," he said graciously. "Thank you for the suggestion."

"You're quite welcome, Sir," Yang told him, and her eyes glinted with satisfaction as she watched him head for the lift.

Citizen Lieutenant Rodham was waiting to play guide again. Thornegrave's initial opinion of the citizen lieutenant had been amply confirmed in the course of the trip from Shilo, and he was amazed and baffled by how someone as unprepossessing as young Guillermo could convince so many different women to sleep with him. The citizen major general still didn't like the citizen lieutenant a bit, but he'd been forced to change his mind about him in at least one regard. He'd figured the smarmy, apple-polishing little bastard to be completely useless, but he'd been wrong. The citizen lieutenant wasn't particularly skilled at his official duties, but he attacked them (when anyone was looking, at any rate) with enormous energy, and he'd displayed a facile wit at borrowing other people's work or at least explaining away his own failures. More to the point, however, he had a quality StateSec occasionally needed badly: amorality.

It grieved Thornegrave to admit that, for he disliked seeing people in SS uniform who were devoted to the Revolution solely out of ambition, not conviction. He despised such fellow-travelers on a personal level, and on a professional one, he regarded them as dangerous soft spots in the People's armor. If they would profess one belief out of expediency, there was no reason to believe they wouldn't embrace conversion to another the instant the winds of advantage looked like shifting.

Yet much as he disliked admitting it, he knew people like Citizen Lieutenant Rodham made the best informers. One had to be careful to ensure that they weren't "informing" on some obstacle to their own advancement simply to get the unfortunate person out of their way, but people who had no convictions would not be led by *mistaken* convictions to risk their own hides to protect others. More to the point, perhaps, they had a priceless gift any really good informer needed: they made people trust them. In Rodham's case, for example, he had not only inveigled Citizen Major Regina Sanderman into his bed, but also into some highly indiscreet pillow talk. Sanderman didn't know it yet, but Thornegrave did. He and his chief of staff were watching the citizen major very carefully, waiting for the actions which would confirm the disaffection her talks with Rodham had suggested.

I really do hate this little bottom-feeder, Thornegrave reflected as, once again, the citizen lieutenant punched the code to summon a lift car, *but the People can't afford to throw away a perfectly useful tool just because its handle is a little slimy. And at least he does know his way around this damned ship better than I do. I wonder how much of that comes from nipping in and out of other people's bunks?*

"Does the Citizen General wish the Citizen Lieutenant to escort him to the observation blister, Sir?" Rodham asked when the car arrived, and Thornegrave looked at him sharply. Rodham hadn't been on Flag Bridge when Yang made her offer, nor had Thornegrave yet told him where they were headed.

It seems I underestimated him. He's got better sources than I thought. But he may be even stupider than I thought, too, if he's going around showing off the fact that he's keeping tabs on me. *Or is he clever enough—and gutsy enough—to deliberately risk pissing me off by displaying that his ability as an information gatherer extends even to my own movements because he figures his demonstrated value will impress me enough to outweigh my irritation with him?*

"Yes," he said after a moment. "Please do escort me to the blister, Citizen Lieutenant."

"Of course, Sir! If the Citizen General will follow me, please?"

Oh, I will. I will! Thornegrave decided. *And I'll give you a little more rope, too, Citizen Lieutenant. You're too full of your own cleverness to last forever, but it'll be interesting to see how far you get before you fall off that cliff you're so busy building . . . and how far you bounce.*

"Hyper footprint!"

Honor looked up as the grav scanner chief of the watch called out the warning. All other sound ceased in the control room, and every eye joined Honor's in swinging to the master plot as the bright red icons of unidentified hyper translations blinked into life. She realized she was holding her breath, counting the sources as they appeared, and forced herself to breathe out and look away, displaying her calmness to the troops.

"Seventeen point sources, Ma'am!" the chief petty officer announced.

"Acknowledged, Scan. Thank you, and stay on it," Commander Phillips replied. She was the CO of Charon Control now, for Harriet Benson was back in space, commanding ENS *Bacchante* while Alistair McKeon commanded ENS *Krashnark* and Jesus Ramirez acted as the fledgling "Elysian Space Navy's" senior officer in space. Honor would have preferred to be out there herself, but her place was here, with the bulk of her people, and between them, Jesus and Alistair made a team which would be hard to beat. Especially with Benson to back them up.

The scan tech said something else to Phillips—a question this time, asked too quietly for Honor to hear—and the commander nodded. Then she patted the CPO on his shoulder and crossed to Honor.

"Any orders, Milady?"

"No," Honor replied, watching the plot once more. "I—"

"Excuse me, Admiral, but we have their probable course plotted," the senior tracking officer said. Honor looked at the woman and nodded for her to continue. "We make it right on six hours for a zero-zero intercept, Ma'am. Their present accel is two-point-one-six KPS squared, which is right on the money for the *Longstops*, and they haven't had time to ask for course directions yet, but their heading is right to take them exactly to Point Alpha. I'd say it has to be the Shilo Force."

"Thank you, Commander." Point Alpha was the entry point for the shortest of the four cleared routes through the Hades minefields. All four entry points were marked on the standard SS charts, which was evidence that those were StateSec ships out there, but Charon Control routinely shifted the actual routes around. That meant the newcomers certainly would ask for course directions shortly . . . assuming Commander Ushakovna was correct, of course.

Honor suppressed a desire to grimace and nobly refrained from pointing out that she hadn't asked Tracking to speculate, and she heard (and felt) Nimitz's quiet bleek of entertainment from her shoulder at her restraint. Commander Ushakovna was almost certainly right, after all, and Nimitz and Honor both knew Honor's fleeting temptation to say something cutting stemmed solely from her own nervous tension.

Well, at least I didn't do it, Honor thought wryly, and tasted Nimitz's agreement over their link. The cat leaned forward in the carrier she wore on her back now, and the tip of his nose whuffled gently through her hair to find the back of her ear while his amused love flowed into her.

"All right, people," she said, turning to look over the staff manning the control room. "We should be receiving their ID transmission within the next ten minutes or so, but it's going to be a long, slow haul before they get close enough for us to make our move. I want you all to take a deep breath and settle down. We only get one shot at this, but we've done it before on a smaller scale, and we can do it again. Commander Phillips."

"Yes, Milady?"

"If you would, please, I want everyone relieved in rotation. We've got the trained personnel. Let's be sure the people who are going to be carrying the ball when the penny drops are rested and fed."

"Aye, aye, Milady. I'll see to it."

✧ ✧ ✧

Citizen Major General Thornegrave paused, his hands resting lightly on his keyboard. The words of the memo on the living conditions to be provided for the forced laborers in Seabring glowed steadily on his terminal, but his attention drifted away from them once more. It wasn't like him to be distracted this way . . . but, then, he seldom had a memory quite so spectacular to do the distracting, either.

The hyper translation had been all Citizen Commodore Yang had promised. He'd never imagined anything like it, and he knew he'd stood there, gawking through the observation blister's magnifying grav lens, as ship after ship followed *Farnese* across the hyper-space wall into the Cerberus System. The sleek battlecruisers had been magnificent enough, with the two hundred and fifty-kilometer disks of their Warshawski sails bleeding blue lightning, but the transports had been even more awesome. They outmassed the battlecruisers by over five-to-one, and despite their weaker drives, the actual area of their sails was much greater. They had flashed into existence like huge, azure soap bubbles, blazing against the blackness like brief-lived blue suns, and the sight had driven home the reality of their sheer size. There were many larger ships in space, yet for the first time in his memory, Thornegrave had been pushed into standing back and appreciating the sheer scale of the human race's dreams. By many standards, the *Longstops* were little more than moderately oversized cargo barges, and he knew it, but they didn't feel that way as they glowed and flashed in the long night.

And if we can build ships like that, surely we also have the capability to complete the Revolution, he'd thought, gazing in awe at the spectacle. But then he'd felt a cold chill as the unsought counter-argument trickled through his brain: *Unless someone equally capable—like the goddamned Manties—manages to stop us.*

It was at such moments that he most missed Cordelia Ransom. Unlike ninety-nine-point-nine percent of his personnel, Prestwick Thornegrave knew what had really happened to Ransom right here in this system. In his personal opinion, PubIn had been wise to announce that she—and *Tepes*—had been lost in action while acting as the Committee's personal representative at the front. It had been no more than true—aside from the minor issues of where and how the ship had been destroyed—and it had given her the status she had so richly earned as one of the Revolution's most revered martyrs. Her loss had still been a savage blow to the New Order, and Thornegrave rather regretted the fact that the delay in announcing her death had required State Security to lie to the survivors of so many of its own personnel—by omission, at least—by concealing *Tepes*' loss. But the Committee had clearly recognized that admitting the Manties and their lackeys had killed her after she ordered that aristocratic, elitist murderess Harrington's execution would have hurt the People's morale—and boosted the Manties'—more than her later, more traditionally heroic "official" death.

Now he grunted irritably as the familiar thought reminded him once more of the People's loss and dragged him back to the present. He glowered at the words on the display in front of him, then snorted and saved and closed the file. His moment of exaltation on the observation deck lay five-plus hours in the past, and it was time he returned to Flag Deck.

"They're coming up on their final course change, Milady," Commander Phillips said quietly, and Honor nodded, never looking away from the plot. Phillips' voice was a bit hoarser than it had been when the Peeps first made translation, and Honor wasn't surprised. The tension had ratcheted steadily higher as the enemy continued blithely in-system, and in an odd sort of way, their very failure to show any suspicion at all only made it worse. It was as if everyone in the control room was holding his or her mental breath, waiting tautly for some indication that all their plans were going into the crapper, and every moment in which that didn't happen simply made the dread that it might that much stronger.

Of course, it isn't all "their" plans; it's all my *plans,* Honor thought wryly. She felt the dryness in her own mouth, and Nimitz leaned forward against her back, resting his chin on her shoulder and crooning almost subliminally to her. Or perhaps it *was* subliminal, something sensed over their link and not heard by her ears at all.

She drew a deep breath and made herself stand motionless, the thumb of her single hand hooked into her belt. She didn't really care for that pose—it felt slouched and unprofessional—but she could hardly clasp one hand behind her in her usual "I'm feeling no tension" mannerism. The thought wrung a genuine chuckle out of her, and she saw Phillips turn towards her in surprise.

She shook her head at the other woman, declining to explain her humor. It wouldn't have done much for her image as a calm, cool combat commander. Besides, she wasn't sure how much of it was a tension reaction. Everyone had felt nerves tighten as Scanning got a better read on the seventeen point sources. They had expected two battlecruisers and three heavy cruisers; they'd gotten six BCs and four CAs, with two light cruisers as a screen. In the final analysis, the additional firepower shouldn't make much difference, but that hadn't kept the increased odds from making them all wonder what other surprises the Peeps might have in store for them.

Not that we don't have a few surprises of our own, Honor thought more grimly. She glanced at a secondary plot, this one showing the two green icons hiding behind Niflheim, the outermost of Hell's three moons. *Krashnark* and *Bacchante* held their positions, concealed from any Peep sensor in the moon's shadow but ready to dash out firing at need. They wouldn't add much to the orbital defenses' sheer weight of fire, but their mobility gave them a tactical value all their own . . . not to mention what the realization that her people had already seized at least two enemy ships might do to the Peeps' morale.

The convoy from Shilo made its last course alteration, swinging just outside the innermost ring of mines and settling into parking orbit. Their short-range active sensors were on-line, but that was no more than a sensible precaution this close to such a massive concentration of mines. It was always possible for the station-keeping drive on one or more mines to fail and send the weapons into what was supposed to be a safety zone, and no sane captain (even an SS captain, apparently) wanted to be taken by surprise when something like that happened. But the incoming ships obediently shut down their wedges as they came up on their assigned orbital positions, and Honor looked up as Phillips leaned towards her tactical officer.

"Any sign of active weapon systems?"

"No, Ma'am," the lieutenant commander at Tactical replied. "And they're powering down the nodes on the freighters."

"Only on the freighters?" Phillips voice started out sharply, but she got control of it by the third word and smoothed it out quickly.

"So far," the tac officer confirmed. "Wait one. . . . We've got node power-down on the cruisers, as well, Commander, but the battle-cruisers are showing standby power readings."

Phillips said something under her breath, then glanced at Honor, who shrugged more calmly than she felt.

"It was always a possibility," she said evenly. "If I were in command up there, I'd probably do the same thing with *all* my ships, not just the battlecruisers. It's the only way they can hope to execute any radical maneuvers quickly enough to do some good if a mine does come adrift up there. But it won't make much difference against the amount of firepower we can actually hit them with."

"Agreed, Milady," Phillips said, and then grinned tautly. "Not that I wouldn't be happier if they'd gone ahead and shut them all down!"

"You and me both, Commander," Honor admitted, then drew a deep breath and stepped over to the communications station. She reached down and took the microphone the com officer handed her. The AI-driven "Warden Tresca" Scotty Tremaine and Horace Harkness had built out of the dead Black Leg's file imagery had performed beautifully during the Peeps' approach, but it was time for a more hands-on approach, she thought grimly, then nodded to Phillips.

"All right, Commander. Pass the word to *Krashnark* and *Bacchante* to stand by, then prepare to execute Flypaper."

"Aye, aye, Ma'am."

"That's odd," Citizen Commodore Yang murmured.

Citizen Major General Thornegrave glanced up from his conversation with *Voyager*'s skipper at the sound of her voice. The big transport's CO went right on talking in response to Thornegrave's last question, but the Citizen Major General wasn't listening. He was watching Yang as she leaned over a waterfall display at the tactical station and frowned.

"What is it, Citizen Commodore?" he asked.

"Probably nothing, Sir," Yang replied, eyes still on the display, "but Camp Charon is still hitting us with an awful lot of active sensors, radar and lidar alike."

"Why should they be doing that?" He heard a small, sharp edge in his own voice, yet there was no real concern in it. Just puzzlement that grew as Yang shrugged.

"They were tracking us all the way in, Sir—as a routine security precaution, I assumed. Why they should continue doing it now that we're in orbit is beyond me, however. Oh," she waved one hand in a dismissive gesture, "I suppose they could be running some sort of training exercise down there. They can probably use all the live tracking experience they can get. It's just that there are a lot more sensors involved than I would have expected, and lidar is normally used primarily as fire control."

"*Fire* control?" Thornegrave half-rose, but Yang turned and shook her head quickly at him.

"Fire control teams need practice, too, Sir," she reassured him, "and the fact that their sensors are active doesn't mean their weapons have been released. In fact, it's SOP for the weapons *not* to be enabled in an exercise, so I'm not afraid of anyone shooting us by accident. It's just that the exercise, or whatever it is, is on a much greater scale than I would have antici—"

She broke off as her com officer jerked suddenly upright in her chair. The woman spun towards her CO, then remembered Thornegrave's presence and started towards him, only to freeze half way. She hovered indecisively, training and desire drawing her one way, the formal chain of command and fear of the SS drawing her the other, then shook herself out of her paralysis. She didn't face either of them directly. Instead, she aimed her eyes at an invisible point midway between them.

"Citizen General, I—" She sounded shaken, almost stunned, and broke off, then cleared her throat. "I believe you'd better listen to this message from Groundside, Sir," she said in a flatter, mechanical tone.

"What message?" Thornegrave growled. "Is it Warden Tresca?" He'd already had a long conversation with Tresca on his way in, and the man had signed off less than ten minutes ago. What could he be comming back about so soon?

"No, Sir." The com officer swallowed. "It's— Here, Sir."

She held out an earbug and Thornegrave blinked at her in astonishment. She was clear across the bridge from him, and he snorted in impatience.

"Just put it on my display, Citizen Commander," he said brusquely. She gazed at him a moment longer, still holding the earbug, then shrugged and turned back to her own console.

"Yes, Sir. Replaying the original transmission now."

Thornegrave leaned back in his chair, wondering what in the world could explain the woman's odd attitude, and then his eyebrow rose as another woman appeared in his display. There was something oddly familiar about her, but the uniform was entirely wrong. Her tunic was sky-blue, her trousers were dark blue, the stars on her shoulder boards were the wrong shape for any of the People's uniformed branches, and she appeared to be missing her left arm. The hair under her bizarre visored cap was a close-cropped mass of feathery curls, and the left side of her face looked almost paralyzed, and he frowned. That face and that uniform rang distant warning bells, but he didn't know why, and at the moment, surprise kept all other reactions at bay. But then a small, sharp-muzzled head appeared over her right shoulder, and air hissed in his nostrils. Grayson! That was a *Grayson admiral's* uniform, and the woman was—

"Attention PNS *Farnese,*" the face on his display said in a cold, hard voice. "I am Admiral Honor Harrington, Grayson Space Navy, and the planet Hades is under my control. I am transmitting this message to the attention of Citizen General Thornegrave over a whisker laser in order to ensure privacy. My purpose is to allow you the opportunity to reply to my transmission before its contents become general knowledge and inspire someone to panic and do something stupid."

She paused, very briefly, and Thornegrave stared at her numbly while his brain slithered and skidded like a man on slick ice.

"I am transmitting from the central control room at Camp Charon," she resumed in that same, diamond-hard voice, "and the targeting systems now locked onto your vessels are under my command. You are instructed to cut all power to your nodes immediately and stand by to be boarded. Any resistance to those instructions, or to any other order from myself or my subordinates, will be met with deadly force. I require an immediate response to these instructions."

Thornegrave fought his horrified shock, but his mind was too stunned to function. It was impossible, a small, cold voice insisted in the back of his brain. Honor Harrington was dead. She'd been dead for weeks before PubIn faked up her execution for the media. There was no possible way she could be looking out of his com screen and issuing ultimatums. Damn it to hell, she was *dead!*

But her grim, purposeful expression was awfully determined looking for a dead woman's.

"My God!" Thornegrave looked up at the whispered half-prayer and saw Yang standing at his shoulder. "That's— It *can't* be her! I saw the imagery of her execution myself! Unless—" She jerked her eyes from the display to stare at Thornegrave, and the citizen major general saw the speculation erupting behind her eyes. But he could only look back at her, his own brain refusing to accept the evidence of his senses, and then the com officer spoke again.

"I'm receiving another transmission, Sir!" she said sharply, and Thornegrave twitched as the citizen commander switched the new message to his display without orders.

"I am awaiting your response, Citizen General Thornegrave," Harrington said coldly, "but my patience is not unlimited. You will comply with my instructions *now*, or I will open fire on your vessels. You have thirty seconds to acknowledge my transmission."

"Sir, we have to do something!" Yang said urgently.

"But we— I mean, I can't—" Thornegrave swallowed hard and forced his brain to function by sheer willpower. "Citizen Commander!" he barked at the com officer.

"Yes, Sir?"

"Is she telling the truth, or is this going out to the other ships, as well?"

"I don't believe it is, Sir. We're receiving an encrypted whisker laser from one of Charon's comsats. I think she meant it when she said she doesn't want anyone else hearing her just yet." The citizen commander paused a moment, then cleared her throat. "Is there a reply, Sir?" she asked.

"No, there is not!" Thornegrave snapped. "I will tell you when I decide—when *I* decide, Citizen Commander!—to respond to any messages. Is that clear?"

"Yes, Sir," the com officer replied flatly, and Thonegrave glared at her. A part of him knew he was lashing out at her as a sop to his own incipient panic, but the rest of him didn't much care. And if using her as a target helped hold that panic at bay and jog his brain back into working, so much the better.

"Citizen General, we don't have time for this!" Yang said in a low, urgent voice. "Her time limit is running out, and we're sitting ducks up here. You've got to respond now!"

"I don't *have* to do anything, Citizen Commodore!" Thornegrave told her sharply.

"Yes, you do!" Yang snapped back. "She's giving you a chance to settle this without bloodshed, Sir. If you throw it away, God only knows what will happen!"

"I am not accustomed to being dictated to by escaped prisoners who—" Thornegrave began, but Yang cut him off harshly.

"She's not an escaped prisoner; she's the person who controls the firepower to blow this entire convoy to hell in a heartbeat!" she told the SS officer in a voice like ground glass.

"Nonsense! You're panicking—exaggerating!"

"No I'm not!" She glared at him, "Sir, this is my area of expertise, not yours, and we are utterly helpless up here. None of us have our wedges up. We can't maneuver, our point defense is down . . . Hell, we don't even have our rad shielding on-line! If we even bring up our fire control, her sensors will spot it instantly, and she can swat us like flies before we lock up a target or—"

"Very well, Citizen General," the cold, flat voice from his com said. "Your time is up. What happens now will be on your head." She looked out of the field of the pickup. "Switch to the all-ships frequency," she said.

"What? What does she mean?" Thornegrave demanded, but Yang had already spun away from him. She ignored him completely, snapping urgent commands for her com officer to get her a link to the other captains. But there wasn't time, and Thornegrave saw Harrington turn back to face the pickup.

"To all units orbiting Hades," she said flatly. "This is Admiral Honor Harrington, Grayson Space Navy. I am in control of Hades and all of its facilities, including its orbital defenses. You are locked up by my fire control as I speak. You will immediately cut all power to your drives, shut down all active sensors, and await boarding. Any delay in the execution of or disobedience to any of those instructions will result in the destruction of the disobeying vessel. This is your first, last, and only warning. Harrington out."

"All ships," Yang was barking into her own microphone. "All ships, this is the Flag! Comply with all instructions from Charon! I repeat, comply—"

"Citizen Commodore—the *Attila!*"

Yang swung towards the master plot, and a spiked fist grabbed her stomach and squeezed as PNS *Attila*'s StateSec CO panicked. She couldn't really blame him, she thought numbly—not when Harrington's demand came at him cold that way. If that idiot Thornegrave hadn't blustered and delayed, it might not have happened. As it was, every captain was on his or her own, and *Attila*'s impellers were still at standby. Yang would never know exactly what Citizen Captain Snellgrave had hoped to achieve. Perhaps he'd thought that if he got the wedge up fast enough, brought his sidewalls on-line quickly enough, he might last long enough to take Charon out with a missile strike before the orbital defenses killed his ship. Perhaps he actually thought he could maneuver clear under the cover of his wedge, though only a fool—or someone driven to fatal stupidity by panic—could have believed anything of the sort. The most likely answer was that he simply didn't think at all; he just reacted.

Whatever he thought he was doing, it was the last mistake he ever made. *Attila* hadn't even moved yet. Her emergency reaction thrusters flared wildly, and her impeller strength shot upward, spinning towards full power, and Charon's sensors must have seen it the instant it began to change. The wedge was only beginning to form, still far too nebulous to interdict incoming fire, when eight remote graser platforms opened fire simultaneously. All eight scored direct hits, and beams that could have ripped through unprotected battle steel at three-quarters of a million kilometers smashed into her from less than two thousand. They punched straight through her hull like battering rams, shattering plating, tearing anyone and anything in their paths to splinters, and the battlecruiser's emissions signature spiked madly as the grasers shed energy into her. Her thrusters were still firing, turning her on her long axis, and the energy fire gutted her like a gaffed shark. And then, with shocking suddenness, her fusion plants let go.

Yang's visual display blanked as the dreadful, white-hot boil of fury overpowered the filters. *Attila* was less than six hundred kilometers from *Farnese* when she went, and the flagship's hull fluoresced wildly as the stripped atoms of her eviscerated sister slashed across her. Only her standard, station-keeping particle screens were up, and those were intended mainly to keep dust from accumulating on her hull. They had never been intended to deal with something like this, and threat receivers and warning signals wailed.

It was only later that Yang realized that only one of *Attila*'s plants had actually let go. The fail-safes on the other two must have functioned as designed. If they hadn't, *Attila* would have taken *Farnese* and probably *Wallenstein*, as well, with her. As it was, the flagship's damage was incredibly light. Her starboard sensors, communications arrays, and point defense laser clusters were stripped away, half her weapon bay hatches were warped and jammed, up to a half meter of her armor was planed away in some places, and she lost two beta nodes out of her forward ring and three more out of her after ring, but her port side was untouched, and the sensors and com lasers on the roof and floor of her hull survived more or less unscathed. Had she dared contemplate resistance, she would actually have remained a fighting force. . . until the grasers which had killed *Attila* got around to her, at any rate.

Wallenstein was further away . . . and partially shielded by the heavy cruiser *Hachiman*. The big *Mars*-class cruiser took a savage beating from the explosion. She was much closer than *Farnese* had been, and the shock front smashed over her on the heels of the energy spike. The fact that any of her hull survived even remotely intact was an enormous testimonial to her designers and builders, but she was turned into a dead hulk, blasted and broken, and none of her people had been in skinsuits or expecting trouble of any sort. Two-thirds of them died almost instantly; of those who survived the initial blast, half took lethal radiation doses not even modern medicine could do a thing about.

But her sacrifice saved *Wallenstein* from *Farnese*'s fate. She came through with only minor damage, and *Kutuzov, MacArthur,* and *Barbarosa*, Yang's other battlecruisers, were far enough out to escape without significant injury. Best of all, all of her other ships' skippers—thank God!—had the sense to do absolutely nothing to draw the defenses' ire down on them.

The rest of the convoy was outside lethal radius of the explosion, and Yang felt a bitter, ungrudging moment of admiration as she realized why "Charon Control" had been so careful to steer the warships and transports into different orbits. The *Longstops* would have been turned inside out by a fraction of the damage *Farnese* had survived, but their positions meant they got little more than a moderate shaking from the explosion. The light cruiser *Sabine* was almost as fortunate; her sister ship *Seahorse* was not. The second light cruiser remained more or less intact, but most of her weapons and virtually all of her sensors were reduced to scrap, her after hammerhead was smashed in and twisted, and half her after impeller ring—including two alpha nodes—was destroyed outright.

It took several minutes for the explosion's interference to fade enough for Charon to punch a fresh com laser through to *Farnese*, and a white-faced Prestwick Thornegrave stared in horror at the face of the woman who had just killed four thousand of his personnel.

"I regret the necessity of that action," she said flatly, "but if any of your surviving vessels fail to comply instantly and completely with any instructions they receive, I will repeat it. And I will repeat it as many times as I must, Citizen General. Is that understood?"

Thornegrave stared at her, and his mouth worked, but no words came. Her expression hardened, and a small tic developed at the corner of her mouth as he gaped at her like a beached fish. He tried frantically, but he couldn't get a single word out, however desperate his effort, and Rachel Yang shot one look at him, then punched buttons at her own com station. Thornegrave's face vanished from the transmission to Charon, and hers replaced it.

"This is Citizen Commodore Rachel Yang," she said flatly. "Your instructions have been received and will be obeyed, Admiral Harrington. Our communications are badly disorganized up here at the moment, however. Please give us a little time to get our net back up so that I can pass the appropriate orders to the other units of the convoy."

"Very well, Citizen Commodore," Harrington replied. "You have five minutes to instruct your vessels to stand by to be boarded. My people will come aboard in battle armor and with heavy weapons. Any resistance—any resistance at all, Citizen Commander—will be met with lethal and overwhelming force."

"Understood," Yang got out through gritted teeth.

"Be very sure that it is, Citizen Commodore, because most of my people have been on Hell for years, even decades. They won't hesitate for a moment to kill anyone who resists. In fact, they're probably looking forward to it."

"Understood," Yang repeated.

"Good." The right side of Harrington's mouth curled to bare her teeth in what might conceivably have been described—by someone other than Rachel Yang—as a smile. "Then there's just one more thing, Citizen Commodore. You will inform your captains that any effort to abandon ship, scuttle their vessels, or wreck their computer nets will also be considered justification for the use of lethal force. Your ships are our prizes, and they are StateSec vessels. As such, and in light of what State Security has done to the prisoners on this planet, neither they nor your personnel are protected in our eyes by the Deneb Accords. They would be wise to remember that."

She never raised her voice. It remained conversational, almost normal, but liquid helium lurked in its depths, and Rachel Yang felt something shudder deep down inside her as she nodded in silent submission.

Chapter Forty-Seven

"Preparations complete, Milady," Captain Gonsalves said formally from the com display, and Honor nodded back gravely. For forty-seven hours, every available hand had labored frantically. Now it was time.

"Very well, Captain Gonsalves," she said just as formally. "You're cleared to depart." Then her voice softened. "Godspeed, Cynthia," she finished quietly.

"Thank you." Gonsalves managed a smile. "We'll see you at Trevor's Star, Ma'am. Don't be late!"

She cut the circuit, and Honor turned to the display on her new flag deck and watched the transports accelerate ponderously out of Hades orbit towards the hyper limit with their single escort. They'd managed to cram just over two hundred and eighty-six thousand people—*her* people now, however they'd become that—aboard those ships. That was a little better even than Montoya had estimated, and the troop decks were packed claustrophobically full. But crowded as they were, their life support—buttressed by the scores of small craft which had been added to their systems—should suffice to see their passengers safely home.

Even now, Honor could hardly believe they'd actually managed to get this far, and she felt a fierce pride as the *Longstops* headed outward.

She deeply regretted the spectacular destruction of *Attila* and (for all intents and purposes) *Hachiman* and *Seahorse*, and not simply because of the loss of life. The explosion had cost her ships she'd needed badly, and it would have been entirely avoidable if that idiot Thornegrave had taken the opportunity she'd given him to surrender without violence. But he hadn't, and she hadn't dared give him more time. For all she'd known, he'd simply been stalling while he used untappable whisker lasers of his own to send messages to the other convoy escorts. It had been unlikely that he could have accomplished anything through active resistance, but he might have made the attempt anyway, in which case she could have been forced to destroy *all* of his ships. A more likely, and almost equally devastating ploy, would have been for him to have ordered his units to purge their computers before she ordered them not to. In that case she would have taken them intact but lobotomized, which would have made the battlecruisers useless to her as warships. She could have copied the basic astrogation and ship service files and AIs over to them from *Krashnark*'s master data banks, but for all her size and firepower, *Krashnark* was simply too small to require all the computer support a *Warlord*-class battlecruiser needed. She could have stripped them down and used them as transports, but she could never have used them in combat.

All of that was true, yet a tiny part of her insisted upon wondering whether she'd really thought all that through before she fired or whether she'd acted before she had to, striking out to exact a horrible vengeance she need not have taken. She supposed she would never know, and the truth was that it didn't really matter. What mattered in the cold, cruel calculus of war was the outcome, and that had been to so terrify the personnel of the surviving ships that they'd almost begged the boarding parties to take them into custody and get them planetside before Honor decided to kill them, as well.

But helpful as it might have been in that regard, there was no way the damage to *Farnese* could be seen as anything other than a serious setback. Her port broadside was intact and fully operational, and Honor's people had managed to clear the hatches on about two-thirds of her starboard weapons (mostly by cutting the jammed hatch covers loose and jettisoning them), but Cerberus simply didn't have the facilities for the repairs she needed. Her starboard sensors were useless and her starboard sidewall would be available at no more than fifteen percent of designed strength. For all practical purposes, she could fight only one of her broadsides, and if anyone got a clear shot at her crippled flank . . .

Still, damaged or not she *was* a battlecruiser, and with her sisters *Wallenstein, MacArthur, Barbarosa,* and *Kutuzov*, she brought Honor's strength in that class up to five. In addition, she had the heavy cruisers *Krashnark, Huan-Ti, Ares,* and *Ishtar*, and she'd hung onto *Bacchante*, as well. The damaged *Sabine* had been sent off with a skeleton crew as Cynthia Gonsalves' flagship and to play scout for the *Longstops*, but even without her, Ramirez's "Elysian Space Navy" was assuming formidable proportions. Indeed, Honor had been hard-pressed to find crews for all of them.

To be completely honest, she mused, still watching the transports and their single escort accelerate away, *I don't suppose I really* did *find crews for all of them.*

She smiled crookedly at the thought. Given the fact that half of *Farnese*'s weapons were useless anyway, she'd reduced the battlecruiser's new company from Caslet's estimated requirement of thirteen hundred to just seven hundred, which had given her (barely) the trained and retrained personnel to man all of the heavy cruisers and put the required thirteen hundred each aboard the other battlecruisers. They'd managed it only by stripping Charon down to naked bone—Charon Control had only a single full-strength watch crew, with just enough other people to make sure there was always a sensor and com watch—and accepting a rather flexible definition of "trained." But none of her subordinates had argued about any of those decisions; they'd reserved their protests for her decision to choose *Farnese* as her flagship.

McKeon had been the first to weigh in, but only because Andrew LaFollet had been a bit slower to realize what she intended. Neither of them wanted her in space at all if it came to a mobile battle, much less on a half-crippled ship! But she'd overridden them both—and also Ramirez, Benson, and Simmons—and despite LaFollet's dark suspicions, it wasn't because of any death wish on her part.

The problem was experience. Harriet Benson's command and tactical skills had come back to her with amazing speed, but she was the only one of Hell's long-term prisoners Honor could really regard as up to commanding a starship in action. Several others were fit, in her opinion, to serve as department heads, stand their watches, and carry out a CO's orders, but they simply hadn't had time to develop the confidence and polish a warship's captain required. Nor had she been able to come up with the required skippers out of more recently captured Allied personnel. With the exceptions of Commander Ainspan and Lieutenant Commander Roberta Ellis, none of them had command experience with anything heavier than a LAC. Ainspan had captained the light cruiser HMS *Adonai* and Ellis had at least captained HMS *Plain Song*, a destroyer, so Honor had assigned Ainspan to *Ares* and tapped Ellis to take over *Bacchante* from Benson.

But that had still left her with eight heavy units, each in need of the best captain she could find. She'd done the best she could by assigning Alistair McKeon to command *Wallenstein*, Benson to command in *Kutuzov*, Solomon Marchant to command *MacArthur,* and Geraldine Metcalf to command *Barbarosa.* That had taken care of the undamaged battlecruisers, and she'd picked Sarah DuChene to command *Ishtar*, Anson Lethridge to command *Huan-Ti*, and Scotty Tremaine to take over *Krashnark* from McKeon. She'd really wanted to give one of the heavy cruisers to Warner Caslet. By any conceivable measure, he would have been the most experienced CO she could have picked for a Peep-built ship, but too many of the liberated POWs still nursed reservations about serving under an ex-Peep, no matter who vouched for him. So she'd made him her XO aboard *Farnese* instead, on the theory that her lamed flagship would need the best command team it could get, and then played mix-and-match in an effort to build something like solid teams for all of her other ships. Jesus Ramirez would be her liberated squadron's second-in-command from aboard *Wallenstein*, but he simply hadn't been able to bring his tactical and shiphandling skills up to the point of handling a warship in a close engagement, and he knew it. In the meantime, Commander Phillips would run Charon Control, and Gaston Simmons would have overall command of Hell.

It was, by any imaginable standard, a ramshackle and jury-rigged command structure from the perspective of current skills levels. But most of the people in it had been given almost a full T-year to get to know one another, and Honor expected their trust and cohesion to overcome a lot of their rough edges.

It had better, anyway, she thought, and turned away from the display at last. Any more Peeps who just happened to drop by Cerberus would almost certainly come in fat, dumb, and happy, just as Thornegrave had. She expected that condition to last for perhaps another two to three months—long enough for Thornegrave and his intervention battalions to be reported as overdue at Seabring—and she intended to use those months to drill her new crews mercilessly.

Unfortunately, if the last T-year had been any indication, there wouldn't be many casual visitors in a period that short. Which meant she wouldn't be able to grab off any more handy transports like the *Longstops*. Which meant that in all probability there would still be better than a hundred thousand liberated prisoners trapped on Hell when the Peeps noticed Thornegrave's nonarrival and sent someone to find out where he was.

She didn't know who or what that someone would be. The logical thing for the Peeps to do would be to send a courier boat to check in with Camp Charon to determine that Thornegrave had arrived and departed. If that happened, she would still have a chance to bluff her way through and convince them he had—that whatever had happened to him and his ships had happened somewhere between Cerberus and Seabring. But even if she managed it, she would be on a short time count from that moment on, because even StateSec was bound to notice eventually that Cerberus had turned into a black hole for anything larger than a courier.

No, time was closing in on her, and she knew it. She would be fortunate to get just the three months she was counting on—or praying for, at least—and every additional day would represent its own individual miracle. Somehow, in whatever time she had left, she had to find a way to grab the shipping she needed to get all of her people off Hell.

And she would, she thought grimly. One way or another, she would.

"All right, people. Let's get to it." Citizen Rear Admiral Paul

Yearman looked around the table in his briefing room and smiled a wintry smile as the side conversations died and all eyes turned to the head of the table. He waited another moment, then glanced at the man sitting beside him. "Would you care to begin, Citizen General?" he invited politely.

"Thank you, Citizen Admiral," Seth Chernock acknowledged, then paused a moment for effect, letting his frigid eyes sweep over the ship commanders gathered around the table. They were a very mixed lot: four in StateSec's crimson and black, and fourteen, counting the two transports' skippers, in the People's Navy's gray-and-green. His senior ground commanders were also present, for it was important for everyone to understand what was planned, and they were an equally motley mix. Citizen Major General Claude Gisborne was SS, but almost half the total ground force—and two-thirds of its senior officers—were Marines.

It was not, Chernock thought grimly, the most cohesive command team imaginable. Unfortunately, it was the only one he'd been able to scrape together, and it had taken him nine standard days to assemble all his expeditionary force's bits and pieces and get it underway. The good news was that he'd managed to put together an escort of no less than ten battlecruisers (although one of them was one of the old *Lion*-class) and six heavy cruisers, and the People's Marines had been able to provide two of their *Roughneck*-class fast attack transports. The bad news was that he'd been able to come up with less than twenty-seven thousand troops to put aboard those transports. Of course, if his warships could secure control of the high orbitals, that should be plenty of ground-based firepower. The prisoners on Hades might outnumber his troops by better than twenty-to-one, but a few kinetic interdiction strikes would take care of that nicely. Perhaps even more to the point, Gisborne was an ex-Marine himself, and he'd gone out of his way to establish a sense of rapport among his subordinates, StateSec and Marine alike. All things considered, Chernock was extremely pleased with the way his ground force command team was shaping up.

He was less enthusiastic about the naval side of things, although that certainly wasn't Yearman's fault. Chernock had drafted the Citizen Rear Admiral because he knew his own limitations. He was primarily an administrator and a planner, and what limited "combat" experience he had consisted of a dozen or so large-scale intervention efforts. That didn't even come close to qualifying him to command a joint space-ground campaign in his own right, so he'd grabbed Yearman as his official second-in-command and de facto naval commander.

And from all he'd so far seen, Yearman had been an excellent choice. He didn't appear to be an inspired strategist, but he had a firm grasp of the tactical realities, and he'd immediately set out to hammer his mismatched squadron into something like a coherent fighting force.

Nine days, unfortunately, wasn't very long. Chernock suspected that an all-Navy task group could have gotten itself sorted out and drilled to an acceptable standard in that much time, but three of Yearman's battlecruisers—*Ivan IV*, *Cassander*, and *Modred*—were commanded by StateSec officers, and so was *Morrigan*, one of his two *Mars*-class heavy cruisers. Those officers, and especially Citizen Captain Isler, *Modred*'s skipper, deeply resented being placed under effective Navy command, even at Chernock's direct orders. Citizen Captain Sorrenson, *Morrigan*'s CO, was probably as resentful as Isler, if less inclined to show it, and it hadn't helped that Yearman's drills had made it painfully obvious that all four SS ships had been trained to a much lower standard than their Navy counterparts. The discovery of their operational inferiority had only honed the StateSec officers' resentment . . . and probably inspired a certain carefully concealed contempt among Yearman's fellow regulars.

Personally, Chernock was glad to have the training differential made clear. As far as he knew, this was the first joint Navy–State Security operation to be mounted, and he had taken careful note of his own service's inadequacies. He already knew his post-mission report was going to be scathing, and he intended to send it directly to Citizen Secretary Saint-Just's personal attention. If, in fact, it became necessary for SS units to deal with rebellious ships of the regular Navy, they were going to need either an enormous preponderance in firepower or far better training, and it was his duty to point that out to StateSec's commander.

In the meantime, however, Yearman had to get his mismatched command team into some sort of fighting trim, and he had driven them mercilessly while the ground force was assembled in Danak. He'd made considerable progress, although Chernock knew he was still far from satisfied, and he'd gone on drilling them on the voyage to Cerberus. Unfortunately, that trip was only forty-five light-years long, and the *Roughnecks* were fast ships for transports. The entire voyage required only eight days base-time, which gave Yearman less than six and a half subjective to get them whipped into shape. After five days of nonstop exercises and tactical problems, even his regulars were heartily sick and tired of it, and the StateSec officers hovered on the brink of rebellion. Yet even Citizen Captain Isler must realize how much they had improved, and Chernock's presence was enough to enforce at least a surface civility.

"I'll keep this brief," he said finally, his voice very level. "We represent a hastily assembled force many of whose personnel have never previously worked together. I realize that the intense efforts which have been made to overcome our lack of familiarity with one another's methods have been hard, exhausting, and often irritating. I know there are short tempers around this table, and I understand the reasons for that. Nonetheless, I . . . will . . . not . . . tolerate *any* display of anger, any hesitation in obeying the orders of a senior officer—regardless of the uniform he or she wears—or any species of insubordination or rivalry. Does anyone require a clearer statement on this issue?"

Several stormy expressions had gone blank as their owners digested the cold, flat, *dangerous* tone in which he delivered his spaced out warning. He waited several seconds, but no one spoke, and he smiled thinly.

"I hoped that would be the case, citizens, and I am gratified to see my hope was not in vain. And now, Citizen Admiral Yearman, if you please?"

"Yes, Sir. Thank you." Yearman cleared his throat, looking both pleased and a little nervous at the unequivocal firmness of Chernock's support. He must, the citizen general reflected, be as uncomfortable with this mixed command structure as anyone else, but at least no sign of that showed in his voice.

"Our exercises to date have given me cause to feel some degree of optimism," he began. "Our coordination still leaves much to be desired, and I'd be nervous at the thought of going into a conventional engagement without longer to polish our rough edges, but I believe we can handle the current mission. I remind all of you, however, that overconfidence is one of the most deadly enemies known to man."

He paused to sweep his eyes around the table, and Chernock raised his hand and rubbed his upper lip to hide an involuntary smile as those eyes lingered just a moment longer on Isler than on anyone else.

"The parameters of our problem are relatively straightforward," Yearman resumed. "We've all studied the data Citizen General Chernock has been able to provide on the orbital defenses, and I'm sure all of us are aware of the fundamental weakness inherent in their design. Aside from the ground bases on Tartarus, Sheol, and Niflheim, all of their weapons platforms are unprotected by any passive defenses and effectively incapable of movement. In addition, their missile defense capability is much more limited than their offensive firepower. They're short on counter-missile launchers, and they have barely a third of the missile-killer laser platforms I would have built into the defense grid. As such, their weapon systems are extremely vulnerable to proximity soft kills, and we can almost certainly penetrate their defenses without resorting to cee-fractional strikes. We may have to take our lumps from the ground bases, but their ammunition is limited, and we should be able to blow a massive hole in the orbital defenses before we have to enter the ground bases' range.

"Blowing away the defenses is, however, a worst-case scenario. I'm sure all of us hope Citizen General Chernock's worst suspicions are unfounded." The citizen rear admiral glanced at Chernock as he spoke, and the citizen general nodded. He was a little surprised

Yearman had had the guts to say such a thing openly, but he couldn't fault the Navy officer's sentiments. Not that he believed for a moment that his fears were baseless.

"In that happy event," Yearman went on, "no attack will be necessary and our force can return to Danak or disperse to other duties. Even if the prisoners have succeeded in taking over Camp Charon and securing control of its com systems, it is still possible that the garrison had time to permanently disable the ground control stations before the prisoners could seize control of the defenses. The odds of that, however, are not great, which is the reason we are all out here.

"Our job, citizens, is to get Citizen General Gisborne and his people safely down to secure control of Styx Island. To this end, I intend to advance with the entire escort, less Citizen Captain Harken's *Rapier*." He nodded to the dark-haired Navy officer. "Citizen Captain Harken will employ her ship as an escort and control vessel for the transports, which will remain at least one million kilometers astern of the main body at all times."

"Is that really necessary, Citizen Admiral?" It was Citizen Captain Fuhrman, CO of the battlecruiser *Yavuz* and one of the regulars, Chernock observed. Yearman raised an eyebrow at him, and Fuhrman shrugged. "Nothing in my download suggested the need for an n-space, in-system escort, Citizen Admiral."

"No, it didn't," Yearman agreed, "and I may be paranoid. Nonetheless, I want someone watching over the transports—and our backs—if we're going to be pegging missiles at defenses as dense as the ones around Hades. I have no desire to see anyone, even a hijacked destroyer, creeping up behind me while I concentrate on the job in hand, and I think we can spare a single heavy cruiser to keep an eye on the back door. Do you disagree?"

"No, Citizen Admiral," Fuhrman said after a moment. "You're certainly right that we can spare a *Sword*-class's firepower—no offense, Helen—" he grinned at Harken "—and it can't possibly hurt anything to watch our rear. I only wondered if there was something in the download that I'd missed."

"I don't believe there was," Yearman replied. "The problem, of course, is that downloads sometimes don't contain all relevant data, no matter how hard the people who prepared them worked at it. So let's spend a little extra effort to make me feel comfortable, shall we?"

One or two people chuckled. Several more smiled, and Yearman smiled back at them. Then he cleared his throat.

"After detaching *Rapier*, I intend to form all of our other units into a single striking force. Citizen Captain Isler, you will be my second-in-command, and *Modred* will take over if something happens to *Tammerlane*. Citizen Captain Rutgers will back you up in turn in *Pappenheim*."

Yearman paused once more, looking at Isler. The SS officer seemed surprised by the announcement, and he glanced at Chernock, as if wondering if the citizen general was behind the decision. But Chernock hadn't had a thing to do with it, and he was as surprised as anyone else. At least two of Yearman's regulars were senior to Isler, and Chernock hadn't anticipated that the citizen rear admiral might be sensitive enough to the rivalries to formally name his most resentful subordinate as his executive officer.

"I understand, Citizen Admiral," Isler said after a moment, and Yearman nodded, then looked back around the table once more.

"If we have to shoot our way in, I anticipate that the heavy cruisers will sit more or less on the sidelines, at least initially, aside from thickening our anti-missile defenses. We'll be going in without pods, which I regret, but we can't always have everything we'd like to have."

Which was especially true, Chernock reflected, when you organized an operation like this with such haste. Neither of the *Roughnecks* were configured to carry the bulky missile pods, and the only interstellar bulk carriers in the system had been two enormous and ridiculously slow old tubs which would have more than doubled their transit time to Cerberus.

"The battlecruisers have the most magazine capacity and the most powerful missiles," Yearman continued. "I intend to take advantage of that capacity and range and hold the lighter ships for the cleanup work after we open the main breach. My staff will coordinate fire distribution from *Tammerlane*, but I want all of you to watch your plots carefully. We've got the capability to tear the defenses apart if we have to, but in the absence of any missile resupply we can't afford to waste what we brought with us, and there's going to be a hell of a lot of confusion when warheads start going off inside a densely packed shell of platforms like the one around Hades. It's entirely possible that you, or one of your tac officers, will see some problem—or potential opening—that we're missing from *Tammerlane*. If that happens, I want to hear about it in time to adjust our fire, not from your after-action reports. Understood?"

Heads nodded around the table, and he nodded back.

"Those are the high points of my intentions," he said. "My staff has put together a more formal briefing, and we'll get to that in a moment. Before that, however, I want to say just one more thing.

"We're a scratch-built task group, people. Some might go further than that and call us jury-rigged, and we all know where our problems lie. I've worked you hard in an effort to overcome them, and I just want you to know that I'm pleased with how well you've responded. I feel confident that we can carry out our mission to Citizen General Chernock's satisfaction, and I want you to pass that expression of my confidence along to your crews, as well. They've worked just as hard as you and I have, and if we *are* called to action, they're the ones who will make it all come together in the end. Please be certain they all know I realize that."

He looked around one more time, making eye contact with each of them in turn, then glanced at his chief of staff.

"And now, Citizen Commander Caine, why don't you get down to the details for us?"

Chapter Forty-Eight

Honor smiled as Nimitz crunched enthusiastically on a celery stick beside her. The 'cat sat upright on the stool to which one of her machinists had added a padded, upright rest that took the strain off his crippled midlimb, and he radiated a sense of vast contentment. The new strength their link had acquired on the planet Enki let her experience his blissful pleasure in full as he devoured the celery, and she'd discovered that the change made it much more difficult for her to ration his supply, even if he couldn't digest Terran cellulose properly.

Well, I suppose you could make a case for too much cocoa being bad for a person, too, she told her modestly guilty conscience, and chuckled mentally. She began to turn to say something to Commander Alyson Inch, her chief engineer, when an admittance chime (actually, it was a buzzer aboard a Peep ship) sounded and she looked up quickly. Andrew LaFollet, who insisted upon standing post behind her even when she ate, turned at the sound and crossed to the dining cabin hatch. He opened it and looked out, then stepped aside to let Lieutenant Thurman into the compartment, and Nimitz stopped chewing abruptly. He, too, looked up in sudden expectancy, and Honor's good eye narrowed as the lieutenant's excitement communicated itself to both of them.

She mopped her lips with her snowy napkin and laid it neatly beside her plate as Thurman crossed to her and came to attention. Since taking command of *Farnese*, Honor had made a point of dining regularly with as many of her officers as possible. It was one of the best ways she knew to become acquainted with them in a short period, and just as she had hoped, they had begun gelling in her memory as individuals. But only ten days had elapsed since Gonsalves' departure with the *Longstops*. That wasn't a lot of time. In fact, it remained a terrifying distance short of the respite she'd hoped and planned for, and she and her people were still feeling their ways into their working relationships.

But it seemed they had just run out of shakedown time, and she felt a ripple of sudden tension, like an extension of her own, spreading out about the table as the other people in the compartment realized that fact.

"I apologize for interrupting your meal, Admiral," Thurman told her.

"That's quite all right, Lieutenant," Honor replied calmly, using formality to help hide her own reaction. "May I ask why you've come?"

"Yes, Ma'am." The lieutenant drew a deep breath, and when she spoke again, her voice was flat. "Commander Warner extends his respects, Admiral," she said, "and we've detected hyper footprints. Eighteen of them."

Like most of the prisoners from long-ago wars the PRH had squirreled away on Hell, Amanda Thurman had been there long enough to become quite old for her official rank. In fact, she was older than Honor, and Honor could feel the lieutenant clinging to her pretense of calm with every iota of that hard-won maturity.

A sledgehammer blow of shock replaced the formless tension which had greeted Thurman's arrival as the numbers hit home with her officers. Eighteen point sources. It was an entire task group, Honor thought with a strange sense of detachment. That many ships couldn't possibly be here for the sort of casual visit which had brought *Krashnark* and *Bacchante* to Cerberus, and no courier boat had warned Camp Charon to expect more visitors on the Shilo model. Which could mean only one thing. But how? Shilo had asked for confirmation of Proxmire's departure for his next duty post, and Camp Charon had provided it. It might have made sense for StateSec to send someone to look more fully into the courier boat's disappearance, but why send this heavy a force even if they hadn't fully bought the explanation or had additional questions? Unless *Krashnark* or *Bacchante* had been missed, as well? But even then, the logical move would have been to send someone to make inquiries and check out the situation—not to reach straight for a short task force like this!

But even as the thoughts tumbled through her brain, she knew the reason wasn't really important. She had to deal with the consequences, regardless of the decision chain that had created them . . . and whatever happened now, the Peep authorities would know something was very, very wrong in Cerberus. Even if her orbital defenses and outgunned squadron should succeed in defeating these intruders and captured or destroyed every one of them, she and any of her ships which survived the battle would remain chained to Hell by the people still trapped on its surface. And when the incoming task group failed to report back, a still larger force would be sent. And a bigger one after that, if necessary. And then a bigger one yet. . . .

"I see," she heard her voice say to Thurman, with a calmness she didn't recognize. "Do we have an emergence locus and vector on them, Amanda?"

"Yes, Ma'am." Thurman tugged a memo board from her tunic pocket and keyed the display, but she didn't need to look at it. "They made a relatively low-velocity alpha translation, right on the hyper limit. At the moment, they're approximately fourteen-point-five light-minutes from Hades on an intercept course with a base velocity of just under twelve hundred KPS." She paused for just a beat, drawing Honor's eye to her face, and then added, "Their accel is only two hundred gravities, Admiral."

"Two hundred?" Honor's tone and gaze sharpened, and Truman nodded.

"Yes, Ma'am. CIC's best estimate is that two of them are in the four- to five-million-ton range, with civilian grade impellers. The rest are obviously warships—probably heavy cruisers and battlecruisers. Given the size of the *Mars*-class ships, it's even harder than usual to distinguish between them at any kind of range, so CIC is uncertain how the ratio breaks down."

"I see," Honor said. Thurman was right, of course. At six hundred k-tons, a *Mars*-class was as big as many an older battlecruiser, and their impellers had brute power to burn. "And their locus?" she asked after a moment.

"Right in the middle of the Alpha Zone, Admiral," Thurman said, and this time there was a sense of something very like exultation under the completely understandable fear the odds had produced in her.

Honor understood exactly why that was, and Nimitz made a soft sound, midway between a growl and a snarl, as he shared her fierce surge of satisfaction.

That has *to be a pair of transports—probably stuffed full of more SS intervention units, or even Marines—and a heavy escort,* she thought. *It's the only thing that makes sense . . . and the fact that there are only* two *transports and nothing heavier than a battlecruiser means someone threw the entire force together in a hurry. Battlecruisers can do the job of blowing a hole in the orbital defenses if they have to, but if they had their druthers, they'd certainly have brought along at least a few battleships, and preferably a superdreadnought or two. And if they put it together* too *hastily, then maybe—*

She closed her eyes for a moment while her thoughts raced. Were those ships SS, PN, or a combination of the two? She would prefer for them all to be SS, given the difference in training standards and general capability, but it might be even better if they were a scratch force from both services that hadn't had time to shake down into an efficient fighting machine. *Sort of like us, in that respect*, a corner of her brain thought wryly.

Yet there was no way she could divine the origin of the task group's units, and she put the thought aside as one worth keeping in mind but not one she could afford to waste time upon. Instead, she felt her brain turning into another channel, following smoothly down the logic tree she'd put together last week. She hadn't really expected to need it this soon, and she wasn't at all sure her crews were sufficiently trained to pull it off even if everything went perfectly. Even so, she blessed the circumstances which had put her in position to at least try it. And if they *could* make it work . . .

Honor had run endless computer analyses of every tracking report in Charon Control's main data base, examining the record of every single arrival in the history of the Cerberus System. She hadn't known exactly what she was looking for—only that no information was ever completely useless and that she needed any data she could possibly get if she was to evolve a tactical approach that might have a chance of dealing with a heavy enemy force. And so she'd set the computers to work, churning their way through the raw reports, and last week, those computers had reported an interesting fact.

Every InSec and SS ship ever to visit Cerberus had translated into n-space at loci and on headings very close to least-time courses to Hell, allowing for h-space astrogation discrepancies . . . and so had the only two regular Navy units—*Count Tilly* and Heathrow's courier boat—ever to visit Cerberus. But they'd all done so from above the plane of the ecliptic. That was unusual. Most skippers tried to make transit in or very close to the system ecliptic because the hyper limit tended to be a little "softer" in that plane. It made for a slightly gentler transit, reduced wear on a ship's alpha nodes by a small but measurable degree, and allowed a little more margin for error in the transiting ship's hyper log position. So if every skipper made a high transit approaching Cerberus-B, she'd realized, there must be a specific reason for it.

It had taken Command Phillips another full day of digging to confirm Honor's suspicion, and the explanation had vastly amused her, for there *was* no reason . . . except for the fact that Peep bureaucratic inertia seemed to be even greater than the RMN's. Honor had always assumed that the Manticoran Navy held the galactic record for the sheer mass of its paperwork, but she'd been wrong, for the Peep arrival patterns went back to a bureaucratic decree that was over seventy T-years old, and as foolish today as it had been when it was originally promulgated.

The very first InSec system CO had taken it upon herself to instigate the procedure as a "security measure," and no one had ever bothered to countermand her orders. As nearly as Honor could figure out, the high transit had been designed as an additional means of identification. Because it represented an atypical approach pattern, Camp Charon's tracking officers would be able to recognize friends even before they transmitted their IDs in-system. Given how much sensor reach and tracking time Charon had, the maneuver was among the more pointless ones Honor had ever come across. The planetary garrison had ample time to identify anything that came calling long before it reached their engagement envelope, and over the years, the high approach had probably cost hundreds of millions of dollars in gradual, unnecessary wear on the alpha nodes of the ships that had executed it.

But it had never even been questioned. Indeed, by now, she suspected, no one had the least idea why the measure had been instituted in the first place. It was simply a tradition, like the equally irrational RMN tradition that light cruisers and destroyers could approach one of the Star Kingdom's orbital shipyards from any bearing, but heavy cruisers and capital ships always approached from behind, overtaking the yard in orbit. No doubt there had once been a reason (of some sort, at least) for that; today, neither Honor nor anyone else in the Navy knew what it had been. It was simply the way things were done.

But if the reason for the SS's traditional approach to Hell really didn't matter at the moment, the fact that it had offered Honor the chance to lay the equivalent of a deep space ambush certainly did, and she'd grabbed it. There was always the chance that someone would break the pattern, but if they followed it, she could make a much more precise prediction than usual of where they would drop into normal-space . . . and of the course they would pursue after they did. That was why she had chosen to hold her ships where they were while her crews worked doggedly in the simulators. She could have kept them in orbit around Hell or hidden them behind the planet's moons, but they could carry out sims as well here as there, and if someone happened to come calling in the meantime . . .

As someone had, she told herself, and opened her eyes once more.

"Their time to Hades?" she asked Thurman crisply.

"CIC makes it roughly six and a quarter hours, with turnover a hundred and eighty-two minutes after arrival, Ma'am." Thurman glanced at her pad, then checked her chrono. "Call it another six hours even from right now for a zero-zero intercept."

"They won't go for a zero-zero," Honor said, and one or two of the people seated at her table looked at her a bit oddly as they heard the absolute assurance in her voice. She felt their reservations and turned her head to give them one of her crooked grins. "Think about it, people," she suggested. "They didn't bring all those escorts along just to say hello to Warden Tresca! The fact that they're present in such force indicates that they have to be suspicious, at the very least. And *that* means that whoever's in command over there has no intention whatsoever of straying into Camp Charon's powered missile envelope."

"Then where do you think they will, stop, Admiral?" Commander Inch asked quietly.

"Right around seven million klicks from the launchers," Honor said positively. One or two other sets of eyes went blank for a moment as people worked the math, and then several heads nodded slowly.

Manticoran missiles and seekers had improved steadily since the war began, and the Peeps' front-line weapons had followed suit, although their improvements had been less dramatic. But Cerberus was a rear-area system whose primary defense had been that no one had the least idea how to find it. Its missiles were the same ones it had been given before the war began, with standard prewar drive options and a maximum acceleration of eighty-five thousand gravities. But by dialing the birds' acceleration down to half that, endurance could be tripled from sixty seconds to a hundred and eighty . . . and range from rest at burnout upped from one million five hundred thousand kilometers to approximately six million seven hundred and fifty thousand. The lower acceleration made them easier to intercept in the early stages of flight, but velocity at burnout was actually fifty percent greater. Just as importantly, it also allowed them to execute terminal attack maneuvers at much greater ranges, and Charon Control had enough launchers to fire salvos sufficiently massive to swamp anyone's point defense.

But ships which stopped outside that range from Charon would be the next best thing to immune to missile attack. Oh, the defenders might get lucky and pop a laser head or two through their defensive fire. But once the missiles' drives went down, they would be dead meat for the attackers' laser clusters, and the orbital launchers, which lacked the powerful grav drivers built into a warship's missile tubes, could impart a maximum final velocity of only a little over seventy-six thousand KPS. That was much too slow to give modern point defense fire control any real problems against a target which would no longer be protected by its own wedge or able to execute evasive maneuvers as it closed. Even worse, the attackers (unlike the orbital launchers) were mobile. They could dodge, roll ship to interpose their wedges, and otherwise make it almost impossible for birds which could no longer maneuver to register on them.

"You really think they'll come in that close, Ma'am?" someone asked.

"Yes," she said simply. "Either that, or they wouldn't have come in at all. If they wanted to be *really* safe from our fire, they would have made translation further out, accelerated to maximum velocity, and launched from several light-minutes out. Their birds would come in at point-nine-cee or more, much too fast for our fire control, and we'd never be able to intercept them effectively."

"Why didn't they do that, then, Ma'am?" the same officer asked.

"Either because they're still not *positive* Camp Charon is now hostile, or because they're worried about accidentally hitting the planet," she replied. "The inner-shell launchers are dangerously close to Hell for that kind of work. Even a slight malfunction in a proximity fuse or a targeting solution, and they could ram a bird right into it. I don't think they'd worry unduly about killing fifty or sixty thousand prisoners, but they've got people of their own down there. Whoever's in charge of this task group doesn't want to kill her own personnel by mistake, and she probably knows all there is to know about the defenses. That means she knows we're weak on point defense and counter-missiles, so she'll come right to the edge of our envelope, stop, and send her missiles in at lower velocities. We'll stop a lot of them—initially, at least—but she doesn't need to score direct hits on us, and we *do* need to score them against her ships."

More heads nodded. Modern warships did not succumb to proximity soft kills—unless, like *Farnese* or *Hachiman*, the proximity was very close and the explosion very violent indeed and none of their passive defenses, like impeller wedges, sidewalls, and radiation shielding, were on-line. Orbital launchers and weapons platforms did. Which meant the exchange rate in destroyed weapons would be hugely in the attackers' favor.

Usually, Honor thought with a shark-like grin, and felt Nimitz's fierce approval in the back of her brain. *Oh, yes. Usually. And maybe this time, too. But I will by God let them know they've been in a fight, first!*

"Lieutenant Thurman, please return to the bridge," she said calmly. "Inform Commander Caslet that the squadron will execute Operation Nelson. He will pass the word to the other ships by whisker, then lay in a course for Point Trafalgar and prepare ship for acceleration. Is that understood?"

"Aye, aye, Ma'am!" Thurman snapped back to attention, saluted, spun on her heel, and hurried away. Honor watched her leave, then turned back to her dinner guests.

"I'm afraid our meal has been interrupted," she said calmly. "All of you will be needed at your posts shortly. First, however—" She reached out and lifted her wineglass, raising it before her.

"Ladies and Gentlemen, the toast is 'Victory!'"

Chapter Forty-Nine

"That," Citizen General Chernock said flatly, "is *not* Dennis Tresca." He jabbed a savage finger at the face of the man still speaking from the main com screen. His own bridge chair was well outside the field of Citizen Colonel Therret's audio and visual pickups as "Tresca" spoke to the chief of staff, and Citizen Rear Admiral Yearman looked at the citizen general oddly.

"With all due respect, how can you be so certain, Citizen General?" he asked quietly. Chernock glanced at him, and the Navy officer shrugged. "Whoever he is, he's fielded every question we've asked him so far, Sir," he pointed out. "And I don't see any signs of hesitation or that he's being coerced."

"I don't think he is—assuming that it's actually a 'he' at all!" Chernock growled, and one of Yearman's eyebrows rose, almost as if against his will. Chernock saw it and barked a short, hard laugh that did absolutely nothing to still the fury pulsing in his heart. Dennis Tresca was—or had been—his friend. But if that wasn't Tresca on the com, then he could only assume the warden was a prisoner or dead. And from what he knew of Tresca's treatment of enemies of the People, it was highly unlikely any of the elitist scum on Hades had been interested in allowing him to surrender.

"My own guess is that we're looking at an AI," the citizen general went on after a moment. Yearman cocked his head, his expression painfully neutral, and Chernock laughed again, this time almost naturally. "I know it's better than we could probably produce, although some of the work at Public Information's special effects department might surprise you, Citizen Admiral!" *Like the imagery of that pain in the ass Harrington's execution*, he didn't add. "But there are quite a few recently captured Manty POWs down there, and their cyberneticists have always been better than ours. One of them, or several working together, could have put together something much more sophisticated than we could."

"But in that case, how can you tell it's a fake at all?"

"Because he hasn't asked to speak to me, even though Dennis knows Therret is my chief of staff and wouldn't be here without me. Besides, the word choice isn't quite right," Chernock told him. "I suspect what we're actually seeing is an AI-filtered image of someone else's responses to our transmissions. Someone is sitting down there in Charon Control ad libbing replies to whatever we send, and the AI is translating them into Dennis' voice, adding his mannerisms, and probably dipping into his personnel records and file copies of earlier com conversations for any background information it needs. But good as whoever built the damned thing was, he didn't quite get it perfect. Unlike the real Dennis would have done, it hasn't made the association between Therret's presence and mine. Either that, or whoever's running it is trying to avoid talking to me because he's afraid I'll trip him up. And either the AI's word selection criteria is a little off the money, or else its override filters aren't sensitive enough, because the occasional 'non-Tresca' word choice is leaking through. At any rate, it isn't Dennis. I'll stake my life on that."

"I see." Yearman looked grave, and Chernock smiled in somewhat caustic sympathy. For all his dutiful attention to detail, the citizen general knew, Yearman hadn't truly believed unarmed, dispersed prisoners, with no tech support whatsoever, could somehow make an open-sea crossing and mount a successful amphibious assault on Styx Island. He hadn't said so, and Chernock couldn't possibly have faulted how hard he'd worked at whipping his task group together, but the citizen general had known that deep down inside, the Navy officer had been essentially humoring him.

Now Yearman knew Chernock hadn't been a lunatic, and he was suddenly thinking about all those orbital defenses with absolute seriousness for the first time. The citizen general watched him unobtrusively from the corner of one eye, wondering if the citizen rear admiral would decide to change his tactical approach now that his threat appreciation had just shifted so radically. But Yearman only nodded slowly, then turned and paced towards the master plot. Chernock watched him go, and then turned cold and bitter eyes on the electronic manikin posing as his friend.

They had been in-system for just over three hours now. Let the damned AI and whoever was running it continue to think it had them fooled. They'd made their turnover to decelerate towards Hades three minutes ago. In another hundred and ninety-two minutes, Yearman would turn to open his broadsides and send the bastard a very different sort of message.

Honor Harrington sat in her command chair and listened to the damage and injury reports coming in from all over her ship. She'd known there would be some, no matter how carefully and thoroughly they'd secured for acceleration. Modern warships simply weren't designed for this kind of maneuver. They didn't have proper acceleration couches at every station, and the people who crewed them weren't used to thinking in terms of locking down every piece of gear against a five-gravity acceleration.

But that was precisely what looked like making this work, she thought, and the reports were both less serious and less numerous than she'd feared when she ordered her ships to do something no warship captain had done in over six centuries.

The reports ended, and she smiled wickedly as Nimitz added his own complaints. He'd been remarkably patient about waiting until the official reports were all in, but he hadn't enjoyed the last half-hour a bit. Treecat *g* tolerances were considerably higher than those of most humans, just as Honor's was, but that didn't mean Nimitz had enjoyed spending thirty-five minutes weighing three-point-seven times his Sphinxian weight. The fact that it had been much worse than that for Honor's human crewmen, and especially the ones who had spent long enough on Hell to fully acclimate to its .94 *g* gravity, hadn't made him any happier about it, either, and he let her know it in no uncertain terms.

He bleeked indignantly at her smile, and she lifted him in the crook of her arm, cradling him against her breasts while she tried to radiate a sufficiently contrite apology. He looked up at her for a second or two longer, then made a snorting sound, patted her live cheek with a gentle hand, and forgave her.

"Thanks, Stinker," she told him softly, and let him slide back down into her lap as she turned back to her plot.

Most of her captains had thought she was out of her mind when she first proposed using *reaction thrusters* to generate an intercept vector. It simply wasn't done. The maximum acceleration a ship like *Farnese* could attain on her auxiliary thrusters, even if she ran them up to maximum emergency power, was on the order of only about a hundred and fifty gravities, which was less than a third of what her impeller wedge could impart. Worse, those thrusters were fuel hogs, drinking up days' worth of reactor mass in minutes. And to add insult to injury, without a wedge, there was no inertial compensator. Warships had much more powerful internal grav plates than shuttles or other small craft, but without the sump of a grav wave for their compensators to work with, the best they could do was reduce the apparent force of a hundred and fifty gravities by a factor of about thirty.

But Honor had insisted it would work, and her subordinates' skepticism had begun to change as she walked them through the numbers. By her calculations, they could sustain a full-powered burn on their main thrusters for thirty-five minutes and still retain sufficient hydrogen in their bunkers to run the battlecruisers' fusion plants at full power for twelve hours and the heavy cruisers' for almost eight. Those were the minimum reserve levels she was willing to contemplate, and they represented the strongest argument against Operation Nelson. Thanks to the huge StateSec tank farm orbiting Hell, they would be able to completely refill the bunkers of every ship afterward, and twelve hours would be more than sufficient to decide any engagement they could possibly hope to win, but none of her ships would have the reactor mass to run for it if the battle fell apart on them.

Well, I told *them it worked for Cortez,* she thought wryly. *Of course, most of them don't have any idea who Cortez* was. . . .

As far as her subordinates' other concerns went, a half-hour at five gravities would be punishing but endurable—most humans didn't begin graying out until they hit six or seven *g*, and heavy-worlders like Honor had even more tolerance than that. And it would take a ship over three million kilometers down-range and impart a velocity of almost thirty-one hundred KPS. That wasn't terribly impressive compared to what an impeller drive could have done in the same length of time, but it offered one huge advantage.

With no impeller signature, a ship might as well be invisible at any sort of extended range.

On the scale to which God built star systems, active sensors had a limited range at the best of times. Officially, most navies normally monitored a million-kilometer bubble with their search radar. In fact, most sensor techs—even in the RMN—didn't bother with active sensors at all at ranges much above a half-million kilometers. There was no real point, since getting a useful return off anything much smaller than a superdreadnought was exceedingly difficult at greater ranges. Worse, virtually all warships incorporated stealth materials into their basic hull matrices. That made them far smaller radar targets than, say, some big, fat merchantman when their drives were down . . . and when their drives were *up*, there was no reason to look for them on active, anyway, since passive sensors—and especially gravitic sensors—had enormously greater range and resolution. Of course, they couldn't pick up anything that wasn't emitting, but that was seldom a problem. After all, any ship coming in under power would have to have its wedge up, wouldn't it?

Stealth systems could do quite a bit to make an impeller signature harder to spot, but they were even more effective against other sensors, and so, again, gravitics became the most logical first line of defense. They might not be perfect, but they were the best system available, and captains and sensor techs alike had a pronounced tendency to rely solely upon them.

But Honor's ships didn't *have* impeller signatures. She had waited two and a half hours, watching the Peeps and plotting their vector carefully before she committed to the thruster burn. The acceleration period had been as bad as she had anticipated, but now her ships were slicing through space at a steady thirty-one hundred KPS, and she smiled again—this time with a predator's snarl—as she watched their projected vector reach out across her plot. Assuming her initial estimate of the Peeps' intentions had been accurate (and their flight profile so far suggested that it had been), she would cut across their base course some three minutes before they slowed to zero relative to Hell. She would be somewhere between six hundred and nine hundred thousand kilometers from them at the moment their courses intersected . . . and their bows would be towards her.

The two transports—and that was the only thing those two big, slow ships could be—had dropped back to ride a million and a half kilometers behind the main task group, ready to hand but safely screened against any unpleasant surprises. A single warship—probably a heavy cruiser, and most likely one of the older *Sword*-class ships, from her impeller signature—had been detached as a close escort for them, but Honor wasn't worried about that. If her maneuver worked, she should be in a position to send enough firepower after them to swat the escort without much difficulty, and all three of those ships were much too far inside the hyper limit for the transports to possibly escape before her cruisers ran them down.

"I see it, but I didn't really think you could pull it off, Ma'am," a quiet voice said, and she looked up to find Warner Caslet standing beside her command chair.

"Between you, me, and the bulkhead, I had a few doubts of my own," she said quietly, and smiled at him.

"You certainly didn't act like it," he told her wryly, then paused and snapped his fingers explosively. Honor blinked as she tasted the bright sunburst of his emotions as he abruptly realized or remembered something.

"What?" she asked, and he looked down at her with a strange expression.

"I just realized something," he said, "and I certainly hope it's a *good* omen."

"What?" she asked again, a bit more testily, and he gave her an odd smile.

"It's exactly two years and one day since you were captured, Ma'am," he said quietly, and both of Honor's eyebrows flew up. He couldn't be right! Could he? She gawked at him for a moment, then darted a look at the time/date display. He was right!

She sat very still for a moment, then shook herself and grinned crookedly at her.

"You should be a little cautious about surprising your CO that way just before a battle, Warner!" She shook her head. "I'd actually forgotten the date."

"Well, you *have* been a bit busy for the last couple of years," he pointed out, "and I figure the Committee of Public Safety is going to be more than a little bit put out when it discovers how you've been spending your time. But it does seem appropriate somehow to kick some 'Peep' butt as an anniversary present."

"So it does," she agreed, and he smiled at her again, then turned and headed back for his own station. She watched him go, then gave herself another bemused little shake and looked back at her plot.

You're so right, Warner, she thought. *I* do *owe these people an "anniversary present" . . . and if we can take them intact, and if they're big enough, and have enough life support—*

She pushed that thought back into its mental cubbyhole. *One thing at a time, girl,* she told herself. *One thing at a time.*

Seth Chernock was a much more experienced interstellar traveler than his colleague Citizen Major General Thornegrave. As a general rule, he rather enjoyed such trips. Unlike many of his fellow StateSec officers, he was a cerebral type, a man who treasured the chance to catch up on his reading, to think and ponder, and he was accustomed to turning what others saw as boredom into profitable—and enjoyable—time in which to do just that.

But there were times he agreed with his colleagues, and this was one of them. Not that he could call the slow, dragging approach to Hades *boring*, precisely. It was hard to feel bored when the acid of fury and the chill of a fear one couldn't quite suppress, however hard one tried, gnawed at one's stomach lining. Besides, this was a time for action, not thought. Thinking was what had alerted him to the problem and brought him here, but what he wanted now was vengeance.

He checked the time display. Another eleven minutes. And whoever was in control on Hades had begun to figure out what Citizen Rear Admiral Yearman had in mind, he thought with cold, vicious pleasure. They were still trying to bluff, but their "com officers" had grown increasingly nervous, questioning the task group's vector and asking for clarification of its intentions. They'd been doing that for the better part of two hours now, and at first, Yearman had dictated a series of glib responses, each of which had seemed to ease their minds a bit, at least temporarily. But for the last twenty minutes, the citizen rear admiral had simply ignored their transmissions, and the bastards had to be becoming frantic.

Good, he thought coldly. *You go right ahead and sweat it, you pricks. You've killed my friend—I'm sure of it now—and for that, I'm going to kill* you. *So enjoy the minutes you've got left!*

"Seven minutes to vector cross, Ma'am," Warner Caslet reported, and Honor nodded. They were right on one-point-three million klicks short of the invisible spot in space she had named "Point Trafalgar," and there was no sign that the enemy had noticed them yet. The capabilities of Peep electronic warfare systems were limited compared to those mounted in Allied ships, but her people were using the ones they had for all they were worth. And given the fact that their sensor hardware, active and passive alike, was identical to that of their opponents, they had a very clear idea of what the Peeps might be in a position to see. So far, the strength of the radar pulses being picked up by their threat receivers remained well below detection values, and unless something changed, they should stay that way until the range had dropped to no more than eight hundred thousand kilometers.

And my estimate of their flight path was just about on the money, too, she reflected. In fact, the intercept she was about to achieve would be a far better one than she'd dared hope for. With only minimal steering burns to adjust her own trajectory, her ships would split the interval between the two Peep forces almost exactly in half: seven hundred and seventy k-klicks from the lead force, and seven hundred and thirty from the trailer. She smiled at the thought, but then her smile faded as she raised her head and looked around her bridge once more.

So far, her plan appeared to be working almost perfectly. That was rare enough to make her automatically suspicious, with the irrational certainty that Murphy's Law had to be waiting to strike and she simply couldn't see it. But even if everything continued to go perfectly, she was very badly outnumbered by the Peeps' firepower, and her people were still hardly what she could call a well-drilled, efficient fighting force.

And most of us don't have skinsuits, either, she thought, then smiled once more, grimly. *This seems to be becoming a habit for me. I suppose I'd better see about breaking it.*

She snorted at the thought, and Nimitz laughed quietly with her in the back of her mind. Not that it was actually all that humorous. But since there was nothing she could do about it, she might as well laugh. It beat crying over it, at any rate!

The problem was that skinsuits, whether Peep or Allied, were essentially custom built for their intended wearers. They were permanently assigned equipment, and modifying one to fit someone else was a daunting task even for a fully equipped maintenance and service depot. But Hell didn't have an M&S depot for skinsuits, because it had never needed one. Her available techs had done the best they could, but they'd been able to fit no more than thirty-five percent of her crewmen; the remainder wore only their uniforms. If one of the Peep ships took a hit and lost pressure in a compartment, the people in it who survived the initial hit would survive the pressure loss; if one of *her* ships took a hit and lost pressure, two-thirds of the people in the compartment would die . . . messily.

And frantically though Alistair McKeon, Andrew LaFollet, and Horace Harkness had searched, they had not turned up a single Peep skinsuit designed for a one-armed woman a hundred and eighty-eight centimeters tall.

Despite her friends' anxiety, Honor was almost relieved that they'd failed. It was irrational, no doubt, but she preferred to share the risks of the people under her command, and she would have felt unbearably guilty if she'd been suited and they hadn't. And there was another point, as well—one she had chosen not to look too closely at even in the privacy of her own mind. Nimitz's custom-designed suit had been confiscated by StateSec and lost with *Tepes*, and he had no emergency life-support module. If pressure was lost, the 'cat would die, and the part of her mind Honor had decided not to examine shied like a frightened animal from the thought of not dying with him.

Nimitz made a small, soft sound, crooning to her as he sensed the darker tide buried deep in her emotions. He might not understand its cause—in fact, she hoped he didn't—but he tasted it in her and snuggled his muzzle more firmly into her tunic while his love flowed into her.

"We'll be coming up on our firing point in five minutes, Sir," Citizen Rear Admiral Yearman reported. "Do you wish to offer them a chance to surrender, or should I simply open fire?"

Chernock cocked his head and smiled at the Navy officer. Yearman had clearly accepted his own conclusions about what had happened on Hades, even if neither of them had the slightest idea of how the prisoners had pulled it off. And he'd become increasingly, if quietly, bloodthirsty as his ships headed in and the people on the ground kept lying to him.

"I believe Citizen Secretary Saint-Just and the Treasury would probably appreciate it if we could talk them into surrendering, Citizen Admiral," the SS general said wryly. "I doubt that they will, though. And if they don't, you can go ahead and blast holes in their defenses to your heart's content, and the Treasury will just have to live with its unhappiness over replacing the destroyed equipment."

"With all due respect, Citizen General, my heart bleeds for the Treasury," Yearman said. It was a daring remark to make to a StateSec general, even for a flag officer, but Chernock only laughed. Then he sobered, and his expression turned grim.

"Between you and me, Citizen Admiral, I agree completely," he said, and his space-black eyes were cold.

"Radar hits from the main body are approaching the detection threshold, Ma'am."

"Understood." The tension on *Farnese*'s bridge was a physical thing now, coiled about them like some hungry beast, and Honor made her voice come out calm, almost gentle, soothing the beast. Her command chair's drive motors whined softly as she turned it, sweeping her gaze across the bridge. With the loss of her left eye, she didn't trust herself to look over her shoulder as she normally would have, and she'd lost some of the peripheral ability to watch the nest of repeater displays wreathed about her chair, as well. But the battle board glowed a reassuring crimson at Tactical—for *Farnese*'s port broadside, at least—and her helmsman sat tautly poised and ready at his station. The impeller board beside him burned the steady amber that indicated nodes at standby, ready to bring up instantly, and Honor inhaled deeply. The oxygen burned in her lungs like fiery wine, and she glanced at Warner Caslet.

"Firing solutions?"

"Locked and updating steadily, Ma'am," he replied, and like Honor herself, there was something profoundly unnatural about how calm he sounded.

She nodded and returned her attention to her plot, watching the icons on it creep steadily closer to one another. Unlike her ships, the Peeps' impeller wedges made them glaring beacons of gravitic energy. Honor's active sensors were off-line—instantly ready, but locked down tight to prevent any betraying emission—but Tactical had run a constantly updated firing plot on passive for over half an hour. The Peeps were dialed in to a fare-thee-well, she thought grimly, and she was about to accomplish something no Manticoran officer had ever managed to pull off. She was about to pass directly between two components of a superior enemy force in a position to rake *both* of them . . . and do it from within effective energy range.

"Two minutes to course intersect," Caslet said, his voice flat with trained, professional calm.

"Stand by to engage," Honor Harrington said softly.

"What the—?" Citizen Lieutenant Henry DesCours straightened abruptly on PNS *Subutai*'s bridge as a single icon blinked into abrupt existence on his display. Then a second appeared with it. And a third!

"Citizen Captain!"

"What?" Citizen Captain Jayne Preston twisted around in her chair, frowning her disapproval for the undisciplined shout from her tactical section.

"Bogies, Ma'am!" DesCours' fingers flew across his console as he brought the powerful emitters of his electronically-steered fire control radar to bear on the suspect blips. It had a much narrower field of view than his search radar, but it was also much more powerful, and his face went white as more points of light blinked to life on his display. "Three—no, *ten* of them! Bearing three-five-niner by oh-oh-five, range . . . *seven hundred and thirty thousand klicks!*"

Raw disbelief twisted his voice as the range numbers blinked up at him, and for just one instant, Jayne Preston's mind froze. Less than a million kilometers? Preposterous! But then the bearing registered, as well, and panic harsh as poison exploded deep inside her. They were in front of her. Whatever the hell they were, they were *directly* ahead of her! That meant there was no sidewall, and with no sidewall to interdict them, the effective range of modern, grav-lens energy weapons was—!

"Helm! Hard skew turn p—"

"*Fire!*" Honor Harrington snapped.

The main Peep force lay fifty degrees off the starboard bow for most of her units as they crossed its course, but *Farnese* was inverted relative to the others. The Peeps lay off her *port* bow, and all down her left side, heavy graser and laser mounts fired with lethal accuracy. Her impellers and sidewalls came up in the same instant, but Honor hardly noticed. Short as the range was by the normal standards of space combat, it was still over two and a half light-seconds. The massive beams lashed out across the kilometers, and they were light-speed weapons. Despite the range, despite the nerve-racking wait for the people who had fired them, the ships they had been fired *at* never saw them coming. They were already on the way before Jayne Preston even opened her mouth to order a course change . . . and they arrived before she finished giving it.

The range was long, but it had never as much as crossed Paul Yearman's mind that he might actually face mobile units, as well as the fixed defenses. And even if he had, surely they would have been picked up before they could get into *energy* range! He'd detached *Rapier* to watch his back, but the decision had been strictly *pro forma*, taken out of reflex professionalism rather than any genuine sense of danger. And because he'd seen no sign of hostile mobile units, the ships of his command had held an absolutely unswerving course for over six hours . . . and Honor's fire control teams had plotted their positions with excruciating precision. Ninety-three percent of her energy weapons scored direct hits, and there were no sidewalls to deflect them as they slashed straight down the wide-open throats of the Peeps' wedges.

The consequences were unimaginable, even for Honor—or perhaps especially for Honor. She was the one who had planned the maneuver, the one who had conceived it and carried it through, but deep down inside, she'd never quite let herself believe she would get away with it. And surely she wouldn't get her first broadsides in utterly undetected and unopposed!

But she had. It wasn't really Yearman's fault. No one had ever attempted an ambush like it, and so no one had any kind of meterstick to estimate the carnage such an attack might wreak. But the dimensions of the disaster became appallingly clear as Honor's fire smashed over his ships like a Sphinx tidal bore.

The battlecruisers *Ivan IV*, *Subutai*, and *Yavuz* lurched madly as grasers and lasers crashed into their bows. *Ivan IV*'s entire forward impeller ring went down, all of her forward chase armament was destroyed, and the ship staggered bodily sideways as hull plating shattered and the demonic beams ripped straight down her long axis. They could not possibly have come in from a more deadly bearing, and damage alarms shrieked as compartments blew open to space and electronics spiked madly. Molycircs exploded like prespace firecrackers, massive bus bars and superconductor capacitors blew apart like ball lightning, trapped within the hollow confines of a warship, and almost half her crew was killed or wounded in the space of less than four seconds.

But *Ivan IV* was the lucky one; *her* forward fusion plants went into emergency shutdown in time. *Subutai*'s and *Yavuz*'s didn't, and the two of them vanished into blinding balls of plasma with every man and woman of their crews.

Nor did they die alone. Their sisters *Boyar* and *Cassander* went with them; the heavy cruisers *Morrigan, Yama,* and *Excalibur* blew up almost as spectacularly as *Subutai*; and every surviving ship was savagely damaged. The battlecruisers *Modred, Pappenheim, Tammerlane, Roxana,* and *Cheetah* lived through the initial carnage, but like *Ivan IV,* they were crippled and lamed, and the cruiser *Broadsword* was at least as badly hurt. *Durandel*, the only other heavy cruiser of the main force, reeled out of formation, her forward half smashed like a rotten stick while life pods erupted from her hull, and chaos reigned as the crews of maimed and broken ships fought their damage and rescue parties charged into gutted compartments in frantic search for wounded and trapped survivors. Yet chaotic as the shouts and confusion over the internal com systems were, the intership circuits were even worse, for one of ENS *Huan-Ti*'s grasers had scored a direct hit on *Tammerlane*'s flag bridge.

Citizen Rear Admiral Yearman was dead. Citizen General Chernock had died with him, and neither of them had ever even known their task group was under attack. The grasers' light-speed death had claimed both too quickly, and with their deaths, command devolved upon Citizen Captain Isler, in *Modred*. But the StateSec officer had no idea at all what to do. In fairness, it was unlikely *any* officer—even a modern day Edward Saganami—would have been able to react effectively to such a devastating surprise. But Isler was no Saganami, and the sharp, high note of panic in his voice as he gabbled incoherent orders over the command net finished any hint of cohesiveness in his shattered force. It came apart at the seams, each surviving captain realizing that his or her only chance of survival lay in independent action.

A few missiles got off, and *Pappenheim* actually managed to turn and fire her entire surviving starboard broadside at *Wallenstein*, but it was a pitifully inadequate response to what Honor's ships had done to them. *Wallenstein's* sidewall shrugged *Pappenheim*'s energy fire aside with contemptuous ease, and despite the short range, point defense crews picked off the handful of Peep missiles which actually launched.

And then Honor's entire squadron fired a second time, and there was no more incoming fire. Five of the enemy hulks remained sufficiently intact that someone might technically describe them as ships; all the rest were spreading patterns of wreckage, dotted here and there with the transponder signals of life pods or a handful of people in skinsuits.

"Cease fire!" she snapped before her gunners could wipe out all of the cripples, as well. And, almost to her surprise, they obeyed. She felt a distant amazement at their compliance, for she knew how dreadfully most of them had hungered for revenge. But perhaps they were as stunned by the sheer magnitude of their success as she was.

She supposed it would go into the history books as the Battle of Cerberus, but it shouldn't. She felt an appalled sense of horror at the totality—as unanticipated on her part as on Paul Yearman's—of what she had accomplished. She had killed more people than this at the Fourth Battle of Yeltsin, but the sheer, blazing speed of it all stunned her. "Massacre of Cerberus" would be more accurate, she thought numbly. It had been like pushing Terran chicks into deep water filled with hungry Sphinx sabrepike. For the first time she could recall, she had fought a battle in which not one single person under her own command had been so much as injured, much less killed!

She glanced at her plot again. The transports had swerved wildly, turning to lumber uselessly towards the hyper limit, but they wouldn't get far. Already Scotty Tremaine was taking *Krashnark* in pursuit of one of them while Geraldine Metcalf went after the other in *Barbarosa*. There would be no one to oppose either of them, for the single Peep heavy cruiser had been the target of the port broadsides of every one of her ships except for *Farnese* herself. The failure of her fusion bottles hadn't blown PNS *Rapier* apart; they'd simply illuminated the splintered fragments of her hull in the instant that they consumed them along with her entire crew.

Honor sat a moment longer, staring at her plot, and then she shook herself, drew a deep, deep breath, and pressed the stud that connected her to the all-ships circuit.

"Well done, people—all of you. Thank you. You did us proud. Now do us even prouder by rescuing every survivor out there, People's Navy or State Security. I—"

She looked up without closing the circuit as Warner Caslet unlocked his shock frame and climbed out of his own chair. He turned to face her and came to attention, and her eyebrows rose as his hand snapped up in a parade ground salute. She started to say something, but then she saw other people standing, turning away from their consoles, looking at her. The storm of their exultation raged at her as, for the first time, they fully realized what their victory—and the capture of the transports—might mean, and she felt the entire universe hold its breath for just an instant.

Then the instant shattered as her flag bridge exploded in cheers. She tried to speak, tried to hush them, but it was impossible. And then someone opened the ship's intercom, and the thunder of voices redoubled as the cheers echoing through every compartment of her flagship rolled out of the speakers. The same deep, braying triumph came at her over the com from the other ships of the squadron, powerful enough to shake a galaxy, and Lady Dame Honor Harrington sat frozen at its heart while the wild tide of her people's emotions ripped through her with all the blinding, cleansing fury of a nova.

They'd done it, the tiny corner of her brain which could still work realized. These were the people who had done the impossible—who had conquered Hell itself for her—and she couldn't think now, could no longer plan or anticipate. And it didn't matter that she'd led them, or that the odds had been unbeatable, or that no one could possibly have done what they had. None of that mattered at all.

She was taking them home, and they were taking *her* home, and *that* was all in the universe that mattered.

Epilogue

*Admiral White Haven sat at his terminal, watching another of the endless, dreary ONI reports which had become all too familiar in the past eight T-months scroll up his terminal. Casualties and damages, ships lost, people killed, millions—*billions*—of dollars worth of industrial investment blown away. . . .*

There had been no more runaway Peep triumphs like the series of attacks with which Esther McQueen had announced the change in the military management of the PRH, for the Allies had not allowed themselves to become that overconfident a second time. But the momentum which had been with the Alliance for so long had disappeared. It hadn't gone entirely *to the Peep side of the board, but it was clearly McQueen and Bukato who were pushing the operational pace now. And unlike Citizen Secretary Kline, McQueen understood she had the ships to lose if spending them bought her victories.*

He looked up from the terminal, running a weary hand through hair streaked with more white since the Battle of Basilisk, and grimaced as his eye lit on the star map frozen on the mural wall display in his quarters. The Barnett System still burned the spiteful red of the PRH, and Thomas Theisman had not sat still. When no attack had come from Eighth Fleet—which had been busy protecting what was left of Basilisk Station until a proper replacement could be scraped up from somewhere—Theisman had nipped out from Barnett to retake Seabring in an audacious raid. He'd hit that system and the Barnes System both, and then gotten his striking force back to Barnett before Theodosia Kuzak learned of its activities and reacted to its absence. It was unlikely she could have gotten permission to uncover Trevor's Star to move on Barnett anyway, given the shock which had temporarily paralyzed the Alliance's command structure and political leadership, but Theisman had been so quick that she couldn't have hit him even if she'd had *permission.*

Which, White Haven thought with admiration-tinged bitterness, only reemphasized the danger of allowing an officer of Theisman's caliber time to recover his balance and plan his own shots.

We should be moving on Barnett right now, *the Earl thought.* Hell, we should've concentrated Eighth Fleet two *years* ago, as originally planned, and damned well hit Theisman then! But even granted that we lost that chance a long time ago, we're still back at Trevor's Star and concentrated again, and why the hell did the Admiralty and the Joint Chiefs send us back out here if they didn't mean for us to carry out our original orders?

But he hadn't been given permission to reactivate his original attack plan, and despite his need to vent frustration, he knew why. The Alliance was afraid . . . and this time it had too much to lose.

He snorted savagely at the thought, yet it was true. He suspected that Queen Elizabeth and Protector Benjamin were as determined as he himself was that the initiative had to be regained, and he had complete faith in Sir Thomas Caparelli's fighting spirit. Lack of courage had never been one of the things he'd held against the burly First Space Lord. But even though Elizabeth and Benjamin were, by any measure. the two most important heads of state in the Alliance, they weren't the only ones, and their smaller allies saw what had happened to Zanzibar and Alizon—and Basilisk—and were terrified that the same would happen to them. Nor had the Star Kingdom or the Protectorate of Grayson maintained as unified a front as their rulers must have desired.

The Manticoran Opposition had been as stunned as anyone else for the first few weeks. But then, as the true scope of the disaster became clear, that had changed. Their leaders had stormed into the public eye, plastering the 'faxes and domestic news services with condemnations of the Cromarty Government's "lax and inefficient," "inexcusably overconfident," and "culpably negligent" conduct of the war. Never mind that the Opposition had done its level best in the decades leading up to that self-same war to ensure that the Star Kingdom would never have had the Navy to survive its opening weeks. Or that it had paralyzed the Star Kingdom's government and delayed military operations for months following the Harris Assassination, and so allowed the Committee of Public Safety to get its feet under it. Nothing in the universe had a shorter half-life than a politician's memory for inconvenient facts, and people like Countess New Kiev, Baron High Ridge, Lady Descroix, and their tame military analysts like Reginald Houseman and Jeremiah Crichton had even shorter memories than most. They sensed an opening, an opportunity to blacken Cromarty and his advisers in the eyes of the electorate, and they'd seized it with both hands.

The political fire on Grayson had come from another source . . . and been leveled upon a different target. A group of dissident steadholders had coalesced under the leadership of Steadholder Meuller, denouncing not the war as such, but rather the fashion in which

Grayson's "so-called allies unfairly—and unwisely—dominate the decision-making process." They knew better than to expect the Grayson people to shrink from the dangers of war, but they had hit a responsive nerve in at least some of their people. Centuries of isolation could not be totally forgotten in a few years, and there were those on Grayson who believed Meuller was right when he implied that their world would be better off if it were to go its own way rather than marrying its military power and policy to someone—like the Star Kingdom—who had obviously miscalculated so hideously.

And listening to all that drivel were the voters of the Star Kingdom and the steaders of Grayson. Men and women who had steeled themselves for the perils of war before the shooting began, but who had become increasingly confident as the actual fighting went on. Few of them had been happy about the war's cost, or about the lives which were being lost, or about rising taxes, reduced civilian services, or any of the hundreds of other petty and not so petty inconveniences they'd been forced to endure. But they had been confident in their navies, sure the ultimate victory would be theirs.

Now they were confident no longer. Esther McQueen had accomplished that much, at least, and the repercussions had been severe. Now all too many voters demanded that the Navy hold all it had taken, as a glacis against additional Peep attacks. They had gotten out of the habit of thinking in the stark terms of victory or slavery, and with the loss of that habit, they had also lost the one of accepting that risks had to be run. That an outnumbered Navy had *to take chances to seize and control the initiative. Indeed, they no longer even thought of themselves* as *outnumbered, for how could an overmatched fleet have accomplished all theirs had? That was why the shock of McQueen's offensives had cut so deep . . . and why the critics vociferously demanded that "the incumbent incompetents be replaced by new, better informed leaders who will let our incomparable Navy safeguard our star systems and our worlds!"*

Which came down in the end to calling the Navy home to "stand shoulder to shoulder" in defense of the inner perimeter . . . which was the worst possible thing they could do.

White Haven scrubbed a hand over his face and took himself sternly to task. Yes, things were worse now than he remembered their ever having been before. And, yes, the Opposition was making inroads into Allen Summervale's authority and popular support. But the Manticoran electorate was not composed solely of credulous fools. In the long run, he estimated, the damage popular trust in the Cromarty Government had suffered might take years to completely heal, but it would be healed in the end. And quite possibly faster than White Haven might believe at this moment that it could be, given the Queen's unwavering, iron support for her embattled prime minister and his cabinet. As for Grayson . . . White Haven snorted a laugh. Samuel Meuller might have assembled a coterie of vocal supporters, but they were a definite minority, and Hamish Alexander knew he *wouldn't care to be the one who challenged Benjamin Mayhew's strength of will!*

Nor was the military front hopeless. Despite heavy losses, Alice Truman, Minotaur, *and the carrier's LAC wing had proved the new LAC concept brilliantly at Hancock, and ONI's best estimate was that the Peeps still hadn't figured out exactly what had hit them, though they must obviously have some suspicions. In the meantime, the new construction programs were going full blast. Within another few months, the first of an entire wave of LAC-carriers would be joining the Fleet, and the new* Medusa*-class—*

No, he corrected himself. Not *the* Medusa*-class. For the first time in its history, the Royal Manticoran Navy had followed the lead of a foreign fleet, and the* Medusa*-class missile pod superdreadnoughts—the wisdom of whose construction no one doubted any longer—had been redesignated as the* Harrington*-class.*

White Haven felt a familiar bittersweet loss as he contemplated the change, but the pain had become less. It would never go completely away. He knew that now. But it had become something he could cope with because he had accepted the nature and depth of his feelings for her. And she would have been proud of the way her namesake had performed at the Battle of Basilisk. Almost as proud as she would have been of how furiously her adopted navy had fought not just at Basilisk but in half a dozen engagements since. The GSN was young, but it continued to expand explosively, and the RMN was beginning to realize its true quality. Manticoran officers had begun to pay it the supreme compliment: they truly were as confident going into battle with GSN units in support as they were with fellow Manticorans.

The Alliance was regaining its balance. It had been knocked back on its heels, but it was still a long way from on the ropes, and while people like Hamish Alexander sparred for time, the massive construction programs behind them were churning out the ships which would take the war to the Peeps again someday much sooner than most people would have believed possible, and—

The chirp of his com interrupted his thoughts, and he hit the acceptance key. Lieutenant Robards' face appeared on it, but White Haven had never seen his aide with an expression like the one he wore. His eyes were huge, and he looked as stunned as if someone had used his head for target practice with a blunt object.

"Nathan? What is it?" the admiral asked quickly, and Robards cleared his throat.

"Sir, I think—" He stopped, with an air of helpless confusion which would have been almost comical if it had been even a trace less deep.

"Go on," White Haven encouraged.

"Admiral, System Surveillance picked up a cluster of unidentified hyper footprints about twelve minutes ago," the Grayson lieutenant said.

"And?" White Haven prompted when he paused once more.

"Sir, they made transit quite close to one of the FTL platforms and were identified almost immediately as Peeps."

"Peeps?" White Haven sat suddenly straighter in his chair, and Robards nodded.

"Yes, Sir." He glanced down at something White Haven presumed was a memo pad display, cleared his throat once more, and read aloud. "Tracking made it five battlecruisers, four heavy cruisers, a light cruiser, and two of their Roughneck*-class assault transports."*

"What?" White Haven blinked. He couldn't possibly have heard right. That was a decent enough squadron for something like a commerce raid, or possibly even a strike at some lightly picketed rear system, but twelve ships, without even one of the wall among them, wouldn't stand a snowflake's chance in hell against the firepower stationed here at Trevor's Star. And what in the name of sanity would a pair of transports *be doing here? They'd be dead meat for any decent warship—even one of the old-fashioned, pre-*Shrike *LACs!—if they moved inside the hyper limit.*

"I assume they hypered back out immediately?" he heard himself say. The only logical explanation was that someone on the other side had made a mistake. Perhaps the Peeps were *planning a major attack on Trevor's Star and the transport echelon had simply arrived too soon . . . or the main attack force was late. In either case, the sensible thing for the Peep CO to do would be to flee back into hyper-space—at once.*

"No, Sir," Robards said, and drew a deep breath. "They didn't do anything at all, Sir. Except sit there and transmit a message to System Command HQ."

"What sort of message?" White Haven was beginning to be irritated. Whatever ailed his flag lieutenant, prying the facts out of him one by one was like pulling teeth. What in God's name could have someone normally as levelheaded as young Robards so off-balance and hesitant?

"They said— But, of course it can't be, only— I mean, she's—" Robards broke off again and shrugged helplessly. "Sir, I think you'd better see the message for yourself," he said, and disappeared from White Haven's terminal before the earl could agree or disagree.

The admiral frowned ferociously. He and Nathan were going to have to have a little talk about the courtesy due a flag officer, he thought thunderously, and after that *they'd—*

His thoughts chopped off in a harsh, strangled gasp as another face appeared on his display. Other people might not have recognized it with the hair which framed it reduced to a short, feathery mass of curls and one side paralyzed, but Hamish Alexander had seen that same face in exactly that same condition once before, and his heart seemed to stop beating.

It can't be, *he thought numbly.* It can't be! She's *dead*! She's—

His thoughts disintegrated into chaos and incoherence as the shock roared through him, and then the woman on his display spoke.

"Trevor System Command, this is Admiral Honor Harrington." Her

voice sounded calm and absolutely professional—or would have, to someone who didn't know her. But White Haven saw the emotion burning in her good eye, heard it hovering in the slurred soprano. "I'm sure no one in the Alliance expected to see me again, but I assure you that the rumors of my recent death have been exaggerated. I am accompanied by approximately one hundred and six thousand liberated inmates of the prison planet Hades, and I expect the arrival of another quarter million or so within the next eleven days—our transports have military hyper generators and we made a faster passage than they will. I regret any confusion or alarm we may have caused by turning up in Peep ships, but they were the only ones we could . . . appropriate for the voyage."

The right side of her mouth smiled from the display, but her voice went husky and wavered for a moment, and she stopped to clear her throat. White Haven reached out, his fingers trembling, and touched her face on the com as gently as he might have touched a terrified bird, yet the terror was his, and he knew it.

"We will remain where we are, with our drives, sidewalls, weapons, and active sensors down until you've had time to check us out and establish our bona fides," she went on after a moment, struggling to maintain her professional tone, "but I'd appreciate it if you could expedite. We were forced to pack these ships to the deckheads to get all our people aboard, and our life support could be in better shape. We—"

She broke off, blinking hard, and Hamish Alexander's heart was an impossible weight in his chest—heavy as a neutron star and yet soaring and thundering with emotions so powerful they terrified him—as he stared at her face. He was afraid to so much as breathe lest the oxygen wake him and destroy this impossible dream, and he realized he was weeping only when his display shimmered. And then she spoke again, and this time everyone heard the catch in her breath, the proud tears she refused to shed hanging in her soft voice.

"We're home, System Command," she said. "It took us a while, but we're home."